The Apex Cycle Book 2

WRITTEN BY

M.T. ZIMNY

Editing by Melissa Ball

Cover Illustration and Special Characters by Maria Mondloch
Back cover photography by Andrew Rossi
Fonts: Cinzel, Marcellus, Roboto, Merriweather

ISBN: 978-1-7356571-1-0 (Paperback)

For Connor.

I know I dedicated the last one to you, but it felt wrong to write about superheroes and dedicate it to anyone else.

TABLE OF CONTENTS

ONE
Writing on the Wall ... 7

TWO
Apparitions in the Sickbay ... 14

THREE
Treading Water ... 23

FOUR
Parasite Days ... 37

FIVE
Old Friends ... 46

SIX
Hephestae ... 56

SEVEN
Turbulence ... 65

EIGHT
Among Giants and Heroes ... 79

NINE
Scourge Queen Revisited ... 91

TEN
Swordplay ... 104

ELEVEN
Qualifying ... 118

TWELVE
Pastas and Premonitions ... 129

THIRTEEN
The Apex Team Games ... 143

FOURTEEN
Foil and Failure ... 158

FIFTEEN
The Regatta ... 168

SIXTEEN
Clash ... 179

SEVENTEEN
A Minor Impalement ... 189

EIGHTEEN
All On The Same Page ... 202

NINETEEN
Living Arrangements ... 210

TWENTY
The Boxes in the Closet ... 221

TWENTY-ONE
House Call ... 228

TWENTY-TWO
All In Frame ... 239

TWENTY-THREE
The Legacy of Paul Fleming ... 251

TWENTY-FOUR
Broken Plates ... 261

TWENTY-FIVE
New Year's Eve ... 269

TWENTY-SIX
Second Act ... 280

TWENTY-SEVEN
Havard's Daughters ... 287

TWENTY-EIGHT
Enter Wavemaker ... 297

TWENTY-NINE
Leaks ... 308

THIRTY
Countdown ... 315

THIRTY-ONE
Northshore Park ... 328

THIRTY-TWO
Duel on the Dock ... 342

THIRTY-THREE
Safehouse ... 352

THIRTY-FOUR
A Very Bad Plan ... 367

THIRTY-FIVE
Maelstrom Under the City ... 384

THIRTY-SIX
The Sisters ... 401

THIRTY-SEVEN
Rat ... 411

THIRTY-EIGHT
Evacuation ... 421

THIRTY-NINE
In the Undertow ... 440

FORTY
Flotsam ... 451

FORTY-ONE
Ruins of a Drowned City ... 462

FORTY-TWO
Hunted ... 476

FORTY-THREE
The Penthouse Dome ... 489

FORTY-FOUR
Father and Brother ... 502

FORTY-FIVE
The Village Girl ... 515

FORTY-SIX
Voice in the Night... 533

FORTY-SEVEN
Ares ... 548

FORTY-EIGHT
Disarmed ... 558

FORTY-NINE
The Last Viking ... 569

FIFTY
Will and Testament... 581

1

Writing on the Wall

My mile time wasn't too bad considering I was, by my count, three times undead. This time around wasn't my best, though, and I watched the unforgiving stopwatch ticking in the corner of my visor screen. If I didn't have to wear all this gear, it'd be no problem. However, the heavy boots weighed on my ankles and the visored helmet felt awkward. But, hey, at least I looked cool.

"Good work, Sammy!" As much as I adored Naomi, I scowled as she chirped in my earpiece. "You made it to Sector Two. Convene with the others in Sector Eleven. You have twenty minutes."

"Sector Eleven?" I gawked at the map floating in the bottom corner of my visor. "That's clear across the island!"

"Then you better run fast. Remi and Erik are coming from Sectors Seventeen and One. I heard what Fleming has planned for whoever is last."

"And?"

"And you *don't* want to be last."

I looked at the tiny map. Remi was closest to the rendezvous sector, but she was in the busiest part of the island. Having to keep to the shadows and away from prying eyes would slow her down. Erik, meanwhile, would be coming from the docks. He'd have no problem getting to Sector Eleven.

I should've been grateful for the training exercise, I mused, as my boots rhythmically slammed against the pavement. I was lucky to be on the team at all considering I hadn't passed the trials. Extra exercises were a small price to pay. Still, though. I was ready for them to be a thing of the past.

I stopped at the mouth of an alleyway, peering into the empty street to make sure no one would see me. Even after running all night, the midnight December air that rolled in from the ocean and down the roadways of New Delos was sharp on my exposed chin and neck. I bounced on the balls of my feet to keep warm as I waited for a car to pass.

"Everything all right?" Naomi asked in my ear. "Looks like you've stalled."

"Yeah, I'm good," I wheezed, sprinting across the street as the car's taillights disappeared around a corner. "You know how unbearable traffic is this time of day."

Someone snorted on the other end of the comm but I couldn't tell which of the other captains it might have been.

A blue light blipped in the corner of my vision. The visor screen flashed, "RAIN DETECTED" at me and I scowled. The temperature was too close to freezing for me to care for rain.

I kept an eye on the clock as I raced towards Sector Eleven, taking notice of the dots on my map that tracked Remi and Erik's progress. Remi was moving slow, as predicted, but Erik didn't seem to be moving at all.

A few more minutes into the run and I didn't need my helmet to tell me it was raining. The onslaught worked fast to make the pavement slick with icy puddles and I struggled to keep my footing.

"Samantha." It wasn't Naomi's bright voice in my ear this time, but Fleming's urgent bark. It was hard to reconcile the militaristic tone with the awkward and nervous history teacher I knew it belonged to. "Report to Sector One to rendezvous with Erik."

Erik's dot hadn't moved since I'd looked at it last.

"Is he lost?"

"We don't know, he's not responding."

I changed course for the northwestern point of New Delos.

"It's probably a helmet malfunction." Justin's voice was reassuring and I felt like the captain was speaking more to Fleming than to me. "There's a chance he won't even be there."

"Cool, but if I'm the last one to Sector Eleven because Erik couldn't figure out how to turn on his helmet, I'm not doing whatever punishment Fleming has planned."

My dot grew closer to Erik's on my map and I frowned as my visor informed me I'd entered Sector One. After being nearly kidnapped at the docks here three months ago, it was my second to last favorite place on the island, beaten only by the museum, somewhere I had also been almost kidnapped and later stabbed.

The museum was the last place I'd seen Dad, too, before I'd put a knife through the skull of the monster who'd taken him in the first place. Adrestus had gone on to make a full recovery, of course, still with Dad locked away somewhere.

Not Dad, I reminded myself. *Vidar.*

It had been almost two months since finding out my dad was actually my brother, Vidar, and I still had difficulty calling him anything but my father. But what was a millennia-year-old viking girl with a lifetime of constructed memories and no recollection of her prior life to do?

I shook my head to clear it, pausing behind a dumpster to catch my breath.

"Why've you stopped?" Fleming's voice rang out in my helmet and I jumped. "What's wrong?"

"Nothing!" I hissed. "I'm almost there, alright?"

I left my respite behind the dumpster and crept along the alley wall between two warehouses. Erik should only be a few blocks away. Fleming didn't need to get his tie in a twist.

The industrial district of New Delos was dead at this time of night. With the road empty, I chanced a diagonal dash across the street rather than sticking to the shadows. I made it to Erik's alleyway and looked down the dark corridor.

I let out a dry scoff.

"Yeah, he's not here."

"You sure?" Naomi urged. "It's weird his helmet would still be transmitting from that location, even if it's turned off."

The streetlights on the main road did little to illuminate the alley but I could still see into the dark with the night-vision my helmet offered.

"Yeah, there's—"

A huddled mass lay limp on the ground. I swallowed.

"Samantha?"

"Hold on." My voice shook as I sprinted towards Erik. "Send a car. I found him."

I skidded to a stop, spraying puddle water over Erik as I did. He didn't react. I knelt next to him and pulled his helmet off, careful to catch his head in my gloves before it lolled back and hit the pavement.

"His breathing is steady, but he's out cold." I shook Erik's shoulders to try and wake him but it was no use.

"Wesley and Everest are on their way. Remi should be there soon, too." Fleming said. I bit back a protest. Wesley and Remi in the same place was the last thing I needed. "Are there any signs of a struggle?"

I glanced around, but the alley was clear and the rain would have already washed away any upset dirt a fight might've caused.

"No signs of fighting." But as I said it, I noticed the mark that stretched across the skin of Erik's neck. "Wait."

I pulled at the collar of his uniform. The bright red imprint of a hand wrapped around the front of his throat, as if someone had grabbed him there and their hand had burnt his skin.

I only knew one person with powers that could do that, but Amanda was a wanted criminal who was currently being held captive by the very man she was wrongfully accused of trying to murder. No one had seen her since the night at the museum two months ago when she'd been locked in combat with her sister.

"What? What do you see?" Fleming demanded. Heavy footsteps echoed behind me in the alley.

"Hold on," I said, turning to look. "I think Remi's here."

But I didn't see Remi. Instead, I saw the sole of a black boot as it struck out, kicking me square in the chin and knocking me back over Erik's unconscious body.

As far as I could tell, I was only out for a couple of seconds. I wasn't even sure if I had even been properly unconscious, like when the power flickers in the middle of a storm and everything goes dark but sputters back to life after a moment or so.

The night sky, dyed a faint orange by the glow of the city, looked down at me, spinning in a way I was almost certain night skies weren't supposed to. What had been solid pavement underneath me now rocked haphazardly. I shook my head, trying to make it be still, but it only made the distortion in my vision worse.

I saw her boots first, firmly on the ground now rather than flying at my face. The puddles around them flickered orange but I couldn't figure out why.

"Remi? What—"

I looked up at the woman standing over me. While her armor was similar to the uniform Remi would be wearing, it wasn't my teammate. A dark cape billowed out behind her and a black mask covered the lower half of her face. Most striking of all, she was perfectly bald. Where hair should have sprouted from her scalp, an orange flame licked at her skin, illuminating the alley and sending embers into the air.

I blinked rapidly, trying to focus on the fiery lady looming overhead.

"Hephestae..."

The word came out of the woman in a strained whisper.

"Samantha? What's happening? Who's there?" Fleming was back in my ear.

"I'm good," I said dreamily. "Fine. I'm fine."

"Hephestae..."

She raised her boot again and I flinched away, but the kick never came. There was a labored grunt as she slammed into the alley wall. Remi had arrived and wasted no time in attacking the mystery lady. I slumped back against Erik, watching Remi dodge a column of flame.

She stumbled back from the heat and the woman scaled the brick wall, pulling herself up by a windowsill and clambering up to the warehouse roof. Out on the street, tires squealed as they pulled up on the curb. The alley flooded with bright, white headlights.

"I'll catch her!"

Wesley barreled out of the back of the car, the number "7" visible on his shoulder armor, but Remi leapt in his way.

"Watch out!" she shouted as fire rained into the alley from the rooftop. Wesley collided with her and both went sprawling across the pavement.

"*You* watch out!" Wesley jumped back up to his feet and sprung up the warehouse wall, kicking off the brick to grab onto a second floor window frame.

"Get down!" Remi called. "We need you here!"

"We *need* to catch her!" Wesley tried to slingshot himself to the next floor, but the brick was too slick with rain. He scrambled at the wall and slid to the ground, rolling as he hit the pavement. He scowled at Remi from under his visor. "Why'd you get in my way? I had her!"

"She would've toasted you and you know it!"

"Hey!" Everest came out from the driver's seat of the car to yell at them, bits of shaggy, black hair sticking out from under his helmet. "Maybe we can fight later?"

He made a sweeping gesture towards Erik and me.

"Yeah, Erik needs help." My words slurred but I nodded importantly.

"Right. Erik is the one that needs help." I could hear the eye roll in Remi's tone.

Wesley helped me to my feet and the world lurched awkwardly as I stood up.

"Careful," he murmured.

"I'm fine."

Everest and Remi carried Erik to the car between them. Wesley put a hand on either side of my helmet and pulled it off. A mess of tawny hair fell against my shoulder armor and Wesley took off his own helmet to look me in the eyes.

It was hard to focus on his face and his green eyes swam in my vision.

"Are you sure you're okay?" he asked. I nodded too aggressively. The alley spun.

"Yeah. But, Wesley," I leaned in close, steadying myself against his chest, "what's that wall say?"

"Wall?" he repeated dumbly, turning to look at the alley wall he'd tried to chase Hephestae up.

Dark letters had been scorched into the brick, sooty residue spelling out what was either a warning or a threat. The black letters bled in the rain, but the writing was still legible.

Wesley read the message out loud, gulping as he did.

"'New Delos will burn.'"

We all stared in the direction the assailant had disappeared to. She was gone, and I knew it was my imagination, but I thought I could still hear the crackle and hiss of her fiery mane.

2

Apparitions In The Sickbay

The Sickbay lights were too bright. I squinted up at them angrily. Naomi sat with me as I waited for the team nurse to finish caring for Erik at the other end of the long room. Naomi's fellow captains, Justin, Marcus, and Jen, sat on the bed opposite mine, whispering. The sound of an argument between Remi and Wesley echoed in from the hallway. I tried not to eavesdrop, focusing instead on Tonka, the unofficial team mascot, who purred in my lap and flashed his orange cat belly at me.

The door slammed open, sending Tonka skittering off the bed and under a cabinet. Wesley marched inside, his face red and his brown hair sticking out at odd angles after having been in his helmet. I gave him a thumbs up and his shoulders relaxed, though he still looked peeved.

"You're okay, right?" he asked.

"One hundred percent!"

"You sure?"

"She's not sure of anything, Wes, look at her." Naomi's tight, dark curls bounced as she gestured at me wildly.

I wrinkled my nose at them both and leaned back against the headboard.

"I'm fine!"

"Yeah? What's the name of your sixth grade teacher?" Naomi asked wryly.

Searching for the memory was like sifting through mud. I laughed and pushed away the sudden panic that gnawed at the edges of my mind.

"Joke's on you," I sang. "Alison must've not given me one."

Wesley flushed red as Naomi squinted at me. I bit my tongue to keep from saying anything else. I'd let Wesley in on my secret Viking background almost as soon as I'd found out, but was still waiting for the right time to tell Naomi.

"See? What's that even supposed to mean? Sammy, you're concussed."

Across the room, Erik's bed curtain slid open and Nurse Everly stepped out, wearing his usual lavender scrubs. He had an angular face and a dark, perfectly bald head that gleamed under the fluorescent lights. Fleming followed, his brown hair pushed back from compulsively running his hands through it, something he did when he got stressed. His glasses dangled from the front of his wrinkled button up.

"Concussed, huh?" Everly said. Wesley stepped back to make room at the bedside and I frowned at them.

"I'm not concussed. I've had a concussion before and it was nothing like this."

Everly held out a hand. Grumbling, I placed my hand in his and felt a familiar rush along every nerve from my fingers to my toes. He tutted and looked to Fleming.

"Feels like a concussion."

"Are you sure?"

Everly crouched so he was at eye-level with me. He held up a single finger.

"Samantha, try to follow my finger with just your eyes."

He moved it back and forth in my field of vision. I looked at Wesley standing just behind him and winked. I was nailing this test. Wesley didn't look so sure.

"I'm going to give you some words and I need you to repeat them back to me," Everly instructed.

"Repeat them. Got it."

The others stared at me expectantly.

"Samantha?" Fleming prompted. I scowled in confusion.

"What?"

"You need to repeat the three words Everly just gave you."

"But he..." I screwed up my face, trying to think. Had he already given me the words? There was a vague memory there. I clawed at it. "Right. Uh, 'cloud' was one of them, I'm pretty sure."

Everly straightened up and looked at Fleming.

"Like I said. Concussion. Judging by the bruise on her chin, her head got kicked back."

I rubbed my chin and winced in surprise. It was tender to the touch.

"How long of a recovery?" Fleming asked.

"It looks severe, so probably two weeks. She'd be out of the Apex Games for sure."

"What?" Wesley exclaimed. "No, she has to compete."

"If she's concussed, Wesley—" Naomi started.

I snorted loudly and they all turned to look down at me.

"I'll be fine. Just let me sleep it off."

"No," Fleming and Everly said together.

"I'm more worried about first semester finals than I am about the Apex Games," Fleming mused, scratching his chin.

"Should I get the Serum or no?" Everly asked.

"Her plus Erik makes two in one night. At this rate, we'll need more spinal fluid from Weaver soon." Fleming pushed his hair back and sighed. "Yeah, give her the Serum."

I held out my arm obediently, ready for the IV that would deliver the miracle cure that Everly kept hidden in the Sickbay. Naomi gently pushed my forearm back down.

"I don't think this one goes in your arm."

Everly disappeared into the back.

"Where does it go?"

Everly reappeared pushing a cart.

"I'm going to need you to turn on your side and bring your knees up to your chest."

I looked at the long, hollow needle on Everly's tray and leapt from the bed, running straight into Wesley. He steadied me as the world churned.

"You'll be fine," Everly insisted. "You've done this before, actually. The difference this time is that you'll be conscious for it."

"It'll hurt."

"I'll numb the area beforehand."

Justin, Marcus, and Jen watched from where they sat across the room and my face became warm at the sight of the captains.

"How long will it take?" I asked.

"Not long, if you cooperate."

I warily got back on the bed to lie on my side with my back towards Everly. He tugged on my shirt to expose my back and something cold swabbed my lower spine.

"Why is it wet?" I exclaimed.

"Just an antiseptic. Hold still. You'll feel a pinch."

Wesley knelt down next to the bed and smiled at me.

"It'll be easier than the IV Serum," he insisted. "You won't have to wait around with it hooked up to you."

"Easy for you to say," I mumbled back. "You're not the one getting a spinal tap."

"If it makes you feel better, I got one, too!" Erik called from his corner of the room. I scowled. It did *not* make me feel better to know I was on the same level as Erik, the guy whose only special ability was to secrete any smell.

Granted, I didn't have an Apex ability at all, so who was I to judge?

"You'll feel some pressure and some slight discomfort," Everly said behind me.

"That's just doctor-talk for 'it's gonna hurt'."

I screwed my eyes shut as something pressed into my lumbar spine. Fingers wrapped around mine and I opened my eyes to see Wesley's hand. I looked to his face to smile my thanks but startled.

A large man towered behind Wesley. His hair was long and matted, his beard pulled into a braid that rested on his leather tunic. Blood and mud had dried across his face. He stalked towards my bed soundlessly. Wesley hadn't noticed him. I tried to shout a warning, but it caught in my throat.

"Samantha, what's wrong?" Naomi's voice was sharp behind me. "She's upset."

"We're almost done, Samantha." Everly said coolly. He hadn't seen the intruder yet. No one had.

The man snarled, baring his yellowed teeth, and pulled a sword from the hilt at his waist.

"No!"

I struck out, pushing Wesley out of the way, and shouted as pain spasmed across my back.

"What's wrong?"

"Someone hold her down!"

"Where's Justin?"

I thrashed against the hands that grabbed me and the man drew the sword back, ready to strike.

"Don't you see him?" I screamed.

"Sammy, there's no one there!" Wes was in my ear. He was wrong. The man was *right there*. Maybe some kind of Apex power kept the others from seeing him.

I pushed away, scrambling backwards on the bed.

A new hand grabbed my arm and everything locked up as Justin's stasis ability took hold over me. I couldn't move. I couldn't shout. I was trapped. I watched the man's hungry face as he tightened his grip on the sword hilt and let the blade arc through the air.

I braced myself, ready for the metal. White-hot iron sliced down the left side of my neck, stopping as it caught on my collar bone.

"Naomi, what's wrong with her?" Fleming asked.

I waited to see the blood spill out onto the white sheets, but it never did. The man dissipated into the air.

"I don't know, but she's terrified."

As long as I was frozen, I couldn't tell them what was wrong. Naomi could read emotions, but not thoughts.

The Sickbay darkened and my pulse quickened. Was I dying? Had the man killed me?

In place of beds, I saw mossy rocks. The curtains and shelves morphed into trees. A creek bubbled nearby. I'd been here before.

"Sammy?"

Wesley's face broke through the image and I blinked, back in the Sickbay and looking at the ceiling. The fog that had settled over my head after getting kicked had lifted but I was coated in sweat.

I lifted a quaking hand to my neck. Instead of an open wound, I found the long scar that ran from just below my jaw and to my clavicle, tracing the exact path the man had cut me with.

"What happened?" Fleming asked. He and Everly stood on one side of the bed. The four captains huddled behind them. Justin was sporting a bloody nose and I wondered if I'd given it to him.

"I think—"

I looked at the others again and Fleming seemed to understand.

"Everyone, out." He pointed to the door. "Erik? How are you feeling?"

"Fine, I guess."

"Good. Out."

Wesley wavered but Fleming glared at him and he followed Naomi and the others through the door. It slammed shut and the two adults spun to face me.

"I thought I saw someone," I stammered, embarrassed at having panicked in front of everyone. "I think...I think it was a memory."

It sounded stupid to say out loud. I'd recovered memories from my past life before, but they'd only ever happened in my sleep, appearing as dreams. This was the first time I'd seen a man from the middle ages walk into a room.

"A possible side-effect of the Serum?" Fleming asked. Everly's dark, bald brow furrowed as he thought.

"Possibly. This Serum interacts directly with the central nervous system. Any damaged or lost memory could be recovered by it."

"I first dreamt about old memories after Adrestus had...you know." I drew a finger across my neck. I didn't like talking about my recent murder, even if I *had* recovered.

"And what did you see this time?" Fleming prompted.

"I told you. It was a man. I think he's the one that did this." I pointed to the scar I'd thought, until recently, had been from a bike crash.

"Closer to the end, then?"

"Yeah. So far everything I've remembered seems to have been just before I went under." There wouldn't be many memories left to remember after that. I'd spent several centuries in a coma, waking up barely a week before the semester started, head full of Samantha's invented life.

Fleming wrung his hands before running his fingers through his hair.

"Great, well, you know what to do." He glanced around awkwardly and I wondered if he was searching for something to say. The poor man hadn't asked to become the guardian of his high school friend's adopted viking daughter and there wasn't exactly a handbook on how to navigate that, either. "Good job tonight. I want your report by morning."

I grunted.

"Sure thing."

Naomi pretended to be asleep as I slipped into our dorm room. I should've crawled into bed but instead I sank into my desk chair and flicked on my table lamp. Floundersen the Betta Fish twisted in his tank under the sudden light and I sprinkled food pellets into his water as I glanced back at Naomi. In the two months we'd been roommates, I'd learned the sound of her breathing when she was properly asleep. Now, she was too quiet. I steadied myself. She couldn't help eavesdropping on the emotions of those around her, but I liked to think I'd gotten good at doing my best to conceal them.

A black notebook rested between two heavy texts on my desk. I wriggled it free and it fell open. The notebook had been Everly's idea. It was supposed to help me organize the few memories of Eydis that had bubbled up in my consciousness.

I made sure to skip the first page, like I always did when I opened it. That was where I'd written about the bodies of Eydis' family— my family. I didn't like thinking about them lying amidst flame and ash, killed by Adrestus. I had no memories of them alive, but it was still easier to keep my emotions neutral when I went straight to page two.

I shot another glance at Naomi, as if she might somehow indicate she knew I was thinking about my murdered family from a thousand years ago, not that she knew about them. I'd been careful to keep the circle of people who knew about my previous life small. Fleming, Everly, the school principal, and Wesley. Naomi had to know I was hiding something. Her powers of perception missed nothing, but she'd at least let me have privacy the last couple months and hadn't asked about it too much.

I did need to tell her eventually, though, and I almost had on several occasions. However, Fleming, Everly, and even Wesley seemed to look at me different since finding out and with my family in hiding and kidnapped, Naomi was all I had left. "Samantha Havardson" still existed as long as she believed that's who I was.

I squinted at the blank notebook page. The spinal tap had left me with a headache that I'd hopefully be able to sleep off. I scribbled out the details of the ghost man who'd attacked me in the Sickbay before flipping through a few of my previous notes and drawings.

This new memory had to have happened just before I'd escaped into the underbrush and collapsed in a creek. My fingers curled around my notebook edge thinking about it. My blood had turned the water red as I'd ripped the wound in my neck open further to hide Adrestus' prized jewel. His Lapis. The small rock that had given him immortality and had then kept me alive for another thousand years.

"Samantha?" Naomi's voice was groggy behind me. "Are you okay?"

I took a slow breath and smiled reassuringly.

"Yeah, sorry. I'm headed to bed."

I flipped the light off and crawled under my covers.

"What were you thinking about just now?" Naomi asked in the dark. "You felt sad."

"The usual. I miss my dad." I burrowed the side of my face into my pillow, facing the wall with my back to Naomi. *Vidar*, a little voice hissed in the back of my head like it always did when I talked about Dad out loud. *His name is Vidar and he's your brother.*

"We'll find him," Naomi insisted.

"I know."

But it had been two months. For all I knew, Adrestus might have already added Vidar to the ranks of family who were dead on my account.

3

Treading Water

In the cafeteria for breakfast, it was clear I wasn't the only one who'd had a poor night of sleep. Wesley trudged in with his roommate, Anthony, close behind. Both had dark circles under their eyes and windswept hair. Naomi and I made room for them at our table and they collapsed into the chairs next to us.

"Again?" Naomi asked as Anthony put his head down on the table, his ears sticking out from a tangle of dark brown locks.

"It wasn't so bad this time." Wesley tried to pat down his hair, but it sprung back into place. Anthony mumbled something unintelligible into the table. "You've been doing well recently. It's probably my fault, stressing you out with that creepy message about the city burning."

"Has Isabelle ever had this problem?" I asked. Anthony looked up, his eyes red with sleep-deprivation.

"No, Isabelle never accidentally created wind tunnels in her sleep." He said his cousin's name as it tasted bad. "Neither did my mom, or my Uncle Lance. Or Grandma, for that matter."

As guilty as it made me feel, part of me was glad to have someone else whose life had been completely uprooted by Adrestus. Sure, the whole team had been affected by the missing students but Anthony had actually been one of the kidnapped kids. Even after we'd brought him back, Adrestus' "blessing" of Apex abilities had made the last few months difficult for him.

"Sometimes it takes a while to get powers under control," Naomi assured him. Anthony's frown deepened.

"Yeah? Figure out how to turn yours off yet?"

"Hey!" Wes bristled and Naomi looked down at her cereal. Anthony's face softened.

"Sorry, that was rude," he mumbled. "I'm frustrated."

"It's alright, I get it." Naomi smiled at Anthony but didn't eat any more of her cereal. "Have you considered telling Bethany yet? It might make you feel better."

Anthony glanced across the cafeteria at the back of his girlfriend's head. She laughed at the cereal bar with a few friends from our year and Anthony's frown deepened.

"It'll freak her out. We've only been together two months. That feels like a three month conversation, doesn't it?"

"You can control it while you're awake, now, right?" I asked. Anthony hadn't run out of class to hide somewhere more suited for hurricane-winds in a few weeks. He shrugged dolefully.

"Mostly. Training's helping, I guess."

While not on the team, Anthony had been granted special training privileges in the Apex facility. Wesley put on a brave smile and tried to look relaxed by leaning back in his chair.

"Isabelle's doing a great job with you, but if you ever want a *real* opponent, I'm—"

Wesley fell back in his chair and slammed against the cafeteria floor. Heads turned and Wesley glowed red as he pulled himself to his feet. I chased after his chair, which skittered a surprising distance across the tiles.

"Whoops," a voice sneered overhead. I straightened up to see Andersen lounging at a nearby booth table. He glared at me from under carefully gelled brunette hair as he leaned against his girlfriend, Jamie. Her arms wrapped around Andersen's waist so that her hands rested in the pockets of his zip-up. "He should probably be more careful."

My hands tightened around the chair back. Wesley's Apex abilities granted him super strength and senses. It wasn't like him to fall out of his seat. Andersen, meanwhile, could manipulate any non-organic material, like stone, synthetic fabric, and cafeteria chairs.

I smiled back, not at Andersen, but at Jamie. She squinted suspiciously. With heavy eye make-up, round cheeks, and a sharp chin, she looked like a haughty raccoon.

"How's the city councilman?" I asked. Her lawyer father was the most outspoken anti-Apex voice on New Delos, but if he were to find out his daughter was dating one of the island's super humans, his disgust would be nothing compared to hers. "Has he outlawed Apex yet? Declared capes to be contraband?"

The corner of Jamie's lip twitched but she mirrored my smile and shrugged.

"Only a matter of time before they're all behind bars," she sang, tightening her arms around Andersen. He scowled a warning at me. "Just wait, once he convinces the other council members, this city is going to change for the better."

"Won't that be nice?" I grinned, looking Andersen dead in the eye. "No more of those nasty Apex."

"Shut up, would you?" Andersen growled. "We all know you're one of the biggest Apex sympathizers out there."

"Or maybe I *am* an Apex," I pointed out, knowing the only thing that would bother him more than having to pretend to hate Apex was bearing the thought of me being the one with super powers.

I spun around on my heel and marched Wesley's chair back to our table. Naomi narrowed her eyes at me.

"You shouldn't get Andersen worked up," she warned. I shrugged as Wesley took his chair. "He'll take it out on you later."

"You saw what he just did! Since when does he need excuses to make us miserable?"

"You're giving him reasons to get more creative."

"You aren't friends with Jamie, anymore." I threw my backpack over my shoulder and gathered my breakfast dishes. "Her and Andersen's happiness isn't your responsibility."

"Other people's happiness has never been my responsibility," she snapped. "Keep that in mind later today when Andersen tries to get even."

The walk to Schrader Hall for class was more awkward than usual after our sharp words with each other and we hunched against the December air that bit at us between the two buildings. Up ahead, Andersen and Jamie walked arm in arm. If I hadn't known what terrible people they both were, they might've looked cute. I fidgeted with an old eraser in my pocket and hoped Naomi was wrong about Andersen wanting to get even.

Fleming was already in the classroom, writing an assignment on the board. I followed Wesley down the aisle of seats to our usual spot in the front row. As I went to sit down, my chair disappeared from under me. Andersen laughed a few rows back.

"He's feeling real original today, isn't he?" I mumbled, holding the chair firmly in place as I climbed into it. "Anyone else sensing a theme?"

I pulled out my World History notebook and slapped it on the table as the bell rang.

"We'll get back at him in gym, just wait," Wesley whispered.

"You plan on drowning him?" Naomi asked. "Thursdays are pool days, not combat practice."

Fleming raised an eyebrow at us as he turned to face the class. My cheeks warmed, but at least it had been Naomi he overheard talking about drowning Andersen and not me.

"Before the lesson, I have some quick announcements," he said, apparently deciding to ignore our talk about murdering our classmate. "First, Paragon Days are being held on the college campus this weekend. The Industry Project finalists from across the city will be presenting Saturday and we need volunteers to help set up and clean up."

Heavy silence fell over the room as we all avoided looking at Fleming in case he decided to take eye-contact as an answer. If I hadn't been staring so intensely at the notebook on my desk, I might not have noticed the spiraled metal binding carefully unwinding itself.

I smacked my hand on top of it, as if that might keep Andersen's powers from working.

"Yes, Samantha?"

I looked up at Fleming and silently cursed Wesley for picking seats in the front row. My pencil wiggled out from under my arm, led by the metal end. Wesley grabbed at it as it made a break for the edge of the desk and scowled at Andersen over his shoulder.

"Wesley and Samantha, thank you for volunteering." Fleming clapped his hands together.

"But Andersen—"

"Great," Fleming continued, glancing at the pencil trying to squirm out of Wesley's hands and putting two and two together. "Andersen is our third volunteer. Anyone else?"

"Mr. Fleming, that's not fair!" The class turned to look at a red-faced Jamie. "Andersen didn't do anything, he's two full rows behind them!"

"Thank you for being our fourth and final volunteer," Fleming clipped, turning back to the board. "You can all meet me after class and I'll let you know where you need to be and when."

I exchanged a glance with Wesley. Being forced onto the clean-up crew for Paragon Days wasn't all that bad, but having to work with Andersen and Jamie?

"I refuse."

"Sorry?" Fleming turned back towards Jamie.

"Paragon Days celebrates the very kind of people I believe should be barred from the island. The Apex are evil and that includes Paragon, whether he saved the city or not."

"Do you even hear yourself?" Heather snarled. The Apex students typically avoided confronting Jamie to skirt suspicion but Heather must have reached her limit. "Was he evil or did he save countless lives? Pick one."

Jamie crossed her arms at Fleming in a silent dare. He shrugged.

"Fine. You don't have to volunteer." A triumphant smile crept across her face before Fleming shattered it. "Instead, detention. You'll serve it helping at Paragon Days."

The class stifled giggles as Jamie blanched, blinking in indignation.

"My father is—"

"A public servant who'd be embarrassed to know his daughter got detention by speaking rudely to her teacher?" Fleming snapped. "The four of you, my desk, after class."

My pencil made another break for freedom, but I let it roll off the table. Fleming deadpanned at Jamie, waiting for her to talk back again. When she didn't, he smiled darkly and finally began the lesson.

"Anyone know what's got Fleming so worked up?" Wesley asked later in fourth period as we treaded water in the center of the training pool. Coach

Reiner with her steel-gray hair stalked along the edge, lecturing us about hypothermia, but we weren't listening.

"He's always worked up," Heather snickered, her long, black hair pushed up into a swim cap like mine.

"Not like this." Naomi mumbled. "I've never seen him give anyone detention before today."

I sank a few inches into the water and exhaled. Bubbles gurgled around me. I had a pretty good idea what was behind Fleming's mood. The others didn't know that New Delos' Greatest Hero, Paragon, had been his older brother, Paul. Of course the island celebration dedicated to him would set our teacher on edge. Jamie calling him evil probably didn't help.

"Is it really detention for Jamie if we're going to be the ones miserable that she's there?" I asked, pushing away thoughts of Fleming's dead brother. "It's more of a punishment for Wesley and me than it is her."

"You really think you dislike us more than we dislike you?"

I sank back into the water as Andersen floated by.

"Drown him, right?" Wesley mumbled at Naomi. "That was your suggestion this morning?"

"No, it definitely wasn't!" Naomi hissed.

Someone cleared their throat and we all glanced at the lanky student taking a seat at the shallow end of the pool. His long, brown hair was knotted in a bun and his legs dangled over the poolside so that his feet and calves were submerged in water. He flashed us a jaunty smile and the other sophomores threw anxious glances at each other.

"In the right conditions, it can take less than ten minutes to become hypothermic!" Reiner's voice bounced off the walls and ceiling. Everly watched from the bleachers, making me feel more anxious than assured. We didn't usually have the nurse supervise our exercises. "Most of you know Sergio."

Reiner gestured towards the boy at the end of the pool. I gave Naomi a confused look.

"He was a senior here last year and is now on the university team," she whispered. Wesley grimaced behind her. If a heavyweight like him was nervous, Sergio was bad news for everyone.

"We'll give Sergio a few minutes to cool down." Reiner grinned, the water temperature already dropping dramatically. "Falling in the water around New Delos in December is enough to kill any one of you, so today we practice being prepared."

"New Delos in September met those conditions," I muttered through clattering teeth. I'd been this cold before, when Andersen had left me floating in the ocean. That had been enough to kill me, though my borrowed immortality brought me back.

"What's the point of cold training if the city's supposed to burn, not freeze?" Remi asked. She treaded water as far from Wesley as possible.

Reiner made a face.

"The message last night could've been graffiti. Plenty of kids like to say things to sound edgy."

"It didn't *look* like someone trying to be edgy," Remi sniffed.

"I heard the perp had a cape," Freddie piped up. "That sounds like a real-deal villain to me."

"If you all want to do fire training so bad, I'll make note of that for next week," Reiner fumed. "For now, who can tell me the first signs of hypothermia?"

"Sh-shivering," Heather chattered. Reiner smiled. Veins of frost ran up Sergio's legs now, grabbing at his knees, but he didn't seem to mind.

"Correct! What else?"

"Vanessa," Everly warned, "you better not be planning on *actually* giving them hypothermia."

"Numbness?" Freddie bobbed near the pool's edge and looked furtively at the ladder.

"Correct again! Don't stop now! I can tell it's starting to hurt. Concentrate through it. What comes next?"

"Vanessa!"

Reiner ignored Everly's warning and looked around at us expectantly.

"Hands off the wall, Chase!"

Olivia kicked off the wall and held her hands up to show she wasn't cheating.

"Coach, what's even the p-point of this exercise?" Remi asked through blue lips.

My teeth clattered against each other and I tried to keep my knees drawn close to my body while staying afloat. It was getting colder faster.

"No amount of training will make you immune to hypothermia, unless you're like Sergio and have an ability that can be honed that way," Reiner explained. "It *is* possible to train how you respond to the cold. The next sign of hypothermia I was looking for was confusion. If you end up in the ocean, you need to find a way out. Staying calm and focused is vital but as your body shuts down, this becomes increasingly difficult. Archer!"

Everest Archer floated effortlessly with his knees drawn up to his chest, bobbing like buoy. He looked uncomfortable, but his ability to change his density had so far allowed him to float on top of the water and retain heat.

"Yes, Coach?"

"Square root of forty nine?"

"Seven?"

"Correct! You get to stay in the water. Miss a question, and you're out. Learn to focus, despite the cold. Last one in the pool doesn't owe me laps next week. And who knows, maybe the water will be on fire since that's what you all apparently want."

We anxiously looked at Everly, but he sat with his lips tightly drawn together.

"As long as one of us outlasts Andersen, I'll be happy." Wesley seemed the least bothered by the icy water. I wondered if his strength-based powers helped him withstand extreme conditions.

"Cripps! Twelve times six!"

"Sixty-six?" Skyler Cripps answered from where he floated with Andersen.

"It's seventy-two! Get out of my pool!"

Skyler scrambled out and let Everly bring him a towel as he sat shaking on the tiles.

"You know," Naomi stared at the warm towel draped over Skyler's shoulders, "I don't mind laps if it means getting out of here."

"You've beat Sergio before," Wesley said. "You'll be fine."

"I only had to outlast his cold for two minutes last time!"

I looked back at the college student sitting at the opposite end of the pool. A thin layer of ice radiated on the water's surface around him. He smiled back, fixing the bun on his head, and seemed to look at me with just his left eye.

"Two minutes?" I asked. "Was your Final Trial against him?"

"Whitlock! Three hundred sixty divided by sixty!"

"Six," Remi answered without hesitation.

"Lewis!"

We paused to see if Andersen passed Reiner's question. When he did, Wesley grumbled.

"Yeah, Sergio was my Final Trial opponent. It was cold, but I m-made it, so here I am." Naomi tried to shrug in the water.

Freddie missed his question and joined Skyler at the bleachers.

"Taylor!" Reiner barked. "No, sorry. I mean Havardson."

Three months on the team and Reiner still called me by Alison's maiden name most of the time. I couldn't blame her. Most people still believed Apex Team alumnus Alison Havardson to be my mother. Most days even I had to remind myself that she wasn't.

"Eleven times nine!"

"Ninety-nine."

"Bradford!"

Naomi frowned, trying to rub heat back into her arms while staying afloat. Behind her, Everest was getting tired keeping his ability activated and was slowly sinking into the water.

"Eighteen plus seventeen?"

Naomi blinked back at Reiner.

"Twenty-five? Wait, no—"

"Out! Hisakawa!"

It couldn't have been longer than a few minutes, but it felt like we'd spent the whole hour in the water by the time Andersen and I were the only two left. Heather hadn't been out long after Naomi, followed by Remi, Olivia, Wesley, and finally Everest. Reiner's questions seemed to be getting more difficult, but maybe I really was just becoming hypothermic.

"Sergio, colder, please!"

The ice layer had crept past the halfway point of the pool and Andersen and I huddled as close to the far wall as we could without Reiner barking at us. Andersen's lips were a faint blue but he kept them pressed together, refusing to so much as let his teeth chatter. The memory of him leaving me in the ocean tugged at me. It had been so dark and cold and I'd been fighting for my life and I'd lost. I tried to swallow both the cold and the panic.

"You need to come back!"

Maybe the cold had started to mess with my head. I could've sworn I'd heard Dad's voice. I couldn't see him, but my heart leapt into my throat.

"Something wrong?" Andersen goaded.

"It's not the first time I've been left floating in freezing waters," I snapped, trying to refocus. Dad wasn't there. He couldn't be.

Andersen glowered, his outline blurring in my vision, and Reiner saved him from having to respond.

"Lewis, what is one half of three fourths?"

The look on his face said I might have him beat, but Reiner clapped exuberantly when he answered, "Th-three eighths."

I could beat Andersen. I needed to beat Andersen.

"Taylor, what is twelve percent of fifty?" I could barely hear Reiner through the wind that had picked up, blowing saltwater spray into my face.

"S-s-s-six." I tried to find the source of the wind. Isabelle or Anthony maybe? Was this a new stage to the challenge?

But something was wrong. The pool water had started to whip around us, becoming choppier and making it harder to stay afloat.

"Is she okay?"

Wesley's voice called out from the stands, but I thrashed in the waves, unable to see him. The edges of the pool were gone, too, replaced by an expanse of icy ocean.

"Samantha?"

I could hear Andersen, but he was gone with the rest of the pool. Searing pain pierced my shoulder and I cried out, salt water filling my mouth.

My legs locked up and the waves pulled at me. Between their crests, I caught a glimpse of someone swimming, striking out against the water. His hair, while pulled into a bun like Sergio's, was much lighter.

"Eydis, hold on!"

Dad...no...Vidar. Vidar was coming.

My fingers clasped around something solid and I struggled to stay afloat with the heavy sword in hand.

Water sucked me downwards, swallowing me. I tried to fight it, but my arms wouldn't move. The pain in my shoulder started to numb. Maybe if I dropped the sword...but...no....it was *my* sword. I'd come all this way to get it. I watched helplessly as the surface got farther, my hair rising up around my face like tendrils in the water.

Arms wrapped around my chest and pulled me upwards and the surface broke across my face.

"I've got you, I've got you!"

"V-V-Vidar!" I coughed. My brother's face came into focus inches from mine. Beads of saltwater rolled off the tawny scruff that he was so proud of despite it not yet being a full beard.

"What are you doing?" he yowled, dragging me back through the waves. "It's freezing out and your shoulder—"

"I got it, Vi," I waved the sword in weak triumph. "Told you I would..."

As the waves buffeted us, I felt something hard and cold against my back.

"Don't tell Father," I mumbled. I couldn't tell if Vidar had laughed or was just spitting water out of his face. "He'll make me throw it back..."

"Sammy!"

"I told you not to push them too far!"

I blinked the salt water from my eyes and flinched when I saw a sea of faces staring down at me.

"What—"

I tried to push myself up off the poolside tiles but Everly put a hand on my shoulder. Relief, confusion, and heartbreak churned inside me. Blankets weighed me down and my head rested on a folded towel.

"That's weird." Reiner consulted her clipboard. "My notes say they had at least another five minutes before loss of consciousness."

"I-I'm fine!" My lips were numb, but I fought my way into a sitting position. Wesley pulled his towel off his shoulders to put around mine.

"You pushed them too far." Everly grabbed my wrist and I felt the familiar rush along my nerves. "You're lucky. It's only a mild case."

"They weren't even in the water for fifteen minutes," Reiner scoffed. "You opened the lesson saying it can take less than ten minutes to get hypothermia!" Everly shot back.

"Did I win?" I asked.

"Tie." Everly said it with a finality that I knew Reiner wouldn't try to override. "Everyone, showers. Now."

Naomi and Wesley hesitated as the others shuffled towards the lockers, but I smiled at them and they turned away. Everly remained at my side.

"What happened?" he asked in a low voice.

"Another memory, probably from the Serum yesterday," I admitted. "I think the water triggered it."

I stared at my toes sticking out from under the blankets. Vidar had looked younger than he had in my other recovered memories of him. Everly frowned and helped me to my feet.

"Add it to the journal after class." He turned towards Reiner, who sat with Sergio at the bleachers. The college student looked up at me curiously from the icicle he was building in his hand. "And *we* are going to talk about changing the lesson plan before the next class gets here."

4

Parasite Days

I stalked out of the locker room, still shivering despite a hot shower. I'd expected residual effects from the Serum, but not whatever *that* had been.

Someone called my name from across the atrium and I looked up to see Andersen scowling alone in a corner.

"What do you want?" My grip on my backpack strap tightened.

Andersen glanced around and shoved his hands in his jacket pockets.

"How'd you do that?" His tone was more suspicious than curious. "There's no way a Beta like you could outlast everyone else."

"Guess I don't mind the cold," I said as if everyone hadn't just watched me pass out.

"Don't think I haven't noticed that you're hiding something."

My stomach knotted but I did my best to look stoic. Even if Andersen was annoyingly perceptive, there was no way he'd figure out I was secretly a viking girl from middle-ages Iceland just because I performed well on a cold water stress test.

"You're one to talk about hiding things when Jamie still doesn't know you're an Apex."

"Leave her out of this." His lip drew back in a sneer but he kept his voice even. "There's something weird going on with you. Forget tolerating cold water, Wesley said you *died*."

I wanted nothing more than to tell him that, actually, I'd died three times, but I held back.

"Wesley just *thought* I was dead."

"Doesn't matter. There's no reason Fleming should have let you back on the team. You lost your trial, end of story. Then you break school rules, nearly get yourself killed *again* and you get to walk back on? I've read the reports. I know Adrestus took your dad and the rest of your family took off."

"Worry about yourself." I wanted to hit him, but I had to keep a straight face.

"Adrestus wanted *you*. Why? What are you to him?"

"Wish I knew."

I turned away. I didn't have to talk to Andersen. I didn't owe him anything.

"Just so you know," he called after me, "if you put any of us in danger by being here, I'll be the first to hand you back to him."

"I thought you wanted to be a hero," I retorted. "But, sure. Take the easy way out. We both know you can't protect anyone."

Picking fights with Andersen was the last thing I should've been doing and I did my best to avoid him for the rest of week, dreading Saturday afternoon. I'd at least have Wesley with me at Paragon Days, but things with him hadn't felt normal since I'd ditched him at the Homecoming dance in October.

When four o'clock rolled around on Saturday and I made my way to the lobby, I found Wesley waiting by the front door, decked out in Paragon's signature colors of red and white.

"Andersen and Jamie already left." He smiled as I came out of the stairwell. "I figure you didn't want to walk with them anyway."

"Not really, no."

An awkward silence fell between us as we set out towards the neighboring campus. I'd been successful in avoiding one-on-one time with him in the past few months, not only because of the Homecoming disaster, but because he was my only friend who knew my big secret. I was afraid one day I might look at him and see him looking back at me like I was a stranger.

The schools were on the east side of the island, facing the mainland. It kept the campuses relatively protected from the bitter winds that rolled in from the open ocean, but I wrapped my jacket around me as tight as I could.

"What did Andersen want after gym the other day?" Wesley broke the silence.

"You couldn't hear him?" Usually Wesley's super-hearing let him eavesdrop.

"I try not to listen in on conversations I'm not a part of, but I did hear him mention me." He fidgeted with the phone in his hands.

"He's suspicious," I grunted. "He knows I'm not who I say I am."

"You *are* Samantha, though. That's all that matters."

"You know what I mean." My stomach twisted. What if Wesley was wrong? Samantha didn't technically exist, so how could I be her? "If Andersen is wondering, then others are, too. There's no way Naomi doesn't know something's up."

Wesley furrowed his brow in response and the high school campus passed behind us as we crossed into the University. There were more buildings here, interspersed with bright, green lawns. On a usual

December Saturday, it would have been barren, but today red and white banners hung between balloon arches and students milled about in Paragon's colors.

Booths lined the main walkway where vendors advertised their Paragon-themed swag and snacks. Steam rose from a table boasting hot apple cider from behind a throng of shivering people.

"Why isn't Paragon Days in the summer, when it's about forty degrees warmer?" I mumbled.

"It's the anniversary of when Paragon saved the city from sinking. Can't really change the date."

"That doesn't mean we have to celebrate on the exact day! Wasn't he doing cool things and saving people year round?"

I jumped as a hand grabbed my shoulder but when I spun around, it was only Fleming. The hot cider in his hands steamed up his glasses, making his expression that much harder to read.

"You're supposed to be in the humanities building already."

"You're not there yet, either," I pointed out. Fleming's frown deepened and he took a long draw of his cider.

"Then you better hurry."

Wesley grabbed my arm and drew me away from Fleming, pushing through the crowds of shivering festival-goers.

"I know he's your guardian now, but you should be careful how you talk to Fleming when he's in a mood."

"If he wants to be in charge of me, then he gets to be talked to the same way I'd talk to my real parents. And by real parents, I mean my parents who aren't actually my real parents."

My smirk died on my face as we entered the humanities building. The exposed brick stretched to the ceiling three floors overhead and dying daylight poured in through massive windows to glitter off a colossal hanging glass sculpture. My gaze lingered on the third floor walkway. I'd been up there once before, to see my dad's office after it had been ransacked.

Andersen and Jamie fought in the lobby, their shouts echoing off the vaulted ceiling. While Andersen wore a red and white school shirt, Jamie donned a navy crewneck that read, "Parasite Days". My stomach clenched. Fleming was already in a bad mood and a shirt calling his dead brother a parasite wasn't going to help.

Jamie waved a navy cloth in Andersen's face.

"I had it made for you!"

"Then you should have given it to me back at school! I'm already wearing this."

"Those are Paragon's colors!"

"They're school colors!"

"Which are based on Paragon!"

"Why do you even go here if you hate the colors so much?"

"I won't have to worry about it after my father makes Apex illegal!"

They fell silent when Andersen saw us approaching. He snatched the shirt from Jamie.

"I'll put it on if I have time," he growled.

She pursed her lips, not looking entirely satisfied but happy he took the shirt all the same.

"Isn't Fleming supposed to be here?" she snapped as we joined them. "The sooner he gets here, the sooner I'm out."

"The presentations don't hinge on Fleming's schedule," Wesley said dryly. Jamie glared at him and collapsed into a lobby armchair right as Fleming came into the building behind us.

"Mr. Fleming!" Jamie leapt to her feet and pulled at the edges of her crewneck. "How do you like my shirt?"

Fleming gave her a withering stare.

"There's a trailer behind the building with the tables and decorations. It needs to be unloaded. Samantha, I need your help with something else."

I looked back at Wesley, not sure which of us was worse off as he followed Andersen and Jamie to the back door.

A cover band started up outside as Fleming led the way to the lecture hall, the first chords of the electric guitar permeating the building. A group of college students studying around a table looked up in annoyance.

Fleming stepped into the room at the end of the hall and flicked the lights on to reveal the amphitheater-style space.

He cleared his throat as he strode down the steps to the front of the room and I followed a few paces behind.

"Do you have things at Alison and Vic's house?" His tone was curt and formal and he kept his eyes on the computer's load screen.

I looked at the carpet thinking about the bedroom Alison and Vic had never gotten around to setting up for me. I'd only been awake for a few days before we moved to New Delos and I didn't remember owning anything that wasn't already in my dorm.

"I'm not sure. Is that important right now?"

"I'm trying to get my place ready for winter break."

It took me a moment to understand what he was saying.

"I can stay in the dorms. I don't mind." I blustered. I knew chances of finding Dad in the next couple weeks and spending the break in the family townhouse were slim to none, but I'd take a lonely holiday in the dorms over an awkward one with Fleming any day.

"The dorms aren't open over the break." Fleming looked just as uncomfortable as I felt. I didn't even know if he had family. He tore his eyes from the computer, and for the first time that week, he didn't look annoyed or angry. Just a little sad maybe. "Sometimes team members aren't able to return home. They stay with Nurse Everly or myself, usually depending on if they prefer Hanukkah or Christmas. Since I'm your guardian, my place *is* your legal home now. We can set up the guest room for you."

I shuffled my feet, ignoring the warmth in my cheeks. Fleming hadn't asked for this anymore than I had, but here we were.

"I don't think I have anything at the townhouse. All of my stuff is in the dorm room." I made a note to ask Wesley and Naomi if they knew who usually stayed behind for break. Being stuck with Fleming for two weeks would be one thing, but if I got stuck with Fleming *and* someone on the team who didn't like me, I wasn't sure how I'd survive.

The hall door swung open and Wesley came in carrying two folded tables under each arm.

"Maybe try being a little more discreet?" Fleming hissed as I went to unburden Wesley. I buckled under the weight of just one table.

"I didn't want to make more than one trip."

"Just hope Jamie doesn't figure out how heavy these are," I wheezed, wrestling the table to the ground at the front of the room.

Andersen and Jamie decorated the main lobby and set up signage outside while Wesley and I tackled the lecture hall. We bent over a broken table together, working to fix a latch with ample amounts of packaging tape when a faint memory wiggled at the back of my head.

"What're the Apex Games?" I asked. "Fleming said something about it the other day."

"Just a big show-off festival at the end of the semester," Wesley snorted.

"Kind of like the Night Game?"

"The Night Game is a very serious and important training exercise," Wesley teased. "The Apex Games are actually games but the Night Game is more fun, if you ask me."

"Why?" I shook my hand, trying to break free of a long strand of tape stuck to my wrist. "A big show-off festival sounds like your kinda thing."

"It's for the parents, mostly, and I don't care about showing off to them. The college team competes, too, so we never stand a chance at winning, or even placing top three for that matter."

Wesley secured the last piece of tape and we flipped the table back onto its legs to test it. It wobbled, but remained standing.

"Oh, look," a voice drawled behind us. A man in a suit stood in the doorway sipping from his signature oversized travel mug. "If it isn't the girl who should've been expelled by now."

"A bit late for coffee, isn't it?" I snarled.

There was no point arguing with Trev Baker. As the sole member of the Apex Team Council who'd voted to expel me in November, any attempt to defend myself to him would be futile.

"You better not be tormenting my students, Trev." Fleming shouldered past Trev Baker, ladened with banners and streamers.

"He wasn't," I chirped. "It's just his bosses that torment children."

Fleming gave me a warning glare as Mr. Baker's cheeks reddened. Anyone who worked for Schrader Industries worked for Adrian Schrader and since Adrian Schrader secretly worked for Adrestus, Trev Baker was essentially the employee of the man we'd been fighting for the last several months.

Wesley took the banners from Fleming and tried to steer me across the room.

"Why is he here?" I hissed at Wesley as he held the banner up against the wall.

"He's a presentation judge, I think. I heard from Heather that Fleming wouldn't let Schrader or Cunningham attend so they figured Trev Baker was a good compromise."

"Why have a judge from Schrader Industries at all if they're run by Adrestus?"

"They're sponsoring the scholarship prize, and as far they're concerned, Adrestus isn't real and he's definitely not their museum curator." Wesley cast a nervous glance at the adults.

"But he is!" I slammed the stapler into the wall, pretending it was Dr. Cunningham's face. *Adrestus'* face.

"No leads yet on the message your students found?" Mr. Baker asked Fleming.

"As soon as we know anything, the Council will know, too."

"Oh, geez," I said loudly to Wesley. "Who do you suppose is threatening the city? Can't possibly be the guy who was kidnapping kids and then stabbed me."

Wesley tittered awkwardly, as if unsure if he should laugh or not.

"We've all heard your outlandish theory about Dr. Cunningham," Trev sneered. "He's been a respected member of New Delos since before you were born."

"Somehow I doubt that." I laughed sardonically.

"That's enough." Fleming stepped between us, clearly fearing I'd be dumb enough to let slip I was a thousand years old for the sake of an ironic joke.

"Cunningham is a good man who's been through a lot in the last few months." Trev's voice carried a warning lilt. "The last thing he needs is some high school brat spreading lies about him."

"You know I'm telling the truth, you just don't care enough to turn against the guy that signs your paychecks!" I fumed.

"Put down the stapler," Wes whispered in my ear. I hadn't realized I was brandishing it in front of me like a weapon.

Anger seared inside me and my hands trembled. Trev Baker was either an idiot or *knowingly* working for the guy who had my father captive. Either way, he was unfit to sit on the Apex Council.

"Stay where you are." I jumped at the sound of my own voice resounding in my head. I touched a hand to my throat, as if to verify I hadn't actually said anything out loud.

Trev's outline blurred to be replaced by that of a much younger man. His beard receded and his hair became dark, wild, and curly. His eyes morphed from brown to stark blue. A bronze sword hung at his side.

Trev Baker was gone. A young Adrestus stood in his place.

5

Old Friends

The stapler slipped from my hand. Another memory. The lecture hall flickered from view. Rocks slick with tidal water slipped underfoot. Adrestus, looking no older than sixteen, stood against the gray backdrop of an icy fjord. A wooden sailing ship drifted out in the water. Wesley grabbed my shoulder, anchoring me back in reality.

"We're done," Fleming said. "Samantha and Wesley, go enjoy the festival. I'll see you for clean up."

"I don't want to hurt you. I just want to talk to the chief of your village," the phantom-Adrestus said. I pushed him away.

I left the banner half hanging on the wall and refused to look at Trev as I left. Wesley scrambled to follow. I'd told the council Dr. Cunningham was Adrestus, but it was my word against his and he had Adrian Schrader along with all the money he gave the Apex teams on his side.

"The chief isn't here, is he?" Adrestus' voice echoed in my head as I burst into the hall. I took several strides before squeezing my eyes shut and pressing my forehead against a wall.

"No, h-he—" Eydis stammered.

"Why else would they send a girl like you? And an injured one at that?"

"Shut up!" I growled through gritted teeth.

"I didn't say anything."

I opened my eyes to look at Wesley. His green eyes were wide behind his glasses.

"Sorry, not you." I leaned back against the wall.

"Fleming said we can leave. Sammy, I'm—"

"Once he's gone, I'll be fine. We said we'd help clean up so we will."

Wesley leaned against the wall next to me and I wished he'd stop staring.

"I just want to make sure—"

"That cider looked really good outside." I cut him off. "Forget Trev Baker. It's Jamie we should worry about. She's gonna freak when she finds out Fleming is letting us take a break."

Wesley pulled his knit cap over his messy hair and pushed off the wall to lead the way to the side exit. I wanted to pretend everything was okay, that I wasn't bothered, but it was hard. I was still shaking with indignation and it took every bit of focus to keep Young Adrestus and Eydis' voices out of my head.

"There's usually a parade, too," Wesley said as we walked out to a walkway lined with propane heaters. They glowed in the dark, casting dark orange shadows across the faces in the crowd. "They canceled it this year, with all the anti-Apex protests and kidnappings."

"I'm surprised Jamie's the only person I've seen protesting. With a whole celebration for Paragon, I thought there'd be more."

"That's why it's on the university campus. Private property. I can hear protesters a few blocks away from the school, but they're being held back."

I looked the direction Wesley had nodded, as if I might see the protesters beyond the brick school buildings.

"They weren't allowed on the pier at the Welcome Back Festival, either," I muttered but Wesley shook his head.

"I can point to six different members of the university team from here." Wesley tilted his head to listen. "Plus, two of ours."

"Two of ours?" I asked, digging money out of my pocket as we approached the cider booth. "Who? Where?"

"I can hear Justin and Jen talking on the humanities building roof. I guess Fleming felt like having some captains around, just in case."

I traded a few dollars for a warm cup of cider and wrapped my fingers around the cup to absorb as much heat into them as possible. The crowd jostled us and we stepped off to the side, shivering under one of the propane heaters.

"Somehow having that many team members ready to go makes me more uneasy."

"It's just a precaution." He bit his lip and glanced around. "Can I ask you something kind of awkward?"

I laughed nervously. Awkward with Wes could mean anything.

"It's about Remi."

My hesitant smile froze on my face and I worked overtime to try to make it look natural. However, Wesley grimaced, so it couldn't have been as convincing of a smile as I'd hoped.

"Sorry," I mumbled. "I just don't know Remi very well."

Even though Wesley's ex-girlfriend was one of two other team members assigned extra training after having not passed the entrance trials, I had done very little to get to know her. They hadn't dated while I'd known Wesley but something about their friendship made me uneasy in a way I wasn't used to. One day, they'd be perfectly happy, the next, they'd be endlessly bickering.

Wesley stepped back onto the path and I followed him as we passed by vendor booths, looking over what they were selling. My mouth watered at the smell of deep-fried treats.

"It's because you don't know Remi as well as everyone else that I want your opinion." He hesitated at a booth selling funnel cakes before digging a few crumpled dollars out of his pocket and trading them for a deep fried dessert. "Is it weird to keep dating your ex?"

"What?" I sputtered, coughing up hot cider. "You're dating Remi, again?"

"No!" he said quickly, blushing wildly under his knit cap. We stepped back off the path to huddle under a new heat lamp while Wesley unwrapped his funnel cake. "I mean, not yet."

"Not yet?" I parroted. I understood their friendship even less than I'd realized. They barely seemed compatible as acquaintances, let alone boyfriend and girlfriend.

"I was considering asking her out again. I know it hasn't worked out in the past but who knows. Things might be different now that we're both on the team."

"So *date her*."

I had to consciously work to keep from making a face. I didn't need to be *with* Wesley to be friends with him, but that meant he was free to be with anyone he wanted. As much as I wished I could, I couldn't run a monopoly on who Wes spent time with and in what way.

"Everyone else will be waiting for us to break up." He picked at his funnel cake and I shied closer to the heat lamp. "It's not easy when no one expects you to make it."

I raised an eyebrow and took a long sip from my cider, glowering at him from over the rim of the lid.

"Oh, no," I said dryly. "I wonder what that must feel like."

"Right, sorry," Wesley mumbled. "But you get it then. It's not exactly the same as trying to get on the team, but it feels like everyone is watching and secretly hoping for the fall out."

I swished the cider in my cup, feeling it swirl and shift.

"I won't be secretly hoping for a fall out." I broke a smile, looking up at Wesley. "If being with Remi makes you happy, you should be with Remi."

I'd thought my words might help put him at ease, even though I'd rarely seen him happy with Remi around, but his brow knit tighter.

"That's just part of it."

"You like her, right?" I wanted to be done talking about Remi. I could force myself to be happy for Wesley, but it was torture having to dissect the pros and cons of them getting back together. "That's all that matters."

"Right, but I like—" He cut himself off and gave his funnel cake a quizzical look. "Yeah. You're right."

We meandered over towards the stage where another local band had started their set. We stood at a high table and I wrapped my hands around my cider cup.

"Are we good?"

My grip around the cup tightened at Wesley's question.

"Yeah, of course." I didn't look at him. "*Are we good*" had been the question burning underneath every single one of our interactions since October.

"I know we're good, but are we *good*?"

I laughed and gave him a funny look, pretending not to know what he meant. I hated that he'd noticed how awkward it was between us lately, too.

"When you had your concussion was the most relaxed you've been around me in months," he said. I took a long sip of cider to keep from having to respond. "Is it because I know?"

"No," I said too quickly, my careful composure slipping. "I mean, maybe. I don't know. It's a lot of things."

"Is it anything I can fix?"

Classic Wesley, thinking he can fix anything and save the day.

"We're fine. Nothing for you to fix." I forced the world's most uncomfortable smile. "Look, I'm relaxed. I'm having fun. I have a warm drink and I'm listening to a very mediocre band with one of my best friends. We're *good.*"

Wesley's shoulders sagged in relief and he smiled back.

"One of your best friends? I don't know if I'm ready for that kind of commitment, but if it means I can steal some of your cider, I might be willing to take on the title."

I laughed, more naturally this time, and pushed the cup towards him. Huddling under the propane heater and sharing a cider, I was happy to pretend everything between us was just the way it had been before I'd died.

Wesley headed to the lecture hall a few minutes before the presentations were due to be finished, but I told him I'd catch up in a little bit. Instead, I climbed up to the humanities building third floor, marveling at the massive glass sculpture hanging from the ceiling.

Dad's office was half way down the walkway. I would've liked to sit at his desk, maybe find something from the short time we'd all been a family, but I knew the door was probably locked. At least the crime scene tape had been removed from his doorway. I reached to try the door handle, but hesitated when I heard the raised voices in the office next to his.

"You know where she is!" a young woman cried. "Why won't you tell me?"

"Leave it, alright? You're better off forgetting my daughter."

Guilt and fury stirred in my stomach at the sound of Mr. Hendricks' voice. Winnie's father was far from my favorite person, but the last time

I'd seen his daughters, they'd been locked in battle against each other. I couldn't help but to feel at least partially responsible for their falling out.

I was about to retreat back down the hall to the stairs when a man with mousy, thinning hair stepped out of the office, followed by a student with long, dark tresses under a Paragon Days knit cap. Mr. Hendricks' eyes widened when he saw me.

"You," he said. I gulped.

"So you're just disappearing again?" the girl demanded, angry tears welling in her eyes. "You have her somewhere, don't you? Is it because she quit the team?"

Mr. Hendricks looked from me to the young woman.

"Brooke, if Amanda wanted you to hear from her, you would have."

"She wouldn't ghost her own girlfriend!" Brooke crossed her arms and Mr. Hendricks curled his lip in distaste.

"Then I guess you aren't her girlfriend, anymore." His gaze flickered past Brooke and landed on me. With a final proclamation that if Mr. Hendricks wouldn't help her, she'd find Amanda herself, Brooke shouldered past him, stomping down the hall, and leaving me alone with Winnie's father.

"Why are you lying to her?" I asked. "You don't know where Amanda is."

He eyed me and I felt like he was sizing me up.

"She's with her sister. She'll be fine."

Fleming or Dr. Weaver must've been in contact with him, then, keeping him updated, which meant they'd also been in contact with my fake mother. I tried to shove away the sudden resentment that gurgled in my stomach.

"I thought you were supposed to be off-island watching Alison and Avery."

"I'm in charge of four classes. I like to come in and make sure my teaching assistants aren't ruining the next generation of linguistic students." A festive explosion outside sent flashes of color bouncing through the windows and off the glass ceiling piece, refracting across the walkway. The fireworks for Paragon meant the night was almost over. "Besides, I was close with Paragon. I like visiting to celebrate him."

Blue light from the fireworks display washed over Mr. Hendricks' face.

"You mean Paul."

His eyes narrowed at the mention of Fleming's brother.

"Yes. Paul. He told you, then."

I shrugged.

"Fleming keeps a picture of you all behind his desk. It wasn't hard to figure out."

Mr. Hendricks rolled his eyes, showing off where his daughters had learned the skill.

"He *wants* people to figure it out. Makes him feel more important than he is," he scoffed. Something like pity mixed with the contempt on his face. "I heard about your trial, by the way, and while I'm sure you gave it your all, it just further proves what Alex Fleming has already demonstrated to the rest of us: Betas don't belong on the Apex Team."

The fury incited by his words curdled with immediate vindication and I grinned sweetly as Mr. Hendricks turned away to lock his office door.

"It's funny you say that," I goaded, "since I'm on the team anyway."

He paused with his keys over his door handle. In the light of the fireworks, the color left his face.

"You're *what?*"

"On the team." I crossed my arms and smirked, daring him to tell me I wasn't.

His cheeks flared red.

"Then it's no wonder my daughters haven't been saved with Alex filling the roster with *flunkies*."

"Your daughters haven't been saved because *you* drove Winnie to follow a madman in his weird conquest!" I retorted. "Or maybe you didn't hear about that? You were such a bad dad that Winnie's been actively trying to get us all killed."

"Winnie's always been eccentric. Amanda will bring her back to us. Lord knows Alex is useless to help, especially letting strays like you on the team."

"Amanda almost *killed* her. You're lucky Vidar was there to protect her. It would've been your fault if he hadn't been." I couldn't help the ice in my voice.

"*My fault?*" His cold composure morphed into fury, maybe from worry over his daughters but more likely because I had the audacity to call him out.

He stepped forward to tower over me but it had been a while since I'd been afraid of anyone like Mr. Hendricks. His eyebrows smoldered, thin streams of smoke rising off of them, and he grabbed the front of my shirt to pull me close.

"Tell me they're okay."

I pulled the collar of my shirt back, glaring, letting him stew in his worry for a moment longer before finally responding.

"They weren't *dead* last I saw, but that was two months ago."

"Vidar," Mr. Hendricks suddenly said. "You said Vidar. You figured it out."

"Most of it." The fact that Mr. Hendricks of all people had known about my secret past-life before me stung, but I shoved my bitterness away as he studied me with regained composure.

He leaned back against his door frame, calming down, though his eyebrows continued to smoke. I kept my hands in fists at my side in case he tried to grab me again, but he retreated into his office. He rifled through his desk before returning to hand me a black cylinder that fit nicely in my hand.

"If Alex is going to insist on letting Betas on the team even after they fail the trials, might as well give you this. Alison used it when she was on the team. Had to get a permit for it and everything."

I clicked a button on the side of the cylinder and electricity sparked on the end.

"A taser?" It was a weirdly paternal gift, even if his reason for giving it to me was a bit backhanded. "I don't need this."

I held it out for him to take back but he ignored me and went to lock his office door.

"You failed the trial. You couldn't defend yourself for two minutes, so how are you supposed to save my kids? You need all the help you can get." A distant look came over him. "I was supposed to give it to Winnie on move-in day and forgot. Now it's collecting dust."

The fireworks crescendoed into a final string of explosions, flashes washed across the walkway, and the sky crackled. We both paused to watch the grand finale light up the sky outside the large windows before it died, leaving us in dark silence.

"You shouldn't be here. It's dangerous with Adrestus at large," Mr. Hendricks finally said. "Let me take you back to school. Alison would worry otherwise."

"No." I recoiled. "I'm supposed to help Fleming clean up downstairs."

"Alex is here?" Mr. Hendricks' face darkened. "Good. I'm gonna kill him."

6

Hephestae

I had to go down the stairs two at a time to keep up with Mr. Hendricks. The main lobby was full of people exiting the lecture hall. I saw Heather walking out holding a large First Place plaque but I didn't have the time to congratulate her.

Mr. Hendricks probably didn't want to *actually* kill Fleming but their interactions I'd seen were nothing short of volatile. Besides, if he yelled at him in front of Jamie, it could be game over for Apex Team.

"Alex!" Mr. Hendricks roared as he marched into the lecture hall. Jamie and Andersen pulled banners from the wall next to the door and Mr. Hendricks faltered at the sight of them. Jamie must've convinced Andersen to wear the sweater she'd made him because now they both donned "Parasite Days" swag.

"Roy, what're you—"

But before Fleming had a chance to gather his bearings, Mr. Hendricks descended on Jamie and Andersen.

"What's this crap?" He poked Andersen square in the chest and Andersen stuck his chin out in defiance.

"It's *truth.*" Jamie crossed her arms.

Mr. Hendricks rounded on Fleming.

"I know you had your differences but the fact that you, of all people, would allow your students to wear such blasphemous—"

"Why are you here? Is Alison—"

"What kind of show do you think you're running here? You trying to make sure I never see my daughters again?" Mr. Hendricks got in Fleming's face but Fleming continued to look passive. He glanced at me in the doorway and then at Jamie.

"Maybe we should go back to my office," he said. "I'd hate to get in the way of clean-up."

Mr. Hendricks seethed but even he wasn't brash enough to endanger the secret of the Apex Team. Fleming told us to load the tables back into the trailer and led Mr. Hendricks into the hall.

"Wasn't that Winnie's dad?" Jamie asked. "No wonder she and her sister turned out insane."

"Amanda's not insane," I snapped, helping Wesley with the folding tables up front.

"No, she's just an unhinged Apex who almost killed a museum curator."

"She didn't—"

"Drop it," Wesley whispered. "Jamie likes getting a rise out of people. It's what makes her and Andersen so compatible."

The table latch snapped on its own accord and we both jerked our hands out of the way as the metal legs collapsed. Andersen snorted behind us.

I bristled but Wesley shook his head.

"Ignore it."

"He could've broken our fingers!"

The lecture hall lights flickered and I glanced towards the light switch. I didn't care what Wesley said. Andersen needed to cool it.

"Andersen, cut it out!" I glared at Andersen pretending to be busy taking down a banner.

"How about you leave him alone?" Jamie shot back. "We're nowhere near the lights."

"If only she knew," Wesley mumbled and I stifled a laugh just before the lights shut off completely.

"Andersen!" Wesley and I both snapped.

"It wasn't me!"

My eyes strained against the dark. Without the green glow of the exit sign over the door, it would've been impossible to see at all. Jamie looked at the ceiling and waved her arms in a wide arc over her head.

"Is it on a motion sensor?" she asked, jumping up and down.

"Seriously, turn them back on!" I looked for Andersen in the dark.

His silhouette threw up his arms in defense.

"I'm not the one who turned them off!"

"Sammy." Wesley grabbed my shoulder and pointed towards the door.

An orange glow flickered in the hallway, casting dancing shadows through the rectangular door window. It steadily grew stronger, flickering brighter and brighter.

In the dim light, Wes gulped.

"Get back!" I shouted.

Andersen at least had the sense to listen. He grabbed his girlfriend's hand and pulled her to the front of the room, joining us behind the collapsed tables. The orange glow outside danced off Jamie's wide eyes as they crouched next to us.

"It looks like fire," she said. "Why aren't the alarms going off?"

"If the whole building has lost power, they might not work anymore." Andersen fidgeted next to me. Despite his usual confidence, even in the face of danger, as long as Jamie was around, he wouldn't be able to use his powers to protect them. Neither would Wesley.

"Then what are we doing hiding from a fire?" Jamie snarled. She stood but Andersen and Wesley pulled her back down as the door handle turned.

Shifting red-orange light danced into the lecture hall and my stomach dropped at the sight of the familiar fiery head. The hall blazed behind her, pushing Hephestae's outline forward, her cape billowing in the heat of the flames.

Jamie leapt over the collapsed table and lunged for the fire alarm on the wall as Hephestae barreled down the steps in a fiery tornado.

"They don't work!" Wesley yelled when Jamie pulled on the fire alarm lever. She shrieked as Hephestae bore down on her but instead of cowering, she grabbed a nearby chair and swung it at her assailant just as Andersen jumped to her defense.

The metal chair knocked him sideways to the floor and Jamie stumbled backwards as Hephestae continued her advance, leaping over Andersen.

Wesley tackled Hephestae into the wall.

"Get her out of here!" Wesley shouted as his shirt smoldered in his struggle to keep Hephestae pinned. I didn't have time to worry about his safety. I grabbed Jamie by the wrist and pulled her past the fight.

"We've gotta go!"

"But Andersen! I didn't mean to—"

"He'll be fine!" I half-dragged her up the steps to the door and she reached out behind us for Andersen.

Flames licked the corridor walls and the hall was full of smoke. We dropped to the ground in search of breathable air. I pulled the neck of my shirt up over my mouth and nose but it didn't help much.

"You need to keep moving!" I coughed, scrambling away from the flames that had engulfed the wall next to us. Jamie paused to look back into the lecture hall.

"My boyfriend is still in there!"

"And so is my friend!"

I grabbed Jamie by the ankle as she clawed along the tiles to get back into the lecture hall. I took as deep a breath as I could and tucked Jamie's legs under my arm to drag her down the hall towards the main lobby.

The hall flickered and morphed, threatening to change from a school building to a burning viking village. I gritted my teeth under my shirt collar. I'd already recovered the memory of my burning home. I didn't need to be reminded of it.

I focused on the tiled floor to stay in the present but over the roaring whispers and crackles of the flames, I could hear Eydis' screams and they tore at my throat.

Jamie kicked at me, but I tightened my hold on her, not letting go until we were clear of the smoke in the center of the lobby. The flames couldn't have been set too long ago since the power had only been out for a few minutes. Hopefully it was contained to the hall we'd just come out of.

"You need to get out of here," I commanded as Jamie gathered herself. The fire was spreading unnaturally fast, probably egged on by Hephestae's powers.

"Believe me now?" Jamie coughed. "Apex are *evil*."

"Shut up and leave, won't you?" I stared at the dark smoke, waiting for Wes to come running out.

What was taking him so long? And where was Andersen for that matter? If Jamie left, I could run back and help, but as long as she was here, she was sure to follow me.

"Ratcliffe..."

We both looked up at the sound of the rasping voice. Hephestae stood on the second floor walkway, her fire-hair lapping at the third floor. Despite the flames, I went cold. If she was here, what had happened to Wesley?

"Who do you work for?" I demanded, stepping in front of Jamie. I squinted at the woman, trying to see through the swirling smoke and the mask covering most of her face.

"I *told* you," Jamie whimpered behind me. "I told *all* of you about Apex and *you didn't listen!*"

"Is it Adrestus?" I asked when Hephestae continued to stare. "Because you can tell him we're done being kidnapped!"

"Not kidnap." Hephestae's voice made the hair on the back of my arms stand on end and I flexed my hands, preparing for a fight. "Kill... Ratcliffe."

Hephestae launched over the railing, hurtling towards the first floor like a comet. Jamie shrieked and I shouted for her to run. I kept my eyes on Hephestae but was relieved to hear the slap of Jamie's shoes on tile as she fled.

I pivoted to keep myself between Hephestae and her target. She lunged and I cocked a fist, ready to strike, bracing for the heat that was sure to lap at my skin when I did.

"Stop!" A heartbroken wail stopped me mid-punch and a fiery fist struck my stomach. I doubled over and the voice cried out, "don't hurt her!"

Hephestae swung again but this time, I threw up an arm to block it. My forearm smarted where she hit me and my sweater smoldered, but she'd left her abdomen unprotected in her attack. If she hadn't given me a severe concussion the other day, I might have felt bad as my foot connected with her navel.

"I said don't hurt her!" Brooke pushed me out of the way, dark hair flying, and she knelt over Hephestae where she landed on the floor.

The flames on her head died as the air was knocked out of her. She splayed out on the tiles, winded, and in the half-second it took her to regain her bearings, I got a good look at her bald head, hair burnt away, and her wide, brown eyes over her mask.

My heart broke. Amanda Hendricks stared up at me.

"It's me!" Brooke tore at the mask on Amanda's face, peeling it away to reveal a blank, faraway look under pupils wide with fear. "Amanda, look at me!"

"Amanda," I said dumbly. "But, why?"

"It's Hephestae now!" She leapt to her feet, throwing Brooke off of her, and I braced to block her a second time. However, instead of a fist, I was met with an open palm. She spun me behind her before making a sprint for the side hall after Jamie.

"No!"

As I chased after her, Brooke right behind me, I found the black cylinder in my back pocket. I tucked my face to protect it from the fire on Amanda's head and jammed the end of the taser against her neck as I switched it on.

She convulsed and fell to the ground, her flames sputtering out once more. I fell against the wall, panting as I waited for her to recover and come at me. However, she rolled onto her hands and knees, coughing in Brooke's arms. When she looked at me over her girlfriend's shoulder, something had changed.

"Samantha!" she sobbed. Her face contorted with fear and pain but, unlike the blank expression she'd held before, it was at least her own. "Help me!"

Her hands grabbed at the back of her bare neck, clawing at something I couldn't see.

"It's okay." Brooke's cheeks were slick with tears as she tried to grab Amanda's hands. Amanda shook her head and pushed her away.

"You need to leave before she comes back." She lifted a hand towards Brooke's face before drawing it away. "Please."

"But I've been looking for you!" Brooke cried. "You *left*! I thought you were *dead!*"

Amanda's shoulders shook.

"I'll find you, okay? Trust me. You need to leave. *Please.*"

"Amanda, I—"

"*Trust me.*" Amanda started into Brooke's eyes with a look that held all the ferocity and love of her promise. "I'll find you, but they'll make me hurt you if you stay. I love you, and you need to trust me."

A beam creaked overhead as fire ate away at its supports. Brooke's neck tensed as she swallowed but nodded. With a final squeeze of Amanda's hands, she stood up and ran out of the burning building.

"Amanda," I hissed. "What's going on? Why are you trying to kill Jamie? Who sent you?"

"It's them, Sammy." She continued to grab at the back of her neck. "It's the woman with the white hair."

Adrestus' right-hand woman had the power to control anyone she touched. If she'd found a way to use her powers at a distance, we were all in very big trouble.

I shivered. Being under her control was terrifying, even in my limited experience with it.

"She's going to come back. I can feel her rebooting," Amanda said. "They're going to—ugh!"

She convulsed again and grabbed her head. I shook her shoulders.

"Don't let them! Fight it! They're going to what?"

Amanda opened her eyes, inches from mine. They welled with tears that spilled over.

"New Delos...they want me to...ah!" She shook her head. "You have to save the city."

"Save it from what?" I demanded. "Amanda, come on, you're stronger than her!"

"You need to shock me again," she begged through gritted teeth. "It might buy me more time. They want to burn...everything..."

I hesitated with the taser in my hand.

"What about Brooke," I said, desperately trying to find something that might keep Amanda herself. "You heard her. She's been looking for you."

Amanda's face broke in anguish.

"Shock...me..." She reached for the taser, but as she took it, the blank expression returned. Her head erupted in new flames and she threw the taser aside, its plastic body melted by her heat.

Amanda's hand shot up to grab my wrist and my skin blistered where she touched me. I cried out in pain and recoiled as she stood, looming over me, completely aflame.

"What did Amanda say to you?" she rasped. "Tell me!"

Fire rained down and I rolled away, narrowly missing the onslaught. The smell of burnt hair mixed with the smoke that continued to fill the room.

Violent coughing echoed from down the hall and my stomach clenched as Amanda turned to face the silhouettes that fought their way through the smoke. Jamie emerged, supporting Andersen with her "Parasite Days" crewneck pulled over her mouth and nose.

"Watch out!"

My warning from where I watched helplessly on the floor was too late. Amanda had already sent a column of flame shooting up the wall and tearing at the ceiling tiles. A mighty splintering sound ripped through the lobby and I watched in horror as Jamie and Andersen disappeared under the collapsing ceiling.

7

Turbulence

Amanda was gone by the time I made it to the rubble heap. Andersen and Jamie may have been some of my least favorite people, but no one deserved to be crushed to death. I clawed at brick, plaster, and metal as I tried to get to where they'd gone down, but the building was still filling with smoke. My lungs burned, my eyes stung, and my head was getting lighter with each movement.

My vision blurred and I saw a neat row of bodies lying in the ash.

"No, no, no!" I paused my digging to press my hands against my eyes. The bodies weren't real. It was more scraps of memories bubbling up at the most inconvenient time *again*.

"Sammy!" Wesley appeared on the other side of the cave-in and bricks scattered as he clambered over the rubble. "Are you hurt? What happened?"

He'd died the remnants of his burnt shirt hung around his face, possibly for what little protection it offered from the smoke but maybe for anonymity's sake as well as he led several college students to safety. Soot mixed with sweat on his exposed chest and pink and red burns peeked out from under the mixture.

"Andersen and Jamie—" I choked.

Wesley balked at the rubble as the students behind him sprinted for the door.

"No!" He threw bricks to the side and I tore at the debris with him. He moved to lift a larger beam but I pulled him back.

"If Jamie sees—"

"Better than her dying under there."

Wesley turned back but before he could lift the steel beam, it shifted. Dust and debris moved as the hunk of metal rose from the rubble to reveal Andersen's outstretched hand, trembling with exertion. He bent over Jamie, whose hands had balled Andersen's shirt into fists against his back. Her eyes widened in both horror and awe as she peeked out from their embrace to watch the metal hovering over them.

It came down with a heavy crash, sending dust up to join the smoke, and despite the fact that the building was still on fire around us, Jamie and Andersen stayed in each other's arms.

Jamie pulled away from Andersen with her mouth agape, still processing what had happened. A timid smile crept across Andersen's face. He looked weirdly relieved. His secret was out. Jamie blinked and her stupor passed, replaced by disgust.

"Get off!"

She shoved Andersen hard in the chest and he fell back against the loose bricks, more out of shock than the force of her push. She scrambled to her feet, stumbling out of the debris.

"Jamie?" he mumbled.

"No!" She spun to face him. Dust and smoke coated her face and her hair was disheveled but she still somehow looked beautiful and intimidating. "You're one of *them*!"

"But I'm not—"

"Not trying to murder me? Not one of the bad ones?" she sneered. "You lied to me! You lied to *everyone*! You knew how I felt and you weren't man enough to own up to what you are!"

"He just saved your life." I never thought I'd see the day where I defended Andersen.

"He's a *liar!*"

"Jamie, please." Andersen was still where Jamie had left him, sitting in the dirt and staring up at her, pleading. Jamie paused, maybe considering going back to him but the walls groaned and the moment passed. I hadn't thought it possible for someone to look so cold and proud as they fled a burning building, but Jamie stalked to the doors with an angrily dignified air.

Wesley reached down to help Andersen but Andersen brushed him off.

"I don't need your help." Andersen stood and clambered out of the rubble. Dried blood coated the left side of his face as he trotted after Jamie towards the door.

I followed Wesley out in a stupor and the outside air was cold but welcome. Firetrucks were arriving and Jamie threw herself sobbing into the arms of the first fireman on the scene. Across the yard, a lone figure sprinted towards us from across campus.

"Fleming's coming," Wesley sighed, nodding at the figure.

I grabbed Wesley's arm. With his shirt in burnt tatters, his bare torso was covered in goosebumps.

"It was Amanda."

I felt him tense.

"So she's a traitor like Winnie."

"No, it's worse than that, but there was something else." I turned back to look at the humanities building. Fire poured from the windows on the right side and I vaguely wondered if my dad's office would be alright. "She said time is running out to save the city."

"Save it from what?"

I shook my head. I wanted to say more, but firemen and paramedics descended on us with blankets and oxygen tanks. I let go of Wesley's arm, and the back of his hand brushed against mine.

The University Apex Team Headquarters hid under the main basketball arena. Wesley and I sat on the floor outside of Professor Parker's office while Fleming paced inside, consulting with his counterpart, the head of the university's Apex Team. I pulled my knees up towards my face, letting my tangle of burnt, smokey hair fall forward to hide me. The image of the dead family lying in the dirt was burned into the inside of my eyelids and no matter how hard I pressed my eyes against my knees, I couldn't make Eydis' memory go away.

"What're they saying?" I couldn't bear the silence any longer.

"They're wondering if Adrestus can turn Amanda into a puppet, what's stopping him from taking control over all of us."

"Is that all?" I snorted. The thought hadn't occurred to me. What if he sent Dad after us next? I would never be able to bring myself to fight him.

"No, actually." Wesley sighed and I peeked out from behind my knees. His head rested against the wall and he stared at the ceiling expressionlessly. The university hoodie Professor Parker had lent him hung off his lean frame. Bandages peered out from under the collar. "They're worried about Andersen."

"Jamie doesn't know what she saw. It was smokey."

"He didn't deny it."

"What about a memory alteration? You and Fleming both threatened me with one when I found out about the team."

"That's just a thing we say to scare people into keeping quiet. I doubt it would work on Jamie." He dug his phone out of his back pocket. "But why would Adrestus want Jamie dead in the first place? Why give her family another reason to hate Apex?"

He frowned at his phone screen.

"What's wrong?"

"Anthony says to check the news."

I scooted closer to Wesley on the floor as he pulled up a live press conference on his phone. John Ratcliffe took up the screen, standing at a podium.

"Turn it up," I hissed and Ratcliffe's voice grew louder.

"...something I have been warning of my entire career and now these animals have threatened my family, which is why I'll be endorsing Schrader Industries' Epsilon Initiative."

"The what?" I asked.

"Shh!"

"The Epsilon Initiative is a new project, aimed at leveling the playing field in New Delos, and perhaps, in the future, across the country. I'll let Mr. Schrader fill you in on the details."

I bristled as Adrian Schrader took over from Ratcliffe at the podium. Camera flashes reflected off his wide, charismatic smile and he scanned the crowd, taking a moment before speaking.

"Schrader Industries has prided itself on being at the forefront of invention and innovation on New Delos since the island's conception. Unless you subscribe to the legend of the Apex Father, we don't know where the Apex first came from but my great grandfather aimed to give them a place they could live in peace." His expression darkened and he looked straight into the camera. "Unfortunately, events from the explosion at St. Thomas Aquinas Chapel fifteen years ago, to the recent spate of kidnappings and now, the attack on Councilman Ratcliffe's daughter mere hours ago have caused the city to lose faith in those we once considered our neighbors."

His voice grated against my mind. It may have been Adrestus' blue eyes that haunted me in my waking hours, but it was the sound of Schrader's voice taunting me as I ran through an empty museum that I heard in my nightmares.

"Tonight," Schrader continued, "I'm proud to announce Schrader Industries has created the technology to gift ordinary people the same powers the Apex have used against us. We will create a brand-new generation of island-sponsored heroes, called Epsilons, sworn to protect our citizens against the Apex who dare use their powers to terrorize New Delos."

The press went wild, every reporter talking over each other to get their questions heard, but I leaned back and shook my head.

"They want to make more Apex?"

"They want to make *obedient* Apex." Wesley dropped his phone and buried his face in his knees. "They did it to Anthony. He was their lab rat."

"But *why?*"

"He's got to be planning something. At least we know why he was after Jamie. It was an easy way to get a City Councilor to endorse his project."

The office door opened and we both scrambled to our feet as Fleming came out with the head of the University Apex Team. Professor Parker was taller than Fleming and her dark braided hair wrapped in a knot atop her head added to her height.

"There's been an update." Fleming's grim frown mirrored Parker's.

"We saw." Wesley waved his phone.

"We don't know if it's related to Adrestus yet, though," Parker warned. All three of us gave the University Apex leader a withering glare but she shrugged. "Even if the allegations against Schrader are true—"

"They are," I interjected.

"*If* they are, Mr. Baker will never allow us to move against Schrader Industries. They fund both programs and are a major donor for both schools."

"So we're going to let Adrestus build himself a super-powered army out of embittered citizens because of school politics? Can we even *trust* the money he's giving us?" I hissed. "Fire Trev Baker! Find new donors!"

"Diane, you can't deny it's worrisome." Fleming turned his frown towards Parker.

"Which is why we'll keep an eye on the situation. We'll talk with Mickey about convincing the rest of City Council to put a stop to the project until we know more about the intentions behind it, but there is good news here." Wesley looked like he wanted to interrupt her but Parker raised a hand. "If this *is* Adrestus, it means he can't rely on controlling us like he has Amanda. Otherwise, why would he need to recruit and create more Apex?"

"Oh, good." Wesley rolled his eyes. "We can all rest easy knowing the only person under his control is the one who could torch the entire city, which might happen if her warnings are true."

"You've both had a long day," Fleming said. "Get some sleep. And I know neither of you are on great terms with him, but Andersen is going to need you to defend him if word gets out about tonight."

I nodded, embarrassed that Fleming felt the need to ask us to keep Andersen' secret safe. He was a terrible person, but there'd be trouble for everyone if his secret got out.

It took less than a day for Jamie to put our promise to Fleming to the test. She spent Sunday morning in the floor common room, surrounded by students asking her to retell the night's events. As Naomi and I passed through on our way to blow off steam with some combat training, Jamie was partway through telling a version of the story where she'd fought Amanda one-on-one, armed with nothing but a chair and a broken stapler.

"As scary as it was," Bethany, Anthony's girlfriend, interrupted, "isn't making more Apex a bit like trying to put out a fire with more fire?"

"How else are we supposed to defend ourselves against them?" Jamie demanded. "This way, we'll have *real* heroes, registered through the city, ready to help. The Apex are cowards, hiding among us, waiting for their chance to strike, like Andersen."

"Andersen's not an Apex," Bethany laughed nervously, twisting the end of her braid in her hands.

"He lifted a steel beam without touching it." Jamie's voice dripped with cold pleasure. "He's one of them."

I was halfway through the door to the stairwell when Jamie's best friend, Madison, called out my name.

"Samantha, you were there last night." She flipped her cherry-red hair over her shoulder. "What did you see?"

I hesitated as every eye in the room turned to me.

"Andersen jumped on Jamie to save her from falling debris. After that, it was so smokey and dusty, I don't know how Jamie saw anything, let alone Andersen using magic."

"It wasn't magic, it was—"

"It was really smokey," I insisted, "and we'd been breathing all that in. It was too disorienting to see anything."

Jamie turned bright red and before she could call me a liar in front of every sophomore girl in school, I spun on my heel and pushed into the stairwell with Naomi right behind me.

"You defended Andersen?"

"It doesn't matter. Jamie will make sure the whole school knows by the end of the day."

"It was smart not to outright say he wasn't an Apex," Naomi said as we twisted down the stairs to the lobby. "If you and Wesley come out too strong against her, she'll tell everyone you're Apex, too."

"It's three versus one! Why would everyone believe Jamie over us?"

Campus was empty, like it was most Sundays, and we walked quickly to get out of the cold. Naomi's phone rang in her bag, sounding louder than usual in the silence of campus.

"As rude as she is, Jamie's a social authority. If she says someone's an Apex, they're an Apex," Naomi explained, fishing out her phone.

"That's stupid."

"Plus, Andersen might not deny it."

"He can't be that stupid, can he?" I raised an eyebrow at her.

"More proud than stupid, but yes." She held her phone up in front of us as she answered the incoming video call. A woman who looked like she could be Naomi from the future knit her brows on the screen. "Hey, Mom!"

"Naomi, are you alright?" Mrs. Bradford fretted. Children shouted offscreen, calling to each other as they played. "You weren't at Paragon Days last night, were you?"

Naomi smiled warmly at her mom.

"Not when the fire happened, no. Samantha was, but she's okay." She adjusted the phone so I appeared next to her in the small box in the screen corner.

"Hi, Mrs. Bradford!" I waved at the camera as we pushed through the doors into Schrader Hall. "I'm perfectly fine and so is Naomi!"

Mrs. Bradford sighed and a reluctant smile inched across her face.

"You know I worry about you kids." She paused when a child shrieked and the camera tilted to the ceiling as Mrs. Bradford yelled. "William! Let go of your sister's hair!"

"Don't worry about us," Naomi laughed as her mom readjusted the camera to reappear back on screen. "Sounds like you're the one dealing with *real* danger over there."

"A straight week of snow." Mrs. Bradford gave her younger children a side-eye. "School's canceled and I can only make them play outside for so long before they're too cold. Send help."

Loud music blasted in the main gym as we entered the Apex facility atrium.

"Hopefully the combat gym is empty," Naomi fussed. "We gotta go, Mom, but thanks for checking in."

Mrs. Bradford beamed at us through the phone, her brown eyes wrinkling kindly.

"Sure thing. I love you both. Keep each other safe."

"Love you, too, Mom." Naomi smiled to herself as she hung up, then grimaced at the door to the combat gym. "This doesn't feel good."

She pulled the door open and a gust of wind swept into the hall.

"Oh, hey, guys." A miserable looking Anthony sat cross-legged in the center of the ring. Wesley and Anthony's cousin, Isabelle, sat with him.

"Close the door!" Isabelle snapped and Naomi and I hurried inside. Though not a full-on tornado, a strong breeze whipped around the room with Anthony at its epicenter. My hair blew around my face and I struggled to pull it into a ponytail.

"We were eating breakfast and Schrader's new project came up on the news," Wesley explained.

"I didn't mean to lose control, it's just..." Anthony hid behind his hands. He'd been the lab rat for the Epsilon Initiative. Anyone in the same situation would've reacted the same way.

"I know someone who might be having a worse day than you." I sat on the mat next to Anthony, abandoning any plans to practice combat with Naomi. "Jamie told the whole floor about Andersen."

"All the guys know, too." Wesley sat on Anthony's other side, looking grim. White bandages peeked out from under his shirt collar, matching the bandages on my wrist where Amanda had grabbed me.

"You didn't get Serum, either?" I asked, pointing at them. Wesley rolled his eyes.

"Everly is officially stockpiling the Serum because of the threats about the city burning, so my burns from last night have to heal the old fashioned way."

"What have you tried so far?" Naomi asked.

"Everly gave me a cream but—"

"Not you," she snapped at Wesley. "Anthony."

Anthony blushed and the wind picked up.

"Isabelle's been going over control techniques but nothing's worked."

"What about yoga?"

"You can't control the wind with stretching," Isabelle snorted. Her hair whipped around her face like dark tentacles in the wind.

"But it's not Anthony controlling his powers," Naomi explained. "It's his stress, which yoga can relieve."

Anthony looked dubious but followed Naomi's movements as she planted her feet and reached forward into downward dog.

"Everyone has to do it," Naomi instructed.

"I'm injured."

She glared at Wesley.

"*Everyone* has to do it."

Wesley begrudgingly joined Naomi's yoga circle and after a few minutes, the wind began to die. My shoulders ached as Naomi moved us through a series of positions and I glanced under my arm at Wesley when we came back to downward dog. He strained to keep his back in line with his arms and made a face at me when he caught me looking. I stuck my tongue back out at him and he smiled.

When Anthony's gale finally subsided, Naomi let us sit. Isabelle and Wesley looked as disheveled as I felt but Anthony and Naomi both looked relaxed. Anthony let out a long sigh.

"Thanks." He looked down at his lap. "Just, the thought of people lining up to have Schrader do to them what Adrestus did to me..."

A soft breeze briefly stirred the air.

"He shouldn't be able to give powers to just anyone, though," Isabelle said, as if that might help. "You already had the Epsilon One gene. It was just a matter of activating it without Epsilon Two."

Fleming had explained the two Epsilon genes to me before, after I'd tested negative for both. As far as I understood, Epsilon One coded for the super ability while Epsilon Two acted as the "on switch". You needed both to be an Apex.

"Plus, he'd need donors to do what they did with me, willing or otherwise."

"Or otherwise?" Naomi furrowed her brow. "You had someone else activate your power?"

Anthony hadn't spoken very much about his time spent as Adrestus' captive. He turned a shade of green and refused to meet our eyes. He drew up the hem of his shirt to reveal a long scar along the right side of his torso.

"Lannie Bryce in my case. She probably had it worse than me." Anthony tried to smile but looked more like he might throw up. We didn't ask any more questions. I didn't want to know what went into using Lannie's genes to activate Anthony's or how it resulted in the ugly scar on Anthony's flank.

"Still doesn't explain how Adrestus is able to give powers to someone *without* the genes, though," Naomi said.

My stomach churned and it was my turn to avoid eye contact. The Adrestus of legend was known as the Father of All Apex and now I knew that our Adrestus and that Adrestus were one and the same.

I also knew he had the Lapis, Adrestus' precious rock that granted immortality. His rock he claimed helped him create the first Apex. The rock that had been lodged in my neck for a millennia before he ripped it out.

It was my fault. I let Adrestus take the Lapis back. Now he was going to build an island-sanctioned army, endorsed by John Ratcliffe.

And he couldn't be killed because of it. Because of me.

I stood up and the others looked at me in surprise.

"What's wrong?" Naomi asked.

"I need to talk to Fleming."

"That's convenient." Wesley nodded towards the hallway. "He's at the door."

Fleming startled when he opened the door to see all five of us staring at him. The bags under his eyes told the story of another sleepless night.

"Naomi and Samantha, with me, please."

We scrambled to our feet as Wesley called out behind us.

"Is it a mission? Did you find Amanda?"

Fleming pressed his lips together as he held the door for us. His expression was the only confirmation Wesley needed.

"It *is* a mission! Do you need anyone else? I'm free."

"You're fine where you're at," Fleming clipped, ushering Naomi and me into the hallway.

I grimaced at Naomi as we followed Fleming to his office and she shrugged back. I was still working my way into Fleming's good graces after my many missteps early in the semester. I hadn't been assigned a mission since going rogue on the last one I'd been allowed on and Fleming hadn't been eager to let me back in the field.

Justin, Marcus, and Jen waited for us, gathered around Fleming's desk. Them, plus Naomi, meant all four captains were here but Olivia hugged herself nervously in the corner, looking just as perplexed as I was to have been called into the meeting.

Fleming swooped around his desk and fell into his swivel chair, pausing to glance over an email on his computer screen before finally addressing us.

"I take it you've all heard about Schrader Industries' new project," he said. My hands balled into fists at my side, my nails digging into my palms.

"This is about how they're going to do it, right?" Justin asked. He leaned over the desk as if trying to get a look at Fleming's screen, eager for more information. "Is it even possible?"

"Yes." I focused on the bite of my fingernails against my skin.

The other students whipped around to look at me where I lingered by the door. Fleming settled back in his chair and gestured at me as if to say, "Go on".

"When I was there in October he told me he was the same Adrestus as the one in the stories." I waited for the others to scoff or call me crazy but living as super humans must've had its effects on what they found believable or not. "He said he made the first Apex with a stone he called his Lapis and he has it again."

"Why weren't we briefed on this?" Marcus demanded, whipping back towards Fleming.

"Because the Council doesn't believe her." As exhausted as Fleming looked with his creased shirt and disheveled hair, his eyes were sharp behind his glasses.

"They don't believe that Dr. Cunningham is Adrestus, either, but you still told us that."

"Adrestus' identity is a matter of student safety. How old he may or may not be isn't, or rather, wasn't. Regardless of who or what the Council believes, we need to learn more about both Adrestus and the Lapis."

It now made sense why Fleming had brought me in, though I still didn't get why Olivia had received an invite. I knew more about Adrestus than anyone.

"What's the mission then? Run an internet search and go to the library?" I asked. It wouldn't be the first desk-work mission Fleming had assigned me.

"Even on New Delos, there's very little written record of the Legend of Adrestus," Fleming sighed. "I've done my best to research it, but it's all conjecture. If Samantha is right and Dr. Cunningham really is the Adrestus of legend, he'll know more about the old stories and what the Lapis is capable of than anyone. We need to go straight to the source. We need to go back to the museum."

8

Among Giants and Heroes

The office suddenly felt very cramped and very warm and I was glad to already be in my moisture-wicking exercise clothes as sweat erupted along my spine.

"You want us to actually talk with the psycho trying to destroy the city?" I gawked.

"No," Fleming asserted and a flutter of relief stirred in my chest. "I want Justin to. You have the most experience with Adrestus, so you'll listen in and watch with Olivia's help."

Olivia perked up at the mention of her name.

"You want us to be invisible?" she asked and Fleming nodded.

"It'll be a busy day at the museum tomorrow," Fleming said. "The hardest part will be navigating through the crowd without bumping anyone but we need to know if it's the Lapis that Schrader Industries plans on using to create Epsilons and if there's a way to destroy it."

"And you think Adrestus is just going to give out information?" Jen crossed her arms in the corner, looking doubtful.

"Maybe not, but he's the only one who knows anything about it," Fleming conceded. He outlined the plan and it was simple enough. Justin would talk to Dr. Cunningham about the Adrestus legend and try to get him to share any information about the Lapis. Meanwhile, Olivia and I would be nearby, listening in and invisible. As straightforward as it was, I struggled to focus on the details.

The thought of going back to the museum, of seeing Adrestus, especially after Anthony had hinted at the horrors he'd gone through at the immortal warrior's hands... My vision swam and I thought I might be having another flashback to my Viking days, but it was Cunningham's manic blue eyes I saw hovering over me as he dug a knife into my collarbone. This memory was much, much more recent.

The meeting ended without me noticing, still thinking about evil curators and ill-fated museum trips. Fleming signaled for me to stay behind and waited until the others had left to speak.

"If you don't want to go to the museum—"

"I'll be fine," I said, even though I wasn't sure. "I'm a little surprised, though."

Fleming sighed and took off his glasses.

"It didn't feel right to send someone in to ask about Adrestus' story without you there. It's your story, too, and who knows. Maybe you'll learn more about Eydis."

It was a surprising gesture on Fleming's part but listening to Adrestus talk about the part of me I couldn't remember wasn't how I wanted to regain my memories.

"Thanks," I mumbled. Fleming stood up behind his desk and adjusted his glasses, possibly so he wouldn't have to look me in the eye.

"Also, your parent-teacher conference is scheduled for next Wednesday at three thirty with Mrs. Young."

"You don't need to go to that." My grades weren't horrible, but they weren't great. Fleming had access to the grade book. He knew this and neither of us needed the reminder.

"I told Alison I would take over as your guardian," Fleming said as matter-of-factly as possible. "That means more than just giving you somewhere to stay over the holidays."

I grimaced.

"Really, it's fine."

"You're right. It is, which is why you'll come to Mrs. Young's classroom at three thirty next Wednesday."

No one saw Andersen for the rest of Sunday, though with an impending trip to my least favorite place in the world, his outed secret was the least of my worries. Monday morning, he slipped into the cafeteria for breakfast after most students had finished eating and walked his plate straight from the breakfast line to the dish pit, shoveling his scrambled eggs into his mouth as he went.

After he walked back out the doors, Wesley and I turned expectantly towards Naomi.

"I'm not your weather reporter for whatever mood Andersen is in."

"Fair, but we gotta know," Wesley prodded, "is today going to be cloudy with a chance of Andersen finally snapping and murdering someone in training? Or is it going to be a light drizzle kind of day?"

"Zero percent chance of murder, but you should both probably steer clear."

"That's Andersen on any day, though." I gathered our dirty dishes.

"Just be extra careful today."

"You act like we're the ones who instigate it!" Wesley grumbled. "Nine out of ten times, he starts it."

"Then don't let today be the one time," Naomi warned through pursed lips.

In class, Jamie sat in her usual seat in the center with her friends crowded around her, casting glances at Andersen, who ignored them from his new corner seat.

Skyler patted Jamie's hand and rubbed her shoulder.

"What's Skyler doing?" I hissed. "He's Andersen's best friend!"

"Sure, but if he takes Andersen's side, Jamie will accuse him of being an Apex, too," Naomi explained in a whisper.

"I'm okay," Jamie sniffed loudly, wanting everyone to hear. "My arm was burned in the fire but it's the lies that hurt the most."

"So it's true?" A boy named Dylan whispered. He craned his neck to look at Andersen in the back corner but quickly ducked when he saw Andersen's face. "He always seemed dangerous to me."

"They could be anywhere," Madison shuddered. "There might be others *in this room.*"

Wesley tensed next to me and Anthony groaned.

"I chose the worst time to spontaneously become an Apex," he whispered. Naomi shushed him. "I'm going to have to break up with Bethany, aren't I?"

"Don't be stupid," Naomi whispered back.

"Maybe there are," Jamie continued, agreeing with Madison, "but you all heard my father. With the Epsilon Initiative, we won't have to be scared of them anymore."

I bowed my head over my notebook. On top of Jamie flouting the Epsilon project that had started with my friend as its lab rat, I was also dealing with the fact that I would be returning to the museum to seek out Adrestus later that day. I would be invisible, of course, but what if Adrestus could still see me? What if he attacked us and took away more of my friends?

Or what if Winnie was there?

When I'd found out that she was behind the mask of Adrestus' loyal henchman, Dion, all the fight had gone out of me and I still wasn't sure if I'd be able to raise a hand against her.

"Mr. Fleming?" Jamie's voice brought my thoughts back to the classroom and I looked up to see Fleming enter. "Can I be excused?"

"Class hasn't even started yet." Fleming set his bag down on the front desk.

"I don't feel safe in this environment."

Fleming looked out over the classroom, taking in the gaggle of friends that surrounded Jamie and then Andersen alone in his corner.

"If you're going to be disruptive, I don't mind giving you detention two weeks in a row."

"I almost *died* at the last detention."

Fleming ignored her as the bell rang and threw the lesson slides up on the front screen. I frowned at the blown-up picture of a long, wooden boat with bright sails and oars sticking out from the sides.

"Vikings!" Naomi grinned at me. "Like Eydis from the stories about Adrestus!"

"Neat." I tried to smile back. Of all the days for Fleming's lesson plan to cover Vikings, it just had to be the day I had to go face my past at the museum.

"You ever think about how much easier our lives would be if she'd done her job right?" Naomi sighed wistfully. "Maybe she should've tried harder and solved our Adrestus problems a thousand years before they started."

I knew she was joking, but my stomach twisted painfully and I slumped in my chair. She was right. I could've saved my friends a lot of grief if I'd taken care of Adrestus a thousand years ago. Naomi of course knew about the popular myth surrounding Adrestus and Eydis, in which Adrestus was the hero and creator of all Apex until the Scourge Queen Eydis struck him down. However, Naomi had no way of knowing that I was the Scourge Queen. Maybe if I'd found the courage to tell her already, she would've kept her thoughts about Eydis' failures to herself.

"What's wrong?" Naomi asked, suddenly serious.

"Nothing," I mumbled. "Just don't want to be here."

"I'm nervous, too." She smiled kindly. "We'll be fine at the museum. Justin will be there."

Fleming looked as uncomfortable as I felt and sped through slides covering brutal attacks on English monasteries by Viking raiders. He glanced at me every time a particularly violent detail about the Scandinavian warriors came up and I wished he would stop.

"Can you go back a slide?" Dylan asked partway through class. "I didn't get everything."

Fleming clicked into the last slide, which detailed human sacrifices, and quickly clicked forward again.

"The slides will be available online after class. You can find them there." Fleming cleared his throat and glanced at the clock as if willing it to go faster. "Not all Nordic people were violent, of course. Plenty were farmers or explorers."

"'Explorers' is a nice way to say conquerors," Madison quipped.

"Yeah, because the English were so innocent," I retorted without thinking. Fleming gave me a warning glare. "I'm not saying Vikings were great, but everyone kinda sucked back then, didn't they?"

"I mean, they did kill a lot of people, Sam," Naomi murmured.

I wanted to signal Wesley to back me up, but stared forward, afraid if I so much as glanced around the room wrong, everyone would figure out my secret.

"Samantha makes an excellent point—" Fleming started.

"You literally just told us Vikings killed their own people at funerals," Olivia said.

"Only the important funerals," Fleming reminded her, as if that might help.

"It's a bit like the Apex, isn't it?" Jamie mused. "The English were like the non-Apex and—"

"Holy crap, can you go *one day* without talking about Apex?" My hair smacked my face as I spun to face Jamie.

"They way you talk—"

"I know," I snapped. "It makes you wonder if I might be one. *We get it.*"

"Maybe it's not that she's an Apex," Madison giggled. "Maybe she's a Viking."

"Yeah!" Jamie lit up. "Havardson! That's a Viking name, isn't it?"

Fleming cleared his throat.

"That's a good point, actually."

I gripped the edge of the desk and watched Fleming warily, my heartbeat screaming in my ears.

"Viking names are very common," he explained. "Havardson, Erickson, Olson. Basically any name ending in 'son'. They were a rough people, but you had to be to survive the conditions they did. Their legacy lives on because of it."

A hint of something like pride passed over his face, but he was careful not to look at me, though my cheeks burned anyways.

The school day dragged by, weighed down by the looming mission to the museum, thoughts of having come from a murderous, violent Viking town, and questions whispered to me in the halls, asking if Jamie was telling the truth about Andersen.

After a grueling training session with Reiner in Fourth Period, Andersen cornered me just as he had last week.

"I don't need you defending me," he spat, blocking the exit into the hall.

"I don't know what you're talking about."

"This morning!" he snapped.

"That wasn't for you." I pushed past him.

"Oh, right. I forgot you're a huge Viking advocate."

I turned to look at him.

"Sure, and why would I care about Apex at all if not for you?"

He scowled and backed off.

"Whatever. Just leave me alone, alright? Everyone else is."

"You're the one bothering me!"

He kept walking, stalking back into the atrium. Wesley passed him on his way out of the locker rooms.

"What did you do to Andersen? Naomi told us to keep away from him."

"I'm trying!" I snapped. "He's not the only one allowed to have a bad day."

"You're nervous about the museum?"

"Aren't you?" We both knew how he felt about me walking into danger. Wesley was always worried, sometimes obnoxiously so.

Wesley blushed and looked away.

"You know what you're doing. Plus, Justin and Olivia will be there with you." He bit his lip and I knew he wasn't being entirely truthful. I appreciated he was trying to downplay his fears, but my insides knotted all the same.

"Yeah, it'll probably be fine." My stomach churned with nerves that said otherwise.

Naomi and Justin left for the museum first to get into position before Olivia and I arrived. Jen led the two of us to the underground parking garage. Of the four captains, she was the one I knew the least. She was tall and lanky and spent a good portion of her allowance on colorful hair dyes that kept her head a rotating selection of whatever had been available at the drugstore that week.

Today it was cyan and I kept my eyes trained on her blue curls as we marched down the corridor to the parking garage in silence.

Usually, when Fleming sent us on missions, we'd suit up in our Apex Team uniforms. However, Jen, Justin, and Naomi dressed in everyday clothes to blend in. As for Olivia and I, she explained when we went invisible, it would turn our clothes invisible, too, rendering the screens on the helmet visors useless.

Jen took the driver's seat of the team sedan and Olivia and I crawled into the back. Despite both being sophomores, Olivia and I weren't close. She'd helped Andersen throw me into the ocean and sure, she'd gone out of her way to be extra nice since then, maybe out of guilt, but we were far from being friends.

We drove out of the parking garage and as we traveled deeper into New Delos, the brick buildings of the university district turned into skyscrapers, which in turn gave way to an expansive park in the middle of the city. Jen pulled into an empty parking lot.

"Come straight back here once you're done," Jen warned.

"Shoot, we were planning on grabbing a bite afterwards." I rolled my eyes. Jen scowled.

Olivia held her palm out over the middle seat and I took it in mine.

"It's a little disorienting because you won't be able to see yourself," she explained. "We'll have to avoid larger crowds, too, since they can be difficult to maneuver through. Ready?"

I nodded and a cold sensation crept over my hand. Our fingers disappeared and as the cold feeling swept across my body, I disappeared with it. I looked down at my lap, but only saw the polyester seat of the car.

"Next stop, the Hall of Heroes," Olivia's disembodied voice chirped. "All good?"

"Yeah." I held out my free hand, marveling at how I could feel it but not see it.

I followed Olivia out her side of the car and into the park, doing my best to keep single-file with her to avoid joggers on the paved trail.

"Watch out for puddles," Olivia warned under her breath. "Even if people can't see us directly, they can see the effect we have on the things we touch."

We passed a newly constructed gazebo, built to replace the one Amanda Hendricks had burnt down in October. I tried not to look at it as we arrived at the edge of the park, across the street from the museum front entrance.

It was a busy Monday afternoon at Adrian Schrader's museum. The opulent white face stretched four stories high, decorated with banners advertising the exhibits inside. White stone turned to skyscraper glass, extending up into the tower that formed Schrader Industries Headquarters, topped with Adrian Schrader's domed penthouse, barely visible from street-level. Patrons milled around the large, stone entrance steps. A group of elementary students on a field trip posed for a picture with their teacher. Naomi sat on the top step, pretending to journal, but I knew she was concentrating, feeling for our arrival.

Her head jerked up and she looked directly at me before typing something out on her phone. She'd explained once how each person had a specific emotional signature. Even though I was invisible, she could pick me out of a crowd.

As we walked through the entranceway, I felt like I was being swallowed. Somehow, I was back where everything had started. Would Schrader's voice follow me through the exhibits again, like it had Homecoming night? I looked around at the walls wildly, as if I might see clues to my dad's whereabouts posted there. This had been where I'd seen him last. Would Adrestus have thought to move him or would he have kept him hidden somewhere in the eighty stories situated on top of the museum?

I stumbled as I caught the back of Olivia's shoe with mine.

"Sorry," I hissed and she shushed me.

We snaked through the foyer entrance, skirting around the center fountain towards the ornate set of stairs on the far end of the room. We dodged students eating snacks on the steps and tour groups going up and down. I brushed dangerously close to an old woman hobbling her way up against the railing and she looked over her shoulder to see who was there.

Up ahead, Justin pretended to read a plaque under an oil painting that hung over the steps. Naomi hurried up the stairs and patted his shoulder. He turned away from the painting to head down the corridor and Olivia pulled me along to follow.

"We're right behind you," she murmured in Justin's ear when we caught up. He ran his hand over his bleached-blond buzzcut to subtly acknowledge us as we approached the Hall of Heroes.

I wanted to close my eyes and block out the room but when I tried, I realized that my eyelids were invisible, too, and I could see right through them. I was forced to look at the two rows of marble statues who watched the room with vacant, pupil-less stares. Last time we'd been here, Andersen had laid waste to most of them but history's greatest Apex had already been reconstructed.

Paragon stood closest to the door, his familiar cape billowing behind him. Someone had laid a wreath at his stone feet with a tiny banner that read, "The City Sinks Without Him". A "Happy Paragon Days" flag stuck out of a bouquet of flowers at the base of his pedestal.

Justin pretended to be interested in Harriet Tubman's statue but I looked to the head of the room. The two statues there were larger than the others. On the right, Adrestus' statue stood ready for battle in his Greek armor and chiseled thighs. It wasn't quite the same outfit he wore these days, but I'd seen him don a similar plumed helmet.

I ignored Adrestus' statue and looked to his right. The statue there swung a stone sword over her braided head, her mouth open in a permanent battle cry. She shouldn't have been any older than fifteen but the artist had aged her up a bit. She looked nothing like the jeans-wearing high school sophomore that I was, but me and the Scourge Queen Eydis, Destroyer of the Apex, were very much the same person.

Justin left the Harriet Tubman statue to slowly walk down the hall, looking up at the stone faces until coming to a stop in front of Adrestus and Eydis. A glass case had been added to the exhibit since I'd been here last, placed between the two behemoths, housing a hilted sword with an engraved blade identical to the one in my statue's hands. I glared at it. It was my sword, kept here as Adrestus' prize.

We situated ourselves behind the glass case to keep out of the way while Justin took his time pretending to be interested in the statues.

"Ouch! Watch your grip," Olivia whispered and I relaxed my hand.

"Sorry."

"Shh!"

The museum curator came around the corner at the far end of the exhibit and shuffled into the Hall of Heroes, beaming up at his prized statues. My throat tightened and I resisted the urge to run away.

Dr. Cunningham wore a navy suit and his salt-and-pepper hair and beard had been neatly groomed. As he turned to face us at the end of the room, I saw his left eye was marred by a thick scar, leaving the eyeball white and foggy. My stomach clenched at the sight of the souvenir from our last encounter. I'd been the one to put the knife through his eye and I'd just as soon do the same to his other one if it meant saving Dad.

He meandered towards Justin, taking the bait.

"Anything I can help you with today?" Adrestus asked, his mouth curling into a benign smile. "I see you've taken interest in the Scourge Queen. She's one of my favorites, too."

9

Scourge Queen Revisited

I should have asked Olivia beforehand what it would look like to others if I puked while invisible. I fought the bile rising in my throat and did my best to calm my breathing.

Adrestus was just feet away on the other side of the glass display case. I would have the element of surprise. I could grab the sword and take care of things here and now.

Except that he probably had the Lapis on him and if he did, no amount of sword swings would do him in permanently. My mind buzzed and I missed the next bit of conversation between Adrestus and Justin. When I refocused, Justin was talking.

"It's just with all this stuff in the news about making new Apex, the Legend of Adrestus was on my mind, you know?" Justin said and I envied his ability to sound so casual. "Him being the Father of Apex and all that."

"According to legend, you mean," the curator chuckled. I hated the sound. "Not everyone believes Adrestus existed."

Justin shrugged.

"Still a cool story, though I don't really understand it all."

Adrestus' one good eye lit up. I eyed the exit.

"What is it that you don't understand?"

"Some versions of the story say Adrestus created the Apex but wasn't one himself. But I thought he couldn't die? Wouldn't that make him an Apex?"

Adrestus laughed, every bit excelling at the role of harmless fifty-year-old man.

"An Apex's power comes from within, genetically embedded into who they are but perhaps Adrestus' immortality was gifted to him."

"Until he died," Justin reminded him and I felt a surge of satisfaction at the flicker of annoyance that flitted across Adrestus' face. Justin pointed up at the Eydis statue. "Because of her. What happened to his gift, then? Why didn't it save him?"

Adrestus took a moment to study Eydis' statue with a solemn, unreadable expression. His blue eye glittered in the bright, exhibit lights.

"He put his trust in the wrong person. The Scourge Queen knew the source of his immortality and the night before setting out on their divine quest to create a more perfect world, she used that secret against him. She stole the source and ran him through with a sword like that one." Adrestus raised a hand to point at the case but it felt like he was pointing through the glass at me. Olivia squeezed my hand and I realized my fingers were shaking.

"But what was the source?"

A grin settled on Adrestus' face and his eye glinted.

"The Lapis, or that's what it was called in Latin. In English, it means 'Stone'. It could give immortality, change any substance into gold, and even create life. It's how he made The Apex and how he lived to be hundreds of years old."

"Then the story can't be real." Justin laughed and the hungry look that had taken over Adrestus' face passed.

"Oh?"

"The Scourge Queen would still be alive!"

Adrestus laughed, too.

"Perhaps she is! She was nastily greedy. They say when her family tried to stop her from going away with Adrestus, she had them killed, all so she could steal Adrestus' immortality."

I shook my head, holding my breath so that Adrestus wouldn't hear it. I didn't kill my family. He had. I hadn't wanted immortality.

But what did I know? What if I had something to do with it? I thought back to the memory of them lying in the dust. I'd been filled with rage and anguish. I couldn't have done that to them.

"I don't suppose she could've destroyed the Lapis?" Justin mused. "Something that powerful probably can't be ruined, can it?"

"Like you said, it's probably all just a story."

"But one you seem to know a lot about. I'm sure you'd know if it was possible to destroy the Lapis."

Justin was pushing too hard. Adrestus squinted at him but smiled.

"Does it matter?"

Justin shrugged.

"I'm just wondering, if Adrian Schrader has found a way to create Apex like Adrestus did, maybe he's also found a way to be immortal. It's an exciting idea for those of us who are ordinary."

Adrestus seemed to relax and looked over Justin for a moment.

"How old are you?"

"Almost eighteen."

"That's too bad," Adrestus tutted sadly. "Project Epsilon is only open to those over the age of twenty-one, but maybe in a few years, you'll make a good candidate."

Justin's face lit up.

"You really think so? Will it still be around?"

"I believe it will be," Adrestus insisted. "Come with me to the office and I can at least see about signing you up for a summer internship."

Adrestus patted Justin's shoulder and led the way back to the entrance. Justin exhaled heavily and shook out his arms. He looked in our general direction and shook his head before following the curator. He'd performed well but was clearly rattled.

Olivia tugged on my hand to signal that we were moving. My legs felt like lead as I followed her out of the Hall of Heroes. Adrestus and Justin walked ahead of us and I tried to keep my breathing controlled.

I didn't have my family killed. I didn't take the Lapis out of greed. I can't have. I knew me. I wouldn't do that.

Maybe Samantha wouldn't do that, a tiny voice hissed at the back of my head. *But Samantha isn't real.*

No. I remembered how I felt at the sight of them. That wasn't the reaction of a girl who'd murdered her family.

But what if the emotions at seeing the memories were Samantha's and just the images were Eydis? What if Eydis hadn't been anguished at the sight of her dead family? What if she'd just pretended to be to fool Vidar?

I wouldn't do that to Dad. I shook my head, blindly following the pull of Olivia's hand to the museum entrance.

As we passed the large fountain in the main foyer, Justin followed Adrestus to the left, towards the museum office. Olivia hesitated, unsure if we should follow while Naomi stood at the front door, watching after Justin apprehensively.

A hand on my shoulder cut my rising panic.

"Don't trust your friends. Adrestus knows you're here," a voice croaked in my ear. Cold dread rooted me to the tiles and I felt a hand shove something into my pocket before Olivia yanked on my arm to hurry me up. "You have forty-two days before the city burns."

I twisted, trying to see who was there, but they had already melted into the crowd. How had they seen me? They'd touched me and my jacket pocket bounced with the extra weight of whatever they'd placed there.

Olivia tried to pull me towards the door, but I resisted, watching Adrestus put an arm around Justin's shoulders as he led him down a side hall. Naomi looked towards us, sensing something was wrong.

"We have to go," Olivia hissed. "He'll be fine."

"He knows!" I said, too loud. A man next to us glanced around, looking for the source of my voice.

"He can't," Olivia whispered.

"He does!"

I yanked Olivia after Justin, shoving through a group of middle schoolers to get to him. We turned a corner and saw the back of Adrestus' navy suit guiding Justin towards a glass office door.

The back of Justin's hoodie wrinkled as I grabbed at it and Adrestus startled as I tugged my teammate backwards.

"Something wrong?" he crooned. I couldn't look away from his marred eye.

"I just remembered, I already have a summer internship lined up," Justin stammered. He didn't know why I'd pulled him back, but he knew I wouldn't have done it without reason. "Sorry, Dr. Cunningham, I didn't mean to waste your time."

Adrestus surveyed him, tilting his head to the side.

"Still, won't hurt to at least look over the paperwork." He gestured towards the office. Justin shook his head.

"Sorry, sir. I need to get back to the school." He stepped back but Adrestus stepped forward and grabbed Justin around the bicep.

"Come now, Justin, you'll regret skipping on this opportunity."

It felt as if the cramped hall had dropped ten degrees as Justin went rigid. Olivia gasped and her hand tightened around mine.

"How do you know my name?" Justin's voice was small and for the first time since I'd met him, the captain looked scared. Adrestus' careful face melted into a sneer.

"I'm sorry, it's not like me to slip up like that," he said seriously. "But, Justin, I think you'll find more opportunities wait for you in that office than elsewhere."

Justin backed away, shaking his head, and a shadow crossed Adrestus' face. Through the glass door behind him, long, white hair flicked out of sight.

Mira. The white-haired woman. The Apex who could control every action of anyone she touched, and apparently, Amanda, too, from a distance. Of Adrestus' followers, she scared me the most.

I chanced a glance back the way we'd come. A ginger woman lingered at the mouth of the hall. I remembered her, too. Esther. Another one of Adrestus' high-ranking followers. She'd tried to kidnap me twice and had watched while Adrestus tortured me on the museum floor. Adrestus was trapping Justin, and us with him.

"Run!" I let go of Olivia and my hands took shape in front of me as I charged Adrestus. I watched his face go from shocked surprise to delighted hatred and while the man had thousands of years of fighting expertise on me, I'd caught him off guard enough to get in a single right hook.

He kept his ground, letting a trickle of blood stream from his nose and his thin lips curled into a smile as we faced each other. Every hair on my arms stood on end as Adrestus conveyed a thousand years worth of hatred in a single stare.

"Samantha," he purred. My stomach curdled. The hall morphed and a much younger Adrestus stood in front of me, frowning in concern.

"What is it, Eydis?"

I felt Eydis' wrist draw across my face, wiping away the ghost of tears from a millennia ago.

"My father," she hiccuped. "He called me the scourge of my people."

"That's not so bad," the boy said kindly, drawing me in. "We can call you Scourge Queen. It sounds powerful."

"I don't want to be a *scourge*, Dres!" I felt young Adrestus rub my back as the older version glowered at me, blood running into his mustache.

"Samantha, come *on*!" Justin roared. I flinched as a hand grabbed mine, tethering me back to the present. The cold of Olivia's invisibility returned and my nose flickered out of sight between my eyes.

Justin fled back down the hall and while Esther tried to stand in his way, a single touch of his hand was all it took for her to lock up, trapped by his stasis ability. Olivia dragged me after him and I followed numbly, too scared to look back and see if Adrestus was giving chase.

Museum patrons shouted as Justin barreled through them towards the front door and signaling for Naomi to run.

They stumbled down the front museum steps together and Olivia and I kept close behind. As we sprinted back through the park, we didn't bother avoiding puddles, splashing haphazardly after Naomi and Justin until we packed into the back of the sedan, panting and yelling for Jen to floor it.

"You two were supposed to take the bus back to campus!" Jen threw the car into reverse and peeled out of the parking lot. I bent over my knees in the middle seat, pulling at my hair. Delayed panic rose in my chest and I fought to keep from hyperventilating. Naomi rested her hand on my back and I squeezed my eyes shut.

"He knew who I was." Justin sounded hollow in the front passenger seat. "How did he know?"

"'Don't trust your friends.'" I repeated what the mystery person had said to me in the foyer. "Someone told me don't trust your friends."

"Back at the museum?" Olivia demanded. "I didn't hear that."

I sat up to see Jen's heavily lined eyes looking back at me in the rearview mirror. I dug in my pocket to find a small plastic box.

"They gave this to me when we were first leaving."

Olivia turned to me in shock.

"But we were invisible!"

The small, gray box had a rectangular screen and a few, unmarked buttons. It beeped shrilly and I dropped it in surprise.

"It's a pager!" Jen reached back to search for it on the floor. The car swerved dangerously, but she straightened up and waved the pager at us from the driver's seat.

"What's it say?" Naomi asked.

"Forty-two." She turned the small screen towards us so we could see the number spelled out on its face.

"They told me I had forty-two days to save the city," I remembered. Adrestus' blue eyes still floated against the back of my eyelids.

"Did you see who it was?"

"She sounded like a woman."

"Amanda Hendricks, maybe?" Olivia suggested. "She said something about the city burning at Paragon Days, right? And there was the message on the wall when she attacked Erik last week."

"Could've been," I murmured, though I didn't think so.

"We can have Remi take a look at the pager once we're back," Jen said. A bus honked at us as she cut the driver off. She waved a sheepish apology out the window. "Maybe she'll be able to find out more or locate other devices it's connected to."

"What if it has a tracker on it?" I asked, more because I didn't want Remi's help and less that I was actually concerned it might be a plot by Adrestus. "If we take it back to campus, Adrestus might be able to find our headquarters."

"Adrestus already knows we're there," Justin said darkly. "He knew who I was. Someone's already told him all about the team."

Trev Baker. Who else could it be spilling team secrets if not the guy on Schrader's payroll? I picked at a hangnail on my thumb as the sky overhead was swallowed up by the garage.

"Sammy?" Naomi whispered, bending in towards me. "It's alright. We're out."

I nodded as Jen parked but when the others climbed out of the car, I stayed in my seat, now pulling at a loose thread in the knee of my jeans. Naomi watched me expectantly.

"I'll be there in a minute," I said. Jen grunted and slammed her door but Naomi gave me a gentle nod before following the others. I listened for the heavy metal door opening and slamming shut and then slid down in my seat, pushing the heels of my hands over my eyes.

My body shook, but the tears didn't come. Good. Most of the team would be waiting inside, hungry for updates. I didn't want them to see me with red eyes when I eventually went in.

For the next fifteen minutes or so, I replayed the afternoon in my head over and over, each time playing through different choices I could've made. What if I'd attacked Adrestus when we were still in the Hall of Heroes? Or pushed past him down by the office? Dad *had* to be somewhere in the building. Maybe if I'd tried harder, I could've found him.

Don't trust your friends.

That had to be about Trev Baker, but which of Adrestus' insiders would tip us off like that? And why?

And, as the minutes ticked by alone in the car, something else nagged at the back of my mind: the memory that had leaked through my subconscious when I'd faced Adrestus. I'd assumed "Scourge Queen" had been an unflattering title given to me by Adrestus' followers, but now I knew, it was inspired by something my father had called me. My *real* father.

The Scourge of my people...

Had Adrestus told the truth in the Hall of Heroes? What if Eydis— what if *I* had been after immortality for myself the whole time? What if I *had* asked for my family to be killed?

And if I did, did Dad know?

Panic welled in my throat and my breath became shaky. I jumped as someone tapped on the window.

Fleming bent over on the other side of the glass, waving grimly. He opened the door, continuing to stoop to look at me.

"Can I come in?"

I shifted over to the far window and he lowered himself into the backseat, keeping the door open with one foot grounded on the pavement outside. I focused on the upholstery of the seat in front of me, wondering when Fleming's lecture would start.

"Are you okay?" he finally asked, tapping his hand against his knees.

"Yeah. Fine."

"I'm sorry. I shouldn't have put you in that position."

"You don't have to do this," I said quietly, leaning against the door. "This whole *guardian* thing. I'm fine. You don't need to worry."

"I'm not— I'd be worried about any student—"

"So I punched Adrestus," I admitted. "It's far from the worst thing I've done to him and things got *spicy* but we're all okay. Let's just forget it."

Fleming scratched his cheek and pursed his lips.

"Consider it forgotten, but my apology stands." He held out a hand, unfurling his fingers to reveal the pager. "I have a mission for you. Kind of."

"Is it to watch this?" I smirked at the gray plastic, taking it from Fleming and turning it in my hands.

"Justin named it the Doomsday Pager," Fleming half-laughed. "It'll probably continue to count down, but check it daily anyway. Remi looked it over. She says it's connected to another device, but communication is one way."

I closed my fist around the pager.

"I'll keep you updated." I pushed the car door open.

"Samantha, if you want to talk—"

I froze with one foot out the door, my back to Fleming. Did I want to talk? I wanted my family. I wanted to be Samantha again. I wanted to forget Adrestus ever existed. Talking might make Fleming feel better, but what if it just made me feel more *broken*?

"I said I'm okay," I insisted. "I'll let you know if the pager changes."

I closed the door behind me harder than I meant to, but disappeared into the corridor towards the gym without looking back.

The next day, I found Bethany sobbing in the bathroom before English class and she fell into my arms, crying that Anthony had broken up with her that morning.

When I asked him about it at lunch, he hunched over his quesadilla miserably.

"It's better this way," he insisted.

"But you like her," Naomi interjected. "I can feel that you do."

Anthony looked up from his plate, angry tears in his eyes.

"You haven't heard the things the guys on our floor have been saying about Jamie. Really mean, horrible things about her and Andersen. It's *gross* and I hate it. What if they find out about me? I couldn't live with myself if they said those things about Bethany."

"You don't get to decide that for Bethany, though," Naomi reminded him. "It's not fair that she doesn't get a say in what she's willing to risk. Now you're *both* miserable."

Anthony shook his head and Wesley patted his shoulder.

"Anthony's got a lot going on," he said gently. His eyes flitted up to meet mine. He'd been careful not to voice his worry over me after the events at the museum, but I could still see it softly broiling beneath our every interaction since the day before. "It's okay to not date anyone right now if it's adding to that stress."

Naomi conceded the point, but Anthony left most of his quesadilla uneaten.

Training that afternoon carried more tension than usual with the news of the Doomsday Pager and Adrestus knowing Justin's name, but there was an odd layer of anticipation I didn't quite understand. The others were on edge, just not in a "The Island Is In Mortal Peril and Only We Can Stop It" kind of way.

Fleming called us all to the middle of the gym as practice ended. He looked annoyed about whatever he was about to announce, but the room buzzed with excitement. Naomi grabbed my arm and pulled me to stand with the other sophomores.

"The Apex Team Games." Heather's eyes lit up and she stared hungrily at the stack of papers in Fleming's arms. "Other kids have their parents watch them play soccer or basketball. Our families get one week out of the year to watch us play in a series of competitions. Might as well have some fun if the Doomsday Pager says the city's gonna burn in a few weeks."

"Listen up!" Fleming shouted. "Most of you know the Apex Team Games are next week, which means you already know what these are."

He handed the stack of papers to Justin and the senior students fell upon them like piranhas.

"Each of you can represent your grade in one of the four contests. Figure out amongst yourselves who will play in what and get the assignments to me by dinnertime tomorrow," Fleming continued. The papers went to the juniors next before Heather wrestled them in our direction.

Fleming continued to go over the rules but it was hard to pay attention while flipping through the packet. Each of the five sections had a header like "Stealth" or "Strength and Endurance". I could easily see my friends with their extraordinary talents being able to compete with college kids, but me? At least I had no family to watch me make a fool of myself.

"How many competitions are there supposed to be?" I mumbled. Fleming had said four, but there were five different contests listed in the packet.

"We're only allowed to compete in the first four," Naomi explained. "You have to be cleared to train with weapons to join in the last, and that's almost exclusively kids from the college."

A weapons contest was probably the only event I would stand a chance in. Strength and Endurance was out of the question and while there were two different Stealth games that looked manageable, I knew I would never compare next to students like Olivia and Heather.

"Looks like we're stuck with the weak link." Andersen glowered down his nose at me. I stuck my chin out at him.

"I've seen you fight, Andersen," I quipped. "I'm *not* the weak link here."

"Big talk from someone who's been knocked unconscious twice this week."

"Good news!" Heather interrupted. "There's four different events, so you guys don't need to *really* work together at all."

I clenched my fists but smiled. The other teams were already deep in strategy talks.

"Alright, fine. Who wants to do—" I glanced at the first competition, "'Stealth and Strategy'?"

"That's easy." Olivia raised her hand but Heather pulled it down, looking around the gym cautiously.

"Maybe we should be a bit *stealthier* and *strategize* somewhere else?" Heather began to lead the way to the lockers. "Shower and dinner, first. Then we plot our victory."

10

Swordplay

Heather, Wesley, and Olivia huddled over the rickety table at the center of the boys' dorm study room, making notes and mumbling to each other while the rest of us took up the mix-match furniture around the space. I sat between Naomi and Everest on the couch closest to the window, ignoring Andersen glaring at me from where he perched on the arm of a thread-bare armchair.

"Do we all get to know the plan?" Freddie asked from the corner. His hay-colored hair puffed around his head in a post-shower frizz halo. "Or are you three keeping it a surprise all week?"

Heather slapped her hands together and spun to face the group.

"Alright, recap. Four events. Two different stealth comps, a strength and endurance test, and a rescue course," she said. "There's ten of us, so that means two to three people for each event."

"I'll take strength and endurance," Wesley offered. Andersen and Skyler both snorted but Wesley ignored them. "It's a boat race and we need two people."

"Great, so take those two and carry the dead weight so the rest of us don't have to." Andersen pointed at Remi and me.

"What did I do?" Remi exclaimed.

"You didn't make the team until Fleming allowed cutting corners." Andersen smacked his packet. "I looked over the events during dinner and there's nothing to do with computers, so, like I said, you're dead weight."

Wesley stood with Remi and grabbed her hand while I pretended to suddenly be very interested in a pen mark on the back of mine.

"They're two-person boats," he said. "Someone has to come with me and you'd be more help than you realize."

She blushed and pushed back a curtain of dark blonde curls. I missed the days when they'd been unable to be in the same room without trying to murder each other.

"Great." Heather made a note on her packet. "Wesley and Remi for the strength and endurance regatta. Next, the stealth comps."

After several minutes of weighing the pros and cons of who would be better in the Stealth-and-Strategy event versus the Stealth-and-Speed race, I ended up grouped with Heather and Naomi for the former. I was happy to be teamed with them but in a game of glorified tag in the pitch dark, I'd be useless next to Naomi's ability to find easy marks and Heather's powerhouse control over darkness itself.

Olivia and Freddie paired up for the stealth race across the island, leaving Andersen, Skyler, and Everest for the rescue course, which, with the exception of Everest, was the last team I'd want to be rescuing me.

With the assignments set, the others started dispersing. Heather, Freddie, and Olivia mentioned frozen yogurt and I looked to Wesley expectantly. He still had Remi's hand in his and he smiled and shrugged.

"You guys go," he said. "We're going to hang back."

So, Wesley was going through with it. He was going to ask Remi out. I didn't feel like eating frozen yogurt anymore, or even *real* ice cream for that matter.

"Yeah, sure." I sounded too happy. "We'll catch you later."

I followed the others out of the study room and out of the dorm into the brisk December night. Naomi brushed my elbow before speaking up.

"I think I'm actually going to skip on Froyo," she said, looking at me.

"Really?" Olivia frowned. "You feel okay?"

"Just tired. Early bedtime for me tonight."

"I'll come with you." I was grateful for the excuse to not join the others. Olivia shrugged and turned away.

"Suit yourselves."

After the others had put some distance between us, Naomi grinned.

"Back to the gym?" she offered.

I ran my hands over my face and groaned.

"Back to the gym."

I paced back and forth across the gym floor while Naomi lay on her back in the center of the room.

"What's wrong?" she asked after letting me stew for several minutes. She'd been kind enough not to ask me about the museum yesterday, but she had to know I was keeping secrets.

"Nothing," I lied. I wondered what Wesley and Remi were doing. I needed to know and I didn't know why. "I'm nervous about the competition. I don't know how to be stealthy or strategize. Or see in the dark."

"Do you want to change events?"

"Sure." I stopped pacing to lean against a punching bag. "Stick me on the rescue team. I'm infamously good at working with Andersen and Skyler."

"We can tie you to the bow of the boat so you can third wheel with Wesley and Remi."

I'd rather die.

"That wouldn't be so bad."

"Stop!" Naomi sat up to laugh and my cheeks burned. I picked my pacing back up, halfheartedly kicking the punching bag as I went. "You'd rather die."

Nothing got past Naomi. Sometimes that was annoying, but now, I was grateful I didn't have to explain myself.

"It doesn't matter." I shrugged helplessly. "Maybe there was a time when I could've had my shot with Wesley, if that's even what I want, but I blew it."

"You don't know that." But Naomi looked nervous. She knew I had no chance of ever being anything more than friends with Wes.

"A lot happened and I ditched him at the dance." I put on a brave smile and tried to look nonchalant. "I should be lucky we're even friends, and friends don't get to decide who their friends date."

Naomi shook out her mane of curls.

"A lot of friends try, even when they don't have a crush."

I halted in mortification and felt every bit of me glow red.

"I do *not* have a crush," I asserted. I changed course, not wanting to talk about Wesley anymore. "What I do have is a problem, because next Monday I'm expected to do battle against a room full of Apex in the dark."

"You won't be doing battle with anyone," Naomi laughed. "It's a stealth comp. You'll be stealing flags."

"That's worse! I'd rather do battle!"

Naomi thought for a moment before flipping onto her stomach.

"Maybe you can." A sly smile played across her face. "How about the weapons comp?"

I snorted.

"Only college students can play in that one."

"Only *weapon wielders* can play in it, which happens to be the entire college team plus Marcus," Naomi corrected. "I'll be surprised if Marcus plays in it, though, since Mr. Dude Ranch prefers to use a lasso and it's a swordplay competition."

I perked up at the mention of swords.

"I like swords."

"I'll talk to Fleming when the captains meet before school tomorrow. I don't see why he'd say no. I've seen you spar before. If we get you permitted by next week, you'd be clear to play."

Even if I got last place, I'd feel better competing in a sword-based competition than a stealth-based one. Naomi thought my sword fighting prowess came from the skills that Alison had downloaded into my subconscious, but I knew they were a remnant of Eydis. It would be nice to put my emerging past persona to use against a room of college kids trying to show off for their parents.

I sat down next to Naomi. As annoying as her powers were, and as aggravating as her leniency towards jerks like Andersen could be, I was lucky to have her as a friend and roommate. It made it all that much worse to be hiding a secret as big as Eydis from her.

"I would really like that."

"Good." She bit her lip, and I thought she might be considering asking me something. However, she must've decided against it as she relaxed and smiled. "You better get first place. I don't go out of my way to help losers."

Sleep evaded me that night. I was too busy imagining fighting off a room full of university kids. When I tried to quiet my mind, thoughts of Wesley and Remi snuck in and I fought them off with fantasies of taking first place next Friday.

Granted, I still needed to earn my weapons permit.

"Weapons aren't toys."

I opened my eyes. Vidar loomed over me against a stark-blue sky. I brushed moss off my face as he reached down to help me up. A waterfall roared out of sight.

"If they're not toys, why is it called 'swordplay'?"

I eyed the sword hanging from his hip. His arms were scarred and scratched from fights while my fingertips were scarred by the whale bone I used to stitch sails all day. It wasn't fair.

"I'm serious." Vidar's scruff was patchy, not quite a full beard. He was lankier than our brother Knut but much scrappier. "If Dad sees you take this again—"

He patted the sword hilt.

"He'll what? Make me sew more boat sails?"

Vidar snorted and drew the sword.

"Fine. But try to take it without asking again and you'll have more to worry about than sails."

I held out my hands expectantly but Vidar hesitated.

"What?"

"No, sorry." He sheathed the sword again. "You're not ready."

"Yes, I am!"

"Who asks for a sword like this?" He mimicked the way I'd held out my hands.

"But—"

He snapped a low hanging branch off a birch tree and threw it at me.

"We'll start with this."

A pillow smacked me in the face and I startled awake. Gray morning light peeked into the room between the window curtains. Kitschy music played on my phone and Naomi raised the pillow, preparing a second attack.

"Your alarm is going off."

I scrambled to stop the music while Naomi shouldered her book bag.

"Must've been some dream you were having."

"Why? Was I talking?" I mumbled, pushing a tangle of hair out my face.

"No, but you felt frustrated."

"Huh." I was tired of Vidar haunting both my waking and sleeping moments, but there was no telling how long the Serum would continue to bring more memories up. If I could, I'd trade in broken memories of a long-gone life for the real Vidar to be safe and out of Adrestus' clutches. Each time he appeared in my subconscious, it was a bitter reminder that I hadn't found him yet.

Naomi lingered by the door, ready to head to the captain meeting. She adjusted her book bag and gave me an odd look.

"You know you can tell me anything, right?"

It was too early to feel this much shame and guilt.

"I know." I tried to smile. She frowned back at me.

"I know you've been dealing with a lot and you don't have to tell me anything you don't want to, but I'm here."

I wanted to tell her. I needed to tell her eventually. But she was on her way out the door. Now was a bad time.

"Thanks," I said instead.

She forced a smile and opened the door.

"Wish me luck, then," she chirped. "If all goes well, you'll be permitted to wield weapons by the end of the week."

By the time class started, I already had a headache from juggling thoughts of Vidar, sword fighting, and how happy Wesley and Remi were at breakfast. My day at least seemed to be going better than Andersen's, who, for the third day in a row, rushed into the cafeteria in the last minutes of breakfast to shovel eggs into his mouth without sitting down.

In the safety of the training facility, Andersen's friends stuck by his side, but during the school day, they kept their distance.

"I heard he has the power to make anyone do anything he wants," a girl whispered at the table next to ours at lunch. "*That's* how he got Jamie to date him in the first place!"

Wesley sat between Anthony and Remi and glared at his tater tots.

"That's ridiculous," Wesley muttered. "No one can do that."

"Avery can."

The others looked at me in surprise.

"Your brother?" Naomi asked.

"You have a brother?" Remi asked.

"Half-brother," I clarified, even though that wasn't right, either. Since Dad was actually my brother, Avery was my nephew.

"You mentioned he was an Apex before, but I didn't realize it was something so..." Naomi searched for the right word.

"Horrifying?" Wesley offered. Anthony elbowed him.

"He's not very good at it," I admitted. "Granted, it's been a while since I've heard from him or Alison."

Remi glanced between us all expectantly, but I didn't feel like catching her up on my family drama.

"Won't you see them at the Apex Team Games next week?" she asked. She was trying too hard to be nice.

"It's unlikely."

"Don't worry," Wesley interjected. "My mom will be here and she's going to love you."

"What makes you think so?"

"You're not an Apex, for one."

Now it was Remi's turn to look dour.

"My dad will love *all* of you," Naomi said. "Just a warning, he'll try to take us to dinner."

"I'm not about to complain about free food," Wesley grinned, "and the more people around to entertain my mom, the better."

As we walked into the gym for fourth period training with Coach Reiner, Skyler swore loudly. Sergio chatted with Reiner across the room, stretching as he did. He wore a black eyepatch over his right eye, even though I could've sworn both his eyes had been fine last week.

"Did I miss the memo for pirate day?" I mumbled. Naomi stifled a laugh.

"No, Sergio only has one eye. He usually wears a glass prosthesis but doesn't like to fight with it in."

"The better question is why is he back?" Heather moaned. "I'm finally feeling warm again after last week."

"Someone go get Everly," Freddie said under his breath. "He'll stop this."

Coach Reiner turned her sharp gaze our way and we froze.

"Taylor, come here." She beckoned me over, using Alison's maiden name as usual.

"It's Havardson," I reminded her as I side-eyed Sergio.

She nodded at Sergio, who grinned like a hungry shark.

"You're going to work with Sergio today."

I tried not to make a face.

"Is this because I passed out in the pool?" I asked. "Because I still outlasted almost everyone else so—"

Reiner laughed, but that only made me more apprehensive.

"Sergio isn't here to ice anyone this time. Fleming told me you're going for your weapons permit. We've scheduled an assessment for you on Saturday morning. Sergio has agreed to train you the next few days to get you ready."

I looked at Sergio in surprise. Even though Naomi had said all of the college students on the team were required to get their weapons permit, I hadn't imagined someone with an ability as powerful as Sergio's would need weapons.

Sergio led the way to the corner where Andersen and Skyler sparred hand-to-hand. They paused as we approached.

"We need this space," Sergio said.

"We were here first." Skyler crossed his arms and stood his ground.

"I need the corner furthest from any doors." Sergio was unfazed. His man-bun added to his already ample height and his arms were lean and chiseled. He held out his hands and two spectacular blades of ice formed, their icy handles wrapping around his fists. "Can't have anyone walking in and getting hurt."

"I didn't realize Samantha sucked so bad that they needed to call in extra help," Andersen sneered.

"I'm here so she can get her weapons permit before the games next week, actually," Sergio grinned. His teeth were white against his olive-toned skin. "If you have a problem, talk to Reiner about it, but this is the safest spot in the gym for sword fighting."

Andersen's eyebrows raised.

"I thought you were doing a stealth comp."

"Depends on how this goes." I tried to look nonchalant. I would've preferred not to have Andersen know I was going for the permit. It would make it that much more embarrassing if I didn't get it.

"Wait!" Wesley called from across the gym. He and Naomi were already going through dodges with Remi but he stopped to look across the gym at me. Nothing got past his super hearing. "You never said you were trying to get your weapons permit!"

I froze as all the sophomores stopped to stare at me.

"You're not doing the stealth competition with us?" Heather asked. My cheeks burned so hot, I thought they might melt Sergio's swords.

"It-it depends."

"I didn't know you knew how to sword fight." Everest looked warily at Sergio's blades. "Is this another one of the skills your mom put in your head?"

"I took fencing classes growing up," I lied, bristling inwardly at the mention of Alison downloading fighting abilities and prowess into my subconscious. Wesley gave my fib a subtle thumbs up.

"Right!" Olivia said. "I forgot you fought off one of Adrestus' men with a sword before joining the team!"

Reiner came to my rescue, yelling that whoever wasn't sparring in the next five seconds owed her laps after school. Andersen and Skyler reluctantly gave up their corner and Sergio faced me triumphantly.

"So you make ice?" I pointed at his swords.

"I control temperature." He demonstrated by turning both blades into steam. "I need a water source to make ice but in a humid room full of people exercising and sweating, it's easy to pull moisture out of the air."

He reformed the swords and offered me one but I recoiled.

"I don't want your sweaty icicle."

"It's just the water content, not the sweat." To prove his point, he lifted the ice to his face and dragged his tongue along its length. He smacked his lips and puckered. "Alright, so maybe it *is* a little salty, but you'll be fine."

I took the ice reluctantly and weighed it in my hand.

"Is this how you...you know." I pointed at my eye. Sergio's mouth parted in a surprised smile.

"My eye?" he laughed. "No swords involved. I had a tumor as a kid. Didn't your parents ever tell you not to ask people about their missing eyeballs?"

I blushed and Sergio laughed harder, drawing looks from the other students.

"Sorry," I mumbled. "I didn't think—"

"Don't be," he insisted. "My missing eye is cool."

Somehow, the smile he gave me made me blush even harder. I cleared my throat and gave the ice-sword a test swing.

"So you fenced, huh?" he mused. "This is more like a double-bladed sword than a fencing saber, so the mechanics will be a bit different than what you're used to."

"Keep your grip loose," Vidar's voice echoed from a long-forgotten memory, but I remained present in the gym. "You'll have better control over the blade if you do."

"I think I'll be alright." Sergio must've been actively using his powers to keep the handle from melting in my grip. It stayed solid as I gave it a test swing.

"We can start with something more saber-like, but the ice will be more likely to break."

"I said it's fine."

"Great." He flashed a haughty grin. "Then show me what you've got."

I lunged.

"Wide, arching movements open you up to attacks," Vidar's voice commanded. I focused on Sergio to keep the room from disappearing and being replaced by whatever memory Vidar was speaking from. "Being too fancy will get you killed."

Sergio parried my attack and the crack of ice on ice drew the attention of the rest of the room.

"If your opponent is long and lanky, limit their movement by keeping in tight," Vidar said.

"You mean like you?" Eydis laughed.

I twisted in close to Sergio.

"Never turn away from your opponent. Fancy twirls—"

"Will get me killed?"

"Yes."

Sergio stumbled away and I jabbed at him again. He locked his ice-blade against mine and forced me back before bringing his sword over me.

"You won't be able to rely on strength like me," Vidar instructed. "You need to be faster than everyone else. Learn to read their movements. Figure out what they'll do next, before they know it themself."

I sidestepped Sergio's attack. He'd left himself open. I slashed at his exposed side but before I could make contact, a second sheet of ice erupted from his free hand, deflecting me.

"That's cheating!" I cried in tandem with Eydis. I could feel the sting of the dirt Vidar had thrown in her eyes.

"There's no such thing as cheating." Sergio's voice mingled with Vidar's as they spoke in unison and I shook my head to clear it.

Sergio's preferred method of fighting was clearly with dual swords. He spiraled towards me, blades whirling, forcing me to defend and dodge at the same time.

Someone cheered for me in support, but I almost didn't recognize the sound of my own name. I wasn't Sammy anymore. I was Eydis and I was going to win.

And Sergio was being fancy. Being fancy would get you killed.

I feigned one way and as I blocked one blade, the other swung overhead in a wide arc. I reached up with my free hand, grabbing his wrist. I delivered a front kick to his abdomen and he fell back. I readied my sword. I'd only have a moment.

He spun towards me, but you should never turn your back to an opponent.

As my blade struck him in the center of his back, it evaporated into steam. Sergio stopped mid-spin and gawked at me with a surprised grin.

"*Ég vinn,*" I declared.

"What was that?" Sergio laughed.

"I said I win," I repeated.

"You definitely said 'eye-vin'." Freddie stood along the far wall of the gym where most of the others had grouped to watch.

"Those must've been some fencing classes." Sergio's dual blades turned to vapor. "I was going easy on you, of course, but you mind giving me the name of your teacher?"

"It was my dad."

"I knew Alison had good taste in men." Coach Reiner appeared behind me. "Sergio, you spin too much."

"I said I was going easy on her, didn't I?"

The door slammed shut. Skyler leaned against the wall next to it, Andersen no longer by his side.

"Good fighting, but maybe just go over what she can expect on Saturday." Reiner patted Sergio's shoulder with a heavy hand. "Fleming wasn't kidding when he said she already had the skills."

As Sergio and I retreated back to our corner, Naomi winked at me and Wesley continued to gawk. He'd seen me sword fight before, but he'd had a poor vantage point from where he'd been motionless on the ground.

Remi tugged on his arm to bring him back to their practice session and I smiled in spite of myself.

Her memories got in the way and Eydis had brought me more baggage than I cared for, but in that moment, I liked how it felt to be her.

11

Qualifying

Over the next few days, I learned that Sergio had, in fact, been going easy on me in our first training session. While my blows vaporized into steam each time I struck him with an ice sword, he did not afford me the same luxury. By Friday, my sides were painted with bruises but Sergio always sent me away from practice with a baggie of ice conjured from the air.

Sergio may have made gym class difficult, but Fleming let up on usual training with Finals looming. Instead, he gave us time to strategize and train for the oncoming competitions. I split my time at the punching bag and working with Naomi and Heather in case I didn't pass the permitting test on Saturday.

I was terrible at fighting blind, but the Stealth and Strategy event would be in total darkness. Naomi pulled a blindfold over my eyes and set me against Heather, who proceeded to whale on me for the rest of training.

I at least seemed to be having a better time than Remi, who spent the two hours on a rowing ergometer next to Wesley. Twenty minutes before dinner, she ripped her feet from the straps and emptied her stomach in a trashcan and collapsed in a pool of sweat.

Junior twins Mike and Desirae sparred nearby and grimaced at the sight of her.

"This is what happens when just anyone is let on the team," Mike muttered, but caught me looking at him. "Not you! It's different. Besides, I heard you outmatched Sergio in a sword fight."

After working so hard to prove I was worthy of the team despite not being an Apex, I thought it would feel better to hear that I wasn't "just anyone" even if I'd made it onto the team on the same technicality as Remi. Instead, vague irritation welled inside me for Remi's sake. She annoyed me, sure, but Mike and Desirae didn't need to make fun of her.

"Doesn't matter if she can't row." Desirae swung a gloved hand at her brother. "Wesley will out-row anyone."

"Out-*row*, sure," Mike said slyly, "but he won't be able to beat—"

Desirae swiped at him again, catching him with an uppercut to the abdomen. He doubled over and she flinched, grabbing her own stomach as their Apex-powered twin link sent Mike's pain rippling through her.

"Don't tell them our strategy, you idiot!"

Naomi and Heather pretended not to hear them but shared a meaningful look. Heather mouthed, "*Isabelle*". Anthony's cousin had a lot more practice with their family's wind-based powers than he had and would easily be able to propel their team's boat across the water while leaving the others in a hurricane.

Training wrapped up with Fleming announcing there would be no after school practice the next week due to parent conferences. With instructions to report to the university arena on Monday evening, he set us loose.

Showered and ready for dinner, I walked out of the locker room with Naomi. Andersen stood in his favorite corner of the atrium, glowering at me. He'd been surprisingly docile all week but never wasted a moment that could be spent glaring.

"What's Andersen's problem?" I whispered to Naomi in the hall. "I'm not the one who announced to the school that he's an Apex. Jamie is."

"I told you already, I'm not your personal Andersen barometer."

"But you'd let me know if he was planning on murdering me, right?"

Naomi made a sound between a snort and laugh.

"I promise Andersen isn't planning on murdering you. As moody as he can be, he's not capable of that."

Little did Naomi know, Andersen *was* capable of murder. I crossed my arms to brace for the outdoor air.

"He could at least stop staring at me."

"He's unhappy," Naomi said simply. "He wants someone to blame and you're an easy target. Don't take it personally."

"Feels pretty personal."

"Leave the feeling to me, then," Naomi joked. "Also, my dad is taking us to dinner tomorrow."

Even though I knew parents would start arriving this weekend, I hadn't given any thought to Naomi's family.

"Just your dad?"

"My sisters and brother, too, since I—" She stopped walking and looked at the ground. She took a moment before giving me an apologetic smile. "I don't go home for Christmas. Or, ever."

"Oh." I gulped. Naomi had mentioned her relationship with her mom was strained but in their many phone and video calls, I'd never seen anything to hint at difficulties between them, let alone anything so bad Naomi couldn't go home.

"My mom has powers just like mine," Naomi explained. "Genetics, you know. Like me, she can't turn it off."

It was a bit hypocritical for Naomi to want to avoid her mom for being able to read her emotions, especially since she knew better than anyone there was nothing she could do to stop it. I bit my tongue, knowing that was the wrong thing to say.

Naomi gave me a smile that was both sly and sad and it didn't matter that I didn't say anything. I, like everyone around her, was an open book.

"It's more complicated than you might think," she said and I was relieved to hear a suppressed laugh hiding in her tone. "Have you ever held a microphone up to a speaker?"

"Sure," I said, mentally thanking Alison for the weird amount of detail she put into my fake memories. "It's loud and high pitched and horrible."

"It's a feedback loop," she explained, "and it's what happens when Mom and I get too close. Growing up was fine, but then my powers manifested. It starts quiet, but I feel her feeling emotions, and she feels me feeling that, which I feel, which she feels, which I feel, and so on. I don't know how to explain it, but even the happiest emotions become unbearable and—"

I pulled her in, wrapping my arms around her and holding her there. I felt her shoulders relax and her head bowed forward to rest on my shoulder. Even if Adrestus had my dad, I could at least hope to get him back. Naomi loved her mom but it was physically too painful to be near her with no way to stop her power. As bleak as both of our situations were, and even though she could still talk to her mom on the phone, I didn't envy her.

"I'll be in New Delos for the holidays, too," I said. "Where are you staying?"

She pulled away and tried to be subtle about wiping a tear away.

"Everly's. I stayed with him last year with Mike and Desirae. He does Hanukkah, which is pretty fun, and has a big family. It feels more like home."

"I'll be at Fleming's," I reminded her. "We'll see each other. And we have all next week to hang out with your dad and siblings!"

"What're you guys still doing out here?"

Wesley and Remi had caught up with us. I tried not to look at their hands clasped together.

"Enjoying the good weather."

Wesley laughed at my joke but Remi looked up at the night sky as if there might be a sunbeam there she hadn't noticed.

We walked to the cafeteria and Naomi laughed and joked with the others. I should've been worried about the permit test tomorrow morning, or the fact that we still had no idea what fiery mess the Doomsday Pager was counting down to. Instead, all I could think about was how Naomi's family had been torn apart by her abilities and how Andersen's powers had made him a social pariah.

Maybe being a Beta made me the lucky one.

I liked the locker room the best when there was no one else there. Sergio had insisted the permitting test would be no problem for me and unlike the Trials required to pass to join the team, I could take it as many times as needed.

I picked up my helmet and took a final deep breath, looking over my reflection. I was secretly glad I was required to wear the full uniform for the test. It made me look like I knew what I was doing and not at all like I was making this up as I went. In a weird way, I'd be relying on Eydis and her experience to get me through this.

I pulled my phone from my locker and went to my most recent outgoing call. I redialed the number. It went straight to voicemail, like it had for months, and I was greeted by Dad's gruff voice recording.

"This is Vic. You know what to do."

I hung up as the message tone sounded and Reiner shouted for me in the hall.

"Taylor!" There was no use correcting her on my name anymore. "We're ready for you!"

Reiner led me out into the atrium and down the hall to the sparring room. A low wall enclosed the matted floor. A small set of bleachers overlooked the ring, and while I'd known the six council members would be there, I was surprised by the small crowd that sat around them.

"Sammy!" Heather shrieked. Most of the sophomores were there, with the notable but predictable exceptions of Andersen and Skyler. Even Anthony had joined, sitting between Wesley and Isabelle.

Isabelle wasn't the only upperclassman there, either. All of the captains had come, as had the twins Mike and Desirae. Sergio sat in a small group of older kids I didn't recognize and my stomach clenched uncomfortably. They had to be university team members.

The Apex Council sat in the center of the bottom bleacher. Fleming smiled uneasily and I withered under the hawkish stare of the gray-haired school principal, Dr. Weaver. She was the only council member other than Fleming who knew who I really was, but never looked particularly happy to see me.

I couldn't blame her. With her self-healing powers, she donated a lot of plasma and spinal fluid for use in the Serum and my recent misadventures had increased demand.

The University Team leader, Professor Parker, sat next to Fleming, her box braids resting over one shoulder. She scribbled furiously at her clipboard even though I hadn't started the test yet.

Officer Allen sat on her other side as the police department representative and was already going over notes with the City Council rep, who I knew by the name Mickey but I wasn't sure if it was his first or last.

Finally, Trev Baker sat at the end. He took a long drink of coffee, squinting at me over the rim of the oversized travel mug that never seemed far. I tightened my grip on my helmet. *Don't trust your friends.* I was still convinced the mystery person at the museum had meant Baker.

"Good morning, Samantha." A rare, coy smile played on Dr. Weaver's lips. "You've drawn quite the crowd."

"You should've charged admittance."

No one laughed. Naomi hid her eyes behind her hand in the back row. I gulped.

"Please note this clears you to *train* with your selected weapon, allowing you to compete with other members of Apex Team in controlled environments. It's the first step to being allowed to wield weapons against Apex threats in the field, but you've got a long road before you are anywhere near ready to do so," Dr. Weaver recited from her notes. "What is your intended weapon?"

"Oh. Uh..." I was too distracted by the crowd. My friends and teammates stared expectantly and I stared blankly back. One of Sergio's college friends stifled a laugh. "A-a sword?"

"What kind?"

"I don't know, the sharp kind?"

Sergio hadn't prepared me for an interrogation.

"I told you this was a waste of time." Trev dropped his clipboard in his lap and leaned forward to look down the line of his colleagues.

"Longsword? Rapier?" Dr. Weaver prompted.

"Like the one at the museum," I said.

"She gets lucky using a sword one time, months ago, and I'm expected to make time for this on my day off?" Trev said.

"No one is forcing you to stay on the Apex Council." I should've been grateful Fleming was sticking up for me, but I was afraid he was giving Baker more reasons to complain.

Dr. Weaver ignored the squabbling men and nodded towards the equipment closet.

"Go ahead and pick out a waster, then."

Sergio had shown me the practice swords called wasters on our second day of training but I'd opted to forgo them in favor of the ice swords. They'd had more weight to them and felt more like the real thing.

I turned towards the equipment room but Sergio called out behind me.

"I've got one!"

He stumbled down the bleachers and gave the council his most dashingly apologetic smile.

"That hasn't been approved—" Trev started but Coach Reiner interrupted.

"Perfect!" She took the ice sword from Sergio and handed it off to me. Like last time I'd used Sergio's ice sword, the handle kept from melting, giving me a non-slip grip on the blade. "Much better than plastic."

"But—" Trev turned red.

"Thank you, Mr. Silva." Dr. Weaver waved Sergio back to his seat. "Let's get this going. Trev did make a point about this being our day off."

Just as Sergio had warned me, Reiner ran me through a series of drills while the council members made notes on their clipboards. Every once in a while, one of them would interject to ask to see a move again.

After I'd nailed every position, lunge, parry, and strike, Reiner nodded in approval.

"Great, now get your helmet. Sergio, I'm going to need one of those."

I secured my helmet and adjusted my grip on the ice. I'd sparred hand-to-hand with Reiner once before and it hadn't been a long fight. However, they'd be hard pressed to find anyone who could best an Apex with the skills to replicate any and every fighting style with ease.

Reiner attacked as soon as my helmet was secure. I stumbled backwards as I parried her attack but if she wanted to defeat me, I'd already be on the ground with a bright, new bruise to add to my growing collection.

And she didn't want to defeat me. She wanted to test me, which meant there would be openings in her attacks, no matter how small. As soon as I saw my chance, I took it, breaking through the onslaught to put her on the defense.

I wouldn't have minded Vidar's voice in my head, but I at least had Eydis' instincts. My nerves melted and it felt less like a test and more like a game.

"Sammy, you got this!"

Wesley's cheer took me by surprise, as did the series of whoops and cries that went up from the other sophomores in response. I kept my eyes on Reiner's sword arm, but in my periphery, I thought I saw her smile.

She cranked up the difficulty. Bits of ice blew off the blades with every blow and after working up a sweat under my helmet, I spotted an opening and lunged.

Reiner sidestepped my attack but momentum carried me forward. The blow to my back knocked me forward onto my knees, but by the sounds of cheering from my friends and the wide grin on Reiner's face as she helped me to my feet, I knew I hadn't lost because I'd failed but because Reiner had decided the test was over.

"Excellent work." Professor Parker grinned at me as the council members filed out of the room to compare notes and decide if I'd passed or not. I pulled my helmet off to watch them go and as soon as the door closed, someone tackled me from behind, knocking me to the matted floor.

"That was amazing!" Wesley cried. He rolled off me and another three bodies barreled towards me as Anthony, Naomi, and Heather rushed the floor, too. A sudden gust of wind ruffled my hair.

"Sorry!" Anthony took a deep breath to regain control. "I can't help it sometimes."

"We don't know that I passed yet."

Wesley held up a hand for silence and tilted his head to one side as he tried to listen, but shook his head in resignation.

"They went all the way to Fleming's office. I can't make out anything they're saying from here."

"We'll know in five minutes," Naomi said. "Are you that impatient?"

"Yes. Naomi, you already know this about me."

The students who'd come to watch the test lingered in the bleachers and the fighting ring. I felt confident, but wished most of them would leave. If Trev somehow convinced the others I wasn't skilled enough to wield a weapon, I didn't want everyone to hear the bad news with me.

As the sophomores chattered excitedly, I caught a snippet of Justin and Marcus' conversation on the bleachers.

"If the sophomores have someone in the weapons comp, maybe we should, too," Marcus said in a hushed tone. "She might actually stand a chance and that might be enough for their team to pull ahead of us."

"You're the only senior who can see in the dark!" Justin protested. "What's the point of picking up a win in combat if we lose stealth because of it?"

"Hey!" Naomi suddenly yelped, looking at her phone. She beamed around at us. "My family's on campus!"

"Are we still on for dinner tonight?" Wesley asked, rubbing his hands together but Remi cleared her throat.

"We're supposed to see my parents."

His smile faltered but he shrugged good-naturedly.

"They need to eat, too, don't they?"

"It'll be fun," Naomi interjected before Remi could retort. "My dad and Mrs. Isaacs get along and he'd love to meet your parents, too."

Remi's shoulders relaxed and she turned to Wesley.

"Fine, but Sunday you're helping me show them around the city."

"Yeah, sure, sure." He leapt to his feet. "We'll talk about it later. The Council's coming back!"

We rushed to the bleachers and my stomach tightened. Fleming led the way in with a smile. Naomi patted my knee.

"They're all very pleased," she whispered. "Most of them, anyway."

Trev lingered in the doorway while his colleagues came into the room. His obvious displeasure was the cherry on top.

"Congratulations, Samantha," Dr. Weaver said. "With a council vote of five to one, you've been granted your permit to train with a double-edged, single-hand sword."

I glowed with pride as my teammates applauded. I'd finally accomplished something to make up for my failure at the Trials. I flinched as someone gave me a hearty congratulatory back-pat right where Reiner had struck me.

"We'll work on developing a tool that isn't quite as lethal as an actual blade," Dr. Weaver continued. "In the meantime, you're free to compete against the college students in Friday's competition if you wish."

I nodded eagerly and Fleming made a note on his clipboard.

I let the others go on ahead as I still needed to change before dinner. Just when I thought nothing could bring me down from the high I was feeling, Trev Baker intercepted me in the hall to the lockers.

"The council made a mistake." Only half the hall lights were on and his face was lost in shadow. I wrapped my arms around my helmet in front of me.

"When they let *you* into their club, maybe," I scowled.

His arms hung loosely at his side, his travel mug empty.

"You still have time to save yourself, Samantha." His words sent goosebumps up my arms. Was he finally going to reveal his allegiance to Adrestus while we were alone?

"Tell your boss—"

"I'm not talking about him," he snapped. "I mean you're going to die. I've seen it."

12

Pastas and Premonitions

Laughter echoed down the hall from the atrium, sounding distorted and distant as the walls swooped around me. I'd died before and the idea didn't scare me, but the haunted look on Baker's shadowed face made me falter. I couldn't tell if he was threatening me or trying to warn me.

"Trev!" Fleming's hand appeared on my shoulder. "Can I see you in my office?"

"I'm not one of your students, Alex, and she deserves to know."

I pulled away from Fleming.

"Know what?" I snapped. Fleming of all people should know how I felt about secrets. His mouth pressed together as he surveyed Baker.

"Mr. Baker's abilities allow him to see the future." He chose his words carefully and Baker snorted in contempt.

"They let me see *death*," he clarified. "Every night when I go to sleep."

I eyed the empty coffee mug and I didn't like the swell of pity that washed over me. I'd probably pump myself full of caffeine, too, if that's what waited for me every night.

He was still a jerk, though.

"And you saw me die?" I asked, my apprehension fading. I *had* died. Whatever he'd seen had probably already happened.

"Multiple times."

Yeah, that sounded right.

"She's fine, Trev," Fleming drawled. "Your visions don't always come to pass."

Baker held out his hand and counted on shaking fingers and his eyes widened in a mania that made me wonder just how many times he'd been forced to watch me meet my multiple ends.

"Stabbed, neck snapped, frozen in the bay, electrocuted. I've seen her die so many times that I'm starting to get *bored* of it! Being on this team *will* kill her!"

"She's *fine!*"

Baker stepped forward and pressed his mug into Fleming's chest.

"It'll be on you," he hissed, spit spraying from between his lips. "Whichever one it ends up being, it'll be your fault."

He shouldered past Fleming and I looked up at my history teacher, waiting for him to turn his frustration on me. He shook his head.

"I hadn't heard the frozen or electrocuted ones yet," he murmured, looking at me like I might drop dead then and there. I'd already frozen to death, even if Fleming was still unaware, but electrocuted? That was news to me.

"You said they don't always come true," I said, trying to make myself feel better. "I'm sure I'm fine."

Fleming nodded, but he'd turned green in the low light.

"You always are, somehow."

I was more than happy to put Trev Baker's death visions behind me, meeting up with Naomi on the first floor of the school. I had to run to keep up with her as she hurried across campus to the dorm lobby, where a tall, dark man waited with two preteens.

"Dad!" Naomi launched herself into the arms of her smartly dressed father. He lifted her off her feet as he hugged her.

"Look at you!" he exclaimed. "More gorgeous every time I see you!"

He set Naomi down and planted a kiss on her forehead. Back on the ground, she was fair game for her brother and sister to latch onto, each wrapping their arms around her and jumping.

"Hey, hey, look!" She pried them off of her and pointed at me. "That's Samantha. And *this* is Will and Zoey."

Zoey looked to be about nine and giggled, hiding behind Naomi as she clung to her big sister's arm. Will appeared slightly older and smiled confidently. Naomi glanced around, her smile fading.

"Where's Joni?"

Mr. Bradford frowned. Zoey and Will looked at each other and then at the ground.

"What's going on?" Naomi pushed away from her family and crossed her arms at them. "Why isn't Joni here?"

"Joni has some good news." However, Mr. Bradford's face said the news was anything but good.

"Dad?"

Mr. Bradford hesitated, glancing at me nervously.

"I can catch up with you guys later for dinner," I mumbled and tried to back out of the lobby, but Naomi reached over and grabbed my arm.

"What good news?" Her face had turned ashen. Her fingers shook where she grabbed me. Mr. Bradford pulled an envelope from his coat.

"She wrote you a letter, but—" he cleared his throat. "She's an Apex, too."

"Like me and Mom?" Naomi's voice cracked. Zoey broke away from her dad to throw herself back at her sister. Naomi let go of my arm to welcome Zoey.

"Yeah," Mr. Bradford said quietly. "She's staying with Aunt Tam until she's old enough to come here. You'll have graduated by then and hopefully there's enough distance between here and the university that you won't have to worry about affecting each other."

Naomi drew the back of her hand across her face and sniffed.

"That's-that's great news. Good for Joni."

Mr. Bradford stepped forward to hug Naomi, sandwiching Zoey between them.

"Have you had any luck, yet?"

"No," Naomi sighed. "Haven't found a way to stop it. Once I do—"

"I know." He stroked the back of Naomi's head. "You'll come home. I know it."

She pulled out of the embrace and took the letter from Mr. Bradford. I watched Zoey and Will run to a lobby couch to play and wondered if someday they'd be pulled away from the family, too, if they had powers manifest.

Naomi leaned against a wall to scan Joni's letter, smiling and laughing sadly to herself at whatever words her sister had sent her. Mr. Bradford turned to me.

"I've heard about you, you know." He had high cheekbones and a wide, white smile that he used to push aside the fact his family was fracturing in front of him. "Naomi has had a lot to say."

I shrugged in embarrassment.

"There's not too much to tell. I'm just Samantha."

"You're crazy is what you are," he chuckled. "I know Naomi doesn't tell us the real scary stuff you kids do, but my wife was on the team once. We know it gets intense keeping Apex threats in the city at bay. I can't imagine joining without any powers."

"Are you...?"

"No." He laughed again but I wasn't sure how he could seem so happy considering the circumstances. Maybe he was used to it. "I'm like you. Hopefully I passed those genes onto Zoey and William, but we'll have to wait and see."

Naomi folded the letter and gently tucked it away in her bag before putting on a brave face and smiling at us from the wall.

"What's for dinner?" she asked.

Mr. Bradford looked around, perplexed.

"I don't know, where are your friends?" He gestured to the empty lobby. "I told you I wanted no less than a small army to feed."

"They're meeting their parents, but we can all get dinner together."

"Of course, and I promise to be on my best behavior for the Councilman." He winked. Naomi scowled.

"Jamie is *not* invited."

"Really?" Genuine surprise spread across Mr. Bradford's face. "I thought for sure you two would've made up by now."

"No, she's worse than ever!"

Naomi launched into the story of how Jamie had told everyone about Andersen's powers and I pitched in details where they were wanted. The distraction was a nice break, but I couldn't help but to feel Naomi was using the story as a way to avoid thinking about her absent sister.

After showing the Bradfords around campus and treating Zoey and William to pre-dinner Froyo, it was finally time to meet Wesley, Remi, and their respective parents downtown for dinner at an Italian restaurant.

Wesley, without a doubt, took after his mom. Mrs. Isaacs had the same unruly brown hair, though longer and grayer. They both had the same long nose and even wore the same style of thick-framed glasses, though I knew Wesley's glasses helped dull his super-sight to keep migraines at bay rather than working to help him see.

As soon as she saw me file out of the backseat of the Bradfords' minivan, Mrs. Isaacs flung her arms wide while Wesley, Remi, and Remi's parents watched from the sidewalk.

"Samantha?" She pulled me into a hug before I could confirm that I was indeed Samantha.

I tried not to look directly at Wesley over his mom's shoulder and instead caught Remi's eyes. They narrowed over a smile that was trying too hard to look sweet. I cleared my throat and pushed away, plastering my own fake smile on my face.

"Mrs. Isaacs, I'm guessing?"

"Yes!" Mrs. Isaacs grinned. "I've heard so much about you!"

I cast Wesley a nervous glance. He'd forgone his glasses for some reason, which always made him look more serious.

"Not too much, I hope."

She laughed in response, steering me towards the restaurant door by the shoulder. When a waiter led us to our table in the back, I tried to vie for a spot next to Naomi, but Zoey and William were too quick. Instead, I ended up between Wesley and his mother.

"Your brother is doing fine, by the way." Mrs. Isaacs leaned over my empty plate to talk to her son. "Do you think you'll make it to his graduation?"

Wesley froze with a breadstick halfway in his mouth, looking back at his mom with wide eyes.

"It would be real nice if you did," she insisted. "You know he'd come if it was yours."

"I might have finals that week."

"Oh, really? Finals? Or are you going to be gallivanting across the city?" She gave him a snide look.

I snorted into my water glass as I took a sip. Mrs. Isaacs raised her eyebrows at me.

"Sorry," I mumbled, wiping water off my face with a napkin. "It's just, I wouldn't call it a gallivant as much as a strut."

"A strut!?" Wesley cried with his mouth full of bread. "I don't strut."

"No, she's right," Remi teased on his other side. "Though, maybe it's more of a swagger?"

Mrs. Isaacs sat back in her chair, giving me back my precious personal space.

"I don't care if you're gallivanting, strutting, swaggering, or sashaying, just try to make it to Benson's graduation."

"You're the one who picks me up from school," Wesley pointed out. "Get me before his graduation and I'll be there."

He grabbed his water glass and it cracked in his hands.

"Wes!" Mrs. Isaacs reached across my lap again to mop up water that leaked from the fissures in Wesley's cup. "You need to be more careful!"

He sat back and stared at the broken glass blankly.

"Are you okay?" I whispered, leaning out of the way of Mrs. Isaacs' elbows. "Did you cut your hand?"

He blinked out of his reverie and looked at his palms.

"I'm fine. Been a while since I've done that." His eyes turned glossy for a moment, but he blinked again, and they cleared. "I've got it, Mom. I'll clean it up."

Remi's dad cleared his throat and turned his attention to Wesley as he tried to stem the water springing from the broken glass.

"Wesley, Remi told us you two are competing together this week." Mr. Whitlock had no hair but lots of beard and rimless glasses that magnified his gray eyes. He looked at Wesley over the top of his menu with skeptical interest. I glanced across the table at Naomi and her siblings. She was helping them complete the maze on their kids' menus.

"Yeah, in the Strength and Endurance competition." He passed the broken glass off to a passing busboy, wiping his palms off on a cloth napkin.

A waitress arrived to take our orders and I tried to speed-read the pasta section without success. By the time it was my turn to order, I panicked.

"Spaghetti?" I sputtered. The waitress paused.

"Are you asking me or...?"

"I—yes?"

Wesley snort-laughed next to me and I elbowed him.

"Did you want a salad or soup with that?"

I felt my eyes widen.

"Yes."

She looked at me expectantly as did the rest of the table.

"Oh, right," I said. "Salad."

"What kind of dressing?"

"S-surprise me."

The corners of her mouth twitched as she wrote something on her order pad.

"It's like you've never ordered food before," Wesley laughed.

The restaurant was suddenly ten degrees warmer and I could hear my heartbeat drumming in my ears. I'd faced an immortal ancient Greek warrior. I'd *died* before. Why was ordering pasta suddenly so terrifying?

"We'll go south first," a disembodied voice crooned in my ear. "You'll love England. It's much warmer there."

I wadded my napkin up in my lap. This was not an ideal time to be visited by memories of young Adrestus.

"I was kidding," Wesley whispered. He rubbed at his eyes, squinting in the restaurant's lights. "I'm sorry. I know you know how to order food."

"No." A manic smile pulled at my face. "I think you're right. I don't think I *have* ever ordered food before."

"What if I don't like the warm?" I heard my voice ask in my head. "What's wrong with the cold?"

"I haven't had feeling in my toes since we came ashore."

William disappeared across the table. Young Adrestus grinned back with rosy cheeks that made his blue eyes stand out more than ever. I blinked him away, focusing on Naomi's brother, trying to mentally stay at the table. Eydis and Adrestus' voices faded and I sighed in relief.

Mr. Bradford and Mrs. Isaacs swapped stories about raising Apex to my left. On my right, Remi's parents continued to interrogate Wesley.

I was relieved when my salad came, doused in a generous helping of ranch dressing. Unfortunately, Mrs. Isaacs had grown bored of her conversation with Naomi's dad.

"What about you, Samantha?" Mrs. Isaacs turned to me. "Tell us about your family."

I prodded at my salad, feeling Naomi and Wesley staring at me.

"They're nice." I finally looked up and smiled at Wesley's mom. "They wish they could be here, but they're, uh, busy."

"If you're not an Apex, then your folks aren't either?" she asked. "Wesley said you're the first non-Apex on the team in a while."

I blushed and shrugged.

"No, my Mom's an Apex," I admitted. "So is my brother."

"Oh." Mrs. Isaacs sat back in her seat. "I suppose that makes sense, too. Where do they live?"

This felt too much like an interrogation.

"On the north part of the island," I said without thinking. Mrs. Isaacs frowned.

"But they couldn't make it this week?"

"Nope." I drummed up an excuse as quickly as I could. "They're helping friends move."

"For a whole week?"

"Yep."

Mrs. Isaacs took a sip of her drink. The straw rattled as it tried to suck up the last of it.

"They sound like good friends to have."

Zoey saved me from further questioning by reaching for a breadstick and knocking over her cup. Mr. Bradford tried to catch the glass, but Zoey and Naomi's salads were already sticky with soda and ice.

"Sorry," Zoey mumbled but Naomi smiled and soaked up the spill with her napkin.

"Is it just your folks, then?" Mrs. Isaacs asked. "No extended family?"

"No, there's more of us," I said automatically. "There's—"

Who was there? I racked my brain.

"Good luck getting Erika to let you take me away," Eydis laughed, reappearing in my head as my blood pressure increased. Adrestus snorted in contempt. I looked around the table, bracing to see him appear, but he stayed locked in my head.

"My mom has a brother and there's my grandpa," I said. Yes, I had a grandpa. I remembered him. "My Grandpa—"

What was his name? I knew his name.

"Maybe Erika can come, too," Adrestus laughed.

"Your Grandpa Max, right?" Wesley offered.

"Yeah!" I speared several pieces of romaine on the end of my fork. "My Grandpa Max. He died a few years ago, though."

"I'm sorry to hear that," Mrs. Isaacs frowned. "How did he...you know?"

"Die?" I asked, maybe too bluntly. Mrs. Isaacs blushed. I gulped. How *did* he die? "I—I don't..."

No, I knew how he died. I remembered the funeral. I remembered the white lilies...the church...it had all been there in my head. Where had it gone?

I shoved salad in my mouth and shrugged an apology as I chewed. It didn't taste like anything.

Why couldn't I remember Grandpa Max?

"Erika would make a good—"

Shut up! I shouted at Eydis and Adrestus. *Shut up, I'm thinking!*

I couldn't see his face but I was certain Alison had put it in my memories. I hadn't even remembered his name until Wesley reminded me.

The room temperature skyrocketed again. Blood roared in my ears but at least it drowned out the sound of Eydis and Adrestus laughing together.

"Sammy?" Wesley asked under his breath.

I stood up and the whole table looked at me. I forced a shaky smile.

"Sorry," I mumbled. "Bathroom."

I pushed my way to the front of the restaurant, not looking back. I couldn't breathe. I couldn't think. It was like my brain had been replaced by white noise that howled along with the blood in my ears.

I thought the cold street might feel nice, but I barely registered the bitter ocean air. Every bit of me screamed to escape or hide, but from what?

I wrapped my arms around myself, as if trying to physically hold myself together.

"Do the boats ever flip?" Eydis and Adrestus were still talking in my head. I let go of my arms to clap my hands over my ears.

"Of course they do," Adrestus said. "You'd know that if you'd ever been on the water."

"So you've had people drown?"

He laughed and I couldn't bear how warm and comforting the sound was.

"No, not my people. We get right back in the boat. You've seen what they can do. An unplanned swim isn't going to drown any of them."

I found a spot in the alleyway next to the restaurant where I could lean against cool brick. An employee stood at the far end of the alley, taking a smoke break, but I knew he wouldn't bother me as I slid to the ground, tucking my head between my knees.

I couldn't remember Grandpa Max. What else was I missing? Alison had family, siblings, my aunts and uncles. I tried to draw up images of their faces in my head but could only see shadowy ghosts. I clawed at the neck of my hoodie. It felt like it was choking me.

"Sammy?" Wesley's sneakers appeared on the ground in front of me. I raised my head to look up at him, wondering if he might be mad I left his mom so rudely. "Naomi said you needed help."

I brushed my hair back and tried to look like I wasn't just hyperventilating.

"It was too warm in there. Had to step out for a second."

Wesley crouched in front me, perching on his toes and balancing his elbows against his knees.

"It's thirty-three degrees out here."

"That's really specific."

"I have super powers, remember?"

I leered at him suspiciously. His face softened and his eyes crinkled.

"I'm kidding," he admitted. "I checked the temperature on my phone before dinner."

I smiled weakly and bowed my head. Wesley fell back against the wall next to me. I was glad he was there, but embarrassment frothed and gnawed at my insides.

"I'm okay," I lied. "You can go back. Remi's probably missing you."

"She has her parents, she's not alone. So, what happened?"

I shrugged, picking at a small tear in the knee of my jeans.

"I'm missing some things."

"Oh," Wesley perked up. "That's fine. I make a great sniffer dog. Tell me what to smell for, and I'll find it."

"Memories," I whispered. "My fake ones. I think they're disappearing."

Wesley deflated.

"That's...that's not something I can smell for you."

"No," I laughed sadly.

"You couldn't remember your grandpa's name."

"I can't remember any of my fake extended family. It's hard to know what else I'm missing if I can't remember it in the first place."

Wesley thought for a moment, rolling a pebble back and forth between his fingers on the pavement between us.

"What about the flash drive?"

"My backup files?" I scoffed.

"That's how I remembered your Grandpa Max," he explained. "We went through those files together. If you go through them again, maybe it'll solidify the memories."

"I don't want the memory of *reading* about the memories. I want the actual memories."

"Maybe it's a good thing?"

"I'm Samantha," I asserted. "I want Samantha's memories."

"You have her memories," he said. "All the way back to the end of August. Those memories are real and they're yours. You're a different Samantha now than you were at the beginning of the school year."

"I'm the same—"

"No." He placed a hand over mine on my knee. "You're not. That Samantha was made of fake memories. *This* Samantha has real memories, real experiences, and real friends."

"I'm sorry," I mumbled. I looked back at my knees and Wesley withdrew his hand, though I wished he'd left it. He sighed softly and massaged his temple.

"For what?" There was a hint of a laugh in his voice.

"You look like you have a headache. I shouldn't have left dinner, I—"

"I *do* have a headache," he smiled, "but it's because I'm not wearing my glasses. Remi doesn't like them but without them, my super-sight is on full blast and it's a lot."

I picked at a hangnail and suppressed my irritation with Remi. Not only did they help him, but I thought he looked nice in his glasses.

"Me being annoying can't be helping. I'm sorry you followed me out here."

"First, you're not annoying. Second, you don't need to apologize about leaving. I've had anxiety attacks before, too."

I screwed my face up at him.

"I didn't have an anxiety attack."

He leaned his head back against the brick.

"If you say so. Do you want to go back to campus?"

"A lot of effort went into ordering that spaghetti," I sighed. "So, no, I'll stay and enjoy the fruits of my labor."

Wesley pushed himself to his feet and extended a hand to help me up. I brushed the dust off my jeans.

"I'll do my best to keep my mom busy talking about other things," Wesley assured me as we walked back to the restaurant entrance. "When in doubt, ask about her spin class."

"How much can there be to say about stationary bikes?"

Wesley nodded solemnly.

"Much more than you'd think."

Naomi was kind enough to not bring up my mid-meal escape that night, though it might have been less out of consideration and more the fact she was deep in thought over her own problems. As I jotted down a few notes in my notebook about the conversation I heard Eydis and Adrestus share at dinner, I registered Naomi in the corner of my vision, sitting on her bed with her knees drawn to her chest, rereading the letter from her sister.

"Your family was nice," I offered. As much as she hated her powers, I wouldn't have minded a quick look inside her head. She'd never looked so forlorn and I felt horribly ill-equipped to reach her.

"They are." She tucked the letter under her pillow and lay down facing the wall.

We turned the lights out early, telling each other it was important to get a good night's rest before finals the next day, but I knew it would be a long time before either of us fell asleep.

13

The Apex Team Games

The first day of semester finals had us slated to test in first and fourth period. In Fleming's class, I tried to ignore Anthony's furious pencil scratching two seats over while Wesley's left elbow jostled against mine. My answers looked short compared to how much they seemed to be writing, but hopefully they'd be enough for Fleming, otherwise Winter Break would be that much more awkward.

In gym, Coach Reiner gave us the extra long finals period to work on whatever we liked. Without Sergio to practice with, I snuck away to the Sickbay instead.

Tonka the cat darted out from under a bed and wrapped his orange body between my ankles. His cushy life beneath the school had put several pounds on the once half-starved stray. Everly peeked out at me from the back rooms.

"What'd you hurt this time?"

"Nothing," I said, surprised at my own defensiveness. "I just had a question."

He raised an eyebrow, wrinkling his bald brow unevenly. Tonka pawed at my knee and I bent over to scoop him into my arms.

"Questions are much more manageable than concussions and knife wounds," Everly said dryly.

"And probably a bit easier than undead students."

I was relieved to see him chuckle at my dark humor.

"A bit, yes. What's the question?"

Everly made himself busy reorganizing the supply cupboard near the door and I meandered farther in, cradling Tonka in my arms as he tried to catch the end of my ponytail with a paw.

"It's the memories," I mumbled. "They haven't stopped."

Everly frowned at a shelf of bandages.

"They continued to come back for a few weeks last time, didn't they?"

"Only when I was sleeping." I focused on Tonka's white belly. "This time, they come back while I'm awake."

"Like in the hypothermia exercise?"

I fell back into one of the bedside chairs.

"Yeah, and a few other times."

Everly abandoned his cupboard to come sit on the bed next to me, but I kept my eyes on Tonka.

"Maybe it's adrenaline?" he suggested. "Any time you're in a frightening situation, enough to elicit a fight-or-flight response, perhaps that triggers it."

That accounted for most of the episodes, but last night, I'd been at dinner. Sure, I'd had a moment of panic, but there was nothing frightening about Italian food.

"I'll keep that in mind," I said. If Everly was right, Friday's sword play competition might get complicated. I scratched Tonka between the ears, thinking back to something Wesley had said. "What do anxiety attacks feel like?"

"Depends. It can be different between people." He kept his voice cool and even. "It's usually that fight-or-flight response I mentioned, but at a time that doesn't make sense."

"Like when ordering spaghetti," I murmured more to myself than Everly. Tonka rolled from my lap to chase invisible enemies across the floor.

"Samantha, we have counseling services—"

"I'm fine." I stood up and marched back to the door. Anxiety or not, I didn't want to divulge my past to anyone else.

"The memories must be frustrating, but I'm sure they'll stop after a few weeks or so. In the meantime, they might help you learn more about Eydis."

"I don't care who Eydis was because she's dead," I said bluntly. I shouldn't have mentioned anything to Everly. What if he turned around and told Fleming? "If anything, I might learn something about Adrestus that could be useful, but everything else is just a distraction."

Everly stayed seated and looked me over thoughtfully as I turned to face him from the doorway.

"Maybe she is dead," he conceded, "or maybe the more you remember, the more you figure out that she isn't."

I folded my arms across my chest and skirted out the door with my head bowed. I didn't care what Everly said. I would make sure I never became Eydis.

After an early dinner, the team gathered in the rotunda at the front of the school to walk to the university campus together. Naomi wrung her hands nervously, excited but nervous to be competing in the first night of the competitions. Anthony showed up with Wesley. He joined us for training so often by now that most of the team regarded him as part of the pack. Besides, anyone who didn't accept Anthony was liable to be thrown into a tornado by Isabelle.

"No Remi?" I tried to sound casual as we followed Fleming and Everly to the neighboring campus. The corners of Wesley's mouth turned down.

"She wanted to study for finals."

Anthony snorted but I shrugged.

"That's too bad."

"I wouldn't blame her if she wanted to skip watching Andersen compete, but tonight it's *Naomi!*" Wesley exclaimed. "She's our friend!"

I nodded, but while Remi and Naomi usually got along, I hadn't pegged them as friends.

The Humanities building loomed ahead and still sported burn marks from Amanda's attack. A fresh wave of yearning for Dad nudged at me when I saw the building he used to work in, but before I could let it bother me too much, we turned towards the sports arena. It was situated next to the water and boasted larger-than-life banners showcasing the various up-and-coming student athletes. While a portion of the arena lower levels housed training gyms and special cafeterias for star basketball and volleyball players, it was the students who *weren't* found on massive posters that were allowed in the part of the lower levels that took up most of the space.

Everly nodded to Fleming and broke away to wait for an elevator while the rest of us filed into a training gym three times the size of ours but with fewer students using the equipment.

"Alex!" Professor Parker waved from the side of a boxing ring where two college students sparred.

"Where is everyone?" I whispered. Naomi looked around the gym.

"What do you mean? The whole team is here."

I looked at her in surprise and she shrugged.

"Not as many students make the college team."

"But I didn't even make the high school team!"

I didn't know why I said it. I had no plans for my future beyond finding Dad and thwarting whatever plot Adrestus had schemed. I could barely see as far as finishing sophomore year let alone college.

The college students stopped their work-outs and drills to wander over to our corner. Maybe I was imagining it, but I felt like they were all looking at me. I focused on the boxing ring, refusing to glance around at them.

"Excellent!" Parker clapped her hands together. "Welcome New Delos Prep! I'm sure everyone knows the rules by now, but bear with me as I give you all a quick recap before we start. Each night this week, you'll have the chance to compete against your teammates as well as members of the other school. Rack up enough points for your team and you might get a medal at the Friday banquet.

"For each event, first place will win their team five points. Second will get three, and third gets one. Everyone else gets the satisfaction of knowing they did their best and, with the exception of my seniors, can try again next year."

Fleming pointed us towards the locker rooms.

"If you are competing in the Stealth and Strategy competition tonight, you're free to go get ready. The rest of you, follow us to the Apex Arena."

Naomi and Heather broke off from the group and I tried to get a good look at who joined them from the other years. Everyone had been secretive about who was competing in what and while we'd speculated who might compete in each event, we wouldn't know until they were up to bat.

"I knew they'd send in Justin," Wesley whispered. "All he has to do is touch his opponent and their flags are his to take."

"But no Marcus?" I'd thought for sure the seniors would pick Marcus to compete in the dark comp. His ability to see heat signatures would've given them an upper hand.

"Guess not." Wesley grinned mischievously. "You know what that means?"

My stomach churned.

"He's competing against me on Friday?"

"That's alright!" Anthony reassured me. "More opponents for you to take out means more chances you get to score points."

"Plus, Marcus can't sword fight," Wesley said. "His weapon of choice is a lasso. He won't stand a chance against an actual Viking."

I felt the color drain from my face and watched as the Wesley's did the same. Anthony gave Wesley a curious look.

"Because, you know, class the other day," he tried to cover. "Because your name is Viking because it's Havardson and-and—"

"Right," I said curtly, thanking the universe Naomi wasn't around to feel the panic gnashing at my insides. "My very distant viking ancestry from a very long time ago is what gives me an edge."

Anthony laughed and Wesley and I sighed in relief.

"That can be your superhero name," Anthony joked. "The Viking!"

"That sounds more like a pro-wrestling name," Wesley said as we walked with the other students out of the gym and down a long, stone corridor.

"They both wear costumes and whale on people. It's basically the same thing," I pointed out.

"Who's the statue next to Adrestus at the museum?" Anthony asked and the panic returned. "If you don't like 'The Viking', use her name instead since you're Adrestus' greatest enemy!"

"I don't know about 'greatest enemy'," I mumbled. "He kidnapped my dad but I'm sure he has bigger fish to fry than—"

I cut off as we walked into the combat arena. The walkway overlooked a space that was roughly half the size of a football field. Instead of green turf, the stands wrapped twenty feet above and around a course covered in large boulders and craggy inclines that dropped off in fifteen-foot high cliffs.

. We followed the other students as they forked out and filled the stands, conglomerating with their team members. The other sophomores led the way to a spot on the far side of the arena, opposite the entrance we'd come from.

A crowd of parents meandered in behind New Delos Prep principal and Apex Team Council Head, Dr. Weaver, who led the way in a pantsuit. Most parents looked around the underground arena in awe but a few seemed right at home.

Zoey and Will hung off of Mr. Bradford as he made his way with the other sophomore parents to join us. He chatted excitedly with a couple I hadn't met yet. The woman had bright, curly hair streaked with gray and white and was taller than her dark-haired husband.

"Heather's parents," Wesley said when he saw me looking at them. "The Hisakawas. Both Apex, both heavyweights. They were on the team before Paragon but didn't make a career of it like he did."

I watched apprehensively, trying to find Wesley's mom in the crowd, but I didn't see her.

Anthony tensed next to me and his hands balled into fists on his knees. A fluttering breeze blew at my hair.

"What's wrong?" I asked.

"Something's wrong?" Wesley whipped around to look at Anthony.

His face contorted into a scowl and he pointed across the arena. I stood up when I saw who had put him on edge.

The last few members of the Apex Council had entered the stands with their special guests. Trev laughed as the handsome, sandy-haired man next to him cracked a joke. I didn't care how much money Adrian Schrader threw at the Apex program. He had no reason to be here.

"Sammy."

I shook Wesley's hand off my elbow. Something feral rumbled inside me. A blond man with greased-back hair stood just behind Schrader. I'd seen him before. He'd stood by while Adrestus cut me open in search of his Lapis and had the power to create horrifying apparitions.

"What're they doing here?" I spat. "No one's wearing their helmets and we know someone is feeding Adrestus information!"

"I'll take care of it," Wesley said, climbing over seats.

"Fleming already is," Anthony mumbled.

Fleming marched across seats to pull Dr. Weaver aside and judging by his wild gestures in Schrader's directions, he was just as pleased as we were about the mogul's presence.

Wesley sat back down begrudgingly, focused on Schrader and Trev.

"But now we know for sure he's working with Adrestus," he said. "Look at his assistant."

The blond man took his seat behind Schrader. He stared out over the arena directly at us. The temperature seemed to drop when I remembered Adrestus threatening to use the man's powers to take away all of my fake memories. What if he could just by looking at me?

Before I could look for an exit, the lights overhead dimmed and the course lit up, shrouding Schrader and his crony in shadows. The last thing I saw across the arena was Fleming and Weaver marching towards the men. Cheers went up around the room as the competition participants appeared in teams at various points around the course, looking around the rocky landscape in varying degrees of awe and anxiety.

Heather and Naomi entered to our left. They each had two flags hanging from belts and their heads bent together as they assessed the crag-filled course.

"Let's go, Naomi!" Will and Zoey shrieked behind us. They stood on their seats on either side of Mr. Bradford, who held up a phone so that Mrs. Bradford could watch the competition via video call. Next to them, Heather's parents clapped politely. Mrs. Hisakawa's icy blue eyes were stoic under her ginger curls but a coy smile played across Mr. Hisakawa's lips.

"Naomi needs to focus," Wesley mumbled. "She plans on 'seeing' in the dark by searching out emotional signatures but she can't tune out the crowd."

Naomi found us in the stands and frowned. Her mouth moved and Wesley shook his head.

"She's asking what's wrong," he said. "We're distracting her."

"Maybe it's a good thing?" Anthony suggested. Wes and I both gave him dubious looks. "She can feel how upset we are. It'll be like an anchor in the dark. She won't get disoriented because we're her compass."

"Our anguish is her true north," I snorted. Wesley laid a hand on my knee.

"You're anguished?"

"No." I pushed his hand away. I wanted to punch something. Anything. "I'm annoyed and a bit mad."

"I'm a little anguished," Anthony mumbled on my other side. Wesley got up to move next to him. He sank in the seat, putting his feet up on the railing that separated the stands from the drop into the arena.

"Don't worry," he said. "Sounds like Fleming has it under control."

"Is he making them leave?" I asked, wishing I could hear across the arena, too.

"I think so. Dr. Weaver is pretty mad. It's hard to hear exactly, but sounds like Trev didn't get permission to bring special guests. I guess there's a process?"

"Students, family, and Apex fans!" Professor Parker's voice filled the arena to the sound of applause. I kept my eyes on Schrader and his assistant. "Welcome to the Sixteenth Annual Apex Team Games! We start our week out with Stealth and Strategy— a game of Flag Tag held in total darkness!"

More cheers. I couldn't find it in myself to join.

I could sneak over while everything was dark. If I somehow could corner them, I wouldn't run away like I had when facing Adrestus the other day. I'd have the upper hand this time. I could interrogate them, ask about my dad and Amanda, too.

"Sammy?" Wesley leaned in to get in my face. "Naomi says you're up to something."

"I'm not planning anything!" For one day, I'd like my friends to not intrude on my thoughts and feelings.

"Fleming is already taking care of it."

"Great." My friends didn't need to monitor me.

Professor Parker began to introduce the teams. I waited for Heather and Naomi to be called and as the sophomores erupted in cheers and whoops, jumping up and down for our teammates, I slipped towards the stairs.

Overhead TVs hummed mechanically as they lowered into viewing position and lit up. The final arena lights cut, plunging us all into darkness and eliciting shrieks of delight from the students.

A green hue took over the screens as they began to stream the course below. I paused as I snuck to the back wall to watch Naomi and Heather take up the nearest TV, their eyes glowing an unnatural white in the night vision camera.

I made it to the back wall just as Professor Parker announced the start of the match. A hand grabbed my elbow and I pulled away.

"Where are you going?" Wesley hissed.

"The bathroom."

"Let's go sit back down, alright?"

The TVs emitted a soft, sickly glow, just enough to light up Wesley's face and I hated how sorry he looked. I'd seen that look from him before.

"They know where my dad is."

A cheer went up on the far side of the arena. Wesley and I glanced up to see Justin immobilize one of the college students and take both flags from his belt.

"You mean they know where Vidar is."

"No, I mean my dad." Another cheer rocked the stands. I didn't have long to get around to the other side to confront Schrader.

"Sammy, we're going—"

"To find him?" I cut him off. "When? We haven't had a lead in months and with the Doomsday Pager counting down, no one cares about looking for him anymore."

Wesley fell silent.

"Naomi and Heather are about to get their first flag," he finally whispered. I glanced at the TV in spite of myself.

Naomi slowly turned from side to side with her eyes closed. She pointed to her right and her mouth moved, giving instruction to Heather. Heather's form dissolved in a way that the night vision didn't seem to make sense of. The image glitched and white noise took over the screen before clearing. When it did, Heather was gone. A different screen glitched and by the time it had cleared, both high school freshmen had been relieved of their flags.

My momentary pride subsided and I tried to look for Schrader in the sea of dim, green-lit faces across the arena from us.

"You're shaking."

Wesley touched my shoulder. As much as I wanted to, I didn't shrug him away.

"I'm angry! Everything is falling apart but it feels like all this team does is try to make everything else into a game. The competitions this week, the Night Game, even training feels like pretend most days, but my life has been *ruined* by Adrestus. He's taken everything."

"I know—"

"I know you know! And I'm excited to watch Naomi play tonight but I *blew* it at the museum last week and now I have a chance to make up for it."

"There's nothing to make up for!"

I was taken aback by the sudden fire in his voice. He pulled me into a nearby row of empty bleacher seats.

"Samantha," he said evenly, sitting me down and holding my shoulders to look me in the eyes. He never used my full name. "Eydis."

I bristled at the use of my *real* name. Wesley smirked but the expression was surprisingly kind.

"We play games because we're terrified." His voice trembled. "I know it doesn't look like we are, but, Sammy, we're *all* scared."

"I know, I just..." I hid behind my hands. "I can't do nothing. My assignment is literally to watch a countdown to the city's destruction and the man behind it all is in the room and we're *playing games.*"

"Life goes on and parents still want to see us beat the crap out of each other. Besides, Schrader isn't in the room anymore. They're in the hall with Dr. Weaver." He dropped his voice and leaned in. "But I get what you're saying, so what's the plan? Tell me how to help."

"I—"

What *was* the plan? The lights would be on in the hall. They'd see us coming. Not to mention, the blond man could ruin my fake memories and Samantha Havardson was unraveling enough.

The answers I needed were *right there* but I was helpless to get them.

"I need Dad back, Wes. If I get him back, things can be normal, again. But what if I lose Samantha before I see him?" It was the first time putting words to what I now realized scared me more than anything. "I want to go back to being Samantha and-and if she keeps disappearing—"

"You *are* Samantha," Wesley whispered. His eyes shone in the TV glow just inches from mine. He'd taken his glasses off to see better in the dark. The sophomores went wild in the stands and we both whipped our heads to see Naomi and Heather's flag collection had grown substantially. Wesley turned back to me. "But you're Eydis, too, and getting Vidar back isn't going to change either of those facts."

The arena air was dry and dusty. I pulled at my shirt collar. I needed to breathe.

No, I needed to get to Schrader.

I leaned back in the seat and pressed the heels of my hands against my eyes.

I didn't know what I needed.

"Let's go sit down," Wesley said, and this time I was tempted to. "I left Anthony back there and he's just as freaked as you are."

I swallowed the bile in my throat. It felt like trying to swallow a rock.

"Yeah, okay."

154

The floor trembled and I grabbed Wesley's arm in surprise, wrapping my fingers around his bicep.

"It's one of the college students," he explained, though he gripped my arm, too. "He has a tectonic ability that lets him move the earth."

"That's not very stealthy."

"Maybe not. But strategic?"

The screen that displayed the student shaking the ground glitched. The white noise cleared, and he was left glancing around and patting his hips for his missing flags.

"Not a good strategy, either, apparently," Wesley snorted.

I rubbed my cheek with the heel of my hand, trying to hide any evidence of tears. Wesley reached and grabbed it.

"It's fine." His hand lingered on mine and I felt him start to pull me into a hug.

"Wes?" Remi's voice cut between us and we froze in our awkward half-embrace. Remi stood behind us, squinting to make us out in the dark.

"You made it!" Wesley let go of me to greet her but she shied away coldly. Wes cleared his throat. "We were just headed back to our seats."

"Looked that way." She stalked past and Wesley grimaced as he hurried to lead her to the seats where Anthony waited.

Anthony attempted a smile as we took our seats on either side of him. Remi crossed her arms and stared out at the dark course rather than the lowered TVs.

"Justin just knocked the last college student out of the competition," Anthony said. "Look, it's just him, Naomi, and Heather left."

Naomi held a stack of flags close to her chest. Her mouth moved and Heather nodded attentively. The next screen over showed Justin with both hands against a rocky wall, shuffling blindly through the dark.

"What are they saying?" Anthony asked.

"Naomi says she can feel Justin getting closer but they're worried about his powers. They want to double-team him, but that's tricky when only Heather can jump through space. Heather says she has a plan, but—"

Wesley stood up to lean over the railing as if to hear better and then abruptly turned away.

He burrowed his head in the crook of his elbow as bright, sudden light exploded across the arena with Naomi and Heather at the epicenter. The TV screens turned white and the crowd cried out.

"What was that?" Anthony shouted over the cheers. Spots burst in my vision but I could make out the blurry outlines of Naomi and Heather running across the lit course towards Justin, who leaned against a boulder with tears streaming down his face.

The other sophomores looked between each other. We'd all seen Heather control darkness but none of us had seen her create light. I looked back at her parents. Mrs. Hisakawa nodded approvingly as she leaned forward with clenched fists.

After a few dazzling seconds, the light dimmed, dissipating back into darkness. After the bright flash, the dark of the arena seemed blacker than before but the TV screens readjusted just in time for us to see Naomi and Heather confront Justin.

The high school seniors screamed from their place in the stands. It was two versus one, plus Heather was a heavyweight. However, Justin was team captain for a reason. Naomi distracted him by attacking head on while Heather flitted in and out of the darkness, causing the screens to spasm with white noise. Justin kept them at bay, twisting and dodging blindly.

As Heather appeared behind him, he spun around and managed to grab her arm. The sophomores groaned and the seniors cheered as Heather's body locked up. Justin had immobilized her. He lunged for her flags but Naomi tackled him from behind and ripped both flags from his belt. There was a reason *she* was a team captain, too.

A buzzer signaled the end of the game and the overhead lights glowed back to life and, despite lingering thoughts of Adrian Schrader, I found it in me to cheer for Naomi along with the other sophomores. Naomi threw her and Heather's captured flags into the air in triumph. They showered down over Justin as he grabbed Heather's hand to remobilize her.

Mr. Bradford, William, and Zoey shrieked behind us. I caught a flash of Mrs. Bradford on the screen of Mr. Bradford's phone as he waved it in the air.

Wesley beamed at me from Anthony's other side, but blushed and turned away as Remi grabbed his hand.

"High School Sophomores take the first win of the week!" Professor Parker shouted over the speakers. "But will they keep the lead after tomorrow's Rescue Course? Competing students, report to the locker rooms tomorrow at five. Everyone else, we'll see you at six!"

The first night was marked with an ice cream fueled celebration in the atrium of our own team base back on the high school campus, but Naomi found a quiet classroom to give her mom a play-by-play over the phone. I filed after Wesley, Remi, and Anthony to the basement, which echoed with shouts issuing from Fleming's office.

"He wants Trev Baker off the council," Wesley whispered.

"We can all hear it this time," Remi snipped. "You don't need to narrate."

As much as I would love to see Baker kicked out, I couldn't help but to feel the damage was already done. Adrestus knew our secrets, whether Baker stayed on the council or not.

14

Foil and Failure

Thoughts of Adrian Schrader haunted me through the night and into final exams the next morning. I turned on autopilot as I worked on my Spanish essay, barely registering what I was writing. Part of me was waiting for Schrader to show up again and I wanted to be ready.

However, Schrader stayed away both during the school day and from the evening's competition. Andersen, Skyler, and Everest departed campus early to report to the university arena as instructed and we followed them with the noncompeting students about an hour later.

Remi stayed glued to Wesley's side. She'd monopolized his company all day, still bitter she'd found Wesley comforting me. They walked ahead of us while Anthony and I lingered in the back of the group with Naomi, who continued to glow over her first place win.

"You're on her bad side, by the way," Naomi giggled, nodding at Remi's blonde curls. Wesley would be able to hear us if he was paying attention but Naomi didn't seem worried. "She's been livid at you both since last night."

"Both?" Anthony said indignantly. "What did I do?"

"Not you, *him*." Naomi pointed at the back of Wesley's hoodie, pulled up to keep his head warm.

"She should've come to the beginning of the competition, then." I didn't care if Remi was mad at me, but I hoped she wasn't being too hard on Wes.

"You don't need to be on the bad side of any more teammates."

I jammed my hands in my pockets as we crossed from the high school campus to the college.

"What's she going to do? Encrypt my calculator?"

"She might," Naomi shrugged. "Maybe don't let her touch it before your math final tomorrow."

"Hands out of pockets, Sammy," Anthony warned. "It's icy and if you fall you'll break your arms."

"You're a worse helicopter mom than Wesley!" I pulled my hands back out my pockets anyways.

"Someone's gotta be the new mom now that he's with *her*."

Naomi rolled her eyes at Anthony.

"Leave Remi alone. She's just trying to fit in."

I screwed my face up, unsure of what Naomi meant, but trusting she understood Remi's inner machinations better than I ever would.

Parents arrived alongside students, filing back to the underground arena. The same rocky, crag-filled landscape filled the course but now a rushing river separated the two ends. Obstacles had been placed across the course and arrows painted on the ground marked the pathway each team would have to take in order to rescue their target.

"It's weird," I said as we took seats in the same spot as yesterday. "I want our team to win, but I wouldn't be too mad to watch Andersen lose."

"He's had a hard time since Jamie told the school he's an Apex," Naomi said matter-of-factly. "He needs a win more than any of us."

I shrugged, wishing Wesley was here to take my side, but he'd found a seat with Remi and her parents several rows back. I wanted to ask Naomi what he was feeling, but I knew she wouldn't appreciate me asking her to abuse her powers that way.

Luckily, Professor Parker whisked me away from thoughts of Wesley and Remi. The arena roared in anticipation as she recapped the rules. Each team would compete one at a time to rescue a volunteer at one end of the course and then return them to the starting point.

The high school freshmen went first, led by Jessa and her ability to lift anything like it was made of styrofoam and bounce weightlessly across the ground like an astronaut on the moon. Her team made completing the course look easy.

Meanwhile, our team made it look near impossible. Whatever win Andersen needed, he wasn't going to find tonight. Skyler's ability to change his appearance proved useless and Everest and Andersen were at each other's throats for the entirety of the course.

A few seats to our left, a man and woman half-hid behind their hands, as if watching was painful. When Andersen accidentally dumped the rescue volunteer in the river, the woman let out a low, "Oh, Andy, no...".

After they finally put us out of our misery and finished the course, they didn't even bother waiting to see their score broadcast on the scoreboard overhead before sulking towards the exit.

In the end, college teams took first and second place while the high school seniors barely scraped by in third. Heather found us after the match.

"All that work Naomi and I put in yesterday!" she complained. "And for nothing!"

"You better beat Marcus on Friday," Anthony said to me seriously. "Isabelle says the seniors are the worst winners."

"I'll do what I can," I assured him, but I wasn't paying much attention to the conversation anymore. The man and woman who'd sat near us in the stands walked ahead with Andersen between them. They must've been his parents, but they looked so normal. I'd always figured

Andersen must've just sprouted from the earth one day, fully formed and ready to reign misery on those around him.

I watched as he shrugged off a comforting arm placed around his shoulders by his mom. I tried to swallow the bitter resentment that rose in my throat. It wasn't fair that Andersen could have a family while mine was broken and scattered.

While Andersen's Tuesday night had been humiliating, Wednesday morning was determined to torture him further. For the last day of finals, Jamie strutted through the halls between classes, waving aluminum foil hats.

"Oh, good," Wesley deadpanned. "Jamie's handing out free garbage."

Jamie smirked and waggled a hat in front of her.

"It's not garbage," she sang. "It's a foolproof way to keep Apex like Andersen from stealing your test answers."

Her friends snickered behind her. Skyler was among them.

"Andersen can't read minds," Wesley drawled, taking the aluminum hat from Jamie.

"Careful," Naomi warned under her breath.

"Even if he can't, someone here might be able to." Jamie spoke loud enough for the whole hall to hear and while some kids paused to laugh along with her, most skirted around, ducking their heads and hurrying past. "And technically, we don't *know* for sure that Andersen can't read minds. We *do* know he's an Apex and that's enough for me to take the extra precautions."

Her twisted smile told us she knew foil hats wouldn't do anything other than torment Andersen but I was willing to ignore her. Naomi and I continued forward and Remi pulled at Wesley's arm to bring him along, but he resisted.

"He's not an Apex," Wesley said, rooting himself to the tiled floor and crossing his arms, crinkling the hat under an elbow.

Jamie's eyes narrowed and her friends tittered nervously.

"I saw him move a steel beam without even touching it," she said in a low voice. "Are you saying I didn't?"

"I'm saying I was there, too. So was Sammy."

I tried to disappear into the wall behind me as the growing crowd glanced my way. I looked at Wesley nervously.

"I'm a liar, then?" Jamie's cheeks grew pink. "Is that what you mean?"

"You wanted an excuse to break up with Andersen because he didn't like the stupid shirt you made him."

"Wes," Remi hissed, pulling at his sleeve. "Andersen's not worth this."

"Andersen Lewis is an Apex and you know it!" Jamie insisted.

"No, he isn't!"

The aluminum hats that Jamie's friends carried suddenly crumpled and flew down the hall, as if bewitched. Gasps and shrieks followed their trajectory and they clattered to the floor at Andersen's feet.

"Yes," he said dryly. "I am."

"I told you all! Didn't I tell you!" Jamie cried as Andersen strode down the hall, sending students scrambling to get out of his way. I'd seen him angry before, but his face burned with rage. It wasn't Jamie he stopped in front of, but Wesley.

A ball of aluminum zipped down the hall at him and he caught it in an outstretched hand. He pushed it into Wesley's arms.

"And I don't need losers like you telling people otherwise."

He pushed past Wesley to continue down the hall.

"I was trying to be nice!" Wes snapped.

"Well, don't!" Andersen shouted without looking back.

"Did anyone get that on video?" Jamie demanded. "I told you! I told you!"

Remi patted Wesley's arm but he pulled away and marched down the hall ahead of us. Naomi bit her lip at me, an unsaid "I told you not to mess with Andersen" plastered to her face.

Jamie and company were quick to make new foil hats and wore them through finals while the efforts of the general student population to avoid Andersen doubled. To Jamie's delight, someone *had* caught him on video that morning and by the time I was leaning against the wall outside Mrs. Young's classroom waiting for my parent-teacher conference, it seemed like everyone had seen it.

I tried not to think about what that might mean for Andersen or Apex Team as a whole and tried even harder not to think about the imminent parent-teacher conference by going over sword fighting moves in my head. I was just about to skewer my imaginary opponent when Fleming interrupted the daydream.

"Ready?" He juggled loose papers in his arms and his glasses were askew, looking like he'd just come from a teacher conference of his own.

I braced myself and followed Fleming into the math classroom, smiling weakly at Mrs. Young. I wondered how much she knew, if she was in on the Apex secret, if she knew why Fleming was now my guardian.

She smiled as we walked in, but I only had eyes for the report card on the desk.

"Alex, so glad you could make it. How've your conferences been?" Gray flyaways stuck out from her bun like a halo.

"The same as always," Fleming sighed, reaching for the report card. He narrowed his eyes at the paper and my stomach clenched uncomfortably. Sure, I wasn't a straight A student, but my grades weren't *horrible*.

"Grades aren't finalized, of course," Mrs. Young said quickly and my palms broke out in sweat. She was running damage control. "Not everyone has had a chance to grade final exams yet, but—"

"But she has a D in Spanish?" Fleming looked down at me.

"I do not!" Spanish was my easiest class, other than gym with Coach Reiner.

Fleming smacked the report card back onto the desk and pointed at Fifth Period. An angry, red "D" glared up at me. The cold sweat moved from my palms to my face.

"That's a mistake," I insisted. "It has to be."

Mrs. Young pressed her lips together and slid a paper across the desk. I recognized my messy scrawl in the header. I'd only taken the Spanish final a day ago. Señora Vasquez couldn't have already graded it, but a large "0/100" splashed across the top in purple marker.

"I failed? How?"

"For one, it's not in Spanish." Mrs. Young folded her hands and frowned at Fleming.

I stared at the essay in horror. I was sure I'd written it in Spanish. I tried to think back to the day before, but I'd been so worked up about Schrader, I barely remembered even taking the test. The words on the paper weren't in Spanish, though they still looked familiar.

"This is completely out of character!" Fleming said, taking the essay from me to inspect it himself. "Samantha, this kind of contempt is unacceptable."

He scanned the page, ripping his glasses off and holding it so close to his face, his nose almost brushed the words.

"It's total...nonsense!"

"No, it's not," I mumbled.

"It's certainly not Spanish," he scoffed.

I didn't know how it'd happened. I'd been so deep into autopilot that Eydis seemed to have taken the final instead. How else could I have written an entire essay in Old Norse without realizing it?

"Luckily, Señora Vasquez understands you've had difficulty settling in this semester—" Mrs. Young started.

"The teachers are all gossiping about me now?" I recoiled away from Fleming.

"Not *gossiping*," he said, "but it's our job to communicate about our students—"

"What's there to communicate? I'm fine!"

"You wrote your entire Spanish essay in *not Spanish*."

"On accident!"

"Then you're not fine!"

"Yes!" I ripped the essay back from him before he could realize it was written in a dead language. I'd rather he think I'd written nonsense on purpose. "I am! Look at my grades, they're all fine except that one!"

"For now!" Fleming exploded. "These are preliminary! What am I going to see when I grade your history final? What's Mrs. Young going to see when she grades your math?"

Mrs. Young cleared her throat, her cheeks tinging pink, and procured another paper.

"I actually glanced over it as soon as she turned it in today and it's fine. I haven't checked your work yet, but it looks like a solid A." She set my math exam down on the desk. I was relieved to see I'd answered in the correct language. "As I was saying, Señora Vasquez understands you're a good student and is willing to let you redo the final after break."

"Why?" Fleming and I asked together.

"Señora Vasquez knows six different languages. She says she's mixed them up her fair share of times and was impressed Samantha knew Norse at all—"

"Norse?" Fleming slowly turned to his head to look back at me, his face unreadable.

"She said it was either Norse or Icelandic."

I held the essay tight against my chest to protect it from Fleming.

"If she wrote it in the wrong language, she deserves the zero," Fleming said.

"If she completed her history exam in the wrong language, you are free to give her whatever grade you like, but Vasquez already has her slated for a retake."

I cradled the essay close as Mrs. Young went through my performance in each class with Fleming. I didn't pay attention, instead trying to conjure up Old Norse words in my head. None came. There was no way I'd been able to write an entire essay in a language I didn't know, but I was holding evidence to the contrary.

Eydis was seeping out in more than just memories, now. She was beginning to bleed into my day-to-day routine and the more she did, the more Samantha would be edged out.

Fleming stood up. The conference had ended without me noticing. I walked ahead of Fleming, hoping to make a quick getaway in the hall, but he stopped me outside the classroom.

"Why would you do that?" he asked. I spun to face him, my Spanish essay now a crumpled mess in my fist.

"Do what? She said mostly good things."

"You sabotaged that essay on purpose!" He struggled to control his tone, but his frustration shone through. "Your parents would be furious."

"Good thing they aren't my real parents, then."

I didn't understand why Fleming was making such a big deal about this when the other teachers seemed fine. Maybe he was already at the end of his rope after handling Andersen's blow-up earlier today, but that didn't mean he got to treat me like trash.

"You know what I mean. I know Alison and I know she'd easily ground you for less."

Heat rose in my cheeks.

"Ground me? Is that what you plan on doing?"

"Alison left me in charge," Fleming said and I could feel my temperature increasing. "I expect you to act how Alison would expect you to act and that includes respecting academics."

"I was the comatose kid in Alison's basement for almost fifteen years," I snorted. "She doesn't get to decide anything for me and neither do you."

"Samantha, I—"

"You want to ground me? Fine. Do it. Winter break is going to suck anyway."

Fleming's face settled somewhere between flabbergasted and furious and I spun on my heel to march away, jamming my crumpled essay into my backpack. I thought Fleming might follow or call me back, but he didn't.

15

The Regatta

With classes officially finished for the semester, Anthony and I met the next morning to make a banner with Wesley's name. Olivia and Freddie had scraped up enough points in the Stealth and Speed competition the night before to keep us in the running to place, though I'd hardly paid attention. I'd been too busy fuming and avoiding Fleming.

"Make sure Remi's name is as big as Wesley's," Naomi instructed from her bed. She had complained until we'd begrudgingly added Remi's name to the banner as well.

"She's not even our friend," Anthony grumbled, slapping her name on the banner in Paragon-Red paint.

"She's our teammate," Naomi pointed out.

"No," Anthony argued, "she's *your* teammate. I'm not on anyone's team. I'm just cheering on my friends, and that doesn't include Remi."

"You really don't like her." I dotted the "i" in her name.

"You don't either," Naomi laughed.

"I don't *know* her," I blushed, "and it's not like she's made much effort to get to know me, either."

"Trust me, you don't need to know her," Anthony shuddered dramatically. "Last year, her and Wesley had a fight in our dorm room when I was trying to sleep. The Resident Assistant on our floor had to escort her away when she refused to leave. Wesley was up all night going crazy and *he* wouldn't let me sleep and then I bombed a test the next morning."

"I sat next to you in that class and distinctly remember you saying you didn't need to study," Naomi smirked.

"What I meant was, a good night's sleep was all I needed."

"But you didn't study?"

"I didn't need to! I had an A before that test!"

I sat back to look over the banner. I didn't like seeing Wesley and Remi's names together but I was pleased with our handiwork. Anthony was surprisingly artistic.

"I can't believe I didn't get a banner from you guys," Naomi joked.

"Maybe you did and you just couldn't see it in the dark." Anthony grinned at her.

Naomi swung her pillow at Anthony but he dodged it and laughed.

Unlike the previous competitions, this one took place along a three mile stretch of water, starting a mile north of the college campus and arching down to the East Pier. We didn't get the chance to see Wesley, Remi, and the other competitors off after dinner, but walked along the boardwalk with the other sophomores, searching for a space to watch from.

Heather found us a spot a mile out from the finish line and away from the other parents and students who'd gathered on the boardwalk in clumps to spectate. Andersen and Skyler kept to themselves a few paces away.

Anthony folded our banner over the railing so that it hung over the ocean.

"Do you think they'll be able to see it from here?" he fretted.

"I don't know. Will our friend with super vision be able to see a giant poster with his name on it?" I pulled my hat down further over my ears. The ocean air cut the island no matter where you were at, but it was particularly bitter right on the water. It would at least keep non-Apex island residents away, letting us compete without giving away the teams.

"I would've made his name bigger!" Anthony cast a furtive glance around the sophomores, not daring to speak ill of Remi in front of them.

"How do we know when they've started?" Olivia leaned out over the water precariously, trying to see up the island coast to the starting line. Night had fallen over an hour ago and evening fog was already rolling in, making it near impossible to see anything. "Freddie, can't you clear any of this?"

Freddie puffed his cheeks out at the fog and he concentrated for a moment. The mist seemed to roll back a little, but it wasn't much of a difference.

"We'll be able to see them when they pass by, at least," he shrugged.

Other students and parents milled past, walking to keep warm while they waited.

"What a cute sign!"

Mrs. Isaacs cut through the sophomores to join Anthony and me against the banister. A puffy, pleated coat dwarfed her form and her glasses nearly tipped off the end of her long nose as she leaned over the bannister to get a better look at our handiwork.

"Did you all make this?" Mrs. Isaacs beckoned Remi's parents forward. "Look, Remi's on here, too."

"Anthony and Sammy made it." Naomi stepped aside to push us forward.

"It's lovely!" Mrs. Isaacs beamed at me and I shuffled my feet.

Naomi drew me back towards the sophomores, leaving Mrs. Isaacs and Remi's parents to idly chat while we waited. Something nagged at the back of my mind, though.

"Naomi," I asked carefully, making sure the others didn't hear, "where's Wesley's dad?"

She frowned at the dark water.

"From what I understand, he's not been in the picture for a while. Wesley doesn't talk about it, though."

I looked back at Mrs. Isaacs, feeling a twinge of new respect. As overbearing as she was, it couldn't have been easy being on her own with two children. Her laugh cut through the night as she talked with Remi's parents.

"Computers, though! That's very practical, and very manageable!" Mrs. Isaacs exclaimed. "Imagine raising a kid who was always pulling doorknobs off and putting things through the sliding glass door."

"Remi was so easy," Remi's mother insisted. "All we had to do was give her a video game to mess with and we were set."

I scowled, my sudden respect fading, and folded my arms on the bannister. As hard as raising Wesley probably was, it wasn't like he *meant* to break doorknobs.

"Are they coming yet?" Anthony bounced on his toes to keep warm.

"Should be." Naomi glanced at her watch. "They'll pass by soon."

I looked up the boardwalk impatiently. It was cold and I didn't like being trapped between Andersen and the parents of Wesley and his girlfriend. I did a double-take and clapped.

"They're coming!"

The bow of the first boat broke through the fog, gliding across the water. It was impossible to tell who it was so far away but the parents and students along the boardwalk cheered regardless. The faster the race finished, the sooner we could all go inside to get warm.

"It's Wesley!" Naomi tugged at my sleeve.

Mrs. Isaacs shouted for her son and Remi's parents clapped politely. Remi took a break from rowing to wave at us from the boat. I begrudgingly waved back as another boat broke through the fog in hot pursuit. Isabelle's long, dark hair whipped around her head and foam rolled off the bow of her boat.

"Is she allowed to use her abilities like that?" Olivia demanded. "Anthony, cancel it out or something!"

"No way." Anthony shook his head vehemently. "I'm not interfering."

Heather shrieked for Wesley to go faster as more boats appeared. We thundered down the boardwalk, trying to keep pace with the boats. I could see Wesley's face strain with the effort of rowing against Isabelle's gale but he was maintaining the lead.

"How much farther?" I gasped between breaths. I hadn't planned on sprinting.

"I don't know, another half mile?" Naomi wheezed.

A shriek echoed over the water and we stopped running to watch Wesley and Remi's boat wobble and flip.

"What happened?" Anthony demanded as we all threw ourselves against the railing.

"Your cousin!" Freddie shot back, pointing at Isabelle as she overtook the capsized boat.

Andersen snickered behind us and I looked back at him and Skyler laughing.

"*You* did this!" I hissed, noting how he quickly jammed his hands into his pockets as if to hide them. "They're on your team!"

"It's what he gets." Andersen shrugged and began walking back up the boardwalk with Skyler.

"Where are they?" Heather shouted. Boat after boat passed Wesley and Remi's flipped hull but neither had surfaced. My stomach knotted and I scanned the dark water for signs of Wes.

"I'm calling Fleming!" Naomi pressed her phone to her ear.

"Isabelle should be disqualified for this!" Olivia hissed. I searched the dark water for Wesley, desperate to see him surface.

"It wasn't Isabelle!" I growled, still searching the water.

"She was throwing wind all over the place! Who else would it have been?"

"I don't know, who hates Wesley and can capsize boats with a flick of his wrist?"

"What happened? Where is he!?" Mrs. Isaacs caught up with us and gawked at the flipped boat. "Wesley!"

Panic welled in my throat and the dark night pressed in around me. They should have surfaced by now. A crowd was growing at the bannister as students and parents conglomerated to stare at the boat, but no one was doing anything to help them. I braced against the railing to pull myself over.

"Stop her!"

I was halfway over the water when arms pulled me back.

"Let go! They'll drown!"

"So will you!" Warm coffee breath broke across my face. It was rare for the fighting skills Alison had embedded in my subconscious to trigger these days, especially as Samantha slipped away, but I felt them take over as I swung an elbow back. Trev Baker wheezed for air, letting me go, but Naomi stood between me and the railing.

"There!" Heather pointed as two heads broke the surface. R e m i ' s blonde hair floated out around her face and her nose and mouth just barely broke the surface as she pulled Wesley towards the boardwalk.

"Help!" Her choked cry floated on the wind and ran through me like electricity. "Help, I can't—"

"I've got them!"

A sheet of ice rose from the water as a figure pushed through the growing crowd to vault over the bannister. Sergio rode his ice-slide to drop the twelve feet from the boardwalk to the water. As he ran, ice formed beneath his shoes, creating a path to Remi and Wes.

"Let me go!" I cried, trying to push past Naomi, but Trev Baker pulled me back again. Out on the water, Sergio helped Remi and Wesley up onto the ice. Remi got to her feet, but Wesley lay motionless.

"Sometimes the best way to help is to stay out of the way," Baker growled in my ear as I stood frozen, staring at Wesley's body. The boardwalk shook. More spectators were arriving, flocking towards the commotion.

"Great." I snapped out of my reverie to shove Baker back. "So stay out of my way!"

"I've seen you freeze to death." He jabbed a finger at the icy water. "I'm trying to *help*."

"Let me worry about how I die. *You* worry about what's going to happen when everyone figures out you've been feeding information to Adrestus."

His face flushed and Coach Reiner's voice shouted over the chaos.

"This! This is why we have hypothermia training!"

"Hypothermia!?" Mrs. Isaacs repeated in a daze.

Fleming pushed his way to the front of the crowd.

"What happened?" he demanded, watching Sergio and Remi drag Wes back to the boardwalk. Water wicked away from their hair and clothes in puffs of steam, presumably another trick of Sergio's. "Samantha, what's wrong?"

"You should keep a better eye on your students, Alex," Baker snarled. "I had to stop this one from jumping in. I already watch her die every night. Don't make me see it in real time."

Fleming stiffened but before he could reprimand me, Sergio lifted Remi and Wesley to the boardwalk on a sheet of ice. Mrs. Isaacs reached over the bannister to pull Wesley towards her, elbowing Everly out of her way. She fell to the boardwalk under her son's weight, but cradled his head in her lap.

"He's got a welt on his head!" She inspected Wesley's scalp, holding him close while Everly tried to pry him away. My heart leapt when I saw Wesley stir.

"Everybody, back up!" Fleming hollered at the crowd to no avail. "Give them space!"

"The oar hit me," Wesley murmured. "One second we were fine, the next, we were underwater."

"It was Andersen," I called to him, trying to push through the crowd. "He's still mad you tried to defend him yesterday."

"You're just *full* of accusations, aren't you?" Trev Baker snorted. "First, my boss, now—"

"You want an accusation?" Fire leapt in my stomach as something snapped inside me, finally broken after months of anger and anxiety. "How about you telling Adrestus all about Apex Team, down to the names of kids involved? You even let Schrader in to watch the competition on Monday when you *know* I heard him the night Adrestus nearly killed me! And you know where they're keeping my dad and won't do anything to save him!"

"Stop looking for your father!" Trev Baker boomed with sudden authority, towering over me. "I've dreamt his death and you're sitting next to him when he goes! Stay away from him, and you'll both be safe!"

The gathered crowd fell silent and I felt a black hole open inside my chest. He'd seen Dad die?

"How?" I whispered. I needed to know. I could avoid it if I knew. "When?"

"What's this about telling someone leaking team member names?" a parent near the back of the crowd demanded. Several others nodded. They pressed around me, driving me back and I fought to push my way back to Baker.

"Tell me how he dies!"

Baker stared at me through the bodies of angry parents, looking like I was something he was both scared of and disgusted by.

"Did she say Schrader tried to kill her?"

"BAKER!" I screamed. No one listened. Fleming caught my eye as he tried to quell the mass. He mouthed my name but I couldn't hear him over the shouting parents and my welling panic. Baker slipped backwards, escaping down the boardwalk and my cries caught in my throat.

"We should leave," Naomi tugged at my jacket. "Let Fleming clean this up."

I was a danger to my dad.

I hugged my knees, repeating Trev Baker's words in my head. The tiled floor of the Apex Facility atrium was cold and most of the lights were off, but a crack of yellow shone out from under the Sickbay door next to me. Carmen, the junior assigned to Call Duty for the night, napped facedown at the call desk.

I bowed my head and lightly tapped the end of Wesley's glasses case against the space between my eyes. I'd made Anthony bring them to me from their dorm, knowing Wesley would have a headache after a night without them but I didn't dare bring them into the Sickbay while Remi and Mrs. Isaacs were still in there.

I smacked a hand against the floor. Trev Baker had to be wrong. Fleming had said his visions were wrong sometimes, and I hadn't died of electrocution yet, so why would he be right about Dad dying with me at his side?

And it wasn't like there was a timeline there, either. It could be decades from now, peacefully, in his sleep. Though, I didn't like thinking about that either.

The Sickbay door squeaked open and I looked up to see Wesley staring down at me. I scrambled to my feet and held out the glasses.

"Oh!" He took the glasses and scratched at the back of his head. "That's why you're out here. I could hear you tapping."

The muscles in his face relaxed a little when he slipped the frames over his nose, but he still looked concerned.

"Sorry, I didn't want to intrude on you and your mom and—" My voice caught and I tried to clear my throat.

"They left through the back a while ago." He glanced towards the exit.

"Oh. Sorry. Did you have to have Serum?"

He walked towards the basement hall outside the atrium and I followed, not sure why talking to him felt so stiff and awkward.

"Yeah, for the concussion." He grimaced and I winced thinking about the spinal puncture it required. "It wasn't super enjoyable, but you know that."

We wound our way up the stairs in timid silence and I hesitated as we exited out the back school hall doors.

"I think it was Andersen, by the way, that dunked your boat."

"Doesn't really matter, does it?" Wesley shrugged.

"I guess not," I said, even though it absolutely did. "Naomi went to Froyo with her family. We might still catch them if we go now."

"Sammy, we're friends, right?"

My stomach churned in a way I didn't like.

"What kind of question is that?" I crossed my arms and his eyes flickered to my neck. I thought he was looking at my scar but he cocked his head.

"You're wearing the necklace I made you."

My hand shot to the bent dog-whistle I'd used against Wesley in the Final Trial, fashioned into a necklace.

"Yeah, I thought it'd bring good luck in the competition tonight. Guess it didn't work."

"Guess not." His forehead creased. "But we're friends?"

"Why wouldn't we be?"

"*Just* friends?"

"I—" I didn't know what to say and gaped at him like some kind of stupid fish. Everything inside me was lead and my knees shook under the weight of it. I shouldn't have worn the necklace because now he knew the one thing I hadn't even had the courage to admit to myself.

He knew I liked him.

"Yeah." My voice broke. "Just friends. That's what we are."

"Sammy, I need to make sure."

I hadn't even made my feelings known to the guy and he was rejecting me.

"Yes, Wesley."

He nodded solemnly, seemingly satisfied with my answer.

"Right, that's what I figured." He glanced back towards the dorms. "I should go to bed. It was a long day."

I nodded, bobbing on the balls of my feet.

"Okay." My throat was tight, making it hard to sound casual. "Goodnight."

He pulled his hood up to ward off the cold and trudged towards the dorms while I lingered at the back steps of the school hall.

"Wait! Wes?"

He turned around and his eyes were big behind his glasses.

"I—"

I like you. I don't want to be just friends.

"I'm glad you're not hurt."

A reluctant smile pulled at his lips and he finally seemed to relax.

"Thanks, Sammy. Goodnight."

"Yeah. Bye."

I wanted to scream.

16

Clash

I didn't have time to worry about Wesley, I told myself as I adjusted my armor in the locker room mirror beneath the University Arena. Two university students suited up on their end of the locker room and I couldn't help but notice how much older and more athletic they looked than me.

I chewed at the inside of my cheek. I hadn't seen Wesley since the night before and the residual nervous butterflies from that conversation waged war against the pre-competition jitters in my stomach.

To make everything just a little bit worse, everyone's families had come to watch them this week, even Andersen's. I would've given my sword arm to have mine there, but Trev Baker's warning about Dad's death cast a shadow over the mere thought of seeing him again.

"Why aren't you excited?" Naomi asked. She sat on the bench that ran between two rows of lockers, helping to outfit sensors on my armor.

"I just wish Vidar was here."

"Who?"

Cold dread gnawed at my chest. It wasn't like me to slip up like that.

"I mean Dad. My dad. Everyone's parents are here to watch, except mine."

"You call your dad 'Vidar'?" Naomi cocked her head at me.

"It's his name," I said, too quickly.

"I thought his name was Vic."

"Vic is short for Vidar." I covered. "He doesn't go by his full name."

"Except for with you, apparently."

"It's an inside joke."

I pulled my helmet over my head as if she wouldn't be able to read my emotions if I was inside. At least she wouldn't be able to see my face.

"You have an inside joke where you call your dad by his full first name?"

"Is that weird?"

I made a show of lacing up my boots, which would have been easier to do before putting the helmet on, but it was too late for that now.

"It's not the weirdest thing I've learned about your family." She frowned and bent down to help me with my laces.

"What can you tell me about the other fighters?" I asked, eager to change the subject.

"You already know Sergio and Marcus. Sergio will use temperature control to make it hard to get close. The other three don't have powers that will be much use. Eli is Everest's older brother, so his powers are probably similar to his. Being able to change his density will help him get around the course, but in a fight, you should be equal."

"And the others?"

"Candice and Boonsri," Naomi frowned. "Candice is essentially the opposite of Heather. Heather makes things dark, with the occasional light burst if she stores up her powers a certain way. Candice can *only* make things bright. As far as I know, she can't teleport the way Heather can, but she'll probably rely on trying to blind you to fight."

"But I suck at fighting blind!"

"You suck at blind *hand-to-hand* combat," Naomi pointed out. "This is sword-to-sword."

"And Boonsri?"

"Plants," Naomi shrugged. "The weapon she's permitted in is a fern. Apparently, it's terrifying what she can do, but since her plant is considered a weapon, she won't be allowed to bring it into the arena."

"The same way Marcus won't be allowed to use his lasso?"

"Exactly."

"But Sergio is still allowed to use ice?"

"As long as he doesn't use them as blades."

I frowned. Sergio was resourceful. There were plenty of ways he could use both cold and heat to gain the upper hand.

"Don't worry," Naomi smiled, handing me my thin competition sword. "You'll do great."

The rocky inclines of the arena hid the other five competitors from view, but at least they couldn't see me either.

I scanned the crowd overhead. Wesley caught me searching the stands and waved. I waved the saber back at him, trying to forget about our conversation the night before. A few rows behind him, Fleming sat with the other council members. They chatted among themselves animatedly, Trev Baker notably missing from their ranks, presumably unwilling to watch me compete.

The saber whistled as I gave it a test-slash through the air. It was more like a fencing foil than the blades I was used to, which could be an issue not only for my prospects in the competition, but also to carry the lie that I'd learned sword fighting by taking fencing lessons as a kid.

"Students!" Professor Parker's voice filled the arena and I adjusted my grip on the saber handle. The lights directly overhead brightened as the lights in the stands dimmed, casting Wesley, Naomi, and the rest of the team in darkness. "Twenty minutes on the clock!"

The scoreboard at either end of the arena lit up with a bright green "20:00". An animated flourish played across the middle of the screen, revealing six names. As the youngest, mine was at the top of list, followed by Marcus then Sergio.

I didn't know much about Candice, Boonsri, or Eli, outside of what Naomi had told me. Sergio had been the one Reiner recruited to help me last week, so hopefully that spoke to his prowess over the others. However, I recognized them as Sergio's friends who'd accompanied him to watch the permit test, which meant they'd seen me fight before, putting me at a disadvantage.

"Remember," Professor Parker warned, "hits to the face will result in automatic disqualification. You get two points per fighter that you defeat, plus three points for being the last one standing, two points for second place, and one point for third. With that said..."

The crowd roared. The sophomores chanted my name but the seniors must've been in the stands directly behind me. Shouts in support of Marcus screamed at my back.

"...swords ready!" Professor Parker shouted. "And, fight!"

The timer on the scoreboard began the countdown, gleaming through the darkness that enveloped the stands. I hesitated in my starting place. Should I venture into the middle and face whoever I found to rack up early points, or should I sneak around the sides and try to increase my chances of making it to the final three?

I crept up the nearest incline to lie on my stomach at the lip of the rocky crag. Sergio apparently had the same idea and he waved jovially from his peak on the opposite side of the arena.

Metal hit metal somewhere to my left, but despite my high vantage point, the terrain was too craggy to see much farther than I had been able to down below.

I slid down the steep side of the incline, glad my gloves and armor kept the rocky surface from scraping me up. A cheer went up in the stands and I whipped around to watch the scoreboard but the names stayed in place. No one had been defeated yet.

"You're better than most my army."

The cool voice in my ear caught me off guard. I twisted to see who was there but I was alone among the rocks.

"You're just saying that."

I recognized my own voice even though I hadn't spoken. I'd known this might happen, but had hoped it wouldn't.

"No, no, no, no, no!" I whispered, knocking the hilt of my saber against my helmet. "Not now!"

I couldn't afford another memory to bubble up right now. It had been embarrassing enough to pass out in the pool in front of the other sophomores. I'd rather quit than have the same thing happen in front of both teams, the entire council, and everyone's families.

"You could come with us," the voice said. Piercing blue eyes swam in my vision, staring at me from under curly, dark hair that framed his porcelain skin.

"You know I can't."

"Yes," he insisted, blue eyes glittering. "You can."

I leaned against a cliffside.

Focus! I blinked away the apparition just in time to see an armor-clad figure bearing down on me from above. The darker colors of the university uniform and the masculine form narrowed it down to Sergio or Eli, and I'd just seen Sergio across the arena.

Eli slammed into the cliffside and I moved just in time to avoid his attack. Chunks of rock broke off and showered around him, so he must've been using his powers to increase his density. Hopefully, that made him slower.

"You're Everest's brother," I said.

"And you're the Beta."

It had been awhile since the word "Beta" had bothered me. Between Andersen and Mr. Hendricks, I'd been numbed to the insult. I wasn't an Apex. So, what?

"My parents think Mr. Fleming made a mistake letting you on the team," he said. I figured he was stalling for time while he sized me up, but his words still made me bristle.

"Are they watching tonight?"

His grip tightened on the hilt. He was left-handed. That might give him an advantage against some, but I'd spent enough hours training against Wesley, who was also left-handed. That hadn't been sword fighting, sure, but the mechanics and feints would be similar.

"They are," Eli admitted.

"Perfect." I grinned. "It'll make it that much more fun to beat you."

His mouth contorted under his visor and I knew he'd want to make quick work of me.

Good.

His lunge was quick, but sloppy. I parried and he leapt into the air. He flipped over me, adjusting his density so that he floated overhead. I ducked to avoid his aerial attack.

"Think of the good we would do together." Adrestus' voice returned. "Eydis, we would change the world."

"But the world is good the way it is." His laugh was callous and cold.

Eli came at me again.

"How would you know?" the voice jeered. "You've never left your village."

"Because they need me here."

I parried Eli, keeping my focus on his left-arm, refusing to be drawn into the argument that Eydis and Adrestus waged in my head.

"No, you only think they do. Why else would they keep you here? How many times have you asked to sail away on the boats that you help make, only to have them send Vidar instead?"

Eli struck out at the cliffside with his free hand as I passed close to it. His hyper-dense arm sent a crack up to the peak and rocks showered over me. It would've been an effective move had it not helped snap me back to reality.

If Eli was anything like Wes, then nothing would trip him up more than fighting another leftie.

Eli lunged. I dodged and deftly exchanged the foil between my hands. He wasn't prepared for my counterattack to come from that side.

My saber lit up as it made contact with the sensors on his armor. A buzzer sounded overhead.

"What?" He looked around dumbly, whipping his helmet off to stare at the scoreboard that showed his name light up in red.

The corner of the stands where I'd seen the sophomores sitting erupted in cheers. I waved my foil in their direction before darting between two crags.

"But why would you want to stay?"

I groaned. The memory was still fighting to be remembered. The more adrenaline coursing through my system, the stronger it would be. When I'd first fought Sergio, I'd been able to channel the memory of learning to sword fight into my attacks, but this new memory was wrought with anxiety and turmoil.

"Because my *family*, Dres!" Eydis snarled. "Of course I don't want to stay! I want to see this world you claim needs to be saved! And I want to save it with you, but I can't leave them."

"I can give you so much more than they can." Adrestus' voice was silk and I wanted to believe him.

Gravel crunched under boots nearby. I held the saber ready. I'd run further towards the middle, so it could be anyone. I needed it to be Marcus. With two points under my belt, I could take him out before he had the chance to win any himself and prevent him from making the final three. It might be enough to help the sophomores pull ahead of the seniors.

However, it was a young woman's voice that called out.

"How about we skip the part where we sneak around?" she asked. "There's only twelve minutes left on the timer."

She stepped out from behind a boulder. Dark, shoulder-length hair stuck out from under her helmet. I was at least a foot taller than her. Between Vidar and Sergio, I didn't have much practice dueling anyone shorter than me.

I took up a fighting stance, ready for her to attack, but she shouted.

"Now, Candice!"

Bright, white light flooded my visor and I cried out in pain. I instinctively struck out with my saber and felt it make contact with the saber of the girl who must've been Boonsri.

I squinted through the light and the tears that had welled in my eyes. A chorus of cheers and boos went up from opposing sides of the stands. Boonsri attacked and I pushed my back up against a ledge. Candice had to be nearby. As much as I didn't want to trap myself in a corner, I needed to limit the number of angles she could attack from.

The blurred outline of Boonsri was joined by a second figure. I blinked rapidly, trying to clear my vision. They blocked my attacks with ease, but I didn't let up. If they got in close, I was done.

The buzzer hummed and I grabbed at my armor. I hadn't felt the hit but the crowd screamed from all angles, a few of them booing.

"What are you doing?" Boonsri shrieked. "We agreed to get the high schoolers first!"

"But you looked like such an easy target!"

I reached under my visor to wipe tears away. My eyes burned but I could see Sergio's saber blinking in blue lights. Boonsri's name turned red on the scoreboard.

Candice took off and Sergio saluted me as he gave chase.

I didn't give myself time to catch my breath. Sergio had helped me out of a tight spot, but I wasn't going to let him take all the glory. I'd spent long enough staring at the rocky maze while watching the week's earlier competitions. I could loop around and catch Candice before Sergio caught up to her.

It worked just as I'd planned. Candice took the corner too fast and ran straight into my foil. My sword lit up and the buzzer hummed. Sergio's team booed, as did Candice's supporters among the college sophomores. The high school sophomores, meanwhile, shrieked in delight. I was in the final three with Sergio and Marcus, with just under eight minutes left.

Sergio came around the corner and Candice pushed him out of the way as she made her exit.

"You should've stuck to the plan!" she hissed at him. He gave her a jaunty smile in apology.

"Sometimes plans change."

He made a flourish with the saber and stepped towards me. I'd taken his quarry and now I stood in its place. The ground between us glossed over with ice. I stumbled backwards and slipped on the slick surface but kept my footing.

Each step he took melted the ice and it rose as steam around his boots. There was an incline behind me. He was trying to trap me and it was going to work. I'd never make it across the ice.

"If you leave me now, you'll regret it." Adrestus' voice returned, more poison than silk this time.

A tight grip wrapped around my wrist but a quick glance told me it was in my head.

"Are you threatening me?" Eydis blurred with Samantha and it was getting harder to breathe.

I retreated further up the incline, trying to quiet the voices.

"No." The voice was suddenly and surprisingly gentle. "I mean your talents are wasted on sewing sails. You'll grow old pricking your fingertips on whalebones instead of living forever, creating whatever world you want."

"*This* is the world I want."

Sergio tilted his visored head at me and I knew he was taking me in with his one eye.

"What's the plan?" he goaded. "I know you're better than this."

Invisible smoke filled my nostrils and choked my lungs as the memory skipped.

Focus!

But the memory gnawed at my edges and Samantha was fraying. Tree branches that weren't there whipped my face as Eydis ran.

I'd made my way to the edge of the incline. The other side was steep but I might be able to escape down it.

My village was on fire. I'd seen this memory before, twice now. It wasn't a happy one.

"But what if your family wasn't a factor?" the voice asked. The memory of the conversation with Adrestus layered over the memory of the burning village.

"Then I would go anywhere with you."

Icy cold gripped my left ankle. Sergio's ice sheet had caught up with me. He grinned as he slowly stalked up the rocky ramp.

"Then for your sake, and the sake of your happiness, I wish them all long, happy lives." Sergio disappeared, replaced by Dres' blue eyes inches from mine. His head tilted forward. His lips brushed mine. My fingers entwined with the curls at the back of his head.

And then, I was back in the smoke. My family's dead bodies lay in a row. They'd been killed before the fire had been set.

Tears welled in my eyes. Sergio's form swam back into focus.

It had been my fault.

I hadn't asked for it outright, but he'd slaughtered them for me. I wiped my mouth with the back of my gloved hand, swallowing the disgust that rose in my throat at the memory of Young Adrestus' kiss.

"Nothing?" Sergio's shoulders fell in disappointment. "Come on, I was hoping for something more from you."

My whole body trembled. Wesley shouted my name in the stands and I came to in time to parry Sergio's attack. I couldn't escape or dodge, though, not with my foot frozen to the ground.

I swung at him haphazardly and he fell back, giving me the time I needed. I bent over and dealt my ankle a swift hit with the hilt of the saber. The ice cracked. Another blow would be enough to wiggle out, but Sergio bore down on me.

An electric jolt ran through my left ankle as I twisted it against its confines. I yanked my foot free and I dropped backwards over the lip of the edge. A collective gasp echoed from every direction in the stands as the ground disappeared beneath me and I fell and twisted into open air.

17

A Minor Impalement

A piercing snap sounded as I landed facedown in the rocks and the pain that shot up my arm from my wrist almost drowned out the hum of the buzzer. My saber landed next to me, flashing blue.

Had I hit Sergio on my way down? I pushed myself up with my uninjured arm and cried out as searing pain tugged at my stomach. I looked down but couldn't make sense of the thin piece of metal that stuck out of my abdomen. The jagged end connected to my saber by a wire that blinked blue.

I'd thought the snap had been my wrist but it had actually been the sound of my foil breaking off in my stomach. I looked at the scoreboard in horror. My name changed from green to red.

"That counts?" I cried.

I leaned back against the cliffside and the stands cried in disgust as they realized part of my saber had been embedded in my abdomen. I pushed myself to my feet but winced as I tried to put weight on my ankle.

The stands lit up and a large "TIME-OUT" animation took over the scoreboard.

"Are you okay?" Sergio called, taking his helmet off to look down at me. Sweaty hair escaped from his bun to stick out awkwardly from under his eyepatch strap.

"Absolutely peachy."

I'd injured myself in three places, I'd lost while Marcus was still in the game, I'd stabbed myself in front of literally every person I wanted and needed to impress, and, while I finally knew I hadn't called for my family to be murdered, I might as well have. Their dead bodies had been an offering to me, like some kind of macabre bouquet.

And Adrestus and me...I wanted to puke.

"I can't say I'm surprised." Everly's tone conveyed a suppressed smile, but as he came around the corner, I kept my eyes down. "Let's get this fixed."

Fleming caught up to us at the elevator and I stared sullenly at the carpeted floor, holding the tip of the saber in place in my abdomen as Fleming asked Everly the extent of the damage.

"Sprained ankle and wrist." He jabbed a thumb in the direction of my stomach. "And a minor impalement."

"What happened?" Fleming demanded as the elevator doors slid open and the university nurse in her mint-colored scrubs hurried over to help me to a bed.

The University Sickbay was more impressive than the one I was used to. While the underground portion of the college Apex facility had a humble nursing station, the actual Sickbay was located in an upper story suite with windows that overlooked the water between New Delos and the mainland.

"I fell," I mumbled. "On purpose, mostly."

"Before you fell, I mean. You looked unfocused."

I grimaced. Had it been that obvious?

"It was more memories, wasn't it?" Everly asked as I sat on the edge of the bed and swung my swollen ankle up so it rested on top of the blankets. "Was I right about the adrenaline?"

"Yeah, a little."

I fell back on the pillows, wincing at the pain in my abdomen.

"This'll need stitches."

"No Serum?" I asked.

"Dr. Weaver has asked us to only use it when absolutely necessary until we know what the mysterious threat facing the city next month is." He straightened up and gestured at me with a sweeping movement. "Besides, when students think they can rely on a quick healing process, they become reckless without cause."

"The honor of the sophomore team was on the line," I explained. "Being reckless was absolutely and indisputably necessary."

He pulled the tip of the saber out in a quick movement and I cried out.

"Careful!" Fleming fretted behind Everly.

"She can handle it."

"Fine, no Serum," I conceded, "but it doesn't need stitches. It wasn't that deep."

"It was deep enough."

"It feels better already."

"That's just Angie." He beckoned over his shoulder at the university nurse. Her long, brown hair was kept in a tight French braid and her arms were marked by battle scars. "She has that effect on her patients."

"It doesn't need stitches!" I insisted. Everly slapped a wad of padding over the wound.

"Tell you what, if the bleeding stops before I'm done with your ankle and wrist, I won't give you stitches."

I willed my abdomen to stop bleeding, but my hopes weren't high. He moved onto fitting my wrist with a brace.

"The memory," Fleming prodded. "Was there anything...?"

He trailed off and I glared at the lump of bandages under my shirt.

"Nothing useful to the team, no. That's what you're wondering, right?" I'd barely spoken to Fleming since our parent-teacher conference. I glared at him and thought I saw him gulp.

"No! Well, sure, but—"

"No information on how to destroy the Lapis. Nothing on how to beat Adrestus." My face burned with shame and I snapped at Fleming just in case he was able to see the phantom of Dres' kiss replaying in my eyes. "I do know I stabbed him in the stomach *eventually* and he seems to have bounced back just fine after a thousand years or so, but I'll keep you posted on if I find anything else that might work."

Everly grunted and moved onto my ankle as Fleming flushed red.

"You're keeping me in a job, at least," Everly grumbled, winding a bandage around the joint.

The Sickbay door slammed open and Angie the University Nurse glared as Wesley, despite his weird mood the night before, led the charge to my bed. It was harder than ever to look at him with my most recently regained memories still swirling in my head.

"You did it!" Wesley exclaimed. "We beat the seniors!"

"But I lost."

"No, you tied for first!" Anthony exclaimed, following Wesley with Naomi.

"I literally took myself out of the game. How could I have tied?"

"You get two points for each player you remove from the game." Wesley beamed. "That includes you!"

"Sergio outlasted you, sure," Naomi explained, "but you had the most hits, taking out three different players, counting yourself."

"And it was enough points to beat Marcus, who had no hits."

"Wait, so..." I tried to do the math in my head but the post-adrenaline crash was making thinking difficult. "Sergio and I both got seven points?"

"Yes!" Wesley and Naomi beamed.

"So we got third overall?"

"If you include the University teams, but first out of the high school!" Naomi said.

I was dizzy with elation.

"My mom is in love with you, by the way," Wesley said. "She would not stop going on about how scrappy you are."

"We're going to be late for the banquet," Remi said. I hadn't noticed her lingering in the doorway.

Wesley looked at the clock and then at Everly.

"Are you almost done?" he asked and Everly chuckled.

"I need to look over her open wound one more time to make sure the bleeding has stopped. I'll send her down once that's clear."

"We can wait if you like," Naomi offered but I shook my head.

"No, you should go. I'll be there soon."

Wesley reached for Remi's hand but she shied away.

"Actually, you go. My shoulder hurts from last night. I want to make sure I didn't pull anything."

Fleming left with Wesley, Naomi, and Anthony, guiding them to the hall, and Everly gestured to the next bed over.

"Angie will look you over once she has a moment," he said.

Remi sat down on the edge of the bed to face me. Everly beckoned for me to lie back and I obliged, acutely aware that Remi was watching.

Everly tutted in disapproval as he inspected the wound.

"Still bleeding. This'll be about four stitches. Hold these bandages here. I need to grab supplies."

"You're serious about the no Serum thing, then?" I craned my neck to watch him disappear into the back. Angie laughed and Everly called at her from the storage closet.

"You laugh now but in another two and half years, she's your problem."

"Samantha." Remi's voice was curt but careful.

"Yes?" Apprehension bubbled inside me.

"Can we talk?"

I glanced between her and the open wound in my abdomen.

"Yeah, sure. I don't have anything going on at the moment."

She took a deep breath and looked at me with round, brown eyes.

"I don't want you to talk to Wesley anymore."

I hated the sound of the awkward, disbelieving giggle that escaped my lips but I had no idea how else to respond. Even when Wesley and I had been at each other's throats in the fall, we'd stood by each other.

"I'm serious," Remi said. Everly came back into the room and under any other circumstance, I wouldn't have welcomed the sight of an anesthetic needle meant for my stomach. This one time, though, it was strangely relieving.

Unfortunately, Remi was on a mission and I was trapped.

"Wes and I dated three different times last year," she continued. "It never worked out for many reasons, but this time is different and I want us to have the best chance."

"Wesley and I are just friends," I promised. Wesley had no interest in me beyond friendship so it was bewildering that I could be perceived as a threat. "I know we went to the dance together but—"

"You and Wes are not 'just friends'," she accused. Everly bit the inside of his cheek and tried to look like he wasn't there. "When you fell —"

She broke off to look at the ceiling. I tried to keep from flinching as Everly's needle dipped under my skin.

"I know you've been through a lot with him and that he worries about you. I'm not saying there's anything going on between you but this is the only thing that'll keep it that way."

Angie approached Remi's bed and reached for her shoulder.

"You said you pulled a muscle?" she asked. Remi shrugged her off.

"No, I'm fine. Sorry if I worried you."

"How's that?" Everly prodded the skin near the wound. "Numb yet?"

"Yes." I lied. The sooner I could leave, the better. I looked back at Remi. "I want Wesley to be happy and he's happy with you. I don't intend on messing that up."

"I'm not worried about you, I'm worried about him."

I gasped in pain and immediately regretted lying about how numb the area around the wound was.

"Then why are you talking to me and not Wes?" It was hard to keep the snarl out of my voice.

Remi bristled, which was pretty audacious of her considering she wasn't the one getting stitches while being interrogated by her best friend's girlfriend.

"I did and he got mad at me. Like I said, he cares about you, and if he won't sever your friendship, maybe *you* will."

Wes' odd attitude made a little more sense now. He was making sure I didn't offend Remi, though I apparently already had. I gaped at her.

"I thought you wanted to have the best chance together."

"I do!" She must've realized how aggressive she sounded because her shoulders sagged and she looked at her lap. "I mean, I do. But as long as you're around, no one else will be as important to him. Please, Samantha. I don't want to be a second-place girlfriend."

Everly pulled the edge of my shirt down over the fresh stitches. He cleared his throat.

"That should do it. Give me a couple steps on that ankle and you're free to go."

I held back a groan as I pushed myself into a sitting position and swung my legs over the edge of the bed. I wobbled to my feet and made a show of taking a few, limping steps to prove I was mobile.

Everly responded with a heavy sigh and turned to Remi.

"And I can trust you to escort her downstairs without locking her in a closet in the name of love?"

Remi's freckles popped out against her blushing cheeks but she nodded diligently.

I didn't know which was more uncomfortable: the wrist brace, wrapped ankle, and stitched up abdomen or the heavy silence that hung over our walk to the elevator.

The doors slid open and Remi punched the button for the lower levels. I recognized the look on her face. It was defeat.

"I know it's a lot to ask of you," she said, "but when you're around, things make less sense for him. If he's going to be with me, I want him to have clarity."

It sounded more like coercion than clarity to me, but I at least could see where she was coming from. Things got confusing around Wesley and he clearly wanted to be *just* friends. I wouldn't be seeing Wesley for two weeks anyway. It could be like a test run. Not to mention, Wesley worried too much about my safety. It might do him some good to be apart while he sorted things out with his ex.

Besides, I wouldn't be able to stomach it if Wesley ever found out about *my* ex. Why would he want to date, let alone be friends with, someone who had *kissed* Adrestus?

"I'll try," I mumbled. Remi's curls bounced as she whipped her head around.

"You will?"

"Yeah," I shrugged. Maybe it would be good for me, too. Wesley had gone out of his way to make sure we weren't anything more than friends. If he wanted what I wanted, he would've done something about it. "Why not?"

Remi smiled sadly.

"I'm sorry, I know he's your friend, but that's what makes it so hard."

"Right." She'd made her point. She could stop talking now. "That makes sense."

The sounds of the banquet echoed down the hall, greeting us as the elevator doors opened. Wesley stood outside the cafeteria. As soon as he saw us, he ran down the corridor, his glasses bouncing on his nose.

"Took you long enough!" He grabbed my arm to inspect the wrist brace. "Don't tell me you had to get the stitches?"

"My shoulder's fine, thanks for asking," Remi teased. Wesley dropped my hand and took Remi's.

"That's good! Did he say if you pulled a muscle or not?"

I stepped away and pointed down the hall.

"I'm gonna hit the bathroom before dinner," I said, trying to find an escape.

"Wait, but—"

"I'll see you in there!" I hobbled away before Wes could stop me.

In the bathroom, I lingered over the sink, wondering how long to wait before going to dinner. Maybe I shouldn't go at all. I'd been skewered, hadn't I? It wouldn't be crazy to think I wanted to go to bed.

I was just about to venture out of my hiding spot when raised voices drifted in from outside.

"It's dangerous, Andy. Your father and I don't mind the risk but with your brother and sister—"

"What's dangerous?" Andersen sounded as if he had a plugged up nose, but he spat the words with vitriol.

"The letters! The threats!" The woman's voice was pleading. "Penny thinks someone followed her home from school the other day."

"She just wants attention! I'm not a danger!" Andersen's voice broke. "I-I want to come home! Please!"

"And you will! After things blow over. I know it's not fair. I went through the same thing once—"

"I don't care."

A thud against the wall rattled the bathroom door and I retreated to the farthest sink.

"Andersen!"

"The letters are probably from kids at school," he cried. "It sounds like something Jamie would do."

"I told you that girl was trouble. If it weren't for her—"

"I don't regret saving Jamie!"

"Honey, I know." The woman sniffed loudly. "Listen, by spring break, things should be better."

"Why don't you admit you just don't *want* me there?" Andersen's voice broke and another thud shook the wall.

Heavy footsteps retreated down the hall but the woman stayed just outside the bathroom, sniffing and taking long, shuddering breaths. The bathroom doorknob turned and I walked backwards into a stall to avoid Andersen's mother.

Mrs. Lewis hovered over the sink, hiccuping softly, and as much as I would've liked to, I couldn't hide forever.

I flushed the toilet for show and limped out to wash my hands, a process made much more difficult than it should've been thanks to the new wrist brace.

"Good job tonight." Mrs. Lewis made eye contact through the mirror reflection and I grinned sheepishly.

"I impaled myself, but thanks."

She dabbed under her eyes with a paper towel.

"My son is lucky to be friends with such talented young people. To be honest, I probably wouldn't have liked you much if I were on the team with you, but that's just my competitive nature." She gave me a smile and threw away her paper towel as she backed towards the door. I fumbled to respond but she laughed. "Don't look so confused, dear, it's a compliment."

The door swung open of its own accord, and she made her exit, leaving me standing over my running sink.

Andersen couldn't have talked to his parents much if his mom thought I was his friend.

I waited another few minutes, giving Mrs. Lewis plenty of time to get back to the banquet before sneaking into the corridor. The banquet was in full swing and even though I tried to tip-toe in, my entrance was ill-timed.

"Fourth place goes to," Professor Parker paused for dramatic effect, "the High School Seniors!"

The seniors glanced around with halfhearted claps and chagrined smiles, although I would've considered fourth place out of eight teams to be a win, especially when four of those teams were made of college kids.

"Sammy!" Wesley waved from the circular sophomore table. I leaned against the back wall to show him I was comfortable standing where I was.

"Which brings us to our top three teams!" Parker gestured at a table of medals behind her. "Third place, the high school sophomores!"

The table of my teammates roared and leapt to their feet to storm the front of the room and receive their medals. My heart sank as Wesley ran to me instead and tried to take my hand. I pulled it away. He drew back, and the look of hurt that passed over his face made me hate myself.

"Sorry," I muttered. "My wrist hurts."

"But your brace is on the other hand." He grabbed my elbow instead and pulled me to the front of the room.

"Right," I mumbled. I flexed my hand, trying to forget the feeling of Adrestus' curls between my fingers. "They're both injured."

I avoided Remi's eyes but could see her leering in my periphery. Naomi clapped me on the back as we joined the others. I winced and grabbed my abdomen.

"Sorry," she giggled. "You made it just in time!"

Wesley made a show of grabbing a bronze medal from the table and lifting it over my head. I leaned away and snatched it from him, tittering awkwardly before slipping it over my head myself.

He made a face but I pretended not to notice as I followed the others back to their table. Professor Parker announced the college freshmen as the second place winners. Sergio looked sour as he walked up to claim his silver medal.

"He was furious when you got points for stabbing yourself," Heather whispered. "He thought he should get the points, claiming he saved you earlier in the match."

"He still got first place." Anthony took his spot at the table. "So what if he has to share it? It wouldn't have made a difference in his team's ranking."

"It's different for the university kids." Olivia pulled apart a dinner roll in the seat next to me. "If they lose to a high schooler, their friends don't let them forget it."

"But he didn't lose to me," I blushed. "He outlasted me and it *was* his fault that I fell and stabbed myself."

"That's what makes it even worse," Olivia shrugged candidly. "We're used to it by now, but the university kids don't want to be on the same level as a...you know."

"A Beta?" I snorted. Olivia shrugged again.

"Well, yeah. Sergio was basically just told he's comparable to a high school girl with no super powers."

I'd thought Sergio had seemed cool when we'd been training. He'd even come to watch my permit test. Disappointment broiled inside me to learn he was just as stuck up about being an Apex as many of the others had been.

"It makes your victory that much sweeter," Naomi grinned, obviously tapping into my feelings. "Plus, he needed to be taken down a few pegs."

"Even if it wasn't on purpose, throwing yourself off the cliff and stealing the satisfaction of beating you was incredible to watch," Heather nodded.

I glanced at Wesley but he was staring at his plate, giving his potatoes a confused look. Remi hunched over, looking annoyed.

The college seniors were crowned the first place champions and we clapped politely as they charged the front of the room. Dr. Weaver stood up to give closing words as the room calmed down and I felt my stomach clench as her eyes briefly met mine and flickered away.

"Students and teachers, it has been an honor to watch our young heroes compete this week. I wish being part of this community could always be as lighthearted and spirited but, as we are all aware, it has been a difficult semester and prospects for next semester are admittedly bleak."

"Oh, this is cheerful," Heather muttered next to me. "Just how I like to end my parties."

"Early in the semester, we fought to bring home students who fell victim to a spate of kidnappings," Dr. Weaver continued. Anthony fidgeted in his seat and I felt my cheeks grow warm. "We know a mysterious man named Adrestus was behind the attacks and while we recovered all of the kidnapped students, Adrestus remains at large."

It was technically true that all the kidnapped students had been rescued, but it still felt wrong to chalk it up as a win. They took Amanda and they still had Dad. I stared at Dr. Weaver, feeling cold sweat break out across my forehead.

"Fortunately, we had one student who was able to offer insight on Adrestus and his cult followers. Before now, the Apex Council thought it unwise to share this information as it was unsubstantiated. However, after many of you became aware of these allegations just last night and with Schrader Industries moving forward with the Epsilon Initiative, I'm making the executive decision to catch everyone up to speed."

The whole room held its breath and my heart hammered in my ears, thundering so loud I thought I might miss what Dr. Weaver said next.

"There is reason to believe Schrader Industries is working for Adrestus under the orders of Adrian Schrader. Effective immediately, we've severed our relationship with Schrader Industries."

18

All On The Same Page

Gasps rippled through the room. Parent veterans of the team cast each other looks of surprise. Adrian Schrader and his family had long funded the Apex program.

"Information has been leaked to Adrestus and Schrader Industries representative Trev Baker has been terminated from his position on the Apex Council. We're sorry for not making you all aware sooner, but with Schrader Industries providing more than eighty percent of our funding, we had a lot on the line. However, I'm convinced this is the right choice if we want to stop whatever it is Adrestus has planned for New Delos and his Epsilon Initiative."

Stunned silence gave way to angry and confused shouts. Dr. Weaver deadpanned at the crowd, refusing to be heckled and looking every bit like the proud head Apex Councilor she was.

"I will not take chances with my students," she asserted. "We've had too many close calls and, if you've been reading our reports, you'll know the city is allegedly one month away from catastrophe. Adrestus is more powerful than we know, which is why I've decided to take the allegations against Schrader Industries seriously."

"Is Adrestus an Apex, too?" Heather's mom stood up with balled fists at the table where the sophomore parents ate together. "Why don't we take him now? He's outnumbered, so where is he?"

"Adrestus is not an Apex," Dr. Weaver said gravely. Several more parents stood with Mrs. Hisakawa, ready to fight.

"We can take a Beta!" a dad in a New Delos University crewneck shouted.

"Not this one."

I gulped. I knew how ridiculous it sounded to say who Adrestus was out loud. Even in a world where anyone might harbor secret super powers, the idea that an ancient spartan warrior had gained immortality from a special, magic rock was ludicrous. If that magic rock hadn't brought me back from the dead several times already, I probably wouldn't believe it myself.

"I'm not scared of some Non-Apex coward!" a man with dark brown hair and large ears protested. Anthony groaned and hid behind his hands.

"That's my Uncle Lance," he mumbled into his fingers. "Isabelle's dad."

"Adrestus isn't scared of you, either." Dr. Weaver looked down her long nose at Anthony's uncle. "While he isn't an Apex, Adrestus cannot die."

A few in the crowd dared to laugh but the sound died fast at the sight of Dr. Weaver's darkly serious face.

"That's not possible!" a mom finally shouted.

"I didn't think so, either," Dr. Weaver admitted, "but I've seen the very thing that grants his immortality at work."

The other sophomores looked at me. They'd all been there when Wesley announced I'd died. Even if I denied I'd been dead, I was sure they were putting the pieces together.

"We believe the source of this immortality is the same tool Schrader Industries is using to move forward with the Epsilon Initiative and we believe it to be an ancient power source that created the original Apex."

The other students stared transfixed at Dr. Weaver's words but many of the parents shook their heads and cast dubious glances around the room.

"This is just a repackaged version of the original legend of Adrestus," Anthony's uncle laughed. He had the same haughty expression Isabelle often wore.

"It's not repackaged," Dr. Weaver said. "It *is* the legend of Adrestus. He knows who our students are and has recently tried to recruit at least one, but he's coming to terms with the fact that we won't stand with him. Now he needs a new generation of Apex who are more willing than we are to work with him, which brings us to the Epsilon Initiative."

"Okay, sure," Anthony's uncle scoffed. "Is the Scourge Queen going to make an appearance next?"

I felt Wesley look at me, seeing him twist his head in my peripheral vision. I wished he wouldn't. With his pointed glance and a heartbeat thundering so loudly in my chest that I was sure the entire table could hear it, I was certain they'd piece it together. I gripped my leg with my uninjured hand to keep it from quaking.

Dr. Weaver could tell everyone right now that they'd all just watched the Scourge Queen of legend impale herself on her own blade. While that wasn't a very inspiring image of fortitude against Adrestus' schemes, she could pull me up next to her as the undead proof she needed to back up her claims.

I was certain she would, even though she'd promised not to tell anyone my identity. Why wouldn't she? My feelings couldn't be more important than convincing everyone that Adrestus was someone we should fear.

However, she scoffed at Anthony's uncle.

"Don't mock me," she clipped. "Adrestus is as real as he is dangerous, even if the Scourge Queen Eydis isn't."

I thought I might slip out of my chair and onto the floor in relief. Somehow, I remained upright.

"I don't enjoy dampening the evening's festivities in this way," Dr. Weaver continued, "but I thought it only fair that we go into the holiday break remembering that we cannot be complacent and we must not be caught off guard. I refuse to see another student harmed by Adrestus and I'm certain our teams have the ability to stop both him and the Epsilon Initiative."

A smattering of clapping echoed through the banquet hall, but it felt hollow. Only a few parents joined in the half-hearted applause. People were either too shocked to have processed Dr. Weaver's words yet or they didn't quite believe them.

"I'm glad they got rid of Baker," Olivia said, as if she'd known the whole time he was trouble. Cautious conversations broke out across the room as each table digested Dr. Weaver's announcement. Wesley still stared at me and, despite my promise to Remi, I met his eyes. He raised his eyebrows at me and I shrugged in return.

Are you doing okay?

As good as I can be.

"Do you think the students staying on New Delos over the break will get special assignments?" Freddie asked. "It would make sense with the Doomsday approaching."

"It's not Doomsday," Everest said. "We don't know what it is."

Heather laughed and wagged her fork in Everest's direction.

"Sure, just that the city is supposedly going to burn. I don't know about you, but that sounds like a doomsday to me. People will get hurt."

"Not if there's extra holiday assignments!" Freddie asserted.

"There won't be," Naomi chimed in. "Not for high school students, at least. Fleming needs a break and I don't blame him."

"Okay, but what if there *are* extra holiday missions?" Wesley said. "I'll be furious if I miss out."

"Right," Skyler snorted. "We all forgot nothing important is allowed to happen if you aren't at the center of it."

"I don't want to be at the center. I just want to know what's happening." Wesley shrank in his seat.

"Man, if only someone had invented something to make instantaneous communication across wide distances easier," Skyler sneered.

"Right, but I still want to be on-hand if I'm needed."

"Why don't you just admit you can't stand the thought of someone getting more glory than you?" Skyler ripped a violent bite of bread from his dinner roll.

"I don't want glory, I want to help!" Wesley looked to me for help and I balled my fingers in my lap.

"Yeah, I'm sure that's what Paragon said, too, but the guy still ended up with statues all across the island." Skyler rolled his eyes.

"Would you both shut up?" Naomi snapped. "Skyler, Wesley just wants to help. Wesley, you sound self-important. Both of you, eat your food."

Wesley blushed but Skyler grunted irritably.

"Shouldn't you be off with Andersen making someone else miserable?" Remi sniffed at Skyler.

"Haven't seen him since dinner started," Skyler shrugged. "Besides, he's not been fun to be with since Jamie socially neutered him."

Even though I'd heard Andersen arguing with his mom, I hadn't registered his absence until now. I craned my neck, wondering where he might be lurking. His parents sat with the other sophomore parents but Andersen himself was nowhere to be seen.

Dessert wheeled out on a train of carts and Heather and Olivia left to bring plates of cake back to the table, leaving Naomi to steal the seat next to me.

"That was pretty intense, huh?"

"Are we surprised?" I whispered. "Skyler's never been a fan of Wesley."

"No, I mean Dr. Weaver's announcement."

"Oh."

Naomi blinked at me with her round, brown eyes. I could almost feel her searching my emotions.

"You had quite the reaction to it."

"I imagine the whole room probably felt like a tsunami to you," I frowned. "It was a lot for anyone to take in."

"True," she nodded. "A lot of people, especially parents, felt unsure. Hopefully they don't try to remove Dr. Weaver from her position."

"They can't do that, can they?"

"No, she has too much support in other places. But I wanted to make sure you're okay."

I needed to tell Naomi about Eydis sooner or later. She deserved to know.

"Yeah, I just wasn't prepared for that, especially after the night I've had."

Heather and Olivia returned with cake, but no one seemed in the mood for dessert. I watched the table of sophomore parents with their heads bent towards each other and their faces serious. Mrs. Isaacs sat back in her seat with a creased brow, looking utterly lost among the other parents.

Andersen's parents were missing from the group, but I found them at the staff table, kneeling next to Fleming. His brow furrowed and he nodded fervently as he spoke with them. I didn't trust Andersen, and while his mom had seemed nice enough, I didn't trust her either.

Fleming stood up and led Andersen's parents away, Everly close behind. They found a spot in the back of the room to talk where Mrs. Lewis could wipe away the tears that trickled down her cheeks in private.

Professor Parker took the spot at the front of the room, tearing my attention away from Fleming and Mrs. Lewis. She gave a quick, concluding speech and while it was much more cheerful than Dr. Weaver's speech, her message of hope felt empty with Adrestus still lingering on our minds.

I followed the other sophomores out of the banquet hall as we finished, hobbling as best I could on my bandaged ankle.

"Need help?" Wesley offered, joining me at the back of the herd.

"I, uh—"

"Samantha, a word?" Fleming called from an off-shooting corridor.

"I'll catch up with you guys," I lied, waving Wesley away. Remi cast me a grateful smile.

"How are you feeling?" Fleming's hair stood at awkward angles like it usually did when he'd been pulling at it. I straightened up despite the sharp pinch in my side.

"I'm great," I said.

"I mean about Dr. Weaver's announcement."

I hesitated. I didn't know how I was feeling. Relieved, maybe, to know that we no longer worked with Schrader Industries and that Baker had been kicked off the Council. Plus, it was oddly comforting to know that everyone was on the same page now about Adrestus and his origins, even if they were hard to believe. However, I felt more on edge than I had earlier. As Adrestus' secrets came to light, it would be harder to keep my secrets in the dark.

"I'm fine."

"I'm sorry I didn't warn you about Baker ahead of time." He scratched the back of his neck and bit his lip. "And I'm sorry about the parent-teacher conference yesterday. It was my first time on the 'parent' end of things and I probably could've handled it better."

"It's fine," I asserted. I didn't want to talk about it.

"Good. So, this'll be your last night on campus before break. I'll pick you up tomorrow after lunch." He looked everywhere but my face, fidgeting uncomfortably. "But there's another thing we need to talk about."

My heart stopped and then double-timed to make up for the pause. Was there news about my dad? Or maybe they'd found a lead on the impending Doomsday threat? Whatever it was, it couldn't be urgent. Fleming was taking his time finding the right words.

"There's a small change in the living arrangements," he mumbled, still not looking at me. "It's a real last minute thing and Everly doesn't have the space for anyone else to stay with him."

The feeling of utter dread that flooded my entire being was more painful than piercing myself on my own sword. I'd heard the argument outside the bathroom. I'd seen Mrs. Lewis pleading with Fleming in the corner during dessert while Everly comforted her.

"Please, don't say it," I begged. Fleming gritted his teeth.

"Andersen will be staying with us over the holidays."

19

Living Arrangement

It was like being stabbed in the stomach all over again.

"But why?" I groaned. "He has a family and a home!"

"Not that it's your business, but his parents are concerned for their and his safety with recent events and—"

"What recent events?" I screwed my face up at him. "Adrestus affects everyone. Andersen isn't special."

"Recent events like rescuing Jamie," Fleming glowered. "She and her father have influence and the Lewises have already received several threatening letters."

"But that doesn't mean he has to stay with *us*!"

"I know you two don't exactly get along—"

"That's putting it mildly," I snorted. "He's a bully. He's like Roy Hendricks."

Fleming's face flushed at the mention of his own high school tormenter.

"I understand it'll be uncomfortable, but this is a time of crisis and
—"

"Right now, he *is* the crisis!" I insisted. "He's horrible!"

"Samantha, I promise I won't let him bother you, alright?" Fleming
sounded more like he was pleading with me than assuring me. "Andersen
has nowhere else to go. I'm sure he wishes he had other options, too."

I rubbed the heel of my good wrist against the middle of my forehead,
trying to release the tension there. As much as I wanted to complain until I
had my way, it was no use.

"I still get a bedroom, right?"

"Of course. It's your apartment as much as it is mine and Andersen is
our guest."

I sighed. I'd survived worse, though this would rank up there as far as
dangerous feats went.

"Fine. But don't expect me to get him a Christmas gift."

Fleming relaxed and stifled a smile.

"I promise, I would never expect that."

Naomi got up early to get one last breakfast with her dad and siblings and I
spent the morning cleaning the room. As much as I wanted to beg her to
change spots with Andersen, it didn't feel right. She'd been in tears while
she got ready for breakfast, explaining she didn't know if she'd ever get to
see Zoey or Will again if they turned out to be an Apex before the next time
they visited. Besides, she was probably exhausted of me and my feelings of
stress and guilt. She deserved a break.

My phone buzzed partway through dusting the dorm and my heart
sank at the sight of Wesley's name flashing across the screen.

"Come downstairs," the text read. "I want to say goodbye."

While I wanted to honor my word to Remi, I couldn't ignore Wesley
when he just wanted to give his farewells. She'd have to understand.

Wesley paced back and forth in the ground floor lobby, forcing
students to dodge around him with their bags as they made their exits

with their families. His face brightened when he saw me, but it turned into a grimace when he saw me limping.

"I can't believe Everly didn't give you any Serum." Wesley wrinkled his nose. "We need you in one piece now more than ever."

He took my wrist brace in his hand and looked it over, as if looking for some hint as to how to make the sprain heal faster.

"I promise I won't let anything exciting happen while you're gone," I assured him. "Although, I might end up murdering Andersen."

"Andersen? Why?" He looked up from my wrist to meet my eyes, his face darkening with concern. I blushed under his sudden scrutiny and the memory of Eydis and Dres tried to force its way to the forefront of my mind again.

I shoved it away by telling Wesley everything from the conversation I overheard between Andersen and his mom to my new living arrangements for the break, and as horrible as it all was, I enjoyed watching Wesley's face go from perplexed to outraged.

"And I thought I had it bad," Wesley shook his head. "What a nightmare."

"Why do you have it bad?"

He reddened and tried to look busy and aloof by scratching his head.

"It was Remi's idea. She wants me to come stay at her house for New Year's."

"But you guys are together again, right?" I asked, trying not to think of shared New Year's resolutions under a sky of fireworks and everything else that went along with the clock striking midnight on December thirty-first. "That's not a bad thing if she's your girlfriend."

Guilt and jealousy festered inside me. Remi had said I confused Wesley when I was around and now he was second-guessing visiting her over break. I should have just texted him goodbye.

Wesley turned an even darker shade of red.

"We're not *together*-together," he explained. "We're not even a *thing*, you know?"

"No," I said seriously, "I don't know. Try explaining that as if I was an ancient viking girl who just came out of a coma."

Wesley scowled but I was sure he was just playing. He at least seemed like he wanted to talk to me, which was a big improvement from two nights ago.

"Let's just say, we'll see how winter break goes," he said. "Although, what's the point of dating if the city is just going to burn to a crisp in a month?"

I took a deep breath and rolled my eyes.

"From what I can tell, Remi likes you a lot and you seem to like her, too. You'll have fun at her house."

"But that's just it!" Wesley said with sudden conviction. "What if she just likes the *idea* of me?"

His green eyes begged for a solution behind his glasses, and while there was a fairly straightforward answer I was tempted to give him, I exhaled heavily and tried to smile.

"I don't know what went down last year, but if you're going to give this another chance, you can't do it halfway. You're either in or you're out."

"You know you're the only one who actually thinks Remi and I could work, right?"

"Other than you and Remi, you mean?"

"Right." He didn't look so sure as he gnawed at his lip.

"Great," I smiled. "So don't make me look like an idiot."

"Wesley, there you are!" Remi charged out of the stairwell, an overstuffed backpack slung over one shoulder. She pushed between us, her backpack smacking me in the side as she wrapped her arms around Wesley. She threw me a warning scowl over his shoulder. I gulped.

"I still need to pack, so I'll let you guys go." I backed away but Wesley broke free of Remi.

"Wait!" He pulled a plastic bag of chocolate chip cookies from his bag. "My mom made these in the common room kitchen for you."

Remi looked like she wanted to murder the cookies as he passed them into my hands. He opened his arms for a goodbye hug that I would have very much liked to accept, but Remi had me locked in a death glare.

Wesley hesitated with his arms out and I froze, looking between him and his not-girlfriend. He cleared his throat awkwardly and settled for patting my shoulder.

"I'll see you soon," he smiled. "Try not to push Andersen out any windows."

"See you." *If Remi lets me.*

He and Remi walked to the door while I lingered awkwardly by the elevator. He pulled his hood up as they exited and he glanced back to cast me one last sad smile.

Remi sent me several texts reminding me about my promise the night before but if anything, I'd done her a favor by talking to Wesley. He'd looked ready to drop their New Year's plans before I convinced him not to. She should've been thanking me instead of chewing me out for "clouding Wesley's resolve".

I typed out, and then quickly deleted, a text response about how she shouldn't want to be with someone whose resolve was so easily clouded. I tried to put her out of my mind. I had much bigger things to worry about and just a few, short hours later, I stood with my bag in the roundabout in front of the dorm, cradling Floundersen's fish tank in my arms.

Andersen sidled up next to me and we waited in silence. He kept sniffing loudly, as if the cold was making his nose run, though mine was just fine. When Fleming finally pulled up in his dated SUV, I thought I would've felt more relieved but there was no escaping Andersen's company now.

Fleming did his best to talk through the heavy awkwardness of the ten minute car ride to his apartment in the middle of the island, but stopped trying after neither of us answered him with anything more than a grunt.

The car ride may have been mercifully short, but I had no idea how I was going to make it through the next two weeks dodging both Andersen and Fleming in a two-bedroom apartment. The high-rise building had a nice view that looked out over the neighboring roofs all the way to the school campus, but wasn't large enough for the three of us to be comfortable for two weeks.

Natural light spilled from the wrap-around living room windows into the adjoining kitchen and dining area. Sparse furnishings kept the space from feeling claustrophobic and a half-constructed plastic Christmas tree sat in the corner behind a large, worn leather recliner.

"Samantha, you'll be down here." Fleming led the way down the hall to the second bedroom. A twin bed and dresser sat against one wall, opposite the desk. It wasn't much but it would give me somewhere to hide from Andersen. "Feel free to decorate however you like. The closet has some old boxes in it, but there should still be room for your things."

Fleming cleared his throat and lingered in the doorway before stepping away to show Andersen his spot in the living room.

Maybe Everly lived nearby and I'd be able to get away to see Naomi. I set Floundersen's tank down on the desk and stood there a moment to watch his fanlike tail furl and twist in the water. He might've been just a fish but it was weirdly comforting to think I, at the very least, had him.

The view wasn't bad either. A wall to wall window stretched across the far side of the room and it looked out over the city. I spent a long time staring out at the adjacent buildings, wondering if the people inside were having a better day than I was.

I stayed in my room until Fleming called me to dinner that evening. He stirred a pot on the stove while Andersen wrestled with the plastic tree in the living room, trying to set it up. I eyed the haphazard string of lights tangled in a glowing ball at his feet, remembering Trev Baker's premonition about my death by electrocution.

"Bowls are on the table," Fleming said, snapping my thoughts away from those of a festive, Christmas-themed demise. "Grab one and bring it over."

After getting my soup and apprehensively lowering myself into a seat at the table, Andersen stalked over and slammed his bowl down, sending potatoes sloshing over the sides. He dropped into his seat and glowered over the steam.

"So what's the deal?" he asked. "When do I get the bedroom?"

Sudden defensiveness rose in my throat. The small bedroom wasn't much, but outside of the dorms, it was my only home. I got ready to dig in my heels but Fleming shook his head as he took a seat.

"I'm sorry, that's Samantha's bedroom."

"Just because she's a girl, I have to stay on the couch for two weeks?"

"It's because I live here. Not just for the holiday. Permanently," I explained. Andersen's scowl deepened.

"So, what, he's like your dad now because you got your other one kidnapped?"

Fleming's eyebrows disappeared into his hairline and I shoveled soup into my mouth, too mortified at him calling Fleming my dad to be mad at his jab. I winced as hot broth scalded my tongue.

"But why *does* Adrestus have your dad hostage?" Andersen pressed.

"That's enough, Andersen." Fleming thought he was helping, but I was sure he was only stoking his curiosity.

"I deserve to know," Andersen shoved his bowl away from him, apparently threatening a hunger strike if we didn't tell him everything he wanted to know. "Am I in danger if I stay here with *her*?"

"I promise that you are always in danger when I'm around," I sneered.

"Samantha, stop," Fleming warned and I rolled my eyes. "Andersen, I promise no one will hurt you here, Samantha included, and Adrestus won't bother us. Who knows, maybe he's taking the holiday off, too."

He grinned at his own joke but it fell flat. Andersen pulled his soup back towards him in defeat while I sipped water, trying to soothe my burnt mouth.

"No homework for two weeks," Fleming said after several full minutes of silence. "No training, either. And I don't have to grade anything!"

"What about our finals?" Andersen asked.

"I was thinking of giving you all B's."

Andersen and I deadpanned at Fleming and he gawked back at us.

"I'm kidding," he said. Andersen grunted. Fleming cleared his throat. "Do either of you have holiday traditions? It's just me here so we can do whatever you like. Sammy, what does your family usually do?"

The color drained from his face as he realized what he'd asked and I bit back a dry laugh. I'd spent the last thousand Christmases or so in a coma.

"Just the usual stuff," I said, digging into my fake memories more to keep Andersen's suspicions at bay than for Fleming's benefit. "We get stockings the night before, which usually have small things like socks, chocolate, and a toothbrush."

"A toothbrush?" Andersen sneered.

"It's practical." I surprised myself with how defensive I sounded.

"The dentist gives toothbrushes out for free. Or have you never been?"

"Of course I've been to the dentist," I snapped, realizing for the first time that I'd never had a real dentist appointment, "which is how I know the free toothbrushes suck. And maybe don't be so superior when it comes to people who don't go to the dentist."

"What about you, Andersen?" Fleming interjected. Andersen pushed a potato chunk around the surface of his soup.

"You don't need to do this."

"Do what?"

"Act like this is normal." Andersen dropped his spoon and it clanged against the side of the bowl. He tilted back in his chair with crossed arms. "None of us like each other, we don't need to pretend that we do."

Fleming squinted at Andersen from across the small, round table, and I knew he was sizing him up.

"For the next two weeks, the three of us are sharing nine hundred and forty-five square feet of apartment. Now, I'm your history teacher, not your math teacher but let me help you out. That is not nearly enough space for us three to hide out and hope we don't run into the others." Fleming forced the world's most strained smile and looked between us. "I'm sorry if human conversation is unpalatable. I promise, I'd excuse you from dinner if your bedroom wasn't five feet away on the couch. Seeing as that *is* the situation, I expect you to, yes, pretend. Now, what do you usually do for the holidays?"

Andersen looked like he might throw his soup bowl, but after a tense moment, he shifted forward so the front legs of his chair hit the floor. He chewed on the inside of his cheek a moment more.

"Hotdogs for lunch."

"I'm sorry?" The corner of Fleming's mouth twitched.

"We eat hotdogs for lunch on Christmas." Andersen glared us as if daring us to tell him that was a dumb holiday tradition.

Fleming nodded animatedly.

"I can probably manage hotdogs."

As valiant as Fleming's attempt at a family dinner for the three of us was, I was glad when the dishes were cleaned and I could disappear into my room. As much as I would've liked to live out of my suitcase for the holiday, two weeks was too long to not unpack.

Half of the closet was taken up with old, dusty boxes and I pushed them to the side to make room for my clothes. The box near the top caught my eye. The corners were torn and it smelt like an old bookshop. Someone had scrawled "Paul" in marker across the side.

I couldn't help myself. A box of things that once belonged to the greatest Apex hero was collecting dust in my closet. My fingertips brushed across the top of the lid but my phone buzzed on the dresser behind me before I could open it.

Sammy, have you imploded yet?

I laughed at the text Wesley had sent to Naomi, Anthony, and I in our group message. My phone blipped as Naomi responded: **I'm pretty sure I can feel Fleming's apartment from across the island.**

I snorted and hoped she was joking. I threw my phone back onto the bed and went to stand in the window. City lights glittered back at me like a sea of tiny stars intermixed with the gold, red, and green festive lights that wrapped around trees and buildings alike. I hadn't gotten a good look at the city from above before now and it was unsettling to think something so breathtaking had been built by Adrestus.

There wasn't much left for me to do with the night other than try and sleep. I ventured out into the kitchen for a glass of water before going to bed but hesitated in the hall.

Andersen and Fleming sat as far as possible on opposite ends of the couch while Fleming flipped through TV shows.

"We can watch whatever you like," he offered. Andersen shrugged and Fleming continued to click through TV shows, looking for something Andersen might enjoy. I snuck back to my room, not wanting to make things even more awkward.

Sleep didn't come easy and when it did, dreams and visions crept into my subconscious to torment me with images of swords, blood, and the family I didn't remember.

A mossy clearing, nestled between two rocky outcroppings, cut through the mess and I stared at a dancing, green sky. A waterfall roared behind me, spraying me with a fine mist.

"We should head back soon," the boy next to me said. He lay on his back and turned to look at me with striking blue eyes that glowed under a mop of dark, curly hair.

"Just a little while longer." I closed my eyes and soaked in the frigid mist that clung to my cheeks. "It'll be too cold soon to do this."

He laughed. I liked the sound. It was cute the way even his laugh had an accent.

"For normal people maybe, but not you." His hand found mine. I opened my eyes to look at him but instead of mossy rocks and the young man, I was staring at the ceiling of Fleming's second bedroom, lit by the city glow permeating the thin, white curtains that covered the window.

I clenched the fingers that had just been in the hand of the boy in my dream. He'd seemed so charming in the memory, like the way he talked and looked at me made me want to make him like me. He radiated importance and power despite not being much older than I was.

But it was a lie. I knew who he was, I knew my sword would end up in between his ribs, and I knew thousands of years later he'd rip apart my family and tear me open on a cold museum floor. As perfect and enticing as he'd been all those years ago, I knew that even at his best he'd been, and always would be, a monster.

20

The Boxes in the Closet

I spent the morning trying to eke out the memories that had resurfaced overnight, but the daylight had forced the brunt of them back into my subconscious. After scribbling out whatever vague details of my dreams came to mind, I pushed my notebook away and stretched. I could only focus on the part of me that was Eydis for so long before needing a break.

I glared at the Doomsday Pager where it sat on the desk next to Floundersen's tank. It leered back at me, a constant reminder that I was running out of time before who knew what. And if I managed to find Dad in that time, would Baker's premonition come to pass? I shook my head. I wouldn't let it. I would keep Dad alive.

For now, I had too *much* time, trapped for two weeks in Fleming's apartment. Luckily, I knew an effective way to both kill time and avoid my new roommates was to hide in the shower and I was about to spend the next twelve days absolutely wrecking Fleming's water bill.

I juggled my shampoos and soaps across the hall to the bathroom and pushed the door open.

"Oh, my god!" My things crashed to the linoleum floor.

"Shut the door!" Andersen howled.

I tried to slam it shut but my shampoo bottle lodged between the door and the frame, sending the door bouncing back open. Screaming and panicked, I fled to the living room, hands over my eyes, the image of Andersen on the toilet with his pants around his ankles seared into my brain.

"What's happening? Who's here?" Fleming bolted out of his room, shaving cream lathered over half his face. He'd thrown on sweatpants and an open robe fluttered behind him, his chest still wet from the shower. He brandished a baseball bat in one hand while his other jammed his glasses over his nose, smearing the lenses with shaving cream as he glanced around as if expecting Adrestus himself to jump out from behind the kitchen counter.

I screamed something that might've been a curse in Old Norse and retreated to the window, hiding my face from Fleming by leaning my forehead against the cool glass while my face burned beneath my skin.

"I'm going to kill you!" Andersen bellowed from the bathroom.

"Why didn't you lock the door?" I howled back, my breath fogging the window glass.

"You're supposed to knock!"

I turned to Fleming, who stood motionless in his bedroom doorway with his mouth agape.

"I didn't see anything," I insisted. It felt important that I make that clear. Fleming put his hands up and backed into his room.

The toilet flushed down the hall and I felt the blood drain from my face.

"Where can I hide?" I hissed. Fleming grimaced and closed his door.

I sprinted to my room before Andersen could come out of the bathroom.

I would have to change schools, I decided as I paced back and forth. Maybe I could leave the island and go into hiding with Alison, wherever she was. I would never be able to see Andersen again. If I did, I was sure to combust from sheer mortification.

Showering was out of the question now, even though the bathroom had been vacated. I couldn't return to the scene of the crime. I sank to the floor on the side of my bed facing the closet and clutched my phone against my face.

I wanted to call Dad. He would make it better. I wanted to hear his voice. I wanted to hear him laugh at me and crack jokes about Andersen on the toilet. A shuddering breath racked my body but I held back the tears.

I scrolled through my contacts and my finger hovered over Wesley's name. Just imagining how he might react made a smile flicker across my face, but Remi's pleas and the lingering shame at having remembered my kiss with Dres held me back.

I hit Naomi's name. It only rang once.

"Sammy? Is everything okay?" She sounded alarmed and I felt bad to have scared her but I couldn't *not* talk to someone right now.

"I walked in on Andersen on the toilet," I blurted.

A long pause crackled through the phone before Naomi shrieked with laughter.

"Stop, no, no, no, you're joking," she wheezed and I felt an intrepid smile tug at my lips.

"It was horrible!" I wailed. "He didn't lock the door!"

"Did you—"

"No! I didn't see anything, thank god. But what do I do?"

Naomi was laughing too hard to speak. I pulled at a strand of hair waiting for her to regain her composure, hoping I might be able to laugh about it someday, too. I closed my eyes in embarrassment but the mental image of Andersen was still plastered against the back of my eyelids.

"You'll have to flee the country," Naomi giggled. "For my sake, of course, not yours. It was already hard to be around you both. Now, it'll be impossible."

I laughed in spite of myself.

"You're right. I can't believe I've done this to you."

"Actually, though, I'm really sorry, but it's too funny."

"Who doesn't lock the door?" I moaned. "I'm going to have to go to the coffee shop downstairs anytime I need a bathroom just to make sure it's safe."

"But was he standing or sitting?"

"I'm *not* painting a picture for you!"

"Pants up or down?"

"NAOMI!" I buried my face in my knees and held the phone out as Naomi howled on the other line.

Laughing with Naomi helped dull my mortification, but after we finished talking and I hung up, I felt worse than before. I missed my friends. I missed the dorm. I missed Wesley. I missed my family.

Living with *Winnie* had been better than this.

I stared blankly into the open closet across the room. The boxes labeled "Paul" peeked out at me.

I inched closer to the closet, scooting across the floor, keeping my eyes on the boxes as if they might disappear if I moved too quickly or looked away. If Fleming cared if I went through them, he wouldn't have left them in my room. And it *was* my room, after all.

And I needed something to take my mind off Andersen.

Still, I felt like I was doing something illicit as I pried the closet door open and pushed my suitcase aside to fully reveal the boxes of Paul Fleming's things. *Paragon's* things.

The dust that layered the frayed cardboard lid of the top box told me Fleming hadn't been through the box in at least a few years. I traced Paul's name with my finger, collecting a coat of dust on my fingertip.

I carefully lifted the lid up and suppressed a cough as a plume of dust lifted with it. It tickled my nose and I sneezed violently.

Sudden pain erupted in my abdomen. I keeled backwards to lean against the bed, biting my tongue to keep from crying out in agony.

Cautious fingers explored under my shirt, feeling for my stitches. They came away wet and sticky with warm blood.

I grimaced at the sight of my red fingers and steeled myself as I looked down at my shirt. A starburst of red blossomed across the gray cotton. An Old Norse swear escaped my lips under my breath.

I reached up for my bath towel where it hung on a wall hook, wincing as I did. I could go search for bandaging later, but I still wasn't willing to venture outside and risk facing Andersen. I folded a corner of the towel under my shirt, the bulk of it trailing out onto my lap, and returned to the box.

A yellowed newspaper showcased Paul Fleming in full Paragon regalia front and center. I recognized the article. A copy of it hung on the third floor of the museum, celebrating the day Paragon stopped the city from sinking into the sea.

I set the newspaper aside and gasped. A black hero mask rested on a neatly folded red cloth. I didn't dare unfold it but was certain it was Paragon's signature crimson cape. Paragon was a city icon. Whatever weird resentment Fleming clearly had lingering about his older brother, Paragon's things belonged somewhere people could see them rather than shoved away in an old box.

I nudged the box, trying to determine if there might be more Paragon paraphernalia hiding inside and when I felt more heft than an old mask and cape were capable of, I wiggled my fingers down the sides to lift the fabric and set it with the newspaper, keeping my free hand firmly pressed against my bleeding abdomen.

Plastic bags of photos took up the rest of the box. A young Alison smiled up at me from the top picture, her blonde hair braided over one shoulder while a teenaged Roy Hendricks struck a face behind her. I faltered at the sight of Alison. I'd last seen her leaving Fleming's office. Leaving me.

The part of Samantha that still existed wanted her mom, as angry as we were with her. I swallowed the emotion and forged on to the rest of the photos. I recognized Alison, Fleming, and Roy Hendricks, as well as the training facility, though the gym equipment was a bit dated. Paragon himself was in very few of the pictures, making me think he was the one who took most of them. High School Fleming looked just as nervous and awkward as adult Fleming and apparently went through a phase where he'd kept his hair buzzed short, making his forehead appear even higher than it already did.

As I made my way through the bags, Fleming and friends got older and Mr. Hendricks smiled less. In one picture, he'd burnt off his eyebrows and I blushed furiously at a mirror-selfie Paragon had taken of himself. He was shirtless with a mask drawn on his face in marker and a red sweater tied around his neck like a cape. I wondered if it was the first iteration of the famous Paragon costume.

I passed over the pictures of people I didn't recognize, but felt a thrill of wonder every time Alison or Fleming popped up. Even if Fleming looked as anxious back then as he did now, they all looked happy, blissfully unaware of the immortal, comatose viking girl hiding in some man's basement. Even as adults, Fleming and Paul seemed close, appearing in holiday photos together as well as birthdays. When Fleming lost his brother in the fire, he must have lost everything.

The last bag had the least amount of photos and the top one made me pause. Fleming, Roy, and Alison sat around a man in an armchair and I startled when I realized it was Paragon. In his other pictures, he'd sported thick, brown hair like Fleming's but here, Alison bent over to plant a kiss on the top of Paragon's gleaming, bald head.

He wasn't bald the way Fleming had looked with his buzzcut in the earlier pictures. It seemed off and unnatural and it took a moment before I noticed it was because he was also missing his eyebrows. Bulging eyes bugged out of recessed sockets and even though all statues on the island boasted Paragon's hulking figure, here he was small and emaciated.

Shaking fingers pushed the picture back into the bag, but before I could throw the photos back, I saw a black case hiding at the bottom of the cardboard box. I lifted it to my face, no longer worried about the bloody towel shoved under my shirt. I flipped it open and then snapped it shut.

I'd enjoyed snooping through Paul Fleming's things, but I felt like I'd crossed a line when I found the diamond ring.

I haphazardly put the box contents back together and shoved it into the furthest corner of the closet.

I crawled to my bed, still thinking about the last picture and the haunted hollowness of Paul's face, surrounded by friends wearing their fakest smiles.

As far as I knew, I was the only student on the team who knew Fleming's brother had been Paragon. I knew Paragon had saved the city from sinking into the ocean. I knew he died in a fiery blaze rescuing an entire building of people. However, I hadn't known that he had, at some point, been very, very ill.

21

House Call

By lunchtime I had to decide if it was worth bleeding to death in secret just to avoid Andersen. I was pretty sure my bath towel was ruined. It lasted most of the morning, curled up in my lap as I sat at my desk, sketching idly in the back of my notebook to pass the time, not daring to go near the other two boxes of Paul Fleming's things.

I struggled to my feet in the early afternoon, hungry and in pain, but only willing to go as far as the bathroom to smuggle toilet paper for fashioning makeshift bandages. I gathered a generous five rolls in my arms and tried to dart back to the safety of my room but Andersen caught sight of me from down the hall.

"What are you doing?"

I froze, staring at him over my mountain of toilet paper, glad I'd changed out the bath towel for an old t-shirt.

"I'm building something."

He narrowed his eyes at me. To be fair, it was a *terrible* lie.

"Where's Fleming?"

He pointed towards the front door.

"Grocery shopping. Do I need to let him know we're out of toilet paper?"

"Why do you care what I'm doing with this?"

"Because I live here, too."

"Yes." I tried to retreat back to my room. "Obviously you've made yourself *very* comfortable."

Andersen turned red and stalked down the hall to follow me.

"You didn't knock!"

"You have superpowers that literally allow you to turn a door lock from anywhere in the room!"

He snatched the top few rolls from my arms but then paused with a funny look as he scanned my face.

"Are you okay?"

"Yeah. I'm fine."

"You look paler than usual."

I snatched the toilet paper back and slammed my door shut.

I figured I had the necessary toilet paper for enough bandages to last me two nights. By then, I was sure the wound would have healed. I lay back to tape a wad of tissue paper over the injury, thinking it might not be a bad thing if Andersen *did* tell Fleming to buy more toilet paper.

But then he'd ask questions and I was determined to take care of this on my own, without help. Sure, Everly had a medical degree and an Apex ability that made him more qualified than anyone to determine if a wound needed stitches or not, but I was going to prove him wrong.

By dinner, I'd bled through several more makeshift bandages, but at least Andersen hadn't brought my new toilet paper hoarding habit up to Fleming. I'd begun to feel woozy, but dinner, as awkward as it would be, was sure to settle my stomach.

I limped out to the kitchen to set the table while Andersen tended to burger patties on the stovetop and Fleming forced conversation about history class. As Fleming set up burger buns on three separate plates in the kitchen, I noticed angry red marks that wrapped up from his wrists to the sleeves of his t-shirt. He only ever wore long-sleeved button-ups to school, so I'd never seen the tendrils of scars that gouged out tracts of red, puckered skin up his arms.

He caught me staring and I quickly looked away. The jerking motion sent another pang through my stomach. I clenched my teeth to stifle a cry. Another stitch had just popped.

I would need more tissues, but Fleming set a plate down on my placemat and motioned for me to sit. I did so as carefully as possible, glaring at my burger and wondering if Andersen had poisoned it.

"Samantha?" Fleming looked at me over the top of his glasses. "Are you alright? You look pale."

"She looked like that earlier, too." Andersen said, already tearing into his burger.

"I'm a pale person," I asserted.

"You're bleeding," Andersen grunted.

"What?" I looked down to see red spreading out on my t-shirt.

"Your stitches!" Fleming leapt up from his seat but I scowled and placed a hand over the bloody spot.

"They're fine."

"Is that why you stole all the toilet paper?"

"You what?" Fleming blanched.

I begrudgingly lifted the hem of my shirt to show the soaked-through tissue. Fleming's expression turned stormy.

"And the stitches?"

I shrugged.

"I sneezed and it didn't work out."

"When?"

"This morning."

Fleming strode into the kitchen and jammed his phone against his ear.

"Armchair. *Now.*" He pointed to the living room as he waited on the phone. "It's me. Samantha's stitches tore. Are you free?"

I glared at Andersen and he took a bite of burger.

"What did I do?" he asked with his mouth full. "Maybe don't fall on your own sword next time."

"I'm sorry, what place did you get in your event?"

He stood up from the table, grabbing his plate.

"Where are you going?" Fleming barked from the kitchen, still on the phone.

"I'm eating in my room."

Andersen crossed the five feet from the dining area to the living room and fell back onto the couch. He threw his feet up on the coffee table and took another large bite out of his burger.

"Fine," Fleming growled. He pointed at me. "Armchair. Before you pass out."

I shoved my napkin against the wound and made myself comfortable on Fleming's recliner. It looked a lot like the armchair Paul had occupied in the last picture I'd looked at, surrounded by his closest friends and looking like death.

I suppressed a shudder as Fleming launched into a lecture.

"This is why I didn't say anything!" I cut him off. "I know I'm fine and I knew you'd do this!"

"Alison left me in charge and that includes making sure you don't bleed out on my watch."

"I'm not going to bleed out. It's only four stitches and I think one of them is still intact."

Fleming continued to berate me, but I was getting better at tuning him out. I stared at the wall behind him, eating my burger, still thinking about the pictures and the engagement ring I'd found in the closet.

When Everly signaled his arrival with a curt knock, Fleming answered the door and Naomi, Mike, and Desirae rushed in.

"Oh, good. You brought an audience," Fleming glowered.

Naomi rushed to my side while Mike and Desirae gawked around Fleming's living room, both of them giddy with curiosity at the sight of their teacher's apartment.

"What happened?" Naomi demanded, lifting the end of my shirt to inspect the homemade bandages. "This didn't have to do with the *you know what* incident, did it?"

She glanced inconspicuously in Andersen's direction, but he was too busy giving the twins a tour of his tiny living space to notice.

"No, it had nothing to do with walking in on Andersen," I mumbled. "I sneezed and they popped."

"Samantha, why am I not surprised?" Everly, as wry as ever, appeared overhead, trying to hide a smile. "You know I don't get holiday pay for home visits, right?"

"Andersen, why don't you show your teammates the bistro downstairs while we take care of Samantha?" Fleming suggested.

"What? No!" Naomi grabbed my hand. "We came all this way for Sammy!"

"Pick up a dessert for us." Fleming fished a few neatly folded bills from his wallet. Mike and Desirae stuck their hands out, but Fleming raised an eyebrow at them as he handed the money off to Naomi.

"That's not fair, we're older!" Mike said as Fleming ushered them to the door.

"She's a captain."

"We're on break! Captaincy doesn't matter when we're on break!"

Fleming shut the door behind them and turned back to Everly and me with a heavy exhale through his nose.

"So, you sneezed and they popped?" Everly asked, pulling on the armchair lever. I grunted in pain as I fell backwards in the seat.

"Is that normal?" I asked. Everly laughed.

"It's not unheard of."

He took hold of my hand and I felt the swooping sensation that meant he was assessing the injury.

"How bad is it?" Fleming asked on my other side. Everly pulled on nitrile gloves and chuckled.

"It's not bad by Samantha standards, but you weren't going to stop it with toilet paper."

He removed the bloody tissues to clean the area while Fleming hovered over his work. Everly pulled a needle from his bag.

"This might—"

"Pinch a little?" I interrupted. Everly laughed and I squeezed my eyes shut as the needle pierced my skin. I wondered if he'd known Paul Fleming or if he'd treated him, maybe while he'd sat in this very chair.

I didn't want to watch Everly sew my skin back together and instead looked at Fleming. He caught me staring and sighed.

"What is it now, Samantha?"

"What happened to your brother?" I didn't know why I asked it, but immediately regretted the question.

I felt Everly's hands hesitate but he kept his eyes trained on his work. I hadn't meant to ask Fleming about Paragon but it was no use now. He exhaled slowly before answering.

"You know what happened to him."

"I mean before the fire."

Fleming ran a hand over his face and rubbed his temples.

"You went through those boxes, didn't you?"

"I'm sorry, I—" I felt worse about snooping than I did about my popped stitches.

"It's fine."

"If it makes you feel any better, they were pretty dusty and are what made me sneeze. So, I guess I got what I deserved."

Everly set his supplies aside and leaned back, surveying my five new stitches.

"That should withstand any sneezes," he said. "If it doesn't, tell someone next time."

He took his tools to the kitchen to clean them, leaving me alone in the living room with Fleming, who fell back on the couch and stared at his hands in his lap. Up close, I could see every callous detail of the scars that marred his arms.

"After saving the city from sinking our senior year of college, Paul enjoyed the pedestal of New Delos' Greatest Hero for a few, happy years. There's never been an Apex like him. Super strength and speed. Flight at small altitudes. Nothing and no one could beat him. Then, he turned twenty-eight and found cancer in his appendix."

"But I thought he died in a fire."

Fleming still hadn't looked at me. His brow furrowed together.

"He did, but he was going to die anyway."

"But the Serum—"

"Didn't work." Fleming's smile twisted with bitter contempt. "Tumors are made of mutated cells. The Serum doesn't recognize them as an injury that needs healing because they're made of body tissue. Paul knew this, but he was desperate. It made the cancer spread faster."

To think someone as incredible and extraordinary as Paragon could be killed by something as un-supernatural as cancer, it didn't make sense. Apex were untouchable, I thought. Unbeatable.

"But he still died a hero." How could Fleming look so resentful over something out of both his and Paul's control? "He saved all those people in that fire."

"Yeah. Thank god for arsonists." Fleming spat. He ran his hands through his hair and forced a smile before I could mumble an apology. "The others will be back soon."

He joined Everly in the kitchen and I pulled the lever to bring the armchair into an upright position, wincing as I did. It was amazing that Paragon had been able to save every occupant of that apartment when he'd been so sick at the time, though now it made more sense how the ordeal had did in someone as powerful as him.

The door burst open and Mike and Desirae paraded in a cake between the two of them. Naomi and Andersen followed and Andersen mouthed the word "thanks" before Naomi broke off to come back to my armchair.

"In one piece again?" she asked.

"For now. What were you two talking about?" I nodded in Andersen's direction. Naomi smirked.

"We used to be in the same friend-group before things fell apart with Jamie for the both of us, remember? And this living arrangement isn't any more fun for him than it is for you."

"Next you're going to tell me he has human feelings."

"Yeah, actually." Naomi's neat frown sent a spike of guilt through my newly stitched abdomen. "He's...really sad."

I scoffed, which was a mistake. I clutched at my fresh stitches.

"Ew, don't cut the cake right next to the Sammy tools!" In the kitchen, Desirae pushed her brother out of the way and transferred the cake further from Everly's sterilizing operation.

"I don't know why you want to cut it at all," Mike retorted. "Can't we grab forks and eat it off the platter?"

"We aren't *animals.*"

Desirae passed plates of cake around and I made room for Naomi in the armchair. Fleming turned on the evening news for background noise as we dug in while Mike and Desirae told us about Everly's townhouse.

The news chyron caught my eye, however, and I lost interest in Everly's townhouse when I saw the anchors discussing Schrader's Epsilon Initiative.

"Initiative Enrollment Numbers Still Low," the chyron read and I wanted to hear more, but as soon as Schrader popped up on the screen, Everly scowled and turned the TV off.

The others hadn't seemed to notice Schrader had been on the screen, but Everly gave me a look that I understood to say, "You're on vacation. Act like it."

But it was hard to feel like I was on vacation a half hour later when Everly gathered Naomi and the twins by the door. The short-lived relief I'd felt at their company disappeared with them as they exited into the hall, leaving me along with Fleming and Andersen again. Andersen slunk back to his couch corner and I snuck back to my room, missing my friends more than I had before.

I kept to myself the next few days and was happy that time was passing without anymore popped stitches or awkward bathroom run-ins. I filled the long hours with more sketching. Since starting the journal I kept for Eydis' memories, I'd gotten better at drawing after hours of trying to recreate memories on the lined pages and now I put the skill to use wallpapering my new bedroom with rough pencil sketches of my friends.

Naomi went up first, followed by Wesley and Anthony. Soon, I had portraits of most of the sophomore team members, then moved onto Dad and Avery and Tonka the Cat. After running out of people to draw on the morning of Christmas Eve, I sketched myself with Wesley and Naomi, smiling at the way I made the graphite capture their smiles. I stuck the paper in the middle of my growing collage, hoping Fleming wouldn't take them down after I moved back into the dorm.

Fleming disappeared for a couple hours that afternoon and returned with large shopping bags that he hurried to hide in a closet. After finishing the dinner dishes that night, he called us into the living room.

Two festive, quilted stockings sat on opposite ends of the couch, misshapen by presents Fleming had jammed inside them.

"What're these?" Andersen grunted.

"Stockings." Fleming rubbed his nose to hide his flushed cheeks.

I picked up the white and red plaid stocking decorated with a "Samantha" name tag.

"They're for us?" It felt heavy. Fleming's face grew redder.

"I didn't get them for myself."

I knelt next to the couch and shook my stocking. A packaged toothbrush rolled out onto the couch cushion. Maybe it was silly, but I felt a thrill of excitement. It was my first real stocking.

"You remembered." I held the toothbrush up.

"Of course." Fleming sat down on the middle cushion. "Don't worry, Andersen, I've got hotdogs and buns for lunch tomorrow."

"What about cream cheese?" he asked.

"Do you put cream cheese on your hotdogs?"

Andersen snorted and went back to his stocking.

"I'll get some cream cheese," Fleming promised with a smile.

Fleming had packed my stocking full with candy, socks, and school supplies. After emptying most of the contents, I found a pocket Spanish dictionary jammed in the toe of the stocking. I lifted it towards Fleming and raised an eyebrow.

"You said you liked practical gifts."

"You fail Spanish or something?" Andersen jeered. Fleming gave him a warning look and Andersen went back to inspecting his gifts.

"There should be one more thing in there," Fleming nodded at me. I searched inside with my hand, wrapping my fingers around something thin. I laughed when I pulled out a pen shaped like a tiny sword.

"I don't need a permit to use this, do I?" I joked.

"Your current training permit should cover it."

For a first Christmas, it wasn't so bad, even if I did have to spend it with Andersen. Maybe Fleming deserved more credit. He was trying, after all.

"And *my* holiday tradition," Fleming said, getting up from the couch and heading into the kitchen, "is a hot chocolate bar. I have a few different mixes and lots of toppings so—"

A knock at the door cut him short and he paused holding a milk jug over a saucepan, leering towards the entryway.

"Were you expecting someone?" I gripped my new pen as if it *were* a sword.

"No."

Andersen stood up and his gifts fell from his lap onto the floor. I scrambled to my feet as well and Fleming tip-toed towards the door. He took his glasses off to peer through the peephole and my stomach clenched when his face turned white and his mouth dropped open. He glanced at me and when I saw him gulp, I did, too.

His hands shook as he unlocked the door and swung it open.

A woman stood in the hall, her blonde curls going flat and a backpack slung over her shoulder. A numb buzz screamed in my ears. She looked past Fleming and into the living room. Her lips twitched as she tried to smile.

"Sammy," Alison said, holding out a crudely wrapped package. "Merry Christmas."

22

All In Frame

My fake mother hesitated in the doorway with the present still outstretched. Last I'd seen her, she'd been in hysterics as she fled the city. Now, her eyes flitted between Fleming and me. Her shoulders hunched forward timidly.

"Alison," Fleming breathed. "How...why...?"

"Are you going to invite me in or not? My bag is heavy and it took a long time to get here."

Fleming stepped aside wordlessly and she entered the apartment, dropping her bag by the door.

"Is Avery okay?" I blurted.

"He's fine." Her smile betrayed hints of embarrassment. "A little annoyed to be left with Roy and Val, but he'll be alright."

She crossed the living room and I shied away as she approached me. There was still a part of me, the part she'd programmed, that wanted to fall into her arms and cry with relief. My mom was here.

But she wasn't my mom. She'd filled my head with lies. She'd left me behind. Heavy bags weighed on her eyes and her skin was ashen, but her smile was kind. I didn't trust it.

"You're hurt," she said with sudden intensity. "Why are you moving like that? What happened?"

I grabbed my shirt over my stitches.

"Alex! She's got a wrist brace on!" She spun towards Fleming. "What happened? Was it *him*?"

"No, it was a training accident." He continued to gape at Alison, as if he couldn't believe she was standing in his apartment.

Her nostrils flared.

"An *accident*? Is she okay? What about the Serum? Where was Everly?" Her eyes scanned over me, searching for more injuries, and she squinted at my ankle brace.

"Is no one going to tell me who this lady is?"

All three of us turned to look at Andersen. He crossed his arms at Alison and she smirked back.

"I'm Sammy's mother."

Mother. She'd *left* me, leaving me alone on the island with nothing more than a bread crumb trail leading to my real identity. Just when I'd lost Dad, she took everything else I had left.

"No." I stepped away, trying to swallow the sudden anger that rose in place of my initial shock. But even as rage broiled, I wanted nothing more than to hide in her arms and tell her everything that had happened. "You're not."

The heartbreak that showed on her face chipped at my heart but I stormed down the hall before my fake memories could convince me to forgive her.

"So is Samantha leaving?" Andersen asked behind me. "Does this mean I get the bedroom?"

I slammed the door to let him know the room was still mine.

Mom was here. No warning. No word from her for months. Now she was in the living room, just in time for hot chocolate.

I pulled at my hair and paced in front of my desk.

"Why now?" I whispered to Floundersen. He flicked his blue tail and swam to the top of his tank, searching for food pellets. Watching his blue scales shimmer as he twisted through the water made my heart beat just a little quieter.

Mom— no, *Alison* had said Avery was okay. I wish she'd brought him with her. Even if I didn't know *what* she meant to me anymore, and even though he was *technically* my nephew, I refused to think of Avery as anything but my baby brother. Hopefully he felt the same way.

I did what I did every time I felt lost and confused. I called Dad. He wouldn't pick up, of course, but my stomach unclenched at the sound of his message recording.

"This is Vic. You know what to do."

"Samantha?" Fleming tapped on the other side of my door. I froze. I could tell him to go away. Part of me wanted to.

"What?"

The door clicked open and Fleming nudged his way through, holding a mug of hot chocolate and my stocking of gifts. My lips twitched and I took the mug, sitting down at my desk. Fleming scanned the wall behind me, nodding to himself.

"Nice drawings."

I hid my face behind the mound of whipped cream floating on top of my drink by taking a long sip.

"Is she gone?"

"She's still here." Fleming raised his eyebrows at me, taking a seat on the foot of my bed. Relief bloomed in my chest, but I was still mad at her. "Her and Andersen are getting along."

I didn't know which of them I felt worse for.

"Are you okay?" he asked, looking back at my wall of drawings.

"I don't know," I admitted.

"You don't have to talk to her if you don't want to."

I picked at the skin around my thumbnail.

"I think I want to," I mumbled. "It's confusing."

"It is."

I looked up at him. I didn't know why he was being so nice, especially when it was my fault his apartment was constantly being overrun by guests.

"How long is she staying?"

"She's planning on staying until tomorrow but I can make her leave if you like."

"No," I said before Fleming was done talking. He smiled, folding his hands between his knees as he leaned forward.

"Should I go get her now? Or later?"

I thought for a moment before deciding it would be best to rip it off like a band-aid. I set my hot chocolate down.

"You can get her now," I said, but quickly added, "but only because I feel bad she has to talk to Andersen."

Fleming nodded and shuffled out of the room. I slurped on the melted foam of my drink while I waited, heart hammering all over again.

"Sammy?"

I drew the heel of one foot up onto the chair to hide behind my knee as Alison crept into my bedroom, holding her backpack. I ignored the pinch in my stitches and she took the spot on the end of the bed.

"Sorry probably doesn't cut it, right?" Alison clutched her bag in her lap.

"Probably not."

"I don't know where to start. We tried to wake you up without the memories and—"

"And it didn't go well. I know. I heard."

She pursed her lips, her eyes scanning me again, but how much of the worry in her face was from guilt rather than concern?

"You left me behind," I blurted, slamming my mug down on the desk. "When they took Dad, you left and took Avery with you."

Alison nodded, brown eyes glistening.

"I needed to get him somewhere safe. His power isn't one we want falling into enemy hands and you..." She shook her head. "You were our best chance at finding Vic and I know you never would've forgiven me if I sidelined you when he needed you most."

I picked at my fingers, turning her words over in my head.

"You left me because I'm not really your daughter."

Her eyes swam and she pushed her bag to the floor so she could kneel at the side of my chair. I let her take my hands in hers even though her intense stare made me uncomfortable.

"You have been my daughter since the day I met you, Sammy. You were always part of the family. I spent hours inventing your memories and we adjusted Avery's as we went. He never went a day not knowing his big sister."

"Does he know?" I whispered.

Mom nodded.

"Yes and he doesn't care. He still calls you his sister. He found out within a month that he was an Apex and half-Viking."

"Every middle schooler's dream," I sighed. Avery wasn't bothered. I was still his sister. He was still my brother. At the very least, *that* much was real. But the memories of growing up with him were slipping. Weekends spent playing together were fuzzier than ever. "My fake memories. They're fading."

Alison bowed her head.

"Have you been recovering memories from before?"

I nodded and she hummed in resignation.

"Can you fix them?" My voice broke and I fought the stinging in my eyes. I didn't want to lose the life I thought I'd had with them.

"I can," she whispered, "but I won't."

"Why not?" I brushed my wrist brace against my cheek, smearing the tears that fell there.

"I invented a life for you so that when you woke up, you'd be well-adjusted. We always intended on telling you the truth eventually."

"But then what does that make *me?*" I ripped my Spanish final from my backpack next to the desk. "I wrote an entire essay in Old Norse without noticing! I don't want this!"

Mom took the paper, crawling back up on the bed, and chuckled to herself.

"You are so much like your...your brother."

I was certain she was about to call Vidar my father before catching herself.

"He writes in Old Norse?"

"He'd speak it when he would get excited or angry. Confused the nurses when Avery was born." She handed back the essay and sighed. "The hard truth of it is, no kid your age feels like they know who they are. Sure, it's a bit weird for you but every high schooler is figuring out their identity. It's hard, but maybe this will help."

She pulled the present from earlier out of her bag and passed it to me. I unfolded the wrappings and when a plain black journal bound in faux leather fell out, disappointment nipped at my insides. I already had a journal to record and make sense of my memories in.

"Thanks," I said meekly. "It's really nice."

"You haven't opened it yet."

I let the front cover fall open and sighed at the sight of Dad's messy scrawl on the first page.

"*My name is Vic,*" it read. "*That's been my name for the last few decades at least. Before that, it was Oliver. I don't remember what name came before that, but I know the first name I ever had was Vidar Havardsson.*"

I flipped through the rest of the pages, each one filled with Dad's penmanship from the first line to the last.

"It's his journal?" I asked, wanting to touch the pages but fearing if I did, his words might dissolve.

"A letter," Mom corrected me. "He wrote this when we first met. When I first woke you up, I thought you were an ordinary girl in a coma. After things went sideways, he tried to explain but I didn't listen. He wrote this, detailing how he'd gotten to where he was with a comatose girl in his attic."

"I always imagined I was in the basement," I murmured, tentatively brushing the page with my finger.

He'd filled every page, down to the last line. I read his last few sentences on the final page.

"*I know it sounds crazy. It is crazy. But you are the only one who can help Eydis. I've been going for so long and I'm ready to rest. It took more than a thousand years to find someone like you. Please, help us. -Vidar.*"

I ran my fingers over the line "*I'm ready to rest*", thinking about how the months following my awakening hadn't exactly been a trip to the spa.

"It details everything from when he found you supposedly dead in the woods to when he met me. You've both been all over the world, looking for an Apex who could wake you." She bent over to zip up her backpack but I caught a glimpse of silver.

"What's that?"

She blushed and reopened the bag, pulling out a silver frame. A lump formed in my throat when I saw the picture behind the glass. In it, I stood with Mom, Dad, and Avery on the deck of the ferry boat that had brought us to New Delos six months ago. I looked horrible, having just unknowingly woken up from my thousand year coma the week before, but it was the only picture of the four of us together.

"You went to Dad's office?"

"I knew he had it there," she said quietly, letting me hold the frame. Dad looked so sullen, but Avery grinned excitedly, his blond hair ruffled by the sea breeze. I missed them both. "I wanted to make sure it hadn't been burned in that fire and when I saw that it was fine...Well, I figured he wouldn't miss it if I took it home."

I gave the picture back and stood up, turning to face my wall. I unpinned one of the middle pictures, staring at it in my hands a moment before turning back.

"I don't have anything else to give you for Christmas." I held the sketch out. "It's not that good, but maybe you'll want it. We didn't have cameras back then."

Mom's lips quivered as she took the portrait I'd done of Dad. It was how Eydis remembered him. Younger, with a patchy beard and long hair.

"This is what he looked like back then?" she whispered, running a finger along the paper. "Sammy, you're really talented. Thank you."

She tucked it into the picture frame behind the family photo. I watched her with arms wrapped around myself, lips pressed tight.

"I can get out of your way if you like. Hopefully Alex has an air mattress somewhere. The recliner out there didn't look comfortable."

"It's not so bad," I swallowed. "Can't say the same about the company."

Mom smiled wryly.

"The boy? Better him than the one you brought to dinner in September."

"What's wrong with Wes?" I hoped she couldn't see the heat that rose in my cheeks.

"Nothing," she shrugged, zipping her bag and picking it up, "but as a parent, a boy my daughter can't stand is safer than a boy she gets along with."

"But you're not my parent."

Mom paused on her way to the doorway.

"I cared for you for almost fifteen years and know more about you than anyone. I'm more your parent than Vic is, or anyone for that matter. Besides, I've got loads of forged documents saying that you're mine."

"Oh, well, if the fake birth certificate says so..." I rolled my eyes but she turned back to me and smiled, the corners of her eyes softly wrinkling.

"More importantly, I say so." She backed into the hallway. "Good night, Sammy. Don't stay up too late reading."

She closed the door with her foot, leaving me alone in my room, sad, happy, and confused but finally, after months of resentment, a little less angry.

I didn't dare touch Dad's notebook that night. Curiosity raged against my insistence to pretend Eydis didn't exist. What if his words brought back more memories, erasing Samantha even further? What if I lost memories of Avery next?

I burrowed under my bed covers. I hoped Mom didn't tell Fleming about the notebook. He would want me to scour it for clues, but it would be useless on that front. Dad hadn't known about the Lapis. He hadn't understood the cause of our sudden immortality.

I turned onto my side to stare out the giant window. I still couldn't believe Mom was in the other room. Was she "Mom" again? Or was she still Alison?

Eventually, my turmoil faded into sleep and hours later, the smell of waffles dragged my consciousness back into wakefulness. I crept out into the kitchen where Fleming, Mom, and Andersen ate waffles at the barstools. Andersen scowled at me and I couldn't blame him. Not only was I keeping the bedroom, he'd had to share the living room with Alison last night.

"Sammy, you're up!" Mom adjusted the phone at her ear, apparently mid-conversation with someone. "Avery, do you want to talk to your sister?"

My heart skipped and she held out the phone for me. She nodded encouragingly and, even though part of me felt like it was a trick, I took it.

"Hello?" I'd barely gotten the word out before he was shouting into the phone.

"Sammy! Mom got me a phone! I've been trying to call you for weeks!"

My face split into a grin at the sound of his voice.

"I dropped my phone in a fountain. I had to get a new one."

"There's so much I need to tell you! Did Mom tell you I'm an Apex? And did you know that Dad's a Viking? Of course you knew that part, because *you're* a Viking! Should I call you Aunt Sammy?"

He laughed boisterously and I took the phone back down the hall, hoping Andersen couldn't hear him yelling through the receiver.

"Please don't." I smiled and clicked the door shut behind me.

"Mom says you're on the secret team looking for Dad!" Avery said. "Tell her to let me come back and help, too. Mr. Hendricks sucks and I want to come home."

"Ew, you're living with Mr. Hendricks?" I snorted.

"Mom's making him homeschool me but all he does is yell and honestly school is pointless when the world is in danger."

"Maybe if you do well enough, you can skip a few grades and join the Apex Team early?"

"Yeah, right. Mr. Hendricks is more likely to send me back a grade, and probably for something as stupid as stapling a paper backwards."

I fell back onto my bed, grinning. I was happy he was safe, but I missed my brother.

"Who cares what Mr. Hendricks thinks," I said. "He's a tool and from what I've heard, he was a sucky superhero."

"Really?" Avery tittered. "Who said that?"

"Try everyone?" Maybe it wasn't exactly the truth, but Mr. Hendricks' reputation wasn't important enough to me to admit it was essentially just Fleming who wasn't a fan.

Silence hummed in the receiver and I sat back up.

"Avery?"

"I'm here. I just...wish I was there."

"You will be. We'll take care of things and then you'll be back."

"Make it quick, please, I miss Dad and I'm tired of Mr. Hendricks setting my essays on fire."

I looked to my open closet, thinking about the picture of Mr. Hendricks with his eyebrows burnt off. If I wasn't so scared to go through Paul's things again, I might've dug through to find it for Avery.

He told me all about his homeschooling as well as the island they were hiding on up north. Unlike New Delos, it was a *real* island, complete with grass, trees, and beaches. Avery did most of the talking until Mom knocked on the door and peeked in.

"The waffles are getting cold," she warned.

"Hey, Avery, I've gotta go," I said. He groaned but I cut off his protests. "I'll give Mom my new phone number. You can text me whenever you want."

"Fine," he conceded. "You better text back, though."

"Always. I love you."

"Ew, don't make it weird, Sammy." He let a pause pass and then, "Love you, too."

Mom took the phone back and shrugged.

"I know he's not happy, but if Adrestus found out he's capable of controlling the whims of others so easily—" She turned back towards the door but froze, looking into my open closet. "Is this..."

She dragged Paul's boxes to the middle of the room, going pale. She threw the lid off the top box, revealing Paragon's cape and mask. She ran shaking fingers over the fabric and I felt like an intruder in my own bedroom.

"Alex!" she hollered, straightening up. She grabbed the cape and its crimson folds unfurled behind her as she whipped into the hallway. I followed her into the kitchen, where she held the cape out accusingly. Fleming blanched and Andersen paused in his waffle chewing, giving the cape a double take. "What're Paul's things doing shoved in a *closet*?"

Fleming glowered, tearing the cape from Mom's hands.

"What am I supposed to do with them? He's been dead for fifteen years."

"Donate them to a museum?" she suggested angrily.

"Oh, perfect," Fleming said sourly. "I happen to know a guy."

"Stop, you know what I mean!" She pulled the cape back from Fleming.

"Is that..."Andersen said slowly, mouth still full of waffle, "Paragon's cape?"

Neither adult answered. They were too busy sizing each other up.

"At least let me take them," Mom finally pleaded. "Roy might like to keep it."

Fleming's face clouded over.

"Roy Hendricks will be the *last* person to keep Paul's things," he hissed, throwing a dirty fork into the sink. "Alison, you *know* he's the reason my brother is dead."

23

The Legacy of Paul Fleming

F leming's words didn't make sense. Roy Hendricks had powers that let him make fires, not tumors. Then again, Paul Fleming didn't ultimately die from his cancer. My disdain for Roy deepened and I bit back the bitter taste that rose in my throat.

"Alex," Mom murmured, "he'd be dead anyway."

Andersen's eyes darted back and forth between the adults, trying to make sense of the conversation. I wondered if it was too late to keep him from figuring out Paragon and Paul were one and the same.

"I always wondered," Fleming fumed, "would you have come to the funeral if it had been the cancer that took him in the end?"

Mom glowered over the cape crumpled in her arms.

"I'm not sure I would have."

"You were basically family and you disappeared after Paul was gone. I didn't hear from you for almost fifteen years until you showed up at school with a family and a daughter I'd never heard of." Fleming looked like he might fight Mom right there in the kitchen, with his fists clenched at his sides.

"Paul saw to it that I never became your *family*." Mom's voice quivered and Fleming's ire broke. His fists loosened and his chest deflated.

"You were my friend before you were his," he said quietly. "What he did to you made no difference to me."

Mom dabbed her eyes with a corner of the cape and Andersen looked to me as if I might be able to explain what was happening.

"I'm sorry I didn't go to the funeral. Maybe if I had, things wouldn't have gotten out of hand, but—"

"Out of hand?" Fleming gawked. "The city hates Apex because of what Roy did that day. A whole city block, *destroyed!* It's a miracle no one *died!* If I hadn't tackled him—"

He broke off to absentmindedly rub the burn scars that painted his arms.

"You shouldn't have provoked him!"

"Then he shouldn't have killed Paul!" Fleming shouted, spraying spit over the kitchen linoleum.

"It was Paul's idea, not Roy's!"

Paul Fleming had been terminally ill but he'd also been New Delos' Greatest Hero. He could go out in a hospital bed or he could die as the hero his city had come to worship. I felt sick.

"Paragon asked Mr. Hendricks to set that fire?" I asked breathlessly. Fleming's eyes gleamed behind his glasses.

"Mr. Fleming?" Andersen squinted at our teacher. "Was Paragon your brother?"

Alison leaned against a counter, clutching the cape as if she was afraid Fleming would try to take it again.

"Might as well tell them. If I've learned anything these last months, it's that secrets are no use to keep."

Fleming ran his hands through his hair, leaving a trail of suds that had been left on his hands after washing dishes.

"Yes, Andersen, my brother Paul was the hero known as Paragon and he was sick," he said slowly. Andersen clamped his mouth shut and his

252

eyebrows shot up his forehead. "When the Serum made his cancer progress, he decided to go out the way he saw fit."

It was no wonder he kept it a secret that Paragon had been his brother. He hadn't died a hero at all.

"Him and Roy were close," Mom cut in when Fleming didn't look like he could talk any further. "Roy had always admired him for his sheer strength and power. So, when Paul hatched his plan, he went to Roy for help and—"

She cut off, too, hugging the cape tighter.

"And Roy set the fire in that apartment building," Fleming finished. "Paul saved every living thing inside, with help from Roy, and in the end, it was too much. When we arrived, we recognized Roy's work and put the pieces together."

Heavy silence weighed on the kitchen, broken only by the distant sound of carolers in the apartment hall. Paul had statues all over the island. He was revered. He was supposed to be the best of the Apex, but he'd died a liar who had endangered the lives he'd sworn to protect, all so he could keep his vanity intact after he was gone. He was the opposite of what Fleming taught us to be.

"So your brother is Paragon," Andersen recapped, "and Paragon faked his death?"

"No, he orchestrated it," Fleming spat.

"And Winnie's dad—"

"Yes, Andersen," Fleming snapped and, for once, Andersen had the sense to fall silent.

"And you." I turned on Mom. "You just left when things got hard? Like you did to me?"

"You couldn't be bothered to come back for the funeral," Fleming said to her. "If you had—"

"You and Roy still would've fought and Roy still would've blown up."

The city had started to turn against the Apex almost fifteen years ago, when an explosion ripped open downtown. My head spun as all the pieces clicked together.

"The funeral, was it at St. Thomas Aquinas Chapel?" I asked quietly.

Fleming and Mom both looked down.

"Yes," Fleming said. "More innocent people hurt. I'd told him beforehand he wasn't welcome, but he showed anyway."

I looked at the burns that mottled Fleming's arms, the ones he kept hidden at school. I'd been wrong to call Roy Hendricks an older version of Andersen. He was worse.

"He moved his family off-island after that," Mom said. "I offered them a place to stay and once Vic trusted them enough, he let them in on our project."

She looked at Andersen again, knowing not to say any more in front of him.

"I already know the kind of help they offered on that front," I said bitterly.

Winnie had been their sacrificial lamb, raised as the second-favorite daughter with no Apex abilities, important only in that she'd become my invented friend.

"We've all made mistakes," Mom conceded.

"Not all of us," Fleming said.

"No, Alex, you always were the best of us." She looked like she meant it, but her words only made Fleming look more miserable.

"Who else knows he was your brother?" Andersen said. He sat frozen over his waffles, looking like he was waiting for someone to yell, "Gotcha!"

"Just those who've figured it out," Fleming admitted. "Samantha, Justin, and a few on the University team."

I blinked in surprise. I hadn't known Justin was privy to Fleming's Paragon secret.

"You know the parents would respect you more if you told them." Andersen crossed his arms.

"Whatever respect I gain should be by my own doing, not my brother's. Alison, you're free to take anything of Paul's you like, just don't give his stuff to Roy, please."

Mom's shoulders relaxed and Fleming beckoned for me to follow him to my room.

"No wonder your stitches popped." Fleming sniffed as he pulled the boxes from the closest, waving away a cloud of dust. "I probably should've done something with these a long time ago."

"I don't think she has room to take all of it," I pointed out.

"I'll toss whatever she doesn't want." He pushed the top box into my arms and picked the other two up himself.

"You can't throw this stuff out!" I protested. "He was still your brother!"

"I've kept his final secret. I've allowed his legacy of heroism to survive despite what he did. That's more than he deserved."

I followed him back to the living room and we set the boxes down on the coffee table. Mom joined us but Andersen stayed on his stool, watching cautiously.

"You should keep the pictures," I insisted. "What if you go bald and want to remember what you looked like with hair?"

"Very funny."

"He *was* a hero, though." I sat on the couch while Fleming and Mom unpacked the boxes. He couldn't have had statues put up all over the island for *nothing*. "Even if he did some bad things in the end, he did a lot of good things, too."

"Hmm."

"He was probably scared, right?"

"I'm sure the people who lost their homes in that fire were scared, too."

"Then it's a net neutral," I argued. "He did bad things, but he saved the entire city from sinking, saving countless lives when he did. Doesn't that count for something?"

"No."

"Why not?"

"It just doesn't!" Fleming threw a bag of photos to the floor with so much force that Mom jumped. Andersen snickered and Fleming blushed.

"It was enough to get him his own holiday weekend," I muttered. "If it counts for the city, it should count for you, too."

"It's not that those lives saved don't count." Mom glanced sideways at Fleming.

"Don't," he warned. Mom smirked.

"What did I just say about keeping secrets? Tell her why saving the city from sinking doesn't count," she insisted. Fleming turned away to go through another box and Mom looked up at me. "Paragon never stopped the city from sinking. We did."

Alison looked like she was daring me to not believe her and Fleming stared unseeing into his box.

"But...but how?" I finally said. Paragon had been powerful. He'd been strong enough to lift cities. Of course it had to have been him. How could a non-Apex and a girl who could invent memories stop a disaster like that?

"Paul was bullheaded," Alison said. "Obviously that never changed about him. When the alarm went off indicating the tidal lift system had malfunctioned and the city was slipping into the ocean, he jumped straight in the water. Swam around for hours trying to figure out a solution."

"But he didn't save the city?"

"No. Alex and I had a different idea. We went under the city and found the main computer for the lift system. Someone had tampered with it. We never found out who, but we were able to reprogram the system. The city stabilized and rose back up. Paul had been flying and swimming all over in his red cape and everyone assumed he must've been the one to save them."

"He didn't correct them?"

"Why would he? Can you imagine a statue of Fleming instead of Paragon out in the bay?" Andersen snorted.

"He had no idea we did anything," Fleming said, ignoring Andersen. "When the city told him that he'd saved them, he believed it. He didn't know how he'd fixed the problem, but he soaked in the praise anyway."

"But what about after you told him what had happened?" I asked. "Why didn't he correct them then?"

"We agreed not to say anything." A sad smile tugged on the corners of Mom's lips. She sorted through the pictures in the bags, slipping them out onto the coffee table. Fleming made a point not to look at them. "The city needed a hero to look up to. Even with the Apex Teams churning out young heroes, no one had stepped up to the plate since Zephyress had retired a few years earlier. Neither of us had the glitz or showmanship to inspire like Paul did."

I folded my arms across my lap.

"Then you can't be mad he took the credit. As far as he knew, he *had* saved everyone. Even in the end, he would've thought he'd made a net positive difference on the city. He did bad things, sure, but you both lied to him about his biggest accomplishment."

"You're right," Fleming shrugged. "And I'm left wondering every day, if we hadn't fed his ego like that, would he have still taken his death into his own hands?"

"Throwing out the last of Paul's things feels like a bad way to come to terms with everything that happened."

Fleming gave me a withering look but Alison suppressed a laugh.

"I'll take what I can," she said, "but Sammy's right. You can't throw it away. Not yet. Andersen, want a Paragon mask?"

She held up an extra black mask she'd found in one of the boxes. He timidly slipped off his stool to take it and Mom glanced into the next box. A haunted look killed the smile on her face.

"What?" Fleming asked, then followed her gaze. "Oh."

She rested the small, black ring box on her open palm and bit her lower lip.

"I didn't know he kept it." Mom opened the box and frowned at the diamond ring.

"What was he supposed to do? Throw it in the ocean?" Fleming scoffed.

She snapped the box shut and pressed it into Fleming's hand.

"I don't want it. The one I've got now is better, anyway." She shoveled pictures back into their bags, still frowning.

A chill passed through the room and I remembered the first time I saw the giant Paragon statue in the bay. Dad's words echoed in my memory: *"He wasn't that great, dear."*

"Oh, my god," I gasped, finally understanding. "You were engaged to *Paragon?*"

Mom avoided my eye but Fleming grimaced at me.

"He broke it off when he got sick." Mom tried to sound nonchalant. "It doesn't matter. Things worked out for the better."

"Wait...Avery...?"

"Good lord, Sammy!" Mom turned red with mortification. "He's Vic's, don't worry about it."

Fleming coughed to cover what I was sure was a snicker.

"Isn't your brother younger than you?" Andersen asked, back at his barstool with the mask in his lap. "Aren't you the one more likely to be Paragon's secret kid?"

My stomach twisted and my cheeks flushed. He'd been so quiet in the kitchen, I'd forgotten he was there.

"Shut up, I'm bad at math." Not true, but I would say anything to keep Andersen from getting more suspicious than he already was.

"I don't have any kids with Paragon," Mom promised, red in the face.

Fleming tucked the ring box into the pocket of his sweats and his eyes lit up as he scanned the table.

"You know, I might keep this one." He held up the picture of Mr. Hendricks without eyebrows and grinned. Mom guffawed.

"I remember that! He got so mad at you that he burnt his own eyebrows off! That might be fridge-worthy."

Fleming grinned mischievously and as he took the picture to the kitchen and stuck it to the fridge, I felt like I was seeing a long-lost, younger version of him. Andersen rubbed his own eyebrows while he watched and Fleming stood back to admire his work.

"You know, Alison, that *does* look nice there."

Mom hung around until after Andersen's hotdog and cream cheese lunch and while I still wasn't sure how to feel about her, I was sorry to see her gather her bags by the door when it was time for her to leave. Paragon's things stuck out of the opening of an old duffle bag that had joined her backpack.

"Ferry shouldn't be too crowded today." Fleming poured coffee into a travel mug, fastening the lid before handing it to Mom. "Do you want a ride to the dock?"

She smiled sheepishly, glancing at the misshapen duffle bag.

"If you don't mind."

I scrambled, searching for a way to keep her with us, even if only for a little while longer. I finally felt like I had a Mom again. I wasn't ready to see her go.

"If you guys were such the dream team back in the day, why can't you stay and find Dad?" I accused. Fleming gave me a warning glare but Mom smiled, pulling me into a timid hug.

"If I leave Avery alone too long, he'll start using his powers on Roy. Last time that happened, I came home to a new pet hamster."

She shouldered the backpack and Fleming helped her with the duffle. I caught a flash of red cape as he pulled the zipper shut. She lingered in the doorway.

"I'll see you soon, okay?" she promised.

"Sure, same time next year?"

"It'll be sooner than that." She shuffled into the hall and Fleming followed with his car keys. "It was nice to meet you, Andersen. Sammy, I know you'll find him. I love you."

"Don't wreck the apartment while I'm gone," Fleming warned, closing the front door. "And don't wreck each other, either."

The door clicked shut and the doorknob rattled as Fleming locked it from the other side.

24

Broken Plates

Alison had only just got here and less than twenty-four hours later, she was gone as abruptly as she'd arrived. I stared at the front door, wishing I had it in me to be angry or sad or maybe even relieved that she was gone, anything to fill the hollowness that took up the space emotion should've been. I'd had a sliver of my family back, and it had already left.

Chair legs squealed against linoleum as Andersen pushed away from the kitchen bar and dropped his hotdog dishes in the sink, adding to the mountain of plates and mugs that had accumulated since breakfast. He slunk away to the couch and I bit back a quip about helping with the mess. Cleaning would be less painful for us both if he didn't lend a hand.

I set my wrist brace on the counter to keep it dry and started the sink as Andersen's phone blared in his lap. He glanced at the screen and tossed it across the couch, where it continued to ring loud enough to be heard over the running water. I gritted my teeth, wondering why Andersen didn't just hang up.

It eventually quieted but immediately went off a second time. Andersen pumped up the volume on the T.V. as the phone rang futilely.

"You can at least turn it off if you're not going to answer it," I said after the phone started ringing a third time.

"You know what I want for Christmas?" He kept his eyes trained on the TV in front of him. "You to not talk to me."

"And I want you to put your phone on silent."

The phone quieted but only for a moment. Whoever was calling Andersen was as intent on getting through as he was on ignoring them.

"She'll stop calling eventually," Andersen grunted. I paused in my dish washing to stare at the back of his head. His hair was a similar brown to Wesley's but lay much flatter.

"'She'?" I repeated. "You're ignoring your mom on Christmas?"

He shrugged.

"If she won't let me come home, she can't want to talk that bad."

The ringing phone said otherwise.

"Oh, no!" I rolled my eyes, turning back to scrub a plate caked in hours-old syrup. "Andersen has a family that loves him but can't see them because he's an idiot who flaunted his powers to half the school and put his family in danger!"

The plate exploded in my hands, sending shards of ceramic throughout the sink and into my palms.

"Watch it!" I yowled, pulling my hands away from the water to inspect the dozens of tiny cuts across my palms. "That hurt!"

The T.V. clicked off and the couch squeaked behind me.

"Then watch what you say."

I spun to face Andersen. He stood in the middle of the living room, silhouetted against Fleming's massive windows. His hands were balled into fists at his side, signaling more of Fleming's dishes were liable to burst.

"I'm glad everyone knows about me." Andersen's voice was low and threatening. "I *am* an Apex and now I don't have to hide and I don't have to pretend to be like *you*."

"You mean pretend to be a Beta?" I sneered. "How awful *that* must've been. Definitely worth having your family stalked if it means avoiding association with people like me."

Andersen stepped up onto the couch cushion and over the back, dropping hard to the floorboards. I crossed my arms at him, refusing to be intimidated but thankful for the kitchen bar that separated us.

"How did you know about that? The stalking?"

"You and your mom were yelling at each other during the banquet. I'm surprised I'm the only one that heard."

"You were eavesdropping!"

"I was in the bathroom!" I snapped.

"Oh, and suddenly you care about not intruding on people in bathrooms?"

I felt my face turn beet-red and Andersen's phone went off again.

"If you aren't going to answer—"

Andersen raised a shaking fist and a metallic pop accompanied a thin stream of smoke rising from the couch where Andersen had abandoned his phone.

"You know," he snarled, stepping towards the kitchen bar. I suddenly became very aware of all the sharp and heavy objects hiding around the kitchen that Andersen could control with a flick of his finger. "It wasn't so bad having to pretend to be a Beta until one showed up in my gym."

"*Your* gym!?"

"Yes." He slapped his hands against the counter. "*My* gym. Because I'm an Apex and that gym was built for me. It was the one place I could be myself, away from the other students, away from Jamie and then *you* waltz in thinking you're some sort of big shot."

"I don't think I'm a big shot, I just want my dad back!"

"Who wouldn't be missing if you hadn't gotten involved in the first place!"

I laughed humorlessly. Andersen had no clue.

"If it's my fault my dad was kidnapped, then it's your fault you can't go home for Christmas. You aren't the only one too dangerous to be near family, or did you not hear my mom? Stop acting like you're special."

I flinched as another plate shattered in the sink behind me. Andersen sneered in triumph and I regained my composure to scowl back.

"I *am* special," he said coolly. "I can do things you'll never be able to do and I made my way on the team without special treatment."

I bristled and tore a plate from the sink.

"You're special, huh?" I spiked the plate into the linoleum. Ceramic shattered and the shards exploded across the floor. "You aren't the only one who can break plates! And I *don't* get special treatment. I work twice as hard and do your job better than you ever have and ever will!"

"You don't do my job, you *meddle*. I did my job when I did what you couldn't and saved Jamie from being crushed to death and now I get hell for it every day while you get an undeserved spot on a team that is better off without you!"

I leaned back against the counter, taking him in. I'd never convince Andersen I belonged on the team.

"You can't keep blaming Betas for everything that goes wrong," I snarled, picking at my palms to dig out ceramic. "We're not all as horrible as Jamie."

"Jamie's not—"

"Not horrible?" I snorted. "Not vindictive and manipulative? You can't still defend her. It's her fault you're here, not mine."

"Don't pretend you're any better than her. Maybe your mom should've stayed with Paragon. She'd be a widow but at least *you* never would've happened."

Cold fury pressed in around me and I paused in my excavation of ceramic bits to look up at Andersen through the curtain of hair that had fallen forward to obscure my face. He'd moved so the kitchen bar wasn't between us anymore but the light coming in from the living room window still cast his face in deep shadows.

"Even if I'm no better than Jamie," I said coldly, "at least I'm not a murderer."

Andersen recoiled in confusion.

"Jamie's not a murderer."

"No. She's not." As infinitely furious as I was, I had to bite back a smile. I'd finally cornered him.

Andersen paused and I went back to digging at my hand.

"I'm not one, either."

Cold vindication rose in my chest. I wanted him to hurt. I wanted him to feel every ounce of misery he'd made me feel since September.

"Sure, you're not." I winced as I pulled a larger piece of ceramic from my hand.

"I'm not!" An edge of panic crept into his voice. I smirked at him from behind my hair and wiped the small streams of blood from my hand with a paper towel.

"You left me in the ocean in the middle of the night." Every word felt good, having carried this secret for so long. "You left me in freezing water in the dark with no way out."

"That doesn't make me a murderer."

"That night on the rooftop, when Adrestus broke my neck, that wasn't the first time I'd died."

In the low light of the kitchen, Andersen's face turned white.

"You said you didn't actually die that night." His voice shook. "You said Wesley was mistaken! No one comes back from the dead!"

"Except me." I couldn't help the wild grin. It felt so good to see Andersen scared. "Adrestus *did* kill me on the rooftop, so he's no better than you, because you killed me first that night on the boardwalk."

"You're a liar!" Andersen snarled. "You know you won't ever compare to *real* heroes so you came up with this bull just to mess with me!"

I pulled the last bit of glass from my hand and flipped my hair over my shoulder.

"Don't believe me, then. But don't go around acting like you're secretly some big hero under a rough exterior. Because, you're not."

I left him in the kitchen, retreating back to my room, the palms of my hands still stinging but my heart thundering with satisfied vindication.

"You aren't, either!" Andersen shouted after a moment. I slammed my bedroom door in response.

The sink started running out in the kitchen and Andersen must've been finishing the dishes and cleaning up the plates we'd shattered. Intrepid guilt tried to gnaw its way into my psyche, but I shook it off. I didn't care how bad a Christmas Andersen was having. He didn't get to take it out on me.

My phone screen flashed on my bedside table and I saw Andersen wasn't the only one who'd missed phone calls. Wesley had tried me twice before sending a "Merry Christmas!! Call me when you can!" text. I scowled as my aggression towards Andersen crumbled into generalized irritation.

I heard Fleming get back a bit later and Andersen explaining the broken plate pieces in the trash as "an accident". I rolled my eyes, settling into the bed pillows with Dad's old notebook propped against my knees. The "accident" that had broken the plates still stung across the palms of both my hands, even though the cuts were, at worst, superficial.

I apprehensively flipped through the notebook. As the pages went on, the level of penmanship slipped, though I was still able to make out the words.

"*At one point in the fourteen hundreds, we both had the plague and I thought that was it. But, that too passed, leaving me with nothing but sore ribs from coughing.*"

I shut the book with a shudder. We'd gone over the Bubonic Plague in Fleming's class and I didn't like knowing that I'd had it.

Still, as I turned the book over in my scratched-up hands, I knew I'd have to read it. Alison had come a long way to give it to me. Maybe there was something helpful, or it would trigger some lost memory that held the key to defeating Adrestus.

My phone buzzed as Wesley sent another text, this time to the group chat. Naomi responded with a picture of a cat in a Santa hat and I swatted my phone away.

Fleming didn't force us to be cordial over dinner despite the holiday, so he must've figured we'd fought while he was out. We sat on opposite sides of the living room, eating our food in silence while Fleming offered lukewarm commentary on the classic Christmas movies playing on a loop on the T.V.

The day paled in comparison to the memories of Christmas I desperately clung to, and the fact that this was my only real Christmas and those were all fake only made me that much more bitter.

When Fleming finally let us retreat to our respective hiding spots in the apartment, I mumbled a final, halfhearted "Merry Christmas" and disappeared, as I already had dozens of times that week, back to my bedroom.

I fell onto my bed and grabbed my phone. Disappointment and relief ran together in a confusing tangle when I saw Wesley seemed to have given up on getting a hold of me. I had no more new messages and felt even lonelier than I had before Alison had so quickly arrived and disappeared again.

I pressed my face into a pillow. Maybe if I was lucky, I could somehow sleep until break was over. But my stomach churned and I knew that school resuming would only bring more problems to the forefront.

I had to retake my Spanish Final, for one. Not to mention, Remi's control over my friendship with Wesley wasn't going to disappear just because break was over. Oh, and the day the city was supposedly going to burn was fast approaching and we still had no clue how to stop it or what exactly it entailed.

I was so busy feeling sorry for myself with my face submerged in pillows that I almost didn't hear the shrill beep on the desk behind me.

I pushed myself up, squinting at my textbooks, thinking I must have imagined the sound before I saw the scrolling text on the Doomsday Pager next to Floundersen's fishbowl.

My heart thundered against my sternum as I stared at the plastic box. I couldn't read the message from where I sat rigid on the bed, but it had definitely changed from the usual daily countdown.

I crept to the foot of the bed, the mattress groaning underneath me. From there, I could see the pixelated letters scroll across the screen and my insides turned to lead as I read them.

"Merry Christmas, kid."

There was only one person who'd ever called me "kid", and that was Dad.

Vidar had sent me a message.

25

New Year's Eve

I paced back and forth in the small space available in front of the bedroom window, cradling the pager in my hands, afraid to accidentally hit a button and delete the tiny "Merry Christmas, kid" but feverishly searching for a way to respond.

Remi had already investigated the device with her powers. She said there was no way to send a message back but she had to be wrong. I needed Dad to know I got his message. I needed him to know I'd seen it.

I needed him to know about Trev Baker's vision.

Agitation threatened to overwhelm me. Dad was alive and apparently well enough to be sending messages. While the voice of the person who'd slipped the pager into my pocket at the museum had been too feminine to be him, he must've had someone helping him from inside Adrestus' ranks.

I paused in my pacing to look at the city lights twinkling through the blanket of fog that settled over the island every night. What was I doing trapped in an apartment with Andersen and Fleming when Dad was somewhere out there?

There was no chance of sneaking out under Fleming's watch. Besides, the only place I had any sort of lead was the last place I'd seen Dad, and even I knew going back to Schrader Tower and the museum was dangerous.

I growled under my breath, resisting the urge to throw the pager into my pillows. Every bit of me ached to respond but I couldn't. My initial elation at the message had quickly given way to roaring frustration.

I stopped pacing to rest my forehead on the cool glass of the window and encased the pager in my fist. I should tell Fleming about the message. I'd been tasked with watching for changes, but this was a personal message. Did Fleming really need to know my dad had wished me a merry Christmas?

But it was an obvious clue to who was behind the pager in the first place. I gritted my teeth and rolled my forehead back and forth, massaging it against the glass. It was a message for me, not the team. It didn't really matter *who* was behind the pager, anyway.

This message was all I had of Dad and I didn't want to share it.

Andersen did his best to avoid me in the days following Christmas, which said a lot since we'd both already been doing our best to keep to our corners of the apartment. Meanwhile, I could barely look Fleming in the eye, certain if I did, he'd know I was hiding the pager message.

The pager had resumed its normal countdown the next morning, so Dad's message was already gone, and part of me felt like disclosing it to Fleming would feel like losing it a second time.

I was finally offered an escape on New Year's Eve when Fleming told us we'd be meeting up with Everly, Naomi, and the twins for a fireworks show downtown. On one hand, I'd get to leave the apartment and see Naomi, but if anyone could guess I was hiding something like a secret message from my dad, it was her.

The downtown boardwalk lined the east side of the island, facing the open ocean and the storefronts glowed bright through the throngs of people pushing their way around the crowd. Stands sat between shops, selling glow sticks and party poppers. Andersen and I lingered behind Fleming, who scanned the crowd for Everly's bald head.

"He'll probably find us before we find him, with Naomi on his side." Fleming grinned at us. We glowered back but his smile didn't falter. He was probably just as relieved to be out of the apartment as we were.

Something heavy slammed into me from behind and dark, curly hair pressed against the side of my face.

"There you are!" Naomi sang, releasing me from her hug as Everly, Mike, and Desirae caught up behind her. She grinned wide at me and chuckled nervously. "Wow, you guys are a cheerful bunch."

"We would've been here faster but there are protesters a few blocks up the street." Everly nodded grimly in the direction they'd come from.

"More Anti-Apex?" Fleming asked.

"Anti-Apex and Pro-Epsilon Initiative, but also pro-Apex and Anti-Epsilon Initiative, and then the real wild card, Anti-Apex and Anti-Epsilon Initiative." Desirae counted them out on her fingers. "So, three different groups that all hate each other. It was a lot of yelling."

Fleming looked as if he'd just swallowed something sour but Everly shrugged.

"They were staying on their respective street corners. I wouldn't worry."

We wove through the crowd and peeked inside the boardwalk stores while we waited for the midnight fireworks. Fleming treated us all to hot chocolates from a coffee shop on the pier. Naomi and I got ours first and wiggled out to wait for the others on the boardwalk. She led the way to a bench at the feet of one of New Delos' many Paragon statues.

I grimaced at the sight of it. The statues were common. There was one right out front of the main school hall and a massive one stood in the bay on the north end of the island, but this was the first time I'd seen one since finding out more about Paul Fleming.

Naomi followed my gaze up to the bronze, blank stare of Paragon and pursed her lips.

"You have a problem with Paragon all of a sudden?"

I shook my head, feeling the puff-ball on the top of my aran-knit hat bobble around as I did. Fleming wouldn't want me telling Naomi about his brother, though I didn't like adding to my ever-growing list of things I was hiding from her.

"There's a lot of these on the island. Isn't it a little weird?"

"Maybe," she pointed at the plaque at Paragon's feet, "but this one was put here because this is where he saved the city from sinking."

"Huh." I snorted. "I thought he saved it while underwater."

"You know what I mean."

I sat next to Naomi, noting how the light cast from the shops behind us caused Paragon's shadow to wash over our laps.

"So," Naomi said with a snide smile that made me nervous, "what the heck did you do to Andersen?"

"Why? Is he moody?"

"All three of you are, but that's not surprising." She took a careful sip of her drink. "He feels sort of embarrassed, though. You didn't walk in on him in the bathroom, again, did you?"

"No!" With everything else that had happened, I'd somehow almost forgotten about the horrific first day at Fleming's. "It's just been a weird week. I'm ready to be back at school."

"Maybe it wouldn't be so bad if you texted your friends back?"

I hunched over my hot chocolate miserably.

"Did Wesley say something?"

"He wanted to know if I'd heard from you." She pulled the lid off her hot chocolate and frowned. "The whipped cream always dissolves too fast. Is there a reason you're ignoring Wesley?"

"I'm not ignoring him!" I said, too defensively.

She snatched my phone from my lap and opened my messages. I grimaced as she flashed Wesley's many ignored texts at me. She cocked an eyebrow and wordlessly raised her hot chocolate to her lips to take a long, accusing sip.

"There's been a lot going on!" I pulled my phone back and hid it in my pocket.

"Oh, yeah?" Naomi laughed. "Like what?"

"My mom showed up."

She sputtered on her hot chocolate in surprise.

"Why?" she coughed. "What happened?"

I gave her the quickest version possible, skimming over the parts about Paragon and keeping details about Dad's journal to a minimum.

"Maybe there's clues in it? We still don't know why Adrestus targeted you."

I gulped.

"Yeah, maybe."

"Unless you *do* know why." Her tone was more accusatory than questioning and despite the biting ocean air, my cheeks burned. "But you don't want to tell me."

I looked to the coffee shop, hoping to see the others. Mike and Desirae stood by the doorway, but Fleming and Everly were deep in conversation inside while Andersen pouted at a lonely window seat.

"That thing Adrestus has, what was it called? The Lapis?"

I nodded carefully, staring at my cup lid.

"You had it, right? That's why he wanted you at the museum? To take it?"

"I..." I didn't know what to say. "I didn't know I had it. I don't really know what it is."

Naomi had become unnaturally stiff next to me. I chanced a sideways glance at her. She was just as focused on her cup as I had been a moment ago and her fingertips dug into the side, bending the cardboard inwards.

"But it's what he's using to give people powers now?"

"I—I think so."

It was coming. The question about Eydis. Naomi was too smart to not have figured it out. My stomach knotted and I braced myself, not sure how I'd be able to lie.

"So," she said slowly, "if it can give powers, do you think....maybe....it can take them away?"

I almost dropped my hot chocolate. Her shoulders bent over her lap as if she was trying to hide.

"Naomi," I whispered, "do you want to get rid of your powers?"

Her lips drew into a tight line and she kept her eyes trained on her cup.

"I don't know yet. You think I'm stupid."

"No." I reached out and pried one of her hands off her cup to squeeze it. "I think you miss your family and I understand that. But you don't know if you'll learn to control your powers better. Without them, we never would've found Anthony and the other missing students."

She pulled her hand back and glared at me.

"And if I'm *not* ever able to control it? I shouldn't *have* to be a hero if it means losing my family." She looked out at the crowd. "Even if my family could handle being near each other with this power, it wouldn't make *this* any easier. Do you know how loud everyone is? I feel every emotion every person here is feeling and honestly, it makes me feel like exploding."

"I know. I—" I what? Was sorry? Understood? I didn't.

"Sammy," she said, her voice straining, "even if I grow up and have kids of my own, someday *they* might get these powers, too, and I'll never get to hug them again."

She clutched herself with one arm and fought back tears.

"It's okay. We'll figure it out. *You'll* figure it out. I know you will."

"Maybe, but it's not worth the risk of never having a family again."

Having gotten my own family murdered, I understood more than she knew, but comforting words evaded me and I could only watch as she worked to hold back her tears.

"Promise me," she said, finally turning to look at me. Her eyes, usually warm and compassionate, glinted with resolve. "If you get the Lapis back from Adrestus, don't destroy it. Not until we know if it can help me."

I swallowed. I hated that rock. Of course, if Dad *was* going to die, maybe it could bring him back. It had saved him from the Black Death, so it should be able to save him from whatever Baker foresaw.

"Unless there's some secret reason you want it gone." Naomi's voice lowered and became uncharacteristically icy. "But that just brings me back to wanting to lose these powers. Everyone is entitled to their secrets, but I get tired of knowing when my friends are keeping things from me."

"Naomi, I—"

"It's fine." She straightened up and forced a meek smile. "Sorry, Christmas was harder than usual this year."

"You don't have to apologize."

She was right. I was keeping secrets. Big ones. Even if I was entitled to keep things private, I knew when the truth finally came out, she'd be hurt I hadn't told her.

But I didn't want to be Eydis and the more people that knew, the more real she became and more Samantha disappeared into the fantasy I knew she was.

Naomi was my friend, though. She might not see me any differently.

"Look," I croaked. "The thing is—"

She stood up abruptly and looked towards the coffee shop. My confession died on my lips.

"Here they come." She shook out her shoulders, as if shaking off the conversation we'd just had. "Let's not think about the Lapis and superpowers tonight, alright? It's been a weird week. We deserve to have fun."

I sat a moment longer on the bench, my heart thundering for the secret I'd been about to share. I inhaled a shaky breath, then exhaled, trying to expel thoughts of Eydis before catching up to the others as they came out of the shop. Fleming rubbed his hands together and looked around the boardwalk, though I noticed he took care not to look directly at the Paragon statue.

"The pavilion is further down," he said. "It'll be the most crowded there, but if there's anywhere to sit, that'll be the best place to see the fireworks."

Live music floated on the ocean wind and despite the conversation I'd just had with Naomi, it was hard to be in a bad mood when the excitement on the boardwalk was so tangible. Mike and Desirae stopped at a booth and when they caught up with us, they'd decked themselves out in glow sticks.

"We all get some!" Desirae sang, crowning my hat with a glowing ring. Andersen scowled as Mike gave him his, but kept the glow stick crown on after he'd stepped away.

Storefronts gave way to man-made grassy knolls that jutted out over the water. Blankets and lawn chairs covered most of the ground and we wove between them looking for a spot. A pavilion sat in the center of the park and a band played beneath its pointed, wooden roof.

"Oh, great," Naomi mumbled under her breath. I gave her a look and she nodded towards a group of adults standing next to the pavilion. "City Council is here."

Sure enough, one of the men in the group turned as we approached the park center. I recognized Mickey, remembering his position on City Council is what placed him on the Apex Council as well. He gave Fleming and Everly a curt nod as we passed.

Careful with Mr. Lewis.

I jumped at the voice that sounded in my head. With my recent spat of memories forcing themselves into my consciousness, I'd have thought I would be used to disembodied voices by now but this was different.

It was Mickey's voice, echoing in the back of my head.

Is John around? Now Fleming spoke, but his mouth didn't move.

"Mr. Mickey's powers," Naomi whispered to me. "He's letting us know that Jamie's dad is here and to be careful with Andersen."

"Can he hear our thoughts?" I asked wildly. I was used to Naomi reading my emotions but I'd rather keep my thoughts private.

"No, you have to respond intentionally," Everly cut in. "But be careful. We don't want anyone overhearing talk of mind-reading."

Fleming redirected our path so that we arched around the pavilion. I craned my neck and saw John Ratcliffe in a thick, wool peacoat laughing with a few important looking people. I wasn't fond of Ratcliffe or Andersen, but I was glad to avoid the chance of them clashing. If Ratcliffe was anything like his daughter, he wouldn't be above causing a public disturbance just to put someone he didn't like on blast.

"How about here?" Fleming stopped at a patch of grass near the handrail that lined the park. I leaned over the metal bar. My glow stick crown reflected off the water twelve feet below.

"Not too windy," Everly nodded. "Good for fireworks."

We settled in the grass and I drew my knees up to my chest to keep warm and make space for the others. Mike pulled out a set of cards and started passing them out but I shook my head when he got to me.

"We've got another fifteen minutes until midnight," Mike said. "You sure you don't want to play?"

"I'm good."

I didn't feel like learning the rules to the game and wanted to take the chance to sit back and watch the crowd. I didn't get to explore the city much outside of the stealth drills Fleming made me run with Remi and Erik and those were usually done after the rest of the city had gone to bed. Now, even though it was still late at night, I could watch the people of the city as they celebrated the oncoming New Year.

A man selling kettle corn walked between the blankets and lawn chairs, followed by a sweet, buttery aroma. Fleming must've seen us tracking the vendor's progress through the park because he smiled and reached for his back pocket.

"You guys want kettle corn?"

"We've got money," Desirae assured him. "You already paid for the hot chocolate."

But Fleming continued to pat his pockets and then jammed his hands into the pockets of his coat.

"Did I hand my wallet off to any of you?"

Everly furrowed his brow at Fleming.

"Did it get picked?"

"No." Fleming cast a resentful look at Everly. "I'd know if someone picked my pocket."

"You probably left it at the coffee shop," Desirae suggested, pulling out her own money as the kettle corn vendor got closer.

Naomi clambered to her feet.

"Sammy and I can go check!" she offered.

Fleming frowned and chewed on his lip but Everly waved us away.

"Hurry back," he said.

I followed Naomi back into the crowd, towards the lights of the storefronts.

"You didn't want to play cards either?"

"Card games are no fun when you can feel who's winning by the way everyone reacts to the hand they get dealt," she shrugged. "Plus, it's nice to get away from the others."

We walked back past the pavilion and grassy park turned back to boardwalk. As we went, Naomi told me about living with Everly and the twins while I gawked around at the crowd. It was hard to believe the island held so many people. I wondered how many were secretly Apex.

A figure in a black hoodie walked towards us, cutting her way through the crowd with purpose. Unlike most of the people on the boardwalk, she wasn't adorned in glow sticks or light up necklaces and kept her head down and her hood up, but my breath caught in my throat. Her angular chin and strawberry blonde hair stuck out from under her hood.

"What?" Naomi twisted to look at me. The crowd jostled her as she did and a man grunted, "keep moving or get out of the way!"

I turned as the hooded figure passed us and disappeared in the crowd. No...I shook my head. I had to be wrong.

"Nothing." I forced a laugh in an effort to steady my voice, but it came off sounding crazed. "I thought I saw Winnie."

26

Second Act

Naomi pulled me out of the way of the crowd that pushed towards the park as midnight ticked closer. She scanned the masses over my shoulder and shook her head.

"Winnie? Are you sure?"

"No, I didn't even see her face, I just..." It couldn't have been Winnie. What would she be doing out here? "It was someone in a black hoodie. I think it just reminded me of how she looked in that ridiculous Dion get up."

Naomi grabbed my shoulders to look me in the eye.

"No mask, though, right?" she asked, referring to the horrifying Greek-Tragedy mask Winnie had taken to wearing since joining Adrestus.

"No mask," I confirmed. I'd only known Winnie for a week, despite my fake memories with her. How was I of all people going to recognize her in a crowd?

"Maybe we should go back. If it was her, Adrestus might be planning something."

"No, it wasn't her," I insisted. I was jumpy after being cooped up in Fleming's apartment for so long. I had to be seeing things. "Besides, we're almost to the coffee shop."

Naomi hesitated, watching my face, and I wondered which of my emotions was giving her pause.

"Sure," she finally said, "but let's make it quick."

I watched every face that passed us as we forged our way back to the shop. A line had formed out the door and Naomi bit her lip.

"There's not a lot of room in there. You wait out here and watch for anything weird while I go in and check."

I nodded. Naomi was a natural team captain. She pushed her way through the crowd at the door, apologizing as she went while I scanned the pier with my back to the shop window.

It wasn't Winnie, I reassured myself. *She would've seen you. She would've stopped.*

I took a deep, wavering breath, exhaling a cloud of fog in the cold, and wrapped my arms around myself for both comfort and warmth, but immediately dropped them again.

Someone in a black hoodie stood across the small plaza on the opposite side of the Paragon statue. Strawberry blonde hair fell forward from the hoodie's confines. Winnie or not, they were the same person we'd passed on the walkway.

She would've had to have doubled-back after passing us and now, even though I couldn't see her face through the shadows, I knew she was watching me.

Wait for Naomi, I told myself, not daring to take my eyes off the figure. She'd feel my agitation from inside the shop. We were better off confronting our stalker together.

A minute passed. Then another.

The crowd outside was dispersing, though the shops surrounding the statue remained full. In the distance, chanting voices counted down, getting louder as the numbers got smaller until, finally, they reached zero and a crackling explosion rang out over the boardwalk.

Bright colors danced and flashed, bouncing off Paragon's bronze head and cape, as fireworks signaled the New Year.

The hooded figure lowered her head further and ducked between two shops. I cast a frantic glance through the window behind me, searching for Naomi, but couldn't see her through the bodies that pressed up against the glass as they waited for their drinks.

I wouldn't follow her far. I'd just pop between the shops and see where she'd gone. After all, Naomi had told me to keep a look out for anything weird, hadn't she? I would be a bad teammate if I *didn't* give chase.

With a final look back at the coffee shop, I darted across the pier and into the shadows. The slim alley lit up sporadically as fireworks burst overhead and by the light of a sudden flash, I saw the figure slip behind the shop.

I tiptoed after her, careful to not thunder my way down the wood-planked walkway, but as I turned the corner, I nearly ran straight into the black hoodie.

I'd thought I'd be angrier, but any hunger for a fight dissipated. Even in the dark, on the slim walkway between the shop backs and the open ocean, Winnie's sneer was unmistakable. My friend. My roommate. My *fault.*

She pushed the hood back and the ocean air caught her hair while fireworks exploded over the water to our left.

"I shouldn't be surprised you're here, *Eydis.*" She looked out towards the park. From here, we could see the pavilion light up, the faces of the crowd changing colors with the fireworks. "Where's your fancy suit?"

"Where's your stupid mask?" I tried to gather my wits and clear my head. "Have the night off?"

The corners of her mouth twitched and Winnie turned to lean against the railing, idly watching the fireworks display with her jaw clenched. She knew I wasn't going to attack her. She knew I didn't have it in me to fight her.

"Where's my dad?"

She snapped her head around to look at me.

"He's not your dad and you're not my friend, so don't talk to me like you are."

"Don't tell me what I am and what I'm not!" The bitter sting of her betrayal rushed back to me and every question I'd wanted to demand of her bubbled to my lips, each fighting to be asked first. "Why would you lie? You offered me up like some kinda sick sacrifice to get into Adrestus' good graces and for what? *Superpowers*?"

She laughed, cold and callous.

"God, Sammy, you're too naive." A flicker of annoyance passed over her face as she realized she'd called me Sammy. "I don't want superpowers. Apex are nothing but tools. I don't want to be one, I want to *wield* them. Just like you do."

She looked back at the fireworks, grinning as I fumbled for a response. Apex weren't my tools. They were my friends.

"Come back with me, alright?" I pleaded. "Fleming can help you."

"Another Beta who uses Apex!" she exclaimed. "Don't you see what a hypocrite you are? We want the same thing, I'm just willing to upset the status quo to get it."

"We do *not* want the same thing!" If she kept talking the way she was, she'd lose the advantage of my unwillingness to hit her. "Adrestus is a maniac! You watched him cut me open at the neck and did *nothing* to stop him! I'd *never* let anyone do that to you!"

"Only because you refuse to let go of the lies that Alison fed you," she snarled. "We aren't friends. We never were. Stop pretending it wasn't all a lie!"

"Because it wasn't!" I yelled. "I followed you to the docks when you asked me because I *cared* about you! After I thought you'd been kidnapped,

I *died* trying to get you back! So don't you *dare* say I wasn't your friend. I was more your friend than *anyone*."

Her hands tightened around the railing and she refused to look at me. Hot tears traced the curve of my cheek and I brushed them away angrily before Winnie could turn and see them.

"You dying for a lie says more about you than it does me." She glanced at her watch. "Act two of three is about to start, by the way, so either get out of the way or don't complain if you get caught up in it."

Her face was somewhere between bored and angry. While I couldn't decide which way she was leaning, I knew either was equally dangerous.

"Act two?" I repeated. There was still time for Naomi to catch up to us if I kept her talking.

"You were there front and center for the first one," she said in the same matter-of-fact tone I'd heard her use so many times. "The attack on Jamie Ratcliffe?"

I looked across the water towards the pavilion.

"What's Adrestus planning?" I demanded. "Winnie, you can still stop it, it's not—"

"Not what?" She backed away. "Not too late? No, Sammy, it is. But, before you go and warn your friends, you haven't possibly seen my sister around here, have you?"

Winnie's face twisted into a cruel grin before she darted down the walkway. As much as I wanted to give chase, she was right. I *needed* to warn the others. If Amanda was here, Adrestus could make her hurt any number of people.

I spun on my heel, sprinting back to the Paragon statue, hoping Naomi would be waiting, but just as I broke through the shops, running out onto the pier to cross to the coffee shop, a column of fire ripped the boardwalk open, swallowing Paragon's statue and throwing me back against a wall.

I crumbled to the wooden planks as screams and flames rent the night. The pier shook as store-goers stampeded from the shops and away from the inferno that twisted with the bronze Paragon at its vertex. I reached up, trying to grab for anything that I might be able to use to pull myself to my feet but just as my fingertips dug into the lip of a shop window, an accidental kick to the back from a fleeing somebody knocked me down again.

The whole pier swayed, though I wasn't sure if it was from the running crowd, the fire eating at the support beams, or the aftereffects of being launched backwards and kicked. I crawled along the floor, clawing my way towards the pavement, but was met with a tennis shoe to the face.

I pulled my arms over my head to ward off any more blows but the pier continued to lurch in an unnatural, dizzy way, spinning so horribly that at one point, I felt like I was crawling along a wooden ceiling, clinging to the planks to keep from falling into the open sky. I clambered away from the heat of the fire, tucking myself under the shop window I'd just tried to pull myself up on.

"Naomi!" I tried to scream, but black smoke filled my mouth.

The pier seemed abandoned, or, at least, no one was running by and kicking me on their way out anymore. However, the screams seemed to only be getting louder and the distant clang of metal against metal rang out amid the snapping and crackling of wood.

A piercing shriek split my eardrums and filled me with dread.

"Eydis!" a woman screamed. "Eydis, where've you gone?!"

"Not now," I said, as Samantha, through gritted teeth. I needed to get off the pier, not lost in another memory.

A pincer-like grip wrapped around my bicep, so aggressively that I thought it must be real, but when I struck out at whoever was there, my fist met empty air.

"It's Eluf's men," the woman hissed, and even though I was alone under the window, I felt her breath against my ear. "They've blocked off the forest. Find Erika and Hjordis, hide them in the longhouse. I'll find Gunhild and meet you there."

It was the first memory I'd recovered of my mother, my *real* mother, and as the world twisted and roared, tears sprung to my eyes as she told me to go find my sisters. No matter when this memory was from, they'd all end up dead. Because of me.

"Sammy!"

Naomi yelled for me from somewhere, but the sounds of Eluf's men descending upon my village grew louder. The fire burned ever closer to my hiding spot under the window and I inched back towards the space between shops.

My mother's grip remained wrapped around my arm as I crawled and when I turned back to look at the fire, it was gone. A village of crude, wooden dwellings had taken the place of the burning pier. My mother helped me to my feet, pulling me up by the arm. Tousled blonde hair escaped the braids that ran down her back and her cheeks were pink from running but her caramel-brown gaze was as steady as ever.

"They should be by the boats if they haven't run to the house already."

"Yes, Mother."

I shrugged off my fur shawl, leaving it in the dirt. Even though winter was fast approaching, I'd move quicker without it. The sounds of fighting were still distant, but getting distinctly closer.

"Hurry, Eydis," my mother hissed. "And, please, don't do anything foolish. You don't stand a chance against Eluf's men."

27

Havard's Daughters

My boots crunched over fresh snow and frost that had covered the village the night before. The pebbled beach was slick with frozen salt-water but I sprinted across the rocks. I didn't have the luxury of being careful. Smoke billowed from the bluffs overlooking the fjord, drifting over the beach from a fire set by Eluf's raiders. If they surrounded the village with flame, we'd be trapped. Those they didn't kill, they'd enslave.

The boats lay up ahead, their hulls tilted on their sides in the black gravel. The beach reeked of dead whale, wafting from the carcass the hunters had brought in the week before. There was still viable meat on the bones, kept fresh by the cold of the oncoming winter. Food would start to get scarce soon. Whatever Eluf had sent his men for, they'd be fools to pass up half a whale.

Which meant if Erika and Hjordis were hiding among the boats, they'd certainly be found.

"Hjordis!" I shouted. There was no need to be quiet. Anyone within earshot would've already seen me racing across the beach. "Erika!"

Erika's wild mane of tawny curls, with its single streak of white hair that sprang from the crown of her forehead before becoming lost in a sea of blonde-brown frizz, popped up from inside the galley of the farthest boat. Hjordis' arm shot up and tried to wrestle her back down.

"It's Eydis!" Erika clambered out of the galley and slid down the boat side. Her fur cloak dwarfed her tiny frame and she struggled to run to me. Hjordis followed, more cautious than our younger sister, casting furtive glances towards the village. The sounds of fighting were closer now. Vidar and Knut would be in the fray but I didn't have the time to worry about them.

"We have to hide!" Hjordis yelled over the wind. She'd done her hair like Mother's that morning and her braids had somehow held up through the chaos.

"Not here." I looked back. Dark figures appeared on the far end of the beach. Erika was still small enough to carry and I scooped her up in my arms. "We need to get home!"

Hjordis ran ahead and I followed with Erika bouncing in my arms, not slowing down until we were off the beach. Snow mingled with the ash that fell from the sky. Hjordis flattened herself against a wall and stared at me with wild, gray eyes.

"We should've stayed where we were!"

"You would've been found. They're raiders. They might take the whole boat." I set Erika down and she kept her hand engulfed in mine as I led the way through the dwellings.

We ducked behind a stack of firewood when two men ran by carrying stolen sheep. If they'd made it this far into the village, missing sheep would be the least of our worries. Some of our men were sure to have fallen.

Don't think about Vidar and Knut, I told myself. *Focus on keeping Erika and Hjordis safe.*

As we approached the house, Gunhild's sharp features peeked out from behind the door and Mother appeared behind her to pull her back. She threw the door open so we could sprint in past her.

"Gunhild, help me with this." Mother pushed a chest in front of the door, though we all knew it would do little to stop anyone intent on entering. Erika clung to our mother's wool skirt, staring at the door with eyes that were almost too big for her tiny, pink face.

After the chest was pushed into place, Mother whipped around and ushered us back.

"Don't just stand there! Hide!"

Even though it was midday, it was dark inside the house. The oil lamps had already been put out so we had to feel our way to the back room where we kept our cots.

Erika and Hjordis disappeared under a pile of pelts. Mother grabbed a long metal spit from the hearth and wielded it like a sword. I wavered in the doorway.

My sword was tucked away under my sleeping mat. Only Vidar knew it was there and if Mother saw and told Father....

I'd be doomed to sailmaking forever.

Something heavy slammed against the door. The dull thud rang out and Gunhild went to comfort Erika and Hjordis when Erika began to softly cry under the pelts.

"Get away from there!" Mother threw me behind her. She was fierce and probably more skilled than I gave her credit for, but if Eluf's men got inside, she wouldn't stand a chance.

"Something's blocking the door," a voice growled.

"Then someone's home."

I stumbled over to my corner of the room and rummaged through the quilts until my hand met cold steel.

"Shh!" Gunhild reprimanded me from Erika and Hjordis' pelt pile. I crouched over the sword, running my hand over the flat of the blade.

Mother pressed against the opposite wall, her outline barely legible against the wood next to the door.

The chest in the front room grated against the floor. I coiled my fingers around the contours of my sword hilt, a familiar shape after so many hours of secret practice with Vidar. I knew I could wield it better than Mother could wield her metal poker, but if it came down to it, would I be able to kill an attacker?

I looked at my three sisters piled across the room.

Yes, killing someone to keep them safe would be easy.

A crack of dusty light slid in from the front room as the invaders breached our meager barricade, accompanied by the screams of our neighbors outside. Mother inched closer to the doorway, ready to protect us.

I held my breath even though my heart raced as if I'd just sprinted across the entire island. I thought my lungs might burst from the effort of it, but I didn't dare make a sound as I listened to the men overturning tables, chests, and chairs in the front room, rummaging through our things.

"Nothing but whale meat," one of them grunted.

"I bet we find something prettier back there. Havard's got four daughters and this is supposed to be his place."

I knelt on my blankets, my sword fully drawn. The others would be able to see it easily if they looked over, even in the dark, but I had a dark feeling they were about to see it anyway.

A hulking man took up the doorway, light peeking through the edges of his tangled hair and beard. The edges of his beard twitched and even though his face was lost in shadows, I knew he'd seen me.

"One of Havard's girls?" he growled and the chill in his voice was enough to make me forget everything I'd learned about sword fighting. He lumbered forward, leering at me.

What would Vidar do?

My grip tightened on the hilt. I could give our sisters and Mother the chance to get away.

But Mother moved before I could and I'd been right about underestimating her. She lunged from her hiding position, driving the meat spit between the man's ribs. He roared in pain and rage. He twisted to face her, ripping the metal handle from her grip, leaving her defenseless.

"Solveig Hildasdotter," he snarled, tearing the iron rod from his flank without so much as flinching. "Havard taught you some tricks."

He drew his hatchet back. Gunhild shrieked from her hiding spot while Mother stood tall and proud in front of the arching weapon.

"No!"

I leapt from my corner. Vidar would've been disappointed in my form. It was sloppy and had the man been prepared for my attack, he'd have easily been able to deflect me.

But he wasn't prepared and I raked the sword across his flank, ripping his tunic and exposing the messy, bloody wound I'd carved there. He howled and turned his hatchet on me but I'd regained my composure. As he raised his hatchet overhead, blood bubbling and spilling between his lips and into his beard, I slashed upwards into his exposed armpit.

The hatchet fell to the floor and the man dropped to his knees. I blanched at the blood that spurted out from under his arm and I froze as he drew his sword in a last ditch effort.

"What are you doing?" Gunhild shouted. "Kill him!"

I closed my eyes, swung, and felt my sword meet flesh.

I stumbled backwards as the man gurgled his final, agonizing breaths and fell forward in a spreading pool of his own blood.

I couldn't look away from what I'd done and in my stupor, I forgot about the second man. Mother drew me back from the doorway as he stepped in, surveying his fallen comrade before turning his bloodshot eyes on me. Blood already spotted the front of his tunic, though it didn't appear to be his, and he was better fitted for a fight than his friend had been with a sword twice the size of mine.

"I don't know if I should kill you," he said with a crooked, wild grin, "or make you my wife."

Mother tried to push me behind her, but Gunhild reached out and pulled her back. I raised my sword.

"We have sheep and a few goats in the back." My voice shook but I held the sword steady. "Take what you want and leave us be."

"We need more than sheep and goats if we want to survive the winter."

"Then go steal it from the Birgers! They have more than us, anyway!"

The man laughed and shook his head.

"We don't stand a chance against the Birgers. They've made a deal with the gods and now they have warriors who breathe fire and move swords without touching them."

He was messing with us, trying to catch me off guard.

"So go find a fire-breathing wife and leave us be."

"Eydis," Mother hissed.

"What? You want me to be nicer to the man who wants to kill us? You think you can come in and take our things? Leave us to starve and freeze to death over the winter?"

"Take your things? Child, where do you think that blade came from?"

I gulped.

"My brother gave—"

"And your brother stole it from a Franc. I recognize the etching on the blade." He stepped closer. "Now come nicely and—"

Erika whimpered under her pelts and the man's grin widened.

"I knew Havard had more daughters somewhere."

"Just take our sheep and leave!"

He tossed his sword from one hand to the other. Behind him, snow flurried through the front door to accumulate in the front room.

"I'm not taking some smelly sheep." He played with his mustache with the tip of his tongue. "What're you gonna do? Fight me in a dress?"

"Yeah. What about you? Gonna fight me..." I'd hoped a retort might come to mind but drew a blank. "Gonna fight me with that stupid face?"

Gunhild groaned behind me. The man chuckled darkly and wagged his sword at me. Mother grabbed a handful of the back of my dress as if that might somehow help.

"Fine, if you want to make this difficult."

I slashed at him before he'd finished talking. He parried easily and I attacked again, trying to drive him away. He stepped back and, in a stroke of luck, slipped in his friend's blood, stumbling backwards over the body.

"Run!" Mother already had Erika in her arms. Hjordis clung to her skirt as they and Gunhild darted from their corner and made a break for the door.

"Hurry, Eydis!" Gunhild called over her shoulder as they tried to maneuver around the overturned furniture and the heavy chest but as I turned to follow, the flat of the man's blade smacked my ankle. He gathered a handful of wool skirts in his fists and dragged me to the blood-soaked floor.

Something like fire drove its way through the back of my shoulder. I howled as the man twisted his blade and yanked it out.

"You're too mouthy to wife, anyway."

I braced for the killing blow. My back, neck, and head were all exposed and I'd just killed his friend.

But his boots thundered past my face as he gave chase to the others. Their shrieks in the front room curdled my blood and I forced myself to crawl forward in time to see Erika, flung over the man's shoulder with her white lick of hair hanging in her terrified face, disappearing through the front door.

I staggered to my feet, grabbing my sword, and fighting through the pain that radiated from my shoulder and down my arm and back. I'd die before I let him steal Erika.

"Eydis, wait!" Mother tried to stop me but I bowled past her, into the path outside the home.

Chaos ruled the village. Snow fell thick, already red with bloodshed. Eluf's men fought my friends and neighbors between dwellings, goats bleated, and men and women screamed. Through it all, I found Erika, bouncing on the back of the man's shoulder as he ran from the fray.

I readjusted my grip and gave chase, dodging men and blades alike as I tried to keep my footing on the slick ground.

Where are you? The stranger's voice in my head was foreign and even though it spoke in a strange language, I somehow understood its question.

The village. I answered back in the same strange language. *They've taken Erika.*

Who's Erika?

The voice was vaguely familiar but Erika's mouth widened in a shriek as she screamed my name. I didn't have time for mystery voices asking stupid questions.

He ran for the birch forest in the direction of Eluf's settlement. I would lose him in the trees. I would lose Erika.

"Eydis! Wait!"

Arms wrapped around me from behind and I screamed in fear, anger, and pain.

"It's alright! You're alright!" Vidar spun me around to face him. Blood painted his face, some his, some not.

"Give me your bow."

My heart dropped at the sound of Father's voice. I turned to see Knut and Father exchange weapons.

The men who'd broken down our door and terrorized us had been large but would've been dwarfed next to Havard Bjørnsson. His wild, tawny beard was barely contained by the plait he kept it woven into and his sinewy arms strained the seams of his cornflower blue tunic as he drew back the bowstring.

"You'll hit Erika!" I shrieked.

He let the arrow loose.

"No," he said, as the arrow buried itself in the back of the man's neck. "I won't."

The man stumbled and fell face forward as Erika rolled free and sprinted back into our father's arms.

Samantha, this is Mr. Fleming. Who's Erika? A new voice intruded upon my thoughts.

Who's Erika? I repeated at the voice. *Who's Samantha?*

Havard turned towards me with Erika still perched in his arms, cowering against his neck.

"Where did you get that?"

I tried to hide the sword but it was too late.

"I gave it to her," Vidar admitted. "Father, I'm sorry, I—"

He turned his storm-gray gaze on Vidar and I felt him shrink next to me.

"Then you'll be the one who throws it in the fjord."

"But we would've been dead without it!" I protested.

"And you were almost dead *with* it." He poked me hard in the shoulder and I bit back the pain that erupted from the wound there. He took the sword and thrust it into Vidar's arms. "As soon as we handle the situation here, it goes in the harbor."

"Please!" I cried.

Knut put an arm around me. I tried to push him away but slumped into his chest.

"We need to get her inside." Knut's chest vibrated in my ear as he spoke. "The wound goes straight through her shoulder."

Fire. I smelt fire.

The village dwellings bled together and the world twisted.

Samantha, focus. Where are you? There was that voice again.

I don't know...

Eluf's men retreated and the fighting was dying. So why was the fire getting louder? Why could I still hear screaming?

Knut lifted me in his arms. I buried my face in his tunic. I could see fire there.

"Miss, are you alright?"

A face swam inches in front of mine and a black sky bled with orange flames. A man in a wool coat tapped my face. He looked familiar.

"What—"

I was on the pier, lying between two shops as fire ate away at the wooden planks just yards ahead. The man was in a long, wool coat and earmuffs.

"John Ratcliffe?" I mumbled.

Samantha, please tell us where you are and what's happening. Who's Erika?

It was Mickey's voice in my head.

Coffee shop.

"Good, you're awake. I was worried you—"

There was another explosion behind Jamie's father and he wrapped his arms around my head as if to shield me. A figure emerged from the flames behind him. I recognized her dark clothes and cape immediately, though her flame-hair blended in with the inferno behind her.

Hephestae raised her hands, as if to rain fire down on us. The flames swelled and I threw my arms over my face, bracing for fiery impact.

Ratcliffe stood over me and threw his arms wide. The pier shuddered and for a moment, I thought we'd fallen into the ocean as water gushed up between the planks like geysers, dousing the flames nearest us and showering me in salt water.

"Stop, Apex!" he cried in a theatrical voice. "You're done terrorizing New Delos for I am Wavemaker!"

28

Enter Wavemaker

Amanda shrieked as freezing ocean water rushed up and over the rail, surging between shops to converge on her. Her fire hissed and sizzled as John Ratcliffe conducted the torrent, stopping only when a rogue wave threatened to sweep me through a burnt hole in the pier.

He grabbed me under my arms and pulled me back. I was too dumbfounded to move on my own. I shook my head, trying to clear the steady thrumming that pounded in my ears before realizing the sound wasn't in my head. The lights of a helicopter shone down on us. I shied away from them but Ratcliffe hoisted me into his arms.

"Let me go!" I kicked out and he dropped me in surprise.

"It's alright, you're safe!"

His waves had doused Amanda's fire, though "Hephestae" was nowhere to be seen. A gaping hole split the pier and while Paragon's statue was by some miracle still standing, Amanda's flames had been hot enough to morph the bronze. Instead of standing proud and tall, Paragon now stooped with his iconic grin melting grotesquely down his chin.

I struggled into a standing position. Ratcliffe kept his hands on my shoulders, pretending to help.

A sudden cacophony nearly knocked me back off my feet and I looked around wildly for the source of the noise. Was it another attack? More fire? Maybe an earthquake.

But Ratcliffe put an arm around my shoulders and guided me forward, my soaked sneakers squishing with every step. A crowd had gathered on the pavement, still decked out in their New Year's lights and flashing hats. For a second, I thought they were yelling at us but then realization and anger dawned on me. They were *cheering*. For Ratcliffe. For "Wavemaker".

He waved as we approached, his arm tight around my shoulders, keeping me at his side. I didn't have the energy to push away. I blinked dumbly in the flashing police lights and sweeping helicopter spotlight.

News crews descended on us, as did several officers and paramedics. A microphone weaseled under a policeman's arm to get in my face.

"Councilman Ratcliffe, Carly Pine with Channel Six. Were you the source of the waves that defeated that villain and her fire?"

"Yes, ma'am," he beamed, leaning closer to the microphone.

"Councilman!" Another body with another microphone bore down on us. "Did you undergo the Epsilon Initiative procedure to gain this ability?"

Camera flashes blinded me. A ringing in my ears was growing louder. I resisted the urge to hide my face in Ratcliffe's sea-soaked coat, wishing I was back with Knut, hiding against his tunic.

"Councilman, can you prove you were the one making the waves?"

Ratcliffe flicked his wrist and I felt all the water in my clothes seep forward, leaving me dry. The water conglomerated as a murky globe in the air in front of us. The crowd shrieked in delight and anger and the reporters pressed in, yelling more questions, flashing more lights and I couldn't escape.

I blinked. The street and the crowd disappeared, replaced by the fjord and Havard and Vidar.

"Throw it," Father growled. Vidar gulped and looked sideways at me, rolling the hilt of the sword, *my* sword, between his hands. "Far enough so she can't get it."

"Please," I begged even though I knew it was useless. "I can help! I can go with you tomorrow to fight Eluf, I—"

The blade whistled as Vidar spun it through the air. My mouth fell open as I watched it soar over the harbor and drop into the water a field's length away.

It was gone.

"Samantha!"

Another flash bulb startled me back to Ratcliffe's side.

"Fleming?" I murmured. The crowd was too dense. I couldn't find him.

"Let me through, that's my— she's with me!"

An officer extricated me from Ratcliffe's arm. Fleming's eyes widened and he moved so fast to reach me that his glasses slipped down his nose and to the ground. He didn't notice as he pulled me away from the officer.

"Sir, are you this girl's father?"

"What? No. Samantha, what happened? Naomi said she left you outside the coffee place."

"We can't let her leave with someone who's not her parent," the officer asserted.

"Yes, that's me. I'm in charge. We're going."

"Miss?" The officer put his hand between us and peered at me under his hat. "Is this man your guardian?"

"I—"

I'd killed a man, I remembered. I'd closed my eyes to deliver the final blow, but I'd done it. My hands shook. I'd fallen in his blood. I reached up for my shoulder, half expecting the sword wound to still be there.

"Can I see some ID, sir?" The officer turned on Fleming.

"It's fine, Brody." Officer Allen pushed his way in. Fleming relaxed at the sight of his fellow Apex Council member. "I know them."

He drew us away, forcing a path through the crowd. Allen and Fleming flanked me on either side but I didn't feel like I was there. I floated somewhere above the crowd, watching them drag me between them.

They're at the bus stop on third.

I hardly registered Mickey's voice in my head. It was just one more after a month of invisible voices clamoring for my attention.

We broke free of the crowd but didn't slow down until we'd passed several streets and could see the bus stop. A small crowd gathered around a bench, all wearing glow sticks.

"The car?" I mumbled.

"The street we parked on is blocked off," Fleming said, his hand still gripping my bicep, much like Solveig, my mother, had. "I'll get the car in the morning."

Naomi broke away from the group and sprinted down the sidewalk to meet us.

"Sammy, I tried to find you!" The dirt on her face was streaked with tears and one of her coat sleeves had burnt through at the elbow. "I'm so sorry!"

Allen stepped aside and she took his spot, keeping pace as we hurried to the bus stop.

Everly stepped out next, extending a hand. I obediently put my hand in his and felt his powers sweep over me.

"She seems a bit dazed," Fleming said. "Maybe another concussion."

Everly shook his head.

"No, just tired."

The twins gawked at me from behind Everly. Desirae wrung her hands while Mike peered from under a crown of flashing glow sticks. Only Andersen had the decency not to stare, awkwardly shuffling his feet to keep warm.

Allen left us to return to the scene Ratcliffe had created and Naomi stayed at my arm, even as the bus rolled up and we crowded inside with the other shellshocked party-goers.

"I'm sorry," Naomi whispered again. We held onto overhead straps as the bus lurched forward. The bus occupants spoke in low voices, buzzing with subdued excitement, but Naomi looked like she might cry. "I couldn't find you. It was like everyone's emotions were screaming and I couldn't see through it all to get to you."

"It's okay," I insisted. Fleming stood with us and while he didn't look at us, I could tell he was listening in by the way his head was angled. "It...I saw Winnie."

His head snapped around so fast that if he hadn't already lost his glasses, they would've been flung from his face.

"Winnie?" he demanded. "When? Where? Is she alright?"

"Alex," Everly warned in a low voice. "Later."

Fleming bit his lip. His mousy hair stuck out in odd directions. He'd probably been pulling on it all night. He rubbed his chin with his hand, still surveying me nervously.

"I'm fine."

"Yes." He nodded curtly. "I know."

Naomi leaned in closer.

"Who's Erika?"

I swallowed and there was no way she didn't feel the panic that swelled in my chest.

"You heard that?"

"Mickey had us all in on the mental link in case we got separated. So who is she?" It was hard to feel like I could hide anything with Naomi scanning me with wide, wavering eyes but I shook my head.

"I'm not sure." It wasn't *really* a lie. I knew almost nothing about the small wild-haired viking girl in my memories. "I think I was just confused."

But it wasn't really the truth, either. This wasn't a great time or place to go into details, but the lies felt heavier than ever. Hopefully, Naomi could at least glean that I was sorry.

The bus squealed to a stop, jostling the passengers against each other. I pressed close to Naomi to let those who needed off to pass.

"Hey!" a gruff voice called out. Naomi and I whipped around to look at a large man stop in front of Andersen after pushing his way to the open door. Instead of stepping out onto the sidewalk, however, he got in Andersen's face. Andersen scowled but stood his ground. "You're that kid from the school, aren't you?"

"Oh, no," Naomi groaned.

"I'm a kid and I go to school," Andersen spat. "What about it?"

"Nah, I saw a video of you online. You're one of *them*!" The man poked Andersen hard in the chest, who, to his credit, didn't waver. "You people couldn't let us have one night, could you? You just had to ruin it!"

"Leave him alone!" a stranger in the back called out. The bus driver looked back warily in the large rearview mirror. "He's a *kid*!"

"He's an Apex!" the man yowled. "It's his fault the waterfront was attacked! It's probably one of his friends who did it!"

Fleming cut between them, forcing the man away from Andersen.

"This is your stop, isn't it?" He gestured towards the door.

"Is he your kid?" The man looked between them. "You one of them, too?"

"We're all tired," Everly said, slow and low. "We all want to get home safe, so how about you leave him alone and move along?"

"No one on this bus is safe with him here!" the man yelled. Most of the other passengers shied away but a few nodded in agreement.

"How about you both leave?" a new stranger shouted. A few others echoed the idea.

"Come on!" the bus driver shouted. "Off or on, I gotta keep going."

The man shouldered past Andersen but before I could sigh in relief, the bus driver nodded at Fleming and Andersen in the rearview.

"You, too. Don't want any funny business on my bus."

"We aren't—" Fleming started to argue but Andersen grunted and stepped out after the man. Fleming looked between Andersen on the sidewalk, the bus driver in the mirror, and me, with Naomi clutching my arm. "Fine. Come on, Samantha."

I pried away from Naomi.

"I'll see you soon," I assured her.

"You, too." She shrank back towards the twins

I pushed through the passengers, keeping my head down but unable to avoid the whispers.

"Is she one of them, too?"

"She kinda looks like the girl Councilman Ratcliffe saved."

"Then what's she doing with one of *them?*"

Everly patted my shoulder before I could step off.

"Let us know if you need anything. Keep an eye on those stitches."

I nodded and joined Fleming and Andersen on the cold sidewalk. We were still at least a mile from the apartment and Fleming mumbled to himself as he tried to download a ride-share app onto his phone.

The man who'd accosted Andersen continued down the street, his friends pulling him along, though he continued to shout about nasty Apex and the degeneration of New Delos until they finally turned a corner and we couldn't hear them anymore.

Andersen stood with his hands in his pockets, staring forward with a passive scowl carved into his face. The only sign he gave that he might've been upset was a few minutes into his reverie when he reached up to rip his glow stick crown from his head and flung it to the ground.

Fleming wordlessly scooped it up to throw away and then resumed his spot between us on the curb where we silently waited for the car Fleming had hailed to come pick us up.

My subconscious was merciful enough to grant me a deep, dreamless sleep. I only wished the stupor could have lasted longer, but just after six in the morning, before the sun was even up, the buzzing of my phone dragged me out of the comfort of unconsciousness.

Everything from the night before crashed down on me like one of John Ratcliffe's waves. Naomi wanting to get rid of her powers, seeing Winnie, Wavemaker's debut, Andersen getting us kicked off the bus, and, of course, the memory of the raid on my Icelandic home, which now felt more tangible than ever.

I clawed at my phone, ripping the charger from the wall as I did, and hid my face in my pillows when I saw Wesley's name lit up on the screen. I couldn't ignore him this time.

I hit answer and set the phone down on the pillow next to me.

"Sammy?" Wesley's voice was tight and nervous. "Sammy, are you there?"

"Yeah." I swallowed, hating how much comfort I found at the sound of his voice, even if he was on edge. "I'm here."

"Are you okay? What happened? Do you know you're on the news? Was it Amanda? And what's going on with Jamie's dad? Did he really save you? Because I find that hard to believe."

I tried to cling to the black numbness that had settled on me the night before, but could feel it giving way, opening me up to the torrent of emotions that lay beneath it.

"Jamie's dad is a hack," I sniffed. "It was a set-up and he just played his part."

"They're still controlling Amanda, then? If I had been there—"

"It wouldn't have changed anything," I asserted, thinking of Andersen being harassed. If Wesley had been there, he wouldn't have hesitated to give up his identity to help me. He'd be forced to become a pariah, too. Maybe it *was* a good thing to distance myself from him.

Wesley was quiet for a moment. Soft, white noise hummed through the phone.

"The video on the news...you don't look like you're all there. You didn't get another concussion, did you?"

I exhaled through my nose.

"No. Nothing like that. I...got stuck. In an old memory."

I was glad he couldn't see me through the phone as tears welled in my eyes and spilled sideways down my cheek to soak into my pillowcase.

"Oh." He sounded unsure of what to say. "Good or bad memory?"

"I got stabbed through the shoulder, so, not great."

"At least getting stabbed is something you're used to."

I laughed but immediately regretted it.

"Sammy, are you crying?" His voice took on a new gentleness. I sniffed in spite of myself.

"No." I wiped the tears from my face. "Why are you up this early? You should still be asleep."

"Remi's house is weird. I don't sleep great here."

I pulled my comforter up over my face and hid there for a moment. I didn't know he was at Remi's house, though he'd mentioned he might spend part of the break there.

"Sammy? You still there?"

"Yeah." I untangled myself from the blanket. "Wes, I...I should go."

His sigh crackled through the phone line.

"You sure? We only just started talking and you didn't answer on Christmas so—"

"Wes!" I tried to keep my tone gentle but firm. "You were the one who told me you wanted you and Remi to work and I told you I believed you could make that happen, but calling other girls at six AM on News Year's Day might not help your chances."

"I—did Remi say something to you?"

"No!" I blushed at the blatant lie. "It's just common sense."

"Common sense is wanting to check in on my very good friend after she shows up on the news being saved by John Ratcliffe of all people!"

"He didn't save me!" I sat up in bed, as if that might help get my point across somehow.

"You watch the news coverage and tell me you wouldn't be worried if the roles were reversed."

"I don't have a single scratch on me," I insisted. "I'm fine!"

"Sure, no scratches, but you were stabbed by a Viking ghost."

I bristled.

"I don't know why I told you that part. It doesn't change anything."

Wesley fell silent and I could almost see him in my head, rubbing his temples in frustration.

"Sammy," he said carefully, "you told me because that's a lot for a person to deal with. I don't know why you insist on doing things alone, but I'm here for when you need me because you're my friend. I don't care if that makes me a bad boyfriend to Remi because I care about you. Which, by the way, we are *not* boyfriend and girlfriend yet."

"Okay, fine." I groaned. "I'm sorry."

"Don't apologize," Wes said. I clenched my jaw.

"Don't boss me around."

"Fine."

I could hear his smile. He was teasing me and I couldn't tell if it was annoying or not. I fell back into my pillows.

"So, John Ratcliffe, huh?" he said after a beat. I snorted.

"Like I said, he's a hack." I crumpled the edges of my blanket in my fist. "Winnie admitted it was all for show."

"Winnie?!"

I filled Wesley in on the details of the night, snuggling into my pillows as the sky outside began to lighten. I kept the phone on my pillow, talking into it with my hands tucked up under my head.

I yawned and Wesley replied with a stifled laugh.

"Are you going back to sleep?"

"Maybe."

"You can go back to bed. I'll call you again later."

I hesitated. I wanted Wesley to stay on the other line until we were back at school.

"Don't," I said softly. "You're at Remi's house. You should hang out with Remi. Be a good boyfriend."

"But I don't want to be a bad friend."

"You're not. You're a very good friend, but you can figure out how to be both. I'll see you next week for practice, okay?"

"Yeah. Okay. I'm glad you're safe."

"Me, too."

He said his goodbyes and I watched the screen, waiting for the line to cut, but it was several long, drawn out seconds before he finally hung up.

My screen went black and I closed my eyes to go back to sleep.

29

Leaks

Wesley continued to text throughout the day and Avery and Mom, now in possession of my new phone number, texted and called, as well. Mom threatened to come back to the island, but I insisted I was alright. She only made things more complicated and I was feeling especially weird about her after recovering memories of my biological mother.

I couldn't help but to feel a little guilty. Even though Alison had betrayed and abandoned me, thoughts of Solveig made me feel as if I was cheating on my adoptive mother. I didn't want to lose my fake memories as Alison's daughter, but at the same time, I wanted to know more about the woman with the blonde plait who wielded metal spits like weapons.

For the most part, though, I pretended my mental excursion to Middle Ages Iceland never happened until evening fell and thoughts of the enemy raider I'd sliced open would creep into the corners of my mind. If it got too quiet, I thought I could hear him gurgling for air, or Erika screaming Eydis' name.

I took to reading my chemistry textbook to drown out the thoughts, falling asleep with it open to a random chapter each night until, finally, at long last, Saturday arrived and I spent the hours after dinner carefully packing my things to return to campus the next day.

Two black journals fell from behind my textbooks and I glared at them. I hadn't yet updated my notebook dedicated to recording recovered memories and the second book was Dad's. I sighed and slid into the desk chair.

I flipped Dad's notebook to the first page, though, after the most recent memory, it was getting harder to not call him Vidar. The Samantha part of me still ached for her dad, but Eydis yearned for her brother.

"My name is Vic. That's been my name for the last few decades at least. Before that, it was Oliver. I don't remember what name came before that, but I know the first name I ever had was Vidar Havardsson.

"My mother used to joke that my name, my first one that is, was a good luck charm. She named me after a Norse god, one that was supposed to survive the apocalypse. She said it meant I'd outlive the rest of them. I don't think this was what she had in mind."

I breathed a shaky laugh. He wrote the same way he talked. Brusque but sensitive. I glanced at the pager, half-expecting a new message to flash across the tiny screen, but it stayed fixed on the daily countdown. Fifteen. I kept reading in a bid to forget it.

"Our village was having trouble with a neighboring settlement. They'd raided our outskirt farms several times and ultimately attacked us head on. We lost people, livestock, and food but when I left with the other men to retaliate, a boy showed up on our shore. If I'd been home that day, I could have sent him away, but it was my sister Eydis who found him on the beach."

I slammed the book shut with a quaking hand, remembering my first encounter with the boy Adrestus on the shore. Vidar blamed me, then, for what happened.

My stomach churned. Of course he did. I blamed me, too, but it still stung worse than a sword in my shoulder to see it written down. And he'd told Mom. No wonder she'd left me in an effort to keep Avery safe. She knew I'd invited trouble into my last home. Who was to say I wouldn't do it to my new one?

I flipped my own notebook open to a random page and slashed a line through the middle. At one end, I scribbled, "stabbed in the woods with the lapis". On the other, "I was born, probably".

I looked at my notes as I worked, piecing together my previous life but between being born and later stabbed, it still felt like so much was missing. Yet the few, meager memories I'd gotten back had already eroded away too much of Samantha. I wasn't sure how much more I could take before I forgot who I was completely.

I flipped through the pages, most of them filled with sketches of memories rather than written word. I always skipped the first page but now I let it lie open, looking at the pencil drawing of my family's dead bodies lying in a row.

Adrestus' voice echoed in my head, repeating the words he'd spoken when he'd captured me at the museum in October.

"Havard is dead, along with Erika and Gunhild and Knut. Hjordis is dead, as is Solveig. Even Sammy here was dead pretty recently."

The murder of my family already haunted me, but now that I remembered them when they were alive, it was torture.

"Samantha, are you packed yet?"

I jumped at the knock at my door and slammed the notebook shut.

"Yeah, almost," I croaked, then cleared my throat.

"We're leaving right after lunch tomorrow," Fleming said from the other side. "Just want to make sure you're ready when we do."

He was just as ready to get his apartment back to himself as Andersen and I were to leave it.

The doorknob wiggled and Fleming's face appeared.

"Everything okay?" Behind his new glasses, his eyes flitted to the notebooks on the desk.

"Yeah." I shoved them into my backpack. "Like I said, almost done packing."

He glanced nervously down the hall, checking for Andersen.

"Did you remember something new?"

I shook my head, zipping the pager into the backpack front pocket.

"Nope. I wasn't writing, just packing."

He opened the door further and shifted his weight from one foot to the other. He ran a hand through his hair, looking past me and out the window.

"I hope you had a good break."

I laughed. I couldn't help myself.

"Yeah, I really enjoyed the part where my crazy ex-roommate attacked me with her sister."

"I meant all the other parts."

I could see on his face that he knew it had been miserable.

"Oh, yeah. It was great."

Fleming drummed his fingers on the doorframe listlessly, still avoiding looking me in the eye.

"Just know this is your home, too, even if it wasn't much fun." He finally looked up but the intensity of his stare made me want to look away. "As long as I'm here, you have a home."

I tried to smile. It was a nice gesture, but probably just that. He knew the destruction I'd caused on my last two "homes" and he'd seen the damage I'd caused his plates in my fight with Andersen.

"Sure," I nodded.

Fleming looked like he might say something else, but must've decided against it. He nodded back, brushed invisible dirt off his shirt and disappeared back into the hall.

Even the weather seemed to celebrate the end of Winter Break. A rare blue sky reflected off the windowed skyscrapers as we drove back to campus after lunch the next day, making everything glitter bright and clean. I clutched Floundersen's fishbowl as we took a sharp turn onto campus and every part of me sighed in relief at the sight of the dorms and school hall.

My brief sense of respite soured, however, while setting my things back up on my bedroom desk. I could hear my name whispered in the hall along with "John Ratcliffe" and "Wavemaker". Of course they would've seen me on the news.

Naomi burst into the room, beaming. She dropped her bags in the doorway and leapt at me.

"We're back!" she sang.

"Don't get too excited." I hugged Naomi despite my warning. "We may be back but the city is supposed to burn down in fourteen days."

She moved her bags to her bed, frowning.

"Is that where the Doomsday Pager is already? Fourteen?"

I tossed her the pager and she inspected it with a grimace.

"Fleming's going to have us on so many patrols," she muttered. "Not that we've seen anything in months."

"Oh, no, you're allowed on patrols." I rolled my eyes. "You know what I'd do to get put on a mission?"

"Go back in time and not make stupid decisions that got you kicked off normal patrols in the first place?" Naomi flashed me a toothy smile and I threw my pillow at her, which she dodged effortlessly. "Your wrist looks better."

I flexed my fingers at her to show off my brace-free hand.

"I'm supposed to go see Everly to give back the braces and let him check and make sure everything is where it's supposed to be. If you're here, then he's gotta be back, too, right?"

Naomi was already grabbing her jacket and jingling the dorm keys.

"We can walk together," she insisted. "I have a captains' meeting I need to get to."

I did my best to ignore the less-than-subtle glances that followed me across campus. Naomi scowled at anyone who looked like they might try to talk to us about New Year's Eve and we made it through the back door to the school hall without being accosted. However, as we took the basement stairs, Naomi's scowl deepened.

"He's really mad," Naomi whispered.

"Who?" I asked, looking down the dingy hall.

"Fleming!" She took a deep breath, pausing at the door, and pushed through.

Fleming stood rigid with his back to the door. He whirled around at the sound of it opening, red in the face and nostrils flaring. Justin leaned against the call desk and he looked away, pulling a hand across his face as if to wipe away tears.

"What's wrong?" Naomi started forward, but stopped when her shoes splashed through a puddle that spread across the atrium floor.

"Everything's ruined." Everly spoke from the door to the Sickbay. Behind him, mattresses were ripped from bed frames and sliced open. Tonka lurked at Everly's ankles, his whiskers twitching. "The gym, the pool, the Sickbay."

"Call a meeting," Fleming growled at Naomi. She nodded and splashed across the atrium to join them at the call desk and log onto the computer. "What do you need, Samantha?"

I gulped and held out the ankle and wrist brace. His shoulders went slack and he bobbed his head towards the Sickbay.

"Who did this?" I tapped my toe in the water.

"We don't know," Fleming snapped.

Voices shouted in the hall behind me and I staggered out of the way as several of the boys from the team barreled in. Wesley came in last, pausing when he saw me. He pulled me into a hug before I could stop him and his bicep tensed against the back of my neck.

"Justin!" Marcus, who'd led the guys in, broke from the group to run to his friend's side. "Are you okay? Do we know who did it?"

I pushed Wesley away. His face was stark white and he looked around nervously.

"What's wrong with Justin?"

"The boys' dorm." Everest wrung his hands behind Wes and he scanned the atrium walls nervously. "Right in the lobby where everyone can see."

"What?" I demanded, looking between them.

"Someone put my name on the wall." Justin's voice rang out but I didn't understand what he meant. "I'm guessing you all saw."

"They're already cleaning it," Wesley insisted. "Not everyone will have seen it."

Justin straightened up and took a shuddering breath.

"Doesn't matter. The whole school will know soon."

"What did it say?" I asked again.

"It said 'Justin Pomeroy is an Apex. Don't let him touch you'." Justin looked at me from across the atrium and a muscle twitched in his neck, but he did his best to smile. "My secret's out, but the more important issue is who'll be next."

30

Countdown

Fleming stood with Everly among the upturned treadmills and scattered weights of the gym. Punching bags emptied their sand through ugly slash marks, which turned to mud in the water that seeped from under the locker room doors. The glass wall between the gym and the pool had been shattered and the pool water dyed red.

The team ignored our shoes slowly soaking as we stood rigid against one wall, waiting for Fleming.

He turned towards us, his face passive and unreadable. Naomi flinched next to me and I knew under Fleming's controlled exterior, he was seething.

"Is everybody here?" he thundered. "Good."

We shrank against the wall.

Everly stood back with his arms crossed, looking over us coolly while Fleming stalked across the floor to the massacred punching bags. He dealt a front kick to the nearest one and it swung to one side before pendulating back and forth, spilling sand across the tiles.

"Every bag," Fleming finally said, "every treadmill, even the showers. Ruined. The pool will need to be drained and refilled. The walls, repainted. If you think this looks bad, you should see the Sickbay. The entire supply of Serum has been stolen. Security footage, of course, is also missing."

Whispers and gasps rose from the crowd and my stomach found a way to knot itself more than it already was. Everly's glower deepened.

"In case you forgot over break, we lost funding from Adrian Schrader, meaning we'll only be able to replace about ten percent of what was ruined."

"Things can be replaced," Everly said, his voice laced with venom as he looked over us. I'd seen him exasperated many times before, but never angry. Now, dark, quiet ire soaked his every word. "The message in the boys' dorm, meanwhile, cannot be undone."

Fleming quit his pacing and took up the spot in the center of the room again, glaring at us all from over the frames of his glasses.

"We know someone fed Adrestus team member names. We assumed it was Trev Baker. We *fired* Baker. But Baker doesn't have access to this gym *or* the boys' dorm, unlike all of you."

Suppressed murmurs rippled down the line as the implications of Fleming's words washed over us. Fleming had to be wrong. No one here, not even Andersen, would tell the school about Justin.

Isabelle laughed and the sound put every nerve in the room on end. Fleming's eyes narrowed.

"That's ridiculous. No one here would do that." Isabelle dared to cross her arms back at Fleming.

"Someone did." Fleming raised an eyebrow.

"Probably the Beta!"

To my teammates' credit, several of them groaned in response to Skyler's theory. It wasn't surprising that he'd suggest I'd made the mess, but my insides boiled all the same.

"Yes," I jeered, leaning forward to get a better look at Skyler where he stood down the line, "because out of everyone here, as the one without superpowers I'm definitely the best equipped to throw heavy equipment around."

"So you're finally admitting you're out of your league?"

I stepped away from the wall to point at Skyler. He stood with Andersen near the far end of the group and glowered back at me under shaggy blond hair that had become unruly over Winter Break.

"I'm sorry, of the two of us, who got first place in their competition a couple weeks ago and who got last?"

Skyler's face burned bright red as a couple of upperclassmen snickered.

"Which of us stabbed themselves and then had to be rescued by John Ratcliffe on live T.V?"

I stepped forward as if to charge Skyler but Naomi grabbed my wrist to pull me back.

"That's enough!" Fleming bellowed. I glared at him, still standing away from the wall. After living with Fleming for two weeks, I wasn't scared of him. "The rest of the afternoon will be dedicated to cleaning the gym as best we can. In the meantime, I'll be talking to *everyone* to figure out when each of you arrived back on campus and where you've been since."

He marched forward and the crowd split to give him a path through the exit. Everly shouted cleaning assignments and we scrambled to get to work cleaning sand, glass, and metal from the floor.

If the impromptu cleaning party had an upside, it was that I got to hide from the rest of the school until evening. Most of my teammates had been kind enough not to mention my "rescue" by John Ratcliffe, though I still caught snippets of conversation around the gym as they worried about Wavemaker and what his new powers might mean for the Epsilon Initiative and New Delos.

I could handle whispers, though. Dinner, meanwhile, was a whole new monster. Justin's secret spread fast and every Apex on the team kept their heads down over their food trays, fearing their names would be posted next. Anthony's silverware shook in his hand as Naomi and I described the state of the gym to him over dinner.

"But what does this mean for everyone else?" he balked. Over his shoulder, I made eye contact with Wes, who ate across the cafeteria with Remi. I quickly looked down at my food.

"We don't know," Naomi admitted. "Good news is, just because the lobby wall *says* Justin is an Apex, doesn't mean he is. He won't get the same treatment as Andersen, either, because he doesn't have Jamie actively campaigning against his existence."

Anthony seemed to relax, but his fork continued to quake through dinner. Whoever was sabotaging the team would know about Anthony's new powers, after all. He was just as liable as anyone else to be accused.

By school's start the next morning, Wavemaker and I were back in the spotlight. The rumors about Justin were just rumors, and he had the benefit of being generally well-liked. Meanwhile, everyone had seen John Ratcliffe swoop to my rescue on the news.

"Ignore them," Naomi said as a group of boys I didn't know pointed at me from down the hall.

"How?" I mumbled. "It's the whole school. I can't just pretend they're all invisible."

"Just pretend *most* of them are invisible." Wesley popped between us, having finally freed himself of Remi, whose first class was on a different floor. "You don't have to ignore Naomi, me, or Anthony."

I bit my lip and tried to smile at the same time. Naomi snorted at the face it made.

Ignoring Wesley over break had been hard enough. Now I had to navigate classes and training with him without setting Remi on a warpath. That on top of the looming Doomsday threat, the mystery saboteur, and my Spanish final retake later that day, and I already felt like screaming.

"Where *is* Anthony, though?" Naomi asked. Wesley sighed.

"He hasn't been able to stop making wind tunnels since yesterday. The sabotage really freaked him out. He has this whole theory about it somehow being his fault and if he hadn't gotten himself kidnapped back in September, maybe none of this would be happening."

"That's ridiculous." I slid into my seat in the front of Fleming's class. "That makes it more my fault because I should've stopped him from getting kidnapped."

"Yes, let's sit around and postulate about whose fault this all really is," Naomi snapped. "That'll solve everything."

She took the seat I'd left between Wesley and me just as something soft hit the back of my shoulder. A wadded up paper fell to the ground. Madison waggled her fingers at me in an insincere greeting.

"Hey, Samantha," she hissed, sounding like she was trying to whisper, but making sure she was loud enough for everyone to hear her. "What was it like being the first person saved by Wavebreaker?"

"Wavemaker," Jamie corrected her out of the corner of her mouth.

"Really?" Madison asked. "Wavebreaker sounds better."

"Ah, well," I smiled as insincerely as Madison had waved, "maybe it's not too late for a rebrand?"

Jamie flushed pink and her fake nails scraped against her desk as she balled her hands into fists. She managed an overly-sweet smile and shrugged.

"Bet you feel silly now. You were against the Epsilon Initiative before, weren't you? Now that one of them's saved you, your tune is sure to have changed."

I laughed and threw Madison's crumpled paper back at them.

"The same way you warmed up to real Apex after Andersen saved *you?*"

"That was different!" she snarled.

"Right," I nodded. "Different because, unlike you, I was never in any real danger since the whole thing was a set-up to make your dad look good."

"You're a liar!" Jamie stood up with her hands on her desk and her curls bouncing around her face. "My dad's a hero and you're an ungrateful Apex sympathizer!"

I folded my arms over the back of my chair and grinned, triumphant in finally making Jamie lose her cool.

"He's a hack and you're a hypocrite."

Deep red blossomed in her cheeks and she opened her mouth for another retort but froze and sat down as Fleming slouched through the door. His withering glare would have been enough to shut anyone up, with hard eyes laden with heavy, sleep deprived bags. He turned his stare on me and his mouth tightened.

"Face forward, please." His command was curt and I spun back towards the front reluctantly. It was just my luck that when I'd finally had Jamie on the defense, Fleming would cut in and ruin it. "Samantha, leave your classmate alone."

Naomi put a warning hand on my knee as I felt my temper flare. I bit my tongue and slid down in my seat.

"Quick announcement before we begin the new semester." Fleming threw his bag down at the desk and turned towards the class. He couldn't have looked more different than the welcoming, happy teacher he'd been on the first day of school than he did now. "Andersen has transferred into a different history class for reasons I'm sure we're all familiar with by now."

A chorus of whispers went up but was quickly doused by Fleming's sordid face.

"Even though he's not in this class anymore, if I hear anyone so much as whisper about the rumors surrounding him or Justin Pom—"

"They aren't rumors," Jamie snipped. "There's a video online."

"Detention. If I so much as hear a whisper, then you'll receive detention. And that, Jamie, is why you should never interrupt, because now your Saturday belongs to me."

As much as I wanted to laugh, I didn't dare. Fleming was clearly still worked up about the sabotage, and I wasn't going to give him a reason to take that out on me.

Maybe it had been Fleming's attitude or Jamie's harassment, but the rest of the day felt sour. I finished my Spanish Final retake in Study Hall, carefully looking it over to make sure I'd used the correct language this time.

While I'd been thrilled to be back at school, as the week wore on, I started to miss the quiet loneliness of my room in Fleming's apartment. On Tuesday, we walked into the cafeteria to the smell of fresh paint and by the end of the day, every student had heard the rumor that Jen's name had been splashed upon the cafeteria wall overnight with the word "Apex".

By Thursday, Jessa, Marcus, and Carmen joined her and Justin, their names appearing in a girls' bathroom, the library, and even painted onto the lawn.

I wish I had the bandwidth to worry about them, but many students had disregarded the rumors. Unlike Andersen, none of them made a show of their powers in the halls so they didn't receive the same level of hate. Not that they were having a *great* time, either, but whatever energy I had left to worry with was put into Wesley, Anthony, and Naomi.

Anthony was convinced his name would be next, even though he wasn't on the team, and his bouts of random gales had come back. Naomi, meanwhile, had been awkward since admitting she wanted to remove her Apex powers at New Year's Eve. She only pressed me about who Erika was a couple times before dropping it. I insisted I'd been confused and had said the name Erika in mistake, but we both knew I was lying.

And then there was Wesley. There wasn't anyone I wanted the comfort of more, and as tempted as I was to go back on my promise to

Remi, every time I looked at him, I thought of Eydis kissing Dres and my shame at the memory kept me in check. It took him a couple days of rejected dinner invites and ignored texts, but he stopped trying by the end of the week and I stopped looking for him and Remi sitting together in the cafeteria.

Even training, which had once been my favorite way to escape, had become tense and stressful. Without our usual equipment, Fleming found new ways to push us after school. If anyone ended up with a black eye, they had to deal with it. Everly and Dr. Weaver were rebuilding the Serum stock but it was slow going. Even with her healing ability, Dr. Weaver could only donate so much of her plasma a day.

The new whiteboard in the atrium was the most stressful change of all. Part way through the week, Fleming handed me a bag of red markers with the instructions to post the countdown number each day. Friday after school, I erased the previous day's number and updated it to a large, red "10". A small crowd gathered behind me to watch.

"Almost to single digits," Marcus grunted.

"Yeah, that's how numbers work." I could hear the eye-roll in Isabelle's voice. "You're a captain, Marcus. Are we any closer to figuring this out?"

"That's hard to say. There's several different factors to take into account and—"

"No," Justin interrupted. "We aren't any closer. At this point, it might be best just to brace for whatever's coming."

I tried to slip away from the front of the crowd but paused when I heard Isabelle ask:

"And can you tell us if Fleming knows who wrecked the place?"

"He's been a grump all week," Desirae said. "If he knew, you'd think he'd lighten up a bit."

"Unless the answer only made him angrier."

I turned to see half the students looking at me and my grip on the marker tightened.

"You guys know it wasn't me, right?"

Isabelle nodded but a few of the other upperclassmen exchanged dubious looks.

"You're newer," one of them, a junior named Harvey, shrugged. "We haven't known you as long so we trust you less."

"And because I'm a Beta?" I spat. "Fleming's a Beta, too."

"Yeah, but we *know* Fleming!"

"And we know Sammy!" Isabelle whirled to face her fellow upperclassmen. "She saved Anthony. She figured out who Adrestus was."

"Which is also kind of suspicious," Harvey mumbled, but he didn't meet Isabelle's eyes.

"Great, Harvey." I flicked the marker at him and he let it bounce off his chest onto the ground. "You update the whiteboard for the next ten days since apparently I can't be trusted."

I stomped towards the locker rooms, leaving the upperclassmen to sheepishly shuffle their feet, but stopped when I heard my name called.

"Samantha." Fleming stood in the main doorway. "My office after practice."

The upperclassmen scattered with their heads down. Only Isabelle looked my way. She rolled her eyes.

"Ignore them. They're all idiots."

"Can't ignore Fleming, can I?"

"No," she shrugged, "but he's an idiot, too."

If there was ever a time I needed to take anger out on punching bags, this was it. Unfortunately, they still hadn't been replaced and I was left to fume over push-ups and lunges for two hours while silently daring Fleming to yell at me for throwing the marker at Harvey.

After showering and defiantly marching from the locker rooms to Fleming's office, prepared for a verbal showdown, Fleming called me in before I could even knock. He'd been angry all week, in both class and training, but now, his voice weighed with fatigue.

I tried to hold onto my anger as I pushed into his office. He might still scold me for flinging the marker. His glasses hung from his shirt collar and an uneaten sack lunch sat next to his computer. He gave me an ashen smile and did his best to straighten up at his computer.

"You handled yourself well before practice." His eyebrows pinched together despite his attempt at smiling, something he seemed to have forgotten how to do in the last week. "I would've thrown more than a marker if it had been me."

I hunched my shoulders in embarrassment at his unexpectedly kind words.

"Is that why I'm here?" I sat down in the chair opposite him.

He wavered and sighed, giving up his forced cheer.

"No. We aren't able to supply you with a training weapon because of the lost funding."

"Weapon?"

"The one you got a permit for?"

It took a half-second to remember.

"Oh, right! The sword."

"Right," Fleming said slowly. "We got as far as half a design when Schrader pulled the money. I tried to find room in the budget but it was either your electrical sword or the medical supplies that got ruined in the Sickbay."

"It was electrical?" My heart sank. An electrical sword sounded cool, though maybe it was for the better considering Baker's premonition about my death by electrocution.

"As soon as we have the money, I promise, we'll get your sword."

"It's alright." I tried to disappear into the threadbare chair, still not sure how to receive Fleming's kindness. "I mostly wanted to fight in the weapons competition and I did that already."

He nodded, but it was as if invisible weights hung from his chin, making the movement slow and labored.

"Still. You worked hard for it. It's not fair recent setbacks should delay what you've earned."

I had nothing to say. I knew I'd worked hard, but I wasn't convinced I'd worked hard enough. Dad was still missing. Names were still being leaked. Fleming studied me for a few moments more and the skin around his eyes wrinkled in an expression that was impossible to read.

"We're going to get Vic back," he said. I swallowed, feeling the space behind my eyes itch and tingle.

"I know," I lied. We sat in silence but the way he stared told me he feared what I'd been scared of for the last month and half.

Whatever Adrestus had in store for New Delos in ten days, it'd be near impossible to get my dad back after it came to pass.

I left Fleming's office stewing in a mixture of regret for my lost electric sword, apprehension for the coming fight, and comfort from Fleming's unexpected kindness.

I watched the floor tiles as I walked down the hall and nearly ran into Remi as she stomped out of the side door that led to the gym. She glared at me and I thought she might chew me out for not watching where I was going. I took several steps back, holding onto my backpack straps.

"Did you just come from there?" She looked at Fleming's office door, her face slack.

"Yes?" I wondered if she was about to add Fleming to the list of people she didn't want me talking to.

Her face contorted and, to my absolute horror, she burst into tears.

"It's okay!" I sputtered. "I mean, I'm sorry."

She leaned against the wall and slid to the floor, drawing her knees up to her face. I looked back at Fleming's office, as if there might be a sign there explaining what I'd done to upset her.

She cried on the floor, holding her phone in both hands and tapping it listlessly against her bowed head. I cleared my throat and knelt down, feeling very much like an awkward parent at a park trying to comfort someone else's kid.

"It was just a meeting about my weapons permit," I mumbled. "Good news, I don't think he thinks you, me, or Erik were the ones who trashed the place. I know some of the upperclassmen might think so—"

She raised her head to glower at me with bloodshot eyes. Clumps of dark blonde hair hung limp in her face.

"I just got off the phone with Wesley," she said. My stomach tightened.

"Is he okay?"

"Probably not considering I yelled at him."

I looked up and down the hall for an escape. I'd already cut back on my interactions with Wesley so much. If she asked me to cut him out any further, I'd have to rearrange my class schedule.

"I thought he was with you," Remi sniffed, disappearing back behind her knees. "He said he couldn't do dinner because he needed to study first and then I told him that he was lying so he could hang out with you. But you were in *there*!"

She gestured towards Fleming's office and her sobs renewed. I slipped my backpack off and lowered myself next to her on the floor. My legs were stiff from crouching and I winced as I stretched them out.

"So call him back and apologize." I hated the guilt that festered in my gut. I knew it wasn't my fault this girl was crying, so why did it feel like it was?

"I can't do that!" She looked up at me with wide, watery eyes. "I'm still mad at him!"

"Why? If he's actually studying and not sneaking off with me, what is there to be mad at?"

"Because I know he *wishes* he was hanging out with you!"

I tilted my head back, letting it tap against the wall. I had no obligation to Remi. I could stand up and walk away and leave her crying in the hall.

"But he *chose* you."

"And now he probably hates me!" she wailed. I glanced back at Fleming's office, afraid he might come out and see what was happening.

"Wesley doesn't hate anyone," I sighed.

"Am I a bad girlfriend?" Remi hiccuped. I recoiled from her big eyes that begged me to answer.

"No," I insisted. "You seem to care a lot, and that's a good thing."

She snorted, a clump of hair billowing up in front of her face.

"I like him, he likes me. We're both on Apex Team this time. It's supposed to be different!"

"Then maybe you guys are just meant to be friends?"

Her eyes hardened and I bit my lip.

"You'd like that, wouldn't you?"

I scowled and stood up, swinging my backpack over my shoulder.

"I would *like* to see you both happy but ever since you guys got back together, neither of you seems like you're actually enjoying yourselves."

I marched away before she could see on my face that she had been right.

31

Northshore Park

As the Doomsday Pager dropped into single digits over the weekend, Fleming boosted scouting trips more than ever. I was itching to get back in my uniform to take to the streets, knowing each day ate away at my chances to find Dad. Vidar? Whatever.

However, Fleming still had me benched indefinitely ever since going rogue in the Fall and when I begged to be put on a single mission, desperate for a way to help, he sent me to Everly to help do Sickbay laundry.

I found a small amount of relief at the fact that my visions of Eydis had subsided since New Year's and I didn't dare open Vidar's journal in fear of triggering more. The dead man on the floor of my family's dwelling still haunted me at night.

Fleming canceled Tuesday training all together, with so many students slated to patrol. I would've loved to go to the gym anyway and run away from my problems on the treadmill, but with my first chemistry quiz looming at the end of the week, I did the responsible thing and retired to my dorm room desk after class to study.

Unfortunately, the new unit made little to no sense. I looked over Naomi's class notes she'd lent me, but my head bobbed closer and closer to the page until I set my forehead down on the cool desk and closed my eyes. It wasn't fair that it took me what felt like hours to fall asleep at night but when I was trying to do something important, it came easily.

A shrill beep jolted me awake and I pushed myself away from my desk so violently that I toppled backwards out of my chair.

I popped up on my knees to stare across my desk at the banner of text that scrolled across the tiny screen of the Doomsday Pager. I froze, drinking in the words, rereading the short message to make sure I wasn't seeing things.

Northshore Park 2300. Come alone.

I staggered to my feet and cupped the pager in trembling hands. It was Dad. It had to be. He'd escaped somehow and now he wanted me to come to him.

But I'd been tricked before. Why wouldn't he have reached out before now? How did he know I had the pager and not Fleming or Dr. Weaver?

No one could have sent that Christmas message other than him, though. I needed to trust it was him on the other end, the same way he was obviously trusting it was me receiving his messages.

I hammered "Northshore Park" into my maps app and felt my chest constrict. The park spread along the northeastern-most point of the island, far from campus but less than a fifteen minute walk from Dad and Mom's townhouse.

I couldn't *not* go. I was going to see my dad tonight. I was going to see Vidar.

If I started the evening off-campus, no one would notice that I hadn't come back. Naomi would be busy with call-duty and wouldn't know the dorm room was empty. I checked the scouting schedule, dully noting

Wesley wasn't on it, but we'd barely spoken in the last week anyway. He wouldn't notice my absence. Otherwise, all assignments for the night were far from Northshore Park. Unless university students were patrolling that part of the island, I wouldn't have to worry about any members of Apex Team lurking in the shadows. I only had to get through dinner with Anthony without raising suspicion.

"You going to a funeral?" Anthony asked over cafeteria lasagna. With Wesley off with Remi and Naomi already reporting to the basement, it was just the two of us.

I looked down at my dark attire.

"I need to do laundry," I covered. "I only had black clothes left."

We piled our dishes together to take them to the dish pit. Once outside, Anthony turned towards the dorms.

"You coming?"

"Nah," I shook my head. "I'm in the mood for frozen yogurt."

"Ew, why? It's thirty degrees out." He crossed his arms at me.

I shrugged.

"Haven't had any in a while and I don't feel like going back to the dorm and listening to Jamie squawk about the Epsilon Initiative and her dad anymore."

"So, you're getting frozen yogurt alone in freezing weather?"

"Yeah, why not?"

"I can come with you, if you like."

I frowned. Anthony wasn't big on frozen yogurt. My plan had hinged on that fact.

"I'll be alright. I know it's not your favorite."

He stood still as he surveyed me and I picked at a hangnail, hoping he couldn't see through my ruse.

"Where are you actually going?"

"Froyo!" I said, too aggressively. He raised an eyebrow at me and I scowled. "Fine. I'm going to a park to meet my dad."

My words fell into mumbles as I finished the sentence, but Anthony's hair fluttered in a tiny wind.

"But Adrestus has your dad."

I stepped closer, so we wouldn't be overheard.

"Yeah, but look at this." I pulled the Doomsday Pager out of my pocket. Even though Anthony hung around the team, he wasn't a member so he didn't know about the secret countdown. Dad's message was still displayed on the screen. "It's him and I'm going to meet him."

"Sammy..."

I shoved the pager back in my pocket and backed away.

"No. No 'Sammy'," I snapped. "I *know* it's him. I'm going to get froyo to kill time and then head to the park and you can't stop me. And *don't* tell Naomi."

Anthony sighed but smiled and began drifting towards the dorms.

"Suit yourself. Stay safe, alright? And enjoy your Ice Cream Lite."

I snorted and turned away.

"And just know that you're crazy!" Anthony called after me. I waved him off.

I had four hours until I needed to be at the park. The froyo shop would close in just under one hour, leaving me over three to travel across the island. I'd used the busses before, but with so much extra time, why not take the long way and see if I couldn't figure anything out about the impending Doomsday?

Was I asking for trouble? Maybe. So what?

The frozen yogurt shop was empty save a lone employee scrolling on her phone at the register. I went through the line-up of flavors and toppings before settling into a corner table to plot my path from campus to the park. I'd only been there a few minutes when a "Low Battery" warning popped up on my screen. I hadn't charged my phone since the night before.

"That's not ideal," I mumbled.

"What's not ideal?"

I dropped my spoon and buried my forehead in my hands. Chair legs scraped linoleum next to me as Wesley took a seat. I hadn't noticed him walk in, but he'd grabbed himself a heaping bowl of mango yogurt while I'd been busy draining my phone's battery.

"Nothing." I exited out of the map on my screen. "What are you doing here?"

"Eating Froyo."

"In thirty degree weather?" I asked dubiously, parroting what Anthony had asked me. A sly smile spread across his face and he took a smug scoop of yogurt.

"That's what you're doing, isn't it?"

I scowled and shoved my bowl towards him.

"Debatably, I'm eating gummy worms with a side of ice cream substitute."

"Are gummy worms good with marshmallow sauce or...?"

I grabbed my bowl back.

"It tastes fine, thanks."

"It's just not a combination I would've come up with."

"Because you lack imagination."

He bit his lip, as if trying to keep from grinning.

"What are we *actually* doing here?"

I bristled. He couldn't read my emotions like Naomi, but I still had to be careful near him. He was annoyingly perceptive.

"Anthony sent you, didn't he?"

Wesley shrugged, stirring his yogurt distractedly.

"He might've asked if I would check on you but didn't say much else."

"Great," I stabbed my spoon into my bowl. "You can make sure I don't choke on a gummy worm."

"If you really were craving frozen yogurt, why did you bring the Doomsday Pager with you?"

"I didn't—"

"It's got this distinctive high-pitched whirring sound," he explained. "Most electronics do and it's in your jacket pocket."

I glanced at the shop employee as if she might be of help but she'd disappeared into the back room.

"I'm taking care of it," I grumbled.

"Taking care of what?" There was an edge of warning to Wesley's voice that rubbed me the wrong way.

I leaned back in my seat, trying to read his face, but he stared back at me as he took stoic bites of frozen yogurt.

"It's personal."

"Anything with Adrestus is personal when you're involved."

"That doesn't mean it has to be Adrestus related."

"Is it?" He sucked a bit of yogurt off his spoon.

I shrugged.

"Don't know yet. You can't stop me, though."

"I wasn't going to."

"Then why are you here?"

"To help." He tugged on his sweatshirt. "I wore black, too, and left my glasses at home."

The message said to come alone. What if Dad didn't show if I brought someone? He wasn't Wesley's biggest fan to begin with, but it wouldn't hurt to take Wesley along if there was trouble on the way. I could make him hide or hang back nearby. Dad wouldn't know he was there.

I exhaled.

"I appreciate it, but I don't know. I'll be out late and with Fleming running triple scouting missions every night, we should keep as many team members well-rested as possible."

His green eyes narrowed at me and he dropped his spoon in his bowl.

"You've been avoiding me," he finally said. My cheeks burned.

"No, I've been busy." Busy avoiding Wesley.

"So this isn't you trying to avoid me more?"

"There's just something I need to check out. It'll be fine. I'll text you updates if it makes you feel better."

"Oh, yeah?" He raised his eyebrows at my phone. "How? Your battery just died."

I tapped on my phone but it didn't respond. Several more increasingly violent jabs proved Wesley correct.

"Alright, fine, no texts." I crossed my arms. "You'll just have to trust me enough to wait until breakfast."

"Sammy."

"Don't 'Sammy' me, Wesley Isaacs!" I shook my spoon at him and accidentally splattered his black hoodie with melted froyo and marshmallow sauce. "Sorry."

"We close in fifteen minutes." The employee stuck her head out of the back room at us.

Wesley stood up and drained the rest of his melted froyo into his mouth. He drew the back of his hands across his lips, looking down at me. "Do what you want, Sammy. I know I can't stop you. I'm sorry we aren't as close anymore, but please, try to be safe."

He stalked out of the shop, throwing his bowl away without looking back.

My face burned. I wanted him to come. Northshore Park was far and the company would've been both welcomed and reassuring, but Dad's instructions said to come alone.

I threw back the last of my gummy worms and followed Wesley out, but he'd made quick work in disappearing back to campus. I hugged my sweater tight around my shoulders. Hopefully the long walk would warm me up.

I'd only made it a few blocks into the darkened city when a shrill beep made me jump. I jammed my hand in my pocket and withdrew the pager, rushing to a circle of light emitted by a flickering streetlamp to better read the message.

I'll be on the private boat dock.

The fact that Dad knew I was on my way emboldened me and I quickened my pace through the streets. I'd done enough drills with Remi and Erik to know how to get anywhere in New Delos by foot and an empty calm settled in my stomach.

I was going to see Dad. Every step brought me closer to him. Trev Baker's warning echoed in the back of my head but I assured myself it would be fine. Dad wouldn't ask to meet if it was dangerous.

About a half hour into my journey, I got the distinct sense that I wasn't the only one making my way to Northshore Park, but every time I spun around, the streets and sidewalks were as empty as they were ahead of me.

I flipped my hood up over my head, as if that might make it feel less like someone was watching the back of my neck. A glass-paned building stood across the street and I turned just enough to catch my dark reflection bouncing off the windows. My hands turned sweaty and my throat closed up when I saw a second reflection following about fifteen paces behind mine.

I took off running without warning and the thundering of a second pair of feet behind me was unmistakable.

Maybe this *had* been reckless. I evened my breathing and took a sharp turn down an alley. Whoever was following me hesitated and I chanced a look back. The silhouette of a head and shoulders peered around the corner, then pulled back out of sight.

I pried the lid off a trashcan.

"I know you're there," I shouted, gripping the lid. "How about you face me instead of hiding from a teenage girl?"

A heavy second passed and I wondered if I'd scared them off, but then, my stalker stepped out from around the corner. I didn't give him another moment.

I hurled the lid down the alley and he shouted in surprise, throwing his hands up to defend himself from the oncoming plastic disc. While he was focused on blocking the lid, I charged.

I caught him off guard, kicking his legs out from under him and spinning him to the pavement. I pinned him there, crouched over his body with a foot against his chest.

"What the hell, Sammy?" Wesley croaked.

"Wes!" I stumbled off him. "You followed me!"

"Yeah, I thought you knew that when you yelled at me to come out!"

"I thought you were a bad guy!" The roaring in my ears subsided and my fingers shook as my adrenaline looked for a place to go. Wesley sat up, rubbing the back of his head.

"You shouldn't be allowed to train with Naomi anymore. That hurt."

"Remi stole my old sparring partner, so it is what it is."

I walked back out onto the sidewalk, leaving him in the alley.

"Hey, wait!"

"Go home, Wesley."

"No." He caught up and reached for my hand, but I pulled away. "I won't try to stop you from whatever it is you're doing, but I can't sleep knowing you're out here alone. Especially since last time..."

"Last time what?"

"Last time you ran off without telling anyone you almost died! You *should* have died!"

"But I found my dad that night, which was what I'd set out to do!"

"Is that what you're doing tonight, too?"

I stopped and jammed my hands in my pockets. I felt the pager there. Dad was calling me to him. I knew he was.

"I think so," I admitted quietly. I pulled the pager out. The screen still displayed the message. "There was a message on Christmas, too. I-I think it was him. It sounded like him."

Wesley took the pager and looked at the message.

"But this is just like last time," he said. "You thought it was Amanda but it was just Adrestus using her phone."

"It's different." I snatched the pager back and continued my walk.

"I'll go back if you really want me to, but please—"

"It's fine," I tried to grumble, but it was hard. I *did* want him there.

"Wait, really?"

"It's too late now, we're halfway to the park."

Wesley fell into step next to me. I could feel him looking at me but I frowned at the sidewalk ahead of us.

"If your dad's escaped Adrestus, why call you to meet him across the island?"

"The park is near his townhouse. He probably can't go far because he's in hiding."

"Then why not just call you to the house instead of making you go to a park?"

"Because what if I'm followed?" I snapped. "He needs me to meet him away from his hiding spot so he can continue hiding there."

"Yeah, imagine if you were followed," Wesley said sarcastically. I threw an elbow his direction but he side-stepped it. "Seriously, Sammy, it feels off to me."

"That's because he's not your dad."

"He's not really yours, either. I want it to be him, too, but if it's not —"

"It will be."

The only sound for a while was our sneakers on the pavement and the wind whispering between alleyways. It felt good to be in Wesley's company again.

"What's Remi up to tonight?" I asked. If she found out about this escapade, she couldn't be mad if I spent the spare moments getting Wesley to talk her up.

"I don't know," Wesley shrugged and I frowned.

"But she's your girlfriend."

"Not yet, she isn't!" he said with sudden defensiveness. "We're still taking it slow, but..."

He kicked at a pebble and it went skittering down the sidewalk.

"But what? You guys spent Winter Break together. Doesn't that make her your girlfriend?"

"I don't think it's what I want."

"Does she know that?" Something like dormant hunger rumbled in my stomach but I ignored it.

"I don't think it's what she wants, either! I just don't know if she's realized it yet."

I grunted and Wes had the nerve to laugh.

"That doesn't make sense." I zipped my jacket so the zipper came all the way up to my chin. "You either want something or you don't. I don't get what's to realize."

A stupid half-smile played across his face and the way the street lights caught his eyes made them glint mischievously.

"What?"

"Nothing." He shook his head. He'd left his glasses at home and his hair fell into his eyes. "You're funny. That's all."

I didn't get what was so funny. I wanted to ask if Remi wasn't what he wanted, then what *did* he want? I bit my tongue. I didn't want to know the answer. Either he didn't feel the way I did, or he *did* and I would have to explain *my* ex situation.

"What's our plan when we get to the park?" Wesley asked after another ten minutes of walking in silence.

"The message said to come alone and we both know how Dad feels about Apex," I said. "You'll have to hang back, but you should be able to listen in and keep watch for trouble while I go to the boat dock."

"Boat dock?" Wesley wrinkled his nose. "That's suspicious. Could be a trap to get you on a boat and kidnap you."

"Adrestus doesn't care about kidnapping me anymore." I rolled my eyes. "Plus, I already told you. It's not Adrestus."

"Sure," he said, though he was starting to look uneasy. My own stomach was doing backflips for different reasons. I was going to see *Dad*.

The path we took to get to Northshore Park led us past the street my family's townhouse lived on. I did my best to pretend it wasn't there, but couldn't help to send a furtive look up the hill to the cul-de-sac where it sat.

A wooded path separated the neighborhood from the park and we wound our way through the transplanted trees of the manmade mini-forest. We both jumped when a dry twig snapped underfoot, then laughed awkwardly to shrug off our jitters.

The trees thinned to reveal a park sitting on a gentle hill that sloped towards the water. A jungle gym stood out against the dark backdrop of the bay and a well maintained lawn divided the sidewalks from boat docks. Several of the moored boats could've easily fit the entire training gym on their massive decks.

We walked to the jungle gym, eying the dock gate. Wesley sat back in a swing and rocked back and forth on his feet. He caught my eye and I smiled nervously.

"He hasn't seen me since the night I found out about Eydis," I shrugged, not sure why I was telling Wesley this. "What if things are weird?"

Wesley lolled his head to one side as he looked up at me. His face softened, but I couldn't help but to feel he was looking at me with pity.

"It won't be. He's still your dad, right? At least, that's still what you call him."

I exhaled heavily through my nose and nodded.

"Right."

"And maybe he can give us a ride back to campus? It's freezing out."

I straightened my jacket and turned to walk down the hill. The grass was slick with frost and I ignored Wesley laughing to himself as he watched me navigate the slippery slope.

As I got closer to the boat docks, my heart drummed harder against my sternum. Despite the icy air rolling in off the water, my palms became sticky with sweat.

Wesley's phone had said we had five minutes until eleven, when Dad said he'd meet.

Five minutes until I saw Dad again.

Until I saw Vidar.

Both the Samantha and Eydis parts of me buzzed with excitement.

A broken lock hung off the dock gate. It creaked eerily as I pulled it open and slipped through, taking care not to look back at Wesley.

The private dock sprawled out across the bay in a maze of yachts that groaned in the water. They moved and shifted as wind blew through their white bows and I hugged my arms, looking around timidly.

"Dad?" I dared to whisper, trying to sound braver than I felt. My heart caught at the sound of footsteps carefully treading over wooden planks, getting closer.

"Sammy, wait!"

I jumped at Wesley's sudden bark. He ran up behind me, shoulders tense and fists balled.

"You were supposed to hang back!"

"It's not your dad." He looked past me, towards the sound of the footsteps.

"No, I'm not."

My knees went weak with disappointment at the sound of the woman's voice and I stumbled back to join Wesley as she stepped out from around a corner. She wasn't Adrestus' most formidable follower and if she was alone, we'd easily be able to take her, but if others lay in wait nearby, we'd have trouble.

I'd last seen her at the museum. Justin had frozen her in the hall when we'd made our escape. Now, her orange hair was swept up into a bun that the island wind hadn't been merciful to. Boots clung to her long calves, all the way up to her knees, where they met with a peacoat. She wasn't dressed for a fight, but I knew that wouldn't let us off the hook.

She dug into her pocket with a leather-gloved hand and pulled out a pager.

"Vidar couldn't make it," Esther said, her face deadly serious, "but he sends his regards."

32

Duel on the Dock

Where's my dad?" I demanded. While Esther had never attacked me head on, she'd been there every time Adrestus had tried to kidnap me or ruin my life, like when she'd stood by and watched as he'd cut open my neck in search of his Lapis.

"I didn't do anything to Vi." Her face registered genuine shock and she threw up her hands in a show of peace. "He's safe, right where he wants to be."

The dock beneath me swayed. Dad was safe.

"Where is he?"

The woman frowned and put her hands in her pockets.

"Adrestus has him. You know that."

"But *where?*" I stepped towards her and my jacket tightened as Wesley tried to tug me back. The woman shook her head. She looked sorry for me.

"Like I said, he's where he wants to be. You know Vi. If he wanted to escape, he would've already."

I fought a surge of angry panic at the idea of my dad being *willingly* separated from his family. Wes stepped forward. He tried to nudge me behind him, but I didn't let him.

"It's Esther, right?" he asked.

I narrowed my eyes at her and watched her neck pulse as she swallowed.

"Yes." Her voice was careful now. She seemed to trust Wesley less. "I know you have no reason to trust me—"

I snorted and she pushed a coil of red hair back behind her ear.

"Why did you bring us here?" Wesley asked.

"I didn't. I asked *her* to come, not you."

"Fine. I'm here." I spread my arms out. "Where's my dad?"

"You know Vidar's not your dad."

I was sick of hearing those words.

"Where is he?"

"The city is going to burn," Esther said, her voice hollow, ignoring my questions. "But you already know that. And thanks to me, you should know it's due to happen on Monday."

She nodded at my jacket pocket, where the pager's outline pressed against the fabric.

I'd been sure it was Dad's pager, even if the voice of whoever had slipped it into my pocket had been feminine. I'd been sure it would be Dad on the docks tonight. Not Esther. Not one of Adrestus' cronies. I exhaled sharply, remembering Esther's ability to sense people's presences. It wouldn't have mattered that I was invisible with Olivia. She would've known we were there.

"Hephestae already warned us the city was in danger." I tried to refocus.

"We know. She escaped briefly, back in December. Shorted the neck implant that Mira uses to control her. She felt it booting up again and with the time she had left, burned that warning into the building side, where you found it."

My stomach flipped. So Mira, the white-haired woman, had created some sort of device to use her powers from a distance. Being under Mira's control for even a minute was terrifying. I couldn't imagine living under it for months.

"Why would you warn us?" Wesley asked. I wondered if he practiced sounding calm or if it came naturally to him. "You work for Adrestus. You know we have to try to stop him if he wants to destroy the city."

"I have people I care about," Esther said. "I-I haven't talked to them in a while, since they think I'm in a cult, but that doesn't mean I want them to die."

"Adrestus is going to kill people?" I asked stupidly.

"You thought he was going to *safely* burn down the city?" Esther raised an eyebrow, an echo of haughtiness creeping into her expression.

"He wants people to join the Epsilon Initiative," Wesley explained. "He can't do that if they're dead."

"He can't do that if no one believes Apex pose a threat, either," Esther said darkly, daring to step towards us. Wesley and I both tensed and she pulled her hands out of her pockets to put them up again. "He's going to use the Hendricks girl, torch as much of the city as he can, martyring John Ratcliffe in the process. The survivors will line up across what's left of New Delos to get powers, all at the low, low cost of unwavering loyalty to Adrestus and his vision."

Wind whistled between boats and for a moment, the dock was all that existed, swaying blithely beneath us and the world reeled.

"He wants to force Amanda to murder people." I felt empty. He had a plan in place. He'd had months to figure it out. Despite all the warnings and clues we'd been fed, we only had six days to stop it.

"John Ratcliffe," Wesley repeated. "When you say 'martyring'—"

"Amanda will kill him in battle."

"That's stupid," I laughed. "Why would John Ratcliffe sign up for a plan where he ends up toasted?"

"Because he thinks the plan is for him to win." Esther's face looked as bleak as her voice sounded. "He thinks he's supposed to replace Paragon as the city's savior, but he's the sacrificial lamb."

Wesley's hand found mine and I relaxed at his touch, letting my fingers lock with his.

"Adrestus has given up on trying to get the Apex to join him. He made this island to gather them, but they didn't want him." She took another step forward. "He wants a following that'll give him the world and now that he has the Lapis, he can build one much more efficiently than before."

"After he murders half the city, you mean," Wesley said darkly.

"Two-thirds," Esther corrected with a whisper. "He wants to kill two-thirds."

Wesley inhaled through his nose and my knees wobbled. We knew Adrestus was bad. He'd experimented on kidnapped kids and had murdered me, but killing two-thirds New Delos was an entirely new level of evil. The fact that he wanted to force Amanda to do the dirty work made it that much worse.

"How do we stop him?" My fingers tightened around Wes'. He squeezed back.

"They're going to start in the city center and—"

A strange look passed over her face and she twisted to look towards the park. Wesley let go of my hand and Esther swore under her breath.

"They followed me."

"How?" I hissed. "I thought your whole schtick was sensing people?"

"There's limitations." Esther crept past us, keeping hidden behind a small yacht. "Two approaching, and a third up on the street. Can't tell if they're together."

"It could be no one," I suggested. "Couple of kids sneaking out, maybe."

Wesley shook his head.

"I hear metal, like armor," he whispered.

The dark of the night seemed to close in around me and I stuck an arm out, searching for something to hold me steady. We only knew one person who wore metal armor.

"I can lead them away," Esther said. "You find somewhere to hide."

"But we need to know how to stop Adrestus!" I said, maybe too loudly, because both Wesley and Esther raised a finger to their lips.

Esther's eyes crinkled. It was weird to see such a kind smile on the face of a woman who'd been my enemy until a few minutes ago.

"You'll figure something out. Vidar, your dad, I mean, he trusts you."

Her words brought a bit of heat to my cheeks and before I could respond she darted out from behind the boat and beelined towards the gate.

"Come on," Wesley pulled at my wrist, tugging us deeper among the boats.

The dock was narrow and the farther we twisted along it, the farther away the street lights of the park became. The deep shadows of the boats offered little comfort, however. If Adrestus found out Esther had told us his plan, he might launch it prematurely, giving us even less time to stop him.

"Did she get away?" I dared to breathe. Wesley paused to listen. His shoulders tensed and he pulled me down into a crouch.

"I think so," he whispered, "but only because I can hear metal footsteps on the dock."

"I thought she was supposed to lead them away!"

We kept low as we ran, scanning the boats for an escape.

"They're getting closer!" Wesley hissed. I pointed up at the bow of a smaller yacht. If we could climb up, we'd be able to hide on the deck, out of sight, until Adrestus passed.

"She said to hide, didn't she?" I could hear the heavy footsteps now, too, along with the clinking of metal. I scanned the side of the boat for a ladder, but Wesley crouched down and offered me his hands.

"I'm right behind you," Wesley whispered as he grabbed my foot. He hoisted me into the air and I grabbed onto the deck railing as I rushed up to meet it. I swung over it and dropped silently to the floorboards.

I moved to make room for Wesley, waiting for him to make the leap up the boat deck. He didn't come. Instead, I heard him call out down below.

"Ahoy!"

I peeked through the railing from behind a tarp-covered lifeboat and raised a hand to my mouth to keep from crying out. Wesley stood beneath me with his back to the boat. Further up the dock, two figures glowered at him. One was a hulking mass of a man with shoulder length matted hair. The last time Wesley had fought Hackjob, he'd been left with a leg broken in three places and a dislocated hip.

But Hackjob was the least of my worries because his master stood close behind, black Spartan-style helmet glittering in the dim night lights and tattered cloak whipping around his ankles. Adrestus himself had come out to play. While Wesley might've been able to take Hackjob, I knew that even with his Apex powers, he didn't stand a chance against the ancient warrior.

"It's a bit late for a child like you to be out," Adrestus crooned. Maybe he didn't recognize Wesley. He wasn't in his Apex gear, after all. They might leave him be.

"I couldn't sleep," Wesley said. "I'm sorry, am I trespassing? I didn't know. I'll leave right away."

"I know you." Adrestus' growl sent shivers through me. "You worked on the Industry Project with Samantha Havardson."

Hackjob shifted his weight from one foot to the other in anticipation. His tongue worked its way from between his lips to lick them.

I pressed against the deck and squeezed my eyes shut.

"Y-yes!" Wesley stuttered, his voice cracking. "Do you know her?"

"I do, actually. I'm sorry if we startled you, but you should head home. It's not safe out here and you might catch cold."

I risked another peek over the tarp to watch Wesley hesitate and then walk towards the men. They were blocking the way back. He'd have to walk past them to get away.

It's okay, I told myself. *Maybe Hackjob doesn't recognize him. They don't know.*

My mouth went dry. Whoever was leaking team information would have *definitely* told Adrestus who Wesley was.

I opened my mouth to scream a warning just as Hackjob landed an uppercut in Wesley's abdomen. He doubled over and Hackjob kicked him back across the dock.

Wesley rolled onto his knees and held up a hand. Adrestus might've read it as a signal for mercy but I knew it was for me.

Stay where you are, it said. *I'm fine.*

I gritted my teeth as Wesley struggled to his feet and Adrestus clapped lazily.

"There's not many people who are able to stand after a hit from Hackjob," Adrestus said. "I've met one or two, though I feel this isn't the first time you've squared up against him."

Hackjob lumbered forward and cocked his head at Wesley.

"Wes," I whispered, barely louder than a breath. "Leave me. I'll be fine."

"No," Wesley said, to both me and Adrestus. "It's not the first time, but he already knows that."

Hackjob licked his lips again.

"Apex Seven, I presume." I hated the sound of Adrestus' voice. Hated it. "What *are* you doing out here all alone?"

"I told you. I couldn't sleep."

"So you came all the way out here? No, I think you were meeting with our little traitor. What did she tell you, I wonder?"

They already knew. The Doomsday Pager didn't matter anymore. The countdown had just run out. Wesley braced himself.

"Take him alive," Adrestus said. "He'll be useful."

Hackjob lunged but Wes was ready. He vaulted over Hackjob like it was nothing and charged Adrestus, who reached for the sword hidden in the folds of his cloak. I slapped a hand over my mouth to keep from screaming, but Wesley was saved from being impaled as Hackjob grabbed him by the back of his shirt.

Hackjob swung him around, flinging him into the side of a moored boat. A metallic clang rang out as Wesley's body slammed into the hull and dropped into the water. My hand shook, but I kept it clamped over my mouth, waiting for Wesley to surface.

Hackjob lumbered to the dock's edge and peered into the water. He looked towards Adrestus and shrugged.

"I said *alive*, you idiot!" Adrestus snarled. "Find him!"

I was about to jump into the bay myself to search for Wesley when the water gurgled behind Hackjob and Wesley leapt up onto the wooden planks, having swam underneath the dock to catch Hackjob off guard.

Hackjob didn't have time to react before Wesley kicked him squarely in the back. He grunted as he lurched, almost falling into the water himself, but regained his balance and sprang at Wesley again.

I glanced around the boat deck for anything that might help. Maybe if they got close enough, I could drop down with the tarp and trap Hackjob. But I peeked back out at the fray to see Hackjob throw Wesley clean across the docks and knew he was too strong to be trapped by a tarp.

Wesley hobbled to his feet and cried out as he put weight on his left leg. I forced myself to look away and keep searching for something, *anything* to help. At the very least, Adrestus had told Hackjob to take Wesley alive. I'd seen him take a beating before. It would suck, but he could handle it.

My hands met metal and I grabbed at the sharp edges of a container. I pulled it out and opened it. It was some sort of emergency kit, with extra water, space blankets, and two flare guns, neatly packed in the corner.

Splashing down below brought my attention back to Wesley. Hackjob had him by the neck, holding him over the dock's edge with his head pushed under the water. Wesley lashed out wildly with his arms. His left leg lay at an odd angle. His other kicked out, trying to find Hackjob behind him. Adrestus watched calmly from a safe distance, his sword still in its sheath.

I leapt up from my hiding place and aimed the two flare guns at Adrestus.

"Hey!" I screamed. Hackjob pulled Wesley out of the water and Adrestus turned to me, whipping his sword out and brandishing it, but the flares were already hurtling towards him, reflecting bright red off his armor.

The first flare missed, colliding with the hull of the yacht behind him, but the second struck him square in the chest. The hit forced him backwards and just when I thought he might manage to maintain his footing, he stepped a foot too far, stumbling backwards into the water.

The gap between the dock and the boat swallowed him and I knew even Adrestus' years of training and fighting wouldn't make him any more buoyant when he was laden with heavy armor.

"No!" Hackjob dropped Wesley and ran to edge where his master had disappeared. I fell from my hiding spot and Hackjob wavered, glancing between me and the water before ultimately deciding to go in after Adrestus.

I ran to Wesley's side, pulling him up as best I could.

"What happened?" Wesley moaned. Blood mixed with salt water on his face and my knees tried to buckle as Wesley leaned against me, unable to stand on his mangled left leg.

"Adrestus is sinking to the bottom of the ocean and Hackjob went in after him." I heaved, pulling Wesley in closer and adjusting my arm under his. "I don't know how long we have."

We hobbled towards the dock entrance. Wesley's haggard breaths warmed the side of my neck and he stumbled several times, but I kept him upright.

"Come on," I said. "You've gotta stay with me. Keep an ear out for Adrestus. Have you got your phone?"

Wesley fumbled in his back pocket and pulled out his phone. I took it and tried to turn it on, but his dip in the ocean must've killed it.

"That's okay," I lied. We passed into the park but I knew we weren't safe yet. No phone, miles from school, and Adrestus would be right behind us the moment Hackjob pulled him out of the water.

Wesley shivered uncontrollably, making it difficult to keep hold of him. We wouldn't make it far, but we needed to tell someone what we'd learned from Esther.

The forested walkway loomed ahead, blocking out the streetlights of the neighborhood beyond its shadows. I adjusted my grip on Wesley and pulled him into the trees, hoping they might hide us if Hackjob and Adrestus somehow managed to catch up.

"Where are we going?" Wesley wheezed as I led the way through the twisting path. The dark of the urban forest made it difficult for me to see, but I trusted Wesley, as injured as he was, to keep a lookout with his enhanced vision.

"The townhouse isn't far from here."

I didn't want to go to the abandoned townhouse that Alison, Avery, and Vidar had lived in before Adrestus ripped us apart, but it was the only feasible option. Not only was his leg definitely broken, but the water had sapped him of his heat. We needed shelter. He needed to get warm.

"I can hear them," Wesley whispered. "They're not chasing us yet. If you put me down, you can go on ahead and warn—"

"I'm not—"

My voice caught in my throat. I'd overestimated Wesley's ability to keep an eye and ear on the shadows around us.

A dark figure stepped out onto the path. Her cloaks rustled in the wind and the dull light that trickled through the trees behind us cast deep shadows across her grotesque Greek tragedy mask. I held Wesley tighter.

"Hey, Winnie," I gulped. "Long time no see."

33

Safehouse

Winnie pulled the mask off, revealing the same haggard look she'd borne at the New Year's Eve festival. She grimaced at Wesley shuddering in my arms, looking more disgusted than sorry.

"Where is he?" Her eyes flickered from Wes to me.

"Bottom of the ocean," I shrugged. "I remember you saying it's, what, five hundred feet deep out here? His armor looked pretty heavy."

Her face twisted.

"You know he can't die."

"Sure, but he can still sink."

Esther had said there was a third person, lingering farther away from the others. I was stupid to have forgotten about it.

Of *course* it was Winnie.

"Go find help," Wes groaned. "I can take her."

He tried to push off of me and was almost successful. As soon as he tried to put weight on his left leg, however, he collapsed back into my arms, shuddering with pain and cold.

"Out of our way, Winnie," I scowled. She looked ridiculous in her long cloaks, meant to emulate Adrestus', but I knew better than to underestimate her.

She looked at her mask lazily, turning it over in her hands and watching how the low light bounced off its silver ridges and curves.

"Why?" she finally said. "You can't beat me and he looks half-dead. Why shouldn't I bring you to Adrestus?"

"For one, he's at the bottom of the ocean," I reminded her, bracing for a fight. "And I don't know how you plan on carrying two people down the street."

"It's not a great plan, but there's no harm in trying." She swaggered forward and Wesley struggled to stand on his own.

"You can still leave him," I said. She faltered and irritation flashed across her face.

"Not this again. Spare me the hero act. I *want* to help Adrestus. I believe in what he's doing."

I wanted to ask if she knew about the plan for next week. If she knew her sister would be forced to murder two-thirds of the city.

But I couldn't show my hand. I couldn't let her know what we knew.

Besides, if she *did* know about the plan, I didn't want to know. Winnie was still redeemable. Misled and angry, but redeemable. Most of my memories of her were fake, sure, but I knew this wasn't her.

"If you want to help him, he's back that way." I jerked my head the way we'd come. "Let us pass."

She cocked her head to the side, as casually as if we were back in class, discussing a difficult homework problem.

"No," she chirped. "I don't think I will."

Her cloaks billowed around her as she went for a kick and I braced myself for the blow. However, it was Wesley she aimed for and her boot slammed against his hip. He grunted as he collapsed, slipping from my arms.

I rounded on Winnie, sudden fury filling me with warmth and bile. I launched at her with both hands extended and we fell off the path into the dirt and twigs of the underbrush.

"He's injured!" I snarled in her ear, trying to pin her down.

"That's what made him an easy target!"

Even with Alison's fighting skills pre-programmed into my subconscious, Winnie seemed to stay a half-second ahead of me, blocking my blows and wriggling out of my armlocks. She flipped me on my back and I landed hard, the air forcing its way out of me.

I writhed, trying to remember how to breathe, scrabbling at Winnie's heels as she stepped back onto the path. She stood over Wesley, who stirred feebly. Her cloak whipped around her as she spun to face me.

"You'll both come with me," she asserted. "Willingly."

She pressed a boot into Wesley's injured leg and he cried out in pain.

"Stop!" I fought my way to my feet, using a tree trunk to regain my footing.

Her bottom lip stuck out in a pout and she made a show of pressing harder. Wesley clawed at the dirt, trying to escape but too weak to move.

"Leave him alone!" I tackled her again, with new vigor, new drive. Whatever bit of pity I had left for her was gone. I didn't care how much her dad sucked or how crappy of a thing it was my parents had done to her.

Winnie disgusted me.

I hated her.

"You can't beat me!" She grunted as I took the upper hand, pinning her against a tree.

"She doesn't need to."

Esther shouldered me out of the way, taking my spot holding Winnie's wrists against the tree over her head. Winnie stopped fighting, realizing she was outnumbered.

"Traitor," she growled. "What did you tell them?"

"I thought I told you to hide!" Esther snarled at me, ignoring Winnie.

"You were supposed to lead them away!"

She shrugged, keeping her eyes trained on Winnie.

"Get him out of here," she said. "I'll keep Dion busy."

I snorted at the mention of Winnie's codename but scrambled to Wes' side. His breathing was shallow but his eyes flickered open to look at me.

"Sammy, just go."

I wriggled an arm under his shoulders and dragged him to his feet. He leaned on me more heavily than before and his shivering had worsened.

"Don't be so dramatic. It's annoying," I muttered. I pulled Wesley past Esther and Winnie, but paused. "Esther, back at the museum, you said not to trust my friends. Who were you talking about?"

Esther's face hardened, but she kept her eyes locked on Winnie.

"I don't know who the leak is, if that's what you mean. Just that there is one."

Winnie's mouth curled.

"More friend problems, Sammy?"

My fingers tightened around Wesley's arm but Esther nodded for us to leave.

"Get out of here before Adrestus realizes where you've gone, and before your friend freezes to death."

I turned away but Winnie called after us.

"I'll tell your dad you say hi, alright?"

"Ignore her," Wesley wheezed. "You need...to get away."

I adjusted his arm over my shoulder and continued down the trail, hoping Esther knew what she was doing. If Winnie got away, she'd hunt us down easily.

The trees thinned and spit us out into the neighborhood. The townhouses that lined the way were quiet and I tried to move as quickly as possible while weighed down with Wesley.

"Won't she find us at the townhouse?" His breathing was ragged and his voice weak.

"She's never been. She might know my family lived in the area, but she won't know specifics."

"But Adrestus sent someone there before. *He* knows."

I swallowed.

"He's got bigger things to worry about right now. Namely Hackjob's diving skills."

My chest constricted as the townhouse came into view. It stood at the top of the hill, a hulking mass wedged between two identical buildings. My calves burned as I dragged Wesley up the hill.

"Try to keep an ear out," I whispered, not daring to look back. He nodded weakly and I picked up the pace, even as Wesley felt heavier by the second.

"Sammy," he breathed, "are you okay?"

"I'm fine, just trying to keep us alive, thanks."

"That's...not what I mean."

I kept my eyes on the crest of the hill. They itched, but I didn't have time to cry over Dad when we weren't safe.

"I'll be okay," I insisted. "So I didn't get to see Dad tonight. I'm sure it won't be long before I do."

But Trev Baker's warning sat heavy in my stomach, almost harder to carry up the hill than Wesley. The sooner I found Dad, the sooner Baker's premonition of his death might come to pass.

My heart rate soared as we approached the house. I set Wesley down on the porch, not letting myself feel relief just yet. Even though he was only half-conscious now, I did my best not to look too winded. I found the hidden house key and let out a grateful sigh when I heard the lock click.

"Keep the lights off," Wesley groaned as I helped him inside. "If Adrestus sees—"

"I get it!" I dead bolted the door behind us. My gaze flickered over the security system, but it was already disarmed. Panic swept through my naval but I reminded myself I'd visited with Amanda a few months back. We hadn't had time to reset the alarm when we left. "We should go upstairs. Feels safer than staying on the bottom floor."

But getting Wesley up the first flight was difficult and we collapsed on the landing near the bedrooms. Wesley curled up on the top step, shivering.

"We need to get you warm." I mumbled.

"Wait." He winced as he tried to push himself into a sitting position. "Thank you."

My shoulders tensed defensively, though I wasn't sure why.

"For what?"

"Fighting Winnie. I know that...it didn't look easy."

I shrugged, forcing my shoulders to relax.

"Adrestus must have her on quite the training regimen. I don't know if I could've beat her, honestly."

"I didn't mean it looked hard in that way."

I blushed and blinked away the warmth that had sprung into my eyes. Winnie didn't matter. Getting Wes warm mattered.

I pulled him to the master bathroom down the hall and was happy to find Alison must've still been paying for utilities because hot water flowed from the bath tap. Candles from under the sink offered us a small bit of flickering light to work by.

"My leg." The pain on Wesley's face as I lowered him into the tub, clothes and all, sent pangs through my chest and my fury with Winnie increased. "You need to splint it."

"Right." I shook Winnie out of my thoughts. Splint, painkillers, dry clothes. "Stay here."

"Where else would I go?"

I didn't let him see the smile that crept across my face. He was starting to feel better if he was up to cracking jokes.

I took one of the candles to raid the medicine cabinet in the kitchen and returned with painkillers, a wooden broom, and duct tape. Wesley had peeled off his shirt and had slipped up to his chin under the hot water. Under the water, a bruise spread across his side, probably from being thrown into the side of a boat.

He raised a hand out of the water and pointed towards the faucet.

"There's a button there. Can you press it for me?"

I hit the button and he grinned as the bathtub jets hummed to life.

"If you'd wanted a spa day, you just needed to say something," I teased. "No need to construct an elaborate plot in which you almost die."

"I wouldn't have died. Adrestus said to take me alive."

"That's somehow less comforting."

I passed Wesley the painkillers and he took them gratefully before blushing.

"You might need to find some scissors. I, um, couldn't get my jeans off over my leg."

"Oh." My voice was several octaves higher than I'd wanted it to be. "Right. Easy."

I shuffled through the bathroom drawers until I found a pair of scissors that looked sturdy enough to handle denim. I turned back to Wesley and snipped them in the air.

"Alright, give me your pants." My cheeks warmed and I laughed nervously. "I don't know why I said that."

But Wesley laughed, too, and I relaxed. I set an old t-shirt and sweatpants of Dad's aside before draining the tub so that Wesley sat in the empty basin in his soaked jeans.

I leaned over his legs and gnawed at the cuff of his pants with the scissors. Once they made it through the seam, they glided through the material.

Any chagrin I had at cutting Wesley out of his clothes was quickly replaced with horror when I saw his mottled, swollen leg.

"It's not as bad as it looks."

I gawked at him.

"You have a lump the size of a softball."

He shrugged, then flinched in pain as I went back to work on his pants.

"It's fine. I'm used to it."

"That's not a normal thing to be used to."

My embarrassment returned the further up Wesley's leg I got, revealing his blue boxers. Wesley laughed as he watched me.

"The good news is help should be on its way any moment. I'm positive Naomi will be able to feel you all the way back on campus."

I brandished the scissors at him and scowled.

"Excuse me for having never cut a man out of his pants before. Is this something you're used to as well?"

"No, this is a first."

I pushed the scissors through the last seam and sat back to look at Wesley's ruined jeans.

"Splint time?" I held up the wooden broom. "Can you break this?"

Wesley took the broom and effortlessly snapped the head off before breaking the handle in half.

"Try and stabilize it through the knee," he instructed and I bent over him armed with the broken broom pieces and duct tape. "The less I'm able to move my leg the better."

It wasn't the best splint and I knew when it came time to remove it, Wesley was going to lose some leg hair with the tape, but it would do for now. I helped wiggle his other leg out of the jeans and looked away to give him his privacy, staring instead at the clump of leaves that had fallen from his sweatshirt pocket.

"Hand me a towel and I can take care of the rest."

I waited in the bedroom, biting my tongue to keep from calling out to ask how it was going. Finally, the door swung open to reveal Wesley leaning against the door frame, dwarfed by the oversized t-shirt and sweats but with his jaunty smile intact.

"Careful!" I rushed to help him to the bed but he didn't have to lean on me as heavily as before. I laid him against the pillows and piled blankets over him.

"Now what?"

"You can sleep if you want. I'll stay up and make sure Adrestus doesn't send anyone to check out the house. There's no landline, otherwise I would call for help."

I jammed a few decorative pillows under Wesley's leg to elevate it and he patted the bed next to him.

"I need to keep look out."

"Just until I fall asleep. I miss talking to you. "

I gave in and crawled onto the bed next to him. The pillows, even though they hadn't been used in months, still smelled like my family.

"You need to leave as soon as it's light out," Wesley insisted. "The team needs to be warned."

"I won't leave you."

"I'll be fine once it's daytime. Adrestus doesn't seem to make moves when it's light out."

That wasn't necessarily true, but he was right that it would be safer. Besides, Fleming needed to know what was coming in a few days.

"I've met your mom," I reminded him, making a shoddy attempt at a joke. "I don't think she'd be thrilled with me if she knew I left you here alone."

Wesley scowled and adjusted the pillows behind him.

"I don't think she'd blame you."

I frowned and even though I regretted bringing up his mother, I couldn't help but to pry.

"What's her deal, anyway?" I asked. "Don't get me wrong, she's nice enough but—"

"But she's completely disinterested in Apex as a whole?" Wesley scoffed.

"Back before she visited, you said she'd like me because I'm a Beta."

"I did *not* call you a Beta." He turned his head to glare at me.

"You know what I mean. A non-Apex."

"Yeah, but I didn't call you—"

"But I *am a* Beta," I said softly. "That's not a bad thing, as much as people like Andersen pretend it is. So, what's up with Mrs. Isaacs?"

He turned away to stare resolutely at the ceiling and I watched the muscles in his neck move as he swallowed.

"I already told you that when I was six, I broke Benson's arm. When my mom heard him crying, she thought it was *me* who'd been hurt. He was two years older and twice my size."

Candlelight danced on the tip of his nose and flickered in his eyes.

"You didn't mean to, though, and that was ten years ago. She can't hold that against you."

He shrugged, then winced at the pain the movement had caused him.

"Her and my dad didn't know we had the Epsilon gene in our family. I guess our particular Apex genetics aren't as dominant as they can be in other lineages. It took a while for them to figure out what I was. By then, I'd broken more than arms. Dishes, doors, toys. Benson wouldn't play with me anymore and my parents kept the neighborhood kids away. They thought I had a temper problem."

"What did you do?" I felt small and selfish for having never asked more about his family.

"I stopped playing." He looked up at the ceiling. "I didn't let other people touch me and I wouldn't touch other people."

"How long until you figured it out?"

"Almost a year." His voice shook. I shifted over so that our shoulders touched and I found a spot on the ceiling to stare at, too. "Turns out, my aunt was an Apex. We only saw her around the holidays and she'd heard about my new so-called behavior problems all year. It wasn't until she saw me that she put the pieces together."

"But if your aunt was an Apex, too, shouldn't your parents have been able to figure it out?"

"My aunt had never told anyone and she was the only Apex in the family before I came along. When she figured out what was happening with me, she told my parents and we went from there. It was too late for my parents' marriage, though. Dad left soon after. Mom won't admit it, but I know it's my fault."

I propped myself up on my elbow to look at Wesley.

"Don't be stupid. It's *not* your fault."

Wesley's cheeks flushed and he turned away. I wanted to find his hand under the covers and hold it, but didn't dare.

"I think she's scared of me," he admitted. "I've tried to ask Naomi before to read her for me but she won't. That's all the confirmation I need, really. To her, I'm not a hero. I'm dangerous and I hurt people and I ruined her marriage."

I looked at him in the flickering light. I knew it wasn't his fault his parents had split, but I also knew that no matter what I said, he'd still blame himself.

"When we get my dad back, maybe he can be your dad, too." My cheeks burned and I leaned back down. "That's weird. Not in a weird way, alright?"

I was terrible at finding the right words to say but Wesley grinned at me.

"He wasn't my biggest fan, if I remember."

"He's no one's biggest fan." I rolled my eyes. "He'll like you if I tell him to. Besides, Alison doesn't think you're that bad."

"You can't offer up Alison as a mom if you don't think of her as yours."

"Who made that rule?" I scrunched my nose at him. "Once I get Dad back, he's still Alison's husband and he's still Avery's dad. It'll be different now that there aren't any secrets, but we'll make it work."

I thought I saw Wesley blush in the candlelight.

"He still might not like me, though."

Wesley wiggled his arm out from under the blankets and held out what looked like the clump of leaves that had fallen from his pockets. I squinted at it suspiciously, rolling onto my side to get a better look and was surprised to see his face was somber and red.

"What is this?"

He gulped.

"A corsage."

I laughed, thinking he must be joking, but the serious look on his face told me otherwise. His jaw set the same stubborn way it had when he'd asked if we were just friends.

"It's for you."

I smiled apprehensively and took the small bouquet of leaves. They were crumpled and wet and he'd used a paperclip to secure them to a hair tie. He must have put it together in the bathroom. I slipped it over my wrist and held my hand out so he could see his handiwork.

"I like it," I said, and I meant it. "But why?"

Wesley shifted under his multitude of blankets and I wasn't sure if it was his leg or my question that had made him uncomfortable.

"I didn't get you one for Homecoming."

I stared at him blankly, the corners of my mouth inching upwards.

"Homecoming was months ago, and you made me a necklace. I didn't need a corsage."

He looked away to glare at the ceiling instead of me.

"I should have gotten you both. Every other girl at that dance with a date had a flower, but you didn't."

"I didn't need a corsage," I laughed.

"I know but—" He struggled to find the words and I let him think, sitting in silence while he gathered his thoughts. "I don't know. I wasn't the best date."

I snorted and rolled onto my back.

"I'm the one who ran away and left you to chase after me," I reminded him. "If either of us was a bad date, it was me. Besides, it wasn't like a date-date. We were friends. We *are* friends."

I was talking more to myself now. It helped to remind myself that's all we were. He didn't like me like that and I had a thousand years worth of baggage that included an ex-boyfriend who had just attacked us.

"Right, but maybe you wouldn't have ran off if I'd been better."

"You beat yourself up too much. It was *months* ago." I waved my corsage overhead again. "But thanks. This is really very sweet."

He chuckled nervously next to me.

"You know what's crazy?" He was trying to sound casual but his voice was strained. "You say we went as friends but part of me at the time wished...I don't know. Maybe not as friends."

I froze, my corsage still in the air. I stared at my hand, not daring to look at Wesley, the ghost of our conversation after the boat race hanging in the air.

"Yeah?" I whispered. "What about now?"

"I..." He paused and I was certain he was listening to my hammering heartbeat. "I want what you want."

My stomach clenched. As far as he knew, I wanted friendship. Was that what he meant? I was right to think I'd blown my chances at the dance but I sighed and smiled. I was happy to be his friend.

"Good."

He smiled back. His eyes glittered in the flickering candlelight and I wished I could tell him the truth.

"I'm really sorry about tonight."

"What for? You kept me safe long enough to come up with a plan."

"No, not the docks," he grinned. "I'm sorry you had to cut me out of my pants."

"Right," I grimaced. "Don't worry, it's only the second most mortifying thing to happen to me."

"What was the first?"

"I lived with Andersen and Fleming for two weeks. Fun fact, Andersen doesn't lock the bathroom door."

Wesley's eyes widened with shock and glee.

"No!" he gasped. "What happened?"

"That's the whole story," I laughed. "He doesn't lock the bathroom door and I learned the hard way. There was a lot of screaming. Fleming thought we were under attack."

"You're lying," Wesley grinned. "You would've told me that."

I shrugged into the pillows.

"I didn't want to get in the way of stuff."

"What stuff?"

"Remi stuff, I guess." I avoided his gaze but could feel his green eyes focused on the side of my head.

"What does Remi have to do with anything?" He sounded more confused than defensive. I adjusted the makeshift corsage.

"She might have said something to me."

"About what?" An edge had crept into his voice and I shrank against the pillows.

"She thought you guys would have the best chance if I stepped back." I didn't know why I was whispering. It wasn't as if Remi would leap out from under the bed. "You like her and I like you so obviously I want you to be happy, and if I made her uncomfortable, maybe there was some merit there, you know?"

"What was that?" Wesley grinned at me.

"What was what?" I reran my words through my head.

"You said you like me."

I rolled my eyes and elbowed him, gently enough to not hurt him but hard enough to make him shut up.

"Yeah, I *like* my friends. Don't flatter yourself."

I chanced a glance at him. He was still smiling, but the corners of his eyes wrinkled kindly.

"I like my friends, too," he said.

I pulled Wesley's top blanket over myself and wiggled closer to him. He settled into me, pressing up against my arm. He closed his eyes and relaxed against me and I let silence fall over us, knowing he needed to sleep. As the minutes passed, his breathing slowed and deepened and I watched the candlelight dance across the profile of his face, pushing long shadows across his cheeks. His hair was still damp. I wish I had a way to dry it.

"Wes?" I whispered. He snored in response. I smiled to myself, nestling into the pillow, still watching him in the candlelight. After the chaos of the night, I clung to the quiet of this moment, not sure when we'd have another like it. I drifted to sleep next to Wesley, despite my promises to keep watch.

Dawn had barely broken outside and tendrils of dull orange light snuck in through the curtains when I woke. Adrestus hadn't found us in the night. With daybreak, I could venture out, find help, and warn the city of Adrestus' pending attack.

Wesley's eyelids flickered and he pulled a face.

"Is your leg okay?" I whispered, hoping it was his injuries that were bothering him and not him remembering the more heartfelt moments of our late-night conversation.

He whipped his head towards me, his eyes wide and wild. I shied away. I must've crossed a line, falling asleep so close to him. I wiggled back and opened my mouth to stutter an apology but his hand appeared from under his mountain of blankets and he pressed a finger to his lips.

"Quiet," he breathed. "Someone else is in the house."

34

A Very Bad Plan

The only sound I heard was the pounding of my heart in my ears, but then, the unmistakable sound of a floorboard creaking overhead brought my heart into my throat.

I rolled out from under the blanket. Wesley struggled to sit up but screwed his eyes in pain. I tiptoed to his side, lifting the blankets to make sure the splint was still in place.

"Sounds like one person," he breathed as I bent over his leg, testing the duct tape with a ginger prod. "Upstairs. No one downstairs that I can hear. Might be Winnie."

"I can take her." I crept to the door, peeking into the hallway. "Stay here."

"You keep saying that as if I could go somewhere."

The white walls of the hall made the second floor landing look brighter than the low dawn light filtering in from a stairwell window should have allowed. They were barren, devoid of family photos, maybe to help skirt questions regarding why I wasn't in any of them.

I tip-toed across the linoleum-wood, afraid the tacky sound of my bare feet peeling from the hard floor with every step might give me away.

The upstairs sink started running as I reached the bottom step. The idea of Adrestus' goons helping themselves to a glass of water from the kitchenette made me bristle as I crawled up the stairs on all fours.

The usual layer of marine fog that rolled in each night muted the light that poured in from skylights. I kept low, hiding behind the banister. The intruder made no effort to keep quiet, rummaging through cupboards and humming to themself.

I rolled my face towards the edge of the low banister wall to look around the corner. It was as if the stairs disappeared beneath me. My mouth dropped open and my foot slipped in surprise. I caught myself on the next step down with a loud *thump!*

The boy twisted around and jolted when he saw me frozen with my face peeking around the corner.

"Sammy?" he cried, dropping his toast. He flung himself across the room and I skirted around the banister so he wouldn't send us both down the stairs when he barreled into me with open arms.

Avery had gotten taller in the few months he'd been gone, no longer fitting snugly under my chin, but his hair was still an unkempt mop of light blond.

"What're you doing here?" I laughed, peeling him off me and basking in my brother's embarrassed smile. "Where's Mom?"

His cheeks glowed pink and he avoided eye contact.

"She's not here." He held his hands behind his back and rocked back and forth on the balls of his feet. "Don't worry about it."

I blinked. *Don't worry about it.* It was probably fine.

"Do you at least have your phone?" I asked. He fished it out of his back pocket and I took it, leading him down the stairs while searching the internet for the school directory.

He followed me all the way to where Wesley lay grimacing on the bed. The look on his face told me he'd heard our exchange upstairs and while he seemed relieved it wasn't Winnie, his eyes narrowed and his lips pressed together.

"Were you here all night?" Avery asked, taking in the pile of blankets and the burnt out candles on the bedside table. "I didn't hear you get in."

"How long have *you* been here?" I dialed the number I found for Fleming's office online.

"Two nights." He shrugged.

"Why?" Wesley pushed his blankets off and flinched his way into a sitting position. "Where's Mrs. Havardson?"

"Don't worry about it," Avery said, echoing what he'd said upstairs. Wesley leaned back against the headboard. A sheen of sweat glistened on his unnaturally pale forehead. He needed Everly.

I jammed the phone to my ear, not sure if I was hoping more for Fleming to be in or out of his office. He'd kill me when I told him what had happened, but I didn't have a choice.

"Yeah, sure." Wesley dropped his questions for Avery. "Who are you calling, Sammy?"

I stared between Avery and Wesley. Avery shuffled awkwardly.

"Did you just use your powers on him?" I hissed. "Just now, when you said not to worry about it?"

Avery turned red and tried to fight back a mischievous smile.

"I'm getting really good at it," he insisted, like that might get him off the hook. "I bet Hendricks still hasn't realized I told him to let me leave."

"Did you use your powers on *me?*" My chest swelled and Avery shrank against the doorframe.

"Alex Fleming."

I froze as Fleming answered the phone.

"Hello?" he prompted.

"I—hello?"

"Yes, this is Alex. Can you hear me? Who is this?"

"Don't tell him I'm here," Avery whispered.

I swallowed hard.

"I messed up." I gripped Avery's phone so that the edges of his case dug into my fingers.

"Samantha?" His voice became sharp. "Where are you? What's happened?"

"My parents' house," I croaked. "Wesley needs Everly."

I stumbled through the details of the previous night. The longer Fleming held his silence, the more I rushed to fill it, telling him everything. The pager, Esther, Adrestus' plan to blow up the city, Winnie. When I finally reached the end, static rustled in my ear as Fleming exhaled heavily.

"Do you have any idea how foolhardy, how *dangerous*—"

"You need to warn City Council. If Adrestus knows that we know, he could attack the city before we can move against him."

"Why, Samantha?" Fleming pleaded on the other line. "Why do you keep doing this?"

"Saving the day? I don't know. It comes naturally, I guess."

Avery and Wesley stared at me while I waited for Fleming to respond.

"How bad is Wesley?"

My eyes flickered over Wesley's leg.

"I'm fine," he mumbled.

"Not great."

"Stay there," Fleming sighed. "Don't open the door for anyone who isn't Everly."

I handed Avery's phone back to him.

"Why didn't you tell him about your brother?" Wesley demanded.

"Avery said not—" I turned on Avery. "You *are* using your powers on us!"

Avery blinked his big, brown eyes at me and pushed his hair out of his face.

"Not on purpose. It just slips sometimes."

"Why are you here?" I demanded. He opened his mouth but I cut him off before he could respond. "*Don't* tell me not to worry about it."

He steeled himself, squaring his shoulders and finally meeting my eyes.

"I'm going to find Dad. Mr. Hendricks said I could."

"Right, because you told him to say that!"

"It's not fair!" The freckles on Avery's cheeks stood out as he blushed. "You get to help and have adventures but I have to hide? I can help, too! I've gotten a lot stronger."

"Obviously," Wesley said under his breath.

"Wesley's leg is broken. That's not us 'having adventures'. That's very bad people hurting us. You're in danger here. The whole city could burn down at any moment."

"And Adrestus will be his most vulnerable!" Avery insisted. "He'll be distracted and sloppy and *that's* when we find Dad!"

"No." I turned back to Wesley. "Do you think you can make it downstairs?"

Avery at least proved helpful in maneuvering Wesley out of the bed. I tried to ignore how he trembled between us. Sweat-stains soaked his shirt and heat radiated from his skin.

We set him on the couch in the living room and I posted up next to him with my knees on the cushions so I could watch the cul-de-sac between the blinds.

"When your ride gets here, don't mention me," Avery said. "I don't want to go back. Mr. Hendricks sucks."

Was he using his powers on me again? Probably. I refused to look back at him, but I couldn't help but to feel I'd been in his shoes before. Desperate to help. Refusing to be sidelined.

When a familiar black car sped up the hill and squealed to a stop out front, I turned back to Avery.

"Go upstairs," I said, still not sure if he was using his powers on me, but feeling like it was the right move all the same. "You should hide."

Wesley gave Avery a weak finger gun farewell before he disappeared into the next room. Wesley rolled his head to look at me. I grimaced at the dark circles under his eyes that stood out in stark contrast to his sickly pale face. Outside, Everly ran from the car to the front porch.

He glowered down at me when I unlocked the front door and stepped aside to let him in.

"Where is he?"

I pointed to the adjoining room and Everly adjusted the medical bag that hung off his shoulder as he swooped into the room.

"It's not Sammy's fault," Wesley murmured as Everly took his hand and furrowed his brow.

"Always the leg with you." He rustled through his bag, procuring a plastic bag of clear liquid and a needle. "You know the drill."

I looked away as Everly cleaned a spot on Wesley's arm and stuck him with the IV needle.

"I can only spare enough to help the fever and fuse the fractures back together, but the bones will still technically be broken." He held the IV bag towards me. "Hold this."

I stepped closer to take it in my hands and Wesley smiled encouragingly, wincing as Everly rolled the leg of his sweatpants up over his knee to reveal the hastily-made splint.

"This isn't a horrible splint," Everly muttered, peeling away duct tape. I chanced a glance and the room churned when I saw Wesley's mangled leg. "You're lucky it kept the bone in place."

The baggie in my hands felt so small. There was no way it held enough Serum to fix Wesley's leg completely, but if Adrestus was about to attack the city, we'd need him in one piece.

"Mr. Fleming's already at City Hall to see what he can do about evacuating New Delos, though our hopes aren't high. Dr. Weaver cancelled class." He sat back on the couch ottoman. "You shouldn't have left campus."

"It was my fault," Wesley offered. I opened my mouth to correct him but Everly beat me to it.

"We all know that's not true. You'll be lucky not to be expelled." He looked at me as he said it.

"Go ahead," I scoffed. "If Adrestus blows up the island, there won't be a school anymore."

"You could have at least let the team know."

If it had been Fleming sitting on the ottoman, I might've pushed back, but seeing calm, stoic Everly disappointed in me made me want to shrivel up and disappear under the couch.

"It was a family thing," Wesley said quietly. I glared at him but he kept going. "She thought her dad was sending the pager messages."

Wesley's IV bag was the only thing keeping me tethered to the room. Otherwise, I might've walked out. Everly nodded slowly and leaned forward so his elbows rested on his knees. Under his thoughtful gaze, I felt like he was using his powers, sweeping over me, looking for the cracks in my head. I waited for him to say something, but he just stared.

"It was stupid, okay?" I finally admitted. "Wesley only followed me because he knew how stupid it was. It's my fault he's hurt."

"It's not stupid to want your family back." Everly rose to his feet and surveyed Wesley. Color had returned to his cheeks and he wasn't sweating nearly as much. "It's probably safe to move you to the car now."

I gave a wistful glance up to the third floor as Everly helped Wesley into the back seat of the sedan. It would be stupid of Avery to watch us from the window and run the risk of being seen, but I wished I could've had a final glance of my brother.

Everly was mercifully quiet on the ride back to the campus. It was a calm, careful silence as opposed to one that broiled with suppressed rage and I used it to mull over Esther's warning as I watched the rising sun turn the city skyscrapers orange.

The dazzling city skyline disappeared as we turned into the parking garage and wound our way into the basement levels. I hoped Fleming was still at City Hall. I wasn't ready to face him.

"You stay here and I'll—" Everly started to say as he parked in front of the door that led to the gym.

"No gurneys," Wes insisted, throwing his door open. It was impossible to tell how much of Wesley's vigor was thanks to Serum and how much was sheer determination.

I hurried to his side to help him but he was able to put more weight down now. The facility door slammed open to reveal Justin and Jen in the corridor.

"No word from Fleming yet," Justin said as we hurried inside with Wes between us. "Everyone's downstairs, though."

He tried to take my spot at Wesley's side but I clung tighter to Wes.

"I've got him."

"You should rest."

"No."

Jen gave a half-grunt and I bit my tongue. The upperclassmen could think what they wanted of me.

"What should we tell the team?" Justin asked. "They want to help."

"Nothing," Everly said, pushing into the Sickbay side door. "They can go back to the dorms if they like."

"They won't," Jen smirked.

The beds that lined the Sickbay were empty, save one. Dr. Weaver sat on top of the covers of the bed closest to the backrooms, propped up against the metal-barred headboard. Gray hairs escaped her bun, framing her pallid face as she wrestled with a set of tubes.

"*What* are you doing?" Everly demanded, all the anger he'd kept so carefully concealed now boiling over. He helped Wesley to the nearest bed and swooped to Dr. Weaver's side, pulling a needle from her grasp.

"We don't have enough Serum," she said blankly.

"And you don't have enough plasma! You've donated too much as is."

"We need to be ready for...ready when the attack..."

She leaned against the headboard, her head tilting back. I wondered how many times she'd donated blood and plasma to Everly's stock of

Serum since having the entire supply stolen. Without the self-healing power locked in her blood, the Serum was useless.

"Not even you can keep up with the amount you've donated this week," Everly said, softening.

"This last one, then," Dr. Weaver insisted. Her gray eyes watched Wesley and me, though her head was still tilted towards the ceiling. "I won't be much help otherwise."

Everly sighed and took the seat next to her bed, organizing the tools on the bedside table. He took her arm gently, and though they looked nothing alike, as he wound her arm to find a vein and stuck her with the needle, I was reminded of a mother and son.

The main Sickbay door swung open and Remi marched in, freckles flushed and blonde hair flying. She looked between us, her face oscillating between rage and anguish.

"Why-what...how could you—"

"You're forgetting who, where, and when." Wesley pressed back into the white Sickbay pillows, as if hoping they might swallow him. "Sammy, I need to talk to Remi."

I stumbled away from the bed, placing a hand over Wesley's make-shift corsage that still sat on my wrist. I cast a glance towards Everly, silently asking for his permission to leave, and he nodded, barely looking up from Dr. Weaver's arm.

I tried to get out before Remi and Wesley could start talking, but as the door swung shut behind me, I heard Remi begin to lay into Wes.

"You *know* how I feel about you hanging out with her!"

The entire team had gathered in the atrium and Justin and Jen were doing their best to navigate questions. Half of them were in uniform, ready to go at a moment's notice.

Heather saw me first. She'd been on patrol last night. Her hair tangled at its ends and fatigue pulled at her face.

"How long do we have?" she asked as I passed. I shrugged and a nearby circle of juniors grumbled amongst themselves.

"Is Wes okay?" Anthony sat nearby with Isabelle.

"He—yeah."

A hand wrapped around my wrist. I twisted to confront whoever'd grabbed me, but relaxed when I saw Naomi's doe-like eyes inches from mine.

"It's fine," she said softly, drawing me away from the crowd. The murmurs continued behind me but I followed Naomi to the locker rooms. I eyed the showers in the back. I could feel dirt crusted in my hair after rolling through the forest trail with Winnie.

However, as soon as the door slammed shut behind us, Naomi whirled to face me. Her eyes, which had been so soft a moment ago, flashed angrily.

"What the hell, Sam!"

She paced between the rows of lockers, pulling at her hair. She'd already put on her uniform. I caught a flash of the number fifteen on her shoulder each time she turned.

"I—I'm sorry."

She shook her head and her curls bounced.

"Sorry won't cut it this time. This is just like before! The messages, the set up—"

"It wasn't a set up."

She stopped pacing to face me again. I sank onto the metal bench between the two rows of lockers.

"Fleming thinks I knew!" she spat. "I could lose my captaincy over this!"

My fingers curled around the lip of the bench.

"Oh, sorry. I didn't realize your captaincy was more important than the city's destruction." I *did* feel bad, but this was the time to be prepping for a fight against Adrestus, not fighting with my roommate.

Naomi shoved a shaking finger in my face, pointing between my eyes.

"Don't," she warned. "You've been keeping secrets for months now and *fine*. You're entitled to that, but *this*?"

"You just said it yourself! You're a captain! You'd have to turn me in!"
Naomi laughed humorlessly and shook her head.

"So you knew it was against protocol—"

"Are you mad I went or if mad I didn't tell you?"

"Both!" Her voice dropped. "Fleming said Adrestus was there."

"I can deal with Adrestus. I *did* deal with Adrestus."

"And Wesley got absolutely destroyed and you had to hide overnight in your parents' house."

"I'm not scared of Adrestus," I lied. Naomi crossed her arms and became deadly still.

"Who are you to him?" she asked. I felt the blood drain from my face. "You and your family showed up right around the same time he started kidnapping people and every time something happens regarding him, it's you, right at the center of it all, whether you put yourself there or not."

I looked away, a tangle of hair falling in my face.

"I'm no one." That much was true. Samantha was fake and Eydis was dead. Naomi breathed heavily, her stare unwavering in my peripheral vision.

"I can feel everything you feel, so why do you keep lying?"

"I'm not." I finally turned to match her gaze. "Adrestus thinks he knows who I am, but he's wrong."

"And who does he think you are?"

The tips of my fingers were going numb from gripping the metal bench so hard.

"Wesley knows, right?" she asked, quiet now. I didn't have to say anything for her to see the answer. Her shoulders sagged and she dropped her hands limply to her sides. "Yeah, he does."

She'd said it herself. I was allowed to have secrets and I was allowed to tell those secrets to who I wanted, yet guilt gnawed my every fiber.

"Fleming and Everly, too," I said, suddenly defeated, suddenly tired of the weight I'd carried keeping Eydis a secret from Naomi. "It's not that

I didn't want to tell you, it's...I don't like talking about it. I like to pretend it's not real."

Not real. Like me. I blinked back tears.

Naomi, always perceptive, sighed and sat down, leaning forward to look sideways at me.

"It can't be that bad."

"Adrestus and I, we go—"

The door behind us crashed open. We twisted to see Heather in the doorway.

"Fleming's back."

My stomach churned painfully. Naomi set her jaw and stood up to follow Heather to the atrium but I faltered.

"It'll be fine," Naomi insisted, waiting for me in the doorway.

"He's going to expel me."

What if he gave up guardianship of me? What if I had to go live with Roy Hendricks in the middle of nowhere, like Avery had, but without the clever powers that would help me escape?

"He can't do that."

"He *can* kick me off the team."

"Sure, but he'll do that whether you're out there or not."

I groaned and tried to run my fingers through my hair, but they caught on knots and twigs. The leaves from the corsage brushed against my cheek and I cupped them in my opposite hand, hiding them from view.

"Also, I'm not going to forget just because we got interrupted," Naomi said without looking back. "About your secret, I mean."

"I didn't think you would."

I tried to tip-toe back to the group, hoping no one would notice my return. Luckily, only Remi looked up, glaring at me from the call desk with red eyes and running make-up.

Everyone else watched Fleming where he stood in the Sickbay door, talking to Everly with their heads bowed together. Everly nodded and

Fleming patted his colleague's shoulder before the nurse retreated back into the Sickbay.

Fleming straightened up and found me at the back of the crowd. His eyebrows furrowed together above his glasses and I could tell by his expression that he was angry about more than my vigilantism.

"Nurse Everly tells me you've all already been briefed. Good." His face was like stone. "City Council has elected to ignore our warnings and will not evacuate the city, nor will they equip it with resources needed to deal with a firestorm."

"So we fight head on?" Carmen asked from the juniors. "We'll catch Adrestus off guard at his stupid museum, before he can attack, and—"

"No," Fleming interrupted her. She clamped her mouth shut and shrank back between her classmates.

"Defense, then!" Christopher, a freshman, nodded importantly.

"No."

Murmurs went up across the room.

"Then what's the plan?" Justin stood up and the concerned whispers hushed at the sight of the captain.

Fleming's mouth tightened into a thin line and he crossed his arms across his chest. His sleeves were rolled up to his elbows and red burn scars splayed across his forearms. He stuck his chin out and looked down his nose at the room.

"The plan is to stay here and stay safe."

I chewed on the inside of my cheek to keep from adding my voice to the protests and angry cries that rose around the atrium.

"We can't just let—"

"People are going to *die!*"

"This is what happens when Betas are in charge!"

Fleming remained stoic and unbudging while Naomi leaned against the wall and massaged her temple with a knuckle.

"This is a mess," she sighed, "and it's going to get worse."

After the team yelled themselves out, Fleming cleared his throat.

"You may not like to hear it, but you're all children." He held up a hand to cut off a fresh wave of protests. "I'd sooner leave the program all together than see any of you get hurt."

"We face danger all the time!" Marcus protested. "It's what we signed up for! To be like Paragon!"

A shadow flitted across Fleming's face, but he kept his composure at the mention of his brother's hero name.

"Adrestus wants to murder two-thirds of the island. I refuse to let any of you be in that head count."

"We can't do nothing!" Heather spat.

"*You* can. The university students as well as the council members able to suit up will be on hand to minimize casualties."

I'd only seen Fleming suit up once before, in a uniform not unlike the students', but in the flashy red and whites of Paragon's old costume.

"What if we try to evacuate the city without City Hall's help?" My voice cut across the atrium and Fleming's eyes darted to mine. I matched his posture, my arms crossed to mirror his.

"Samantha, I think you've—"

"There's an alarm system that goes off if the tidal lift system fails. I read about it for my industry project."

Fleming's shoulders heaved as he took a deep, steadying breath.

"We're not sinking the city," he said.

"We don't have to! If we find a way to set the alarm off without sinking the city—"

"City Hall will announce it's a malfunction and then what?" Fleming shook his head and I dropped my arms.

He was probably right but my mind raced to find a solution.

"Then we just sink it a few feet! The control panel, you said it's under the city."

Fleming narrowed his eyes at me.

"Told you guys she was working with Adrestus," Erik muttered nearby.

"I've been on the team longer than you!" I snapped. Erik rolled his eyes and mouthed the word "*Beta*", which was real rich considering Erik's Apex ability was to make *smells*.

"We *aren't* sinking the city," Fleming pressed forward. "The campus will be on lockdown. You'll all be sequestered to the dorms but I'll keep the captains updated—"

"We're, what, twelve feet over the water?" I interrupted. "We wouldn't have to drop it into the ocean, just enough to scare everyone into evacuating."

Fleming stared at me silently for several long, drawn out seconds but I didn't back down, meeting his gaze. Finally, without looking away from me, he addressed the room.

"Everyone is dismissed to the dorms. Captains, hang back. You," he pointed at me, "a word. Now."

The students already in uniform slunk back to the locker rooms to change and Naomi left to find the other captains. I took my time working my way to the front of the atrium to meet Fleming.

"We'll talk when this is all over," he said. I tried to keep my face passive. It wasn't an immediate expulsion from the team. I should consider myself lucky.

"Is Wes okay?" I asked.

"We can't spare the resources to fix his leg or ribs completely, but the bones are at least fused back together."

"Ribs?" I gulped. I'd been so concerned with Wesley's leg, I hadn't thought about other injuries he might've sustained.

"Alison called about an hour after you did."

I dug my fingernails into the palms of my hands.

"And?"

"Avery's missing. She thinks he might be in New Delos to find Vidar."

I tried to look genuinely concerned at the news but Fleming knew me too well at this point.

"Out with it," he said. I scuffed my foot against the floor.

"He was at the townhouse."

I must've pushed Fleming past his breaking point. He didn't look angry, like he had in front of the team, just tired and a little sad.

"Why didn't you say something?"

"He told me not to."

"Did he use his powers on you?"

"I don't know," I said honestly. "Is there a way I'd be able to tell?"

The city was about to be destroyed and I'd let Avery run into it. I wouldn't blame Fleming for kicking me off the team. *I* would kick me off the team.

"His powers are subtle, so I doubt it."

I jammed my hands into my jacket pockets.

"Adrestus is going to attack the city but why do I feel like it's my fault?

If I had been able to keep the Lapis safe..." I lifted a hand from my pockets to absentmindedly rub the long, ragged scar on my neck. "And if Eydis...if *I* had been able to destroy it when I first stole it a thousand years ago..."

I trailed off and Fleming drummed his fingers on the Sickbay doorframe.

"You broke curfew and left campus without permission. You didn't update the team when you got new information, rather taking matters into your own hands. There is a *lot* you should feel bad about from the last twelve hours." Despite the admonishment hiding in his words, Fleming rested his hands on my shoulders. "You *don't* get to feel guilty about *anything* Adrestus has done. You are not responsible for the actions of a grown man and *nothing* he has done or will do is your fault."

"People are going to die," I whispered.

"Maybe." Fleming let go and straightened up. "I'll be out there, doing my best to make sure they don't."

I couldn't bear to admit it, but if something happened to Fleming out there in Adrestus' firestorm, I'd be lost. However, I nodded, relieved Fleming wasn't immediately kicking me off the team, but certain he'd cook up some horrible punishment when and if we made it through the next few days.

"I don't want you leaving the dorms." He moved towards the captains grouped around the call desk.

"Can I check on Wesley first?"

"Do what you need to."

I reached for the Sickbay door, but my name echoed from behind me.

"Samantha."

I took a steadying breath before turning around to face Andersen. The hood of his jacket was pulled up over his head and he glowered at me from underneath it.

"What do you want?" I braced myself for whatever attack he had ready for me this time. He'd been suspiciously quiet earlier, when the other students had questioned my loyalty and I wasn't ready for whatever verbal assault he'd been saving up since then.

He glanced around the room, his scowl deepening, before looking back at me.

"It was a good plan."

"What?" I asked dumbly. It was a trick. It had to be.

Andersen screwed his face up, as if the words caused him physical pain to say out loud.

"Your plan to make the city sink. It was good." He shrugged. "And, I'm in."

35

The Maelstrom Under The City

He had to be joking and I waited for a punchline that never came.

"Fleming said no," I finally said.

"That's never stopped you before." Andersen thrust his hands into his pockets and looked around to make sure no one was listening. "You don't get to save the day all on your own anymore. You're planning something and I want in."

"I'm flattered," I held out my hands, as if to show him no secret plans were hiding in my sleeves, "but I never have a plan. Things just happen to go wrong when I'm around."

Andersen grunted and turned towards the exit.

"It would work. That's all I'm saying."

He disappeared through the exit door and I wrapped my arms around myself. He'd gotten me riled up enough to run headfirst into danger before and he wasn't above dirty tricks.

I shook off thoughts of Andersen and pushed into the Sickbay. Everly watched Wesley taking practice steps on his freshly healed leg, still in Dad's baggy sweatpants. Anthony sat nearby, waiting patiently for his roommate.

Wesley made a show of balancing on his healed leg when he saw me.

"Look! It's like I wasn't even smashed into a boat last night!"

"Careful," Everly warned. "It won't be completely healed for another couple weeks."

"It feels fine!"

Wesley's eye flitted to the leaves on my wrist and I rushed to fold my hands behind my back.

"Can I walk you to the dorms?"

"Everly's clearing me to leave right now." He stood still as Everly lifted Wes' shirt to inspect the purple and black bruise that painted half of his back. When I'd had a hairline fracture in one rib, it had been painful enough to take my breath away just bending over. My stomach churned imagining how much pain Wesley had to be in.

"And you're to *stay* there," Everly warned, dropping Wesley's shirt over the mottled skin. "Hopefully the lockdown is over sooner than later. I'd hate for Adrestus to keep us waiting."

I walked Anthony and Wesley to the boys' dorm and while I was relieved to see Wesley looking so much better despite a lingering limp, I was stuck turning Andersen's words over in my head.

It was a good plan. It *was* a good plan.

"You coming up?" Wesley asked at the boys' dorm entry. Students lounged in the lobby, confused by the sudden class cancelation but not complaining. They hung in clusters on the couches, laughing, unaware of the oncoming firestorm.

"Actually, yeah," I said. "There's something I want to talk about."

Anthony and Wesley grinned at each other, leading the way through the lobby.

"Told you," Wesley said to Anthony.

"Told him what?"

"That you'd have a plan. I called it," Wesley said smugly, punching the elevator button.

I'd been to the study room on Wesley and Anthony's floor several times, but this was my first trip to their room. The elevator opened to a hall lined with open doors. Students milled between them, basking in their day off, though Freddie and Everest stood by the bathroom, talking together in hushed tones. Anthony and Wesley ushered me to their room at the end of the hall before our teammates could notice us passing.

Anthony fell back onto the bed on the right side of the room, overlooked by a wall decorated with soccer jerseys and tea-lights. Wesley's wall was more barren, sporting nothing but a cork board over his bed. Old photos showed a young Wesley clutching the arm of an older boy, grinning shyly.

I stepped closer, keeping my arms close to my chest to avoid accidentally brushing up against Wesley's bed. The other pictures on the board showed Wesley through the years and I snorted at his middle-school haircut that hung almost to his shoulders. In the middle of the board, I recognized a wrinkled sketch of Wesley and me, sparring like we used to before Remi became his go-to gym partner.

"Hey!" I pointed. "I drew that!"

"Yeah," Wesley blushed. "It fell out of your notebook."

"You didn't give it back?" I smirked at him.

"I tried but you ignored me." He winced as he settled back on his dark gray comforter, putting his glasses on. "Besides, I liked it."

He glanced at the corsage on my wrist before locking eyes with me.

"So," Anthony rubbed his hands together eagerly, "the *plan?*"

I shook my head, trying to clear the blush from my cheeks.

"Right. You've already heard it."

Anthony's grin fell from his face and Wesley winced again, either from pain or disappointment.

"But Fleming—" Wesley said.

"Fleming has his own reasons for not wanting to sink New Delos."

"Reasons like maybe threatening the city is a bad way to handle other threats on the city?"

Reasons like an undying bitterness towards his brother, but now wasn't the time to hash out Fleming-Paragon drama.

I fidgeted, feeling exposed and uncomfortable standing between their beds while they waited for me to say the magic words that would save the city.

"Andersen said it was a good idea." I pressed on despite Wesley's dry laugh. "If Andersen is willing to admit it's a good plan, then I'm sure there are others who agree."

Wesley rolled his head back and forth against the wall.

"Sorry, Sammy, but if Andersen thinks it's a good idea, then he has to be up to something."

"I'm not asking you to trust Andersen. I only need you to trust *me*."

Anthony and Wesley shared a look. The shadow of a smirk pulled at the corners of Wesley's lips.

"How would we do it?" He tilted his head at me.

"There's a control panel," I said. Fleming and Mom had stopped the city from falling into the ocean all those years ago, using the same control. "It's under the city, but if we could reach it, maybe we can figure out how to tell it to drop the city slowly, giving everyone time to evacuate, and just twelve feet or so, so that the city doesn't actually sink, everyone just thinks it is going to."

"You barely know how to log onto the school computers," Anthony laughed. "How are you going to hack into something like that?"

Someone knocked on the other side of the door, slamming their fist against the wood. Wesley turned pale and covered his face with a pillow.

"Wesley! Please let me in! I want to talk!"

A smile forced its way across my face. I yanked the door open.

"Wes, I—" Remi stopped with her mouth open, dumbstruck for a moment before her face contorted into a snarl. "What you doing h—"

I grabbed her wrist and pulled her inside.

"Perfect timing," I grinned. "We need you."

That afternoon, I stood at the head of Wesley and Anthony's dorm room, wringing my hands. Remi pouted at Anthony's desk and even though she kept stealing bitter glances in Wesley's direction, she'd agreed to help. Andersen leaned against Anthony's wardrobe looking bored, which I decided to take as a sign he wasn't interested enough to rat us out to Fleming.

"You're sure you don't want Skyler?" he asked.

"We need to keep the group small," I insisted. "It'll draw less attention and it minimizes the chances of someone snitching."

"Skyler wouldn't."

Wesley snorted and Andersen glared.

"Whoever goes or knows we're going will probably get kicked off the team," Remi said matter-of-factly. "You're saving him his membership."

"Are *you* fine getting kicked off?" Wesley asked her. "It's what you wanted for so long."

An angry retort built in her mouth, apparent on her red face, but then, she sighed and shrugged.

"I thought it was. No one seems to care or notice that I'm there, though. This seems as good a way to leave the team as any."

Heavy silence suffocated the room as we all mulled the implications of what we were about to do.

"Andersen?" Anthony asked carefully. "Are you okay risking your spot? I can try to come up with alibis for you all since I'll still be here but..."

Andersen laughed and I was surprised at how relaxed the sound was.

"Everyone knows what I am. I don't need Apex Team to hide me anymore."

We silently turned towards Wesley. He pretended to clean his glasses on his shirt.

"Wes?" I asked. He forced a lopsided smile and shook his head.

"We might not get kicked off."

"The chances aren't great and you aren't any more special than the rest of us." Remi leaned back in Anthony's desk chair as she pouted at Wesley.

Wesley squinted at his glasses, rubbing at smudges we all knew weren't there. With his injuries, he shouldn't have been going anyways. His leg seemed fine now that he was relaxed on his bed, but something as simple as mis-stepping could snap it.

"Are you sure you don't want to tell Naomi?" Anthony asked. I frowned at the carpet. She'd be furious and I wasn't sure how much more strain our friendship could take, but she had said it herself. She was a captain. If she found out what we were up to, she'd have to tell Fleming.

"She's got her hands full with captain stuff." I twisted a lock of hair around my finger. "Besides, this is as good a team as any."

The soft patter of rain on the window filled the silence. The only thing left to do was the plan itself.

Sheets of rain rolled over the city, turning everything gray. Hopefully the weather would buy us more time against Adrestus, since it might be hard to burn down the city in a downpour. With classes at the high school and university canceled, the surrounding streets were devoid of traffic. Wesley and I lagged behind Andersen and Remi to break up the group and try to look less conspicuous as we marched towards the city center.

Wesley clutched a crudely sketched map of the underground canals, pulled off of our presentation poster from October's Industry project. It had been hiding in Wesley's closet since the project fair. The lift system looked like a spider, with one large, circular room in the center of the city with canals shooting in all directions. All we needed was to find a manhole in the city that would drop us down. After that, it was a matter of getting Remi safely to the computer so she could reprogram it with a touch of her hand.

"You good?" Wesley asked, his sneakers squelching in the rain.

"Yeah." My voice cracked. I rubbed my wrist, now bare after taking off the makeshift corsage before leaving. I'd worked so hard to get to this point with the team and I was about to throw it away. But then I had let Avery loose in the city, knowing full well he was in danger of being caught up in Adrestus' assault. Avery was powerful, but he wouldn't be able to reason with fire.

I needed to stop Adrestus, even if it meant losing my spot on the team. I bowed my head against the downpour.

"You sure we can trust those two?" Wesley whispered. I looked up at him, feeling rain splash against my cheeks. He always looked so much older without his glasses, but maybe that's because he never wore them when he had to be serious.

"Andersen, yes." I didn't put it past him to try something, but for the time being, I wasn't too concerned. "Remi's the one I'm worried about. She did just get broken up with."

Wesley sighed.

"Yeah, I know but we can't do this without her."

"How did it go, by the way? The break up."

"It was okay. I think it's what she wants, too. She was mad, obviously but she also seemed a little relieved."

I watched the back of Remi's hood. I could tell by the way it bobbed around that she was talking with Andersen. Wesley would be able to hear them, but I didn't ask what they were talking about.

"You can be relieved and mad at the same time, I guess," I said. "I feel bad I didn't realize she feels like the team doesn't like her."

"They don't."

I looked back up at Wesley, surprised he could be so casually cruel, but his mouth was drawn into a firm frown and his eyes wrinkled with worry as he watched Remi ahead of us.

It was true that she didn't seem to have friends on the team, and when I thought about it, I'd never seen her hanging out with many of our classmates, either. It sounded all too familiar. I should've been nicer to her.

"They also don't like me too much lately," I smiled. If I acted like it didn't bother me, maybe it wouldn't.

"They're scared. They want to help but they don't want to end up like him." Wesley nodded at Andersen.

"Or the others," I said darkly.

Wesley pulled me away from the sidewalk edge as a car passed and sprayed up water.

"You don't really think it's someone from the team posting the names, do you?" he asked.

"Who else could it be?"

He stopped to rub his temples with the heels of his hands.

"Sorry," I said quickly, "it might not be. It could be anyone."

"It's not that," he smiled through the rain, still massaging his head. "I haven't been wearing my glasses much since yesterday."

"Oh, right." In the chaos of the twenty-four hours, I'd forgotten about the headaches that came with his power. "You could've brought them."

He smirked, then frowned and tilted his head, as if listening to something far away. He whistled and Andersen and Remi spun around.

"Is it Adrestus?" Remi hissed, backing up against a brick building to survey the street.

"No, I think there's an entrance this way.

Wesley led us down an off-shooting alley, stopping over a round manhole cover, three feet in diameter and made of dense metal.

"How do you know it's not the sewer?" Andersen grimaced at the disc. "I'm not climbing down into sh—"

"It sounds different than a sewer," Wesley cut him off, glaring. "Not to mention, it smells like salt water, not sewage."

Andersen held out his hand. The metal disc rattled and lifted out of its nook before shifting to the side, hovering over the pavement. It clattered to the ground and we all froze, waiting for someone to have heard.

"Nice going," Wesley hissed. Andersen grunted and dropped into the hole, clinging to the ladder bolted to the concrete wall. A dull, orange light emanated at the bottom of the long shaft.

"I'm going first," Andersen insisted. Wesley rolled his eyes but stood back as Andersen began the descent into the city's lift system.

I nodded at Remi and she went next, following a few feet above Andersen.

"Are you able to close the cover?" I asked Wesley. He wrinkled his nose at me.

"Of course." However, when he followed me down the ladder, I looked up to see him wince and stop to take a breath as he dragged the metal back into place.

Cold air drafted up the shaft and I shivered as I hugged the cool steel of the ladder, climbing down after Remi and Andersen. The ladder well opened into a wider underground alley with a five foot drop from the last rung. A corridor of water thundered through the adjoining passageway, from which a dusky, orange light filtered into our offshoot.

I dropped to the concrete floor and watched anxiously as Wesley followed suit. He wavered on his landing, tilting to the side as his left leg buckled, but he caught himself on the stone wall.

"That way." Wesley pointed towards the sound of gushing water. Andersen scowled at being told what to do, but Wesley and I had been down here before. We knew the way.

We crept towards the underground river, keeping close to the wall and one by one filed out into the larger corridor. The walkway was a few feet wide with a metal railing separating the path from the water that gurgled violently through the canal. There was an ebb and flow to the sound of the water, as if we were walking through a sleeping giant whose snores echoed off the high barrel ceilings. Sconces on the stone walls lit the space with muted orange and yellows. Wesley held our map up to the nearest one.

"Left," he said. He went to take the lead but Andersen shoved his way to the front.

"I'm not watching you limp the entire way there. Keep up or go home."

Wesley's shoulders tensed but I grabbed his forearm and he relaxed. I wished he *would* go home, though. He leaned on the railing for support and his breaths looked shallow, probably in an attempt to keep from agitating his rib injuries.

We walked in a silent, single-file line. I took the back of the group, watching Wesley limp after the others, and matching my breathing with the pulsating of the water's thundering.

The corridor followed a gentle curve towards the center of the island and I tried to count the minutes in my head. We had at least another mile to go when Wesley ushered us into another narrow offshoot. We crouched in the dark for several minutes, waiting, before two men in hard hats and reflective vests passed by the mouth of our hiding space.

Remi hid behind her knees and Andersen reached up for the ladder overhead, ready to make an escape, but the workers didn't notice us in the dark.

"Will there be more?" I whispered.

"Don't know. Let's just hope the control room is empty."

Andersen ripped the map from Wesley, holding it up in the dim light.

"Are we even going the right way? We've been walking forever."

"I can hear it getting louder." Wesley pointed to the center of the map, at the large circular space. "The underground rivers meet in the middle of the island, where the water is sucked downwards. The control room is suspended over the vortex, so that's where we need to be."

"Suspended?" Remi repeated, blanching and leaning back against the wall, still on the ground. "You didn't say anything about that before."

"Is that going to be a problem?" I crossed my arms down at her as Andersen and Wesley crept back to the main corridor, both vying for the lead position.

"Heights aren't my favorite." She staggered to her feet, looking more green than pale now. She hesitated, watching Andersen and Wesley jostle to get out of the alley first. Andersen won when Wesley's leg spasmed, forcing him to rely on the wall for support.

"No offense," I said slowly, "but why *did* you rejoin the team?"

Remi stared after Wesley as he turned the corner, the orange light bouncing off her eyes.

"To prove that I could. It was stupid. I failed the trials. I should've known that meant this wasn't for me."

She followed the guys, hugging herself.

"I don't think that's stupid." Even though she was talking about herself, I couldn't help but feel offended. It was exactly what I had done, too.

Remi shrugged, leading the way back onto the canal.

"If everything goes according to plan, it won't matter I rejoined the team." She shivered, but didn't look back at me.

The water grew louder as we continued to walk and white light bounced off the water-slicked wall up ahead, washing out the orange glow from the sconces. Andersen quickened his pace and Wesley used the metal railing as a sort of crutch, pushing off it with his hand to keep up.

I faltered as we turned the corner. Our crude map hadn't done the center of the lift system justice. The corridor opened up into a large, vaulted dome. The size of the space was bigger than the sports field at school and perfectly circular. Rivers of ocean water poured into the frothing maelstrom that took up the bulk of the area, swirling downwards, sucking the water into its depths from which a wet, mechanical gurgle rattled.

A hexagonal booth hung suspended from the top of the dome, reachable only by a flimsy set of catwalk stairs that stretched from the wall to our left, over the massive water drain, to the roof of the control booth. I saw Remi swear, but it was impossible to tell if she'd muttered the curse out loud with the water roaring from all angles.

Wesley clamped his hands over his ears and Andersen forged forward, keeping as close to the wall as possible. The path couldn't have been wider than two feet and I made the mistake of peering over the metal railing. My stomach lurched, feeling very much like how the water twenty yards below looked.

Remi kept her back to the drop-off as she walked and dragged her forehead against the wall as she went. I looked up at the rickety catwalk we'd have to climb. If Remi couldn't handle walking *to* the catwalk, I had no idea how we were going to get her *up* it.

Andersen hesitated at the first steps up the metal walkway. It hung, suspended on wires, from the ceiling, climbing up to the space between the control booth and peak of the dome. He tapped it with the toe of his shoe and looked back at us to shrug.

Remi shook her head vehemently before leaning over the railing to vomit. Wesley reached for her, trying to draw her towards the catwalk but she shook her head again, cowering against the wall.

"No way," she shouted over the water. "I'm not walking up that! You figure it out without me."

Andersen furrowed his brow and pushed past Wesley to reach her.

"We did not come all this way just for you to chicken out!" He tugged at her arm but her feet were firmly planted. "We need you!"

"Let her go!" Wesley put a hand on Andersen's shoulder. He shrugged him off but released Remi. Andersen took a breath, closing his eyes, as if about to tap into some secret power. When he opened them, a strained smile spread across his face.

"Remi," he said as gently as he could while still being heard over the water, "you can do things that none of us ever could. No one is making you climb up there, but if you do, you will be saving thousands of people from being burned alive."

The smile didn't move from his face, but his eyes looked like they were trying to scream at her. She slowly turned to look up at the control booth.

"I can't, I—"

Andersen put his hands on her shoulders and got in her face, still smiling.

"If I can let these two morons march me for miles under the city just so we can work together to pretend to destroy New Delos, you can handle a little height." His grimace relaxed and he continued, very seriously, "I promise, if something goes wrong, and I can only use my powers to save one of you from falling, it'll be you."

I shared an exasperated look with Wesley but Remi shuddered and nodded. She stepped towards the metal, let Andersen go first, and carefully followed close behind with her eyes screwed shut.

Wesley stepped aside to let me pass. The metal quaked underfoot as I stepped onto it. I swallowed hard, looking at the water churning beneath my shoes. One wrong step and even Wesley and Andersen's powers combined wouldn't be enough to save me. Besides, Andersen had already promised to help Remi first.

I didn't know if the railing was wet from water spray or if my palms were sweating, but I was able to slide my hands up the metal bannister as I followed Remi's painstaking progress to the control booth. As the water vortex got further beneath us, the dome seemed to spin. I matched my breathing to the groaning of the water pumps below to try to calm myself and focused on the back of Remi's frizzing curls.

When I finally stepped off the catwalk and onto the top of the control booth, it was hardly a relief. We had to stoop to keep from bumping our heads against the roof and Remi crawled to the center on her hands and knees, towards a latch in the floor.

"Why didn't we come in through here?" Andersen patted a circular door cut into the ceiling.

"It's under City Hall," Wesley explained. "We never would've gotten through."

Remi clawed at the latch on the floor, pulling at a heavy lock.

"It's locked!"

Wesley crouched next to her, cupping the padlock in his hand. He gave it a sharp tug and the booth rattled beneath us, bringing Andersen and me to our hands and knees.

"Sorry," Wesley mumbled. Remi retched. Andersen scooted forward to hold his hand over the lock. His fingers twitched like he was playing a tiny piano and when he gave the lock a pull, it clicked.

He smirked as he opened the latch and dropped in.

"After you." I gestured towards the hole and Remi slipped in next, making use of the ladder rungs that hung into the room.

I lowered myself in after them. The ceiling was higher than I expected, so it was a good thing a ladder hung from the entry to help us get out. Giant windows took up all six sides and looked out over the converging channels. A large control panel stretched beneath two of the windows and Remi hovered her trembling hands over it. A single stool stood next to her.

I steadied Wesley as he fell in next to me. He looked around the room, balking at the view, and cautiously tip-toed to a window. I stood with him, looking straight down in the maw of the whirlpool.

"This thing can hold all of us, right?" I asked in a low voice that Remi wouldn't hear. Wesley nodded dumbly.

"It should."

Remi cleared her throat. She still looked green but there was a determined furrow in her brow as she gave us a thumbs up.

"You're already done?" Wesley asked. Remi scoffed, shaking her hair back behind her shoulders.

"No, I've only disabled the security. No one will know we're here until it's too late. The next part will take at least a couple minutes. There's several layers to it and I need to program it so they can't just turn it off or hit reset." She rubbed her hands together and looked around at us. "Are we sure we're doing this?"

"I didn't come for the view," Andersen snorted.

My heart accelerated. This was it. There'd be no turning back after Remi reprogramed the lift system. I looked at Wesley and he nodded, but the skin around his eyes creased.

"Do it," I said. Remi gave us one last grim grin and spun to face the controls. The panel was covered in buttons, levers, and small screens that showed water levels around the island. If we hadn't got Remi up the catwalk, I would've been at a loss at where to start. However, as soon as she laid hands on the machine and closed her eyes, the top row of lights flashed from green to orange.

"Is that bad?" Wesley asked.

"Shut up," Remi mumbled back, her eyes rolling back and forth beneath her eyelids. "There's several levels of clearance I've got to break through."

We held our breath while we watched and, finally, the lights flickered blue. A nervous smile spread across Remi's face.

"That's a good smile, right?" I looked to Wesley for confirmation.

"If you want to call sinking the city 'good', sure," Remi said. "Looks like we're at high tide right now, I can sink the city to water level over twenty-four hours. Is that long enough to get everyone to safety?"

"It'll have to be," Wesley said.

"Last chance to not do this," she warned.

"I wouldn't be suspended over a giant whirlpool with my least favorite people if I thought there was any chance we *weren't* doing this." Andersen stared out the far window, perched on the stool.

"Aw," I muttered dryly and rolled my eyes at Wesley. "I'm touched."

The panel whirred and clicked and I inched closer to the glass wall. Wesley limped up next to me and we stared down at the swirling water together.

"How's your leg?"

"Never better."

"Liar."

He pressed his forehead against the glass and laughed to himself, but didn't argue. I resisted the urge to reach for his hand, though I would've liked the comfort of his fingers around mine.

Instead, I watched as each of the gaping tunnels that fed into the vortex began spitting water harder and faster than before. The glass rattled from the sound alone and I stepped away.

"It won't fall," Wesley assured me. "We're safe."

"Until Fleming kills us, you mean."

"He won't." He glared at the water, biting his lip to keep it from trembling.

"What's wrong?"

His breath fogged the glass as he let out a shaky laugh.

"Are we the bad guys?"

"What? No," I snorted. "We're saving the city."

"But they don't know that." The swirling waters reflected off his green eyes. "I don't want to hurt anyone."

"You mean like your brother?"

His eyes darted sideways to glare at me.

"Yeah, like Benson."

"You were a kid, Wes. This is different."

He shrugged and looked back down. We watched in silence as the gaping whirlpool beneath us swelled, foaming and churning harder with every second. The water glowed red as alarm lights blinked to life around the dome.

"Hey, Remi," Wesley warned, "I thought you disabled security."

"I did," she snapped. "Whatever alarms or lights you're worried about are the city's alarm system. You know, the thing we need to work to convince everyone to *leave*."

"Great," Andersen jumped off the stool, making the booth shudder. He stalked to the center and reached up for the ceiling ladder. "Then we're almost done?"

"Just making sure it can't be reprogrammed. We don't want anyone cleaning up behind us and making this all for nothing."

"And you made sure it'll stop before *actually* sinking?" Wesley asked.

"Yes," she snarled. "Now leave me alone. This is harder than it looks."

Wesley's hand wrapped around my wrist with surprising force.

"It's fine," I whispered. "She's just trying to focus."

"No, not that."

I turned to look at Wesley but he stared past me at the open trapdoor in the ceiling, just over Andersen's head.

"I smell fire," he hissed.

Orange sparks wafted down into the booth. Andersen stumbled back as heavy, black boots dropped in overhead. Hephestae with her flame-hair and dark cape fell into the booth, landing catlike where Andersen had just been standing.

"Remi, don't stop," I barked, stepping between Amanda and the control panel where Remi still worked with her eyes closed. I raised my fists.

"What's happening?" she demanded.

"We have a visitor," Wesley said grimly.

"Yeah." A snarl issued from above and a pearly tragedy mask peered down at us from the roof of the booth. "Just one or two."

36

The Sisters

The booth creaked as Winnie dropped down next to her sister, looking both threatening and ridiculous in her mask and black robes. Amanda stared blankly next to her, her haunted eyes reflecting the red lights that flashed outside. The flame flickering from her head licked the ceiling, turning the tile black.

"Go away, Winnie," I said. "You and Amanda need to get off the island."

"Before you sink it?" Winnie goaded. She stayed in the center of the booth with Amanda, scanning the space. Andersen, Wesley, and I had them surrounded but if we weren't careful, the booth might not be able to handle the damage. Winnie's mask tilted towards Wesley. "You look better. How's that? I thought the Serum was stolen."

So whoever had been sabotaging the team *was* connected to Adrestus. My chest constricted. Had the saboteur seen us leave campus and warned him? But how could they have known where we were going? Unless...

My eyes flitted towards Andersen and that was all Winnie needed. She dove for Wesley, kicking his bad leg out from under him. I lunged after her and Andersen grunted behind me as Amanda went his way.

Wesley fell back against the window and I tackled Winnie to the ground before she could deal any further damage to his injuries. I pinned her arms behind her back, but she writhed on the floor, kicking out and making it difficult to keep her down.

Across the room, Andersen twisted out of the way of flames as Amanda came after him over and over, heating up the small space. Andersen's face contorted and the booth shuddered dangerously. Remi squeaked in horror, but kept working at the panel.

"You ruined my life!" Andersen screamed. The metal stool across the room rose into the air and crashed into the side of Amanda's head. She hardly moved, not bothering to absorb the blow.

"Don't hurt her!" I shouted. "She can't help it!"

"It's her fault everyone knows about me!" Andersen outmaneuvered Amanda's assaults to kick her. She barely flinched and as Andersen's frustration mounted, the booth quaked harder.

"What's happening?" Remi shrieked. "Andersen, stop shaking the place!"

"They're going to kill all of us if you guys don't back off!" I hissed in Winnie's ear. She twisted beneath me and I grunted as her boot collided with my stomach. I fell back and doubled over, gagging for air.

Winnie leapt to her feet and her boot swung into the side of my head. Pain exploded in my temple and black starbursts danced across my vision. I waited for the next hit, but Winnie grunted overhead. My vision cleared and I saw Wes pressing her against the window, knocking her mask askew so that she glared at me with one eye. She struggled against his grip but was helpless against his strength.

She let loose a guttural shriek of frustration, fogging up the glass, unable to fight back against Wes.

"I'm fine." Wes nodded at me. "Help Amanda."

The ceiling on Andersen's side of the booth had completely blackened and continued to smoke thanks to Amanda's fire. A large burn hole marred his jacket sleeve. He'd been forced onto defense, having ripped the ceiling ladder from its bolts to fend her off.

But in a break in Amanda's attacks, the metal stool wobbled behind her, where she couldn't see it.

"Andersen, don't!" I leapt between Amanda and the stool as it hurtled towards the back of her head. My arms took the brunt of the attack, but I fell back into Amanda as the stool smashed into me. The ends of my hair singed and I patted out embers that landed on my sleeves.

"Stay out of the way!" Andersen howled, dodging another column of flame.

"She's controlled by a computer in her neck!" I said, remembering what Esther had told me about Mira's control-device. "Don't hurt her if she can't defend herself!"

"She's doing *just fine* defending herself!"

I tried to pull Amanda's arms back, but she didn't seem to register I was there.

"Winnie, make her stop!" I shouted. The booth shook again, more violently than before and I fell back, disoriented and unable to keep my footing. "Andersen, you're going to get us all killed!"

"She's trying to barbecue me!"

The booth creaked ominously and my stomach backflipped as the floor violently shifted.

"We lost a bracket," Wesley said grimly. Winnie stopped struggling against his hold and the swirling water below reflected in her wide eyes. "If we lose another, this booth goes down."

"Winnie?" I begged. "Make her stop!"

"I can't!" she wailed. "Mira's controlling her!"

Amanda lunged at Andersen again and the booth shook once more.

"Andersen!" Remi and Wesley both shrieked.

"I can't help it!" He swung the broken ladder at Amanda. The window behind him popped and shattered, showering him in broken glass. He looked back and his eyes widened. His fear only stoked his abilities and the booth quaked harder still.

"Stop!"

I jumped between Amanda and Andersen, pulling him away from the gaping window and tackling him to the floor. The shock of my attack made the booth fall still and creak as it settled against its metal wall anchors.

Amanda bore down on us, her whole being alight with flames. I ducked my head behind my arm, unable to look at her through fire, and braced for the heat. However, the onslaught never came.

I peeked over my arm to see Remi with her hand clamped over Amanda's neck despite the flames, digging her fingers into the muscle. Amanda locked up and tears of pain rolled down Remi's cheeks, but she refused to let go.

"Computer in her neck," she gasped. "I found it."

"Stop-p-p!" A raspy gurgle issued from Amanda's throat. She twitched, but was otherwise unable to move. A strangled scream ripped its way out of her and she exploded in white-hot flames.

Andersen and I scrambled away but Remi and Amanda remained standing, both screaming as Amanda's flames spread across the ceiling and out the ceiling door.

"Remi, let go!" Wesley yelled, still holding Winnie against the window.

But Remi held on, bowing her head into the crook of her elbow while the flames gnawed at her arm. The acrid smell of burnt hair and flesh stung my nose. A loud *crack* rang out over the sound of the fire and Andersen shouted a warning. Cracks splintered across the remaining windows, shattered by the sheer heat. Wesley pulled Winnie back from the glass just before the whole thing crumbled, raining into the water.

"Grab Remi!" Wesley shrieked.

I staggered to my feet, but just as I went to pull Remi away, Amanda's fire snuffed out and both girls collapsed to the ground. Remi cried softly, cradling her arm. I braced myself, waiting for Amanda to attack but she rolled onto her back and ripped her face mask off, breathing heavily. She threw an arm over her eyes as a dry sob shook her body.

"Amanda?" I bent over her. "Can you hear me?"

She shook her bald head, rocking it back and forth on the dusty floor. Tears tracked through the ash that clung to her face.

"God, I hate capes so much," she choked.

Winnie stared sullenly at her sister with her mask still covering one eye and Wesley held her arms behind her back. I helped Amanda into a sitting position. Her fingers scrabbled at the back of her neck and a weak, relieved smile broke across her trembling lips.

"She's gone," she said, looking as if she barely believed it. "I don't feel her coming back."

"And she shouldn't." Remi coughed, curling around her arm. "I disabled the chip completely."

Amanda's eyes widened and she crawled towards Remi, prying her arms open to look at the damage she'd done. My insides lurched and bile rose in my throat. I turned away, but not before catching a glimpse of the burnt, bloody mess that was left of Remi's arm.

"I'm so sorry," Amanda whispered. "You shouldn't have done this."

"It doesn't hurt that much, actually," Remi hiccuped.

"Sure, because I burnt the nerve endings away." Amanda tore the cape from her neck and Remi flinched as she wrapped the black cloth around her mangled arm.

The sound of groaning metal brought us all to our feet. Something creaked menacingly overhead and we froze, staring through the trapdoor at the remaining metal fixtures that held the booth in place. The one I could see was charred black.

A blood-curdling snap made the hair stand up on the back of my neck and Wesley cried out as he crumbled to the ground. It had taken a single well-aimed kick to his injured leg for Winnie to free herself.

I rushed to Wesley's side as Winnie flew at Remi. Andersen leapt between them, covering Remi with his body but Winnie ignored them, instead grabbing the fallen stool and smashing it into the control board.

Fire erupted around Amanda's fists as she launched at her sister, her face contorting with months of pent of rage and resentment.

"You let them do that to me!" she shrieked. Winnie rolled out of the way and Amanda's flames lapped across the panel.

"Stop! You'll ruin the controls!" Remi shouted, still in Andersen's arms.

Amanda didn't seem to hear and went after her sister with everything she had left. Winnie laughed callously as she sidestepped Amanda's barrage of attacks, dancing dangerously close to the open edge.

Them fighting like this was what had gotten Vidar stuck with Adrestus. He'd tried to break them up. He'd ended up under a pile of rubble for it. Anger rose inside me and Wesley tugged at my jacket.

"Don't—"

But before I could get between the sisters, the stool rose with a flick of Andersen's wrist and swung into the side of Winnie's head. She crumbled to the floor.

"We're leaving." Andersen jerked his head towards the trapdoor in the roof. "After you, *Hephestae.*"

"It's Amanda," Amanda snarled, but stepped back from where Winnie struggled on the ground. With Andersen having ripped the ladder from the ceiling, she set the stool up under the door and gave her sister one last contemptuous look before using the stool to climb up and out of the booth.

I helped Wesley to his feet as Andersen boosted Remi to the roof with Amanda helping up top. The latch at the peak of the dome, the one that led to the basement of City Hall, already hung open. It must've been how Winnie and Amanda reached us.

"Come on, Winnie," I spat. She struggled to a sitting position, shaking her head as if trying to clear it. Andersen crawled up next and Wesley scowled when Andersen reached down to help him.

"Watch the leg," he mumbled as Andersen pulled him through. Amanda and Remi looked down from the second latch, already waiting for us in the City Hall basement.

Winnie's mask had fallen to the floor and her strawberry blonde hair stuck out at odd angles.

"Come on." I patted the stool. Wesley and Andersen grunted as Amanda helped pull them up through the second latch. "You can't stay here."

Her lower lip trembled but she clenched her jaw to steady it.

"Fine. Whatever."

I reached to help her to her feet but just as she took my hand, metal splintered overhead and bolts popped. One half of the booth dropped, along with my stomach. Winnie shrieked as we swung, the vortex whirling beneath us. I held Winnie to my side as I clung to the control panel and watched the stool fall into the maelstrom.

Wesley screamed my name overhead but I barely heard it, too transfixed by the frothing water to look away. The booth shifted again and Winnie swore loudly next to me, her arms constricting desperately around my neck, but instead of dropping us further, the floor tilted back upwards, leveling out. I looked up and through the doors, I could see Andersen with both arms outstretched, grunting through gritted teeth as he willed the booth upwards.

The floor overcorrected so that we tilted slightly in the opposite direction. A hand reached in and grabbed the edge of the doorway, bending the metal around its grip.

"Hurry!" Wesley shouted. He'd lowered himself onto the roof to hold the booth in place with Andersen's help. "We can't hold it for long!"

"You first," I said, dragging Winnie to the center and forcing her boot into my hand. Wesley's face strained overhead. He had one hand holding the booth and the other gripping the next latch, from which Andersen stared down at us with his hands outstretched and sweating profusely.

Winnie obeyed silently, letting me boost her to the roof.

"Help me up!" I reached for the doorway. My fingers only grazed the lip. Without the ladder or stool, I'd never be able to pull myself up. Winnie looked down at me, her eyes wide.

"Come on, Winnie," Wesley grunted. "She's your friend."

Winnie knelt down and extended a shaking arm. But then, she withdrew it, swallowing hard.

"Sorry, Sammy. I just...I can't," she whispered and bolted towards the catwalk. I watched her run down the metal steps, not bothering to look back.

"Jump!" Wesley begged.

I leapt wildly, grabbing the edge of the doorway and tried to pull myself up but I was too exhausted.

"Hurry!" Andersen howled.

"I-I can't—" I looked up at Wesley. He shook his head at me.

"Try again," he begged. My arms shook. There was nothing left. "Come on."

"I have to let go!" Andersen's voice broke. The metal around Wesley's hand bent and peeled as Andersen began to lose his telekinetic grip on the booth.

"Don't drop me," I whispered, barely audible to myself over the water below.

"Never."

With the last bit of strength I could muster, I dropped one hand and then swung myself up to grab Wesley's wrist.

"Drop it," I said, reaching up with my other hand, entwining my fingers together around Wesley's arm. Metal snapped. The booth fell away from me. I made the mistake of looking down to watch it be swallowed by the vortex.

"Eyes up here." Wesley hung from the latch by one hand and his legs dangled next to me. He smiled. "We're okay."

He lifted me towards his chest and I dared to let go with one hand to wrap my arm around his neck, followed by the other. He pulled us both up through the latch into a barren, white-walled hall lit by harsh fluorescents. The latch slammed shut and sirens wailed in the distance.

Hands reached for me and pulled me away from the hole in the floor as Wesley followed. Andersen leaned against one wall, panting into his knees. Remi sat next to him, still cradling her swathed arm and staring blankly at the opposite wall, trembling.

"Did Winnie make it?" Amanda pulled Wesley to his feet. He cringed and shifted his weight to his uninjured leg. "Did you see?"

He nodded breathlessly and she let him go, pacing in the short space between the two walls. The fluorescent lights bounced off her perfectly bald head, highlighting purple bruises, and she rubbed the back of her neck where Remi had disabled the tiny computer installed there.

She stopped mid-pace to whip around to stare at us.

"Which of you was it?" Wild hostility leapt into her face and she looked at each of us accusingly. Her fists disappeared in balls of flame.

"What are you talking about?" Andersen glowered from behind his knees. His hair was singed and ash dusted his cheeks. Amanda smirked as if she had him cornered, and put her hands on her hips, the way Winnie used to, though when Winnie did it, there was less fire.

"Which of you let slip to Adrestus that you were coming here?"

I looked between the other three. It couldn't have been Wesley. Remi was unlikely since she'd just torched her arm to save Amanda. My gaze fell on Andersen.

"It wasn't me," he said before I could accuse him.

"Who else could it have been?"

"You're the one who had the idea to come here!"

Remi cleared her throat. Her face was devoid of any color and her voice shook.

"We have bigger things to worry about," she whispered, still staring at the wall. "The control booth...it-it's gone."

"So?" Amanda scowled. "You fixed it to stop sinking at a certain point, didn't you? I heard you."

A soft, desperate laugh parted Remi's lips.

"Yeah, I did, but I got a good look at the programming and codes when I was inside the computer. If the connection between the controls and the booth is severed, the lift system defaults to whatever setting was in use at the time of disconnection."

Wesley shook his head.

"No, that can't be right, because the last setting—"

He fell silent and the only sound in the corridor was the distant scream of sirens.

My head spun. I braced myself against the wall.

The city wasn't going to stop. It was going to keep sinking.

We had just destroyed New Delos.

37

Rat

Wesley scrambled to reopen the floor latch, as if looking back down in the dome could somehow un-doom the city. Andersen buried his face in his knees and Remi continued to deadpan at the wall opposite her. Only Amanda seemed unbothered, limping as she paced, bending her arms and flexing her fingers, as if testing that she really was back in control of her own body.

"But you told it to stop," I stammered. "So, it *should* stop."

"I programmed the stop as a separate setting." Remi's vacant eyes watered. "It was faster that way. I...It's my fault. I shouldn't have cut corners."

"It's not your fault, it's *his*!" Wesley turned on Andersen.

"You always think it's my fault and it never is!" Andersen sneered, getting to his feet.

"If you hadn't sold us out—"

"I didn't sell out anyone!"

"This was your idea! You set us up!" Wesley hobbled towards Andersen but his leg gave out and he collapsed to the floor.

"My idea?" Andersen scoffed. "This was Samantha's plan. She announced it to the whole team."

"But if you hadn't—"

"Both of you, shut up!" Remi's voice echoed through the hall. "If we hadn't tried, *she* would've killed a whole chunk of the island! No offense."

Amanda stopped her pacing to shrug.

"Wouldn't have been my fault, but sure. Personally, I'm a big fan of how things panned out down here." She kept her voice light and sarcastic, but her eyes were sunken and hollow.

"We can fight when we're back on campus," I said, pulling Wesley to his feet, "but, we can't stay here. Maintenance will probably be on their way."

"No," Amanda said darkly, helping Remi up. "They won't. Adrestus knows he doesn't have me anymore. His whole plan is shot. His best bet will be to use *this* disaster instead, so he'll have his plants in City Hall keep anyone from trying to fix it. What you need to focus on now is getting everyone out of the city in the next twenty-four hours."

She put a protective arm around Remi and marched her down the corridor to a metal door. Andersen rolled his eyes but followed, leaving Wesley and me behind.

"Is your leg okay?" I asked in a low voice.

"Better than it was last night." He limped forward after the others.

"Broken is still broken."

He grunted. I hovered next to him awkwardly, wanting to help, but unsure if he'd accept it, but then he leaned into me for support. I put an arm around him and he murmured a thanks.

"This is what I was afraid of," he whispered. "We *are* the bad guys."

"Don't be stupid."

"I wanted to save people, but now, they might drown because of us."

I wished I had a response. After everything he'd told me last night about his family, I felt worse than ever for putting him in this position.

Were we the bad guys here? How was this any different than what Paragon had done?

Amanda stopped at the door and peered into the stairwell before ushering us in. The sirens were louder on this side of the door, wailing a single, sustained note. Red flashed overhead. Amanda's eyes shifted back and forth as I passed her, and she jumped as the door slammed shut behind us.

"This'll take us up to the main floor of City Hall," Amanda said, still glancing around wildly. "It's going to be a bit chaotic, so stay close and make for the front doors."

We nodded and hurried up the winding staircase, listening to frantic shouts get louder overhead. My heart screamed against my ribs, threatening to burst through bone.

Paragon had thought he was the good guy and he'd burnt down an apartment building so he could go down with honor. Roy Hendricks, too. Were we as bad as them?

When we tore through the main door, I had to remind myself to keep moving. City Hall was adorned in marble floors and matching walls. Corinthian columns supported the vaulted ceilings. People poured from the elevators to our left, no one taking notice of the bald college student in a black latex costume leading the pack of singed and injured high schoolers.

They hurried across the floor, shouting and screaming over the sirens. Series of double doors lined either side of the chamber and people in suits and pencil skirts rushed between them, calling to one another.

"Is the system on the fritz?" one shouted.

"Real deal! We've already dropped half a foot!" her colleague yelled back, pushing past us while throwing on her coat.

The main doors stood straight ahead, leading out onto a paved pavilion. Rain continued to barrage the city and I bowed my head to it as we reached the front stone steps of the building. A man in a suit helping usher people down the stairs caught my eye. Councilman Ratcliffe stood at the bottom step, pointing people down the street, telling them where to go. His eyes met mine and his face darkened into a scowl.

We'd robbed him of his shining, heroic moment.

Granted, we'd also saved him from being Adrestus' sacrificial lamb, but he didn't know that.

He was too busy playing the role of Good City Councilman to stop us as we fled towards the street. We were passing the fountain in front of the building, sporting yet another one of the city's Paragon statues, when a hand clamped over my shoulder.

Mr. Mickey glowered down at me, rain clinging to his stubble.

"With me," he growled. "All of you."

Amanda tried to slink away, but Mickey gripped her shoulder and steered her down the road to the right. Cars sped past us, throwing sprays of rain water up into our faces but Mickey marched us forward.

"Oh, crap," Wesley moaned.

Mickey turned down an alley and we were greeted by yellow headlights. I blinked through the light and my insides turned to lead. Between swipes of the windshield wipers brushing away curtains of water, I could see Fleming's face at the driver's seat, set like stone, and impossible to read. My stomach fluttered when I saw a familiar, blond head in the passenger seat, grinning cautiously.

"Avery," I breathed. "He found him."

Fleming stepped out of the car but stayed behind the open door. I thought I saw his careful composure falter when he saw Amanda standing with us, but he kept his scowl plastered to his face.

"In. All of you."

The five of us squeezed into the back, not daring complain there wasn't nearly enough room for us across the three seats. I jammed myself against the window furthest from Fleming and Wesley wedged himself next to me. Remi lay across our laps with her boots in my face.

Fleming slammed the door shut after Amanda squeezed in and stayed out in the rain to speak with Mickey. Avery twisted around in the front seat, leaning into the back and gawking at us.

"Was it really you guys?" he asked, his face and voice full of awe that we didn't deserve.

"Who's the kid?" Andersen grunted.

"Sit down, Avery," I said quietly, ignoring both of their questions.

"You sold me out, didn't you?" he accused, still smiling, and making no indication he was going to sit back down.

"Could I have?" I raised an eyebrow and he blushed, knowing what I was implying. "Mom knows you ran away. She called Fleming."

Avery sighed and dramatically fell back into his seat.

"I would've found him, you know."

"Mickey's telling Fleming to go easy on us," Wesley mumbled. We all looked at him in surprise.

"And?" I asked. Wesley tilted his head to better listen to the men outside.

"And he doesn't want to."

Dreadful silence fell over the car, save the sounds of rain pattering against the metal roof, the blaring of alarm bells, and Remi's haggard breaths. Finally, the driver door swung open and Fleming slipped inside. The car shuddered to life and without so much as a glance into the back seat, Fleming peeled out of the alleyway, turning onto the main street and accelerating through a yellow light.

I held onto Remi's ankles to keep her from jostling around too much as Fleming fishtailed around corners. No one dared speak, although Avery tapped out a beat on his knees in the front.

Outside the car window, I saw a city in chaos. Sirens wailed through the streets as people hurried through the rain. They cried and screamed and guilt burned my insides.

It was my fault.

These people were scared because of what I'd done.

Fleming drove to the front of the school rather than the parking garage, mounting the front passenger tire on the rotunda curb. Paragon's bronze statue smiled overhead from his spot in the fountain. I couldn't bear to look at him. A fake hero. Him, Roy, John Ratcliffe, me. All frauds.

We followed Fleming out of the car and up the steps to the main door as fast as we could with the injuries the group had sustained. Avery fell in with me, helping Wesley navigate the stone stairs. At the top, Fleming held the door for us. He waved the others in but stopped me.

"We'll meet you down there," he said to the others. Avery and Wesley gave me a final glance before hobbling into the building. Fleming let the heavy door close and it was just him and me on the top step. I hadn't noticed it before, but the ground seemed to vibrate as the city dropped into the ocean, bit by painful bit.

"I'm—" I started.

"It's only a couple feet, right?" Fleming asked. His voice shook but I didn't know if it was from fear or anger. "You wanted to just drop the city a couple feet. Tell me there's no real danger."

I blinked back the warmth that sprung to my eyes.

"That *was* the plan."

His carefully passive face cracked. He turned away as anger deepened the lines around his eyes.

"Samantha," he snarled. I resisted the urge to step back. He faced outwards, towards the darkening city, and screwed his eyes shut. "Eydis."

The name cut in a way I hadn't expected. Eydis had gotten her family killed. I had destroyed New Delos. As much as I liked to pretend we weren't the same, the ghastly similarities had wormed their way to my attention in new, horrible ways every day since I'd learned the truth.

Fleming opened his eyes, looking out at the skyline of the city I'd doomed.

"If anyone, any single person, doesn't make it off this island, it's on you."

He turned away, ripping the door open and stalking into the halls. I stayed on the top step a moment longer, shaking and alone. He was right, of course. Whatever happened next, it would be my fault.

The halls of the school building were dark and I shrugged against the shadows as I hurried to the basement. When I reached the bottom floor, I could hear the team before opening the door.

The atrium was a sea of dark uniforms and helmets, running to and fro, dividing into teams to go out into the city and facilitate evacuation. I put my head down and cut through the crowd towards the Sickbay. A hand grabbed my arm and I stopped, too afraid to look and face whoever had stopped me.

"Sammy?" Even through the voice modulator in her helmet, I recognized Naomi's voice. I looked up as she pulled her helmet off. Her brown eyes were bigger than ever and a sad frown pulled at her face.

"I know. I shouldn't have gone."

"You should've told me," she said seriously.

"You said it yourself this morning," I shrugged. "It would've risked your captaincy and I didn't want to get you kicked off the team."

"I could've helped." Hurt etched across her face and I shrank in on myself. "You went with *Andersen*, Sammy. You hate Andersen! You can't seriously trust him more than me?"

"It wasn't about trust," I insisted, grabbing her gloved hands. "Andersen said he has nothing going for him on the team anymore and I'm not sure I do, either. But you? This team needs you. You're too good for us."

She scowled but her shoulders relaxed.

"Everly wants to see you," she mumbled and followed me into the Sickbay.

Everly bent over Remi's arm in the farthest bed while Anthony fretted over Wesley in the bed opposite them. Avery watched from one of Everly's wheeled stools, spinning listlessly and scooting back and forth. Andersen sat far from the others, turning his helmet in his hands, as if eager to join the chaos in the atrium. A curtain had been pulled around one of the beds and I wondered if Amanda was hiding inside.

Anthony's eyes lit up when he saw me and Wesley waved.

"No Serum for me," Wes shrugged. Everly grunted without looking up from Remi's arm. "Apparently I've put enough strain on the stock for one day."

"They'll need you to help evacuate the city, though," Naomi frowned. Everly grunted again and this time it sounded more like a sardonic laugh.

"I don't think they want my help," Wesley said quietly. He gave Naomi a sad smile. "What're they doing out there?"

"Justin's got everyone splitting into teams. Coastguard is sending boats so we're going to work with the university team making sure every building is emptied and helping people get to the water." She put aside whatever anger she was feeling towards us to force a smile. "Whatever happens, it'll be better than what Adrestus had planned."

Curtain rings grated against metal as the drapery around Amanda's bed shifted. She leaned against the headboard and quickly drew the back of her hand across her face before any of us could get a good look at her. However, between Fleming and Dr. Weaver, who stood over her, I could see her eyes were red and swollen.

She'd put on such a brave face back at City Hall but I couldn't imagine what it must feel like to finally be free after months of being imprisoned in her own body.

"The team outside can handle keeping the people of New Delos safe for now," Dr. Weaver announced to the room. "We have our own problem to handle in here."

I swallowed. This was it. Time to kick us all off the team.

Dr. Weaver stalked forward, her heels clicking on the linoleum. Everly straightened up as he finished bandaging Remi's arm. Naomi shifted towards the door and Fleming held up a hand.

"We need you for this part." His brown eyes glinted dangerously and Naomi shied back to my side.

"But she didn't know!" I looked between the adults. I wouldn't let Naomi go down for something she didn't do. "I made sure not to tell her so she wouldn't get in trouble!"

"How noble," Dr. Weaver said flatly. "We'll handle your punishments later. This is about something else."

She stepped aside and gestured towards Amanda, who swung her legs over the side of her bed.

"Someone told Adrestus where you were going today and he sent Winnie and me to stop you." She ran a hand over her hairless head and prodded at the bruises there. "And I know someone, probably the same person, has been feeding him information for the last several months. Whoever it was is probably in this room."

"And you guys want me to sniff out which of my friends has been sabotaging us?" Naomi balked. Fleming remained impassive, looking every bit like a teacher with all the time in the world to wait for his class to settle down.

I bit my lip, taking care not to look to Andersen, though I hadn't ruled out Remi, either. She'd been fighting with Wesley just this morning. Why wouldn't she try to sabotage his efforts to save the city? And if it had just been the last several months that Adrestus had been getting inside information, it lined up with when she rejoined the team.

"Oh, no," Naomi breathed. She lifted a quaking hand to her face. She looked at Fleming and Dr. Weaver with wide, pleading eyes. "Don't make me do this."

Amanda looked away.

"What?" Wesley demanded. "Naomi, who is it?"

"Please don't make me say," she begged. Fleming closed his eyes and Dr. Weaver pressed her lips together.

"We need to know," she said.

"I'm sorry, Naomi," Fleming murmured. "I hate to use you this way. You know who it is, don't you?"

Tears spilled from her eyes.

"Yes." Her whisper dripped with bitterness and loathing.

A faint wind stirred my tangled hair. Anthony stumbled back from Wesley's bedside and his chest heaved with labored breaths as he tried to keep his powers in check. His face drained of color.

"Anthony?" Wesley whispered. Naomi and Anthony's silence confirmed it and something like molten lead settled in my stomach.

"No," I shook my head. "That's...why would Anthony sell us out?"

I refused to believe it. Anthony was our friend. It had to be Andersen somehow.

"I'm sorry." Anthony inched towards the back door. "I never wanted to betray any of you."

38

Evacuation

Everly stepped towards Anthony and placed a gentle hand on his shoulder.

"It's alright," he murmured. The faces around the room said it was anything but. Wesley recoiled on the bed when Anthony looked to him and a fresh wind stirred the room.

"Wesley, I'm sorry!" he insisted.

"We could've died tonight!" Andersen spat.

"My arm might be permanently damaged!" Remi sat forward in her bed, hugging her bandages.

Anthony shrank backwards, bumping into Everly. His throat constricted as he swallowed hard and his eyes swam with tears.

"Everly told me there was nothing he could do to fix me but Adrestus said if I gave him what he wanted, he'd undo all *this*."

A gust of wind whipped my hair around my face.

"What've you told him?" Fleming's voice was dark and hard. A strange flicker of relief blinked in my head at not being on the receiving end of his ire, though I knew it was only a matter of time.

"I told him about the mission to the museum." Anthony's voice dropped to a whisper. "I trashed the gym when he asked me, too. I told him when I thought Samantha was up to something last night. I-I gave him names. I painted them on the wall for everyone to see when he told me to."

He looked to Wesley, whose whole body quivered. Naomi shook her head.

"How many names did you give him?" Dr. Weaver asked. Anthony was quiet a moment before replying.

"All of them," he gulped.

"You should've said something." She closed her eyes. "We could've helped."

"I didn't mean for anyone to be in any danger!"

Andersen laughed callously. Anthony met my eyes and I felt my face contort. First Winnie, now Anthony.

"The other night, I sent Wesley after you," he explained. "Even though I told Adrestus where you were going, I also told Wesley, to keep you safe."

"Wesley broke his leg and almost froze to death." I didn't recognize the venom in my voice. "And what about today? I nearly fell to my death because of what you did!"

"I knew you'd be okay, though!"

"Are we?" Wes' voice shook with pain and anger. He stepped off the bed, standing on one leg and we all fell silent as he faced his roommate. "Are we really okay?"

Anthony looked around the room wildly and his eyes landed on Amanda.

"We saved Amanda!" he pointed out. "If I hadn't sent her—"

"*Remi* saved me," Amanda corrected him. "You helped Adrestus use me as a weapon."

Anthony hung his head.

"I'm sorry," he said again. "I'll...I'll do whatever you want me to."

"You'll evacuate with the other students," Dr. Weaver said. "I'll escort you to the dorms."

Anthony crossed the Sickbay towards Dr. Weaver and we watched in silence as she led him out. Wesley fell back onto the bed and buried his face in his hands.

Fleming pulled his fingers through his hair. He looked around the room, avoiding my eyes.

"The others have already had a chance to pack a bag," he said. "You're each to go to the dorms and grab *only* what you need. Samantha and Andersen, I can't believe I'm saying this, but as soon as you're done, suit up. You'll be in charge of evacuating the dorms. One thing I *did* learn today is that the two of you *are* in fact capable of working together so I trust you can at least do this."

I stuttered out an awkward, "yes, sir."

"I want to help, too," Wesley insisted.

"Not until I'm through with you." Everly's words sounded like a threat as he kicked Avery out of his seat to look over Wesley's leg.

"You're injured because of your own foolhardiness," Fleming snapped. "I won't have you running through the city and endangering yourself and others because you can't even *walk*."

"What about me?" Avery piped up, now standing over Everly to watch him set Wesley's leg. "I can help. Or, if you let me—"

"You're staying right here. Alison will kill me if I let you run off again." Fleming finally looked me in the eyes but I wished he hadn't. Disappointment and loathing looked back at me. "Why are you all still here? *Go.*"

Andersen and Naomi scrambled to leave the Sickbay but I looked back at Wesley. He had his arm over his eyes, lying back on the bed while Everly tended to his leg. His shoulders shook and I made to step towards him.

"He needs a moment," Naomi said in a hushed voice, drawing me away. "Anthony's his best friend."

If Fleming hadn't been glaring, I might've argued, but I hurried away before he could change his mind about letting me help.

Naomi melted into the groups of uniformed students in the atrium and someone brushed past me, headed for the exit, fluorescent light gleaming off her head.

"Amanda!"

She folded her arms across her chest and kept walking. I caught up to her in the basement hall.

"Leave me alone. You have stuff to do."

"Fleming's just letting you leave?"

She stopped to look at me and I flinched away from the haunted look in her eyes.

"He can't make me stay," she shrugged. "There's people I care about on the island that I need to make sure are safe."

She took the stairs two at a time to the first floor and I jogged to keep up.

"Brooke?" I asked, remembering the girl who'd stepped between us at Paragon Days.

Amanda heaved a sigh and pushed out the back doors of the school.

"She's my girlfriend and she probably hates me for disappearing," she mumbled, "and I need to make sure she's not about to drown or be swept out into the ocean."

"She didn't seem mad at you at Paragon Days," I said softly.

Amanda stopped with her back to me. Rain bounced off her head and she hunched her shoulders as she rubbed her arms. When she turned back, there were tears in her eyes.

"I know what you did tonight was stupid," her voice cracked and she looked away. She dropped to a whisper. "But thank you. Even if it wasn't me in control, I—I don't know what I would've done if I'd been forced to —"

"It's okay," I nodded, not wanting to make her say it out loud. "You don't have to say anything."

Her chin quivered. Out here, I could hear the sirens, again.

"Your dad is okay, by the way," she said. "I saw him a lot. He was all I had in there."

"Where—"

"He's where he needs to be," she frowned. My stomach knotted. Those were the same words Esther had said to me. "You need to focus on getting people out of New Delos before it's too late. Besides, Adrestus has probably already evacuated him."

She hesitated, looking over her shoulder in the direction of the college campus, where Brooke waited. She looked back at me and, quickly and suddenly, as if wanting to do it before changing her mind, her arms were around me. My whole body locked up in surprise before relaxing into Amanda's embrace.

"Thank you, Samantha."

She released me as suddenly as she'd grabbed me and turned to run into the rain, towards the university.

Rain spewed from darkened skies and I leaned against the brick of the school building, letting the lip of the roof shield me from the shower. I stared across the lawn towards the boardwalk, where a rescue barge pulled up to the railing while floor assistants led their wards out of the dorms and into the downpour. No one noticed me sulking in the shadows.

I watched the map on my visor screen. Little red dots spread across the digitized island, each one representing a team member. I clicked the button on the side of my helmet for audio and immediately regretted it.

"Sector seventeen is almost clear—"

"One of the ferries broke down, but two more are on the way—"

"Is anyone free to come to—"

I hit the button again and the voices in my earpiece went silent. The audio transcriptions still scrolled across the top of my screen but were easier to ignore.

"Don't get in my way, alright?"

I looked up to see Andersen exiting the back door of the school building. Where my uniform showed the number "12" on the shoulders, his said "8".

"That's funny." I adjusted my gloves. "I distinctly remember you doing a rescue based competition at the Apex Games and coming in last place."

"And I remember you stabbing yourself."

I followed him forward, towards the lawn. The university students weaved between the dorms to join the high schoolers on the grass. They hunched against the rain and held their backpacks overhead. A University Apex led the way and I recognized the ice blades in either of Sergio's hands, waving in the air to help guide the students behind him.

"We're even now, by the way." Andersen stopped at the edge of the grass.

"Even how?" I snorted.

"I saved your life." For a moment, I thought he had to be kidding, but his jaw was set firm under his visor. "Earlier. When the control booth collapsed."

"Wesley helped, so don't feel too important."

He stepped forward.

"No, he helped *after*. It broke and swung and was about to break completely but I caught it and I lifted it until Wesley was able to grab hold, too. If I hadn't, you'd be dead."

I crossed my arms.

"Are you looking for a thank you?" I asked, legitimately confused as to why Andersen was bringing this up now.

"No," he shook his head. "Just need you to know we're even. I saved your life."

His meaning clicked into place. I remembered our fight in Fleming's kitchen.

"You mean because you killed me?"

The skin his helmet left visible flushed red and his hands curled into fists.

"But today I saved you. I didn't— I'm supposed to be—" He struggled with the words and I watched him flounder, getting a sick satisfaction out of it. "I'm a hero, okay?"

I shrugged.

"Yeah, okay. Friendly reminder, though. This," I gestured at the students huddled on the lawn, "is our fault. I wouldn't go throwing around the word 'hero' just yet."

"I don't want anyone to die."

"A very noble stance, for sure."

"I'm serious!"

With his helmet on and his voice coming out of the modulator sounding like a robot, it was hard to read him. I put up my hands in a show of relinquishing.

"Great, you're serious! Thanks for saving me, but that doesn't mean you didn't do what you did in September. That doesn't just go away because it worked out that I'm not dead and you got a second chance."

"I—"

I braced for his blow-up, but he deflated.

"I know," he said. "I'm..."

He trailed off and we stared at each other through our helmets for a moment longer before he spun around and fast-walked towards the boardwalk. I watched him leave, nonplussed and a little angry that he thought he could erase what he'd done.

"One backpack only!" I shouted for the twentieth time. I perched on the rescue barge gangway where it rested on the wooden railing. Sergio stood nearby, freezing the water around the barge to keep it from shifting and knocking against the boardwalk while we loaded students.

Andersen helped the floor assistants corral the students, pushing the high school freshmen forward to load first. The Coastguard did most of the work, ushering students into the boats after I helped them up onto the gangway.

"My sister's a senior," one girl cried as Andersen shoved her forward. "I want to go with her!"

"Too bad!" Andersen turned away and I tried to show a little more compassion as I gave her my hand to help her up into the boat.

"Your sister will be right behind you," I promised.

Thunder rumbled overhead and I looked up at the cloudy night sky cautiously. If a lightning storm rolled in, it wouldn't be safe to keep students lined up in the open grass.

I held out a hand to help the next student in but she batted it away.

"Apex creep," she spat. "We all know this is your people's fault anyway."

She stomped past me into the boat and I tried to shake it off. I wasn't an Apex, but she wasn't wrong. It *was* my fault.

"Don't worry about them," Sergio assured me. Sweat beaded and rolled out from under his helmet, dripping off his chin. "Not everyone hates you."

"Just most people," I mumbled.

"Not the University team!" His icy holdings on the boats crackled and steam rose off his shoulders as he refroze water to seal the splinters. "Before you did this, Parker was going to force us underground. Didn't want us getting hurt in the fire. Half of us had already resolved to sneak out anyway to help, then the alarms went off and we were told to suit up. You put us back in the game."

I frowned as I helped up the next student.

"I wish *my* team saw it that way."

Andersen helped usher the sophomores forward. Jamie dragged her heels at the back of the group, laden down by several bags.

"No way am I getting on whatever *they* want me to." She stopped to point at Andersen. "My father is *saving* the city, *right now*. We don't need to evacuate!"

I ignored Jamie's fit and helped my classmates into the barge.

"Have you guys seen Heather?" I heard Bethany whisper to her friends as they filed past.

"No, Remi and Olivia are gone, too, apparently."

"You don't think..."

Most of the students had never seen an Apex in uniform. They'd been gawking at us since we'd arrived. I ignored their curious stares to help the next student.

My stomach clenched. Anthony clung to his backpack, unable to look me in the eye as he stepped up to the gangway. His eyes grazed the number twelve on my shoulder and his face fell.

I took his hand to help him up and a tear mingled with the rain on his cheek. Remorse and anger boiled together. It was hard to be mad at someone who looked so miserable, but his betrayal was still fresh.

"I'm—"

"Don't." I didn't want his apologies. I wanted him gone.

"Just tell him I'm sorry. Please."

He filed into the barge and, for better or for worse, Jamie's ongoing meltdown pulled my attention away from Anthony.

"My father is going to save the city, just like Paragon did!" she shouted on the grass. A floor assistant from the guys' dorm had joined Renee and Andersen in their appeals to get her to board the boat. "I'm not going anywhere!"

The students stopped to watch and I had to snap at them to hurry up and continue boarding. Light flashed in the sky and thunder shook the island. The storm was right on top of us now and Trev Baker's list of the ways he'd seen me die rattled off in my head. I eyed the sky with distrust.

"Move!" I shouted at the stalled crowd. "Of course being electrocuted would save you from being drowned, but I'm not sure the trade-off is worth it."

Jamie sat down in the wet grass in a show of stubbornness and refused to move while the upperclassmen and college students waited for their turn to board. I recognized Amanda hand-in-hand with her girlfriend, a knit cap pulled over her bald head, and standing so her shoulder brushed up against Brooke's.

"Fine!" Andersen shouted. He ripped his helmet from his head and threw it in the marshy grass. A chorus of gasps went up from the other students.

"You!" she shrieked. "I knew this was a setup! You're behind all this, aren't you? Don't lie, I know you're one of them!"

"Everyone knows I'm one of them! You made sure of that!" Andersen snarled. He bent over Jamie and threw her over his shoulder. She kicked and squirmed but he kept his grip on her as he carried her my way.

"My things!" she screeched.

A single bag hovered above the pile she'd left in the lawn, suspended in air by its zipper. It floated blithely after them.

"Happy?" Andersen spat, walking her up the gangplank and depositing her in the boat. Her bag landed with a thud in front of her and Andersen pushed his way through the last few students who waited on the boardwalk.

"Let's keep moving!" I shouted, drawing their attention away from Jamie as more lightning split the sky.

A snippet of dialogue caught my eye on my visor screen. The words "Schrader Tower" drew my attention and I hit the audio button to tune into the other team members.

"—completely evacuated except for the top ten floors or so," Marcus was saying. "Surrounding buildings are empty, too."

"Do you think it's him?" Naomi's voice asked in my ear.

"Who else would it be? Guess it means he's not leaving the city."

Dad. Adrestus was bunkering down in the top of his tower and Dad would be with him.

"Nobody tell Samantha," Fleming's sudden bark echoed through my headset. I froze, perched on the gangway, breathing heavy through my nose as I tried to contain my anger."Understand? We can't have her running off again."

"No, someone please tell her," Jen snorted. My face burned.

"Isn't she on this channel?" Naomi asked carefully. "She might be listening."

Silence crackled on the headset.

"Hold—"

I smacked the button and pulled the next student up maybe a little too aggressively. He rubbed his arm and scowled but I didn't pay him any attention.

They'd found Vidar and they weren't planning on telling me. I probably could have *guessed* Schrader Tower, but attacking Adrestus' building head on because of a hunch would've been foolhardy, even by my standards. Now that I knew for sure, though...

"I'm here," Sergio said, speaking to an unseen someone in his own earpiece. "Oh, yeah, she looks pissed. Why?"

"Who are you talking to?" I demanded. He gave me a blithe thumbs up.

"Make sure she doesn't leave?" he repeated. "I'm on it."

"I wasn't—"

Sergio shrugged and went back to tending the ice around the barge.

"Going to run off? Do what you want, Twelve. We both know I can't stop you."

I boiled under my helmet. I wasn't going to run off in the middle of an assignment, as much as I wanted to. I didn't know what made me angrier: Fleming thinking I needed a babysitter or Fleming telling the rest of the team not to give me updates on Vidar.

Sure, my track record for going rogue wasn't stellar by any means, but I'd hope Fleming would trust me enough to stick around and help clean up my own mess.

The storm above mirrored the storm that raged in my head and we pushed to double our load time. It was well after midnight by the time we got the last student on board and I stood on the boardwalk to watch the boat disappear over the water, accompanied by the lights of another dozen vessels, each carrying as many citizens as they could to safety.

Whatever happened, whatever I'd done, at least I'd helped them.

Every muscle in my body ached as I made my way to the basement. It had only been twenty-four hours ago that I'd been helping Wesley into my parent's townhouse. I'd fought Winnie twice in that time, reunited with Avery, doomed the city, almost died...

The atrium echoed with the sounds of wet boots squeaking on linoleum. The team members who'd returned grouped together under the dimmed lights, solemnly eating sandwiches laid out by Everly.

"We're seventy percent evacuated!" Justin announced and a tired cheer went up. "We'll rotate teams through the night. Everyone needs to be on the boardwalk for evacuation tomorrow no later than three."

Avery sidled up to me at the sandwich table.

"Mom's gonna kill you," I said with my mouth full of turkey and bread. Avery shrugged.

"This is the coolest thing to happen to me in months. I don't care what she does."

"People could die, Avery."

"Still cool. I bet Dad is still out there."

I glared at him over my sandwich.

"No," I warned. "You're staying here with Everly."

Avery pouted, picking the meat out of his sandwich to eat plain.

"The city is getting emptier. The closer we get to when the city submerges tomorrow, the better chance we have at finding him."

"Amanda said he's fine." Usually I was the one desperate to take action. It felt weird to be on the other end, trying to rein in Avery's determination.

"But you aren't even trying to find him!" Avery's face turned pink and he pointed an accusing finger at me. "It's not fair! You had a thousand years with him, I've barely had more than a decade!"

I pressed my hand against his mouth, looking around to see if anyone had heard.

"Could you not tell the whole room I'm from the tenth century?" I hissed. "Dad's fine. If Adrestus wanted him dead, he'd be dead. Amanda says he's still alive and our best bet at finding him is to also stay alive."

I dropped my hand, revealing a dark scowl on Avery's face.

"I'm tired of adults telling me what to do."

"Join the club. Having powers doesn't change the fact that you're only twelve."

"Thirteen."

I raised my eyebrows at him.

"I thought you were twelve."

"I turned thirteen a month ago." He puffed out his chest, as if that made all the difference in his argument.

I frowned. I couldn't remember his birthday. My fingers went numb. I couldn't remember *my* birthday. Samantha was slipping away every day and I wasn't even noticing.

The call rooms that housed extra bunks for late night missions were already full so I was forced to find lodging in the Sickbay, which was probably what Fleming wanted. It would be harder to sneak off under Everly's watchful eye.

The Sickbay lights were low and half the beds were taken up by team members, each of them curled under blankets in the black underclothes of the uniform with their armored pieces piled at the foot of their beds. Wesley waved from the same bed I'd left him in at the far end of the room.

Whispered bedside conversations stopped as I passed and I did my best not to look back at the stares that followed me. Remi sat up in bed across from Wesley, picking at her sandwich.

"Did you eat?" I asked, sitting down on the empty bed next to Wesley's.

"I was first in line. You think a few broken bones are gonna keep me from food?" His smile was a facade and it cracked as I slipped out of the outer shell of my uniform. I dropped the armor on the floor and leaned forward to rest my head in my hands. "What's it like out there?"

"Quiet," I whispered. "Or at least now it is. The sirens turned off about an hour ago. I guess they figured everyone had got the memo."

A beam of light poured in from the atrium as Fleming marched Avery into the Sickbay. He pointed to the bed next to mine, and Avery crawled under the covers obediently. I glared at Fleming, daring him to look at me, but he didn't. Instead, he crossed to check on Remi.

"I can hear it," Wesley said. He was on his back with his head turned to look at me. "The city. I've listened to it all day. It sounds like it's drowning."

"It is."

Remi and Fleming spoke in hushed tones and Wesley cast them a careful glance before looking back at me.

"Sammy?" he whispered. I crawled off my bedside to kneel at his. "Last night, I—"

He cut off and I blushed. We'd talked about a lot of things last night.

"It's okay," I prompted.

"I don't want to be what my mom thinks I am."

It may have been dark, but his eyes looked glassy.

"No," I said softly. "She loves you, Wes."

"I've tried for so long to make her proud but now I've—" He swallowed and looked to the ceiling. I could hear Fleming and Remi across from us.

"Look, it's not so bad," Fleming whispered. He'd rolled up his sleeves to show Remi angry red tendrils of scar tissue that climbed up his arms. "Of course, I've got gross man arms, so your burns won't look nearly this bad."

434

Remi laughed weakly, holding her bandaged arm up to compare to Fleming's.

"But what if the nerves don't heal? What's the point of being an Apex if I can't interface with computers anymore?"

"Then we'll teach you to interface with your feet," Fleming rolled his sleeves back over his burn scars. "It'll be alright."

Fleming looked up and caught my eye and I quickly turned back to Wesley, who struggled to find whatever words he was looking for on the ceiling.

"When you join Apex Team," he said slowly, "the goal is to be like Paragon. He *helped* people. But have I really done that? I feel like I only ever get people hurt."

I smiled grimly. Paragon was hardly a role model now that I knew the truth about him purposefully putting people in danger, which, ironically, we'd now done as well.

"The city was going to burn. We did what we needed to do."

"But now if anyone dies, it's not Adrestus' fault. It's ours." He shifted under his blankets. "Sounds like he's not even bothering to evacuate."

"I know," I said darkly. "I overheard on the comms. Schrader Tower."

"Do you think your dad—"

"Probably."

I looked back at Avery, but his back was to me, rising and falling with his slow, deep breaths. Tonka leapt onto his bed and curled up in the crook of Avery's knees, his orange tail flicking sleepily.

"Are you—"

"I'm not going to do anything," I promised. "I have to help evacuate in the morning. I just have to trust that he'll be okay."

Wesley smiled weakly and I knew he was relieved. He nestled into his pillow.

"We'll come back for him, okay?" he said. "Just wait. When this is all over, we'll get your dad back."

The rain died down by noon the next day and I blinked at the empty street through the afternoon mist. Lazy light filtered through the overcast sky, diffused by the fog that enveloped the city, giving every abandoned car and building a haunted, gray glow. Most of the city had been evacuated by breakfast.

Naomi walked ahead, slowly turning her head back and forth as if listening for something. She and Isabelle, who lagged behind us, were some of the few team members willing to work with me. Isabelle had refused to speak to anyone since finding out about Anthony but had nodded obediently when Fleming ordered her out with us. I followed Naomi in awkward silence, wondering how long she could go before chewing me out over what I'd done. So far, she'd mostly pretended I hadn't done anything, but her cool exterior was too formal and polite. I knew she was seething.

The island hummed louder now and when we passed a manhole cover, it rattled in its nook. Water gushed in the chamber below, gurgling angrily.

"I don't feel anyone," Naomi sighed, craning her head to look up the face of an apartment building.

Isabelle pulled off her helmet and cupped a hand around her mouth. "Hello? Is anyone left? Superheroes, here to save the day!"

Her voice echoed off the buildings and seemed to amplify in the gray haze. She gave us a cheeky smile and shrugged.

I checked the map on my visor. Blinking spots dotted the streets, moving quickly, but none as fast as Marcus. He hurtled through the streets in the team car, using his thermodynamic sight to check for stragglers.

"This was all because some lady told you Adrestus was going to kill people?" Isabelle asked suddenly. Her face was blank and tired.

"Yes."

"And you trust her?"

"Yes." My stomach flipped. "She helped us fight off Winnie."

"And you trusted Winnie at one point, yeah?" She looked back up the face of the building. "You trusted Anthony, too."

"We all trusted Anthony," I said. "And he's still your cousin."

Isabelle's hair flared and I felt her breeze stir through the ponytail that hung out the back of my helmet, but she turned away.

"He's not a bad guy," I said, but the words tasted like dirt in my mouth. "Anthony just wanted to feel like himself again."

"He sold us out."

Water crashed up ahead and through a break in the buildings, I could see ocean waves smash against the boardwalk to lap at the island. Water sprayed into the air.

"Fifteen, please report." Fleming's voice crackled in my earpiece.

"Nothing to report, sir," Naomi responded, her hand pressed against a button on the side of her helmet. "There's no one left."

"Great. We're loading the final barge. Get back to campus. I want *all* of you here in ten."

I scowled at the way he said "all". I knew who he meant.

But Isabelle walked forward, staring between two buildings at the waves as they exploded against the side of the island.

"Maybe it's a good thing you sank the island," she murmured. "Nothing good happens here and I'm tired."

Her shoulders dropped with a sigh and she turned back, pushing past me towards campus.

The team assembled on the lawn, like the other students had the night before. High schoolers mixed with university students, everyone still in uniform with the exception of Remi. The rescue barge was smaller than the one we'd used to evacuate the schools and it bobbed in the water, waves knocking it against the boardwalk while Sergio did his best to conjure ice to hold it still. The waves shattered his ice sheets as quickly as he made them, but he kept at it while Everly balanced on the gangway, carrying bags and supplies into the barge.

"Grab your things and let's go!" he howled over the smashing of waves. Water oozed up between planks of the boardwalk, soaking the pile of backpacks and belongings that had been gathered on the nearby grass.

I hurried to grab mine, throwing it over my shoulder and holding Floundersen in his tank close to my chest. I recognized Wesley's backpack. He was probably already on the boat with Avery, so I added it to my load on my back. Wood splintered and I stumbled back as the barge smashed into the boardwalk.

"Come on! High schoolers first!" Professor Parker grabbed several backpacks from the pile and signaled us to load as Marcus joined the group, panting.

"Everything's clear except—" he paused to look at me. "Yup. Everything's clear."

Everything's clear *except Schrader Tower.*

But it was far too late to go look for Dad now. The boat bumped dangerously against the lawn, chewing up the boardwalk with every jostle, but Sergio kept the ice thick enough to hold it in place while we boarded.

Heather smiled wanly at me, her helmet under her arm. Tired shadows on her face seemed to pull at her features as if she hadn't been able to shake the darkness her abilities allowed her to control.

"I traveled into *so many* apartments in the last six hours. Lots of closets and pantries that were dark enough for me to pop into and check to see if anyone was home," she sighed, leading the way across the gangway. "No one was, of course. The city starts sinking and people clear out pretty fast."

The lights inside the barge were dim and rows of benches filled the main cabin. Fleming stalked between them, tapping the shoulders of the students who dared to lay down.

"Make room for the college students!" he barked. "We all need to fit inside!"

"There has to be somewhere we can nap," Naomi groaned.

"Wesley's probably got us a spot already." I readjusted Floundersen in my arms, scanning the galley. Andersen sulked in a corner and the other sophomores sat silently nearby with their helmets in their laps. Remi leaned against a window, staring at the white caps blankly with Tonka curled in her lap. College students pushed past us as they filed in and I stepped out of the way. I couldn't find Wesley.

I couldn't find Avery.

My pulse quickened. They should already be on board. They should've been the first ones on. Wesley could barely walk. Where else could he *be?*

"It's alright," Naomi said quickly. "Maybe there's another room."

The boat lurched under us and I fell back against the window.

"We've got to go!" Professor Parker shouted from the doorway.

"Remi!" I shoved Floundersen's tank into Heather's arms and marched over to the sophomores. "Where is he?"

"Who?"

"Who do you think?"

Naomi touched my shoulder and I shrugged her off.

"He was with your brother last I saw him," Andersen grunted. "Kid wouldn't shut up about the Schrader building at lunch."

Icy dread settled over me. My head spun but I didn't know if it was from panic or the lurching of the barge.

"That should be everyone!" Everly called. Professor Parker slammed the heavy, metal door shut.

They were gone. We were evacuating and they weren't here.

Wesley and Avery were still in the city.

39

In the Undertow

The boat hummed as the engines pushed away from New Delos. Panic ripped me from the inside out and I slammed myself against the door.

"Let me out!" I screamed.

"Samantha!" My arm yanked backwards as someone grabbed it from behind. I looked up wildly at Fleming. He towered over me, his jaw set and brow stormy. "What is going on? It's too late to go back, I'm sorry about your father but—"

"Wesley and Avery!" I shoved him in the chest. He could blame me for the city sinking but *this* was his fault. "They're still on the island!"

The color rushed from Fleming's face.

"Did we forget students?" Professor Parker demanded.

Fleming twisted to scan the galley.

"No, they were here," he insisted. "I saw them load, I—"

"I don't feel them onboard," Naomi said quietly.

The whole boat stared at us and my body went cold. They would die. Wesley and Avery would *die.*

I ripped the door open and stumbled onto the boat deck. We were already twenty yards out and gaining speed. Waves gnawed at the edge of the island as it slipped under the water level.

I ran to the back deck, ocean wind whipping my hair around my face, and held the railing as the choppy water rocked the barge up and down.

I would swim. I couldn't leave them.

"Stop her!"

I turned, one leg already over the railing as Justin lunged for me on Fleming's orders. One touch, and I'd be frozen in his stasis.

"No!" Naomi pulled him back. Her eyes turned wide as Justin froze her, her face stuck in a silent plea. Wesley was her friend, too.

"Samantha!" Fleming screamed over the wind. "Don't you *dare*—"

I launched myself out over the water and braced for the icy cold. However, before I could plunge into the waves, one of them rose to meet me, freezing under my feet.

Sergio leaned over the boat railing, giving me a thumbs up as Professor Parker tried to wrestle him back.

The ice cracked and shifted beneath me as I ran and the closer I got to the island, the thinner it became. I slid the last five yards, stumbling as my boots hit the grass, but I kept my stride, the wet grass squelching beneath my feet as I sprinted.

The lawn shifted as I ran and the school building rumbled to my left. The whole island shook as the ocean lapped at its edges, but I ignored it, sprinting past the school hall, past the Paragon statue, past the frozen yogurt shop, into the neighboring streets, not bothering to look back at the barge.

Water spurted violently up through storm drains and manholes, flooding the streets as the skies opened back up, ending the tentative pause in the storm.

"Samantha!"

I staggered to a halt in the middle of an intersection, more from exhaustion than from any desire to obey Fleming's command. I hadn't noticed he'd given chase.

I doubled over, my lungs screaming for air. Fleming splashed through the water to meet me and his fingers dug into my shoulder as he spun me around to face him.

Water dripped from the end of his nose and the traffic lights overhead reflected red in his eyes as he glared down at me. For a second, I thought I saw a hint of the man who was worthy of being what was left of Paragon's legacy.

"Why, Samantha? Why couldn't you listen just this once?" He'd never sounded like that before, with his voice cracking as he said my name. I was horrified to see tears in his eyes.

"I won't let them go down with the city."

"And I won't let you kill yourself trying to do something you can't!"

I backed away, my resentment mounting.

"I know where they're going. I can get them."

"And then what? Swim them to the mainland?" Fleming flung his arms out wide.

"I don't know."

"Fly them to safety?"

"I don't know!" My voice reverberated off the windows of the surrounding buildings. Dirty water swirled around my boots, still gurgling up from beneath the city. Fleming's nostrils flared wider at me and I responded with a look of loathing.

I hated him for being right. I didn't have a plan but that didn't mean I could leave them.

"Go back," he pleaded. "Everly's there with a lifeboat. I'll get them."

"And what? Swim them away?" I parroted. His angry facade broke, leaving behind tears on a tired man's face. "You said it yourself. If anyone is left on this island, if anyone dies, it's on me."

Fleming shook his head, sloshing through water to close the distance I'd put between us.

"No," he croaked. "I didn't mean that. I could never mean that."

"You did, though! And you were right!" There was a warm pinch behind my eyes. I swallowed, trying to keep the tears at bay but they filled and fell, hot and wet, onto my cheeks. "If I had never woken up, none of this would be happening. There'd be no Epsilon Initiative, no reason to destroy New Delos. Everyone was safer when I was asleep and that stupid rock was still hidden in my neck."

"Samantha, no."

"I should be dead." My hands trembled at the thought. "Not because of the times I've died and come back since last summer, but because I was born over a thousand years ago and I should have died over a thousand years ago. What does it matter if I put myself in danger trying to save people who are only at risk because I didn't die when I was supposed to?"

"But you're alive," Fleming said. He was right in front of me now, a hand on either of my shoulders. "Why or how doesn't matter. What matters is that you value that gift."

"I'm not alive," I whispered. "I'm a ghost."

Fleming searched me with his eyes and I stared back defiantly, silently daring him to try and find anything real about me. Fleming finally dropped his arms and looked over my head at the city that loomed over us.

"It's my fault they were left behind. I should've watched Avery closer. I know how the Havardsons can be. I'm sorry."

"They're on their way to Schrader's building." I looked over my shoulder. Schrader's penthouse, still another mile or two away, towered higher than any of the surrounding skyscrapers.

Fleming sighed, letting an irritated growl tear at his throat as he did.

"Then let's go. We don't have long until the waves come."

We ran through a half-foot of water, towards the museum. Fleming took the lead with a surprising level of endurance. Each street we passed without any sign of Wesley and Avery made my chest constrict. My heart pounded harder. A buzzing screamed in my head, white noise threatening to drown me, until—

"Help!"

Water pulled at my calves but I ran faster, lifting my boots out of the water with each stride.

"Wes!?"

"Sammy? We're down here!"

Wesley's voice pulled me forward but the water deepened. A rushing torrent tore through the street ahead. Up a few blocks, a geyser of water shot up from under the city, surging thirty feet into the air. Fleming pulled me back before I could run into deeper, stronger water and we held onto a streetlight to keep from being swept up.

"There!" He pointed down the block. A delivery truck was turned on its side in the middle of the street, water gushing around it. Avery and Wesley clung to the hood, drenched and calling to us.

"We're coming!" I called.

"What were they thinking?" Fleming growled under his breath. He hugged the buildings, holding whatever grip he could find as he slogged down the street. I followed, feeling the water trying to pull me away from the wall.

"Here." Fleming waded through waist-deep water to hook his elbow around a light post. He held out a hand to me and I took it. The water ripped me from the wall, but Fleming's grip on my wrist kept me from being swept away.

He swung me out into the street and the water rose up to my chest, reeking of salt and city grime. Wesley watched anxiously from the truck hood, Avery tucked under his arm. My stomach constricted when I saw Avery's blond hair streaked with blood.

"The city!" Wesley yelled at me. "It's dropped below sea level! You should be gone!"

"You should be, too!" I shouted back. Wesley maneuvered a crutch out from between his and Avery's bodies and extended it towards me.

Fleming's fingers slipped against my wrist and his grip tightened as my free hand scrabbled for the crutch handle.

Wesley gave it a gentle toss and my hand wrapped around the handle. Wesley lunged, pushing off the truck and carrying Avery with him, and latched onto the other end. The sudden weight pulled at my shoulder but I gritted my teeth and kept hold while Fleming reeled us in. I kept my eyes on Wes and he stared back at me with relief and regret.

Fleming swung us towards the street edge and the four of us collapsed together against a building. Wesley threw his arm around me and Avery stirred, still conscious but still bleeding. Fleming pulled him over his shoulder.

"We're so close to Dad," Avery mumbled as Fleming carried him to an alley where the current wasn't as strong. "I can feel it."

"What happened?" Fleming demanded, setting Avery down to bend over him and inspect his injuries. Wesley leaned against me. His hair stuck to my face and his whole body heaved with the effort of breathing.

"As soon as I realized he'd left, I went to find him," Wesley explained, coughing up water between breaths. "Everyone else was busy and I thought I could bring him back but as soon as I caught up..."

He shook head.

"He convinced you to go with him," I finished darkly.

"The water came out of nowhere and swept him up. He hit his head but I was able to go after him. We were stuck on that truck for a while before I heard you coming. I thought..."

He trailed off and his arm tightened around my shoulders.

"Let me go," Avery mumbled, pushing Fleming away. "Let me—"

Fleming clamped a hand over Avery's mouth.

"If you use your powers on us and get us all swept to sea, I'll kill you." Fleming hoisted him over his shoulder in a display of strength I didn't know he was capable of. "If we hurry, we can still make it."

"I'm sorry," Wesley said in my ear as I helped him follow Fleming out the other end of the alley. "I shouldn't have let him leave at all, I—"

"It's fine," I snapped. "Focus on getting back to the lifeboat."

We turned out of the alley onto a street. Up ahead, Avery bounced against Fleming's back as Fleming hurried him back towards campus. Fleming stopped to look at us. I didn't want to admit it, but Wesley, with his broken leg and broken ribs, was slowing us all down.

"Go!" I insisted, waving Fleming on. "I've got Wes."

Fleming's dark scowl returned and he looked like he was going to march back to us.

"He's Alison's kid, too!" I protested, pointing at Avery. "Let me take care of myself. It's better to bring her back one kid than two drowned ones."

Fleming was too far away to read but he turned back and continued down the street towards campus at a surprising pace considering he had a middle schooler thrown over his shoulder.

"I'm sorry," Wesley mumbled again. He was getting harder to support as water swirled around my calves. "Avery...he's convincing."

I thought Roy Hendricks was supposed to be teaching him how to use his powers responsibly, though, looking at his track-record with his own kids, maybe it was a bad idea to have put him in charge of Avery's training.

"It's okay." I spit salt water out of my face. "It's not your fault."

"Is everyone else safe?"

I nodded. Fleming turned the corner up ahead. It was just Wesley, me, and the abandoned city.

"The boat left before we knew you were gone." A grim laugh parted my lips. "I abandoned ship pretty quick after that."

We continued down the street, fighting the water that was almost to my knees now. It pulled us forward as it rushed towards the ocean. I tasted salt water on my lips and I counted our steps as if that might make them count for more.

"Sammy, move!"

Wesley suddenly shoved me out of the way as a car, rolling freely in the torrent, careened towards us. It knocked him off his feet and I screamed his name. The car continued to tumble through the water and I rushed to help Wesley up.

"I'm fine!" he sputtered, spitting water out of his mouth. "It's going to take more than a sedan to do me in."

However, as he regained his footing, his face went blank. He blinked water out of his eyes and heaved the kind of sigh that told me he was bracing himself.

"Sammy." He grabbed my hand, squeezing it in his. "I think it might be too late."

I shook my head.

"We have plenty of time."

"I can hear waves," he whispered. "They sound big, Sammy. *Really big.*"

I put my arm around him to drag him forward.

"It's not too late if they aren't here yet."

But I could hear it, too. The crashing roar of heavy water bearing down on the city, gushing through skyscrapers and alleys, overturning anything its path, rattling the streets. The water around our legs sucked away, receding like a tide just before a tsunami hit.

"Sammy," Wesley coughed. "I just wanted to make things right, I didn't want...I couldn't let..."

I dared to look back and froze in awe. Surging water pressed forward to tower several stories high, casting the street in mottled shadow as light bent through the face of the wave. Tendrils of foam frothed upwards, clawing ravenously at the sides of skyscrapers.

"Hold on," I grunted. I wrapped one arm around the pole of a streetlight and the other around Wes. I locked my hands together behind his back, pressing into his chest. "Here it comes."

The roar of the water echoed against the buildings. I opened my eyes to watch over Wesley's shoulder as it bore down on us, pushing cars out of its way, unstoppable in its attack.

It hit like a brick wall and swallowed us whole. My feet lifted up, flying out behind me as we became suspended in the water. It pulled at us and my fingers began to slip but Wesley kept a tight hold around me while the world crashed around us.

When the wave spat us out on the other side, we dropped to the pavement. The water reached past our waists now.

"There's another coming," Wesley gasped, coughing up salt water. "They shouldn't be that big, there's no way."

"Okay, okay." I struggled to find my footing, sliding in the undertow. My legs shook. I didn't have much left in me. What if the waves never stopped coming?

I stared up the street, watching the next wave swell and form. The silhouette of a man conducted it from the lip of a rooftop. Wavemaker. "We can't stay here."

"I know, just wait!"

Wesley pulled me in and the second wave hit. I was less prepared this time. The water tried to rip me from Wesley's arms and while suspended in the nothingness of the water with my eyes screwed shut, unable to scream or breathe, I felt his hands scrambling to keep me close. He locked onto my wrist and just as I thought my shoulder would dislocate, the wave passed.

"We need to move," I panted, gagging on dirty salt water.

"The alley!" Wesley was already hobbling to the gap between two buildings. "We can climb a fire escape, get to the roof."

I pulled him in close, wedging my shoulder under his arm, heaving him towards safety. The water pulled at our waists, dragging us back from the alley and I gritted my teeth.

I would not let Wesley be hurt anymore. Not because of me.

But the roaring of the water swelled as it bore down on us a third time.

"Too late!" Wesley cried and I felt his arms around me.

We were like rag dolls at the mercy of the wave as it carried us down the street. We writhed and twisted as the water and Wesley's arms constricted around me, refusing to let go.

My head broke the surface and I gulped for air. Wesley kept his arm around me, trudging forward as best he could on a broken leg, fighting to get us close to another alley.

"It's Jamie's dad. It's Wavemaker," I choked. The wet had turned Wesley's brown hair dark and it clung to his forehead. My boots slipped against the pavement with each step we took. "It has to be."

Another wave tore through the street behind us and we collapsed against another streetlight post just before it swallowed us. Wesley was the only thing that existed in the middle of the wave and my fingers dug into his back, reaching around the pole to grab him.

As soon as it passed, we scrambled for the alley, ignoring the burning of salt water in our throats and sinuses. A car lodged lengthwise in the mouth to the alleyway and shifted as water pulled at its frame. Wesley and I helped each other over the hood in the narrow space between the two buildings. The undertow wasn't so bad in the alley and now that we were clear of the main street we moved faster through the water. We stopped beneath a metal fire escape, secured to a brick wall on a second-story window.

"We can't get up there," I panted.

"Sure we can." Wesley turned his back to the wall crouched so that the water reached his chest. Beneath the surface, he interlaced his hands together. "I'll boost you up, then jump up after."

"But your leg..."

"It's fine." He flashed an assured smile. I didn't know how he could look so calm with the city sinking around us and with the injuries I knew he was hiding. "I can make it."

There was no other way. If I boosted him up, I wouldn't be able to jump high enough to reach the fire escape. Water sucked at the edges of the car in the alley entrance and metal scraped against brick. I steadied myself and put my hands on Wesley's shoulders. I lifted my knee towards his chest, placing my boot in his hand.

My face was inches from his and he looked at me with the same settled smile, his green eyes reflecting my haggard face back at me. The empty city and the ocean and all its wrath slowed as I took him in.

He dared to tilt his head back, lifting his chin, watching me as he did. His lips barely grazed mine, but they felt soft and his shaky breath was warm and smelt like salt. He lingered, his mouth hovering just millimeters away.

"Wes—" I whispered. His green eyes threatened to swallow me and even as tears welled in them, he kept smiling.

"Tell my mom," he croaked. "I want her to know I was a hero."

"What—"

Air whistled in my ears as I flew upwards. I reached out for the metal railing and threw myself over to look down at Wesley. He stepped away from the wall, looking back at me with the same damn smile.

"Come on!" I called, leaning as far over the railing as I could, stretching my arm down towards him. The car groaned and metal crunched as the oncoming wave sucked it free. "You can make it!"

But he shook his head and, his smile finally faltering, mouthed something at me, inaudible over the ocean's roar and my own pleading scream.

Wes kept his eyes on me as white foam lifted the car at the mouth of the alley. Even as the wash hurtled towards him, he didn't look away, not until the wave had consumed him.

The wave passed. He was gone.

40

Flotsam

I shrieked Wesley's name, desperately trying to find him in the wash. The car cartwheeled through the alley, smashing against either wall. He had to be in there, in the foam, fighting the water.

"WES!" His name ripped my throat and I screamed it over and over, begging the ocean to give him back. It couldn't have taken him far. He had to be nearby still.

But he'd been swept up with that car. He could be unconscious underwater or sucked out into the next street over, too injured to get back to me.

And each wave was bigger. Another surged through the alley, reaching as high as my fire escape, ripping at the rusted bolts. I scrambled up the rickety metal stairs as it collapsed behind me, caught in the wave. Water tugged at the loose metal and I sprinted up a few flights before falling to my knees.

Wesley was still down there. I could reach the roof, scan the street for signs of him, find a way down to reach him or a way to get him up to me.

I crawled up the next few metal steps.

I shouldn't have let him help me up. I should've known he'd do something stupid and heroic.

The roof was slick with rain water and I sprinted across the top, slamming into the low, concrete wall on the opposite side, leaning over, searching.

"Wes!" I screamed. The streets were completely flooded and the city seemed to be sinking faster now that we'd broken sea level. Upturned cars and dumpsters floated in the brine. Dangerous and haphazard currents drew white lines in the ocean foam that reached from one side of the street to the other. Waves crashed against building sides but as the water got deeper, they seemed to get smaller, looking less like uniform tidal waves and more like ocean chop on a stormy day.

And there was no Wesley. I collapsed against the low wall, still screaming his name, but, like the dying waves, each shout had less energy than the last until they broke down into exhausted, dry, painful sobs and I hoped the city would devour me, too.

In the three days that had passed since the city sank, I'd forgotten what silence sounded like. The closest I'd gotten to it had been several days ago, on the long ride in the lifeboat to the mainland when a loud, numb buzzing in my ears had drowned out the sounds of the boat motor, the ocean, and Fleming's questions.

But here in the middle-school-gym-turned-emergency-shelter that housed a good portion of the displaced people of New Delos, nothing could quiet the constant stream of murmurs that hummed like a beehive. Even in the dead of night, people whispered to each other from their cots, wondering when and if the city would be raised from the ocean, where they might go if it wasn't, and who could've done something as cruel as destroying the city we all loved.

It hadn't slipped completely under the ocean and could still be seen glinting on the horizon. Apparently the lift system had become waterlogged and stalled. The city had drowned, but only the first few stories were actually underwater.

Anyone with anywhere else to go had already left, including most of the team. Anthony had left with Isabelle to go stay with family. He'd broken down at the news about Wesley. Isabelle and Naomi had to hurry him outside before he caused a full-blown tornado in the shelter. After that, Fleming was quick to arrange the cousins' departure.

I caught glimpses of Justin across the gym from time to time, staying with his evacuated family. Naomi, Mike, and Desirae had cots next to Everly's halfway across the gym from my cot with Fleming and Andersen, but I hadn't spoken to any of them in the three days we'd been there.

Other than Fleming and Alison, who'd been waiting for us at the shelter when we first arrived, Wesley's mother was the only person I'd spoken with. She arrived the day after the city sank, her older son at her side. Benson was taller than Wesley and had darker hair, but he looked a lot like his brother. His presence felt like sacrilege. He was almost Wesley, but not the one I wanted. I gave the Isaacs his last message and, detached and unfeeling, watched them cry into each others' arms.

Because it couldn't be real. Wesley couldn't be gone. Mom joined Fleming and sat down with me on our first day in the gym.

They told me what I already knew. Wesley was missing. Then they told me what I refused to believe. He probably wasn't going to come back. The news about Wesley had quickly spread through the broken ranks of New Delos, helped along by the projector screens airing national news coverage of the city's destruction. Everyone knew about the lost boy and several search and rescue teams had gone out by boat and helicopter without results. Wesley was presumed gone.

Gone.

I refused to even think the other word I'd heard the others whispering. The word the news anchors tossed around on the projector screen TV. Gone wasn't necessarily permanent. Gone meant he could come back.

Gone was something I could fix.

So I lay on my cot, unable to eat, unable to sleep, unable to feel, losing myself in the dull white noise of a gym full of whispering people, clutching Wesley's glasses to my chest, having stolen them from his things, knowing he'd have an awful migraine when he finally showed. I waited for Wesley to come in through the double metal door, dripping wet with sea water and limping but smiling his infuriating, cocky smile.

But he never did.

I curled around a bowl of dry cereal on my cot while I stared up at the sports banners that decorated the gym walls. I'd memorized the names of long-since graduated middle schoolers who'd placed in decades-ago state competitions. I read them and reread them and reread them, finding a small bit of comfort in the task.

That morning, there'd been talk of a more permanent housing solution for the people I'd displaced. Adrian Schrader meandered through the cots, talking with and encouraging citizens. Adrestus may have stayed behind, but he'd sent his lapdog to be with the people.

He avoided my corner of the gym.

"Sammy?"

I twisted my fingers around the case of Wesley's glasses at the sound of Mom's voice.

"Hmm," I grunted.

"Last chance."

I twisted my head on the pillow and lifted my eyes to look at Mom through a tangle of unbrushed hair. My stomach clenched. Every time I saw her, I felt like I'd added another name to my growing list of people who needed saving. Winnie, Dad, Amanda, Wesley.

Avery peeked at me from behind Mom, trying to keep out of view.

"I'm not leaving."

"You can't be comfortable here. We have a house and you could—"

She swallowed hard when I lowered my eyes to glare at Avery. If he hadn't run off, if he hadn't used his powers to get Wesley to help him, if he hadn't come to New Delos in the first place...

He'd done everything I might've been stupid enough to do. I never wanted to see him again.

"Right," Mom sighed. "Can I at least have a hug goodbye?"

I rolled from the bed and stood rigid as Mom carefully wound her arms around me. I looked at Avery over her shoulder but he avoided my eyes by looking at the ground.

"Mrs. Havardson, Amanda's almost ready."

Amanda's girlfriend, Brooke, wrung her hands behind Fleming's empty cot. Her and Amanda were leaving with Mom and Avery. Apparently her aunt lived on the same rural farm island they'd been hiding out on. Shiny, dark hair fell past Brooke's shoulders and even though she looked nervous, her amber eyes were warm.

Mom pulled away and it wasn't until her arms let me go that I realized I didn't want her to leave. I swallowed the feeling.

"Avery and I'll get the car and meet you guys out front." Mom adjusted her backpack. "Avery, say goodbye to your sister."

He peered at me from under his blond mop of hair. A bandage stuck to his forehead where he'd needed stitches.

"Bye, Sammy," he mumbled.

I held Wesley's glasses case with both hands against my chest as I sat back on my cot.

"Bye."

Mom took Avery's hand and led him away. I thought I saw him try to look back at me as they forced a path through the crowd and cots.

"I'm Brooke," Brooke smiled. "I don't know if we've officially met."

"We kind of did at Paragon Days." I sat back on my cot, wishing Brooke would go find Amanda and let me wallow in my emptiness.

"We're getting ready to leave but I wanted to say thank you for bringing Amanda back."

"It's Remi you want. She did most the work."

"Yes! I did meet Remi."

I narrowed my eyes at her. She seemed nice and warm and I *wanted* to like her, but I didn't know why she was here. She sat back on Fleming's cot and my shoulders tensed.

"Amanda told me you lost someone close." Brooke's amber eyes were soft but I recoiled. She was going to say what everyone else was thinking.

"Don't bother." I held the glasses closer. "I don't want to hear it."

"I thought Amanda was dead." Her voice dropped to a whisper and she looked embarrassed to say the words out loud. "One night, she said she had something she needed to do and then she never came back. I thought maybe Mr. Hendricks knew something I didn't but then, I don't know. I stopped hoping until Paragon Days. "

But Amanda *hadn't* been dead. She'd just been *gone*.

"All I'm saying is don't give up hope on your friend." She flipped her thick hair over her shoulder. "You brought Amanda back and from the things she's told me about you people, your friend sounds like he can withstand a bit of surf."

I dropped the glasses case in my lap. I wanted to believe her. I wanted to hope Wesley was okay.

"'You people'," I repeated softly, remembering something Mr. Hendricks had said in their argument. "You're not an Apex."

Brooke's tanned cheeks turned rosy and she looked away.

"No, I spent the first three months of our relationship thinking Amanda didn't want me to meet her parents because I'm a girl. Turns out, it was because I'm a Beta." She looked back at me, blushing harder. "Not that she's ashamed of that! It's just that her dad—"

"Has a complex?" I finished for her. "I've met Roy Hendricks, too, remember?"

"Brooke, we need to go."

Neither of us had heard Amanda creep up to the cots. She hid her bald head under her favorite tattered ball cap and had done her make-up to make her fake-lashes look less out of place. The back of her head, where she wasn't covered by the cap, sported mousy, brown fuzz where her hair was growing back.

Brooke stood up and took one of Amanda's two bags and smiled at me encouragingly.

"You can be sad," she said, "but don't let it make you immobile."

Amanda chewed her lip, looking like she wanted to say something to me, but gave me a curt nod instead, and walked hand-in-hand out of the gym with Brooke.

I mulled over Brooke's words for the rest of the day and somehow found the energy to join Fleming at the dinner line in the outdoor basketball court. As soon as the hot soup touched my lips, I gulped it down, realizing how hungry I'd become after not having an appetite for three days.

Fleming watched me eat with cautious relief but I tried not to look at him too much. His eyes were rimmed red. I was afraid he'd been crying and didn't want to confirm my fears by staring at him for too long.

Andersen joined us, sitting on the next cot over. He hadn't spoken to me since before we'd evacuated the schools together.

"You can still change your mind." Fleming sounded groggy. He wore the same old university hoodie he'd lived in for the past three days and, like me, I was sure he hadn't slept since leaving New Delos. "I can always call Alison to come back and—"

"I'm sure." My voice was hoarse from lack of use.

"I don't mind you staying with me, but as it stands I don't have an apartment. Alison has a house and—"

"No."

I would not leave this cot until Wesley came through those doors.

"Samantha, can you look at me?"

I wanted to hate Fleming. He should've noticed Wesley and Avery were gone. He should've sent them away when the non-Apex students had evacuated. But instead, I only felt sadness.

"I'm fine with continuing to be your guardian," he said slowly. Andersen slurped his soup, not paying us any attention. "I don't mind, but things won't be the same moving forward."

"I'm sorry," I said blankly. "I'll try to listen more and not destroy any more cities and get any more of my friends—"

I swallowed.

"No, not like that," Fleming frowned. "I mean, yes, I won't complain about you being more receptive to instruction but I'm talking about something else."

He stared at me expectantly, as if he didn't want to say aloud what he was thinking and if I could just figure out how to read his mind real quick, that'd save him a lot of grief. I responded with a blank stare.

"After this, I'm quitting."

The words didn't register quite right. I didn't understand.

"You don't like teaching?"

A reluctant but sad smile crept across his face.

"I don't mean teaching."

It felt like actual electricity zapping my stomach.

"The team?" Andersen demanded, suddenly interested in the conversation. "You can't quit the team!"

"Yes, I can, and I'm going to. I never should've lost track of my students, not when they ran off to Northshore Park, not when they snuck under the city, and not when they escaped back into the city without me noticing." He shrugged and even though I could tell he was trying to seem nonchalant, it looked like the weight of the world was on those shoulders. "I'm not cut out to be in charge of Apex Team."

"That's not fair," I snapped. "All of those things are my fault."

"And me," Andersen insisted. "I helped. Kick us off, keep your spot."

I scanned the room for Dr. Weaver. I could convince the Apex Council head not to accept Fleming's resignation. Instead, I found Schrader. He caught my eye and smiled and my anger tripled.

"I haven't told Dr. Weaver yet," Fleming said, seeing me looking around the room. "I already discussed things with Everly, though, and he understands."

"That doesn't mean he agrees." The team would be lost without Fleming, as annoying as he was sometimes.

"No," Fleming conceded, leaning his elbows against his knees and cradling his soup in his hands. "But he understands it's my choice to make. City engineers sailed out this morning to assess if and when they can raise the city. Once everyone has somewhere to go, I'm stepping down."

It wasn't fair. It was my fault. I would *love* for it to be his fault, or Avery's fault, or Remi's fault even, but it wasn't. It was *mine*.

"But who will replace you?"

Fleming looked at his calloused hands.

"That's for them to figure out. Roy Hendricks applied last time the position was open. Maybe he will again."

I stood up so fast that my soup nearly fell off my cot.

"If Roy Hendricks wasn't such a horrible dad, we might not even be in this mess!" I shouted. Fleming signaled for me to be quiet and I lowered my voice but stayed on my feet. "He drove Winnie to Adrestus' side, which got Amanda captured and turned into a weapon. Look what he did with Paul! Roy *hurts* people!"

"I said he *might* apply," Fleming said slowly. "That doesn't mean he'd get the job."

The hollowness returned to my stomach and my rage drained away. I fell back onto the cot. Fleming's fault. Roy's fault. My fault. I forced soup down my throat in an effort to squash the guilt.

"Anyway, I was asking if you were sure about staying because there's a motel opening up tomorrow," Fleming said, blowing on his soup while sitting cross-legged on his cot. "More people are clearing out and I was going to try to get us a room."

The three of us hadn't fared well in a two-bedroom apartment together, but even a musty motel room with Fleming and Andersen sounded better than a crowded gym. I wasn't in a place to complain about lodging, either, having rejected Mom's offer to go with her and Avery.

"What about the others?" I asked.

"Everly is going to try for a room for Naomi and the twins, I think." Fleming spoke carefully. "Others will stay with their families."

"And Wesley's mom and brother?"

Fleming's spoon clinked against his bowl and he stared at its chunky contents.

"They have a hotel room in the next town over." His forced nonchalantness set my teeth on edge. "She's staying there until we have a chance to search the city after the engineers are able to get it lifted again."

"Searching for what?" Andersen deflated on his cot. "Are we searching for Wesley or for his..."

My bowl shook in my hands.

"Searching for *Wesley*," I snipped. Andersen shrugged dolefully without looking up from his soup.

"Samantha," Fleming said slowly, draining me of what little hope Brooke had allowed me to feel earlier. "We talked about this."

"I came back," I reminded him. "I've come back three times!"

Andersen burned red as Fleming screwed up his face, trying to remember the third time I'd died.

"This is different," he finally said.

"I was dead!" I didn't recognize the hysterical voice that came out of my mouth. It wasn't me talking. It was someone else. "I was slashed open, I had my neck snapped, I've had hypothermia, I-I-I..."

My lip quivered and I watched as my soup swirled and distorted behind a film of tears. Why had I let Wesley help me up first? Why hadn't I tried harder to help him?

Why had he been selfish enough to kiss me when he knew I'd never get to see him again?

I was acutely aware of Andersen and Fleming both staring at me. I wanted them to stop, but didn't know how or what to say or where, if anywhere, to run.

But then, Adrian Schrader's voice on the loudspeaker spared me having to find an escape.

"Citizens of New Delos," he simpered, "it is my absolute pleasure to announce Schrader Industry's private engineers ,with the help of Epsilon Hero Wavemaker, have successfully begun the lift process."

A smattering applause bounced off the high gym ceiling and Schrader scanned the crowd with his stupid smile plastered to his face. He found me in the crowd and his smile widened.

"We may have a long road ahead of us, New Delos," he continued, "but I assure you, we have saved the city."

41

Ruins of a Drowned City

T he salty wind nipped my nose but I welcomed its bite. It reminded me of the wind in the city, blown in fresh from the ocean. I tightened my wool blanket around my shoulders and curled in on myself, hugging my knees on the large slab of rock where I sat, watching the waves crest and crash against the beach. The sun rose behind me, throwing my shadow across the sand.

It was the first time I'd been out of the gym since arriving at the shelter and while other evacuees walked along the dawn-dyed beach, I was happy to lose myself in the sound of wind and waves.

New Delos glinted on the horizon, like a shard of glass rising from the sea to catch the early morning sun. It was impossible to tell at this distance, but I imagined the buildings pushing up into the sky as the engineers reversed the damage I'd done.

"Any room for me?"

I jumped at the sound of Naomi's voice. She lowered herself onto the rock next to me and I offered her half the blanket. She smiled as she took it, draping it over her shoulder.

I stiffened next to her. She'd avoided me since we'd come to the shelter, not that it was hard to avoid someone who refused to leave their cot. Wesley had been her friend before he'd been mine and I couldn't bear the thought of facing someone else I'd hurt.

"It's good to see you outside of the gym," she said when I stayed silent. "I can't stand it in there with Schrader lurking."

She shuddered and I swallowed the lump in my throat.

"Your powers still don't work on him, then?"

"Nope," she sighed. "I might as well be trying to read the wind's emotions. He's a black hole of feelings."

I pulled the blanket tighter around my shoulders and focused on the sounds of the waves.

"Rumor has it Fleming wants to send some people back to search."

I ripped my eyes away from the waves to stare at Naomi.

"Is it a rumor or insider captain knowledge?"

She shrugged against my shoulder.

"Rumor. Sergio heard him talking with Professor Parker," Naomi murmured. I hunched further over my knees. "I don't blame you, you know."

"You should." Ocean wind blew sand into my eyes and I hunkered under the blanket.

"He was always stubborn. You couldn't have stopped him."

"Is," I corrected her softly.

"Sorry?"

"You said he *was* stubborn. He *is* stubborn."

I felt her deflate.

"Right. *Is* stubborn."

I fidgeted as she went quiet, thinking about all things still unsaid between us.

"All these people have been displaced because of me."

"Or they could've been torched," Naomi said bluntly, "but we'll never know. The best thing you can do is assume it was for the better."

I watched a woman down the beach show off a bit of beach glass to her partner.

"You're still mad at me, though."

Naomi's laugh was hollow.

"Of course I am. You left me out *twice*. But right now, I'm too sad to hold it against you so I'll just be mad at you later if that's okay."

"Any idea who Fleming is considering to go back?"

"Sergio claims Everly is going for sure," she said. "And if Fleming's working with Professor Parker, there might be university students going."

I grumbled incoherently into my knees. He would never send me, but I still needed to try.

"Last I saw him was the court checking in with families at the breakfast line," Naomi said. "Better go catch him before he makes up his mind on who's going."

I took a moment to stretch out my legs, letting my half of the blanket drop over Naomi. She wrapped it around herself and smiled wanly.

"It really is good to see you off your cot," she said. "I'll come by later to give this back."

She tugged at the corners of the blanket and I nodded in embarrassment before setting up the concrete steps to the middle school.

I took them two at a time, already forming an argument in my head. Fleming *needed* to let me go. I tried to tell myself it was a good sign he was sending Everly. It meant he anticipated the mission needing medical attention and maybe it meant that he thought Wesley was injured, but still alive.

The basketball court bustled with activity despite the early hour. Steam rose off of large vats of oatmeal, curling in the sea breeze, and people huddled with thin blankets over their shoulders like capes as they sipped watered down coffee.

Fleming stood with a family near the gym doors. Justin's parents nodded along with whatever it was Fleming was saying while Justin looked between the adults blankly. A younger girl, maybe Avery's age, hung off his arm.

"They have plenty of room," Fleming was saying as I got closer. "I got off the phone with them a half hour ago and it's not a permanent solution but they'd be happy to house you."

"But the city is lifting," Justin's father said. "Schrader said we can go back soon."

"I'm not sure that's the case." Fleming shook his head. "The damage still needs to be assessed, which could take months. It won't be safe to move back for a while."

"You'll like Marcus," Justin insisted to his parents. "His family is nice."

Justin's mother stroked her son's shoulder.

"Thank you, Alex," she said quietly. "We'll think about it."

Fleming nodded and saw me as he turned away. His lips tightened, pressing together disapprovingly, as if he knew what I'd come to ask.

"Have you had breakfast?"

"Yes," I lied. I ran my fingers through my knotted hair in a last ditch effort to look put together enough to send to a sunken city.

He stalked past me, back towards the gym and I followed eagerly.

"I haven't made any decisions yet," he growled before I could make a play. I scrunched my nose up at him and crossed my arms.

"What's it matter if you're just going to quit?"

The gravel at his feet shifted and crunched as he came to a halt. He looked around at the surrounding people before leading me away from listening ears, back towards the beach.

"You understand why it's a bad idea to send you, right?" The ocean wind blew his hair to the side but he still looked unshakably stern.

"Yeah, but it's like I said back there." I jerked my head towards the water, towards New Delos. "I don't belong in this millennia. If I'd died a thousand years ago, when I was supposed to, if I'd just taken care of

Adrestus back then, none of this would be happening now. There'd be no threats to the city, there'd be no kidnapped kids, and Wesley—"

My voice caught and I frowned, trying to hide my shame behind a gruff facade.

"We've been over this," Fleming said, surprisingly gentle. "You might be older than any of us, but you're still just a kid."

"I'm expendable." I tried to sound matter-of-fact. "You said if a single person didn't make it off the island—"

"I know what I said!" he snapped and I shrank away from his sudden outburst. "I'm sorry. I shouldn't have said those things, I was angry and... and it's my fault he's gone, not yours. I should've paid more attention. They never should have been able to run off."

"Let me fix it," I begged. "I can't stand it here. I can't stand doing nothing."

Fleming looked out over the bluff, staring sadly at the water.

"But you don't know what you'll find."

Even as my heart constricted and my stomach dropped, I shook my head.

"I don't care," I insisted. "I have to find him."

"And if you find something you don't want to—"

"I don't care!" I shouted it this time. "How long do you think I'll be on the team once you quit? If you get replaced by Roy Hendricks, he'll kick me out, first order of business. This is my last chance to do *something*. One last mission. *Please.*"

Fleming drew in a breath that seemed to last forever, and then let it out, just as slow.

"You can't go near Schrader Tower," he said blankly.

"I won't," I promised, heart racing. Had it worked? Was I going?

"I'm serious, Samantha. You can't go looking for Vidar."

"I know," I nodded eagerly. "When do we leave? Can we go today?"

"City should be raised enough by tomorrow morning. You'll head out before sunrise."

My stomach was in knots all day, but I finally found the energy to shower in the locker rooms and eat three full meals. I pulled my backpack into my lap at my cot and dug through the front pocket, shifting past the flash drive that outlined my fake memories, past the two black journals, and to the bottom of the canvas. Cool metal rolled between my fingers and I pulled out my necklace, the one Wesley had made out of the dog whistle I'd used to fight him in the Final Trial.

The whistle was bent into a "V" from when he'd crushed it in his hands and I traced the shape with my finger. It still worked despite being bent out of shape. I'd used it in October to help Wesley find me when I was at the museum.

Maybe it could now help *me* find *Wesley*.

Even if it didn't, it felt good to have something from him around my neck. I'd told Fleming and Mom exactly what had happened just before the surf took him. I told them how he'd lifted me up, despite his injuries, how he'd said to tell his mom he was a hero, and how he'd disappeared in the foam.

But I hadn't told them how he'd lifted his chin to mine and how he'd mouthed something indistinguishable before going. That light kiss and those last words, whatever they had been, were for me and I carried them in the small piece of bent metal on the chain that I now clasped around my neck.

As I went to put the backpack away, the black corner of Vidar's notebook stuck out. I stared at it a moment before begrudgingly pulling it into my hands. I ran my fingers over the cover.

I couldn't run from Eydis forever and it had been a couple weeks since her memories had butted into my head.

I flipped it to a random page near the front and felt queasy when my name jumped out at me.

"*When I woke up, Eydis was missing and I knew where she'd gone. We'd seen Adrestus' camp and I knew what she'd left to do. I knew how many men* *with strange abilities would leap to their master's defense if she tried anything and if anything was certain, it was that she <u>would</u> try something."*

I smiled in spite of myself. It was somehow comforting to think that whoever I was, Sammy, Eydis, or otherwise, I was and always had been a pain in the neck.

My smile dissipated with the next words.

"It was too late when we found her. We found the stream first, running red with blood. And then, there she was, up a few yards, on her back in the water, slashed open at the neck. The last of my family.

"Against all odds, she lived, waking up long enough to scream in agony, although whether that was from the pain, the loss of our family, or at having put a sword through her friend, I wasn't sure. We waited for her to die, but she refused, and eventually Eluf used his new powers to put her to sleep.

"She had a pack in the woods that we found. After she'd been injured, she must've been trying to reach it and very nearly did, though the things kept inside made little sense. A few strips of smoked salmon, a decorative dagger, a blanket, and a skein of vinegar."

Vinegar? Why would I have brought vinegar with me? My stomach tightened. Adrestus had said any liquid the Lapis touched would be turned into the elixir that granted immortality. What if I *had* planned on stealing it for myself all along?

"You ready for tomorrow?"

I slammed the journal shut and whipped around. Naomi stood over me, carrying the blanket I'd left with her that morning.

"What? Yes! Tomorrow." I slipped the journal into my backpack and I felt her eyes follow me as I did. "I still can't believe Fleming is letting me go."

"Me, neither," she shrugged. "It's you, me, and Sergio. Everly, too, but he'll have to watch the boat."

"A solid team," I smiled. It would be good for Naomi and I to be together if we found the worst. Her eyes lingered on my backpack.

"What were you reading?"

"My journal."

"You felt stressed."

I kicked the backpack under my cot, nearly taking out Floundersen's tank as I did.

"I've had some stressful things happen," I countered. "Rereading them was just as stressful."

"Right." She didn't look convinced but held out my blanket. "I brought this back. Thanks for letting me use it."

I folded it over my arm and smiled in thanks but her brow knit together.

"Do you remember back before the city sank? In the locker room?" she pressed. A nervous sheen broke out on her forehead. I scratched at the canvas of my cot absently.

"Yes."

"Did you want to continue that conversation?"

I balled my hand into a fist. Did I want to admit to her who I was? I'd been ready to, or at least thought I'd been. But with everything that had happened since, I already felt like I was drowning.

"Yes." I gulped and met her eyes. "Just maybe it should wait. Once we have Wes back, I'll tell you everything."

"Sure, Sammy." Her face fell and before I could apologize, she walked away with her head down.

Maybe it would be easier to tell her about Eydis once I was officially kicked off the team, but right now, the world felt too heavy to bear opening that scar back up.

The boat launch was a half mile north of the middle school and Fleming and Professor Parker walked Sergio, Naomi, and I up the beach before sunrise to meet Everly. We wore our uniforms under big coats, carrying our helmets in front of us.

The waves breaking on sand seemed louder in the dark than they did during the day, but I liked the sound. I matched my breathing to it, trying to empty my head and feelings, but the knot in my stomach refused to unclench.

Everly waved at us from a lagoon sheltered from the waves. He lifted a duffle bag from the dock and threw it into the bed of a thirty-foot boat. Most of its length was taken up by the pointed bow, but there'd still be plenty of room for all four of us in the back. I was glad I had let Naomi pull my hair into a braid before we'd left. The cab that rose around the driver and passenger seats didn't look like it'd keep the wind out very well.

"Radio me as soon as you reach the island," Dr. Weaver instructed, her gray fly-aways escaping her bun to flutter in the breeze. Everly nodded, doing a final engine check. The principal turned to Naomi, Sergio, and I. "Stay away from Schrader Tower and stay away from the engineers and *Wavemaker*."

Her face soured when she used John Ratcliffe's alias

"They'll be close to City Hall, so you'll want to avoid that neighborhood, too," Professor Parker offered.

Sergio jumped into the boat and Everly scowled as it rocked with the force of his landing.

"Don't worry about us." Sergio adjusted the black patch he wore over his missing eye. "I'll keep everyone in line."

"You sure you didn't have anyone older?" Fleming asked Parker. "Maybe Boonsri? Or Eli?"

"They've all gone home to family," Parker frowned. "Besides, I trust Sergio and he's equipped to handle the water that's sure to still be in the city."

Sergio smiled smugly and fell back into the passenger seat, leaning back and crossing one leg over the other. Naomi let Everly offer her a hand as she stepped down into the boat. I went to follow but Fleming reached for my elbow.

"Be careful, alright?" The single dock light overhead cast orange shadows across his face. "You're my responsibility, remember, and I don't need Alison mad at me for anything else."

I forced a smile.

"What is there to worry about? We'll poke around a bit and come right back."

I saw his throat constrict as he swallowed a lump.

"Right. And remember, whatever you find, it'll be okay."

I hugged my helmet tighter against my chest.

"I know."

"Remember what Alison and I told you. The odds that he survived—"

"I *know*."

I jumped into the boat after Naomi and turned to look up at the three adults on the dock. The two women looked grave but Fleming had an odd expression on his face.

"Whatever happens and wherever Wesley is, just know he's proud of you." Fleming's voice came out strained. "And I am, too."

My cheeks burned in the dark and I took the seat behind Sergio's. It swiveled as I sat and as I tried to mumble my thanks to Fleming, Everly ignited the engine and it purred with life.

I lifted a hand half-heartedly in a weak farewell. Dr. Weaver nodded as we pulled away from the dock and putted out of the lagoon.

The boat bounced over ocean swells and I clutched the edges of the worn cushion seat. I was certain if I didn't, I'd fly out the back and get lost in the dark water. It didn't take long before the wind forced me to pull my helmet down over my head in a bid to keep warm. Naomi and Sergio did the same.

The world felt massive out here, with ocean stretching into night sky ahead of us. Behind us, the first light purple hues of daybreak began reaching into the clouds over the mainland while New Delos got closer and closer.

Maybe I was seasick or maybe I was nervous about what we might find in New Delos, but I had to fight the urge to lean over the side and puke into the boat spray.

Light percolated through the clouds like brushstrokes of sunrise, racing us to the island. Paragon's massive bronze statue still stood tall in the north bay and as we got closer, I recognized the pier to the south where we'd had the Welcome Festival back in September. I'd ridden the ferris wheel with Winnie, just before meeting Wes for the first time, hiding under a table.

We approached the high school campus from the water as the sky turned early-morning orange. The sides of the school buildings were stained with seawater and the lawn was still submerged.

But the city was silent. No crashing waves. No dreadful humming as the lift system dragged New Delos under the surface. Just the gentle slap of water against brick and stone, interrupted by the splash of a seal slipping into the wash from the front steps of the girls' dorm.

Everly puttered the boat past the school hall, but let the engine die as we reached the Paragon fountain at the front. He stood up and surveyed the barren, flooded streets and took a long, slow breath.

"It gets shallower past here and I don't want to risk ruining the engine on the concrete." He turned to look at us and nodded gravely. "I need constant check-ins and be back in time for a lunch break. I packed sandwiches."

Sergio leapt from the boat, catching himself with a sheet of ice and struck out down the street, not bothering to look and see if we were following.

I grimaced at Naomi and she shrugged before swinging herself overboard, dropping into knee-deep water. I scrambled to follow her as she slogged after Sergio.

"You don't have to come if you don't want to," she said cautiously.

"Of course I want to!" I glared at the number fifteen on her shoulder armor, annoyed she'd even suggest something like that.

"Sammy, I don't mean it that way."

Ahead of us, Sergio formed and reformed the ice under his boots so he stayed on top of the water while we splashed after him.

"I want to be here," I insisted. "I begged Fleming to let me come."

"You just might not like what—"

"I get it!" My voice echoed over the water. I gritted my teeth. "I know you all think Wesley is dead!"

Dead.

It was the first time I'd said the word out loud since Wesley had disappeared. I tugged on the necklace chain around my neck, feeling like I couldn't breathe.

"And if you are coming with us, I hope you understand that it's a possibility."

"I know."

"Then why'd you bring his glasses?"

I blushed under my helmet and my hand fell from the necklace to the glasses-shaped lump in my uniform leg pocket.

"He could still be alive and if he is, he's probably got a migraine."

"Samantha!" Sergio called from up ahead. My heart leapt painfully. What had he found? "Where was the last place you saw him?"

Oh.

"It was down a bit further." I waded past Naomi, eager to put her behind me.

"Do you remember the street?"

I suppressed the flicker of irritation that flared inside me. Of course I didn't remember the street. I'd been actively trying not to drown, not taking careful notes.

"No, but I lost him in an alleyway."

The water level dipped and deepened as we went, which surprised me since I'd never thought of New Delos as anything but a perfectly flat manmade city. However, we'd be waist deep one moment and then on dry pavement the next.

I toyed with the necklace around my neck, rolling the bent-up dog whistle between my fingers. If he was alive and conscious, he'd be able to hear it from a mile away, maybe further. I caught Naomi looking and quickly shoved it under my armor.

"That's a good idea," she said gently. "It'll help him know we're looking for him."

She was just being nice but I lifted the whistle to my lips and blew. A faint sound emitted from it but it would be enough for Wesley.

"He's got super-hearing," Naomi explained to Sergio, who pursed his lips in confusion. "It's a dog whistle and it's helped before."

I kept the whistle balanced between my lips as we walked, sounding it off every twenty steps or so, but had to put it away after my teeth wouldn't stop chattering. Even though the uniforms did a good job keeping heat in, we'd been walking through wintery ocean water for nearly two hours and the cold was getting harder to shake.

Around mid-morning Sergio led the way up a stone stoop so we could take a short rest. He pulled his helmet off and let his long hair shake loose over his shoulders. Naomi and I leaned against a door and watched as Sergio turned the water trapped in our armor to steam, rising from our legs and boots in hot wisps.

I shuddered as warmth returned to my legs and Sergio handed out granola bars. I held my helmet between my knees, eating in silence and staring down the watery street, hoping for some sign of Wesley. A group of seals sunning themselves on a stoop a few blocks over barked, but other than that, there was nothing.

We only had the day to look for him and I felt like we'd barely made progress. The city was so big and with the waves that had flooded the city, he could've been swept anywhere.

"Let's keep going." I pushed myself to my feet.

"We just sat down," Sergio grumbled over the granola bar that stuck out between his teeth while he rubbed under his eyepatch. "Another minute won't make a difference."

"*Every* minute makes a difference." I flicked the butt of my granola bar at him. I didn't have the stomach to finish it.

"As team leader—"

"Naomi's a captain, not you."

"I'm a university student!" He glared at me from the corner of his eye.

"A *freshman*," I sneered. "We're sophomores, so technically—"

"Technically nothing!" Sergio screwed up his face, as if he wasn't sure if he should be angry or confused by my argument. "You're *high schoolers*."

"Fine, but we outnumber—"

"Stop!" Naomi interjected, pulling at her curls. I shied away, feeling guilty having not realized our spat might agitate her empath abilities.

"Sorry," I mumbled. But she doubled over, clutching her head as tears streaked her cheeks. I gently pushed her into an upright position. She stared into space with pin-prick pupils and her shoulders shuddered as gasps and sobs racked her body. "Naomi?"

"I feel...I'm feeling..." My grip on her shoulder tightened and I felt my whole body ice over.

"What? Naomi, what do you feel?" I demanded, trying to get her to look at me.

"Screaming," she whispered. "He's screaming in my head."

"Who?" The sound of my roaring heartbeat in my ears made me feel like I could hear screaming in my head, too.

"Guys," Sergio whispered. He stood at the edge of the stoop, summoning an ice sword in both hands. "Is that Paragon?"

He pointed a sword down the street and I followed his gaze to the red-caped figure standing knee-deep in the ocean water. Where Paragon's uniform had been white, this one was black, but the style, the cape, and the mask were all the same. Messy brown hair stuck out at odd angles.

I stumbled down the steps, splashing into the water, the absurdity of the sight not registering as relief and joy and desperation choked me.

It wasn't Paragon.

It was Wesley.

42

Hunted

Wesley was alive. I'd refused to believe he was dead, but the relief that blossomed in my chest forced its way out of me through heavy sobs as I sprinted through knee-deep saltwater to get to him. I couldn't get to him fast enough and shouted his name.

"Sammy, *no!*" Naomi shrieked behind me.

Wesley barreled forward and grabbed me by the shoulders. For a tiny half-second, the world was normal again. I'd found him. He was alive. We —

His knee jammed into my stomach and I fell forward into the water, retching.

"Wes..." I gasped between gags. He lifted me by the collar of my uniform and it choked up against my neck. The bent necklace swung free but he ignored it as he forced me to look him in the face. "Wes, I'm sorry, I —"

The passive look behind his mask was familiar, calm and empty except for the wild fear in his eyes. Amanda had worn the expression as Hephestae.

No...

Ice shot up from the water, restraining Wesley's hands and arms. He dropped me to fight against the icy shackles but Sergio re-froze it faster than Wesley could break it.

I reached out for his face in a numb disbelief as his dilated pupils screamed for me to run.

"Wesley," I choked, holding his face between my hands as gently as I could. "Give him back! He's not your puppet, you cowards!"

"Eydis..." His voice tore from the back of his throat, guttural and forced. "I'll bring...you...to your master..."

"Get out of there!" Sergio bellowed behind me. "I can't hold him for long!"

"I won't leave him!" I wrapped my arms around his neck.

"S-Sammy..." Wes gasped, and I knew it was him talking, not his captors. "Run...please..."

Ice splintered and Sergio yelled again. Hot steam shot upwards and I screamed and stumbled away, throwing my hands over my face to shield it from the heat. Between my gloved fingers, I saw Wesley surge forward.

Instinct took over as I rolled out of his way just as several sheets of ice rose up to trap him in a prism.

"WES!" I shrieked again. "Don't hurt him!"

A thunk reverberated from inside Wesley's ice prison and I pressed my hands against the cool surface, unable to see inside. A second thunk sent cracks spiderwebbing across the plane.

"Samantha, we're leaving!" Sergio bellowed. I looked back at him helping Naomi off the stoop, stopping when she retched into the water. "We'll come back for him, I promise, but we can't fight him!"

"He's in pain!" I screamed. When we'd left for the island, I'd braced to find the worst, but hadn't been prepared for *this*. "I won't leave my friend!"

"*She's* your friend, too!" Sergio pulled Naomi through the water and flinched as Wesley hit against the ice prison again, creating more cracks in the surface.

I looked between Naomi and the block of ice. Whatever Naomi was feeling, she was picking up from Wesley, who would only continue to feel worse the more he was forced to attack us. I stepped away, blinking back tears, knowing I couldn't fight him but feeling my heart splinter at the thought of leaving him.

"I'm sorry, Wes," I croaked. "I won't let them make you hurt me."

I splashed through the water towards Sergio and Naomi and hot, stifling steam filled the street.

"What's happening?" I demanded, slipping myself under Naomi's other arm, trying to look back through the vapor to see Wesley's prison.

"That was me." Sergio panted while Naomi trembled between us. "He'll have a harder time finding us in the steam."

"He has super hearing. Or were you not listening to Naomi?"

"*He* has super hearing. Doesn't mean whoever is controlling him does. And speaking of things I thought he was supposed to have, where's his broken leg?"

The steam clung to my face, but it was too late to go back for our helmets. For all the dumb things I'd done since waking up last summer, even I knew we didn't stand a chance against Wesley when he finally broke free of Sergio's ice.

But he was *alive.*

We could come back with Remi, if her hands were healed, and set a trap. We could get Wesley back and then I'd destroy Adrestus for what he'd done.

"Get us off the street," Naomi growled through gritted teeth.

"We need to get back to the boat," Sergio argued. The fog was so thick, I could barely see him on the other side of Naomi's frizzing hair.

"There's more of them," she panted. "I can feel them. We need to hide."

Sergio was too far from Wes and too tired to hold the prison together any longer. Ice cracked and splashed into water as it finally caved and the air was ripped in two as Wesley screamed in rage and agony behind us.

"That's *him*," I cried. "He's resisting her!"

Wesley had been able to talk to me, even if it was only a few words and now he screamed defiance. Amanda hadn't been able to do that. Maybe Wesley's abilities were helping him fight the control, even if only a little...

We stepped off the street towards a glass-faced building. Sergio placed a hand against a window showcasing shelves of waterlogged, salt-stained designer purses. The glass shimmered and warped before bursting into a million pieces.

"Not too subtle, but we'll be fine," he muttered, helping me pull Naomi through the window. The plush carpet squelched under our boots and a bit of kelp hung from a glitzy chandelier in the center of the shop.

Naomi leaned against the cash register, regaining her breath and I cradled my stomach where Wesley had kneed me. Steam wafted into the purse shop and Sergio grunted as he lifted a metal gate out of the way, opening us up to a multi-level shopping mall.

"We can't stay here," he said, holding the gate up. "He'll know where we went as soon as that vapor clears and I can't boil it forever."

It was wrong to be running away from Wesley after everything that had happened. We came here *for him* and now, when he needed us the most, we were running.

"Sammy, come on." Naomi winced as she ducked under the metal gate. Wesley howled again outside and I locked up with indecision. "We can't fight him."

"I—"

I looked back out into the steam but the next scream that ripped its way from Wesley's lungs wasn't his voice.

"EYDIS!"

"Samantha!" Sergio hissed. I turned away from the street with fingers balled into fists to keep from shaking.

"I'm coming."

I ran after them into the mall. The shopping center was built like a well and the food court that made up the main floor had been turned into a wasteland of overturned chairs and tables. Each of the ten or so floors rose in circles overhead, connected by a network of escalators.

"Where to now?" Naomi grabbed at her head. "He's getting closer."

"Up?" I suggested and we slid across the puddles that dotted the floor to reach the nearest escalator.

"Eventually, we'll run out of 'up'," Sergio argued, but he led the way up the decommissioned escalator. "And the further we get from water, the less useful I'll be."

"You can heat and freeze more than water, can't you?" I snapped. Naomi waved me off as I tried to help her up the stairs and she leaned against the railing to support herself.

"Everly will figure out something's wrong when we don't check in," she said, grimacing with every step. "We'll hunker down somewhere, and he'll send backup."

"But how are we supposed to warn him about Wes?"

"They'll figure it out when they get here," Sergio said grimly.

"But what if they hurt him?"

Sergio stopped half a floor above me to glare.

"Then they hurt him. He's a tank. He'll be fine."

We found a lounge four floors up and Naomi collapsed onto a broken massage chair while Sergio broke open a vending machine and passed around waters.

My heart jumped when I saw the water in my bottle quaking and thought the city might have started to slip back into the ocean before I realized it was just me, unable to keep my hand still.

All Wesley wanted was to be *good* and they'd turned him into a weapon.

But he's alive! And his leg is fixed!

I screwed my eyes shut, unable to handle the dueling emotions of relief and rage.

"It's okay to be confused," Naomi said from the massage chair. She leaned her head back and stared at the massive skylight six floors above us. "He's confused, too."

"*I'm* not confused," Sergio said proudly, attempting to fix his long hair into a bun. "I know we came to find him, but as far as I'm concerned, he's the enemy now."

He tried to puff up his chest, but after being forced to use his powers as much as he had to contain Wesley, he looked pale and gaunt. Sweat still dotted his forehead.

I crossed the lounge to a large window to survey the street below. Sergio's steam had dissipated and several figures trudged through the murky water. I recognized Hackjob's hulking shape approaching the broken purse shop window below and I stumbled away.

"What is it?" Sergio demanded. I ran from the window to the railing that looked into the food court and four floors below us, Wesley stood with the Paragon cape hanging off his shoulders.

"We have to keep going," I hissed as Hackjob and a woman I didn't know joined Wesley at the court's center. The woman had a wool shawl buttoned at her shoulder and her hair was cropped short in a pixie cut. She lifted a hand and unclasped her shawl, revealing a tank top underneath. My stomach backflipped when four leathery wings the same color as her skin unfurled from her back. "We *really* need to keep going!"

I rushed to help Naomi up and the sound of wings beating against air thundered behind me. Sergio's face went slack as he looked past Naomi and me and I twisted to see the winged woman perched on the railing. Her lower set of wings folded against her body while the upper ones spread out on either side of her, spanning at least ten feet.

"Give us Eydis." Her voice was cool and assured but her eyes glinted with an unspoken threat.

The plastic bottle in Sergio's hand split as the contents froze and lengthened into an ice javelin.

"Run!" He hurled his spear and the woman leapt off the bannister, beating her wings against the air to keep suspended.

"I've found them!" she called as Sergio made another spear and Naomi and I took off to the left. Wesley's red cape billowed behind him as he raced up the escalators with Hackjob right behind him.

Sergio threw his second javelin and the woman howled when it nicked her wing, but she stayed airborne.

"Keep going, I'm right behind you!" Sergio yelled as we reached the next escalator. "I'll take care of her!"

Hot air dried my face as I took the escalator steps two at a time. The winged woman dove towards us but a sudden gust of wind blew her off course.

"Did Sergio do that?" I exclaimed, watching the woman get buffeted to the opposite side of the mall.

"Sure did!" he called out behind us. "Change the air temperature and you change the air flow. The bigger the temp difference, the stronger the wind current!"

The woman steadied herself in the air, several floors above us, but Sergio kept an updraft going that made it impossible for her to fly at us.

"What do they mean 'Eydis'?" Naomi panted behind me. "They keep saying they want Eydis."

"She's the Scourge, right?" Sergio asked. "From the original legend?"

I led the way up the next escalator.

"She's got a statue next to Adrestus' in the museum," Naomi said.

"Is she even real, though?" Sergio snorted. "I'm not sure if I'm even ready to believe *this* Adrestus is *that* Adrestus."

Adrestus wanted me. That wasn't too surprising. He'd tried kidnapping me before, but I thought he'd given up that quest now that he had the Lapis.

Surrendering would be an easy way to find Vidar and maybe save Wes. Plus, Naomi and Sergio could get away, but my stomach churned when I remembered what Adrestus had said to me last time I'd been in his clutches.

"Now that I have what's mine, it's your turn. I will watch you die every day until you know the pain you put me through!"

I shuddered, knowing he'd keep his promise.

A thud sounded behind me and the escalator rattled. I spun on the top step, expecting to see Wesley or Hackjob, but the sound had been Sergio collapsing on the stairs.

"Sergio!" Naomi bent over him but he waved her away.

"I'm alright," he panted. The hot air that blew my hair upwards weakened and Sergio had turned pale. "Not used to keeping my powers activated for so long."

Naomi tried to help Sergio to his feet, but fell next to him with her eyes screwed up.

"Wesley's getting closer," she whispered. "I can't stand it."

Wesley's greatest fear was hurting the people he loved and now he was being forced to hunt them. Of course Naomi was in agony.

The winged woman shrieked and dove again, straight for me at the top of the escalator.

"Move!" Sergio struggled to his feet and sprinted up the last few steps to push me out of the way. He leapt up and over the rail and Naomi and I shrieked as he tackled the winged woman out of the air.

"Sergio!" Naomi cried and I ran to meet her where she'd fallen. Sergio and the woman dropped out of sight but we didn't have the time to see where they'd landed. I dragged Naomi to her feet and up to the next floor, scanning the shops for somewhere to hide.

Up ahead, a blacked out window sported neon signs advertising laser tag and was the only shop without a gate. I pulled Naomi through the turnstiles and into the dark laser tag lobby.

"Sammy, what does it mean?" Naomi groaned. "What do they mean by 'Eydis'? You know. I can feel that you do."

Tears welled in my eyes as I glanced around the lobby for where to go next. I'd waited too long to tell Naomi and now here we were, being chased because of the secret I'd been too selfish to let her in on.

"I wanted to tell you," I whispered, leading the way into the darkened laser tag course. Low walls and massive foam blocks wound through the space, their shapes only made discernible by the LED glow lights that stuck to the walls and floor. "I didn't know how and I guess I didn't want it to be true."

I found a corner near the back of the room. If Wesley wasn't able to use his super senses, we might be able to wait out for help. We'd missed lunch. Everly would know something had happened. Help would be on the way.

"Is this the big secret?" Naomi asked, rubbing her temples. Faint lights dyed the edges of her face orange in the dark, catching every corkscrew curl of her hair. "Do you have something else of Adrestus' besides the Lapis or..."

She trailed off as I shook my head. I adjusted my position so that I faced her and took her hands in mine.

"It's me," I said, feeling the secret bubble up in my chest, ready to pop. I focused on her forehead rather than look her in the eyes. "I'm Eydis."

"Like, symbolically?" she asked.

"No. I mean literally."

The corner of her mouth twitched and I thought she might laugh. I pulled my hands out of hers.

"You're a thousand years old?"

"It's a long story."

"Yeah, I'd say that's a pretty long time, too." She shook her head, scowling. "This whole time, you were playing us?"

"No!"

"The whole 'Beta' thing was just a ploy, then?" She shifted away from me and for a horrible moment, I thought she might hand me over to Wesley and Hackjob herself.

"Naomi, please!" I begged. My two best friends were here with me and one was being used as a weapon and the other was disgusted I'd had the gall to call her my friend. She tucked her hands up into her armpits, as if afraid she might accidentally brush against me. "I didn't know until Homecoming night!"

Her eyes narrowed and a curl fell in her face.

"That doesn't make it better."

"I didn't tell you because I didn't want it to be true!" I shouted. We both froze, listening for sounds of Hackjob and Wesley but the laser tag course remained silent. "You know how much it sucks to find out your entire life is a lie programmed into your head? And that your real family all died because of something you did?"

"Yeah, actually!" Angry tears filled her brown eyes and the orange LED glow highlighted every line of her frown. "I do know what it feels like because I have to feel you feeling it everyday!"

"How's that my fault?"

"It's not! But I'm tired of always taking the high road in everything I do just because I always see where everyone else is coming from! Just once, can someone think about what I feel like?"

"That's not fair!"

"None of this is fair!" Naomi shuffled away, glaring through her tears. "What the hell, Sammy? You're an immortal viking queen and didn't think I should know?"

"Not technically a queen," I mumbled, pulling my gloves over my face. "'Scourge Queen' was just a nickname."

"That's not the point!" Her voice bounced around the laser tag course and I flinched.

"I'm sorry I didn't tell you, but this isn't the time to fight about it!"

"Well, gee, if only it had come up sooner!" Naomi's eyes glistened with resentment.

"I tried!"

"You told *him!*" She pointed towards the exit. "You told Wesley! You see a boy you like and of *course* you'll tell him your secret! Whatever it takes to seem interesting, right?"

"I'm—"

Heartsick tears welled in my eyes and Naomi's look of anger turned to one of mortification. She reached out for me but I pulled away.

"No, Sammy, I didn't mean that last part." The tracts of tears on her cheeks glistened orange. "I just thought you and I...You told me I deserved better friends than Jamie but then you keep something like this to yourself...I'm sorry, Sammy, I really am but I'm so mad!"

"Eydis..."

We both jumped at the rasp that sounded from the exit.

"Move," Hackjob grunted. "I'll drag them out."

I put a hand over my mouth to keep from breathing too loud.

"I'm sorry," Naomi mouthed. She bowed her head and her shoulders shook.

"Me, too." I pulled her in, holding her tight as Hackjob thundered through the course, bumping into every wall and corner.

"We know you're in here," he teased.

"I'll draw them away," I whispered to Naomi. "It's me they want. They'll leave you alone. Stay hidden until Everly comes for you, okay?"

"Sammy, no—"

But I slipped away, crouching behind low walls. If I could make it to the exit, I'd have a way out and could call them after me. They'd leave Naomi alone. I'd be the only one in danger. I could—

Naomi's muffled cry went through me like a stake, pinning me to the spot.

"We have your friend, Eydis!" Wesley's cool rasp hissed. "Come on out or I'll break her arms."

Hackjob chuckled from the shadows. I couldn't let Naomi be hurt because of me. I couldn't let Wesley go through the trauma of breaking her arms.

"You have three seconds before I snap her at the elbows." Every one of Wesley's words was labored, as if the white-haired woman was pulling them out individually with pliers. He fought every syllable but it wouldn't be enough. Naomi's arms would break. "Three. Two—"

"Don't touch her!" I stuttered, jumping up from my hiding space. Wesley stood with Naomi locked in his arms while Hackjob lurked behind them. "I'll go, but don't hurt her, please!"

"Sammy, no!" Naomi glared at me from Wesley's arms. She shook with the pain of being so close to him.

"Naomi, I'm sorry I didn't tell you the truth. I'm going to make it up to you. At New Year's Eve, you said you wanted the Lapis so you could use it to stop being an Apex. If I go with him, I can find it."

She shook her head and Wesley's grip tightened.

"Drop her and I'll go with you," I said slowly. "Wes, I won't let them make you hurt Naomi. I won't force you to hunt us any longer."

He responded with a haunted stare behind his Paragon mask but I knew he was screaming at me to run. Everything about him made me want to scream, but I smiled

"It's okay. It isn't your fault, Wes." I dropped my voice to a whisper. "I'm so sorry."

I put my hands up and Wesley dropped Naomi. She fell, clutching her head and crying. Wesley stepped over her body to reach me.

I reached for my pocket and Wes' hand shot from his side to grab my wrist.

"I have something for him. It's *fine.*" I spoke directly to the woman I knew was in control.

"Show me first," he rasped.

I waved his glasses in front of my face, unsure of where his puppet master was watching from. There must've been some kind of camera hidden in his costume.

"His glasses," I said. "He gets headaches without them."

Wesley stood as still as the statues he was dressed to look like as I unfolded the glasses and slipped them over his cloth mask. In the light of a green LED, his eyes glittered though his face remained stony.

"Better?" I asked, knowing he couldn't respond. "Great. Let's go see Adrestus."

43

The Penthouse Dome

Outside the laser tag gym, the mall felt quiet, though it was hard to hear anything over the blood screaming in my head. Agreeing to go to Adrestus wasn't a permanent solution. He might make good on his promise to kill me over and over, maybe making Wesley be the one to do so.

My stomach clenched. No, this was a very bad plan, but Wesley's hand clamped around my bicep and only the woman controlling him could break a grip as strong as his. But, he was alive and, even if only for the next few minutes, he was okay.

"Samantha!" Sergio staggered to his feet as we passed him on the bottom floor. His bun had come undone and dark hair fell in his face, obscuring his eyepatch from view. A sickly pallor washed out his skin and he clutched his ribs in pain, but the air around him rippled with heat as he prepared for a fight. Hackjob growled in delight.

"It's okay," I stammered. The winged woman limped out from wherever she'd been hiding to join us, scooping her wool shawl off the ground and throwing it over her shoulders. "Naomi's upstairs. You guys find Everly, I'll—"

Wesley yanked on my arm in what I assumed was a warning to stop talking and I grimaced at Sergio, mouthing an apology. He and Naomi would be okay. Everly was sure to be looking for them already.

Outside, afternoon fog rolled in between the skyscrapers of New Delos, turning everything gray. I slogged through the water next to Wesley while Hackjob and the winged woman followed.

"Scourge Queen," Hackjob jeered, jumping ahead to walk backwards in front of me. Limp, tangled hair hung in his face and when he licked his lips, I caught a glimpse of his strikingly white teeth. I hid behind a jaunty smile.

"Hey, how mad is Adrestus about the whole flare gun thing the other night, on a scale of one to ten?"

Hackjob curled his lip.

"No talking," Wesley rasped. His cape dragged in the water.

"Just trying to make conversation."

"Talk again, and I break your bones."

I gritted my teeth but held my tongue. We rounded a corner and I scowled at the large stone steps up ahead. Schrader Tower sat on top of the museum, stretching higher than the surrounding buildings. It was impossible to see the top through the fog, but that was where Adrian Schrader supposedly lived in the glass-domed penthouse.

The grand foyer of the museum was dark and I was grimly satisfied to see the adjoining exhibits had been emptied to save the artifacts from the flood. The walls, floors, and fountain in the center of the foyer, however, were streaked with sea grime.

Wesley marched me down the same hall Adrestus had led Justin down, towards the glass-doored office. Even though the office carpet was wet with salt water and the computers had been destroyed, the elevator chimed when the winged woman held a keycard to its panel.

I glanced sideways at Wesley. He must've hated himself right now. I wanted to comfort him, but knew Adrestus would love a reason to force Wes to break my arm, so instead, I lifted a hand to my bicep and rested my fingers over his.

The elevator dinged and its door slid open. I stepped inside and the glass box gave us a spectacular view of the concrete elevator shaft walls. The winged woman stopped Hackjob from following us in and he scowled.

"Stay," she clipped, "in case we were followed."

"But I want to see the master break her!"

"Next time, Hackjob."

My breathing constricted and I thought I felt Wesley's fingers twitch under mine. I squeezed them and the lift jolted.

The elevator traveled up the windowed side of Schrader Tower and the glass walls looked out over the island. The park across the street shrank at my feet as we got farther, and then it was swallowed in fog as we continued to rise through gray mist.

We broke through the low-hanging marine layer as we continued to ascend, and the surrounding skyscrapers stuck out from the fog like columns in a sea of cloud. Light bounced off their sides, only to be reflected by the next building over, creating a dazzling array of sunbeams.

We bumped to a stop and the movement flipped my stomach and lightened my head. With the streets shrouded in mist, it was impossible to see how high up we were. For all I knew, we might've left the Earth completely. A firm hand on my shoulder drew me away from the window and I let Wesley steer me out of the elevator and into a lavish lobby.

Silver sconces lined gray walls, casting their light up to the intricate crown molding. A balding man in black sat at a sleek desk, flipping through a magazine and he looked up at us lazily as we exited the elevator. The corners of his mouth curled into a sneer and I flashed him a toothy grin in return. I'd had my fair share of run-ins with Miles and I hadn't missed him much.

"They're upstairs." His voice grated against my ears. Wesley pushed me forward and the winged woman fell back, staying with Miles at the desk. I led the way into a long, sconce-lit corridor and immediately bumped into an invisible wall.

Miles laughed at the desk and as much as I seethed inwardly, I didn't dare say anything.

"Watch your step," Miles chortled. Of course he would taunt me with his ability to create force fields. Maybe he was still bitter about what Amanda and I had done to his eyebrows a few months back. The invisible barrier dissolved but I walked with my hand just slightly forward, feeling for more secret roadblocks.

The corridor stretched towards the center of the building. Oil paintings of historical figures decorated the walls between sconces and I recognized each of them from Adrestus' Hall of Heroes exhibit.

Paragon's portrait lived at the far end of the hall and I hesitated before walking into the next room. He grinned on the canvas, wearing his mask and cape, puffing his chest out, but I only saw the sick man in the photo I'd found in the closet, shrunken and pale.

Wesley shoved me and I stumbled into a circular room with a round hole in the high ceiling, through which I could see a glittering glass dome overhead. A winding staircase of black metal stretched from the gaudy, red carpeted floor, up into the domed penthouse.

"Climb," Wesley growled. The stairs rattled with each shaking step I took. I rolled the dog whistle on my necklace between two fingers, trying to find comfort and bravery in the small bit of metal.

The glass dome stretched to every edge of the penthouse room, creating a vast, open space. The only furniture was directly across from us, near the glass perimeter to allow whoever decided to lounge there a nice view.

Mira, the white-haired woman, sat up on a chaise lounge, a tablet screen propped up in front of her and her hands decked out in sleek, electronic gloves. Despite the snow-white mane that hung to her waist, her face was that of a young woman and she looked me over with hungry eyes. She waggled her fingers at us as we stepped from the staircase to the marble floor and Wesley mirrored the movement.

I balled my hands into fists, my fingernails digging through the tips of my gloves and into my palms.

"They're here," Mira crooned to the man behind her.

Adrestus stood with his back to us, staring out the glass dome as if there was anything to see other than an expanse of gray clouds. He'd chosen a suit today rather than his ostentatious Greek get-up and he kept his hands folded behind his back.

I glared at the low gray sofa, where Winnie hunched her shoulders over the ugly mask in her lap. A blond man leered next to her. He was the same man who'd accompanied Schrader to the first night of the Apex Games, the one Adrestus said could destroy my fake memories. I shied closer to Wesley, pressing my shoulder against his.

"Look who's joined us!" Adrian Schrader stood up from his end of the couch, deftly buttoning his cream suit jacket as he did. He'd *definitely* been at the shelter last night. How'd he get here so fast, and without us seeing him on the water? "Do you need anything, Samantha? Water? Tea? Wine? Oh, drat, you're still just a kid, aren't you? Well, if you don't tell, I won't!"

He pulled a wine bottle up from behind the couch but set it down as Adrestus turned around to face us.

I flinched in horror at what had become of his face. The last I'd seen his eye, it had been fogged over and scarred, but now deep purple veins cracked his face, spiraling out from the socket that housed an eye with a blood-red iris. The scar still marred the space between his lid and eyebrow, but the eye, despite the macabre color, was clear once more.

"Eydis," he said softly. His voice was different. Less baritone. Younger, maybe? I took in the rest of his features, trying not to focus on his left eye. His once salt-and-peppered hair and beard were less gray than before and his skin, despite the throbbing veins, was smoother.

It was as if he'd de-aged twenty years since I'd seen him last.

"Enjoy your swim the other night?" I goaded. Mira flicked her wrist and Wesley gripped my upper arm.

Adrestus raised a hand to signal it was alright, and Mira tentatively had Wes let me go.

"I don't think I like the glasses," Adrestus murmured, taking in Wes' glasses-and-mask combo.

He walked across the marble floor to get closer to him. I watched with bated breath, every muscle tensed and feeling like my chest might explode. He may have looked younger but the change made him all the more repulsive. His hair wasn't just darker, but fuller, too, and in his suit he looked like a successful, young businessman on the rise.

Or, at least he would if it weren't for the single, blood-red eye. It made his right eye look all the more blue and I didn't know which one I hated more.

Adrestus raised a hand to Wesley's glasses and I acted instinctively, batting it away.

"Don't." I glowered at him and reached for Wesley's hand. I enclosed his wrist in my grip, even though Mira could have him break my arms at any moment.

Adrestus' audience watched, waiting to see how their master would react. He studied me and I wished I would stop shaking. His calm exterior didn't fool me. I'd seen him go from serene to raving in the blink of an eye.

"He matters to you," he stated, leaning back and stroking his chin. "That much is obvious. I mattered to you once, too, not that you would remember."

I swallowed, hoping my face didn't reveal that select memories had returned.

"And yet I still stabbed you in the gut and stole your pretty rock."

Adrestus' eyes glinted dangerously but he nodded.

"True. Quite the opposite of what you did for Mr. Isaacs."

He stalked back to the couches and made himself comfortable next to Winnie. She stared at the mask in her lap, her knuckles turning white around its edges. Adrestus gestured towards the second couch and I glared at the empty seat next to Schrader.

"No, thanks. I don't plan on staying long."

Mira smirked and Wesley forced me into the seat next to Schrader, who wiggled the wine bottle at me again. I ignored him.

I did a quick head count. I didn't know how well Schrader could fight but Naomi had dealt with the blond man swiftly when we'd fought him last. Adrestus, Mira, and Winnie, meanwhile, would've been tough opponents even if they'd been alone. Plus, they had Wesley, along with anyone else in the building, including Hackjob, Miles, and the winged woman.

Even if I *could* somehow free Wesley, we were horribly outnumbered. Naomi and Sergio and Everly could burst through the domed ceiling and it still wouldn't be a fight we'd win.

"You see there's no escape, yes?" Adrestus said softly, reading me. "I can even the playing field if you like."

He nodded and Winnie, the blond man, and Adrian Schrader all stood and walked towards the stairs while Wesley took the seat next to me.

"Thanks for leaving me in that booth," I spat as Winnie passed. Her cheeks colored but she kept her eyes down as she disappeared down the spiral stairs into the floor below.

Mira flexed her hands on the chaise lounge. Wesley did the same next to me. There had to be a way to free him. I hated how much I needed Remi here with me.

"So," Adrestus said coolly, extending his arms along the couch back as he leaned into the cushions. The arms of his suit hitched up, revealing a glittering, silver watch. "How'd you do it?"

"You know how." I felt like I was trapped in a snow-globe. As the gray clouds dimmed outside the dome, floor-lights blinked on, lighting the dome from the marble tiles. "We snuck into the lift system control booth —"

Adrestus struck a face and waved his hand at me, as if shooing away a fly. He didn't just seem younger, but more aloof, too, as if his youthful appearance had injected him with new arrogance.

"No, I don't care about *that*. I care about *him*." Blue and red eyes narrowed at Wesley.

"Good. Me, too." I stood back up to face Adrestus, but Wesley pulled me back down. I glared at Mira. "He *isn't* your plaything so give him back."

A smile played on the edges of Adrestus' lips and his mismatched eyes wavered between Wes and me. He placed a hand over his heart in a show of faux-scandalization.

"We're the ones who fished him out of the brine and fixed him up. Where were you?"

"*We* could've fixed his leg just fine—"

"His leg, sure, but it's a wonder he was alive at all. Wavemaker threw everything he had at you two and not even Mr. Isaacs could survive in the surf." The blue eye twinkled maliciously. "Bleeding from the head, water in his lungs, a bit of rebar through his abdomen. Even with his abilities, he should've been dead."

My heart broke at the thought of Wesley injured, bleeding, and alone in the wash while I sped away on a lifeboat. Horror rose in my throat like vomit and I looked at Wesley, but he stared blankly at the far glass wall.

"You used the Lapis on him?" My voice shook. Wesley *had* died?

"No!" Adrestus laughed as casually as if I'd just told a particularly good joke about the weather. "It doesn't work like that. You have to connect with the Lapis' elixir *before* you die for it to work. I explained this to you once, a long time ago."

I tried to connect the dots and see how Wesley had survived, but seething rage made it hard to think.

"We didn't have any elixir," I said through gritted teeth.

"That's what I thought." I hated the smug lilt in his voice. He stood up to stalk back to the window, looking over the darkening city. "If the Lapis so much as touches liquid, you've got Life Elixir. For a thousand years, I wasted it on wine and water but you? You shoved it in your neck and let it steep for a millennia. And what are you and every other person full of?"

Liquid. I reached for Wesley's hand on the couch as Adrestus came back around towards us. He crouched so his eyes were level with mine. Up close, I could see the white of his reddened eye was more of a lilac color.

"Even the air you exhale carries tiny bits of it in the water vapor in your breath and it doesn't take much elixir to sustain someone. How else would Vidar have survived with you? Still aging, but very, very slowly. Just breathing the same air as you was enough."

Adrestus turned his eyes to Wesley and I thought I saw a shadow of the madness I knew him to be capable of.

"Leave him alone," I hissed, inching closer to Wes.

"But breath only carries so much of the elixir and it's been a few months since you've had the Lapis. Your cells are turning over and you're slowly losing your immortality. It seems it was enough, though, since Mr. Isaacs is sitting here with us and not floating in the ocean." He turned his snide grin my way. "It was a kiss, wasn't it? Probably right before he would've died? I mean, you would have had to breathe *right* in his face for it to work."

Mira snickered. Adrestus smiled and straightened up. As he turned away, I saw my chance and lunged from the couch, my right fist cocked and ready to strike.

And then, the dome spun and marble pressed against my face as my shoulder screamed against its socket. Wesley's glasses clattered to the floor next to me as he pinned my arm against my back.

"Good save," Adrestus murmured to Mira. "You know, I think I *do* like him better without the glasses."

"He looks ridiculous," I grunted into the marble. "They all do."

"My new Pantheon? I let Dion pick her own outfit. She'll be devastated to hear you don't like it." Adrestus leaned over us and I had to strain my eyes to look at him with one half of my face still pressed against the floor and Wesley's hand on the back of my head. Adrestus ran the hem of Wes' cape between his fingers. "And *this* belonged to Paragon himself. Your friend should be honored to be wearing the cape of New Delos' greatest hero."

"That's not his cape," I growled. "I've seen it."

"He had more than one," Adrestus grinned, dropping the fabric and standing up. "He let me keep this one when he worked for Schrader Industries."

Adrestus gave Mira a signal and Wesley lightened the pressure against my back. I pushed up to my knees. Fleming hadn't mentioned Paul working for Schrader.

"Paragon wasn't a hero," I spat.

"No, but he was irritating. Can't tell you how many times I offered him my right-hand spot," he mused, glancing nervously at Mira. "Other than Mira, of course. She's hard to replace and I'm not sure even Paragon would've been as useful as she's been. Either way, it doesn't matter since he wasn't interested in my vision for the world, even when I offered him immortality and teed him up the way I did."

"*You* sank the city the day Paragon saved it?"

Adrestus rolled his eyes- or rather, eye. His red one stayed immobile while the blue eye lolled in his head.

"Let's not get hypocritical, alright? So we've *both* sunk the city. I at least built it. *I'm* the one who designed it so that it even *could* sink so I'm free to do so as I see fit." He picked lazily at a fingernail. Even his knuckles looked younger. "But Paragon didn't want what I had to offer and instead went and lit himself on fire. Turns out, both Fleming brothers were disappointments."

"Fleming..." Wesley gasped above me.

"I told you to keep him quiet." Adrestus glared at Mira.

"He used a lot of neurotransmitter. It might need a refill." She scowled at Wesley. "At least this one doesn't keep bursting into flame."

"Wes?" I begged, pivoting on my knees and grabbing his clenched fists. "Let me talk to him! Please!"

To my surprise, Adrestus nodded at Mira and she shrugged her long, white hair over a shoulder. I felt my heartbeat in my throat as she tapped her tablet screen. Wesley gasped and I clambered to my feet with his glasses in hand.

He continued to stand rigid but his green eyes blinked in bewilderment and they wavered as they oscillated between mine.

"Sammy?" Tears welled in his eyes and I could feel them in mine, too.

"Wes, I'm so sor—"

"Run, Sammy!" he cried. "Leave me here, I'll be—"

I pressed his glasses back onto his face and his chin quaked as he held back sobs.

"I knew you were alive," I whispered even though I knew Adrestus would still be able to hear. "Everyone thought you were dead. Not me."

I tried to give him a coy smile.

"Because you're too stubborn." His voice was a shaky laugh. "But please, you need to go."

"Not without you."

"Please, Sammy!" The tears fell faster down his cheeks and I rubbed them away with my gloves. His voice rose into a shout. "Run before they make me—"

"Alright, alright that's enough!" Adrestus clapped his hands. "Can't have any of that."

Wesley's face glassed back over and his mouth clamped shut.

"Give him back!" I yelled, still dabbing at his face with my gloves.

"No, I don't think I will." Adrestus dragged me off of Wes and my whole body locked up as he held me by my shoulder armor. "I own you both now and I still haven't forgotten what you did to me, even if you have."

I curled my lip at him.

"I remember pushing my sword into your gut after you killed my family and it's going to feel so good when I get to do it again."

Adrestus pushed me away and I bumped against Wesley's unresponsive chest. His face contorted and I thought he might put my supposed status as a walking, talking life elixir to the test right then and there, but instead, he looked to the stairs.

"Dion!" Winnie's masked face popped up from the staircase entry when Adrestus called her name. "Escort Eydis to her room. I'm done with her for the night."

"I'm not leaving Wesley!"

A heavy backhand took my breath away and Adrestus' fancy watch grazed my cheek. Winnie dragged me away from the couches, away from Wes. I was too dazed to resist.

"Wesley!" He couldn't even turn to watch me go. "Wesley, I won't leave you!"

"Sammy..." He rebelled against Mira's control with every letter.

"Take him to recharge," Adrestus said to Mira. "The last one went a full week between charges, this one barely lasts a day."

"Wes!" I cried, wishing he would turn back so I could see his face again.

"Also, Dion," Adrestus called after us. "She called your costume stupid. Maybe it's time for an upgrade?"

Winnie shoved me hard from behind and I stumbled down the stairs.

I only tried running from Winnie once as she led me through the halls of the floors beneath the dome. She easily swept me onto my back, knocking the wind out of me. I lay gasping on the tiles while her mask swam overhead.

"You really suck, you know that?" I wheezed as the air returned to my lungs.

"You really are stupid, aren't you?" she snarled. "You have any idea what Adrestus will do to Wesley if you try to run?"

She yanked me to my feet and pushed me forward.

"Don't act like you care about Wesley. If you cared for anyone other than yourself, you wouldn't still be wearing that stupid outfit."

Winnie's face turned stormy but she chewed on her lip to keep from replying. The corridor she led me through looked more like that of a hotel than a prison, with fancy tiling, silver sconces, and ornate crown molding along the high ceiling.

"We're here." Winnie stopped in front of a gray door. She slid a keycard into a slot while I eyed the end of the hallway. "Remember, run off and Adrestus makes Wesley walk off the roof."

The door swung open and she pushed me into the darkened room.

"Don't you dare touch him!" I shrieked. "I'll kill you all if anything happens to Wesley!"

She slammed the door in my face and I wiggled the knob, but it was locked from the outside.

Something inside me broke and I fell against the door, letting the sobs work their way out. Captured by Adrestus, Wesley weaponized against me, and Fleming...

He'd be so disappointed in me.

I curled up against the door, my whole body shaking as I cried. I'd come up with a plan later. Right now, I let myself whimper into my knees.

"Eydis?" The voice in the dark was cautious and I jerked my head up to scan the room. A light flicked on to reveal a well-furnished, upscale suite and a bewildered man stood in the center of a small living room, his eyes unbelieving over his tawny beard. "Oh, my god, Sammy?"

I flew across the room and flung myself into his chest and my cries redoubled as his large arms constricted around me, his embrace proving he wasn't some sort of cruel mirage. He held me close, stunned and overwhelmed, as I shook in his arms.

The circumstances weren't great and there was no telling what Adrestus might do to us, but, for better or for worse, I'd finally done it. I'd found Dad.

44

Father and Brother

Dad held me out at an arm's length to take me in, as if he couldn't believe I was in the living room of his prison cell.

"What happened?" He ran a finger across the scrape Adrestus' watch had left on my cheek. "Why are you here? Are you hurt?"

I shook my head and drew my hand across my face to wipe the tears away. He looked...*well*. Not just okay and alive but healthy and taken care of. I'd expected to find him bruised and gaunt with starvation but his beard was neatly trimmed and his button up shirt looked freshly ironed.

Even his prison, if it could be called that, was *nice*. Nicer than Fleming's apartment. Floor to ceiling windows, marble countertops, sleek furnishings...

"They have Wesley," I choked. "I came back to look for him and they made him hunt me."

"I know." He nodded along as I spoke and his brow knit together while his eyes raked over me. "You were never supposed to come here. I'm so sorry. For everything."

Dad frowned and pulled me back into a bear hug.

I stiffened against his embrace and pulled away.

"No, it's not safe!" I scrambled back, pressing against the door as I tried to get as far from him as possible. "Trev Baker saw you die in a dream!"

Dad's lips parted in a confused smile.

"I don't know a Trev Baker. What are you talking about?"

I sank to the floor, overcome with renewed sobs. He was going to die. Wesley was under Adrestus' control, Naomi hated me, I was captured, and Dad was going to die.

"He's an Apex! He has dreams and—and—"

"Look at me!" He pressed my face between his hands, crouching next to me. "I'm fine! I'm safe! *You're* safe!"

I collapsed back into his arms and after regaining my breath, I choked out an accusation.

"You lied to me. You and Alison both."

"I know. I didn't know what else to do. I'm sorry. Are you hurt?" he asked again. I let him barrage me with questions. Had I really sunk the city? Is Amanda okay? What about Avery and Alison?

After I answered to his satisfaction, he ushered me into the kitchen and put a kettle on the stove. I stood with my back to the ceiling-height window, still not sure he wasn't going to combust into nothing before my eyes. He let the silence between us fester until I finally said:

"Vidar?"

He looked up from the stovetop, his storm-gray eyes crinkling at their corners.

"You used my old name."

"Just trying it out," I mumbled, blushing. He smiled.

"In that case, yes, Eydis?"

"I remember bits and pieces," I said quietly. He nodded, a little too curtly.

I thought when I found him, I'd get my dad back but Eydis clawed at my subconscious. Vic and Vidar bled together. Father and brother.

"What do you remember?"

I slipped onto a stool at a small, high table that pressed against the window.

"You taught me to sword fight."

He chuckled sadly, turning his back to me to tend the kettle.

"You were a fast learner."

"I remember Eluf's men breaking into our home."

The mugs in his hands clinked together.

"That's a name I almost forgot," he said, his back still towards me.

"Probably better that way," I snorted. "After what he did—"

"He died fighting to save you." He finally turned to face me, two steaming mugs in hand. I recoiled in surprise.

"No, he didn't, his men attacked us and—"

Vidar shook his head, smiling sadly behind his beard as he set the mugs on the table. My eyes grazed his arms below the rolled sleeves of his buttons up. His tattoos there were that of a modern man, not a Viking.

"That was two years earlier. After we, you know, found you in the stream, Eluf was the one who put you in your long sleep. One of the first Inculcators."

"He was an Apex?" To be fair, I had zero regained memories of Eluf himself but he still *felt* like an enemy based on the one fragmented memory I had of his men.

"An Epsilon," Vidar corrected, taking the stool opposite mine. He stared at me over his mug, his eyes crinkling as he took me in. I wanted him to be my dad. I *needed* him to be my dad.

But I only saw Vidar. I hated Eydis for it.

"An Epsilon?" I repeated. "So he wasn't born with powers, Adrestus gave them to him?"

"Exactly. Like he did with Seidon."

I scrunched my face in confusion.

"I don't remember a Seidon."

He laughed. I'd missed the sound.

"Right, sorry. *Wavemaker.* He was supposed to be Seidon but went rogue and gave himself a new name in the moment."

I snorted.

"Both names are dumb."

Vidar nodded emphatically.

"But they fit Adrestus' Parthenon theme, recreating the Greek gods how he sees fit. Seidon and Poseidon. Dion and Dionysus. Hephestae and Hephaestus. Even 'Mira Aimes' is supposed to be a take on Artemis."

I scanned his face, looking for traces of Dad. I'd wanted to find him for so long, and now that I had, it felt like there was one last barrier keeping us apart. I swirled my tea around in the cup and it struck me as odd that Vidar would have *two* mugs. It was strange that a prisoner would have one at all, but two?

"Do you get visitors?" I asked.

"Sometimes. They'd let Amanda come by when she was here and there was a woman named Esther, but she's gone now, too, so it's mostly Adrestus who comes to see me."

I pushed the mug away, not wanting to use anything Adrestus might have touched. Dad nudged it back.

"Adrestus doesn't like tea. He's never used it."

I continued to scowl at the steaming cup.

"But he still comes by? Why?"

He shrugged and looked around the small kitchen uncomfortably.

"He likes the company, I think. We've both been around for so long and seen so much. Who else can he talk to about the War of the Roses or the Revolution? No one else was there except us."

I wrinkled my nose. He must've been pretty bored and lonely to be able to stomach Adrestus sitting in his kitchen with him.

"Don't give me that face," he laughed. "If I wasn't nice to him, he wouldn't have let Amanda visit. Besides, complacent enemies are easier to handle."

"You seem comfortable here." I didn't mean to let so much bitterness seep into my voice. "It's cozy."

"If you think, even for a second, that I'd rather be here than with you, Avery, and your mother—"

"Not my mother," I said wryly. "And you're not my father."

Dad and Vidar dueled in my head, and the man in front of me felt more like a stranger. Loneliness weighed in my chest.

"I might as well have been." The corners of his beard lifted in a cocky smile and Vidar clicked into place.

"You threw my sword in the bay."

His cheeks reddened under his beard.

"I gave it to you in the first place. And Havard made me. You should've hidden it better."

I balked at him, feeling the ghost of a derisive laugh building in my chest.

"We were cornered and Erika was *kidnapped*!"

"Oh, crap, I forgot about that!" His mouth dropped open. "It's been such a long time."

"*You* forgot?" I shook my head in indignation. "I have like five memories but this is one *you* forgot?"

"Like I said, it's been a while. Forget Erika being kidnapped. I barely remember *Erika*." His face grew serious, and maybe a little sad. "And things that happened afterwards made it easy to forget we'd ever been at odds with Eluf."

I blew a strand of tangled hair out of my face and leaned an elbow on the table to look out the window, but the kitchen light was too bright and my own bedraggled face stared back.

The things that happened afterwards.

The things I didn't quite remember but knew enough to know it was probably my fault.

"You remember them, then?" Vidar asked, and in this moment, he *was* Vidar.

"Yeah," I said softly. "Just a little but I remember Mother, Gunhild, Hjordis, and Erika and I remember being afraid I'd lose them."

"What about Havard? And Knut?" he pressed.

"Havard was Father, right? He kinda sucked. I don't remember Knut well, but he seemed alright. Most of the memories I have are of you."

Or Adrestus...

"You said sword fighting?" He grinned. "I remember that."

"Yeah, and a little bit of drowning."

"I remember that, too."

I curled my fingers around my mug.

"And I remember—"

The words caught in my throat. I wanted to be casual. It was so long ago, after all. Rings formed on the surface of my tea as my fingers shook.

"Bad things?" Vidar offered. I gulped and nodded, trying to clear my throat.

"The fire," I whispered. "And what, I mean who—"

Their bodies in the dirt, strewn in a neat, deliberate line. Erika so little...

Vidar nearly pulled me off the stool as he wrapped me in another hug.

"Of all the crappy things to remember," he murmured into my hair and just like that, he was Dad again.

"It's fine. I remember getting stabbed in the neck, too."

"So just the cheerful things, then." He tried to pat my hair but his fingers became ensnared in a tangle. "Maybe it's best you took a shower. I'll call and see if they can't bring you fresh clothes."

We talked long into the night after I'd cleaned up, sitting in his small, though posh, living room. He asked about Avery and Alison some more, then about classes, and friends. He told me how he'd befriended Esther and how they'd worked together to get the Doomsday Pager into my hands, how she'd let him send a Christmas message.

"I'm sorry things with Avery aren't going well." He sat in a large recliner and despite it looking like a chair that would be very comfy to lean back and disappear into, he sat forward with tense shoulders. "I'm sure Roy is doing his best to train him."

I scowled from the sofa corner, where I curled up in a blanket in a set of clean clothes that had appeared in a box by the door. A platter of half-eaten pizza bagels sat on the coffee table, and while I'd been about to grab another, Dad's flippant remark about Roy Hendricks made me lose what was left of my appetite.

"For someone who's always been outspoken about Apex, you've sure chosen a real winner to make an exception for."

"Arguably, I made the exception for Alison. Roy just sorta tagged along, but he's not as bad as you think."

"Yes, because his kids turned out *great*."

Dad grimaced.

"Either way, I liked him more than the Flemings."

I bristled under my blanket, though I wasn't sure why. I knew Paul Fleming had been a fraud, though, to his credit, it sounded like he'd turned down Adrestus' offer of helping him create a new world order. And sure, Fleming the History Teacher was annoying and overbearing, but he was better than *Roy*.

"Roy helped kill Paul," I mumbled darkly into the blanket folds. I flicked my eyes towards Dad, but he shrugged. "You knew?"

"Alison told me years ago. Paul was a fake. Roy was just helping his friend."

"Mom didn't even go to his funeral."

"Why would she? The guy broke off their engagement."

I sat up too fast, swinging my legs free of the couch and kicked pizza bagels across the room.

"So you knew they were engaged?"

Dad's face reddened and he finally leaned back in his seat.

"Well, sure. Typically when you marry someone, they tell you about the other people they've been engaged to."

"Is that why you hate Paragon?"

"It's hard to hate a dead man, Sammy. Trust me, after living a thousand years, I know a lot of them."

I settled back into the couch and glanced in the direction of the door. As relieved and overwhelmed I was at having been reunited with Dad, it was hard to focus knowing Wesley was trapped upstairs in his own body.

"He'll be okay," Dad said, following my gaze to the door. "Your friend is tough. Adrestus came by for dinner the other night and told me the shape they found him in."

"Did you see him?" I tightened the blanket around my shoulders.

Dad didn't look like he wanted to answer, but he nodded reluctantly.

"I was with him when he woke up. Told him to stay calm and that I'd take care of him as much as I could, though we both knew there's not a lot I can do."

I remembered the night spent hiding in the townhouse with Wes, telling him my dad could be his dad, too. The role seemed to come naturally to Vidar, having taken care of Amanda for months as best he could, and the only reason he was here was because he'd thrown himself on top of Winnie to save her from falling rubble.

And even if he was my brother, he'd carted me around for a millennia. My fake memories could fade to nothing, but it would still be hard not to see him as my dad because that was what he *was*. Not just to me, but to everyone. Even in my oldest memories, Vidar acted more fatherly than Havard did.

"Sammy?" he prodded. I blinked, trying to clear my eyes.

"It's nothing," I mumbled, pulling my blanket up around my face. "I just missed you."

His face grew dark and he shifted in his seat.

"You sure you didn't just miss the fake version of me in your head?"

"No, most of those memories are disappearing."

"Are you okay with that?" He squinted at me. "It took us years to create them and they only lasted six months?"

"I miss them," I admitted. "It's scary not knowing what's going to be missing next. I don't remember when my birthday is."

He pushed himself off his chair and stepped around the pizza bagels that now littered the floor. I pulled my legs in close to make room as he sat back on the couch next to me.

"I don't remember what we put on your birth certificate and Vikings didn't keep good calendars," he sighed, "but it was early summer, maybe late spring. I was pretty young still, but Gunhild was thrilled to have a sister."

He kept his hands in his lap and the floor lamp behind me cast a glow across his face.

"Early summer," I repeated, smiling to myself. "I haven't missed it, then."

"No." Orange light glittered on a tear that he thought I didn't see. "You haven't. We're getting out of here, alright? And we're bringing that boy with us and we're going to have the biggest birthday party."

I laughed, but it sounded more like a sob.

"Yeah, okay."

"I'll even let that dumb teacher come. First birthday in a thousand years, it's literally the event of a millennium."

I nodded, trying to imagine my friends and family safe and happy and healthy.

"How old am I turning?"

"Sixteen," he beamed. "About time, too."

Dad insisted I take the bedroom for the night, but I knew his six and half foot frame would never sleep comfortably on the sofa, so I rooted myself to the spot until he begrudgingly brought me a spare pillow.

However, I spent the night with my eyes wide open, taking in the living room in the moonlight that streamed in through the window behind me. Dad proved himself as stubborn as me and also refused to sleep in the bed. Instead, he made camp on his recliner and I watched his beard stir as he snored.

Trev Baker said he'd seen Dad die and that I would be next to him when he did. I clutched my blanket close to my face, still watching Dad. I'd barely gotten him back, but if Baker was correct, my being near him put him in danger. His prison was safe before I'd been tossed in it with him.

I would just have to make sure Trev Baker was wrong.

I already had enough to worry about without Trev Baker's dark warnings. I hoped Wesley was okay. I hoped he would be able to sleep tonight.

I hoped Naomi didn't hate me. I hoped at the end of this, I was still Samantha to her.

And I hoped Fleming didn't give up on me. How many times had I run off for him to chase after me and clean up the mess? He had to have a breaking point and while I didn't know where that point was, I felt like I couldn't be too far away.

Dad snorted in his sleep and I watched his outline in the dark before flitting my eyes towards the door. I knew I wouldn't be able to sleep before I tried *something*, so I swung my legs off the couch and shifted my weight to my feet.

I tiptoed around the pizza bagels on the floor and felt the low carpet change to tile underfoot. I pressed against the metal door handle. The silence of the room made the sound of the lock clicking against its constraints seem a thousand times louder than it should have and I looked over my shoulder at the back of Dad's chair. His low, slow breaths went uninterrupted and I turned back to the door.

I ran my hands over the hinges and along the door's bottom edge, hoping to find some weakness, some way to slip out. If I had Andersen's power, I could unscrew the bolts around the door without even touching them. If I was like Wesley, I'd have already ripped the door from its frame.

Of course, if I was like *either* of them, or like anyone else from the team for that matter, I probably wouldn't be trapped in the first place.

Defeated, I crawled back to the couch and slipped back under my blankets.

"Eydis?" Dad startled awake, glancing around the room. I flinched at the name.

"I'm fine," I croaked. He squinted at me as his eyes adjusted to the dark but nodded assuredly and settled back into his chair.

My investigation of the prison suite in the morning proved just as fruitless as my late night door inspection. There was no convenient laundry chute, no large air ducts, and even if the windows *did* open, we were near the top of the skyscraper.

Dad watched with melancholic resignation, knowing I wouldn't stop until every apartment corner had been explored and I wondered if he'd done the same when he first arrived.

"I made pancakes," he said from the kitchen table. "They taste better warm."

I stalked past the table, cramming half a dry pancake into my mouth without stopping as I moved on to inspect the bedroom for the third time.

"Wesley is counting on me," I mumbled through the pancake.

"Then I'm glad I'm not Wesley."

I spun on my heel to glare at him and slammed the bedroom door in his face. When I came out a minute later, I'd changed out of my loaner clothes and back into my uniform. Dad struck a face.

"They left jeans for you, you know."

"I'm on the job." I shoved the other pancake half in my mouth.

He handed me a glass of orange juice and I tried to throw it back too fast, spilling a good deal of it down my chin.

"You're a prisoner." There was a hint of a laugh in his tone and I glared.

"Dress for the job you want, right?"

He shrugged, scraping butter over his pancakes.

"Take it from a guy who's been here a while, but sometimes even pretending to be agreeable will get you further with Adrestus. Something about your uniform doesn't exactly scream that you're willing to cooperate."

I took another swig of orange juice, this time straight from the jug, staring Dad dead in the eye as I did.

"I'm *not* willing to cooperate. You know what he did to Wesley! And you were there in October when he said what he wants to do to *me!*"

Dad cringed as he remembered Adrestus' threats to make me die for every day I'd forced him to age.

"All I'm saying is, Adrestus has an ego. If you feed it, he's less likely to hurt you as badly as he would otherwise. He might even let Wesley visit us."

"We don't have to worry about *visits* because I'm getting us all out of here."

Dad smiled sadly.

"I know you will."

I knew he was lying.

A knock thudded against the door and I tensed, ready to spring out of the kitchen. Dad frowned and shook his head as he stood up from his stool.

The door opened without invitation and Mira grinned like a cat leering at a cornered mouse. Hackjob lurked behind her in the hall.

"What does he want today?" Dad grunted.

"Just Eydis," Mira crooned, beckoning me forward. I stayed back near the kitchen, eyeing her warily.

We could take them. In my uniform, most of my skin was covered and to use her powers, she needed skin-to-skin contact. Hackjob would be a little trickier since he was built like a rhino and was just as powerful, but we could just—

Dad stood with his back to Mira and Hackjob, his eyes wide in a silent plea. *Don't*, he mouthed.

"I thought we had clothes sent up for Eydis." Mira scanned my uniform.

"They didn't fit," Dad lied.

Mira fixed her grin on her face, but her eyes narrowed.

"We'll have new ones sent. For now, *that* will do, I guess."

She beckoned again but I stayed rooted to the kitchen tile, unable to move as my brain whirred, looking for a solution. A way out. A way to find Wesley and get him out of here.

Mira's smile cracked and her floor-length skirts whooshed around her ankles as she swooped into the room. I braced for her, ready to dodge, but she stepped aside and made room for Hackjob.

He lumbered into the room and, with a single sweep of his arm, smacked Dad against the wall.

"Don't—!"

Mira wagged a finger at me as Hackjob slammed into Dad a second time, cracking the drywall. Both men were massive, but Hackjob was an Epsilon, aided by powers Dad would never dream of even wanting.

"Vidar's been such an agreeable prisoner," Mira purred, "and I'd hate to have to break a few of his ribs on your account."

She held out a hand, inviting me forward. I hesitated and Hackjob drew back a fist.

"Don't hurt him, I'm coming!"

I stumbled forward before Hackjob could deal Dad the next blow. Mira's long, spindly fingers wrapped around my hand and every muscle in my body tensed against my will. I was under her control.

45

The Village Girl

E very muscle screamed against Mira's commands, but she had total, effortless control over my every move. She clicked her tongue in satisfaction and nodded at Hackjob to release Dad. Hackjob scowled in disappointment, but let Dad go. He steadied himself against the dented wall and I followed him with my eyes as long as I could before Mira guided me out into the hall.

She kept a hold on me for the entire walk up to Adrestus' floors. My feet worked against my will as they took orders from Mira, transmitted from her hands to mine.

I could barely stand the sensation of being made into a puppet for five minutes. Wesley had to endure it every moment. Amanda had to suffer through it for months. If Naomi was right and there *was* a way to use the Lapis to take away Apex abilities, Mira was at the top of my list.

"I never got the chance to tell you, it's very good to see you again, Eydis," Mira said in the elevator. "I feel like it's been so long. You look just the same."

She grinned her unsettling grin. I wanted to remind her it had only been two months since I'd seen her, but my mouth was sealed shut under her control.

We passed Miles at the desk and veered down a hall to the right rather than going straight down towards the spiral stairs. I strained against Mira's powers, fearing whatever unknown threat waited for me on the other side of the heavy, carved door at the end of the corridor. What if they were going to put a thing in my neck to control me with, like they had with Amanda and Wesley?

"Stay," Mira growled at Hackjob before directing me through a door. He took up guard and we entered what looked to be Adrestus' dining room.

The room curved, following the outline of the domed penthouse on the floor above and morning light reflected through the windows and bounced off the three glass chandeliers that hung over the long dining table. The trajectory of the windows continued into the next room, where a sitting area much like the one upstairs was situated to look out over the city.

Dark, orchestral music crooned from somewhere beyond the sitting room, and if I'd had control over my eyes, I might've rolled them. Adrestus was definitely trying to set the tone, but it came off as forced and a little tacky.

He appeared in the next room, looking the most casual I'd ever seen him in slacks and a button up under a batter-stained, blue-striped apron. His new youth caught me off guard even though I'd seen it the night before.

"Just in time." His smile was insincere under his blood-red eye. "I hope you haven't had breakfast. I just pulled muffins out of the oven."

Mira filed me through the dining room and the glint of silver caught my eye on the wall opposite the windows. My heart snagged at the sight of a polished, silver sword mounted against the white wall. *My sword.* The one I'd used to kill Eluf's warrior in my family's home and the one I'd risked freezing to death to retrieve from the bay after Havard had made Vidar throw it in the ocean.

And, though this memory was fuzzier than the others, I was pretty sure it was the same blade I'd sunk into Adrestus' gut.

"I see you've noticed your sword!" Adrestus called as he disappeared around the corner. "Had to move it up here after the museum levels flooded, but I rather like its new home."

The smell of fresh blueberry muffins washed over me. I didn't care how tantalizing the scent was. I'd never trust anything Adrestus had baked.

The sitting room gave way to a large kitchen with a double oven and a large, marble-topped island that any chef would happily die for. Adrestus hummed along with the music as he used a fork to pop muffins out of their pan. The blond man lurked in the corner, twisting a large kitchen knife in his hands and the winged woman with the pixie cut leaned against the far end of the island, her wings hidden under a large, floral cardigan. A bag that looked suspiciously like the one I'd seen Everly carry with him sat next to her with a bit of tubing sticking out of the top.

"Did we not send you new clothes last night?" Adrestus whisked strudel icing, looking at me with concern. "Those uniforms can't be comfortable."

Mira forced me into a kitchen island stool and my left arm raised and laid itself on the counter, palm up.

The winged woman ducked around the island, taking the knife out of the hands of the blond man as she approached me. I strained my eyes against Mira's control to watch her warily.

"Hold her still so I don't nick her arm."

Mira scoffed but the woman ignored her, pinched the fabric around my bicep, and pushed the tip of the knife through. Once she had a cut, she set the tool down and used her hands to rip the sleeve so that my arm was exposed from the bicep down.

"You'll remember our conversation from last night, I'm sure," Adrestus said off-handedly, now drizzling icing over the tops of the muffins. "We need to test my Life Elixir theory and to do that we need a small sample. I promise Lana isn't going to hurt you."

The woman, Lana, smiled and her eyes crinkled kindly, but I still didn't trust her as she tied off my arm. I wanted to kick out against the counter and fight back but I was helpless as I watched her draw my blood.

The music crescendoed and if I could have gritted my teeth, I would have.

"Gregor, turn that down, would you?" Adrestus pointed vaguely and the blond man disappeared to the sitting room. Adrestus nodded importantly as he watched the tube attached to my arm fill with red. "Mozart. It's a shame you slept through his career, Eydis. I was convinced he had to be one of mine. An Apex, I mean. He wasn't. Some of his contemporaries were, but it's always annoyed me that *he* wasn't."

Lana finished her work while Adrestus picked at a muffin. My head spun and Mira released me without warning. I gripped the edge of the counter, but slipped off the stool to my feet.

"Be good," Mira warned, running her pinky over her red lips.

"Where's Wesley?" I demanded, backing up against the window, ready for a fight that no one else seemed interested in. Gregor was still in the other room after having turned down the music. Lana packed her medical bag and Adrestus handed Mira a muffin on a plate. He looked up at me, annoyed.

"The boy? He's sleeping until we need him. Have a muffin." Adrestus came around the island to offer a blueberry muffin and I batted it out of his hand. It fell to the tiles and Adrestus curled his hand into a fist. A muscle in his jaw twitched and his blue and red eyes flashed dangerously. "Suit yourself. Mira, Lana, leave us."

"But, Master—" Mira looked at me nervously and Adrestus waved her away.

"I can handle her."

Mira slinked out of the kitchen, followed by Lana but I kept my guard up. Mira and Lana being sent away improved my odds, but it still didn't look good. Gregor lingered in the entryway to the sitting room, the knife from before somehow back in his hands.

Adrestus pulled the stool out from the island and leaned against it, brushing his hands off on his apron. If it weren't for the red eye, he would've looked ordinary.

"What happened to your face?" I blurted. "You aren't old anymore."

"The Lapis!" His face brightened, as if he was happy I'd noticed his new youth. "It took some trial and error but the stone remembers me. The same mechanism that allows it to grant immortality also works to move back the clock to the form I existed in when I first came into contact with it. Of course, my eye wouldn't have healed had we not stolen that Serum from your little hideout."

I grimaced, wondering if Adrestus would stop de-aging now that he was a thirty-something-year-old or if he'd revert back to his teenage self. The thought unsettled me, though I didn't know why.

"So where's the Lapis now?" I asked. Adrestus smiled coyly.

"Safe, but good try. I made a large enough batch of elixir to create a new generation of Epsilons and then stored it away." He blinked slowly. It was impossible to look away from the ruby iris. I could tell he was examining me, maybe trying to calculate my next move, waiting to see what I might try. Dad said to be a good prisoner but I wanted nothing more than to smack Adrestus upside the head with the muffin tin.

"If the Elixir is what gives people their powers, why am I still a Beta?"

"Good question," Adrestus nodded and licked muffin icing off his finger. "The stone will turn any liquid into Life Elixir, but there are a few more steps and ingredients before it's able to create Epsilons. You don't remember when I first told you about all this?"

I pressed my palms against the glass behind me. Gregor balanced the knife between his two index fingers while Adrestus continued to study me.

"You really don't remember *anything* from back then, do you?" he murmured when I didn't respond. "No, I find that hard to believe. You've got to remember *something*. Perhaps I can jog your memory?"

He went for another muffin and peeled the wrapper from its base, keeping his eyes on me.

"It's no use," I shrugged. If I could convince him I didn't remember being Eydis, maybe he'd stop *seeing* me as Eydis. He wanted revenge on her, not Samantha. "I've tried to remember but I can't."

His lips curled and he leaned forward on the stool.

"Not even your family?"

I shook my head, but I could feel the lie written in the panic on my face.

"I'll tell you about them. Havard and Solveig and their six children. Your youngest sister was Erika. She was so little and so perfectly adorable with that funny tuft of light hair. And she broke *so* easily. I killed her first."

The muffin tin was in my hand before I realized I'd launched myself across the kitchen. I shrieked as I swung it at Adrestus' head but he lithely slipped from the stool.

"You *do* remember, then!" Cruel lines pulled at his features as he snarled in triumph. I charged at him, wielding the tin like a shield but he kicked me in the stomach with a slippered foot. I fell back against the kitchen floor wheezing for air and vengeance. "Yes, I killed them, but you tried to kill *me!*"

"You killed them first!" I gasped, pulling myself to my feet. "You didn't need to but you *did!* My family!"

"I did it for you!" he bellowed and the wild gleam in his eyes told me he thought I should be grateful. "They were tethering you to that island! We were going to save the world together but you couldn't bring yourself to leave them. So, I freed you."

"You *ruined* my life!" I grabbed a stool this time and tried to use it like a battering ram. Adrestus sidestepped the attack, grabbed the stool legs, and swung me into the wall. I cried out, but stayed standing, leaning against the wall for support. "The world didn't need saving, you just wanted to turn it into your plaything, like you did my village."

Adrestus turned his back to me to look out the window. He clasped his hands behind his back as he surveyed the city.

"A naive sentiment," he whispered to his reflection. "How many wars have been fought? How many countries overrun? How many children dead from plague and famine? Just because it looks alright from up here doesn't mean the world doesn't need me. A thousand years ago, you declined my offer to help me save it. Fifteen years ago, it was Paragon. Now that I have my Lapis back, I'll just create a new following. A new legion. A new *order*. I've been here longer than anyone. The same way your brother took responsibility of you, I must take responsibility of the world, before it kills itself."

He may have had his back to me now, but Gregor stood between us, knife still in hand.

"The world doesn't need *you*," I spat.

"You thought it did, once upon a time. Gregor?"

The kitchen dissolved around me. Rocks rose from the floor and the tiles turned to slick pebbles. Gregor disappeared and Adrestus stood facing me now, his red eye gone. He was several inches shorter and his cheeks were clean-shaven. He couldn't have been older than sixteen. The window he'd been standing in front of had been replaced by a frigid bay and salty spray rolled in on the breeze.

"You're definitely injured!" Adrestus' clear, blue eyes raked over me and dull pain spread from my shoulder. I clasped a hand over the sword wound, several days old, but healing poorly. I wasn't great at resting.

"No, I'm—"

"I was told this was a well protected settlement, but you're the best they have? An injured girl?"

His skin was like fresh snow but dark curls fell in his face. He maybe had a year or two on me, but I was almost as tall as him and his knuckles looked unbruised. I could take him.

"You're not welcome here." I leveled the tip of my blade between his eyes.

A ship bobbed out in the bay. He may have come ashore alone, but he'd have back-up.

"Let me heal you," he said. "I have a friend—"

"*No.*"

"He's very good at what he does. You won't feel a thing."

"I'm also very good at what I do. Leave now, and *you* won't feel a thing."

He pursed his lips, like he was trying to hide a smile. Indignation simmered inside me. He thought I was a *joke.*

"Come back here after nightfall. I'll bring my friend. Chase us off if you like, but not until you've let him look at that shoulder. If it doesn't heal right, you'll lose range of motion in your arm."

He waded back into the surf towards a small rowboat, smiling openly now. The water morphed around him and the sky darkened, giving way to a new memory. The tide was further out and I sat on a rock, my sword at the throat of a strange man who prodded at my shoulder.

The boy stood back, like I'd told him to.

"It doesn't feel better," I growled. "You said—"

"He's not done yet."

Warmth spread from my shoulder and the torn muscles and tissue writhed under my skin. I pressed my sword against the man's neck and he put his hands up in surrender.

"It shouldn't hurt," he said quickly.

He was right. There was no pain, though the sensation was far from pleasant. I stared at my exposed shoulder in horror as the skin melded together.

"The gods—" I gasped.

"Whatever pantheon your people follow, I promise they had nothing to do with this power."

I stood up from the rock, sword still at the ready in one hand while I stretched and tested my healed arm. It was as if the injury had never even occurred.

"Then where did they come from?"

The boy grinned in the moonlight.

"They came from me."

Kitchen tile bruised my knees as I collapsed to the floor. The room jolted back into existence and Gregor leered down at me. Adrestus still stood by the window, watching with polite interest.

"Did you see anything? Oh, I think you did."

My stomach lurched and I gagged, but nothing came up. I leaned forward on my hands, though my elbows wobbled, threatening to give way under me. For all the times I'd been bombarded by sudden memories, they'd never left me feeling this ill.

"What was that?" I gasped between heaves. Gregor chuckled darkly overhead.

"That was Gregor," Adrestus said simply. "An Inculcator, like your non-mother and your nephew. I told you once I could restore your memories by stripping away the false one and that's what Gregor has done."

Panic crept within me like sludge and I ran through my remaining memories of growing up as Samantha, but how was I supposed to account for what I didn't know wasn't there?

"What did you see?" Adrestus asked. "Your family maybe? No, it was me, wasn't it? I can tell by the look on your face."

I clawed the air above me, searching for the lip of the counter to pull myself up, but just when I finally had a grip, Adrestus murmured:

"Again, Gregor."

My insides flipped as I landed in the darkened interior of my family's dwelling. Havard paced the length of the main room while my sisters huddled in the corner with Knut. Vidar sat behind our father and when I locked eyes with him, he shook his head in a warning.

"I want them gone," Havard boomed. Several of the town leaders that had packed into the house nodded in agreement but a few glanced around, unsure. "We don't need their help."

"You saw what they did to your girl's shoulder!" one of the leaders protested. My cheeks burned as he gestured towards me and I pulled my wool blanket up over my shoulders as if to hide. "And he's saying he can teach us to do the same!"

"But why?" an older woman snapped. "At what cost? There's got to be a drawback."

"They already taught the Birgers!" the first man protested. "How long before they teach Eluf's raiders? How long before we're the only ones who can't breathe fire or sail a boat with the strength of only a single man?"

As they continued to squabble, Havard stopped his pacing to eye me. I'd been the one who'd invited the stranger in while they'd all been away. This was my fault.

The scene changed and I stood barefoot in a mossy grove surrounded by birch trees. Water bubbled nearby, fed by the thawing snow. Dres had his biggest fur cloak on, but I was warm in my dress.

I brandished my sword at him.

"You'd put up a better fight if you took that off." I nodded at the cloak and he shook his sword back at me. It was bronze instead of silver, but I liked the way the springtime sun caught its edge.

"I have a thousand years of fighting experience on you," he boasted. He grinned behind his helmet. I thought it looked stupid, but he said it came from his home, in Sparta, wherever that was.

"Then why do I keep winning?"

"You do *not*—"

I lunged and he tried to parry and maybe it was the cloak and stupid helmet, or maybe I actually was a better swordsman than him, but he stumbled back, breaking through the undergrowth that encircled the grove and slipped down the ravine.

"Dres!"

I abandoned my sword and chased after him through the bushes but when I got to the stream at the base of the slope, he was nowhere to be found. I spun in a circle, searching for him and was about to retreat back to the grove when arms wrapped around my waist from behind.

"No!"

The world lifted sideways and I splashed into the ice-cold creek. I shrieked with delight and cold, pulling Dres in after me.

The water washed away, leaving me heaving on Adrestus' kitchen floor. I stumbled away from Gregor, duly noting the light in the kitchen had shifted. The day was slipping away and it was impossible to tell how much time had passed.

"Stay away from me!" I shuddered, clawing my way across the kitchen floor to escape Gregor. My stomach clenched, threatening to empty its contents and sweat dripped off my chin.

"Oh, is she awake again?" Adrestus called from the next room over. "Make sure she doesn't scuff up the floor too much. I just had it polished."

My arms gave out and I collapsed against the tiles. They spun beneath me and spat me out onto the pebbled beach.

Vidar paced in front of me, looking very much like Havard. Rocks and shells crunched under his boots.

"He *lied* to us!" he spat, gesturing out at the water where Dres kept his boat moored. "He said he wouldn't teach Eluf's clan his *tricks*."

"We don't know that he did!" I pleaded. The setting sun was warm against my back.

"Eluf's oldest son was seen moving mounds of earth just by waving his hands! Who do you suppose taught him that?"

"The Birgers!" I suggested wildly. "Or there's that other settlement
—"

"You *know* it was that boy!"

I crossed my arms at Vidar.

"When are you going to start trusting him? He's been here long enough."

"I'll trust him when he keeps his promises." Vidar looked back at the massive hull of Dres' ship. "How does he do it? Has he shown you?"

I picked at a scab on the back of my hand.

"No," I whispered. "I've asked, though."

"He won't teach you?"

"He doesn't want me to change."

Vidar fumed silently for a moment before bursting.

"Then why's he trying to convince the rest of us to learn?"

I shrugged helplessly. Vidar marched across pebbles to get in my face.

"Figure it out, alright? You invited him in last winter, now find out what he wants us for."

The scene changed again. Green light bounced off walls of ice and I watched it glint off Dres' dark hair as he looked up at the dancing sky through a hole in the roof of the ice cave.

"Are you really a thousand years old?" I asked.

"No," he admitted. "I'm nine hundred and thirty-seven."

I tried to disappear into my pelt. When he'd first told me his age, I thought he'd been joking.

"How?"

His shoulders shook with gentle laughter but I glared at him as he continued to watch the lights in the night sky. Havard, Vidar, Dres. No one took me seriously.

"Is it like your men? The ones who can do magic?" My voice sounded small inside the cave.

"It's not magic and no. It's not like what they can do."

"Then what is it?"

He finally looked at me and his blue eyes caught the green of the light.

"I told you. I won't teach you."

"At least tell me!"

He walked towards me and didn't stop until our faces were a foot apart. He hadn't grown at all since we'd met, and I'd almost overtaken him in height. He grinned coyly and reached down the front of his shirt, pulling out a pouch fastened around his neck with a leather string.

"You can't tell anyone."

"I won't."

"Eydis."

"I *won't*."

He shook a pebble into his hands. It's uneven edges were rounded and smooth and it was so blue that it almost seemed to glow.

"What is it?" I whispered. It was pretty, sure, but other than that, it looked remarkably unremarkable.

"It's my Lapis." He laughed at the look on my face. "Lapis means stone in Latin, but this is a special stone."

"Ooh," I cooed. "A *special* stone."

He curled his fingers around the rock.

"Don't mock it," he hissed. "You have no idea how many scholars have tried to make their own over the centuries but *I* have the only one."

"How?"

"I made it."

He reopened his hand to stare at his Lapis and the blue of the rock reflected in his eyes.

"And it keeps you from dying?"

"*And* aging!" He slipped it back into the pouch and back under his tunic. "And it lets me give gifts to those I meet."

I frowned and stepped away, my heart sinking.

"But you won't give me a gift."

If I could fly or move the earth, Havard would *have* to take me seriously. No more sewing sails. No more waiting at home while Vidar went on the adventures.

Dres' eyes widened and he reached for my hands.

"No, you're too precious for that." He drank me in and I could see my stark expression reflected in his pupils. "I want you to live forever with me instead."

I pulled my hands away so he wouldn't feel them shaking.

"Forever's a long time," I whispered.

"It is," he nodded. "I don't want to be alone for it all."

Forever. My brain buzzed with elated panic. Forever with *Dres.*

"And we'd save the world together?"

"Yes," he whispered back emphatically. "And when our work is done, we can live forever in the empire we've made."

I glanced back towards the mouth of the ice cave.

"What?" A new edge crept into his tone.

"That all sounds great," I insisted, "but I can't leave yet."

"We leave tomorrow."

My heart plummeted and I gawked at him. His face became cold and stony.

"What? You can't!"

"We'll be back in the spring. Your people have been generous in supplying us with food and shelter for the past year, but have otherwise been uncooperative in aiding us in our more long term goals."

"They don't trust your *gifts,* you mean," I accused. "Just because they're naturally suspicious —"

"I may have forever, Eydis, but the world doesn't!" It wasn't like him to raise his voice and he looked immediately sorry for it. "There's more settlements to the north. They'll be desperate for our help with winter rolling in. After that, we'll come back. *I'll* come back."

The cave disappeared and I was back in my family's longhouse. Snow howled outside and I huddled in the corner with Erika and Hjordis, a protective arm around them both. The leaders of our village sat around our father's long table, weapons lying in the open next to their mead.

Eluf was taller than my father, but lacked his brawn. His face was long and strong cheekbones stuck out from his dark, wiry beard.

"I'm telling you, I've never seen so much gold in my life," he was saying, unperturbed by the unwelcoming gazes of the village leaders. "He offered it all to us if we attacked you again before the snow began to melt."

I shook my head. I would know if Dres had that much gold. I also knew he'd never attack the people who'd housed and fed him for a year. He'd *protected* us from Eluf and his men. Why would he ask Eluf to attack us?

"Then why aren't you attacking us?" Havard glowered.

"What good is gold to us? As helpful as Adrestus' gifts have been, and while we've had our *differences*, we won't turn on our fellow Norsemen for the gain of a foreigner."

Havard turned to glare at me and I tightened my grip on my sisters.

"You're the one who brought this curse on us," he growled. The rest of the room followed his gaze to me and I stuck out my chin out in defiance.

And suddenly, I was bobbing in the ocean chop, gritting my teeth as I struck out against the water with my oars. The boat was meant for two people, but I'd have to manage on my own if I was to intercept Dres in time. I needed to warn him. If he came into our harbor, I wasn't sure even his Lapis could protect him against what Havard had planned for him...

The ocean morphed into tents and I walked through Dres' new campsite. Without Havard's protection, he'd had to set up a camp of his own a safe distance away.

"They said you betrayed us to Eluf," I said, chasing after Dres. He looked the same as he had when he'd left before winter, but his shoulders were tenser and I couldn't get his brow to unfurrow.

"That's a lie. Eluf is trying to turn you against me because he doesn't want us protecting you."

"He said you have gold."

He stopped to gesture around at the tents.

"Where? I don't see any gold here. You told me Eluf attacked your village a year ago. Why would you believe anything he said?"

The next memories washed over me in a disorganized clamor. Images of Adrestus' New Delos apartment spliced between scenes, so I was never sure of where, or when, I was. Secret walks with Dres through the forest, listening to him talk about the world he wanted to create. Trying to escape down a hall while Gregor followed. Sword practice in stolen hours with Vidar. Mozart's Requiem swelling overhead. Havard yelling that I'd never leave the village again as long as he lived. Plush carpet pressed against my face. The acrid scent of my burnt village.

After the fire, Vidar carried me all the way to Eluf's settlement and Eluf welcomed Vidar and me into his home. Someone shoved food into my unfeeling hands. Women who'd survived the attack wailed outside, mourning the loss of our home.

Dres couldn't. He wouldn't...

But I knew he had.

He'd killed my family.

All I had left was Vidar.

The next morning, I shoved food into my satchel and rummaged through Eluf's rations until I found a skein of vinegar. I wrinkled my nose at the smell and added it to my bag.

The last thing I grabbed was my sword.

I walked alone through the woods, choking on whispered apologies to my brother and sisters and mother and father. I would make it right. I might even see them soon.

Orange and purple tinged the sky when I finally walked into Adrestus' camp. The men at the camp entrance nodded at me and I smiled back.

Adrestus' tent was at the middle of camp. He was already awake, studying a map of the surrounding settlements. He looked up as I entered and readied himself.

"You've killed them," I said blankly.

"I had to set you free." He studied me carefully but I smiled.

"Yes, thank you. You've made everything easier."

He relaxed.

"You'll come with me?"

"That's why you did it, right?"

"It was part of it." He smiled coyly and came around the table to greet me properly. "And now you're mine. I don't have to share you."

I put a hand on his shoulder, still smiling. I reached for my waist with my free hand. Metal slid against leather as I drew my sword.

"All yours. Your Scourge Queen."

I watched my smile crack in the reflection in his eyes. I plunged the tip of my sword between his lower ribs without thinking. Without feeling. Blood welled between his lips.

"Eyd—"

"Shh." His snow-white face blurred behind a screen of tears. I left the sword lodged in his body and reached for his neck, ripping the leather string, pulling the pouch out from beneath his shirt as he watched in horror.

I shook the Lapis into my hand.

"You took everything from me," I droned, watching the blood bubble from his mouth, "so now I'm taking your *forever* from you."

"Eydis..."

He stumbled back, clawing at the sword hilt that protruded from his torso. I ducked out of the tent. No one had realized what I'd done, but they would soon.

"She's coming around."

Adrestus' voice was deeper. Something soft supported my head but my hair stuck to my face, sticky with sweat. My eyes flickered open and I stared at the white pattern carved into the apartment ceiling. Hunger pains ripped at my stomach and I struggled to sit up, dazed and unsure of where I was.

"Maybe that was too much that time?"

I jerked to the side to get a better view of the room. Adrestus and Gregor sat across from me, silhouetted by the evening light that filtered into the room. I scrambled into a sitting position, but my stomach flipped and I leaned over to retch.

All I had left was stomach bile and Adrestus cringed as it splashed across his Persian rug.

"You *must've* seen something that time," Adrestus crooned. "You've been out for hours."

"I saw you die," I gagged.

Adrestus leaned back in his leather chair, rocking idly side to side, as if thinking.

"It didn't have to be this way, Eydis," he murmured. "We were going to save the world together."

"You wanted to use me to convince my people, my *family*, to join your sick crusade!" I struggled to my feet but the room swooped around me. Had I really been unconscious all day? How many memories of Samantha had Gregor erased to deal that kind of damage? I tried to think, but my mind was too clogged with fresh images of Eydis' life. "And you...you were a thousand years old, treating me like a *plaything*."

"I was sixteen until you stole my youth from me! Forced me to live off the few bottles of elixir I had left, aging between sips!" He stood up from his chair.

"It doesn't matter how young you looked! You were a gross old man giving a young girl attention to get what you wanted!" I scanned the room for something, *anything*, that could be used as a weapon. I lunged for a piece of iron-wrought art hanging on the wall behind Gregor, but the man grabbed me by my wrists and I crumbled in his arms, weak with fatigue and hunger.

"Take her back to her room," Adrestus hissed and Gregor dragged me through the dining room towards the door. My sword glittered on the wall. "Welcome back, Eydis. Now that you've returned in full, I look forward to breaking you."

46

Voice In The Night

I passed out somewhere on the walk between Adrestus' apartment and Vidar's prison suite. High-rise skyscraper hallway morphed into birch trees as my tiny, child-sized feet carried me across the moss.

"Knut, don't!" I shrieked, knowing my brother was hiding somewhere out of sight.

"Raaaaawh!" He howled like an animal and leapt out at me. I screamed and giggled as he grabbed me around the waist and lifted my tiny frame into the air. "A tasty child like you will make a great meal for a bear like me!"

Air whistled in my ears as Gregor dropped me in the entryway of Vidar's apartment. I slumped against the wall and the door slammed shut next to my face.

"Sammy!" Vidar's arms wrapped around my shoulders. "What happened to your sleeve?"

I looked down at my bare arm.

"I'm remembering," I mumbled. My brain scrambled to find any trace of Samantha and I locked onto a memory of a long-past Christmas spent during a power outage. I remembered Dad singing an off-key version of What Child Is This, insisting it helped set the mood as we opened presents in the dark. I leaned into Dad's chest, sighing in relief. Samantha was still there. She wasn't gone yet.

"Can I leave now?" a voice asked from the living room.

I straightened up and pushed Dad away, every hair on my bare arm standing on end. A board game took up the coffee table, save a corner where textbooks and notebooks lay in a pile. Empty dinner plates stacked on the floor to make room for the game pieces.

Dad had told me Adrestus let him entertain visitors, but I didn't think that included Winnie.

She sat in the dark hoodie she'd worn at the New Year's Eve festival and, despite crossing her arms in an act of defiance, shrank back into the same couch I'd spent the night on.

"What's *she* doing here?" I staggered to my feet and Dad put his hands up in apology. "You know what she's done!"

"I know, I know! But she's still a high school student, I'm still a professor, and Adrestus values an educated following."

I looked back at the textbooks on the coffee table. Dad's betrayal somehow made my newly recovered memories feel more raw. Dres had betrayed me, too.

"You could've said something!"

"I was going to but then they took you away and—" He steadied me as I swayed. "Are you okay?"

It was a stupid question and I shoved him away from me.

"No!" I pointed at Winnie. "You, get out!"

"Sammy—" Dad placed a hand on my shoulder.

"It's fine." Winnie collected her textbooks and binders.

"We haven't finished the game!"

"Oh, yeah, that looks *real* academic," I snorted, glaring at the colorful game pieces that were strewn across the table.

Winnie pushed past us, hugging her things.

"You'll miss dessert," Dad warned her.

"You have to stand back before I open the door."

Dad sighed and pulled me away from the entrance. Winnie slipped her keycard into a slot just over the handle and pushed into the hallway. The door slammed shut.

I stumbled to the kitchen, aiming a swift kick at the coffee table as I went. Game pieces rolled to the floor and Dad frowned after me.

"Winnie's only sixteen. She's just misguided."

"She enslaved her own sister!" I tore through the cabinets, looking for something, anything to eat. My stomach screamed for food. "She tried to get me kidnapped *twice*. She attacked me and Wesley *and* left me to fall to my death when *I* helped *her!*"

Dad wavered in the space between the kitchen and the living room.

"What happened today?"

I smashed a bag of chips in my fist.

"I told you! I remembered things."

I opened the bag too violently. Crushed chips flew across the kitchen table and scattered onto the floor. White noise filled my head. I stared at the ruined snack, feeling a tightness creep up my legs, to my stomach, to my neck.

"Sam—"

"I JUST WANTED A SNACK!" I threw the remains of the chip bag to the floor, but it didn't make nearly a satisfying enough impact so I knocked a chair over, too. "You have this whole *stupid* apartment where you can feed Winnie dinner and dessert and I can't eat a freaking bag of chips!"

"Hey, hey, hey! It's alright! I have more snacks!" Dad reached out for me, but I slapped his hands away and retreated to the far side of the kitchen. "Why don't you tell me what happened?"

I hated how his forehead creased with worry. I hated how I didn't know if I was looking at Dad or Vidar. I hated knowing I'd ruined his life.

"Come on," he coaxed. "Please, Eydis."

The name felt like fire and I backed further into my corner to try to escape it.

"I'm *not* Eydis," I spat, no longer able to keep the tears from springing to my eyes. "I don't *want* to be Eydis!"

Dad's brow furrowed with hurt.

"Of course you're Eydis, don't be ridiculous. Why would you *not* want to be her?"

I shook my head, searching for the words that had evaded me since discovering who I was.

"Because," I croaked, "I hate her."

"Why?" His voice leapt with unexpected defensiveness and he looked ready to fight me for speaking so ill of his sister. "It was Adrestus—"

"She trusted him!" I beat on my chest armor and tears flecked the kitchen tile. "She *loved* him and that makes her an idiot! I *can't* be her, Vi. I..."

Dad caught me before I fell to my knees, hands over my face.

"He tricked you. He was manipulative and he tricked you and you can't blame yourself for the actions of a bad man," he murmured as I shook in his arms. "You *are* Eydis, though. I see it in everything you do. The faces you make, the way you talk, the way it's impossible to change your mind because you're so damn stubborn."

"He forced me to remember." I squeezed my eyes as he tucked me under his beard and held me there. "It was all my fault."

"Nothing that happened was your fault."

"Yes—"

"*No.*" He held me out, pressing my face between his hands, and his thumb swiped a tear from my cheek. "Without Adrestus, Eluf *would* have wiped us out. He kept us safe for a whole year and sure, he was working with Eluf, too, and playing his own game, but that's *not* your fault."

I looked up at his storm gray eyes. They were the same ones that looked back at me whenever I looked in a mirror. They were the same eyes our father once had.

"I think Samantha's almost gone," I whispered. Dad's shoulders heaved as he sighed.

"*You* are Samantha, not those fake memories, and you're Eydis, too, and that's *wonderful*."

I wrapped my arms around him, sniffing into his shirt. He was both Dad and Vidar in my head, so why was it so hard to make room for both Sammy and Eydis?

"Can I have some dinner?" I mumbled. He pulled me towards the table and smiled.

"Of course. So what happened to your sleeve then?"

I clamped a hand over the inside of my arm where my blood had been drawn.

"Adrestus thinks I'm full of his stupid Life Elixir. He said he wanted to test my blood to confirm."

Dad's gentle expression morphed into one of fury. I gulped.

"He *what?*" He grabbed my arm, fervent but gentle, to inspect the small needle wound. "Why?"

I shrugged, not knowing why I suddenly felt like I was in trouble.

"The stone, his Lapis, apparently changes any liquid it touches into the stuff that keeps him immortal. He thinks when I put it in my wound way back when, I accidentally turned *myself* into Life Elixir and that's how I stayed alive."

"I'm going to *kill him*," Dad seethed, rubbing the light bruise on my inner elbow. "I'm going to break his damn rock and I'm going to *kill* him."

"*Can* it be broken?"

"Better be," he murmured, breathing heavily through his nose. "Sammy. Eydis. Promise me you won't ever let anyone use you, alright? I won't see you turned into his own personal Fountain of Youth."

"He said as my cells turnover, it'll likely fade," I muttered, not looking at him. He reached for my face again. This time, he was the one with tears in his eyes.

"I've fought to give you a second chance at life and now that I've finally secured one for you, I'll die before I see it ripped from you just to feed someone's immortality."

My second chance at life...

But I hadn't forgiven Eydis, I hadn't forgiven myself, and it wasn't a second chance I was sure I'd ever deserve.

Dad slept on the recliner chair again and, like the night before, I stayed awake long after he'd succumbed to snores. At some point, the sound lulled me into a fitful, sweaty sleep and the aftereffects of Gregor's attacks reverberated through my subconscious.

"Show me." Eydis' voice was painted with excitement. Dres' face took shape in the dark. He held the Lapis up for me to see, glittering blue in light of our oil lamp.

"Like this." He dropped it into a copper mug. I grabbed it from him, unable to contain myself. I stared at the dark liquid, waiting for it to bubble or change color.

"It's not doing anything."

He laughed, and took the cup back.

"Not *visibly* maybe, but this is now the most precious cup of wine in the world."

He swirled it in his hand before throwing the drink back, rock and all. He grinned at me and spat the Lapis into his hand, smacking his lips. The rock had turned from blue to blood red but slowly faded to purple as I watched.

"I want to try it!"

"That was the last of my wine."

I looked around the crowded storeroom, but the lower decks of Dres' ship offered little light.

"What about this?" I grabbed a jar of vegetables suspended in liquid from a shelf. I uncorked the lid and Dres balked, closing his fist around the Lapis.

"Put that back!"

"What?" I sniffed the juice and wrinkled my nose at the smell of vinegar. "I don't mind. I want to try the Elixir!"

"No!"

"I thought you wanted me to live forever, too!"

"Neither of us will if you put the Lapis in that! I used to have two, a long, long time ago."

"And?" I prodded, giving the pickled vegetables another sniff.

"And then I tried to turn vinegar into Elixir and the stone dissolved."

I clamped the lid back over the jar.

"Oh."

"Yeah. *Oh.*"

I shoved the jar back onto the shelf, glad it was dark enough that Dres wouldn't see my cheeks glowing red.

"When do I get to try it then?"

"When you finally come away with me." He put the stone back into its pouch and led the way to the stairs.

Samantha.

My eyes flew open and I sat upright on the couch. Dad was still asleep. Had I dreamt I'd heard my name? I scanned the room, straining against the shadows.

Samantha, can you hear me?

The beating of my heart against my eardrums threatened to drown out the voice and for the first time since willingly handing myself over to Wesley and letting him bring me to Schrader Tower, I felt something akin to hope.

Fleming? I called out in my mind.

Holy crap, we found her. I recognized Apex Councilman Mickey's voice in my head. It sounded just like it had the night of New Year's Eve when he'd linked us all telepathically.

I leapt from the couch, trying to remember where I'd discarded my uniform. If they were here, it was time to go.

Samantha, first, are you all right? Fleming's disembodied voice echoed in my head.

Yes. What's the plan?

Are you somewhere safe?

I looked over at Dad, still asleep.

For now. I'm in an upper floor of Schrader Tower. I'm with my dad.

Excellent. Stay there.

I pressed against the window glass, as if I might be able to see Fleming on the streets below. However, the city was dark and a layer of fog shrouded the pavement.

How long? I asked. *They have Wesley. We can't leave without him.*

I know. We're formulating a plan. We have to move slow so he doesn't realize we're here. Even in my head, Fleming's voice had a warning edge to it.

I looked back at the door. I was ready to go *now* but I didn't have much of a choice at the moment.

He might move me in the morning.

Out of the tower?

No, but...

I tried to think of an excuse, anything to make Fleming act sooner rather than later.

We don't want to mess this up, Sammy. Naomi's voice was calm and casual, if slightly reprimanding.

Who all is there? I asked, trying to remember who all had been left at the shelter when we'd left. *Do you have Remi?*

I listened to the hum of the refrigerator as I waited.

No, Remi's arms haven't healed all the way. Fleming finally said. *But there's enough of us here to save Wesley, I promise.*

Who?

Fleming listed them in my head. Him, Mickey, and Professor Parker from the Apex Council, along with Sergio, several other university students, Naomi, Andersen, Justin, Freddie, and the twins. Everly was stationed back at the school, keeping hidden.

I ran through the abilities I knew they had in my head. Sergio and Andersen, as much as I hated to admit it, were powerful foes to be reckoned with. Naomi and Justin were both highly skilled, as the other university students were sure to be. Freddie's presence explained the thick fog that had rolled in. He'd probably summoned the mist to keep them better hidden.

But with all their powers combined, was it enough for them to storm Schrader Tower?

I frowned, still trying to squint through the fog.

Probably not.

Do you know what floor you're being kept on? Mickey asked.

No.

Do you know what kind of defenses are in place?

No. I was useless. *What if you asked Wesley? He's in the building, if Mickey could add him to the psychic link—*

Doesn't work like that. Mickey cut me off. *I can only link with people I can see or those who I've linked with before. Just sit tight. We'll try to have a plan in place by tomorrow evening.*

Anything could happen in that time.

Don't hurt Wesley. My voice was small in my head.

We can't guarantee— Mickey started.

Don't. Hurt. Wesley. I rapped my knuckles on the window as I thought each word. Dad snorted in his sleep behind me.

We won't. Fleming assured me. *You have my word.*

I sighed in relief. If Fleming said they wouldn't hurt him, they wouldn't.

Get some sleep. We'll check back in when it's morning.

I stayed at the window long after the psychic link broke off. Fleming and the others being on the island should've put me at ease, but I felt more anxious now than I did before. Last time they'd attacked Adrestus head-on, he'd ended up with both Amanda and Dad in his clutches.

Goosebumps erupted down my arms and I didn't know if they were from the nighttime chill or the anticipation of a fight. I finally crawled back under the blanket on the couch, shivering. I pressed a hand under my pillow to better support my head and flinched when my fingertips found the edges of cool plastic.

I slipped my hand back out from under the pillow. A white keycard pressed between my fingers and I stared at it in elated horror. It looked identical to the card Winnie had used to leave the suite earlier in the night.

I didn't know how it had gotten there. Maybe she'd had a spare in her pocket and it had slipped under the pillow during her board game with Dad? It didn't matter.

Fleming? I tried to call out in my head. *Mr. Mickey? Naomi?*

Nothing. The link was cut. Only Mickey could reconnect it.

I pushed myself back off the couch, wearing my blanket like a cape as I tip-toed to the door, just as I had the night before. Fleming said to stay put. That had sounded easy enough when I didn't have an escape key.

I twisted the keycard in my hands and crouched down so that I was at eye-level with the key slot. What if it worked? I didn't have a plan. When I'd run back to find Wesley and Avery as the island sank, Fleming had yelled at me about not having a plan. My lips turned dry and I held my breath as I raised the plastic card.

A large hand wrapped around my wrist and I jumped. Dad had come up behind me so silently.

"Where did you get this?"

I flipped the card from my fingers and into the palm of my hand.

"Found it." I kept my eyes on the card slot, refusing to turn and look at him.

"Give it."

I waited a second too long and he pulled my arm back as gently as he could and turned me so that he stood between me and the door. I hugged my blanket tighter around my shoulders, holding the keycard close to my chest.

"I just want to see if it works. I wasn't going to leave." That wasn't necessarily true. I had no plan. Dad loomed over me. His hair stood up on one side of his head and dark shadows hung under his eyes.

"And what if Adrestus gets an alert every time a door is unlocked?" he asked quietly. "What if there is someone stationed out there right now, ready to separate us if you so much as think about trying anything?"

The edges of the keycard cut into my hand as I gripped it tighter. Vidar was supposed to be a Viking. Even when I thought he was a normal dad, he'd seemed sterner, so why was he so unwilling to make a move?

"I forgot we were playing by Adrestus' rules," I snarled. "I just wanted to see if leaving was an option. Don't worry, I still plan on being a *model prisoner.*"

"It's *not* about being a model prisoner!" Dad stepped forward, driving me away from the door. I stumbled on the hem of my blanket. "It's about being *smart.* Let's say the key works. Then what?"

"Then we make a plan!"

"I know you think you're invincible but you and I don't stand a chance against Adrestus' followers."

"What if it's not just us?" I asked. Dad's brow furrowed and I felt a hint of satisfaction at having information he didn't.

"Wesley is—"

"Not Wesley."

I turned back towards the window and my blanket billowed out behind me dramatically.

"Who?"

The fog was even thicker now and rain splattered the other side of the glass.

"Fleming is here with some others. There's no plan yet but—"

"How do you know?"

Dad tugged on my shoulder but I remained resolute, continuing to stare out at the dark city.

"One of them can send mental messages. They woke me up to let me know they're here."

"And the keycard—?"

"I just happened to find it under my pillow."

Dad marched to the couch and ripped my pillow from the cushions in investigation.

"It's not there anymore!" I rolled my eyes.

"Winnie," he murmured. "Why would she leave it here?"

I leaned back against the window, letting the glass cool my shoulders.

"On accident?"

"Or because she knew you'd try something." He shook his head. "It's a trap."

"Or it's our lucky break!"

He threw the pillow back on the couch and stomped into the kitchen. He pulled out the drawer under his coffee pot and stood to the side so I could see three identical keycards.

"Winnie leaves them every month or so," he said, "but I'm not leaving until the rock that my family was murdered over is destroyed."

"You've been able to leave this whole time? And you chose to stay?" I felt tiny standing in the dark kitchen. Amanda and Esther had both tried to warn me. They'd said Dad was where he was supposed to be. They meant he was here by choice.

"I'm going to stop him from living forever and stop him from making any more Epsilons. Please, Sammy. You aren't safe until it's gone."

"He's already got the Elixir made!" I rolled my head back and forth on the glass, letting it massage my scalp.

"So we stop him from making more!"

I glared at the keycards in the drawer. He'd had a way out the whole time.

"Even if I'd used them, it's probably some kind of trap or test," Dad scowled. He pointed into the drawer. "So drop it."

"You're not my real dad." I didn't sound nearly as venomous as I'd meant to.

"I'm the closest thing you got." He raised an eyebrow and I scowled at his open palm. I slapped the card into his hand and he dropped it into the drawer and slammed it shut. He swore quietly and began pacing the room.

"What? I gave it to you!"

"If Alex is here, we can get you and Wesley out," he mused, "but I still don't know where the Lapis is, or how to destroy it. I can stay behind, but Adrestus will be suspicious if I don't leave with you."

My stomach fluttered and I flicked the kitchen lights on. Dad winced as light flooded the space. I ripped open the cabinets, letting my blanket fall to the floor while I searched.

"What are you doing?"

"Vinegar!" I hissed. "He told me how to destroy it once! *Vinegar!*"

Dad crossed the kitchen and dove into the fridge, pulling out a jar of pickles.

"Would this work?"

"Does it have vinegar in it?"

"It's *pickles*." When I didn't respond he continued with, "Yes, there's vinegar in it."

I grinned. Maybe Dad being a good prisoner and being allowed snacks and pickles *hadn't* been such a bad thing after all.

But then, my last words to Naomi came crashing back and the pickle jar looked less like a weapon to use against Adrestus and more like a broken promise.

"Wait," I said. "We can't."

Dad's face turned sour and his right eyebrow hitched back up his forehead.

"Why not? We just need to find out where it is and work it into whatever plan your English teacher dreams up."

"Fleming teaches history and you know his name." I glared at the pickle jar as if it was its fault I'd even thought about breaking my promise to Naomi. "My friend needs that rock and I told her I'd get it for her."

Dad's face went blank and then slowly contorted into an expression of angry confusion.

"Yeah, I'm sure lots of people would like the magic rock that makes them immortal, Eydis!"

I blinked at him, shrinking backwards out of the kitchen.

"I mean Samantha. Sammy." He sat down at the table and buried his head. "I'm not leaving this rock in one piece knowing what it can do and has done."

"She needs it," I whispered. I'd failed Naomi in so many ways. I needed to at least do this. "When she's done with it, we can destroy it."

Dad laughed callously.

"No one is ever *done* with immortality. It has to be taken from them."

"She doesn't want to be immortal!" I snapped. "She wants to get rid of her powers!"

Dad blanched.

"Well, that's...I mean, I'm sorry, I wouldn't want powers, either, but..." he reached for the pickle jar and fished out a spear. "Do we even know the Lapis can do that?"

He crunched into the pickle.

"No," I admitted, "but maybe we don't need it if Adrestus is right and I'm filled with Life Elixir."

"Absolutely not." The pickle jar shook as Dad slapped the table. "You won't become a resource for these people."

"She's not *these people*, she's my friend!"

"I'm sorry. I know. I don't care who it is, I won't let you be used anymore than Adrestus already has."

I gathered my blanket up off the floor.

"Whatever," I mumbled. "We have time. Fleming doesn't have a plan yet and we don't even know where the Lapis is hidden."

"Right. One thing at a time." Dad finished off his pickle and put the jar back in the fridge. "If things get sticky tomorrow with your friends storming the building, the first thing we should worry about is getting sleep."

He flicked off the kitchen light and I slunk back to the couch.

"How am I supposed to sleep?" I pulled the blanket up over my head, listening to the recliner chair creak as Dad settled back in.

"Think about your birthday," he suggested.

"That's months away."

"First birthday in a thousand years needs months of planning." There was a smile in his voice and I smiled to myself, too.

"Can I have sushi for dinner on my birthday?"

Dad laughed until I giggled, too, poking my head out from under my blanket to look at him in the dark.

"You can have all the sushi in the world as long as you share with me." His eyes reflected what light was available and I knew he was looking back at me. "I love you, Sammy. And I love you, Eydis. It'll all be okay, whatever happens."

I buried my face in my pillow, feeling the pounding in my chest and the pounding in my head subside at his words. *It'll all be okay.* And if Dad said so, it had to be true.

47

Ares

I pretended to be asleep the next morning as Dad shuffled around the kitchen. It was a miracle I'd slept at all, but it still hadn't been enough. My stomach ached and my eyes felt full of lead.

Samantha?

I pulled my pillow over my head as Fleming's voice cut through my thoughts.

What?

Good morning to you, too. Any updates?

Actually? Yes.

I told Fleming about the keycard and the mental link became so silent, I thought Mickey might have severed it.

Are you— I prodded at the aether with my mind and jumped when Fleming's voice snapped at me psychically.

Don't do anything. Stay where you are.

I scowled.

Save it. I already got this lecture.

"What is it?"

I pulled my head out from under the pillow to look at Dad. He stood in the kitchen, wringing his hands around a spatula.

"What is what?

"You're growling."

I grunted and the sound did sound a bit like an annoyed growl.

"It's just my dumb teacher in my head."

Dad tapped the spatula against the palm of his hand.

"He has a name, you know," he said, repeating what I'd said the night before.

I threw the pillow at him and he swatted it away.

"Watch it! I'm making frittatas!" He straightened his apron and shook the spatula at me. "Ask Alex if there's a plan yet. I want to know anything and everything."

I strained, trying to listen for Fleming, Mickey, or even Naomi's voice in my head.

"I think they've gone," I mumbled. "Where'd my uniform go?"

Dad returned to the stovetop, tending to his frittatas with one hand and pouring coffee into a mug with the other.

"It's starting to smell and you're missing a sleeve. Also, while you were gone yesterday, Adrestus had more street clothes dropped off for you along with the message that if you refused to wear them, he'd have Wesley — never mind. It's best I don't say." He tried to sound aloof as he passed on Adrestus' message, but his face darkened and he jabbed at his frittata a little too aggressively.

I knew better than to assume Adrestus would make an empty threat and as I changed into the jeans and t-shirt that had been left for me, I couldn't help but feel empty.

I was useless to Wesley. I couldn't even tell Fleming where they were keeping him. In street clothes, I felt even more helpless. At least in my uniform, I knew who I was. Apex 12. Team member. *Someone.*

In jeans and a t-shirt, I was either the ghost of a dead girl or the shadow of a girl who didn't exist, though I couldn't figure out which. Since

Gregor had messed with my head the day before, it felt like Samantha Havardson was an old tape on rewind, and the more she rewound, the more the tape tangled and frayed.

I was disappearing.

As the morning wore on, it seemed to get darker outside and I wished our apartment faced west rather than east so I could watch the storm roll in over the ocean. There wasn't much else to do. Dad wasn't allowed a TV and I wasn't interested in his collection of boardgames.

Fleming checked in every hour until just after lunch, when he told me they were about to go silent.

We've stayed out of sight, but Naomi says Adrestus' patrols are getting suspicious. We have to retreat until it's safe and you'll be out of range of Mickey's powers.

I stared out the rain-splattered windows, playing with my necklace and wondering which of the buildings that rose like pillars from the fog they were hiding in.

What do you need from me? I asked, already knowing the answer.

Stay where you are. Stay safe. We'll be in touch soon. You won't be there much longer.

Adrestus must've had his fill of tormenting me the day before, because as the afternoon crept away, Dad and I were left alone, me staring out the window from my perch on the couch back while he played solitaire and hummed to himself until I finally couldn't take it any longer.

"Tell me about home."

Home. The word electrified me. I hadn't meant to say it.

"*Fallegur.*" He moved a stack of cards on top of another. "*Kaldur.*"

Beautiful. Cold.

"Do you miss it?" I drew a finger through the fog I'd breathed onto the window.

"*Daglega.*"

Every day.

"Tell me about our family."

His recliner creaked behind me and he heaved a sigh.

"I thought you remembered them."

"I do." The window squeaked beneath my fingertip. "But it's all in pieces."

"Our mother was beautiful. Solveig. Our father Havard would do anything for her. In their youth, she fought by his side and when she was injured and almost killed, he vowed he'd never let any harm come to her or any of his future daughters." He laughed to himself and playing cards slapped against the table as he moved another stack. "So the gods cursed him with four of them."

I twisted my head to look at him and he grinned at me.

"Cursed with one in particular it seems," I sighed.

"You didn't want to be kept at home."

"I don't care about Eydis." I looked back out at the gathering clouds. "Tell me about Knut."

The couch shifted as it took Dad's weight. He swung his legs over the couch back as he joined me at the window.

"Level headed and paternal, which he had to be as the oldest of six. Havard may have taught me to wield a sword, but Knut taught me how to know when to use it or not."

"Gunhild?" I asked next, going down the line. He cleared his throat. It sounded painful.

"Spitting image of our mother. Our father wouldn't let her marry unless whoever asked for her hand could best him in a sword fight. He said there was no point in marrying his daughter off to someone who couldn't protect her as well as he could."

"And then us."

"And then us. Vidar and Eydis."

"You got me a sword." I dragged my finger back across the window pane.

"It's upstairs now. As horrible as he is, at least Adrestus knows proper sword care."

"I saw it." The Vidar of my memories was slighter and younger and his beard much patchier, but I could see his shadow in the man next to me. "Vidar was nice."

"I was." He turned his storm gray eyes on me and it was my brother sitting next to me on the couch back. "We were middle children together. Had to watch each other's backs."

"Tell me about Hjordis."

"Can't tell you about Dissy without telling you about Erika. Erika worshipped her and Dissy loved the attention. Erika liked having someone she could look up to. No one ever saw them separated."

I drew another line in the fog of my breath that clung to the window before folding my hands in my lap, smiling at my work.

"What's that?" Vidar leaned over to look at the row of stick figures. All eight of them smiled like the bumper sticker families on the back of minivans and Vidar sniffed loudly.

A tear traced the curve of his cheek and my cheeks glowed red.

"I'm sorry." I raised a hand to wipe them away but he grabbed it before I could.

"No. Don't be. Please." He smiled and the first peal of thunder rumbled in the distance. "It's the first time I've seen us all together in a long time."

I sniffed, too, and he wrapped an arm around my shoulder and pulled me in to kiss the top of my head.

"I can make you a permanent one," I promised. "I've gotten pretty good at drawing. It might not look perfect but—"

"Thank you," he whispered. I blinked before he could see the tears in my eyes.

A single knock echoed on the other side of the door and we both jumped, simultaneously jamming our knees against the window. Dad swore and rolled backwards onto the couch as the door swung open. Winnie glowered from the doorway, her black hoodie pulled up over her head.

"You've got a dinner invite." She jammed her hands into her hoodie pocket.

"Give me a moment." Dad hurried to clear his solitaire game but Winnie shook her head.

"Just her again."

Dad froze, looking at me still perched on the couch. My insides curdled. I didn't want to see Adrestus and I didn't want to see Gregor. I wasn't ready for Samantha to disappear completely.

"When will she be back?" Dad demanded. Winnie shrugged.

"After dessert?"

I slid off the couch back and tried to smile reassuringly at Dad. He grimaced back.

"I'll be fine," I insisted. "You said it yourself last night. It'll all be okay."

"Right." He nodded curtly, but his eyes wrinkled in concern. "I'll see you back here."

I reached out mentally, calling for Fleming, trying to let him know I was moving. I was met with silence and the hum of my own brain going numb with anxiety.

Winnie stepped aside as I followed her into the hall. As soon as the door slammed behind me, she clicked her tongue.

"You were supposed to run."

Anger writhed inside me.

"Why? Adrestus doesn't need an excuse to torment me."

"Idiot, Adrestus didn't want you to escape. I did."

I looked sideways at her but she remained stoic until we were in the elevator.

"You don't know what he has planned." Cold, taciturn, bitter Winnie tried to hide the quake in her voice and I didn't want to know what could be so bad that *she* was shaken.

"I couldn't leave Wesley behind."

"You'll wish you did." She finally turned to look at me and her green eyes wavered. "Sammy, you should've run."

The elevator door slid open to Adrestus' penthouse lobby and she whipped around to face forward. Miles sneered from the desk and I ignored him as Winnie led the way to the right. She stopped at the door to Adrestus' dining room.

"Enjoy," she mumbled, swinging the door open and standing to the side to let me enter.

Adrestus sat at the head of the dining table, an impressive and mouth-watering spread laid out before him. His white suit matched the white table cloth, making his black hair seem blacker and his red eye redder. He lit up as I stepped into the opulent dining room.

"Finally! You have no idea how hard I worked on this meal for us. Come and sit." Adrestus gestured towards the empty place setting in front of the window, but I looked instead to the seat across from it. Wesley sat unnaturally rigid at his plate. My sword glinted on the wall behind him.

"What are you waiting for?" Adrestus clapped his hands together. "Sit! Ares and I have been waiting!"

"Ares?" I looked to Wes and he grimaced. "His name is Wesley."

"All those who are blessed enough to join my pantheon get new names worthy of their new status," Adrestus beamed. "It seemed fitting Mr. Isaacs would become my god of war, don't you think?"

"Wes," I croaked, taking my seat. Soft, classical music wafted in from the sitting room but the rain against the window behind me nearly drowned it out. "Are you okay?"

"You shouldn't have come back for me." His lips twitched and I knew he must've felt the same way I did. Relieved to see each other, terrified of what might come next. His stiff posture signaled that Mira was hiding somewhere, keeping him under control. I'd have to tread carefully if I wanted Adrestus to continue to allow him the use of his voice.

"Ham?" Adrestus held up a platter on his end of the table. He kept his head tilted at an odd angle, as if trying to look at us both with his blue eye.

Without invitation, he stood and began dishing slices of ham onto both of our plates, standing over Wesley and then leaning over the table to dish mine. I hated how good it smelled.

"They let you wear your glasses." I couldn't look away from Wesley. I felt that if I so much as blinked, Adrestus would somehow make him disappear. His face looked hollow and his eyes haunted but he managed to smile at me from behind locks of brown hair falling limply in his gaunt face. He looked horrible, but at least Adrestus had allowed him to attend dinner in jeans and a t-shirt instead of the Dark Paragon get-up.

"Thanks for bringing them. They help." His eyes flitted to the dog whistle that rested above my shirt collar. "Nice necklace."

Adrestus fell back into his seat at the head of the table, an awkward and cold distance from us both. There was more food than three people could ever hope to eat in one sitting and my stomach was so knotted I thought I might never be hungry again.

"This is nice! We're having fun, aren't we?" Adrestus sang. "You did so well yesterday, Eydis, I thought you might enjoy a nice dinner with your *friend*."

The way he said the word "friend" sent a chill down my back and I eyed the sword on the wall.

"What happened yesterday?" Wesley demanded. "What did you do to her?"

"It's okay, Wes. I'm fine," I said, but he kept his eyes on Adrestus.

"Just helped jog her memories is all! No need to get defensive." Adrestus took a large bite of ham and then looked at me to talk with his mouth full. "Though, I wonder, how'd we do? Is there even any Samantha left after all that?"

I hesitated, not wanting to let him know there was more left for him to rip away from me, but not wanting to worry Wes.

"Sammy?" Wes' voice was tiny, as if afraid I might not respond to the name anymore. I looked at him sadly, wishing I could tell him somehow that Fleming was on the island. He was coming to rescue us.

"Yeah, I'm still here."

Adrestus grunted in irritation but shrugged.

"Perhaps I'll have Gregor come back after dinner."

My stomach flipped and if Wes hadn't been at the table, I might've tried then and there to run away. But there he was, sawing at the ham on his plate awkwardly. He wrinkled his nose as his arm lifted it to his face against his will. It made me sick to watch him being force-fed by his own body and as he moved, I noticed the small bruise on the inside of his arm.

"What's that?" I asked.

Adrestus clapped.

"Yes!" he said, his mouth full of mashed potatoes. "I'm so glad you asked. *That's* you! We got the idea from your principal, actually, the way she donates plasma to share her Apex ability. Yours isn't an Apex ability of course, but the concept's the same!"

"The Elixir..." I frowned at Wesley and he made a weird movement, as if trying to shrug with his face. "Why give it to Wesley?"

"You mean *Ares,* and we'll get to that! First, eat up! You've barely touched your food!"

Instead, I reached for the sparkling cider set next to my plate. It fizzed against my tongue and I set the glass down and pushed it away. It tasted more like metal than apples.

"Tell me about school. How is your friend Anthony adjusting to his new powers? I know it was a bit of a shock to discover them so suddenly, but I had hopes he'd come to appreciate what I'd done for him."

"Go to hell," Wesley snarled.

"Careful." Adrestus waved a reprimanding fork in his direction, emphasized by a well-timed flash of lightning outside the window behind me. "I'd hate to go through an entire dinner having taken away your speaking privileges."

He sat with his head turned at a jaunty angle, so that his blue eye darted between us. In a strange way, it reminded me of Sergio and how he would tilt his one eye towards his opponent while sparring.

"So you don't want to talk about Anthony?" Adrestus continued. "Fine. Tell me about your teacher, Mister Alexander Fleming. I know some fun facts about him that would blow you away."

"We know about Paragon," I deadpanned. Wesley squinted at me behind his glasses and I tried to shake my head. "Besides, you literally called them the Fleming brothers two nights ago."

"You don't want to talk about Paragon *or* my favorite student at New Delos Prep? Maybe I should call Gregor up early," Adrestus suggested. "Ares might like to watch. Just how much *have* you told him about your true identity?"

"I know she killed you," Wesley sneered.

"That she did!" Adrestus stood back up, letting his chair topple backwards. He crossed back behind Wesley and lifted the sword, *my* sword, off its place on the wall. I tensed in my seat, apprehensive over how close the sharp edge was to Wes' face as Adrestus waved it through the air. "With this! But I ultimately survived my assassination and continued to live on for centuries, giving me a long time to think about how I might punish her should our paths ever cross again."

My fingers dug into the edges of the table. He'd given this speech before.

"You're going to kill me," I said plainly.

"No." His mismatched eyes become bulbous with excitement. He ran a hand along the flat of the silver blade. "You're going to do exactly what you did a thousand years ago and betray the person closer to you than anyone. *You're* going to kill *him*."

48

Disarmed

Absolutely not!" I stood up, grabbing a butter knife as if it might stand a chance against the silver sword. Adrestus shrugged and set the sword down on the table in front of Wesley, whose eyes had grown wide behind his glasses. "Don't worry, Wes, I'd never—"

"He'll be *fine*," Adrestus smirked. He procured a bandage and began wrapping it around Wesley's upper arm, fixating his blue eye on his work. Wes craned his head away the best he could, but he was trapped.

Fleming? I struck out with my mind, searching for Fleming or Mickey or Naomi or even Andersen, but they were silent, still too far away.

"You see," Adrestus purred, leaning down to get eye-level with Wesley's bruised arm, "if I'm right and you *are* made of Life Elixir, Ares should be fine. Your breath alone was able to save him from death before. With a sample of your blood running through his veins, he'll come back. Let me test my theory. You owe me that much. If you need a little encouragement, I could have *him* try and kill *you,* but you won't let him do that. You know it'll hurt him less to die at your hand than it would to become one of your murderers."

"What if you're wrong?" I demanded, trying to buy time. "What if I'm not Elixir, and I die for real?"

His red eye, I realized, was the exact shade the Lapis turned when in use. In my memories, it had been blue when dormant, but once activated, it turned the color of rubies. The color Adrestus' eye now donned. He flicked his hand lazily towards my drink.

"You drank some proven Life Elixir already. You're good for at least a few days with the sip you took, but if the threat of Ares killing you isn't enough motivation, we can add an extra bit of fun. If you wait too long, he'll bleed out his supply of Life Elixir and he *won't* come back. Mira, please dull the boy's pain receptors. We can't have him passing out."

I shook my head in confusion and Wesley's mouth widened in a shout as Adrestus scooped up the sword from the table. Horrible realization washed over me too late. Silver flashed through the air, lightning bouncing off its sheen as Adrestus brought the sharp edge down over Wesley's right arm, just below the elbow.

My brain couldn't register what I was looking at. White tablecloth turned red and Wesley screamed, unable to move, while his severed forearm lay on the table between his plate and a bowl of corn, his fingers curling inwards towards his palm.

"The tourniquet I tied should buy you a little time, but—"

Feral rage propelled me up and over the table, scattering plates, cups, and Wesley's arm. I brandished the butter knife in one hand and grabbed Adrestus' face in the other, tackling him to the ground and pinning his arms beneath my knees. However he'd thought I would react to him slicing off Wesley's arm, this was not it. He goggled up at me, immobilized with shock as rage brought my butter knife swinging down.

Because of what he'd done to my friend.

Because of what he'd done to my family.

Because of what he wanted me to do.

And, because I knew where his precious Lapis was hidden.

Warm blood spurted between my fingers, turning the knife slick, but I kept my grip until his eyeball popped out with a squelch, dangling over his cheek, still tethered to the socket by nerve and tendon. Knife edge scraped against stone and the Lapis, red with blood and power, rolled into my hand.

That's why he wanted to know the extent of my immortality. He was trying to do the same to himself, with the Lapis tucked behind his eyeball.

He shrieked up at me in a language I didn't understand, blood running down his face, onto the floor tiles, into his gaping mouth. It hadn't been that long ago that our positions were reversed.

I gagged as my shirt collar bunched up around my throat. The room spun as I lifted off my knees, slammed into the table, and skidded across the top, taking bloody tablecloth, dinner plates, and Wesley's arm with me. I stumbled off the far end of the table, the bloodied Lapis still in my hand.

"KILL HER!" Adrestus bellowed. Wesley stood, his face hauntingly passive, his left arm cocked in a fist, while his right ended in a bloodied stump. If I wasn't so terrified, I might've sobbed at the sight of him.

"You have to *fight* it, Wes!" I begged. He threw his chair out of his way and it cracked against the window. I backpedaled into the sitting room.

"You will pay for what you've done!" Adrestus pulled himself up behind Wesley, using the table for support with one hand and cradling his dangling eyeball in the other. Half his face ran with blood and I couldn't look away from the gaping hole where I'd plucked out his eye.

I was trapped. I could run deeper into the apartment, somehow find a way to signal for Dad to come help. Maybe if I screamed loud enough, he'd use one of his many keycards and come running, but I remembered Baker's warning and nixed the idea. Dad would be in danger if he came to help. I was on my own.

Samantha, we're back. Fleming murmured in my head. *We have a plan but—*

WESLEY JUST LOST HIS FREAKING ARM, FLEMING! GET UP HERE NOW BEFORE HE LOSES HIS OTHER ONE!

Fleming barraged me with questions but I didn't hear any of them. I was too busy watching red spots bloom on the white, plush rug of Adrestus' sitting room as blood spattered from Wesley's arm.

"I know you can fight it!" I pleaded, watching him lumber after me. "Fight her, let me help you."

Wesley screamed as he tried to reclaim his body but Mira forced him to lunge and I turned to run farther into the apartment. Adrestus' screams echoed after me, outlining all the horrible things he was going to do to me, then Wesley, then Vidar.

Samantha, what's going on? Where are you? Fleming's voice finally cut through the noise of the apartment and I found enough of my wits to think-scream a response.

Floor beneath the penthouse! Hurry!

Wesley kept the same slow, deliberate pace. The hall past the kitchen continued to follow the curve of the window and I passed heavy wooden doors to my left. Rain smacked against the glass to my right, the wind carrying it at a nearly horizontal angle. The light from the sitting room behind me waned as I ran and the hall was only lit by intermittent flashes of lightning. I tried a door, was relieved to find it unlocked, and slipped inside.

Before closing the door, a flash of lightning from behind illuminated the room for a second, showing it to be some kind of fancy study with a heavy desk and fine, wooden cabinetry.

I focused on the wall of cabinets, locking it in place in my head as the room plunged back into darkness and I crept blindly until I found the cupboard door with my hands.

I squeezed inside and held my breath.

Fleming? I thought.

Yes?

My stomach loosened.

I just wanted to know you were still there.

Wesley's heavy footsteps sounded in the hall, interspersed with the crashing of thunder.

We're almost in the building. We'll have to take the stairs, but yes, Samantha, I'm here.

Hurry.

It's eighty-seven stories.

Hurry.

The door clicked open. Wesley would be able to hear me with his super senses, but Mira didn't have access to those.

I listened to his footsteps outside the cabinet.

"Blood on the door handle," Wesley rasped. "Very sloppy."

I flexed my hands in the dark, feeling my fingers stick together with Adrestus' blood. I tightened my grip around the Lapis. It was sticky, too, and emitted a soft heat. A shadow passed over the slit between the hinges.

"Fight it, Wes!" I launched myself out of the cupboard, aiming to tackle Wesley. He must've had every muscle tensed, though, because I bounced off him. He squared up and I flinched as Mira swung his arm.

It would've made contact, and probably would've cracked my skull, too, had she not swung with the fist that no longer existed. Blood splattered from the wound and whipped me across the face.

I fought the bile in my throat and sprinted out of the room, back towards the kitchen, through the sitting area, and to the gory dining room. Adrestus was gone, but the sword still glittered on the floor, next to Wes' arm. I tried to ignore his curled fingers that had so many times held mine. My stomach churned and my head went light but I grabbed the hilt of the sword, not to fight Wesley with, but use against anyone who stood between me and Mira once I found her.

Wesley charged after me, faster than before and I chanced a look back at him running over spilled food and stained tiles.

I wanted to run to him. I wanted to tell him it was all going to be okay. I was going to save him.

But I had to keep going.

Updates? I demanded as I ran back towards the elevator.

Floor fifteen. We're going as fast as we can.

I scowled. It was Andersen's voice.

Where's Fleming?

I'm busy!

With what? I shouted in my head.

They know we're here!

The hall curved towards the elevator. I could hear Wesley thundering behind me and the thunder clapping overhead. I skidded to a stop as Miles appeared, leering behind his desk, a twisted smile curling his face.

I had to try, but I already knew what would happen. Before I reached the elevator, I bounced off one of Miles' invisible walls. He guffawed behind me.

"It's funny every time! You wouldn't think it would be, but it *is!*"

I pivoted, ignoring Miles, ducking under Wesley's outstretched hand, and sprinting down the adjacent hall, past the portraits, towards the spiral, metal steps.

Lightning flashed outside and the flickering light poured into Adrestus' glass penthouse dome, flooding the stairway before going dark again. Metal clanged as I ran up the steps two at a time, holding the sword ahead me and jamming the Lapis into my back pocket.

Wesley leapt from below, crashing into the railing halfway up the spiraled steps. He held onto the railing with his left hand while his right arm waved as if trying to grab at me.

I stumbled up into the empty penthouse. The storm outside raged from all angles with me at its center. Each peal of thunder shook the glass and lightning reflected and magnified against the dome's curves.

I'd hoped Mira might be up here, but I was alone.

Until Wesley joined me.

I brandished the sword in front me, hoping Wesley knew I'd never use it against him.

"Wesley," I pleaded. His mutilated arm hung loosely at his side. "You have to try to fight it."

"Kill..." he groaned, "...me..."

I tightened my grip on the sword.

"Never." I needed Remi. I needed her powers. I was useless. The best I could do was keep him from bleeding out before help arrived from below. "And I won't let you hurt me, either. Promise."

He charged and I dodged, ducking away, but he didn't give me time to even catch my breath before I was dodging his next attack.

When I faced Wesley in the Final Trial back in October, when I'd been trying to make the team, I hadn't stood a chance against him.

I still didn't. If Mira had the use of both of Wesley's hands, I wouldn't have made it this far. No one would have. Lightning forked overhead, splashing across Wesley's face and sending our shadows cascading across the tile. I was running out of space to move as I tried to out-maneuver him.

Glass bumped against my back and Wesley pulled back a fist. I rolled out of the way at the last moment and his knuckles cracked against the dome.

It was a hit that would've done what Adrestus had told Wesley to do. Cracks in the glass spiderwebbed out from Wesley's fist and as he drew his hand away, blood dripped from between his fingers.

"Wesley, whatever happens," I panted, "it's not your fault. I know this isn't you."

I ducked away from his fist. Every time I tried to move towards the stairs, he drove me back against the glass.

How had I fought Amanda when she was under Mira's control? The first time, she'd kicked my face and gave me a concussion. But the second time? I'd bought a few moments with the stun gun. It had shorted the control chip and forced Mira to reboot.

I didn't have a stun gun on me, though, and it wasn't as if I could hand Wesley a fork and convince Mira to have him stick it in an electrical socket. Besides, maybe it would be best if I avoided electricity all together since Trev Baker had said it would kill me.

Except I'd had Life Elixir for dinner. Even if I was struck by lightning, I wouldn't stay dead.

"Sammy, *please*." Sweat and blood splashed the tiles at Wesley's feet as he came after me with attack after unrelenting attack.

"If you can talk, you can fight! Fleming is here, coming up the stairs. Just hold on a little longer!"

But he screamed in agony.

"It *hurts!*" He faltered in his fight and his face twitched. A raspy voice took over as Mira regained control of his vocal cords. "Turned his pain receptors back on. He's much more agreeable now."

Wesley lurched forward and I eyed the tourniquet around his arm.

"It's okay, Wes." My voice cracked but I pretended it didn't. "It's not your fault. You did so good."

I pressed my back against the glass.

"It'll be less painful for him if you just give in," Wesley growled. "Let me make it quick."

The sky outside the dome crackled and I slowly raised my hands in surrender, holding the sword handle so the blade pointed down. A jagged crack ran along the glass next to my head.

"It's okay, Wes," I nodded. "Trust me."

He readied his fist.

"I can't wait to kill you again tomorrow."

He lunged and I rolled away. Glass splintered where he made contact, adding to the fault lines he'd already created in the dome, and while his weight was off center, I dealt him a swift kick to the side. He stumbled, knocked off balance, and in the milliseconds I'd bought myself, I plunged the sword into the glass split, throwing all my body weight behind it, wedging it clear through to the other side.

Lightning forked and thunder shook the dome as Wesley's arm wrapped around my shoulder from behind. The sword acted as a lightning rod and the dome lit up as electricity rippled across the surface. I twisted into Wesley as the lightning struck, pushing him to the ground, trying to cover him from the explosion as best I could.

Then, numb silence and blinding hot pain that seared across my body, the smell of something burning, twitching arms, every hair on the back of my neck standing straight up. The sky burned and shattered, raining shards of glass over us, but I barely noticed it through the pain. My body spasmed and something hot sliced into my back and through to my chest. The metal of my necklace seared against my skin and I screamed until it was like a lightbulb burst in my head and the sounds and lights extinguished.

All of forever was forced in the span of mere seconds and when my vision cleared, wind whipped at my hair and rain splattered the back of my head. The floor of the penthouse glittered with shattered glass.

"Wesley?" I choked. I rolled off him. His eyes were closed and a burn mark splayed out across his chest, perfectly mirroring the burn on mine. I'd tried to protect him the best I could. I wasn't sure we'd survive a direct bolt of lightning.

Wind pulled at me and I tried to drag Wesley's limp body further from the edge but stopped after I saw the trail of blood that stemmed from his arm.

I hadn't wanted to kill him. This wasn't the plan. I shook his shoulders, fighting through muscle spasms and pain.

And then—

"Sammy?" he murmured. His eyes flickered open. "What smells so good?"

"Wesley?" I broke into a sloppy grin. My dog whistle necklace dangled in his face as I leaned over him. "Can you—"

He lifted his hand to my cheek and the gentle touch of his fingers seemed to pull me closer.

"She's gone," he whispered. "I—"

He grunted and screwed his eyes shut as he spasmed.

"I'm so sorry, Wes. For everything. For Adrestus, for—" I looked back at his stump of an arm. He was still losing so much blood. "Fleming and the others are going to save us. We're going to be okay."

He smiled wanly and let his hand drop from my face.

"I'm so tired, Sammy. And it hurts..."

My fingers found the Lapis in my pocket and I shakily tried to hold it over him, as if whatever rain it managed to catch might roll off and onto his face, keeping him alive. Its surface had faded back to blue, but it flashed purple and red wherever the rain touched it.

"Why's it always you and me on a rooftop, huh?" he said dreamily.

"Wes, stay awake. Everly can help you. You just need to—"

His eyes sharpened with sudden fear.

"Sammy, run."

It was too late.

"So you ruined my newest pet?" Adrestus stalked towards us from the stairway. His eye no longer dangled from his face but the empty socket still bled freely, staining his white suit. He hunched like a snake coiling itself before the strike.

I shifted through the glass on the floor to put myself between him and Wesley, but my body shook with fatigue. A heavy backhand, laden with rings and his silver watch, met my face and I fell back. He grabbed me by the collar and dragged me to the edge of the rooftop as I screamed for Wesley, kicking feebly. He scooped my sword out of the glass, dropping me to the ground as he did.

Wind howled at my back but I tried to look at Wesley rather than think of the eighty-seven story drop to the pavement, but he looked to have finally lost consciousness.

"You think you're clever?" he snarled. "Eydis failed a thousand years ago. Why is Samantha any different?"

"She's not!" I yelled to be heard over the wind.

"Then I'll take the same amount of pleasure in scraping you off the sidewalk in the morning as I would have back then." He balanced the toe of his shoe against my chest but movement back at the staircase caught my eye.

Vidar appeared, illuminated by another lightning flash. He sprinted across shattered glass. *No.* He would die. He would...

"Maybe I'll reboot your friend and make him be the one to clean you up," Adrestus crooned. Dad wrapped his arms around Adrestus, ready to pull him back, but it didn't matter.

Adrestus' foot pressed against my sternum and the world opened up beneath me as I tumbled backwards into rain and space.

49

The Last Viking

Lightning spread out above me like bright white and blue veins crisscrossing against a black marble sky. As I hurtled towards my next death, the Lapis still warming my hand, I could only think of how each millisecond ripped me farther from the roof where Wesley was bleeding out and Dad grappled with Adrestus.

I'd died before. That wasn't what scared me. What *did* scare me was the thought of waking up in a world without Wes or without Dad and I screamed in protest as gravity hurtled me away from their sides.

A sudden, mighty groan rose from the building and something hard and sharp slammed into my back. The face of the building twisted away from me as metal tendrils wrapped themselves around my arms and legs, spinning me as I fell.

I cried out in pain and shock, spinning with the metal until I was falling slower and able to see the lines of steel that had peeled themselves off of Schrader Tower to catch me and slow my fall. I came to a stop halfway down the building face, my arms pinned to my side by torqued metal. My hair and necklace hung around my face as I gawked at the flooded sidewalk another forty stories below.

Steel creaked and unfurled, curling me upwards until I could see a broken window several floors above me. Naomi clung to the shattered-out window frame, her toes dangerously close to the edge and her hair whipping wildly in the storm.

"She's almost here!" she called out. "You've got her!"

The metal lifted me towards the opening and Naomi's arms pulled me into the dark hallway. My knees gave out as soon as my feet felt solid floor and I collapsed with my face in Naomi's armored shoulder.

"He's going to kill them." My voice was strangled and muffled. "On the roof, he has Wesley and my dad."

"It's okay." Her arms tightened around me, trying to quell my trembling. "Fleming and the others will save them. They're almost there."

"I'm sorry." My fingers curled against her back. "I should've told you everything as soon as I found out."

"Sammy—"

"No! You were living with a thousand-year-old undead viking girl and you deserved to know just as much as Wesley did!"

"Sammy!"

"I won't hear it! You were right to be mad at me!"

She pried me off of her, a nervous smile on her lips. Her eyes glanced behind me. Someone cleared their throat.

"Yeah, I knew there was something weird about you."

I scrambled to my feet and my stomach plummeted as if I was falling from the rooftop all over again. Andersen leaned against the hallway wall, doing his best to look bored with his uniform helmet under his arm, but his cheeks tinged red in the dark.

"How long have you been there?"

He scowled.

"Who do you think caught you? That's *twice* I've saved your life now."

"That still doesn't make up for—"

"I *know*," he snapped, a bleak expression overtaking his face. He looked to Naomi. "I just updated the others. They're still trapped about fifteen floors up, but Fleming says to get her out of here."

I stepped away, squaring up, the feral beast Adrestus had unlocked in me threatening to rear its head again.

"I'm not leaving them."

Naomi gulped and wrung her hands.

"I can't go up any higher than this floor without Wesley making it difficult."

"He shouldn't be as agitated now," I insisted. "I think he lost consciousness from blood loss."

"His arm," Andersen grunted. "It's not really..."

I struck a face and both Naomi and Andersen blanched.

"You don't have to come with me," I said. "It's dangerous and you'll get in trouble."

Naomi shook her head.

"We can't just let you *go*, either! He'll throw you off the roof again and I'm not going to be responsible for that."

I rolled the Lapis between my hands. In the calm of the hallway, I thought the stone felt and looked different than it had when Adrestus had extricated it from my neck. It didn't look whole, like bits of it had been chipped away, though that was something to worry about later.

"I'll come back if he does," I said quietly. I unfurled my hands to show her the stone. It glimmered softly, emitting an azure glow. I extended it to Naomi. "Here. As promised."

Her chin quaked as she surveyed the Lapis.

"Is that...?"

"I don't know how to use it for what you want but yeah. It is."

She took it between two shaking fingers and her cheeks glowed blue as she raised it to her face to inspect it. Naomi was wonderful and spectacular for many reasons, not just her Apex abilities, but sadness tugged at my edges thinking about her throwing that part of herself away.

"Thank you, Sammy." She flung her arms around my neck. "I'm going to figure it out and I'm going to see my mom again. I'll come with you to the roof."

My stomach clenched and I pulled away, glancing around the hall for a stairwell, though I wasn't sure how my exhausted legs would manage to carry me up at least forty flights.

"It's fastest if you take the elevator."

We all jumped at the sound of Winnie's voice. She stepped out from around a corner down the hall, back in her black cloaks and theatre mask. Naomi and Andersen rushed to throw their helmets back on but Winnie shrugged.

"Don't bother. Anthony already told us who you all are." She raised a gloved hand and pushed the mask up over her head, revealing her haggard face. "Do you want my elevator key, or not?"

Winnie, who'd been a spitfire even in my fake memories of her, looked defeated, with heavy eyes and a tired frown.

"It's a trap," Andersen warned. "Why would you help us?"

"Why does it matter?" Winnie balled her fists. "Do you want the key or not?"

Both Andersen and I turned to Naomi, who shook her head.

"She feels genuine," she admitted. "And a little guilty."

"I'm not guilty of anything!" Winnie snapped. She pointed at me. "Sure, I don't like *you*—"

"I already told you, it's not my fault!" I snarled.

"I don't care whose fault it is!" Her voice bounced off the barren walls and Naomi shifted forward to put herself between us. "I don't *like* you and I didn't care for most of my classmates, but—"

She faltered and I saw her swallow hard.

"You don't want anyone to die," Naomi said slowly. "That's okay, Winnie. We don't, either."

Winnie deflated, looking like a lost kid more than an enemy.

"Adrestus *believes* in me and I still believe in him, and Wesley was weird and kind of annoying, but never mean. Adrestus told me what he was going to make you do and..." She inhaled deep before continuing. "Tell me you didn't? He's okay, right?"

It was hard to feel bad for Winnie, especially as she stood here telling us she still believed in Adrestus and his vision.

"Your guy chopped his arm off. Last I saw him, he was bleeding out on the roof," I said tersely.

Winnie put her hands up in surrender, holding a keycard in one.

"Just help him, okay?"

Andersen marched forward and snatched the card. I slinked past, headed towards the elevator down the hall, giving Winnie as wide a berth as possible.

"Wait," she cried after we'd passed. Lightning flashed in the broken window behind her. "You have to hit me."

Naomi and I recoiled but Andersen grunted.

"Okay. Why?"

"He'll think I helped you!"

"You *are* helping us!" I didn't have time for Winnie's whining. Wesley and Dad needed us.

"Yeah, but I can't have Adrestus thinking so!"

"We aren't hitting someone who isn't attacking us," Naomi sniffed, pulling on my arm to draw me away. Andersen, however, sauntered back to Winnie.

"Fine, but you have to hit me back."

"Oh, my god!" Naomi growled. She dragged me down the hall, the sounds of grunts echoing behind us. Andersen's boots slapped against the floor as he hurried to catch up. "You idiot."

"What?" he snapped, stopping outside the elevator door. He held one hand up to stem his bleeding nose. "She had a point."

We filed into the elevator and Andersen and Naomi were so taken aback by the view the glass walls offered of the city, that I had to remind Andersen to swipe Winnie's key over the card reader.

The elevator rocketed us upwards and I bounced on my toes in anticipation.

"Miles, the one with the force fields, might be in the way, but Dad got past him somehow, so maybe he's taken care of." I looked at the ceiling as if concentrating there would help us go faster. "There's also the chance someone will have come and taken up his spot if he's injured."

You better be on your way out of the building.

I jumped at Fleming's voice in my head. The looks on Naomi and Andersen's faces told me they'd heard it, too.

"Ignore him," I muttered.

Samantha, we'll handle it from here! Get out!

The elevator door slid open and I braced to face whoever had taken up Miles' post. My knees went weak. Mira sat on the desk with one leg bent up towards her face, her heel on the desk edge. The other dangled lazily in a swirl of long skirts. The tablet she'd used to control Wesley rested on the counter next to her.

"Thought you might be back," she murmured, brushing long, white locks behind her shoulder and leaning her cheek against her knee. "You've broken two of my favorite toys."

Metal and thunder alike clashed up ahead, the sounds coming from the broken penthouse. If Dad and Wesley were fighting Adrestus, at least one of them, hopefully both, were still alive.

"I've got her," Andersen growled, pushing forward to face Mira.

"What's that on your shoulder? A number eight?" Mira slipped off the desk and tilted her head at Andersen. "You're the one whose secret got out, right?"

"Because of you!" Andersen pulled off his helmet and threw it at Mira. She lazily sidestepped it and it soared behind the desk, crashing into the wall. "You were in control of Amanda that night! *You* tried to kill Jamie!"

"Sounds like it's *Jamie's* fault your identity leaked, not mine." Mira placed a hand over her chest in fake indignation. "But if it's a fight you want..."

She pushed up her sleeves and flexed her fingers.

"Shouldn't have thrown your helmet!" Naomi hissed. "She controls people with skin to skin contact!"

"Shouldn't be a problem."

Naomi and I jumped away as the elevator door wrinkled and creaked behind us. Andersen balled his fists and a sheet of metal peeled itself away from the elevator door. It collided with Andersen's back and creaked as it bent to encase him inside.

"Go!" Andersen's voice was muffled under the metal armor he'd fashioned for himself. Mira scowled and tried to maneuver between us and the hall but metal pipes ripped from the ceiling to wrap around her waist and pull her back.

I led the charge down the hall. Andersen's metal echoed behind us, metal clashed overhead, and the metal of the spiral stairs clamored as I ran, with Naomi hot on my heels, up to the penthouse.

The storm had carried the lightning past the tower but heavy rain continued to barrage the roof with sheets of water. Silver met bronze as Dad battled against Adrestus, brandishing the very sword he'd gifted me so, so long ago and parrying the attacks of Adrestus' weapon. Adrestus' suit was in bloody tatters but he was unrelenting in his attacks on Dad.

"Oh, my god, Wesley," Naomi breathed. Glass shards scattered as she sprinted to his side.

He was right where I'd left him, still bleeding from his arm, looking horrifyingly lifeless. Wind ruffled his rain soaked hair and Naomi pushed it out of his face. She clamped a hand over her mouth with her free hand, taking in his mutilated arm and the burn that spread across the front of his shirt.

"YOU!"

I spun around and squared up, ready to protect my friends. Adrestus stood across the open penthouse. His suit hung from his shoulders and flashes of undershirt and bloodied torso peeked from between the tears in the white fabric of his jacket. Rain matted his hair and the left side of his face was coated in a mass of blood. He pointed a bronze sword at me, his face contorting.

"WHY AREN'T YOU DEAD?" he bellowed. "WHERE IS MY LAPIS?"

He charged and I braced to catch his sword in my body, knowing I couldn't die and I had nothing to fight it with.

Dad bolted between us, my silver sword flashing in his hands. He intercepted Adrestus' assault. Sweat, rain, and blood mingled on his face and he chanced a glance back at me. His clothes were as shredded as Adrestus' and a long cut traced his forehead.

"Sammy." A relieved grin cut through the strain on his face. "You impossible kid, get your friend and *go!*"

He grunted as he pushed Adrestus back, but the Spartan charged at me a second time. Dad stayed between us, forcing Adrestus away as he hurled curses in ancient Greek at us.

"Not without you!"

He exchanged blows with Adrestus before landing a kick square in Adrestus' stomach. He stumbled back and doubled over. His shoulders heaved with the effort of the continued fight.

"Give me my stone!" he wailed. "I don't care how many times I have to throw you off my building! I. WANT. MY. LAPIS!"

He straightened up, catching Dad off guard to clip him under the chin with the hilt of his sword.

I shrieked as he fell backwards, my sword clattering from his hand to the floor. Adrestus swung his blade overhead, preparing to bring it down through Dad's chest and Trev Baker's voice reverberated in my mind.

I've dreamt his death and you're sitting next to him when he goes! Stay away from him, and you'll both be safe!

"NO!" I tackled Adrestus around the waist. As we fell to the ground, his head whipped back and smacked the tile. His sword sprung free of his hand, spinning through the glass until it disappeared over the edge of the building.

I struggled to my feet and he gaped up at me as he gagged for air.

"You...were supposed...to rule...with me..." he choked. "My army...will assemble...and kill...all of you..."

"Sammy." Dad's hand rested on my shoulder and we stood over Adrestus as he continued to heave for air. "Thank you."

The warrior flipped onto his stomach and clawed his way to his knees, his blue eye glaring through the dried blood that painted his face. Dad gave him a final kick to the chin. Adrestus keeled forward and landed facedown in the glass, where he stopped moving.

"Sammy, we need to go!" Naomi cried. "Wesley's fading!"

We spun away from Adrestus' unconscious body and Dad charged across the floor to reach Wesley. I followed in a daze. I'd done it. I'd saved Dad.

"Keep his arm lifted!" Dad barked. Wesley hung limp in their arms as they carted him across the rooftop, their feet sliding in the loose glass that covered the tiles.

"Let me help," I pleaded, reaching to support Wesley's head. His stump rested on his chest, bleeding into his lightning-burnt shirt. I held a hand to his mouth, making sure I could still feel his breath. "Dad, how did you get out? The keycards in your drawer—"

"Winnie sprung me after she heard Wesley screaming. But you... how are you not dead? You come back every damn—" Dad's head whipped to the side. "MOVE!"

He shoved us out of the way, throwing Wesley into our arms. Naomi and I collapsed under the sudden weight, scrambling to protect Wesley's head as it lolled back. Glass scraped the palms of my hands and cut through my jeans and into my knees.

"What—?" I looked up at Dad. A strange look crossed his face and tears filled his eyes as he looked down on us. "Dad, why—"

When I saw the blade sticking out from his chest, it was as if I could feel it in mine as well.

"DAD!" I shrieked, abandoning Naomi and Wesley on the ground to catch all six and half feet of him as he toppled forward.

Adrestus howled with laughter, limping backwards, leaving the sword, *my* sword, the sword *Vidar* had given me, lodged in Dad's back.

"This isn't over, Eydis," he screeched, withdrawing to the building's edge. Wind played with the tatters of his suit as he lifted a hand in a sick salute. "I'll burn this whole world to the ground if that's what it takes to save it!"

He held out his arms before toppling backwards over the edge. A dark mass rose from where he'd fallen and I recognized the four wings and neat pixie cut of Lana as she carried Adrestus away, teetering on the wind.

"Dad?" I sobbed. He looked up at me, blinking slowly. I tried to keep the blade still, balancing him on his side. "It-it's okay, alright? Naomi?"

Naomi watched in horror, on her knees, with Wesley in her lap.

"Y-yes?"

"The Lapis! I need it!"

She froze, not understanding, and then—

"Oh!" She dug in her pocket and revealed the small stone. It rolled in her hand but she watched me apprehensively.

"I'll give it back! Please! He'll die!"

She held it out on a shaking hand and I leaned across Dad to take it.

"I-I've got it," he grunted softly. "Eydis, give it to me. I've got it from here."

I shoved the stone into Dad's hand. He would know how to make it work. He groaned as he reached back to his own pocket and procured a vial.

Yes. Of course. We needed a liquid to—

He uncorked the vial and the stench of pickle juice wafted upwards.

"No!" I went to slap the glass from his hand, but he'd already dropped the Lapis.

The vial clattered to the floor, foaming red, purple, and blue. I clawed at the liquid and I cried as it burnt my hands.

"What? What did he do?" Naomi demanded.

"Why?" I sobbed, pulling at the front of his shirt. He chuckled softly, laying his head against the stone tile.

"I wanted it gone," he whispered. "Took a few months, but I finally did it."

I looked at the blade that stuck out of his heaving chest, slick with blood. Maybe Adrestus was right. Maybe I had the power to save him. I raised my arm to the blade.

"Grab her!" Dad barked with sudden ferocity. Naomi abandoned Wes to grab my arms and tackle me backwards. I screamed in protest. "I told you, you are nobody's resource. Not Adrestus', not mine, not anyone's!"

"NO! Let me save you!"

"Eydis!" His voice reverberated across the rooftop. He coughed and blood stained his lips. My brother. My father. My only family. I thought I'd saved him. I thought we were going to be okay.

"Dad, please..." I begged.

"Sammy." His mouth hinted at a smile. "Why do you think I carried you around all those years if not to give you a second chance at life? My work is done."

Metal clanged behind us as people made their way up the spiral steps. Dad's eyes flickered over me.

"But I don't want a second life if you're not in it!"

"Samantha?" Fleming's voice broke me and my shoulders shook with unrestrained sobs. Naomi released me and Fleming took her place.

"I protected you for a thousand years," Dad continued. "I've done everything I can for you."

"No..." It was like a giant hand had grabbed my chest and was squeezing the air out of me. The rooftop spun. This wasn't real. This couldn't be real. "But Avery and Mom..."

Tears bled down his face and he showed the first signs of regret but he swallowed and steeled himself.

"They have each other and they have you," he coughed. "But I miss *them*. I haven't seen our family in so long, Eydis."

"They can wait a little longer!" I didn't want to be alone. I *couldn't* be alone. "Vi, please."

"It's time to go." His voice faded, but he smiled through the blood and tears before looking to Fleming. "Watch her for me? I've got her this far. The rest is up to you."

His smile waned and his eyes turned glassy and I shrieked as if that might bring him back. But as much as I screamed, I couldn't bring him back to the rooftop. It didn't make sense how a man so big and so strong could look so small and empty, lying with a sword through his chest.

"I've got you," Fleming cried in my ear and I fell into his shoulder, hiding there, shaking and sobbing until I choked on air. "You're okay, Sammy. I've got you."

50

Will and Testament

It was a good day for a funeral and Dad had waited long enough.

Waves whispered down in the cove, the sound mingling with the voices of those setting up for the ceremony. It was the first warm day since we'd arrived on the rural farm island more than two months ago, nice enough to coax me out of the house Fleming had bought and onto the back porch to watch the afternoon sun gleam off the ocean. The long grasses that grew along the windy bluff bowed and danced in the breeze that played with my hair.

Gravel crunched in the driveway and my stomach clenched. I didn't want to look and see who it was. I didn't want to see Alison or Avery or the small wooden box of ashes I knew they'd be carrying with them.

"Sammy?"

My throat constricted and I spun to look up at Wesley. His hair had become shaggier in the weeks since I'd seen him and he flashed me a timid smile.

"He let you come!" I exclaimed, throwing my wool blanket aside and launching myself into his arms. He embraced me back and I pushed away with sudden realization. "What is this?"

I grabbed his right arm, running my fingers over the red plastic. He showed off by flexing his fingers. They worked in tandem with each other and there was a small, mechanical whir as they moved.

"Everly just got it in last week," he beamed. "It's not as nice as a carbon fiber one, but it was printed to fit me exactly!"

I tried to ignore the burning in my eyes and forced a smile to match his.

"It's wonderful, Wes." My smile broke and the tiniest sob escaped my lips. Wesley pulled me back in with his real arm and practiced patting me on the back with the other.

"Don't feel bad, Sammy. Please. I can't bear it." He tugged at his prosthesis and I winced. A lock of my hair was caught in his knuckles. "Shoot, sorry."

I gave a wet laugh and focused on the darkness of his shoulder as he pressed around me trying to untangle himself from my hair.

"What's it like with Roy?" I asked, leaning my cheek against his collarbone as he worked. He'd gotten so much taller since I'd seen him.

"Horrible," he snorted. "The campsite is nice enough but it would be better if you were there."

Roy Hendricks' first order of business after he'd taken Fleming's position as head of Apex Team was to kick me off. No Betas. Even though we were all hiding on the same island, he wouldn't even let me visit the campsite the teams were living on along the south coast and it was rare for him to let any of the students leave, either.

I couldn't be too mad at him about that, though. Adrian Schrader had declared New Delos a free state as soon as the city was deemed safe to return to. Within weeks, he'd secured treaties with the world's most powerful nations and suddenly, unregistered Apex were illegal across the globe while Epsilons were not only encouraged but also granted automatic citizenship on New Delos. The power to turn anyone into an Epsilon proved a powerful bartering chip for Schrader.

Luckily, there had to be a breaking point somewhere. Adrestus no longer had the Lapis. There was a finite number of super soldiers he could create. For the time being, though, my friends weren't safe.

"What about you?" Wesley asked. "It seems nice here."

"I hate homeschooling," I shrugged, "and my tutor is a bit of a hothead. Watch it!"

I slapped a hand to the back of my head and Wesley burned red.

"Sorry," he mumbled, withdrawing his prosthesis to pick out the hair he'd pulled from my skull. "I thought it was free."

I watched him concentrating on his plastic knuckles, studying the way he flinched when the fingers suddenly extended.

"The red is cool," I mumbled. He smiled.

"You think so? If I get a carbon fiber one, I want black, so I figured I'd get something more fun for this one since it's cheaper." His cheeks turned the color of his new arm and he looked up at me with sudden horror. "It's not too flashy, right? For tonight? I mean, everyone's going to be in black."

"No!" I insisted. "It's perfect! He'd like it. Besides, you should see what I'm wearing."

He turned an even darker shade of red and I felt my cheeks tinge pink.

"Hey!" He pointed at the scar centered just below my collarbones, shaped like a small, upside-down "V". "We match!"

He pulled at his shirt collar to reveal the same mark on his sternum.

"Yeah, it's from the dog-whistle necklace you gave me." I tucked my hair behind my ears. "Sorry, I was wearing it when the lightning struck. It must've branded us both."

"Please don't apologize," he said quietly, letting go of his shirt collar. He rubbed at his shirt, over the burn scar, and looked out at the ocean, the muscles in his throat constricting.

"Are we...um..." I scuffed my bare foot against the wooden planks of the porch. "It's probably not a good time to talk about it, but the day we sank the city..."

He looked back at me and grabbed onto his fake arm where it connected to his elbow.

"What about it?" His voice cracked.

"When you saved me, right before you hoisted me up, you..." I abandoned the topic. I couldn't bear to mention the kiss. What if he didn't remember? Adrestus said they found him with a head injury. My cheeks burned hotter. *Oh, my god, what* if *he* didn't *remember?* "I mean, right after. You said something but I couldn't hear you. Do you remember what you said?"

Wesley's mouth turned into a thin line as he pressed his lips together.

"Samantha!"

I scowled as Fleming called me from inside the house.

"I'm busy!" I called back.

"You need to get ready! People are starting to arrive!"

I looked back at Wesley, relieved to see him smiling again.

"Yeah, I remember what I said, but let's concentrate on the things on hand first." He laughed when I frowned at him and he reached forward with both hands to take mine. His new fingers flexed aggressively when they met mine and I laughed as he scowled at them. "When this is all done, I'll find you and I'll tell you what I said. We've got work to do first."

I nodded as Fleming yelled for me again.

"Sorry." I grimaced.

"Your roommates are as fun as mine," Wesley grinned. "Try sharing a cabin with Andersen and Anthony."

I wrinkled my nose. I was still bitter Anthony had been let onto the team while I'd been kicked off. Roy would rather have a traitor than a Beta training under him. I understood there wasn't anywhere else for Anthony to go, but *still.*

"I'll see you down at the beach," I sighed. Bile lodged in my throat and Wesley's arms were back around me.

"It'll be okay. You're going to do great."

He held me by the shoulders as best he could with the prosthesis. He screwed up his face and before he lost his nerve, he deftly bent in and kissed my cheek.

I blinked in surprise, raising a hand to the spot where his lips had touched.

"Sorry, I hope that was okay, I—"

I pushed up onto my toes and kissed his cheek back. It was perfect and sweet and wonderful and I liked the way his cheek felt against my lips but my eyes filled with tears, as did his.

"I wish he could've been my dad, too, like you said he would be," Wesley whispered. My throat locked up and I nodded, unable to speak. "Remember when you had us over for dinner last fall? I never told you, but I overheard him say you better not be dating me."

A strangled sound somewhere between a laugh and a sob burst from my throat.

"I figured you did." The fingers of his left hand found mine and his thumb stroked my knuckles.

"He was there, at Schrader Tower, when I woke up." He watched our hands instead of looking at me. "I was scared, but he said it was okay. He was probably lying, but it still helped."

I squeezed his hand back, unable to speak. It wasn't fair.

"Samantha!" Fleming yelled again. Wesley let go of my hand and gave me his bravest smile.

"I guess I'm keeping you, huh?" He waved his red hand at me and backed down the porch steps. "I'll see you down there."

I watched him disappear around the side of the house before I slipped inside to the kitchen. Fleming brewed tea at the stove, wearing a black suit and his scruff neatly trimmed.

"Naomi's waiting for you in the bathroom," he said.

"I didn't think she'd come."

"Of course she came." Fleming looked up from his tea. "Have you seen Amanda? If she's not ready yet, either..."

He stalked into the next room, calling for Amanda.

I took a moment to breathe before climbing up the narrow staircase to the cramped upper floor, which housed three rooms. A low ceilinged hall connected my bedroom, which overlooked the front yard, to Amanda's on the other side of the house. Light poured from the bathroom door, which sat in the middle of the floor.

Naomi poked her head out and she brandished a hairbrush at me.

"Been a while." She tried to smile.

"Feels like it."

I sat in the stool in front of the bathroom mirror and Naomi wasted no time in getting to work on my hair. She propped her phone up on the counter to scroll through reference photos.

"I spent all week looking up how to do Viking hair."

"It doesn't need to be too crazy."

She began twisting the hair above my left ear into a braid.

"Let me have fun, okay?"

I watched her fingers braid my hair back into a ponytail, which she then teased with the comb. It did look nice, in a strange, wild way. It would've made Dad smile. Naomi chewed on her lip while she worked and after she was satisfied, she turned to my meager make-up collection.

"You didn't have to come today," I said quietly as she rubbed foundation over my face.

"You're my friend." The make-up brush jabbed me over the eye.

"You're not mad?"

She threw the brush in the sink.

"I'm livid. He took the only hope I had of ever being able to spend more than five minutes with my family. In a way, this is kind of like their funeral, too, even though they're still alive."

"Then you shouldn't torture yourself by going to the beach after this."

"Are you kidding?" Her words were angry, but the look on her face was one of pain and longing. "I feel everything you feel, Sammy. I know how much it hurts and I know, as selfishly selfless as Vic was at the end, he was a good guy."

She dabbed under her eyes, trying to spare her mascara from the tears.

"But you hurt, too, Naomi." I wrapped an arm around her neck and pulled her in. "Even if I can't feel your hurt the way you feel mine, I know it's there and I'm—"

"No!" She laughed suddenly. "You *can't* say you're sorry. Wesley and I agree you say it too much."

She cleared her throat and returned to the make-up bag.

"Fleming says hurry up." Amanda walked past the bathroom. She'd gelled back the inch of mousy brown hair that had regrown over the last two months and looked stunning in her black dress.

"It's *make-up*," Naomi hissed. "It's *art* and I refuse to be rushed."

After Naomi finished my hair and face, she went ahead to the beach while I finished getting dressed in a long black dress that felt too formal and too dark for Dad's taste. He would have grumbled at the fuss we were all making.

I pulled on sandals and tried to buckle the straps with trembling fingers. The sun was getting lower on the horizon. It was almost time.

"He hates me," Eydis' voice broke through my thoughts. There weren't many memories left for me to remember, but every once in a while, they snuck in, filling in the holes I didn't know were there. Eydis' voice was higher pitched this time, as if younger, and she sounded like she'd been crying.

"No, he doesn't." Vidar. Dad. He sat on the twin bed and his young, bare-faced smile carried the trace of a laugh. "He loves you."

"Not as much as he loves Gunhild!"

He laughed outright now.

"Oh, well, everyone loves Gunhild the best!" He looked around conspiratorially. "But actually, you're just as good as Gunhild, Eydis."

I looked at my hands, shame flooding my insides.

"No, I'll never be like her."

His arm wrapped around my shoulder.

"No, you won't." His storm gray eyes that matched mine shone with pride. "I didn't say I want you to be like her, just that you're as good as her. Good in a different way. And Father *doesn't* hate you. He loves you, and even if he won't say it, I will."

He squeezed my shoulder.

"I love you, Eydis."

I wiped my tears away.

"Love you, too, Vidar."

"Sammy?" The memory broke. My hands were still wrapped around my sandal buckle and a tentative hand brushed my shoulder. Fleming's voice was slow and gentle. "Everyone's ready."

I buckled the sandal and stood up. Fleming's eyes were already red and somehow, that brought fresh tears to mine.

"Alright."

"You can take a second if you need."

I looked back at the twin bed, where I'd seen the Vidar of my memories sitting.

"No, I'll be okay. It's time we sent him off."

Fleming followed close behind as I walked down the steps carved into the hill that led to the cove. The beach was small but private, lit by white candles flickering in the sunset.

Naomi and Wes stood nearest the steps and I was surprised to see Andersen standing with them. He gave me a curt nod as I passed and I tried to work my lips into a smile. Behind them, Amanda leaned against

Brooke. Dad had been her only friend when they'd both been imprisoned. She hadn't taken the news of his loss well.

Roy and Valerie Hendricks stood back a little farther, near the clay wall carved into the cove by eons of waves breaking against the beach. Roy had been Dad's friend and while his presence was less surprising than Andersen's, he was somehow less welcome.

Esther, Adrestus' deserter and the woman behind the Doomsday Pager, stood alone, the dying sun catching her ginger hair spectacularly. Dad made friends wherever he went, despite being naturally suspicious of almost everyone. Of course he'd made new friends even when he was a prisoner.

Finally, Alison and Avery stood at the edge of the water, a canoe between the two of them with its stern pulled up onto the sand. Avery looked like a mannequin in his suit, his tie so tight, it looked like he was holding his breath. The few times I'd found it in me to visit him and Mom, he'd hid in his bedroom, refusing to even see me. Now, he avoided my eye and instead I looked at the carved box in his hands.

Dad.

Mom smiled wanly, her blonde hair pulled into a bun. She clutched a bulging folder against her chest and made room for me by the boat. Lilies and tulips filled its body, surrounding a small pedestal at the boat's center.

Mom cleared her throat.

"Thank you all for coming," she said, her voice wavering. I stared at the sand, begging myself not to feel. It had been two months. How could it still hurt so much? "Vic wouldn't have wanted anything too fancy, but I do have a few words before we send him off."

She broke off and looked to the sky to steady herself. Fleming stood on her other side and pried a hand from her folder to hold in his. She cleared her throat a second time.

"You've heard it said in countless eulogies, the list of what someone was. A husband. A father. A brother."

I closed my eyes. Naomi had worked so hard on my make-up. I didn't want to ruin it.

"And yes," Mom continued, "Vic, like countless men before him and countless men to come, was all of those things. Husband. Father. Brother. While he wasn't the first or only man to hold those titles, *no one* took the meaning of those words to heart as he did. They were sacred charges that he carried for centuries. He was born to protect and he made damn sure that's what he did, all the way to the very end."

Her voice broke and she nodded to Avery. His shoulders hunched up towards his ears in discomfort as he waded into the ocean. His slacks soaked up to his knees and he wavered over the boat, clutching Dad's ashes to his chest. Pain etched itself into every detail on his too-young face as he lowered Dad onto the pedestal. His hands hesitated on the carved wood and then he ripped them away, as if afraid he'd lose his resolve to let him go.

"The greatest Vikings were buried with their most prized possessions," Mom murmured. "As we send Vic on his way to reunite with the family he lost so long ago, the greatest thing I can offer him to take on his journey is this."

She opened the folder and pulled out a photo in a silver frame. I clenched my jaw. It was the photo Mom had retrieved on her Christmas trip to New Delos. The one Dad had kept on his work desk, the four of us, posing for a family selfie on the ferry ride to New Delos. The only picture of the four of us together.

Mom set it on the box, running her finger along a corner of the frame. On the other side of the boat, Avery bowed his head to hide his face, but his shoulders shook violently and his hands balled into fists at his side.

"I'll see you in Valhalla, my love," Mom whispered. She kissed the side of the boat, kneeling in the salt water, her face contorting in pain. Fleming drew her away as Amanda stepped forward and pushed the boat out into the water.

We gathered along the water line to watch it drift away. Each of Mom's sobs ripped at me and I tried instead to focus on the sounds of the small waves lapping the shore, but as much as I wanted to pretend I was somewhere else, I couldn't.

"Sammy," Amanda whispered. She pressed a wooden bow into my hands.

"What if the boat doesn't burn right?" Sudden panic flared inside me. What if I ruined this, too?

"I'll make sure it does."

Once the boat floated to the middle of the cove, I nocked the arrow Amanda handed me into the bow, pulling the string back. We'd practiced all week but I hadn't counted on my hands shaking so horribly.

She held a hand over the oil-dipped arrowhead, and it lit up in her palm.

I tried to aim through blurry tears but as soon as I let the flaming arrow loose, I knew I'd missed. However, the arrow arched through the air, seemingly caught on the wind, and found its target.

I thought I saw Andersen hurriedly slip his hands into his pockets as the floating pyre lit up and Vidar made his final ascent.

By the time the fire burned out, I was dizzy with sadness and fatigue, but I'd agreed to do one last thing for Mom. Fleming had arranged for a small monument to be put up on one of the bluffs overlooking the ocean. It didn't resemble Vidar in the slightest, but I liked the stone Viking that looked out over the water, letting anyone who got too close know that those hiding here were protected.

I hesitated in the sand at the bottom step, looking up the stairs that led back out of the cove.

"What's wrong?" Plastic brushed against my hand, and even though they weren't real, I still found comfort when I grabbed Wesley's mechanical fingers.

"I don't want to go. I don't want to say goodbye." Mom and Avery were already half-way up the stairs.

"It's okay," Wes whispered as I went to follow Mom and Avery out of the cove. "I'll come find you when you're done. I'm here."

I held onto that promise as I forced my legs to climb after Mom and Avery. My arm was heavy with the burden I carried for I'd been tasked with bringing the last piece of Vidar up to the stone Viking: the sword he'd armed me with. The sword Adrestus had jealously hoarded like a trophy for a thousand years. The sword that had killed my dad.

I caught up with Mom and Avery and we finished the climb together in silence. The wind blew harder here than it did in the cove and Alison showed me the slit in the stone pedestal in front of the Viking figure. I slid the sword into the hole so that the hilt rested just below the statue's clasped hands and I felt it lock into place. This was a good place for it to rust and disappear, in the stone hands of Vidar's effigy.

"I know you're both grieving in your own ways," Mom said, standing in front of the stone man and staring up into his face as purple dusk fell around us, "but it's important that we heal together, as a family. I know that will take time, but Vic loved both his children. He would want to see us together."

Avery grunted, standing as far as he could without being an awkward distance away. Mom looked away from the stone Viking to try to smile at me.

"I understand why you want to stay with Alex and Amanda," she said. "I know things are weird with most of your fake memories gone, but you're still my daughter and Avery is still your brother. If you ever feel up to it, we will always have space for you."

I nodded.

"Thanks."

"You two haven't spoken since you arrived on the island." Mom looked pointedly at Avery. "I'm going down to help set up dinner, but try and talk, alright? You love each other. Your father wouldn't want to see you like this."

Avery wrapped his arms around himself and I stood stoically as Mom kissed my forehead before she went back down the hill to the glowing lights of Fleming's house.

"I don't care what she says." Avery's voice was brittle and acidic. "You are *not* my sister."

I bit my lip, not sure how to respond. To me, he was still my brother.

"But I want to be."

"No!" His blond hair fluttered about his face as he yelled. "I went to New Delos to *save* Dad but you didn't let me! And now he's dead *because* of you!"

Malice dripped off every word. I stared at Avery in shock, wondering how long he'd harbored this resentment.

"Avery, I—"

"Don't!" he shouted. "You said you would save him! You promised! And now he's dead! He lived for a thousand years but as soon as you woke up, you killed him! *You* did this!"

His hand shook as he pointed it at me.

"If I could bring him back—"

"You already *had* a dad! And you already got *him* killed." Tears streamed down his face, catching the rising moonlight. "Why'd you have to kill mine, too, huh? I want him *back!* Give him back to me!"

He fell to his knees, sobbing into the dirt and pulling at his shaggy, blond hair. I watched in stunned silence, not knowing how to help, wanting to pull him close, knowing he'd never let me.

"Why didn't you let me save him?" he wailed and his voice cracked. "I could've saved him!"

"Avery, please." I stepped forward, but he stumbled to his feet and staggered away towards the path back down the hill. "I'm sorry. I miss him, too."

"Shut up," he said flatly, trying to regain his composure. "I don't want your stupid apologies. You know what, Sammy? Just forget it. Okay?"

He whipped around and ran down the hill. I watched him go as he passed a figure on its way up to meet me in the dark.

Just forget it.

Forget it.

My heart thundered and despite the cool wind, I broke out in sweat.

Forget it.

Forget what? I didn't remember. It was like waking up and trying to hold onto a dream, but the harder I tried to remember, the faster it slipped away.

The figure on the path ran to me now. He was taller than me and wore glasses on his long nose.

"Sammy?" He grabbed my shoulder with one hand, green eyes afraid. I stumbled back. "Sammy, what's wrong?"

I stared at him blankly, perplexed.

"I don't know," I murmured, trying to remember why I'd been so panicked just a moment ago when everything seemed fine now.

Forget it.

There had been a boy here. I remembered that much, and those had been the words he'd said to me.

Forget it.

And so, I did.

ACKNOWLEDGEMENTS

Considering you have found your way to the Acknowledgements page of a sequel, chances are you've now read both my books. So, I'd like to start by thanking you, Reader. When I first decided to publish The Apex Cycle, I told myself it'd be worth the trouble if a single person found joy in Samantha's story. If you are one of them, these books happened because of you.

But there are others who made these books possible. My author friends I've made along the way, like TR, Lauren, and so many others, thank you for letting me share my story with you and inspiring me with yours in return.

Thank you to my early readers, especially those who gave attentive feedback that helped Samantha shine. Every one of you helped make DELTA into what it is, but I'd like to extend an extra thanks to Lydia, Sally, Madi, Kayla, Andrew, A.D., and Gigi for your diligent note-taking and typo-finding. (And an extra-extra thanks to Andrew, for entertaining my husband with Monster Hunter when I needed to get writing done).

Next, I must thank Julia and Ben. If you two hadn't spent countless hours playing pretend with me growing up, I'm not sure I'd have the passion for storytelling that I do today. Mom, Dad, and Danny, you all did your part, too.

And then there's Melissa, 50% hype-woman, 50% supportive Mom friend, and 100% editing goddess. There is no one else who has been with Sammy every step of the way. Your enthusiasm for these disastrous kiddos is boundless and single-handedly fueling the march to the end.

Finally, Connor, the husband and friend who has never doubted me and is always there to remind me to take a break. Thank you for encouraging me, thank you for pushing me, and thank you for supporting me. I caribou.

Samantha Will Return

In

The Apex Cycle
Book 3

CHARACTER GLOSSARY

THE SOPHOMORES OF NEW DELOS PREP

Samantha Havardson: The main character who, unlike her friends, isn't an Apex despite being on Apex Team. Also unlike her friends, she recently discovered herself to be a viking girl from the middle ages.

Wesley Isaacs: An Apex with super strength, super senses, and super bad communication skills. He wears glasses to stave off the migraines that come with his super-sight. He's one of Sammy's closest friends.

Naomi Bradford: Sammy's close friend and roommate. She's an Apex with empath abilities and feels everything those around her feel - but she can't turn it off. She is one of four captains on Apex Team.

Andersen Lewis: High school Apex with telekinetic control over non-organic material. He has a superiority complex the size of New Delos itself and a grudge against Sammy.

Anthony Schultz: Friend to Sammy and roommate to Wesley, Anthony enjoyed a powerless life up until Adrestus turned him into an Apex against his will. His new wind-based abilities control him more than he controls them.

Remi Whitlock: Wesley's ex-girlfriend with computer-interfacing Apex powers. Like Samantha, she failed the trials to make the team, but was allowed on if she engaged in extra training.

Heather Hisakawa: Apex teammate and powerhouse who can control and travel through darkness. She is known for always wearing a bow in her hair.

Skyler Cripps: Apex teammate and best friend of Andersen. His ability gives him control over the appearance of his face. He doesn't believe Samantha should be allowed on the team.

Everest Archer: A dark haired and reserved Apex teammate with the power to change his body density.

Freddie Williams: Apex teammate with the power to create and disperse fog. He has fluffy, hay-colored hair and freckles.

Olivia Chase: Apex teammate with the ability to turn herself and those she touches invisible.

Bethany Valente: A non-Apex classmate of Sammy and girlfriend to Anthony. She is unaware of Anthony's new Apex abilities.

Jamie Ratcliffe: A classmate of Sammy's who is dating Andersen. Like her father, John Ratcliffe, she hates nothing more than Apex and lets everyone know. She's unaware that her boyfriend is an Apex.

Madison: Jamie's best friend. Like Jamie, she has no powers and is happy to go along with her friend's many Anti-Apex tirades.

The Apex Team Council

Alexander Fleming: History teacher, Apex Team coach, and Samantha's stand-in guardian, this man does it all and *without* Apex abilities. His late brother was city hero Paragon, but he keeps this, along with his brother's other secrets, close to his chest.

Dr. Diane Parker: The head of the University Apex Team.

Dr. Penelope Weaver: The principal of New Delos Prep and the head council member of the Apex Team Council. Her healing ability allows her to donate blood plasma to the team to be used in treating injuries.

Trev Baker: Council Representative from Schrader Industries. Sammy believes his boss, Adrian Schrader, is working for Adrestus and that he shouldn't be trusted. In turn, Baker thinks Samantha doesn't belong on Apex Team.

Mickey: Is it his first name or his last name? Sammy isn't sure. He's the city council representative on the Apex Team Council and has telepathic abilities.

Officer Allen: The New Delos Police representative on the Apex Team Council.

Other Apex Faculty

Everly Jacobi: School nurse who doubles as the Team's doctor. His powers that allow him to assess physical wellness and injuries serve him well when caring for injured team members.

Vanessa Reiner: Team Combat Specialist and Apex PE teacher. Her Apex abilities allow her to perfectly replicate hand-to-hand combat techniques.

Angie Le Roux: The team doctor for the University Apex Team. She has the ability to dull the pain of those around her.

The Villains

Adrestus: Also known as Dr. Warren Cunningham. Adrestus is older than the middle-aged man he appears to be. Having reclaimed the mysterious stone that has kept him and Samantha alive all these years, he is bent on using its power to create a loyal Apex following.

Adrian Schrader: New Delos celebrity and business mogul, head of Schrader Industries. However, he's secretly working for Adrestus. Despite not being an Apex, Apex abilities don't seem to work on him.

Winnie "Dion" Hendricks: Samantha's former roommate who has joined Adrestus under the alias "Dion". She's a non-Apex, bitter at having always been her father's second-favorite daughter.

Mira Aimes: Adrestus' right-hand woman with the power to take control over the motor function of anyone she touches.

Gregor: One of Adrestus' followers with powers that allow him to manipulate memories and create illusions.

Hackjob: Another follower of Adrestus. His raw strength and durability make him a difficult opponent.

Miles: A follower of Adrestus with the power to make force fields.

Hephestae: A caped and fiery new follower of Adrestus. Very little is known about her.

Esther: A follower of Adrestus who has the ability to sense the presence and location of others.

John Ratcliffe: City councilman known for his Anti-Apex views. His daughter Jamie attends New Delos Prep and is dating Andersen.

Families and Parents

Vic "Vidar" Havardson: The man that Sammy believed to be her father but is actually her one surviving Viking brother, Vidar. He's been captured by Adrestus and Sammy is determined to get him back.

Alison Taylor-Havardson: Vic's wife who Samantha believed to be her mother until recently. Alison used her powers to give Sammy fake memories of a normal life with them and is currently in hiding with her son, Avery.

Avery Havardson: Samantha's fake brother who is technically her nephew. He's in hiding, learning to use his powers of manipulation responsibly.

Roy Hendricks: Winnie and Amanda's father. In his youth, he was on the team with Fleming and Alison and has strong opinions regarding whether non-Apex should be allowed to join.

Valerie Hendricks: Mother to Winnie and Amanda. She's currently in hiding with her husband, Roy, as well as her friend Alison and Alison's son, Avery.

Amanda Hendricks: College sophomore and older sister to Winnie, Sammy's former roommate. Her fire abilities made her formidable on the Apex Team, but she's quit and was recently captured by Adrestus.

Gabriella Bradford: Naomi's mother. Naomi has admitted that her powers strain their relationship but hasn't said much else on the matter. They video call often.

Other Students on Apex Team

Justin Pomeroy: A senior with the ability to lock those he touches in a stasis. He's one of four team captains on Apex Team.

Marcus McDougall: A senior with the ability to see heat signatures. He's one of four team captains on Apex Team

Jen Reeves: A junior and one of four team captains on Apex Team.

Isabelle Abarca: Junior on Apex Team and Anthony's cousin. She shares in their family's wind-powers, though, unlike Anthony, she was born with hers.

Desirae Sheffield: Twin to fellow junior Mike. They share a telepathic link.

Mike Sheffield: Twin to fellow junior Desirae. They share a telepathic link.

Jessa Davidson: A freshman on Apex Team with the ability to alter gravity's effects.

Christopher Prescott: A freshman on Apex Team with amphibious abilities, including webbed fingers.

Erik Hart: A junior on Apex Team with the ability to create smells. Along with Samantha and Remi, he failed the admission Trial and must complete additional training.

Harvey Hernandez : A junior on Apex Team.

Carmen Hawkins: A junior on Apex Team. Her abilities allow her to anticipate several seconds into the future, making her a difficult opponent.

Jeanie Little: A junior on Apex Team who can turn invisible in rain or fog.

University Students

Sergio Silva: A college freshman with the ability to control temperature. He uses his power to create ice-swords out of the moisture in the air. He's missing his right eye and goes between a glass prosthesis and an eyepatch depending on whether he's fighting or not.

Candice Lloyd: A college sophomore who can bend and control light.

Eli Archer: A college senior and older brother to Everest. Like his brother, he can change his body's density at will.

Boonsri Malee: A college junior with the ability to control plants. She likes to keep a fern on her person at all times that she uses to subdue her opponents.

Brooke Graham: A Non-Apex college sophomore and girlfriend to Amanda. She's been searching for Amanda since her disappearance.

Vikings

Eydis (AY-dees): Sammy's forgotten alter-ego, who she is slowly recovering through broken memories. In modern lore surrounding Adrestus, she is known as The Scourge Queen, the ruthless warrior who murdered the immortal Adrestus of Legend. In reality, however, Eydis was just a teenaged sailmaker with dreams to see the world.

Havard (Hah-verd) Bjornsson: Eydis' father and a leader in their village. He was protective of his family to a fault.

Solveig (Sul-vay) Hildadotter: Eydis' mother. She was both gorgeous and deadly.

Knut (Kah-noot): Eydis' sturdily-built oldest brother. He was the oldest of six children.

Gunhild (Goon-hild): Eydis' older sister. She resembled their mother.

Vidar (Vee-dar): Eydis' older brother and the sibling closest to her in age. After Eydis slipped into her thousand-year nap, Vidar cared for her and eventually posed as her father after he continued to age into his forties despite his immortality.

Hjordis (Hyore-dees): The second youngest and Eydis' younger sister.

Erika (Air-ika): The youngest of Eydis' siblings with a lick of white hair despite the rest of her man being tawny-colored.